Volcano in the Ocean

Laurie de Vere

Paperback: 978-1-966652-92-2
Hardcover: 978-1-967820-29-0
eBook: 978-1-966652-93-9
Library of Congress Control Number: 2025906786

This is a work of fiction.

Ordering Information:

Prime Seven Media
518 Landmann St.
Tomah City, WI 54660

Printed in the United States of America

These are the other books I have written:

One Bead of Gold by Lorraine Stanton – a story of abused children in 1950s New Zealand

And to come **A String of Pearls**

All by Laurie Campbell – a story of Prussia in the 1860s

Prussian Yarns
A Stitch in Time
Tincture and Tantrums
There is a Season
Viennese Yarns
And to come **Orchids** and **Still Snow**

The Fire in the Fern Four by Laurie de Vere – a story of a non-violent society being attacked by a violent society

Volcano in the Ocean

And to come - **Ignition in the City, Smoke in the Forest, Fire in the Fern**

Acknowledgements

With many thanks to Randy Foley for going over the book repeatedly, for giving me ideas and encouragement, and for knowing the GR so well. Randy gave me information about the landscapes, and corrected my worst mistakes.

With thanks to Carlos Ruiz Checa for the Mexican slang.

With gratitude to the Campbell family: to Richard Campbell, Vernon Campbel, and Susanne Campbell for Ahnstan, Winson, and Ahnya. To Harry Campbell and Gwen Campbell snr for their parenting. To Doug Campbell, Gwen Campbell jnr, Steven Campbell and Jennifer Campbell for Donstan, Violet, Violstan, and Donet.

And to all of the Sunday crowd; Mark Faccin, Donald McDonald, Oriano Biagini, Michelle Gaudet, and Richard Bodnar, for being Ahnstan's friends.

Table of Contents

CHAPTER ONE

Hatoe

Before dawn Hatoe Amaru was already on his way down to the docks. He strode along, head down, shoulders hunched up to his ears, to stop himself from glancing back at his lifeless home. But nothing could block the dull thud of the front door swinging shut behind him. The sound was a jolt, pounding home to him how hollow his house was now.

In his mind he could hear Annie whisper, "Hattoooeee," to get him to look back so that she could blow him one last kiss without waking the boys.

He jerked his shoulders higher, his head lower, and marched on. He couldn't bear to look back, couldn't bear to see the balcony empty. Annie was gone. She'd died in his arms three years ago. It wasn't a dream.

And now the boys were gone, too. Hatoe had let the younger one, Kiritoe, go off to university. He could be proud of that. Annie would have been pleased. And who knows, maybe Kiri would make something of himself after all. The boy was a bit of a drifter, with no idea what he wanted to do, and no aptitude for the sea. He might as well be off studying.

It was the older one, Anatoe, which hurt. Nat had loved the sea his whole life, had never talked about doing anything else but being a seaweed farmer like Hatoe and, one day, inheriting the family boat, the Laughing Dolphin. He'd even begged Hatoe to let him leave school early to take his apprenticeship. Then, last night, he'd taken off, not for any reasonable seaman's reason, but to wander the countryside playing music for handouts! He didn't want to sing good music the way his mother had, or teach music; he wanted to go busking – he wanted to be a busker!

That Hatoe could not bear. He never would have believed that it was possible to be any more devastated than he had been when Annie had died, but he was. Just as it had then, the desolation crashed down in overwhelming waves. What made it all that much worse was the bewilderment, worry, and anger about Nat. Guilt pressed down on top of everything else: he'd failed Nat; he'd let Annie down. Annie would have been able to talk sense into Nat's thick head. He lifted his head and whispered to the wind, "I'm so sorry, Annie."

He got a face full of run-off from the palm and fern fronds and tree branches that arched over the path. "Good aim," he said to them, but softly so he wouldn't be heard. The pounding rain from the storm over night had stopped, but it had left puddles on the path and great splotches fell from the leaves and fronds overhead.

Hatoe splashed on down the hill, grumbling, shaking the water off and feeling it drip down his neck. A house he was passing lit up, so he stopped splashing, going on as quietly as he could so that he wouldn't have to talk to anyone.

The darkness was comforting. He knew the path by heart, so he activated no lights along the way. The warm light that began spilling from the windows of the houses of the other sea folk just made him want to hide.

On the path the air was rich with the scents of just washed vegetation and damp earth but when Hatoe stepped out into the open, the wind hit him suddenly enough to make him gasp, and pulled strongly at his rain slick. It was blowing at about thirty knots, he guessed, lifting his head to sniff the air, and to listen.

He didn't need the news to tell him this storm had come straight up from the south. He could smell that in it, and feel hidden within it a bite of chill from the Big Ice, the South Pole. The smell of stirred up salt marshes and mud flats, and torn up seaweed, told him it had been strong enough to do damage. He could hear the splashing and thumping of the boats being thrown into each other and the dock, their bumpers slapping together, the rigging and mooring lines creaking. But no gulls. *Must still be sheltering inland*, he thought.

The sky was still heavy, black, and low, so there wasn't enough light for him to make out the forest of masts swinging back and forth. He knew it was happening more than saw it. It was only the boats' fluorescent eyes and designs bouncing erratically up and down that showed him that they were pulling and jerking at their ropes like tethered seals leaping and straining to be free.

That the marina was in complete darkness told Hatoe that he'd got his wish. He was the first one there. He wouldn't have to face anyone. That's the way he liked it: alone with the Laughing Dolphin, with no sound but the ocean.

He gave a huge sigh of relief, and lifted the cover from the touch pad on the railing at the start of the ramp down to the dock. As he put the palm of his hand on it, light paint lit up in the carvings all the way down the railings and newel posts of the ramp, spreading from his touch.

His way lit by the eerie green light, he jogged on down the ramp to the docks. The Laughing Dolphin's mooring was the first one on the north side of the second pier. On the dock he stopped for a moment just to be alone with the sea. He stood with his eyes closed, filling his lungs with the fresh, clean air, feeling the thumps through his feet as the boats were thrown into the bumpers that lined both sides of the pier. He could feel the loneliness and anger leaving him, soothed away by the sounds of the sea.

As much as Hatoe had adored Annie, his partner, the sea was his mistress and always had been. He was in love with every curve and mood of her. Even when her mood was harsh, cruel, or deadly, still he loved her. She was his life, his blood, his true happiness. Being out on the deep was his bliss.

Then, over all the crashing, banging, groaning, splashing, creaking, and the wind, he heard the faint squeak of a spinner off kilter.

"If that's the only damage we took, we're away laughing," he said, opening his eyes and looking around. The greenish light from the ramp made the spray arcing up over the edge of the pier into a ghostly lace.

At first he thought the sound was coming from one of the little spinners powering the light paint on the docks, but when he went to the carved and painted pole at the foot of the ramp to activate the light paint along the pier, the squeak didn't come from there.

He pressed on the bright white that lit up the pier from every surface that wasn't handled or walked on. It dazzled him for a moment. Hopefully he looked over at the great dark hulk of the Kaumoana on the south side, across from the Laughing Dolphin, but there was no avoiding it; the failing equipment was his. "Ah, you rotter," he scolded it, stepping off the dock down onto the heaving transom of his little weed collector as easily as he would have if it had been standing still.

As he untied the awning so that he could get on board, a sudden gust of wind tried to snatch it from his hand. "None of that, now!" he told the wind firmly, vaulting over from the transom down into the stern deck of his stubby thirteen-metre-long boat. He leaned over, took a strong grip of the canvas and fought the wind for it, his slick blowing about and getting in the way. "Knock it off, Tawhiri, I'm in no mood to play!" he challenged the wind, yanking the canvas back into place.

There was plenty of light from the dock, now, for him to see to lash the canvas down strongly.

At once the wind got under the secured awning, lifting it from the inside and making it bell outwards, rattling and thumping. Hatoe stooped down under the awning to make doubly sure that it was secure, then made his way to the bimini where he could stand upright to slip off his rain slick and his ruck sack.

The ruck sack had been kept dry by the rain slick, but his sandals and lower legs were soaked. He hung his rain slick on a hook in the wheelhouse, leaving it to swing as the wind tossed the boat back and forth, and to make puddles under the dodger while he took a hold of the handhold under the dodger to steady himself so he could slip his precious fuel cell out of its pocket in his ruck sack. The weatherproof cover over his touch pad concealed an ingeniously hidden fuel cell slot in behind the touch pad. He had an ordinary fuel cell slot like everyone else inside the companionway, with the usual beat up looking fuel cell that would be expected for the kind of income a seaweed farmer with a tiny little boat would make.

Lifting the entire touch pad up, he clicked the good fuel cell into its slot and locked it in, even though he knew he didn't need it right then. Hours of a wind that strong should mean that the on-board battery was fully charged, even with one spinner on the blink, and not enough light for the solar panels. He put the touch pad back in place, resealed it, and thumbed it, noting with satisfaction that the Laughing Dolphin obediently lit up along the railings and mast, and under the dodger and the bimini.

Anxious to go below before anyone else arrived, Hatoe slipped off his sodden sandals, held them and his rucksack in one hand, lifted out the storm panel, set it to one side, and opened the companionway doors. His bare heels thumped down the companionway, the rocking of the boat making the companion doors slam open into the downstairs with bangs. The door handles smacked into their holders which held them snugly so that the doors didn't bounce shut again.

Hatoe left the doors open behind him. Now that the boat was lit up he couldn't pretend he wasn't there. He had to activate the light paint, since he couldn't see down below in the dark, so he just had to go with it.

As he ran down, he tossed his sandals into the wet locker to deal with later. The first thing he did when he got down below was touch the lower level of the painted decorative pattern that encircled the inside cabin walls. The bright white light shining down from the ceiling paint dimmed slightly. Hatoe touched the decorations again, aiming for the soft red that would be more restful, but he went too far, deactivating the light paint. Muttering, "I just can't do anything right today," he moved his fingers higher in the dark, touching the upper level of the decorations, reactivating the paint to the level he wanted, the 'sleeping level,' which gave him dim spots of soothing red light; enough to see things that he already knew were there.

Over the noise of the wind banging the boats about, Hatoe could hear voices and the thudding heels of the other boatmen and women walking on the pier to their craft. Much as he didn't want to, he might as well go up top and face everyone. If he didn't, they'd be coming on board to make sure he was okay, which would be even harder to deal with.

He emptied his backpack, stowing his kit in his locker one step down from the table on the starboard side, the food in the narrow galley one step down from the table on the port side, took a deep drink from his thermos to buck himself up, picked up the tool kit to work on the spinner, and the decoy fuel cell, then stepped up from the galley to head back up on deck.

He was on the stairs when he felt the Dolph's stern dip under the weight of someone coming aboard. "Let it be Ben," he prayed.

They met under the dodger, Ben shaking the rain out of his black hair as he stood up under the shelter after ducking under the awning.

"Wonky spinner," Ben said by way of greeting.

Hatoe grunted acknowledgment, lifting the tool kit to show Ben. He clicked the old fuel cell into its slot as Ben thumped down the companionway. His brother's son, Benatoe Westimaru was growing into a seaman after Hatoe's own heart. Lean and wiry like Hatoe, the same crinkled, farsighted, dark eyes, the same instinctive feel for the ocean and her moods. And now it looked as if he was developing the same intimacy with the Laughing Dolphin. Ben even looked more like Hatoe than either of his own sons did.

The wharves had transformed in the time Hatoe had been down below. There was a fine, misty rain; the paths, all the ramps and all the piers were brightly lit; there was noise and activity on every pier; and several of the boats were outlined by brightly shining masts, railings, and portholes. Light reflected off the heaving water showing how active it was and making the nearby white-caps gleam.

The Harbour Master's hut was occupied, and the wall unit was blaring the marine forecast, "This is downgraded to your classic 'foul weather;' the winds're 25 to 30 knots with gusts up to 45 knots, showers with occasional heavy rain and squalls, and small craft warnings."

The largest craft in Matapihi, the Kaumoana, was still a huge, dark, unlit hulk, but her owner, Bram, and his family were standing on the pier talking to Hatoe's cousin, Sue, who moored at the harbour end of the pier, and the busy-body, Ted, who had no boat of his own, but was hired day to day by people like Bram and Sue who needed crew. "And now me," Hatoe thought bitterly, realising that now Nat was gone he was going to have to hire someone.

Spotting him, Sue turn to face him, her fair hair blowing wildly in the wind. "Hey, Hatoe, watch the wallie this morning?"

"Now what?"

"A kelpie's not back from going out yesterday in the Raukawa Moana."

Relieved to talk about something other than how he was, or where Nat was, Hatoe snorted. "The storm was right on top of them yesterday. What doze goes out in a light little boat in the middle of a storm like that?"

"Ah, that wasn't a real storm," Bram scoffed. "She only got up to about forty-five knots. You don't call it a storm until she hits forty-eight knots."

Hatoe gritted his teeth and tried to speak civilly. "It was stronger yesterday before it made its way up here, and they don't call Raukawa Moana 'the Washing Machine' for nothing,"

"They were a small craft," Sue pointed out. "Small craft warnings, remember."

"They live there. They should know how to deal with it," Bram shrugged.

"If they stay in every time there's a bit of a blow, they'll never make a living off kelp," Ted added, moving slightly to peer around Sue at Hatoe, his long nose gleaming white.

Hatoe ignored Ted, but he felt fed up with young Bram's smugness. The sight of the handsome young metal hunter with his big powerful craft, his broad muscular shoulders, his overgrown self-confidence, was irritating in itself, but seeing his pretty, slim, dark-eyed partner with their toddler on her hip and the bulge of a promise of another child brought home forcibly to Hatoe how full of hopes and dreams he and Annie had been when she was pretty and young with Nat on her hip and Kiri just a bump, in that very spot on the pier. He wanted to shout at Bram, "You won't always have everything your own way!" But he didn't say anything like that. Instead, irritably, he declared, "They live there. They should know better than to take chances with the roughest patch of water in these three thousand islands. You couldn't pay me to live there."

Ted chimed in, shifting his feet as he shifted his point of view, "Anyone dumb enough to go out on the Raukawa Moana when she's in a ship-eating mood is asking for what he gets."

Bram's partner, Hine, yelped, "Hold up a mo, Ted! The boat is <u>missing</u>. There's a crew missing. What about their families?"

Sue nodded, "It could happen to any of us!" She gestured behind her where the Kaumoana's bulk bobbed in the dark. "Even in that thing."

Bram protested in defence of his pride and joy, at the same time as Ted tried to say that the kelp farmer could be holed up somewhere, or might have gone out to sea out of reach of the storm, but Sue ignored them both, "Are you going out?" she demanded of Hatoe.

Hatoe held up his repair kit. "I'll fix the spinner first, and see what she's doing then."

Sue nodded. "Reckon I'll do repairs and maintenance for a bit, too," and loped off down the length of the pier.

Bram snickered. "Too rough for you?"

Hatoe knew Bram was goading him, but he could feel himself rising to the bait anyway. Forcing his voice into what he hoped was a nonchalant tone, he shrugged in an effort to look casual, and answered, "You know I like to keep her in tip top condition." He looked over at the dark hulk of the Kaumoana, as if implying that she might not be.

He knew his bait was taken when Bram retorted, "One wonky spinner is all it takes to keep you in?"

Hatoe started to climb up from the stern deck to the starboard walkway. "It's just time, that's all," he smiled, knowing he was irritating Bram as much as Bram had irritated him.

Bram ordered Ted, "Light her up and start setting up for a full day's work. I'll pull in a full crew. We don't have to stay in like these little weedies."

But as they turned towards the big metal hunter the little girl on Hine's hip erupted into ear piercing shrieks.

Ben came bounding up on deck to see what was wrong. He stood under the bimini watching Bram and Hine try in vain to calm Mere. Nothing either parent did would get that child to allow them to carry her on board the bucking boat, even after it was lit from stem to stern, the heavy davits decorated with coloured lights. She struggled and screamed, kicking, squirming and arching her back until her mother nearly dropped her. Only turning away from the Kaumoana settled her. Eventually Hine gave up and left the pier with her child.

"Good set of lungs on that one," Hatoe called to Bram. "She could get a job as a new tsunami siren." Then he sped to the bow, holding the safety harness in his hand until he got to the spot, then leaned over the side to work on the spinner before Bram could come up with a retort.

He felt better, remembering the maxim: 'you can't be depressed and irritated at the same time.' Yet Bram's comments rankled enough that he patted the Laughing Dolphin, caressing the smooth finish of the faux-wood fibreglass 'planking' of her bow, purring to her so softly not even Ben could hear him, "You're a little beauty. If only he knew half of what you've got, he'd laugh out of the other side of his face."

He had attached the safety harness to the safety line along the boat, and clipped the repair kit to the harness, intending to lean over the side and see what was wrong with the spinner. But the Laughing Dolphin wasn't only tossing up and down on the waves, she was also occasionally smacking her port side into the bumpers of the boat beside her, and her stern into the bumpers on the pier. One of those jolts threw Hatoe right off the deck to dangle headfirst down the side in the harness.

Ben arrived beside the safety harness in seconds. "Does it need replacing?" he asked, leaning down with his own safety harness holding him in place.

"Dunno yet." The angle Hatoe was on meant he saw Ben upside down. Even so, he could see that his nephew's usually good-natured expression was uneasy. Hatoe instantly felt ashamed of himself. He had no call to be taking his troubles out on Bram, and certainly not to be involving the innocent baby. He was angry with Nat, not with Bram. A sudden toss of the Dolph's bow ducked his head in the water. "I deserved that," he thought, shaking the harbour out of his eyes and winking up at Ben to show he was okay. "Never got a good look at it, what with Dolphy here washing my hair for me." He patted the bright designs on the side of the boat as he turned himself right-side up in the harness.

"She doesn't want you mucking with her spinners," Ben grinned.

"She needs her eyes repainted; she can't see what she's doing," Hatoe returned. He opened the protective frame over the spinner, then decided the best thing to do was remove the vane so that he didn't have to listen to the squeak, and seal off the aperture so that salty moisture couldn't get into the circuits and ruin them. The offending dolphin shaped, glittery vane was less than the width of his palm across, so he intended to tuck it into the tool kit and take it up with him, but it stuck on the spindle from being off-centre, so he couldn't slide it off smoothly. The moment he applied the least force it flew off. "Oh, for pity's sake," he complained as the vane vanished under the waves. Those brightly coloured, translucent ones had been chosen by Annie, who'd loved pretty things. Every time he lost something she'd picked out, it felt as if he lost a little bit more of her.

"Well, we need a new one now," Ben pointed out.

"Got one. We'll hook it up after she settles down."

The sound of a chant reached them over the noise of wind and waves. Hatoe started to haul himself up asking, "Who's going out?"

Ben reached over the rail to give him a hand. "Dunno."

"Ta." Hatoe was glad of Ben's youthful strength as he was hauled easily back to the deck.

They stood in the bow craning to see. The first boat out left from the pier to the north of them, light paint outlining masts and cabin, but also davits. "A fishing boat," Ben said, still straining to make out more detail through the mists.

"Yeah, but which one?"

"It's a bird's wing," Ben supplied, as he sorted out the details of the light paint on the sides of the hull, then triumphantly realised which bird wing he was seeing. "The Sea Hawk."

"Keisha," Hatoe said. "No surprise she gets away first."

Other chants broke out all over the four piers, calling invocations to Kiwa the god of the sea and Tangaroa the god of life in the sea, asking permission to take from the sea and asking for safety while they did so, as others with undamaged boats and full crews followed Keisha's lead.

"Skite!" Ben blurted out as Keisha started to raise a sliver of sail.

"She's never going to go under wind power in this!" Hatoe exclaimed in amazement.

Ben was saying something along those lines, but his voice faded away from Hatoe's mind as he watched the brightly lit outline of the little fishing boat whisked out of sight into the pre-dawn darkness. His spirit went with her, flown along like a bird on the wing across the Matapihi Harbour into the bigger Tauranga Harbour and along that to the mouth of the open ocean. He knew every millimetre. He longed to fly off like that, to get away, to leave and never come back. "Why can't I go?" his heart cried to him, straining in his chest, battering on his ribs to get out. "I can't," he thought to himself, turning to look up at the path to home. "I can't go home tonight. I can't face the house." The image of that yawning cavern of a house flashed across his mind's eye, in contrast with the openness of the deep blue. He turned back to stare into the misty rain and darkness towards open sea. So fixed was he on the images in his mind that he didn't notice the other boats chugging sensibly under motor power after the rash Keisha, their light gleaming off the white caps, and showing how their outlines and decorations laboured up and down the waves.

Ben's voice penetrated. Hatoe somehow knew he'd been saying something for a while that Hatoe hadn't heard.

"What?" he asked, trying to haul his mind back to the present.

"If we're not going out, I can see them off, then come back and get stuck into the work."

Hatoe looped the harness over his arm and wore it back to the stern. He knew Ben wanted to take part in the chants. He was about to let him go to do that; but made an impulsive decision instead. "Go below and make us some tea," he said. "I have to talk to you."

Ben's eyes widened in surprise, but he turned without a word and made his way along the narrow walkway to the stern, lifting his safety harness so the carabiner wouldn't catch on the lifeline along the boat.

Hatoe took one more look around, checking inside himself to be sure he'd made the right decision. "It's time," he said out loud, and followed Ben, unhooking his harness, and shutting the companion door behind him when he went into the galley.

The first thing Ben said was, "Where's Nat?"

Hatoe hauled himself along the bench on the starboard side of the table until he could lean his back against the wall and stretch his legs full length along the bench. "He buggered off, eh?"

Ben put the teapot into its holder in the middle if the table. "What do you mean, 'buggered off'?" He pulled the tea-cosy down over the pot, handed a mug to Hatoe, and put one for himself into the cup-holder on his side of the table, asking, "You mean, he took off? Where to?"

"He's tramping over the islands, eh? Busking."

Ben's jaw dropped so wide Hatoe thought he could hear it hit the table. "Y'wot?"

"He's 'not cut out to be a seaman.' His 'real calling' is music."

Ben crossed his legs up on the bench, tucking his feet comfortably up under his calves, his voice an astonished squeak, "Unc . . ."

Hatoe cut him short with a look. No one ever called the skipper, "Uncle." it wasn't done. The skipper was, "Skipper," regardless of the relationship. He had never called his father, "Dad," when he'd been crew to him, any more than he'd called his brother, "Bro," or his grandmother, "Nana."

Ben corrected himself and continued, "But, Skip, he's always been 'cut out' for the sea. When we were apprenticed to Bram, Bram was forever telling me, "Watch your cousin and do it like him, he's a natural." How can he say his real calling's music? He never studied music. Kiri studied music."

"Yeah, well, I said all that, didn't I? Fat lot of good it did me. What did you make?"

"Manuka tea. She's got to steep for a bit."

"Good oh." Hatoe reached behind his head to lower the light slightly. Ben had raised it from the low level Hatoe'd had it.

"When did Nat come up with this?" Ben asked, picking up the tea pot and rocking it to mix the steeping tea inside it.

"Dropped it on me when we got home last night, eh? We had a bit of a barney over it and he bailed." Hatoe took a deep breath. "Yeah, that's why I was so cranky with Bram this morning."

Ben nodded, pouring the tea. "I understand."

"Ta." Hatoe watched the hot stream of tea pouring into his mug, feeling wretched. "I should never have made a crack about the baby."

Ben grinned. "She does have a set of lungs on her, doesn't she? She's not scared, you know, she just hates being tethered."

Hatoe picked up his mug to sip his tea. "Nat hated being tethered, too. Kiri never cared, but he never got his sea-legs, either. Fished that kid out of the drink more often than I've pulled up the anchor."

"Hope when mine's born, he or she doesn't scream its head off when we try to take it on board."

"It'll be a boy, you know. Our family only has boys."

"Miki says there's always an exception to a rule."

"Better hope she's not too disappointed when she doesn't have a little girl. Look, Ben, our family has a secret."

Ben went still, his eyes fixed on Hatoe over the rim of his mug. "Something that stops us from having girls, eh?"

"What? No. Pay attention, this is important. Ever notice we do pretty well for weed collectors?"

Ben nodded.

"Ever wonder why that was?"

"Your parents taught you and Dad to manage really well."

"You've got to have the beads first before it matters sand how you manage them."

"We've got beads coming in aside from harvesting weed?"

"You could say that."

"How? I've taken the harvest into the processor myself. I've seen the total that we get and how we portion it out. I'd know if we got any extra."

"No, you wouldn't, Ben. It wouldn't be a secret if it was that easy to spot, eh?"

Ben watched Hatoe's eyes, saying nothing.

Hatoe took a deep quaff of his tea, put his mug in its holder on the side of the table, then looked Ben in the eye, telling him, "There's an island out in the deep blue. 10 days or more away. It's shaped like a metal claw peen hammer head. There's a sort of squarish part to the south like the sleeve that fits over the hammer handle. There're two wrecks there, way down deep; one on the corner of the southern coast, one on the east side. To the west there's the long, curved, claw part, which makes a beautiful big bay. There's a shipwreck there, right up on the beach. To the east there's a shorter, club-shaped part like the strike face of a hammer head. The north coast is a long sloping curve like the top part of the hammer. There's another shipwreck there on the rocks."

Ben's mouth was agape again. "You don't mean we've been hunting metal? In a weed collector?"

"Not exactly. We are descended from the last family to live on Rangitahua, the Bells, from my grandmother's side. We are also descended from the Ngāti Kurī from my grandfather's side. They had family stories about the Bells' life there and leaving because of an eruption, and the Ngāti Kurī erecting a pou whenua there. My grandparents decided when they were young that, because they had ties to Rangitahua from both ancestors that it was their duty to tend the pou whenua."

"They went out on the blue? How far?"

"Over a thousand kilometres to the northeast of Otou."

Ben nearly choked on his tea. "So far? What if we're not the only ones who survived the Big Freeze? What if there are others out there? What if they were followed? What if others bring back the violence that ended the last civilisation?"

"I wasn't born then, Ben. I had no say in it."

"No. Right you are. Have you ever been there?"

"Your Dad and I were both taken out when we were old enough to keep our mouths shut. I went out with Annie once, before the boys were born, but your Mum's never been told about it. You know what a worrier she is. She would have fretted herself to a froth if she'd known what we were doing, and she'd never have come with us. Your Dad and I decided we'd better wait until you kids grew up before we told any of you about it, and our Dad and Mum decided the same. You know what kind of nuisance it would be if anyone heard about it by mistake, or heard enough to figure it out. We don't get much metal when we go, and we sell it slowly over a long time so that there's never a big influx of funds. Just we've always got enough to take care of things, and we've always been that way for three generations now, so no one notices anything different. We've got the best quality equipment, and we keep it in tip top shape, but nothing flashy, nothing to attract attention, nothing to make you kids stand out from the other sea kids."

"There's been talk that our family must have found a wreck somewhere, but I never believed it. No wonder no one ever knew where we went. What's out there?"

"Islands, and some rocks in the ocean. Dunno why they're there. Looks like a joke Kiwa set up to weed out the ones that had a right to be out on His waters from the ones that didn't, because some of them are just under the surface so you can't see them. A good joke, too, judging from the pile of shipwrecks there. She gets pretty deep right by there as well, too deep to dive, so I reckon there's lots more we'll never see. Some of the wrecks have been down so long there's hardly anything left except the shapes in coral and anemones."

"Where do you reckon the wrecks came from?"

"Well, they've got to be from before the Bad Days, and before the Big Freeze, don't they?"

"You reckon it's true that huge ships used to cross the ocean like it was a lake?"

"When we get there, you'll see the size of those things, and you'll know it's not just myth."

Ben looked at Hatoe from the corners of his eyes. "They say before the Bad Days our ancestors flew in the air, too."

"Dunno 'bout that. 'They' say a lot of things. All I know is a lot of sailors lost their lives on those rocks. We show them proper respect when we pick up the metal they left for us."

"Too right! And we thank Kiwa, too, if his teeth don't bite us!"

"You betcha! And Tangaroa for letting us live to get it and get home with it!"

"When was the last time you went there?"

"We go every year or two or three. Got to keep the pou whenua tended to, and it shouldn't be left untended for more than five years at a time after the long time no one went there. It's only wood, you know. It'll rot away if no one takes care of it. We reckon it was untended for a hundred years through the Big Freeze and the recovery. If our family can do it, it won't be left like that again. Someone in your generation had to know, to take care of it, and you're the one."

"Me?!"

"Do you see anyone else here?"

"You want me to go over a thousand klicks out into the deep blue?"

"It's time. I can't do it by myself. We need three on board, minimum, to run shifts around the clock. Eight hours on, eight hours off, eight hours sleeping, in rotation. Do you think Miki would come with us?"

"I . . . er . . . no. She'll be busy with Hine and Bram's baby today. Either Hine will be there with her, or Hine will have convinced her to baby-sit Mere for the day, eh? Anyway, she's got such bad morning sickness she's staying away from the boats for now. You didn't really mean right away today, did you?"

"Yeah, I do."

"The storm?"

"The system's moving straight north, eh? It's going right past us. It's already clearing down in Otaki. It's going to settle down here, just you wait. Fourish the sky'll clear. Wind's slowing down now. Water'll settle by lunch."

Ben's voice cracked. "How long do you reckon we'd be away?"

Hatoe smiled reassuringly at him, remembering how stunned he and his brother had been when they'd been told. "Ten days to get there, a couple of days there, ten days to get back, depending on conditions. That's twenty-two days, minimum. Better to say we're sailing up the coast for a couple or three weeks to put everyone at ease. I'll file the real chart with my parents and your Dad, and put on enough food for three or four weeks at sea to give us leeway just in case. I'll file a coast trip to buy a new spinner from Tāmaki-makau-rau with the Harbour Master. You go, pack for a long trip, tell Miki you're going to be away to get the spinner, and see if you can hire Ray."

"Ray?"

"My Granddad had two sons, and they each had two sons, and we each had two sons, but I've got to hire someone outside the family. Something's gone wrong, somewhere. Yes, Ray. He's the one bloke who'll keep his mouth shut no matter what. If you can't get Ray, see if Sue wants to come. She wasn't going out today, anyway. She's a cousin of ours on my mother's side, so she's whanau. If you can't get either of them, we'll just stay in and do maintenance."

Ben blinked. "We're going to cut metal? How can we do that with weed cutters?"

"We've got metal cutters."

"Y'wot?"

"The Dolph's got her own secrets, eh?"

"I grew up on this thing! There's no way there's a single thing on or in this boat that we wouldn't have found as kids!"

"I know, my brother and cousins and I thought that way, too. It wouldn't still be a secret if kids could find it, would it?" Hatoe got to his feet. "Once we get out on the blue and no one can see me do it, I'll let you in on all of Dolphy's secrets. Rattle your dags, there. You've got to get to Ray before Bram does; he was pulling in a full crew today."

Ben jumped to his feet and ran up the companionway, saying, "Ray or Sue or no-one."

"Got it in one," Hatoe concurred, heading up himself.

* * *

When Ben got back, saying Ray would come with them, Hatoe sat down at the table. Ben sat at the other side of the table, his lean legs crossed lotus-style up on the bench with his bare feet up against his thighs.

"Here, now, you look," Hatoe told Ben, laying the tools out on the table. "I'm going to show you how to do the sols. This time I'm not having you just scrub her and go over the lines for signs of chafe, eh? And we're not going to collect seaweed, we're going on a real journey, so we need to give her a proper update. You've proved yourself to me, so you're going to learn how to check the power fittings."

Ben looked up in sudden intensity. Hatoe could see in Ben's eyes that he realised the amount of trust he was being shown, even if Ben didn't say anything. Many of the boatmen hired professionals to check electrics. It was such a delicate, painstaking task, that it required knowledge was outside the forté of most boaties.

"If you show a bent for this, I'll talk to your Dad about getting you some courses in electrics, what say?"

"Thanks, Skip. I know Dad'll go for it, eh? He thought it was a good idea before, but I couldn't see it."

Theirs was a seafaring family that had made a living from the ocean even back in the days before their isolation. Hatoe and his brother had studied electrics so that they could take care of their own solar panels and spinners, just as their father and grandfathers had. Hatoe's broad brown hands were gnarled and stiffened by a lifetime of hard work in cruel conditions, but they could do delicate work for him if he took his time with it

The mother of Hatoe's sons, Annie, had been a musician, not a seawoman. The older son was following in Annie's footsteps, now; the younger one didn't know what he wanted to do. As devastated as he had been when Annie had died, and as sad as he was that Nat and Kiri were not seamen, Hatoe had no regrets about partnering outside of the close-knit seafaring community.

As he looked at Ben's face, Hatoe realised he was thinking of Ben as his successor. His attitude towards his nephew had changed. He made a mental note to talk to his brother, Rota, about that, as he told Ben, "We're going to go over every sol and every spinner. See, I've got spares of the spinners and standard sols, but we better hope none of the odd shaped sols are cracked or corroded, because I have to order those special. Now, first you have to take the covers off the sols." Hatoe demonstrated to Ben what needed to be done. "You've got to not break the seal, eh? The sea corrodes the wires like nobody's business if they're not sealed right. Solar panels don't work worth a heap of sand if the wire starts to corrode, never mind the expense of new wire!"

*　*　*

As they worked they paid attention to the sounds of the boaties who were ready to leave calling invocations to Kiwa, the god of the sea, and Tangaroa, the god of life in the sea, asking permission to take from the sea and asking for safety while they did so. Then their concentration was broken by the sound of Bram's voice beginning the traditional chants right beside the Laughing Dolphin.

Hatoe took a big swallow of his tea at the first notes of Bram's chant, and set his mug down in its holder on the table, getting to his feet. He scooped everything back into the ditty bag, saying, "Come on, then, son. We'll see Bram off, then I'll watch you do this until you get the hang of it."

Hatoe and Ben stood up in the bow, their voices joining with Bram and the Kaumoana crew. Even in as big a boat as the Kaumoana, the electric motors made only a quiet hum, almost drowned out by the noise of her screws beating the water.

The Laughing Dolphin wasn't the only boat that stayed at the dock that day. The other sailors who'd decided not to go out mostly spent the morning tending to their boats, and were gone from the marina by afternoon.

Hatoe stayed all day, watching the sky as he and Ben gave his vessel a thorough going over. The closely fitted small solar panels were wired in parallel so that if one didn't work it didn't affect the others. It seemed as if everything except the one spinner was in good working order until Ben called, "Here, Skip. This one's cracked."

Leaving the spinner he was checking, Hatoe went to look at the solar panel Ben was indicating to him. "And you can bet Maui had something to do with that, too!" he muttered in disgust when he saw the spider's web of fine cracks across the surface of the glass. "It couldn't have been one of the standards, could it? It's got to be one of the odd ones that I have to order and wait for. Leave it in its place, if you take it out, it'll leave a gap. I'll have to look up its number to order a new one. We need the exact position it's in, then we look it up on the chart, and order it by the order number in that position on the chart. If we get it wrong, we order again and wait for it to come in again. It's easier when we can chart up here and re-check, but I'm not bringing the chart up in weather like this. If it blows away on us, we're sand. We can live without the sol until the order comes in. One cracked sol's not going to make any more difference than one wonky spinner."

They checked and double checked the position of the odd-shaped solar panel, then went down below so that Hatoe could show Ben how to order a replacement.

"I'm going to want you to go to town today," he told Ben. "Put the order in when you're there." The solar panels on the boats were made of a special glass that gleamed, but didn't shine brightly. The last thing anyone wanted was to be blinded by sunlight shining off glass into their eyes. Some of the boaties paid extra for their sols so that they could have colours other than the standard slate so that the vivid colours of their vivid boats would be continued in the sols that covered every surface possible.

Ben hadn't questioned Hatoe's decision not to go out to sea, even though the weather wasn't that bad, and showed no surprise at spending the day working on the boat even after everyone else who had done the same had gone home and the marina was deserted. He didn't even raise an eyebrow when they stopped for lunch when they could easily have walked home to eat. But when he saw the amount of food stuff being delivered, he finally spoke up. "Sure you ordered enough here, Skip?" he asked, with a grin, jumping up onto the dock and grabbing a package from the delivery guy.

"Need enough for three weeks. Need extra just in case. We have to check the water-maker, too." He took his eyes off the skies for only long enough to heft a package, then exclaimed with satisfaction when he looked overhead again, "Oh, now, there she is!"

It was a break in the clouds to the south, showing that the end of the weather system was approaching them. "Ben, I've made out a list of supplies for you to pick up in town that I couldn't get delivered. Check that the order for the sol went through, too, and see if Ray's ready, would you? If he didn't go out with Bram, that is."

"No, I didn't see him. Bram had his Mum and Dad and a couple of dailies, but I don't think Ray was one of the dailies, unless he showed up while we were down below, and wasn't on deck when they left. Ray told me he'd be willing to come with us."

"Ray's not always the most reliable guy. We can still get Sue if Ray's changed his mind."

"What about Ted? He didn't go out today."

"No, not Ted. It's got to be someone who can keep his mouth shut, as well as knowing what he's doing. Or what she's doing, in the case of Sue."

Ben set the last package of groceries on the deck. "You're never going out agin the tide!"

Hatoe shrugged. "Only way to ride on the tails of this one." His sweeping gesture took in the whole sky.

Ben stood beside Hatoe, looking up at the sky, doubtfully. "Everyone else stayed close in today," Ben stated, noncommittally.

Hatoe grunted, moving the groceries down the companionway.

"Are you going to take her south, away from that?"

Hatoe indicated the strip of light that was strengthening into shafts of sunshine beaming down from the dark clouds south of them. "Nah," he shrugged. "That's breaking up. We're going to catch the trailing edge of the wind and use it to speed us up."

Ben could 'see' the water as well as Hatoe could. He knew how to see the minute differences in colour and intensity that meant deeper water, or shallower water, or ocean eddies, or something looming under the surface. However, he was learning how to read the sky. He peered around the sky from south to north and east to west. "You're out of your mind, you know that?"

"You don't have to come."

"Just try and stop me!" Ben loped off towards the town, tucking the list into his pocket.

Hatoe took the groceries below one by one, and stowed them, talking to his boat. "Can you handle a run on the tail winds, my beauty? We'll take a heavy ballast; give you a bit of weight. That should do it, eh?"

Everything's a trade-off, he thought. A light fibreglass boat like the Dolph could go like stink, but had no substance. A heavy vessel like the Kaumoana could take the open ocean better and was built to collect metal, but was as slow as a wet week. He'd never get all the way there in ten days or less on the Kaumoana, even if it would be a bonus to have her davits and metal cutting machinery. Besides, the Laughing Dolphin was rigged as a sloop and could be run twenty-four hours a day with a crew of three. If he wanted to work with something like Bram's boat, he would need more crew, and that would mean more expense and more complication. He decided he was happiest with his light, fast thirteen metre sailing trawler. He had, after all, purchased the very latest, most powerful solar panels and wind collectors to keep the batteries charged so that he had engine power as well as sail, and his electric motor was capable of more power than Bram had in his twenty-metre schooner.

Everything was as ready as he could get it when Ben returned with Ray and the rest of the provisions. "Ah, good-oh, mate!" Hatoe greeted Ray, pleased. "You could make it!"

"Sue's over at Hine's helping her get ready for the baby," Ben told him.

Hatoe started the motor before the men were on board. It made very little sound, just a faint whine that soon settled into a soft hum that was almost drowned out by the screws frothing the water. Ben set the bags of provisions down on the dock, jumping aboard and turning to Ray. Ray dropped his gear to the dock so that he could give the bags of provisions one at a time to Ben, then scooped his gear up and tossed it onto to the deck and went to cast off. Once he'd lobbed the last mooring line to the deck, Ray jumped aboard.

As Hatoe eased the Dolph gently away from the pier, his crew stowed the lines neatly, then they all chanted the traditional invocations to Kiwa and to Tongaroa before Ben and Ray carried the food and gear down below. They hardly spoke, working smoothly together from force of habit.

It was a bit bumpy, going out of the narrow mouth against the tide. Foam splashed right up over them once or twice. Hatoe kept the speed, taking it gently, keeping towards the rocks at the base of Mauao, the loan mountain, to keep away from the sand bank, Ruahine, between the Laughing Dolphin and Matakana Island. When he was sure they were safely past Ruahine, he called to his crew to bring a piece of food up on deck. Ray reached up the steps, handing Hatoe a bag of taro crisps. Hatoe opened the bag and threw a handful of crisps towards Kuia Rock at the base of Mauao to show respect for the power of the sea, gratitude for safe passage through the rocks between Matakana and Mauao and past Ruahine, and hope for a safe return. Then he set a heading northeast.

When they left the sheltered harbour waters of Tauranga Moana, the wind buffeted them and an easterly swell made the boat roll. Settling into the rhythm of the ocean, feeling the movement of the water, Hatoe called to his crew, "You fellows flip a bead to see who takes first kip, and then make us some kai."

When they worked for more than one day at sea, they slept in shifts so at any stretch of the 24 hours one was asleep and two were awake. Once the bead had been tossed and it was Ben who was going to sleep first, he made their evening meal because he would be sleeping when it was time for the midnight shift to eat, so the midnight meal would be Ray's responsibility. They shared the cooking chores evenly.

Freed for the moment, Ray went up on deck and stood beside Hatoe. "Where are we going, Skip?"

"My secret spot."

Ray looked at the heading. "Is it northeast of here, or are you laying a false trail so no one can follow you and find out where it is?"

Hatoe laughed. "I like the way you think, son." Despite the fact that Ray was older than Ben, a partnered man with a family, they were both still youngsters to Hatoe. "Nah, I reckon no one's going to follow us today. They all stayed close to or didn't go out at all. If anyone sees us, they'll be heading home, and they won't have the provisions to follow us the whole way, even if someone did take it into his head to try it. Who knows it's worthwhile to follow me, eh?"

"There's been talk that you have found a wreck somewhere. Ben said we'd be out a fortnight or even three weeks."

"Like as not. Ten or so days to get there, depending on how she goes, a couple there, and ten or so to get home."

"Tangaroa in the sea! Where are we going? There's nothing on this heading once we've gone past Tuhua Island."

Just as he'd told Ben, Hatoe said, "1,600 klicks, give or take, there are some rocks in the ocean. Dunno why they're there. Looks like a joke Kiwa set up to weed out the ones that had a right to be out on his waters from the ones that didn't, because some of the rocks are just under the surface so you can't see them. A good joke, too, judging from the pile of shipwrecks there. And you know how deep the ocean gets, way too deep to dive, so I reckon there's lots more we'll never see. Some of the wrecks have been down so long there's hardly anything left except the shapes in coral and anemones."

"Metal?" Ray breathed in awe.

"Lots of it, and some good stuff. I wanted you for the third man because I reckon we can trust you to keep it to yourself."

"Too right, mate! You've got my word on it," Ray promised fervently. He exclaimed as they shook hands on it, "Rangi in the sky! <u>This</u> is how you've done it all these years?"

"Now you know."

"I'm the only one outside your family who knows?"

"Only one ever. Only ever sailed out with my brother or my parents until my brother got scleroderma, and now my parents are a bit past it I figured I'd better find someone we could trust."

Ray was speechless for a moment. Hatoe was afraid he was going to ask about his partner, who had died, or his brother's partner, who was terrified of the isolation of the trip, but Ray asked quietly, "Where do you reckon the wrecks came from?"

"Well, they've got to be from before the Bad Days, and before the Big Freeze, don't they?"

"You reckon it's true that huge ships used to cross the ocean like it was a lake?"

"When we get there, you'll see the size of those things, and you'll know it's not just myth that the iron ships were bigger than the biggest interisland ferry."

Ray looked at Hatoe from the corners of his eyes, but he didn't say another word.

Hatoe kept his eyes on the surface of the ocean as they talked. He watched the white caps that showed where the wind was strong and headed for the ruffled water that had no caps, where the wind was lighter. The boat was still rolling slightly in the swell as he worked her towards the trailing edge of the weather system.

They could feel it the moment he found what he was looking for. The Laughing Dolphin came alive as the right wind caught her. Ray leaped towards the lines, and Ben dashed up from the galley. Without a word from Hatoe, they both knew from the feel of the boat that the sails should be raised. Quickly and smoothly, they pulled on the halyards, sending the mainsail up the mast, where it filled with wind at once. Hatoe shut the screw off, letting the sail take over. As they trimmed the sail to take them the way he wanted to go, he decided that the jib sail could also go up.

He tested the feel of the boat, with both sails up, reset his course, then told the crew, "She can take over now."

They set the wind vane up, Ben getting the part out and taking it to Hatoe, who told Ben to set it up, and stood ready to adjust the sails to Ben's instructions. When it was adjusted just right, she seemed to lift so that she planed across the blue water like a bird coasting on the air currents. "Oh, you little beauty," Hatoe purred at her. As if she could hear him, the Dolph picked up even more speed and they were off and running before the wind.

As was traditional, the sails bore the swirling motifs that told of Hatoe's family. The sails were red, the motifs were black, the same motifs that were in red on the white sides of the boat. Some boaties had the same motifs that were on their boats chiselled into their faces, where they were known as 'moko'. Not everyone could wear a moko, which was a spiritual declaration as well as a family record and identification.

Nearly all the boaties had their motifs tattooed on their shoulders if they did not have a moko on their faces, so that they could be positively identified if anything terrible happened at sea. When the tattoos were not considered moko, they were known as kirituhi, 'skin art'. The motifs on the Laughing Dolphin told anyone finding the boat that she was a part of Hatoe's family, just as the moko on Hatoe's shoulders told who he was.

The time came for Ray to take the helmsman's position so that Hatoe could have a break and eat his meal. The day had never been very warm, and now, in the evening there was a definite chill in the air, so Ray was wearing a heavy pullover and a windbreaker. Bringing himself out of his reverie with difficulty, Hatoe asked, "What did you make for kai?"

"Got to use all the fresh fruit and veges first, eh? Ben did some mushies with onions and kumara in his secret sauce. Filling and hot. Salad with pretty near everything in it but the kitchen sink, and fruit for pudding."

Ray turned his attention to the boat. "Boy, Skipper, she's got blood in her nose, hasn't she?" His eyes widened in awe at the speed they were making. It was a local sailor's term, referring to the burst of speed a shark could produce when it smelled blood.

Hatoe grinned and nodded, showing Ray the current that was helping them. Even in the fading light Ray could make out the difference in the surface of the water caused by the interaction between the water of the eddy going in one direction and the rest of the sea going in other directions.

Hatoe liked to run his shifts from nine at night to five in the morning, five a.m. to one in the afternoon, and one p.m. to nine at night, so Ben had time to relax that evening between eating his meal at six and going to bed at nine. The meals were at 6 a.m., 12 noon, 6 p.m., and 12 midnight. While Hatoe ate, Ben cleaned up the galley, then came and sat back at the table in his usual lotus position. The two of them talked quietly while Ray was up on watch, Hatoe explaining to Ben that he wanted him to know where the metal was so that he could continue to harvest it after Hatoe was gone, "Because you know, don't you, that neither Nat nor Kiri will ever take to this life."

Ben's eyes opened wide. Normally when they were on the Dolph Hatoe was 'Skip' to Ben, but at that moment he said, "Uncle Hatoe, what if your sons come on later?"

Hatoe shrugged. "If one of them does come to it later it won't hurt for both of you to know about it. If not, at least you know, eh?"

"Isn't it their heritage? Shouldn't you have them along?"

"It wouldn't be safe to make a trip like this with either of those two landlubbers. Everyone on board's got to have good instincts and full strength to make a trip like this. Even if your mother hadn't made old Rota promise not to come again, he couldn't anyhow with that scleroderma doing his hands in."

When he finished eating, Hatoe put on warmer clothes, then went back up on deck, telling Ray, "I'll take the first shift tonight." A normal shift at the helm was two hours, so that they were fully alert when everyone's safety depended on them. No one on Hatoe's boat got straight out of bed and on the helm but had an hour or two to wake up first, so some shifts were three hours to adjust the times around people getting up and going to bed. Except in emergencies, he wouldn't allow anyone on the helm for more than three hours. Hatoe was one of the more popular skippers among the sailors who didn't have their own boats, the 'dailies', because of the way he spread the workload.

Ray went back down below. He and Ben played cards for a bit, then Ben took out his guitar and Ray took out his harmonica, and the two whiled away the evening playing music until Ray took his helm shift and Ben tumbled into the hammock. There was only one hammock. If they needed more sleeping space, they used the padded benches that they sat on for meals. With the table winched down and padding put on it, the eating area became a sleeping space the size of a double bed.

At dawn the conditions were little different from the previous evening. Ray slept from five am until one in the afternoon, when Hatoe was only too pleased to sack out. Hatoe was surprised to find the wind had stayed with them, he'd expected to outrun it during the night. "So long as the storm doesn't come with it, we've got no worries," he said, accepting his good fortune complacently.

With nothing to do other than relax and wait for hundreds of kilometres of ocean to pass beneath them, their mealtimes took on great significance. They planned each meal with minute detail, arguing over what they wanted and how it ought to be prepared, each man fussing over the preparation when it was his turn to cook, and indulging in extensive post-mortems after the meals were eaten.

In their time off-duty they gave themselves over to pure laziness. The ocean was that lovely deep blue colour that told of clarity and cleanliness. The wind held through to the second day, so they didn't turn the motor on, but glided along in a silence broken only by the occasional slap of the water, or creak of the rigging. Never a talkative bunch at the best of times, under those circumstances the sound of a voice was almost startling, so they spoke even less, and then quietly.

The sea became almost glassy as the wind eased off in the afternoon, the light breeze making only shallow ripples on its surface. They took down the genoa and stowed it and raised the spinnaker. Without the sound of the wind in the sails the quiet became huge. They couldn't even see or hear any gulls anymore. They could look over the side in between their two-hour stints at the helm and get a good view of the lives being lived below them. Mostly they saw jellyfish and salps, but sometimes fish or squid. The squid, especially, seemed to enjoy the small bow wave, and sometimes propelled themselves out of the water. Dolphins, too, escorted the boat, playing in the bow wave and entertaining the men.

They tried their hand at fishing, celebrating when they got one, and planning in detail how they'd prepare it for the evening meal.

As Hatoe slept, Ben and Ray saw flying fish launch themselves into their short flights, and counted how long they were in their air, estimating that the longest flight was twelve seconds. After that they saw the big dorsal fins of sunfish flopping lazily about. It was late in the afternoon, when they were having their tea up on deck, that Ray called excitedly, "Ben! Marlin!"

Checking the wind vane to make sure he could leave it for a moment, Ben leaned on the transom with Ray to watch the beautiful fish until it sped away from them out of sight. "Look at the size of that thing. I bet it weighs more than a ton," Ben guessed.

The sound of the sail luffing brought them both at the run. It took only a minute adjustment for the sails to be taut again, and the little boat sailing true and quiet. The two men held their breath waiting to hear a roar from Hatoe, then grinned at each other like mischievous children when the lack of reaction told them they'd got away with it.

"Must've been too tired to hear it," Ben supposed.

"Close, though. You'd be in the lee scuppers for a week," Ray grinned.

The next morning greeted them with continuing fine weather. The wind was at 10 knots and had shifted to the east, so they weren't running before it, but they were still making good time, even if it was nothing like the speed they'd had at first. There was even less to see or to do that day. Hatoe saw some mahi mahi after breakfast, but they didn't stay long enough to be caught and were out of sight in a short time, ending that little diversion before it had provided any more than a momentary distraction. Ben told Hatoe, "This gives me a new appreciation of just how much ocean there really is. You don't feel how massive it is when you're within a day of land all the time. Being out here, knowing you could sail for weeks and never see land, is different from just hearing about it."

Hatoe winked at him. "We haven't gone anywhere yet. Think about our ancestors crossing this for weeks. Think about diving down as much distance straight down as we can see straight ahead and still not being at the bottom. It's a lot of water."

"When do you reckon we'll get there?"

'Tomorrow night, if all goes well, knock wood."

They both knocked on the wood of the wheel.

It was during the night, on Hatoe's shift, that the wind picked up out of the west. Ben was sleeping, Ray was in the galley making the midnight meal for himself and Hatoe. Ray came up on deck with hot soup in a covered mug and put the mug in a holder built behind the wheel, then worked the halyards to reset the sails. "I take it you won't want to go below and eat when she's freshening like this."

"Thanks. It's more than just freshening. Look at the bloody stars."

Ray searched the sky. He knew at once what Hatoe was grousing about. There were patches of sky southwest of them where there were no stars. "Bit of black," he commented as he took over the helm.

"Nah - yeah, and look where it is, too." Hatoe stood looking up at the sails in the moonlight. He adjusted the halyards slightly so that the sails moved a little, and the boat increased speed.

"You reckon that's the same storm?" Ray watched the sails, adjusting the helm to take advantage of Hatoe's adjustments.

"Don't care one way or another. Clouds are coming our way and the wind's picking up. We've got another day to go to get to shelter, and two days to go back to shelter, and guess where the shelter behind us is?"

"Right through that."

"Got it in one."

"These rocks we're going to. They can shelter us?"

"Aside from the ship-eating rocks, there're thirteen islands with vegetation on them, but only one's got reliable fresh water on it, so we'd be best to make straight for it if we can."

"Want me to put her under the screw?"

"Not just yet. We're likely going faster under sail at the moment. I'll wait and see if it turns into anything. Might just be a bit cloudy with nothing to worry about. Keep a sharp eye on the water from now on. Out here I don't want to risk racing across anything I can't see if I don't have to. Last thing I want to do is prang her so far from help."

At the end of his helm shift Ray quietly went down below and put on his survival suit. He didn't do it all up and seal it, but he put it on, including his ship shoes. Hatoe didn't say a word. The next day, at one o'clock in the afternoon, Ray got up and hunched sleepily over a dish of Hatoe's cooking, turning what had been lunch for the other two into breakfast for himself. As he did every spare moment he had, he fiddled with the radio to try to get a signal.

* * *

It was past four o'clock in the morning, just after Hatoe had taken the helm back, and Ray had gone down below to use the head, when there was a mighty crack across the sea, as if a huge log had been thrown hard into water. Ben and Ray both bounced up onto the deck with, "What?! What?! What happened?"

"That'd be a big whale beating its flukes on the water close by," Hatoe told them, not letting on that he'd pretty nearly been airborne himself. "They like to do that at night out here."

In the dark before dawn, they could see no sign of whales.

"Ah, well, I won't get back to sleep now," Ben sighed, rubbing the back of his neck. "Anyone want a cuppa?"

"Yeah, righto, mate. Ta." Hatoe accepted the offer.

By first light they could see the whales off the port stern. The wind was coming at twenty-two knots off the port quarter, with occasional gusts up to thirty knots. The chop was picking up, but they were making good time again. It meant looking right into the wind to watch the whales, which made their eyes tear up so that it was hard to see them, but they couldn't resist.

They did see one smash the water surface with a massive fluke, making a startling crash, but that seemed to be a night-time activity to be stopped once there was no-one left to wake up.

Then another one surfaced only about 5 metres from the Laughing Dolphin. The loudness of its blow was astounding so close to them. It was more than twice the length of the boat. Ben's exclamation of "Love a duck!" from the sudden noise turned into "Cor!" as they all turned away, ducking down, putting their hands over their faces, from the overwhelming fish-oil stench of whale breath, which the wind generously brought right to them.

The wash from the whale surfacing and diving rocked the Laughing Dolphin so much that Hatoe called, "Furl!" Ben and Ray leaped into action, hauling the sails down as Hatoe started up the motor. "Last thing we want is one of those boys any closer than that!" he exclaimed, getting all the speed he could out of the little boat.

Sure enough, Ray claimed to see one surface right where they had been. "What would have happened if we'd still been there?" he wondered.

"We would have had a _really_ close look at it," Hatoe told him.

Ray was heading for the hammock when Ben called, "Look, look!" A whale came vertically up out of the water with such force that daylight showed under its tail before it fell over and crashed back making a stupendous splash.

Hatoe patted the wheel, "Come on sweetheart," he urged the boat as the wake from the whale jump rocked them. "Wee ones can't be in the same pool when the big boys play rough."

The bow was slapping on the chop as they sped away, so as soon as the whales were a safe distance behind them, Hatoe eased up. They set the sails again, because they actually made more speed under sail in the brisk wind. Hatoe had used the motor so that he could be sure to stay on a straight course away from the whales, and not be affected if the wind changed direction or slacked off.

Ray took his turn in the hammock, Ben had his morning ablutions and made breakfast. He took it up on deck to eat with Hatoe instead of taking turns down below. "Want to hand her over early?" he asked.

"Port bow," Hatoe said instead of answering.

Ben looked. A school of porpoises was racing towards them. Impatient to be near the boat, they were coming at tremendous speed with huge jumps with ten or twenty in the air at the same time. "What a sight!" Ben exclaimed.

"Now it's light enough that we'll be able to see any whales or rocks in the way. I want to make all the speed we can to outrun that fellow," Hatoe said, gesturing at the cloud bank on the horizon behind them.

"It doesn't look as if it's coming this way," Ben mused. "Think it's any closer than it was when I got up?"

"Hope not."

After they'd eaten Ben took his two hours at the helm while Hatoe sat at the table down below and brought his log up to date. Before he went back up on deck, he put his survival suit on. He didn't do it up because the lining in it would have made it too hot, and he put his ship shoes in his pocket, but it was faster to do it up after he was already wearing it than it would have been to get it and put it on, then do it up. He noticed Ray was sleeping in his, footwear and all, as he went up on deck.

When Hatoe took the helm back, Ben put his suit back on without a word about it, leaving his feet bare. He asked, eyeing the sky when he rejoined Hatoe, "Reckon we'll out-run it?"

"Might. We can't get much shelter from Tapu Tapuatea. She's not really an island; she's a rock sticking straight up about 70 metres. She's only about 250 metres across, which doesn't give much in the way of shelter in a storm: no beach, no mooring, no bay, no anchorage, real deep water, and the teeth of Kiwa hiding just under the surface all around. That's no place for us in rough weather. If we can do it, I want to carry on to the islands. We should reach them by morning."

They were still under blue sky, the clouds staying astern of them, but the wind was not easing off. "Don't think the winds were sustained like this in the system before we left, were they?" Ben asked.

"Either she's a different storm, or she's picked up steam over the water."

"Nice," Ben said in a flat, disgusted tone.

"Yeah."

"Anyone know where we are?"

"I left the course in my desk."

"Not with the harbour master?"

"Don't want nosy old Bert to know where I go. The family needs to know if they get worried, but no one else. Your Dad and your grandparents have been out here a few times, they'd know exactly where we're going if they saw the course."

Ben stared out at the porpoises playing in the bow wave. "That's why you didn't say much to Bram the morning before we left."

"That's right. I was thinking if the Dolph was in good enough shape to do the trip, and if the weather cleared at the right time, and if we could get the right person to come with us, that I might give it a go. I didn't want Bram or anyone else to think I might be up to anything other than a quiet day in dock."

In a low, level voice, Ben asked, "What are the chances anyone could find us out here?"

Hatoe answered equally quietly, "What do you think?"

"Great." Ben's voice was still flat.

"Yeah."

Ben turned to face Hatoe, and leaned on the gunwale with studied nonchalance, stretching his legs straight out in front of him. "How'd you know about it, then?"

"From family stories."

"I don't remember anyone talking about this."

"We don't talk about it. Too much chance youngsters will let something slip without meaning to. I grew up with the same stories you did, about an ancestral family of ours by the name of Bell who tried to settle on an island in the middle of the ocean about three or four hundred years ago. They must have lived there for something like forty years, but they got chased off by volcanic eruptions."

"That's out here? I always thought that was an offshore island, like Whakaari or something."

Hatoe laughed. "That makes sense you know. Whakaari is erupting all the time, and she did kill everyone who ever tried to live there. Even Tuhua has a reputation for that, and the whole island was tapu because of it for a long time. But our ancestors weren't all killed by the volcano, or we wouldn't be here now, would we?"

"I s'pose not." Ben shifted to sit on the lockers that lined the entire stern deck.

"No, it wasn't an offshore island, it was a deep-sea island."

Ben stared around them, "One family all alone way out here?"

"It wouldn't be my first choice," Hatoe admitted.

"How did you know where to look?"

"My grandfather got a feeling from another story that Bell's Island might be a long way away. Do you remember learning about the great ocean-going canoe, Kurahaupo, that brought some of the first ancestors about a thousand years ago? Its seams opened, and it took on water, so they took it ashore on an island called Rangitahua in the middle of the ocean. Many of the settlers from the Kurahaupo were taken by the Aotea to Aotearoa, but some stayed on Rangitahua to repair the Kurahaupo. When it was sea-worthy, they headed west accompanied by the Ririno. Do you remember learning about that?"

"I think so. Wasn't the Ririno lost with all cargo and most of the settlers?"

Hatoe was pleased. "You do remember! It was wrecked on a reef in the ocean. When my grandfather was a youngster, younger than you, he wondered if Rangitahua and Bell's Island might be the same island."

"What would make him think that?"

"Well, I started wondering how many islands there were all by themselves in the middle of the ocean. They couldn't have been part of an island chain, or the Bells would have gone to a nearby island to wait until the volcano settled down. The only reason he could think of for them to abandon the home they'd worked so hard for so long to make was that they had no choice – nowhere else to go. And to him it was obvious the Kurahaupo was beached a long way from other land. Even if they had been two days from an inhabited island, they would've picked up a work crew and taken them to fix the canoe, wouldn't they?"

Ben thought about it. "One reason for staying there like that could be that it was too far to go anywhere else and back."

Hatoe nodded. "Then, when they did leave, they sailed into the setting sun for days and came across a rock reef in the middle of the ocean. What are rocks doing sticking up in a place like this where the sea floor is thousands of kilometres below? Never mind with a current strong enough to pull one of those mighty ocean-going wakas to its death."

"I still don't see what made him think they were the same island."

"It was the thought of how unlikely it would be for two habitable islands to be so isolated in the same general area. The Bells were ten days north-east of Aotearoa, the Kurahaupo sailed into the setting sun for four days to get to Aotearoa – that would be west. It seemed unlikely that they were two different places. If they were the same, he figured he'd find records or stories of a big volcano alone in the ocean to the northeast, with strong currents around it and rock reefs lurking just below the surface. It also had to be fertile enough that one family could survive for years by themselves, though volcanic soil is like that. He didn't think it was possible to find it, to be honest with you. When he found ancient sea charts of a volcanic island chain way out here with only one inhabitable island and rocky shoals all around it, he was so excited he didn't know what to do with himself."

"How did all of you keep it secret?"

"That's where luck comes into it. He thought no one would believe him, so he told no one but his Dad."

"And they came all this way?"

"No, not then. He was sworn to secrecy and made to promise not to come out here by himself looking for it. Everyone knows that the survivors in the rest of the world will find us one day. Maybe not in my lifetime or yours, but some day people will sail over the ocean again, and they'll find us, and then our isolation will be destroyed. Just because it's inevitable doesn't mean we have to make it happen. Aside from the fact that the Dolph is not a blue water boat, my grandfather's Dad didn't want him to sail so far out in case there was someone out here who saw him and followed him back. I know some people think no one else survived the Freeze, but you never know, eh?"

Ben was quiet for a while, looking all around the great expanse of ocean that stretched to the horizon on every side. He glanced at the clouds to make sure they weren't any closer. Diffidently, he asked, "Did you come out here without Granddad's permission?"

"Nah." Hatoe chuckled. "I might have been a hothead and full of damned-fool ideas, but I wasn't as bad as all that. No, Dad changed his father's mind after he read about the shipwrecks out here. The Dolph might not be equipped to hunt metal, but if there was any here that no one knew about, then Dad figured it was ours by heritage as much as by discovery rights, because we descend from the settlers who were on the Kurahaupo as well as from the Bells. Dad had the Dolph built to his specifications and sailed her out here."

"So, the Dolph was built for this?"

"Yep."

"And he did find something, didn't he?"

"We certainly did! Shipwrecks with brass screws."

"Cor." Ben was speechless.

Hatoe winked. "The most value we could have found per kilo. No need to try to haul huge chunks of iron in a little weed-boat. No need to try to cut huge chunks off wrecks without metal hunter's tools, either. All we had to do was cut a small piece off and take it home. We didn't say a word to a soul. They bought a metal cutting blade from that first little piece they had cut with hard work, a lot of sweat, and ruined all the hacksaw blades. The blade we bought is powered by the fuel cell, and it paid for the really good fuel cell I've got now. It goes through the brass like cutting paper. Come to think of it, that blade has bought us the refitting of the Dolph, the really good spinners and sols we have, and just about everything else we've got that weed farmers usually can't afford. It was another time they came out here, after they'd bought the metal cutting blade, that they took a big chunk back and showed it to my Mum."

"What did she say?" Ben sat forward, leaning his elbows on his knees.

Hatoe was quiet for a moment, reflecting. It had been many years ago. He'd been nineteen and his brother, who was now Ben's father, had been seventeen. Their parents still had black hair, and no one could have foreseen that Hatoe would get a beautiful partner who would die so young, nor that his big, strong, younger brother would end up behind a desk, kept from sailing by scleroderma.

His parents had continued to harvest seaweed into their seventies, but as they drew closer to their eighties they were starting to slow down. That was another reason he'd grabbed at the chance to go to Rangitahua that day: neither of his parents were on the Laughing Dolphin, but Ben was. As dangerous as the trip was, strong young people had a better chance of surviving a mishap than an elderly couple did.

"We didn't tell Mum how far we were sailing." he admitted with a penitent grin. "She was pleased we'd found a wreck we were sure no one else would ever find. She isn't a suspicious soul, your grandmother. It wasn't until she wanted to come with us, and we kept ducking the issue that she started to wonder. When she found out we were bringing a little coastal weed boat out over the blue she about had a bird. But, you know, by that time we'd made the trip a lot of times, and we'd survived it enough times to convince her we were being careful, and she was benefiting from the extra income we were bringing in. She insisted on coming with us, and after that she made us promise to only come out here when the conditions were top notch, and then only with the best crew. No one who wasn't fully adult and licenced."

"Nan didn't make you promise not to come out here?"

"No. Only your mother did that. Your Nana came with us a few times. She made the rules. Don't take any unnecessary chances; never take the whole family at the same time; always take more supplies than you think you'll need; check the whole boat stem to stern and don't go unless she's in perfect condition."

"You put in a new spinner, but we've still got a cracked solar panel."

Hatoe shrugged, "Well, I had the spinner and not the sol, didn't I? I know she's not a hundred percent, if you want to get picky about it, but you know as well as I do that just one sol isn't going to affect anything. If that weather catches up with us, we'll have more than one cracked sol to worry about."

"Yeah."

They both turned and looked at the horizon.

"It's closer," Ben said.

"Yeah."

"The worst part is waiting, watching it, not knowing what it's going to do," Ben complained, getting up and walking over to Hatoe.

"You'd better hope it keeps us waiting for a while yet," Hatoe suggested, dryly, checking the time and seeing that it was time for Ben to be the helmsman for two hours. He stepped away, adding, "Like another day or even two," as he thumped down the companionway to make their midday meal.

Hatoe took the lunch to Ben the way Ben had taken breakfast to him. "Thanks, Skip. I've been wondering; we can't dive down and get brass out of the water in a storm, can we?"

"Not likely. Don't worry, there's all sorts of stuff on land, too. We leave the land pickings for times like this. They had all sorts of things that have lasted 250 years. There're big stainless-steel slabs that we don't even have to cut. They had some kind of room made of it."

Ben stared. "A room made out of stainless-steel? Why? Who would use a metal for building at all, never mind one so valuable?"

"Don't forget the rest of the world could get metal more easily than we can. Presumably if there's anyone still alive there, they still can. We never did have veins of iron ores to dig up like they did, so we always had to get most of our metal from them, so it makes sense that we value it differently from them."

"But to make rooms with it!"

"Judging from the racks in them, it's my guess that they were walk-in fridges, or a fridge and a freezer, made from metal instead of ceramics. Except for being metal they look exactly like our fridges and freezers do."

"Made out of metal?"

"Stainless steel."

"Even given that they had lots of metal, that still doesn't make any sense. How could they insulate it?"

"I don't know, Ben, I'm a seaweed farmer, not a scientist or an archaeologist. I'll show them to you when we get there, and you tell me."

"Do you think our ancestors made those?"

"No. They were long gone by the time anything we'll find was taken there. It seems there were scientists there when the Bad Days happened. It makes sense that they would have had a big fridge and a freezer to keep their supplies fresh. I wondered what happened to them, so I hunted it up. Seems thirteen people were rescued from what they used to call 'The Kermadecs.'

Hatoe thumped down the companionway and into the galley. As Hatoe dumped ti-tree leaves in the teapot to make a fresh pot of tea, Ray woke up and gestured vaguely at the swinging hammock he was in and asked, "Pretty brisk?"

"Not easing up," Hatoe told him.

"We can't get anything but static now," Ray's voice was tinged with distress.

Hatoe shrugged.

"But we never even found out if they found the missing boat."

"We'll find out when we get home."

"But if we can't get anything, that means no one can hear us if we need help."

"Been out here lots of times and never needed help before. Grab your brekkie and bring it up. I want to talk to the two of you before I get my kip."

They took the tea and Ray's breakfast up on deck. The wind was making the Laughing Dolphin creak. The clouds were definitely closer. No one mentioned them, but they all looked, periodically.

"Now, listen," Hatoe said, pitching his voice to carry in the wind. The three men stood closely together so that they could hear. "We should reach the first rocks before I get up. Tapu Tapuatea should be on the horizon off the starboard bow in the next few hours. You'll know it when you see it, it looks like a hump of black rock rising straight up out of the sea, not like an island. Keep a close eye on the charts. Don't go anywhere near it. Keep west of it, no closer than twenty kilometres. There are rocks and shoals under the surface. There's one big one, barely visible at low tide, about eight kilometres west-northwest of Tapu Tapuatea. Once you see it, you'll know we've only got another 210 kilometres to go to Rangitahua. Keep a watch on the water at all times for any sign that there might be something under the surface. If you spot something, wake me up. Got it?"

Ray nodded. "Aye Skipper!" sounding suddenly totally awake.

Ben assured Hatoe, "Sleep well, Skip. We won't take any chances."

Satisfied, Hatoe went to sleep.

While Ben was on duty, Ray went to the bow and spent the time looking intently at the surface of the ocean all around them while Ben also checked the ocean. When it was Ray's turn on duty, they swapped places. The one on duty also kept his eye on the water, at the same time as he watched the wind, the sails, the heading, and everything else that was required of a helmsman. The only times they took their eyes off the water were when they tended to the sails or their own physical needs. The wind vane steered for them, but they still called the one on duty the helmsman.

There was one distraction, shortly before nine o'clock, when Ray was on the helm and Ben saw a whale shark. Ben pointed it out, but he barely glanced at it. Ray was awed by the stunning size of it. "I've never seen anything like that," he told Ben. "It's not a whale, but it's bigger than the Dolph."

"Don't let your attention wander!" Ben frowned. "Last thing we want to do out here is prang a submerged rock."

"There she is!" Ray called, pointing not at the whale shark, but off to the south-east. All at once, where there had been nothing, there was a rock poking up out of the ocean in the middle of nowhere. It stood like a sentinel against the evening sky.

"Finally!" Ben took his eyes off the sea for only a moment. "Skipper will be pleased."

"At least we know for sure that we're where we're supposed to be." Ray muttered, returning to his tasks.

"Did you have any doubts?" Ben was amused

"Not really, but I've never done anything like this."

"Me either, but I'm going to do it again." Ben declared as he made his way in from the bow, "Do you want to come with me, when I come back out here, or have you had enough?"

"I don't know, mate. I'll have to think about it after I've been home for a while. I'm flattered that you blokes trusted me with your family secret, and I'll never let on, but this is a bit much for me. Days at sea out the back of beyond, past the black stump. No one can hear us if we call for help, no one knows where we are; flares not worth a heap of sand this far from where anyone could see them if we prang her." He patted the Laughing Dolphin affectionately, continuing, "Bloody Teeth of Kiwa all around us trying to get a bite; freaking storm hovering over us like a hawk over prey; another two hundred klicks to sail with that thing sneaking up on us; and when we get there, then what? We dive down to a wreck in that storm to cut metal from it? I don't mean to winge, mate, but it's not on, you know? And never mind about doing it all again in the other direction to get home!"

Ben chuckled. "If she's a bit rough when we get there, Skip said there's metal on land that we'll pick up instead of diving."

"A <u>bit</u> rough? A bit!?" Ray pointed at the sky behind them. "Look at that thing! She's turned into a full-fledged storm!" Not only were the clouds murderously black along the horizon, but the sea under them was equally dark, and there was the kind of dark line from the sky to the sea that told of heavy rain. Where they were was still clear and warm, despite the brisk winds, but the storm was threatening to change all of that.

"It would be nice if it didn't hit us in the middle of the night," Ben commented, mildly, as he headed downstairs to take his turn in the hammock. "Bloody oath!" Ray exclaimed in vehement agreement.

After his eight hours off, Hatoe was pleased by the progress they'd made while he'd been sleeping. "That's her alright," he nodded, looking behind them at the rock they'd passed.

"It's unnerving to have a rock sticking up out of the sea all by itself like that," Ray muttered.

"Hate to tell you, mate, but he's not totally by himself. You just can't see his friends, is all."

"Yeah, right, because they're hiding right under the surface waiting for us like flaming octopi waiting in the reefs for a likely victim to snag," spat Ray. "Look at the surf around that thing! There's shallow water all around it, and I can bet there's no sandy bottom anywhere near it. It's all rock, isn't it? We'd be smashed to pieces in surf like that."

Hatoe raised one eyebrow. "I'll be right back as soon as I've woken up a bit and been to the head and had a cuppa. Want one?"

"Yeah, ta, Skip."

Hatoe glanced at the storm as he went back down below, but didn't comment on it.

By morning the winds were no more than fifteen knots, which was a relief. They had passed two small islands with grass and a few trees on them. These were interesting but the crew of the Laughing Dolphin paid more attention to any birds they saw flying around the islands. There were a number of different kinds of petrels, which the men watched closely to see whether or not the birds were going about their normal business or looking for shelter.

"You know," Hatoe muttered hopefully. "I think the storm's moving north. It might give us a miss."

"You think so?" Ray perked up.

"I hope so."

As they went past to the west of the two little islands, they could see the signs of a shoal just under the surface of the one closer to them. Looking back after they'd gone past they could not only see that there was an even bigger shoal under the surface north of the islands, but the bigger island which had looked flat on top was now revealed to have a big bite out of its northern coast, with steam rising gracefully in the shelter of the crater before being whisked away to nothingness when it reached the open winds.

"Tangaroa on the sea!" Ray shouted. "It's a freaking volcano!"

Hatoe shrugged. "They're all volcanoes, mate."

"Even the shoals?"

"Don't know about them, but the old charts have the place riddled with undersea volcanoes as well as the islands."

The sea was very blue, showing an active sea life, including many sharks. "We're not going to dive with that lot, are we?" Ray asked, pointing at the sharks.

"Yeah - nah, mate, we won't dive at all. I don't trust that fellow." Hatoe pointed to the storm. "We'll shelter until she settles down, pick up some metal on land, then we'll head home."

Ray watched the surface of the sea without comment, though Hatoe couldn't mistake the relief in his eyes.

"Next island we come to is bigger, with a couple of coves we could shelter in if we had to," Hatoe offered by way of comfort.

"Is that it?" Ray pointed to a smudge on the horizon ahead of them.

"That'll be the one," Hatoe confirmed.

"They're closer together than I thought." Ray looked so pleased that Hatoe didn't have the heart to tell him that Rangitahua was 120 kilometres further away.

They passed the small island early in the night and continued towards their goal. By first light they could see bands of cloud, and the wind was blowing from the north-east at eighteen knots.

Ray started to fret. "Don't tell me that's turned into a cyclone!"

Hatoe resisted a wicked impulse to say, "Okay, I won't tell you that." Instead, he said calmly, "No worries, Ray. We'll be at Rangitahua before she gets here, if she comes this way, which it doesn't look like she's going to. Put the kettle on, would you? It's nearly five a.m. Time for Ben to get up and you to kip."

"I'll kip on deck this shift."

"No, no, no, mate. You won't get proper rest."

"I won't be able to sleep down there."

"Give it a go, mate."

Reluctantly Ray went down below. Ben tumbled out of the hammock, heading straight up on deck before he was fully awake. "How're we doing, there, Skip?"

"She's dropping off a bit. If she dies down too much, I'll put the screw to her and run for Rangitahua."

Ben stood, staring at the sky. "Yeah, too right, Skip. I'll be right back." He ran quickly down the stairs, returning in short order ready for his day's work, carrying covered mugs of tea for himself and Hatoe.

Without speaking after Hatoe had thanked Ben for the tea, they resumed the positions of a man at the helm and a man watching the ocean until Ben went back down below to cook their breakfast. He reappeared with steaming hot wedges of vegetable omelette that they could hold in their hands to eat. "Oh, good choice, mate, this is corker!" Hatoe exclaimed, sucking air in around his mouthful to cool it.

"Yeah, ta, Skip. Ray's a bit tense, eh?"

"Sitting up, is he?"

"Nah, he's out like a light."

Hatoe laughed, quickly putting his hand to his mouth so that he wouldn't lose crumbs of his breakfast. "And he reckoned he couldn't sleep down there!"

Ben didn't laugh, he frowned. "Have you ever seen him like this before?"

"I've never sailed with him before. Not that I've ever heard of, though. Everyone who's ever hired him has said what a good sailor he is. But then, he's never been out of contact with home before, has he?"

"Well, neither have I."

"No, but Ben, it's really freaked him to be out of touch. Some people are great when everything's familiar, then come unglued when they come up against something strange. Looks like Ray's one of those. Great sailor, reliable bloke, in coastal waters where he can see his way home. Out here it's different. Thousands of kilometres of water below us, hundreds of kilometres from the sight of land, no one knows where we are, no hope of letting anyone know if something goes wrong. It's got to him. No way of knowing that's going to happen to a bloke. Just does sometimes. We've all got our tender spots. When you're skipper of your own boat, it's one of the things you learn to watch for. Besides, it's our family who know where we really are, none of his do, and it's our treasure, it's not his. It's different for him. He doesn't get out of it what we do."

"But we'll give him some for himself, won't we? Over and above his ordinary pay, I mean."

"Of course, but it's still not the same thing. He gets paid to come out here. We can come any time, it's ours."

"I asked him if he'd come with us again, but he said he wouldn't."

"It's still not the same. Imagine if we didn't have our own boat. How would you feel about the risks then?"

"He could get his own boat if he doesn't like being a daily."

"Ah, Ben, my boy, I think young Raethew Perenara is a bit too fond of living high to save up for a boat. Until he gets the hang of saying, "No," to himself, he's going to be a daily worker. This trip would give him a running start if he handled it right, but how much do you want to bet everything he takes home will be gone with nothing to show for it inside of a week?"

Ben watched the sea in silence, until they'd finished eating. He took their dishes down below, then came back up ready to take his helm shift. To prepare to take over he studied the charts, the gauges, the compass, the sky, and listened to Hatoe's instructions with quiet intensity.

"And one more thing," Hatoe said. "Don't worry about using up the battery if you need to use the motor, because if the battery runs out remember we're not dependent on that old fuel cell. You see this dial? If the old fuel cell runs out it'll flip from empty back to full, and you'll know she clicked herself over to the good one."

Ben said nothing, watching how Hatoe resealed the light pad.

"Remind Ray. He'll need to remember if it all goes kumara shaped when he's at the helm."

"The wind's dropping," Ben observed, looking upwards again.

"If she gets below ten knots, we're turning on the motor."

"Reckon that's a cyclone?"

"If she is, that next band of wind will be from the north. We really want to be tucked up in Boat Cove before that happens." Hatoe didn't feel the least bit playful anymore. He handed the helm over and went below for a moment.

They were motoring with all the speed the electric engine could produce when the time came for Ray to get up and Hatoe to get some sleep. All around the sea and air were unnaturally calm, the huge black clouds moving ever closer, the darkness threatening them and making the air seem cooler than it was. There was no mistaking that the blue sky was being overwhelmed by the cloud cover. Even where they were, in the waning blue, it was crossed by bands of white high clouds heading south-west at tremendous speed.

Ray stumbled around, groggy and disoriented when he got up.

One sniff of the electrically charged air, one look at the clouds, and Ray was fully alert. "We should have put in at the other island!" he yelped.

"Rangitahua's safer. We'll make it. You'll see it in a couple of hours. Watch for shoals and submerged rocks. Keep out of the big bay on the west side, there are all sorts of hidden rocks and shoals in and around it, and strong tows. There's a wreck on the beach. Head south to go around the head to the south of the big bay. Wake me when you're ready to make the turn. I'll have to take it around the south coast myself, and I'll need you both to watch for rocks under the surface."

Rangitahua appeared on the horizon ahead of them two hours later; first a faint blur that might have been a torn wisp of cloud between sea and sky, then a phantom island which hour by hour took definite shape, until the high peaks raised jagged fingers up to the sky, as if pointing upwards to warn them what was overhead. Ben and Ray watched as it slowly took form, several times the size of the other islands they'd passed.

"What's that?" Ray asked, pointing.

"Cloud?" Ben suggested.

Ray didn't answer. He watched intently, glancing up at the island frequently as he kept a close watch on the performance of the Laughing Dolphin.

Ben watched the surface of the water raptly as Rangitahua drew closer, but he spared a glance now and then for the odd cloud they caught sight of periodically over the highest peak of the island. It was a change of wind direction that told them what they didn't want to know. By the time Ben put it into words they both knew what they were seeing. "Smoke! It's erupting!"

Ray put his hands up in front of him as if to fend off the island. He was trembling. "Tangaroa in the sea! We're going to shelter from a cyclone in an erupting volcano?! We had an island with coves and no smoke, but we went right past it because this one was safer!" His voice went up to a squeak. "Now it's a whole day behind us, through that!" He pointed at the storm. "We couldn't get back to it if we had the waka of Maui!"

Ben spoke more quietly. "Take her easy, mate, you're throwing a bit of a wobbly there."

Ray swallowed hard. "Sorry, mate. Nothing fazes you, does it?"

"Well, of course it does, but man, you knew this was a risky life before you set foot on a boat for the first time. What's got under your skin?"

"I don't know. This is different from working off the coast. A storm comes up there, we take her straight in. Even if we can't get home, we're never more than a few hours from another island. There's someone there to see our flares or hear our radio. If a volcano goes off, we get <u>away</u> from it, we don't sail right under it because there's nowhere else to go!"

"We're not going to go into the crater! All we have to do is stay upwind of it."

"And if that puts us in the path of the cyclone?"

"The Skipper will know where we can shelter."

"We've got to get him up."

"Not yet. Don't lose your nerve, mate. We'll get him up when we're ready to go south, like he said."

"Think about it a bit, Ben. The smoke's heading east. The best place to keep out of it would be the west bay, but we were told to stay out of the bay. We've got to sail right into it."

"No, we don't. Look at where the storm winds're coming from. The north. If we go into the west bay, we're going to be right in it if it reaches here. We'd be better going around to the south like Skip said, where we can be in the lee of those hills and ridges."

"Look at it!" Ray shouted. "Will you <u>look</u> at it?"

Ben turned and looked at the island. "Looks like a bit like Kapiti," he said. "It's a bit bigger, about six and a half klicks, I'd say, but it's the same general shape and covered in bush just like Kapiti Island." He resumed his search for underwater hazards but stayed in the stern so that he stayed right beside Ray.

"Not that, I mean the point that reaches out to the north side of the bay. We could tuck in there; it gets hundreds of metres high. The smoke'd be on the other side of the island, and there'd be a chunk of land between us and the winds."

Ben stared at the island coming ever closer. He studied the ocean, the clouds, and the volcanic plume.

Impatiently, Ray pressed him, "I'm right, aren't I?"

"I've never been here before, and you've never been here before. Skipper has. We have to go with his plan."

"That's why we've got to get him up. He doesn't know about the volcano. It changes everything."

Still Ben hesitated. He could now make out breakers, and that there were also lines of white far out from the shore of the bay. "So far everything he's said has panned out," he started, hesitantly. "I think, unless we're in immediate danger, we should stay with what Skip said to do."

"By that time, we'll be past the bay!" Ray's voice was shrill. "We should go in there <u>now</u>, where we know we've got a chance! Skip can always get us to carry on later if he wants to. Meantime we'll be in the lee of this bay right now, before that hits. What's to stop us?"

"That for one thing." Ben pointed at the white water at odd spots in the bay. "And look how steep that beach is. Look at the size of that wreck on the beach. It's bigger than the interisland ferry. If it came to grief here, what chance do we have?" He hadn't paid much attention to the ocean behind them because making sure the Dolph didn't hit anything in front of them was the priority. Now, searching for a way to convince Ray, he looked all around. "And that for another," he said, pointing.

Ray followed Ben's line of sight, and his eyes went wide. The wind had made a straight line across the ocean from north to south. On the west side were high seas with breaking waves, on the eastern side were calm seas with barely any transition between the rough and the calm. This wind did not peter out gradually, it blew hard with abrupt edges.

"We've got to wake him, now," Ray mumbled, automatically checking all the seals of his survival suit.

"Yeah. As long as it stays out there it's no problem, but we've <u>really</u> got to stay way away from those rocks. We'd better turn south now so if that reaches us it can't push us into them. Oh, and look. The bay won't be the place to go to keep away from the eruption." There were faint wisps of steam coming from the surface of the bay. Some of the white water they were seeing evidently wasn't only from wave action on submerged rocks. There was also a steaming, smoking heap of rock in the north of the centre of the bay, like an islet of scoria and lava. "Skipper didn't tell us anything about that," Ben pointed out.

Ray went silent and stiff. They were both so busy staring at the sight of steam rising from the surface of the bay and the islet that they didn't see anything coming. The wind slammed into the Laughing Dolphin, hitting her broadside, making her heel over suddenly to starboard, nearly knocking them both off their feet.

"What?! What?!" Hatoe bellowed, landing on deck, sealing his survival suit and reaching for his safety harness. The wind was screaming around them, spray hit them like pellets of hail, the boat was rolling hard. Hatoe took the helm from Ray, roaring against the wind, "Seal the ship! Seal your suits! Furl the sail!" As they raced to make sure their suits were sealed and there wasn't a porthole, door, or hatch open anywhere on the boat, and to furl the sail, Hatoe took off the wind vane and turned her south so that her stern was to the wind. As abruptly as it had hit them, the wind was gone, that column snaking away across the ocean west of them again. They could see the path of it written in the turbulent water where it passed, but the sky over them was still clear. There was no sign it had been there, except for the roughened water, which took several minutes to settle.

Hatoe headed south as fast as he could get the Dolph to go. "Looks like we're not going to escape it," he said. "Both of you get up in the bow.

One watch port, one watch starboard. If she hits us that hard while we're near the rocks they'll eat the Dolph. If you get in the water, go straight for the island. There's food, water, and shelter there that'll keep you going for years. If you keep your head, you'll be found when Rota comes looking for us."

"She's erupting," Ben told him.

"What?"

"Rangitahua. You can't see it now, those cliffs are hiding it from us, but we saw a column of smoke from the hills, and there's steam coming from the surface of the bay."

Hatoe looked back at the bay. Even with the waves stirred up by the wind, they could see steam rising from it. "Mother Papatuanuku," he breathed. "She's made a new lava island."

"What are we going to do, Skip?" Ray's voice trembled.

"Go where I planned to go. The other crater's on the other side of the mountains from there. Watch that water and the sky and keep your eyes peeled for rough patches. We'll sort it out after the storm's gone."

"Here she comes!" Ray suddenly shouted.

"Brace yourselves!" Hatoe just had time to call before the high winds pounced again, shaking and worrying the Dolph like a seal pup in an orca's mouth. This time it did not have them broadsides, it was coming over the port quarter. Skilfully Hatoe eased the Laughing Dolphin over until the wind was dead astern. The boat pitched as the seas rose, but once Hatoe found the right angle, she didn't roll any more. There was no point in the crew watching for rocks once the seas started to break because they couldn't have seen them if they had come across any. Clinging tightly to the grab rails they made their way back to the stern, fighting wind and water.

Ahead of them they could see the high band of cloud speeding to the south-west. It bent towards the west as it dipped out of sight over the southern horizon. Where they were the wind was driving south-east. Further east the seas were calm. It took every last fragment of seamanship that Hatoe had ever learned for him to shift the boat over to the east without giving the winds purchase on her. Finally, hours later, they broke out of the wind-stream into the calmer waters.

At once Hatoe swung in a tight U-turn so that if the winds reached over and grabbed them again, they would meet them head on. They had been driven far south-east of the island in the hours they had been fighting the wind and had to motor back to it. The formidable cliffs of the square base of the south coast faced them, with the long-pointed end of the hammer claw to the west, and the shorter club end to the east. From that angle they could see the complicated wind pattern. The stream of high clouds heading south-west at tremendous speed, down at sea-level almost no wind, and up above 600 metres light winds heading east carrying the plume of volcanic smoke away in almost the opposite direction from the high clouds. To the west of them the vicious winds of the edge of the cyclone right down to water-level, the cloud bank rising up unimaginably high above them.

They could see the smoke from the volcano just east of the middle of the island, but the steam rising from the western side was concealed by the southern hammer handle of the south coast.

They were all silent. They knew without saying anything about it that if they ended up in the water that far from the island their chances of reaching it were miniscule. The lifeboat they had was inflatable. What would happen to it in winds like that not a one of the men wanted to think about. There was no rain as yet, but they could see the blackness under the clouds that meant it was pouring rain on the sea to the west of them.

Nightfall came earlier because of the heavy cloud cover over the south-western sky. Long before the sun normally went down it disappeared behind the clouds, leaving them with low light right when they needed brightness. It wasn't until the moon peeped out that they could tell how much further they had to go. Ben should have been sleeping, but there was no way they could follow their routine. He volunteered to go below and make them all something to warm them up and ease their thirst. "Broth," Hatoe told him. "We should have something to keep the blood sugar up, too. That'll do both."

Ben slipped quickly down, was as fast as he could, and shot back up on deck again in record time. He was lucky, the band of winds didn't hit again while he was down below.

"Ta, mate," Hatoe said.

"Ta," Ray mumbled, carefully dogging the door shut before taking his thermos of broth.

"I made tea, too," Ben told them, indicating a ditty bag of thermoses. "I put honey in them all."

"You're a corker," Hatoe told him.

No one was able to go down below again after that, because the wind found them. They battled on through the darkness and high seas, not able to communicate except by finger-speak, until they broke out of the wind again.

There was no moon as they drew close to the island. Breezes and puffs of wind blew on them now and then, and fat drops of rain splattered down here and there. The seas were restless, and they could hear breakers smashing against the rocky cliffs. Hatoe got out the search lights, and sent a flare up ahead of them so that they could see the rocks and submerged shoals. The winds carried the flare north-east where it vanished uselessly over the land, which told them that the winds above them had changed direction, though there was nothing much defined at sea level.

As they passed the bottom of the handle part of the south coast and began to motor up towards the club part of the hammer head, they came to calmer seas. Another flare aimed lower along the water showed them islets and rocks to avoid. Once they had made their way up to the curved coast on the east side of the bay, they could see where it bent back towards the west. Hatoe was pleased to see Ray calm down as he could see for himself that they really would be sheltered. The tall, steep sides of the mountain ridges of the hammer head base kept the winds from them, and the storm hadn't been going on long enough to drive the seas up into the cove. There were swells, but as yet nothing like the seas they'd had to deal with. The searchlights were enough to show them where the rocks and shoals were. Hatoe took it slowly so that they could be sure of everything they saw before they hit anything.

They stayed close to the coast, going in between the steep shore of Rangitahua and the islets until they came to a small cove. The club shape, curving around to poke back towards the west, plus the great sweep of coast up the east side of the hammer head base to the eastern arm made them as close to enclosed as they could be. The terrain was less cliff-like there, too. The islets, sitting outside the mouth of Boat Cove, acted as a breakwater. Even Ray couldn't say they could have done any better.

Hatoe gave the order for the anchor to be lowered off the bow. Once it was down, he motored gently backwards until they were sure it was firmly stuck, and the cable was taut. The sea was too rough and dark to dive on the anchor, so Hatoe decided they'd put out four lines as well. Ray and Ben secured four lines, one on either side of the stern and the bow and dropped them into the water. Then they inflated the dingy, launched it off the transom, and Ray got on board so that Ben could lower the stern anchor to him.

There wasn't much wind in behind the club of the cove, but the swell made the Laughing Dolphin and the dingy move up and down independently. Hatoe decided to have their supplies on board the dingy while she was tied to the Dolph. They quickly loaded the dingy, then the crew set off to lower the stern anchor while Hatoe checked to make sure the Dolph was as watertight as possible above decks. He was the last man down below. He collected extra bits and pieces that he thought they might need, over and above the normal survival supplies the crew had automatically taken. Then he went up on deck and sealed the door so no water would leak in around it and slipped the storm door over the companion way doors, then took his precious fuel cell and tucked it into his rucksack, leaving the old one in place. He passed the items to Ben and Ray, when they returned, then took the awning from the seat locker, unfolded it and fastened it over the stern deck, ignoring the men bobbing in the inflatable boat off the transom urging him to get a move on. Finally, doing up the end of the awning as if the Dolph was at home in her dock, he backed off the transom and into the inflatable. "Now you be a good girl," he told the Laughing Dolphin. "Don't do anything stupid." He patted the hull.

They used the small motor on the lifeboat and putt-putted slowly out the back of the boat, placing the second stern anchor, and tying the other line to a branch that over hung the water. Then they putt-putted slowly back and along the hull to the bow, where they picked up the two mooring ropes and pulled them up from the sea into the inflatable, coiling them into the bottom of the lifeboat. Then they made more speed to shore, making sure the lines played out without fouling.

While Ben guided the lifeboat and Hatoe watched the lines, Ray played one of the searchlights on the shore so that they could see where they were headed. It was more rock than beach and some of it was simply cliff, so they were careful not to snag their craft. Ben shut the motor off before they hit the rocks, and they took the oars out to fend the dingy off the rocks.

They found a shallow spot where Ben could jump out first to steady the craft and guide it further in. Ray and Hatoe climbed out and all three lifted the inflatable by the ropes along its sides and carried it up onto the rocks, groaning under the weight of it filled with their supplies.

Once it was right out of the water, they weighted it down with rocks then went in search of something to tie the two mooring lines to. There was one tree close enough for one, but nothing within reach of the other. They went back down to the shore and searched among the rocks for a likely candidate. When they found one that it took two of them to move, Hatoe pulled the line as tight as he could while Ben and Ray rolled the rock onto it. Then they tied the line off and put other heavy rocks against it so that it couldn't be moved. By the time they finished the Dolph was held fast both fore and aft so that she could be neither driven up onto the rocks nor out away from shore, plus she couldn't swing around on her moorings. It was only then that they went back to their dingy, freed it from its weights, and carried it on up as high as they could.

The shore might have been less cliff-like than the rest of the south, but it was still extremely steep, the ground shuddered with periodic tremors, and the footing was not stable. Some of what they were trying to climb on seemed to be a rockslide that had not had time to be packed together or filled in with soil. In the moonless night, with the winds picking up and rain threatening, the earth refusing to lie still, and the rocks shifting when any weight was put on them, the chances of a broken leg or twisted ankle loomed ever higher. Finally, they decided that the best thing to do was hunker down with their backs to a small cliff and wait for morning.

As soon as they found a clearing that looked big enough to put the dingy down on the ground, Hatoe set about collecting wood to make a fire with the aid of Ben holding the search light. This involved a lot of hacking shrubs and twigs and bad language.

Ray emptied the boat so that they could carry it further up, putting the supplies in piles beside the boat. Ben joined him as soon as he was no longer needed to hold the light for Hatoe. They lashed the lifeboat down and weighted it with stones.

The sight of the fire was cheering and comforting. Once it could be left untended for a moment, Hatoe joined in moving the supplies to sheltered places among the rocks, making sure that the manuka leaves and the billy were among the first items. He'd carried enough water with him to make tea for them, thinking that they could find fresh water in the morning, so by the time they'd finished there was hot tea ready for them. He rolled kumara into the bottom of the fire to roast in their skins. They had them as is, hot from the fire.

Sleeping the first night was a simple matter. Since the fire had been built on rocks, they didn't worry about it getting away from them. They rolled out a ground sheet by the light of the fire, held it down with stones, emptied the stones out of the boat, untied it, and tipped it upside down over the ground sheet, and lashed it back down again. They slept in their survival suits under the boat, which kept them warm and dry even through the torrential rains that arrived before dawn. The comfort of sleeping on the rocks with only a cushion a piece was another subject, but they were warm and dry.

In the morning the dingy was fighting its tethers, the Laughing Dolphin was straining at her moorings, the rain was lashing down, the wind was coming down the cliff-face with a vengeance, and a swell was coming in from the ocean, breaking over the islets and crashing up on the rocks below them. Even with the downdraft off the cliff, the spray reached them from the breakers as soon as they poked their heads out from under the life-raft. In the heavy rain they could not see past the islets.

"Tangaroa in the sea! We can't stay here!" Ray exclaimed.

"What would you like to do, Ray-boy?" Hatoe tried to sound patient. "You want to go back to the Dolph and sail in this?"

Ray looked around. "You said there was shelter here."

"Yeah, there is. We've got to climb up this to get to it."

Ray looked up at the steep slope beside the cliff. "Nice," he muttered. "We've got to climb that in this?"

"No, you don't have to. I'm going to, but you can stay down here and wait for the weather to clear if you want to."

Ray looked around again. His shoulders slumped and he started to pick up their belongings from under the rocks where they'd been stashed for the night.

"Just a small load first," Hatoe suggested. "It's a steep climb and everything's wet, so we don't know how slippery it'll be, never mind that she'll be trying to shake us off the trail like water off a duck's back."

Peering hopefully into the bush, Ben asked, "There's a trail, eh?"

"After we cut one, sort of, yeah. Most of the trees in this corner are pohutukawa and nikau palms, so I don't know how much help they'll be in terms of hand holds, and the footing could be a bit tricky if it's mostly dropped palm leaves. Take some light lifelines and tie them to trees and rocks for hand holds to make the next trip down easier and a bit safer."

"Safer?" Ray's voice was shrill, his eyes wide. "This is your idea of safe? At any moment we could be buried by hot rocks or lava or snuffed out by a pyroclastic flow!"

Hatoe didn't think it did anyone any good to let Ray's fear get the better of him. "Look, Ray, I reckon we've got two chances: slim and none. On an island with a volcano on the other side of a six-hundred-metre-high ridge we've got a bit of a chance if we keep our wits about us. Out on the open ocean in a cyclone in a little seaweed collector our chances drop right off. If I don't make it, it won't be because I didn't give it a good go. How about you?"

Ray hung his head and didn't answer.

Hatoe had to be satisfied with that.

They turned the dingy back over and filled it with rocks and stones, took some light, brightly coloured lines with them, put on their ruck sacks, making sure they had the manuka leaves, the billy and some food with them, then set off to climb the slope in the pouring rain and punishing wind, and recurring tremors.

At the top they trudged off, following Hatoe, hacking their way through the thick bush with hatchets. Volcanic ash had recently fallen. The rain was mixing with it, covering the forest floor with cement. Under the heavy forest cover there was hardly any wind, but the rain poured down off the leaves washing the ash off them down onto the men.

"This will be lovely for the spinners," Hatoe grumbled. "I picked up a wind full of ash the last time Whakaari threw some around. Ground the gears out of every spinner on the Dolph. Every single one. Everyone who was out that day lost their spinners. Our insurance went up. Took them forever and a day to pay up, too. Spinners are not essential, you see. We've got sols, sails, and fuel-cells as well. Cost me two trips out here to replace them all without waiting for the insurance. That's when I got the souped-up ones we've got now, and the corker fuel cell."

They pulled their rain slicks out of their packs and pulled the hoods forward to protect their faces from the ash, taking off the survival suits with relief. They hadn't worn the slicks while they were climbing because of their tendency to flap in the wind and get in the way. The survival suits kept them dry, but they were constructed to keep bodies alive in the open ocean, not for scrabbling about on rocky shorelines. The suits had become hot, restrictive prisons, even though the three men had each opened theirs as much as they could without having to carry them. The tropical rain was warm, so taking the suits off didn't chill them. The pleasure of feeling air on their skin again after the heat of wearing the survival suits was enough to make them all groan.

When they finally did reach the hut, it was lying flat. They stood, staring at it, in sodden misery. Ray asked, quietly, "Is this a new definition of 'shelter' that I haven't heard before?"

Ben grinned. "I've been called skinny, but even I can't fit under there."

"Earthquakes. There must have been big earthquakes before she blew her lid," Hatoe guessed.

"What's her name?" Ben asked.

"Mo . . ." Hatoe had to think about it. "Moumoukai. No, wait. I think that's the name of the tallest peak. The volcanoes are Denny – no, Denham Caldera and Raoul Caldera. This one is Raoul, I think. Him. His name is Raoul."

"Aue Raoul," they chanted, greeting the volcano respectfully. They sang to the volcano itself, then, after a moment's hesitation, sang to the God of volcanoes. "Aue Raumoko."

"With any luck neither one will mind if we stay alive here until the storm's gone," Ben said. They decided it would be a good idea to pay homage to Rangi, the God of the sky, and Tawhirimatea, the God of wind and storms, as well.

The singing and chanting had made them feel better, but they were still hungry and thirsty and without shelter.

"Let's go back under the trees out of this wind," Ben suggested.

Out of the wind they had a better chance of hearing each other speak. "The place is pack full of nikau palms," Hatoe said. "Let's cut enough to make a roof, then at least we won't have this rain and junk falling on us."

"What are we going to do about water, though? This stuff will be falling into all the water," Ray complained.

"You're just a bundle of joy, aren't you Raykins?" Hatoe groused. "One thing at a time."

They chanted to Tanemahuta, the God of the forest, asking permission to cut branches from his trees. Then they slashed off or pulled down nikau palm leaves and arranged them in the branches of other trees and shrubs until they had a canopy which shed water. Squatting under that, they were at last out of both wind and rain.

"Right, now. There's good water in this place, but the lakes are on the other side of the ridge and in the crater, so I'm betting they're evaporated. Even if they're not, I don't fancy slogging over there to see, do you?"

"It's not really high on my list of favourite hobbies," Ben admitted.

"Rain water's usually clean, but this lot's full of junk," Ray complained.

"What can we do about that?" Hatoe asked.

"Can't we find some streams?" Ben asked.

"Oh, right. They'll have junk in them too, won't they? Won't that put us right back where we are, only more tired after slogging through that out there?"

"Well, then, we put something out to catch rain, and let it sit, then use the top part when the junk has settled to the bottom," Ben suggested.

Hatoe nodded. "That should work."

Ray protested. "Didn't we bring any water from the Dolph?"

"I brought enough for the tea last night. Did you bring any?"

"No." Ray glared at Hatoe. "You said there'd be water here. I didn't think we had to carry it."

"Well, Ray, we could have put in at that other island like you wanted to. We'd be there now, in the thick of the storm instead of out on the edge, with no tree cover and no water at all except what we had on the Dolph."

"The storm is moving north. We could have just gone south below it and just waited," Ray pointed out

Hatoe shook his head. "There's nothing south of here. No islands. I haven't found any charts showing anything this side of the Ice."

"I brought a thermos full," Ben told them.

"Why didn't you say so?"

"It's down at the shore."

Hatoe got to his feet. "That's what we do first, then. We go down and bring up everything we can. If we can get out to the Dolph we get some more water."

They set their ground sheet out to catch rain while they were gone and set off.

The wind wasn't as bad down at the shore as it had been first thing in the morning, and there were fewer tremors, but the rain was so heavy they could barely see the Laughing Dolphin. The swell had evolved into huge breakers that splashed all the way up to where they had spent the night. The lifeboat was full of sea water, even as high as it was. They added a few more stones to it to make sure it didn't go anywhere without them, checked the mooring lines for the Dolph to make sure they hadn't loosened, then took the coverings of stones off the supplies and chose what they could carry, covering the rest back up again. "One or two more trips and we'll have it all," Hatoe estimated.

They had to help each other to make it back up the steep climb. They lay down on the damp ground in the little shelter and rested before they did anything else. They shared Ben's water between them, cold, and ate cold food. Still, it was enough to give them the energy to plan what they could do next.

They set out the containers they'd carried up to catch rainwater and drained the ground sheet into others that they set down under the shelter out of the rain to sit undisturbed, then left the shelter of the forest and took another look at the collapsed building. The building was so old that some of the wooden parts were rotted. There didn't seem to be a stone chimney still standing upright, but they could see where there'd been a fireplace. The walls were corrugated iron, some of which were rusting. They stripped the good sheets of metal off, took pieces of timber that were usable, and lugged everything they needed back into the deep forest.

There they constructed walls and a roof, laying nikau palm leaves over the roof to shed the rain and making sure that there were two Pohutukawa branches accessible so that the hammock could hang inside. They cleared the floor of leaves and twigs down to the earth, and smoothed that as much as they could, then spread the groundsheet over it, which gave them a dryer floor than the rain-soaked earth and ash. They made a shelter over the doorway and hung palm leaves down as a kind of curtain over it. Then they set about finding a way to have a fire that wouldn't be drowned by the rain if outside or suffocate them with its smoke if it was inside.

At last, they had a shelter that kept them dry enough to be passably comfortable, and with a fire so that they could have their manuka tea and something hot to eat. They slept as if they'd been slain after they'd eaten their fill.

In the morning Ray wanted to see if he could find a stream with better water than the rain they'd been collecting. The rain tasted sulphurous, even with the ash settled out of it. The winds had shifted again so that ash no longer blew over them, which meant they could collect purer water, but it still tasted of sulphur. Ray was sure that a stream would not have the sulphur taste.

Ben agreed to go with Ray because he wanted to find some kawakawa berries to quench their thirst in case they didn't find any untainted water. Hatoe had told them that the kawakawa berries growing on the island were larger and juicier than the ones at home.

Hatoe stayed at the shelter to get more sleep.

He was rudely woken a short time later by his crew bounding back, banging on the sides of the hut, shouting, "Skip! Skip! Wake up!"

The panic in Ben's voice jerked Hatoe right up out of the hammock. He stood for a moment staring around their shelter, confused about where he was.

Ben's shout of, "You've got to see this!" had him outside the shelter before he was awake.

"What?! What? What's happened?" Glancing around the forest Hatoe struggled to sort out what was going on. The trees looked just the same. It wasn't raining as much, and the ground seemed to be keeping still. Other than that, nothing had changed.

Hatoe couldn't understand the panic until Ben pointed a shaking finger and said, "We don't know. Ray saw something over there."

Then Hatoe knew he was being had. He'd been the butt of a great many jokes in his time and had pulled quite a few himself. He knew a prank when he saw one. It was the right time for it, the crew had gone through a lot in the last few days, it was only to be expected that they would let off steam now that they were safe. The trouble was, they weren't safe yet, and Hatoe was too tired and too aware of the dangers to fool around with them or to have patience with them. "Saw something? Great Tanë in the Forest! You scared me out of ten years growth because Raykins <u>saw</u> something? I thought at least there was lava on the way! What did you see, Ray? A tree sprite?"

Ray flinched but insisted, "No, really Skipper. There's a – something to the northeast of the island."

Hatoe's arms dropped to his sides. He took a deep breath, looked Ben right in the eye, and in carefully measured tones, said, "I get it. It's your idea of funny to see if I'll fall for it. Well, you'll be pleased to know I levitated right up off the hammock and wasn't even sure where I was for a bit there. That enough for you? Can I go back to bed now? The next man who scares me better have a real emergency or he'll be swimming home, got it?"

Ben stepped in front of the entrance to the shelter, barring Hatoe's way. "No joke, Skip. I reckon we should stay in the trees and take a look-see before she sees us. That's if there's anybody on board to see us."

Hatoe stared at the lean, weather-beaten faces of his crew. It was dawning on his overtired mind that they might not be pulling his leg. He shook his head to clear it. "What?" was all he could manage. Knowing that sounded dumb, he added, "Maui the trickster been at you?"

Ray leaned forward, the intensity in his voice making Hatoe uneasy, and told him, "Yeah - nah, she's solid enough. Making an almighty wake. I've never seen anything like that. Smoke coming out of chimneys. Ghost ship I reckon. Something Tangaroa threw back, or worse, eh?"

Hatoe looked around. There was a steady drip down from the heavy forest canopy, but little sign of wind. He couldn't tell if the volcano had settled down or not, since he hadn't felt its trembles in the hammock. All he could say about it was that he hadn't noticed any shaking since he'd been up. He looked at Ben and Ray again. They were serious. "I suppose you'd better show it to me," he said, ducking back into the bivouac to get his rain slick. If he'd had any doubts, the relief on their faces convinced him that they really did think they'd seen something supernatural.

"Bring your binoculars," Ben advised.

Raising an eyebrow, Hatoe did so.

They led him along a trail they'd blazed through the thick, jungly forest of trees, palms and ferns hung with vines and decorated with mosses. It was less than a kilometre across the narrow spit of land between Boat Cove and the ocean to the east, but the going was tough because the land was steep, with uneven footing and dense foliage. On a mound over a bluff that looked east Ben and Ray stopped. "Reckon the rain slicks might show up against the green," Ben said.

Feeling silly, Hatoe crouched down and peered at the sea through the screening plants. He couldn't see a thing, and was about to protest that they had made a fool of him after all, when he realised they were looking north-east, not east. He turned to look in the same direction. The rain was so heavy on the ocean to the east that he couldn't see past the edge of the downpour. He could hear occasional explosions to the north of them that he hadn't been able to hear before. If the winds eased a little the hiss and roar of a lava flow hitting the ocean reached him. They were far enough away that they couldn't see the lava, or feel the heat, but he knew what it had to be. "Raoul's bleeding into the sea," he told Ben and Ray. "Hear it? The wall of the crater is lowest to the north."

Ben and Ray nodded, but they remained intently focussed, so Hatoe explained, "The only way to get from this part of the island to the wreck on the north coast is to walk along the crater rim. If it's been blasted away it's going to be tough to get across after this eruption."

They didn't respond, so he settled down to wait patiently. The rain eased off which increased their visibility, but all Hatoe could see was small islands to the northeast of them.

Then Ben gasped, "Tangaroa of the Sea!" and pointed.

Hatoe looked at the direction that Ben was pointing, peering into the distance past the islands, trying hard to make out anything at all except the grey ocean and falling rain. Then he saw it.

Lights. He felt the hairs go up on his arms and the back of his neck. There couldn't be anything there. He'd seen to the east of Rangitahua. He knew there was nothing over there. It couldn't be house lights. There was nothing to build a house on. The lights were further out than the arc of islets and small islands – out where there was nothing but open ocean, thousands of kilometres deep.

It took a bit before it registered with Hatoe's stunned brain that the lights were being thrown up and down by the heavy seas. Surely that had to be a ship, yet there was no outline of masts or decks, just round points of lights like a string of glowing pearls. He took the binoculars from under his slick, now that he had something to focus on. He estimated that it was approximately twenty kilometres offshore.

It was like no ship Hatoe had ever seen. It had no eyes. It was wallowing like a blind thing. It was not outlined with light-paint, so it was hard for him to judge through the gloom and the distance, but he guessed it was as long as, or longer than, the interisland ferries, though not as wide. He also couldn't identify it because it had no image in light-paint on the side of its hull.

Why would anyone run their boat dark? That was not only risky, it was illegal. Everyone had to make sure their boats could be identified at a distance. Why would this owner want to keep his ship unknown? They couldn't be poaching from some poor sod's seaweed patch – there were no farmers out here, not to mention no seaweed in the deeps!

On the other hand, they weren't trying to be invisible – they had lights. Light streamed from it, but it didn't seem to come from paint, but from points, like glowing balls. The lights wavered, some of them going off then back on again as if something passed in front of them.

Completely confused, Hatoe concentrated on the hull. There was no sign of solar panels, spinners or motifs. The superstructure was very strange. It was too high, for one thing, and all in the bow, so the ship looked out of balance. There were two high, oval structures in the stern which were belching smoke. Ray was right, there was a wake so big that he could see the white line of it stretching out from the ship despite the distance and the stormy sea. No ship should look like that.

"Is it on fire?" Ben asked.

"No, Ray was right, those are chimneys," Hatoe assured him.

"It hasn't moved very far since we first saw it. It must be very slow," Ray observed.

"What do you reckon it is?" Ben asked. "Is it a throw-back from Tangaroa, or did Kiwa put it here, or is Maui playing his tricks on us?"

Hatoe handed Ben the binoculars, and stared out to sea, thinking. "I don't think it's a throw-back," he mused. "If Tangaroa had thrown it back there wouldn't be any life on it, and I think it's not dead. See if you can see anyone moving on it."

"What sort of ghost ship is it, then?" Ray asked. "If there's life on it, it can't be from Kiwa, and you don't think it's from Tangaroa. What does that leave?"

Hatoe shook his head to clear it. He felt as if he had to be dreaming. This couldn't be really happening. "And you know what? I don't think its Maui, either. I think it's real."

Ben gave the binoculars to Ray and turned to Hatoe. "There are people on that thing. I saw light when a door opened, only the door swung loose, it didn't latch. I saw movement, as if a person went through the doorway."

Realisation hit Hatoe so hard he bent forward and let out a breath as if he'd been hit in the stomach.

"What?" they demanded in alarm.

Hatoe scrambled for words. "You know those wrecks I was going to show you before the cyclone came? Like the one on the beach in Denham Bay? It's one of those! It's a bit different, but it's the same thing! Our ancestors used to use fire for fuel. There were ships like that one everywhere before the Dark Days, before the Freeze. It's an iron ship. It's from overseas." He got up and started back along their trail.

Ben followed him, calling out, "What do you mean?"

"You know how before we left you were talking about others who might have survived the Big Freeze? Well, it's happening. That's them."

Ray fought his way through the thick vegetation to catch up. "Is it a spirit ship?" he called.

"No, it's strangers."

"Strangers? What kind of strangers? From where?"

"From somewhere that's not here. Someone aside from us did survive. After two hundred and fifty years, they're back on the oceans again."

"What do you think they're doing?" Ben wanted to know. "You said there's nothing that way until you reach The Ice."

Hatoe shrugged. "Probably staying away from the rocky coast until the weather clears, then they'll turn and come here to see if they can get fresh food and water, if they're not too scared of the volcano. That's what I'd do, anyway. I'm just guessing."

"Are we going to stay here to meet them?" Ben asked.

All Hatoe's years of keeping Rangitahua secret kicked in at once. "No."

"We're never going out in that to meet them!" Ray exclaimed.

"No."

"What are we going to do if they turn and come here, then? Hide?" Ben snickered.

"No, we're going to head home before they come here."

Ray was aghast. "Skipper! The worst might be over, but the cyclone's not gone yet! We'll have no chance, like you said – and we'll have fried spinners now."

"It'll be a bit rough, but if we slip away tonight, they can't see us and follow us home. They might not find Aotearoa if we don't show them the way. If they're going to take a look here and they're not avoiding the volcano, they'll try to come ashore in a day or two. That could be why they're going so slowly; they're not motoring past; they're sticking around until it's safer. Meantime they're taking a good look. They couldn't have missed the island with the way Raoul is putting up a column of smoke that could have been seen east of here all the way to the other side of the black stump before the clouds moved in. They've never found Rangitahua before, there's never been any sign of life any other time we've been here, and we've been over every millimetre of the whole 2,925 hectares over the years."

The rain started again over the island. They could hear it thundering down on the leaves overhead, though not much reached them at first.

"That's good," Hatoe said. "They won't be able to see us in that. We'll make a good bit of kai for lunch, have a good feed and keep enough for tonight. They'll never be able to see our cooking smoke in this. Anyway, who's to say it isn't part of the volcano if they do?"

"What do you plan to do?" Ray sounded worried.

"We'll haul everything to the trail as soon as we've eaten. We'll take some metal, too. That'll help pay for this little jaunt when we collected no weed to sell. We'll pull the bach apart so that it just looks like fallen palm fronds. We'll take down our ropes from the trail, so it doesn't look as if anyone was here. We'll load the Dolph and slip away at dusk. If we head back around the west side with no lights on, they won't be able to see us. At the speed they're going, they won't have reached the south by tonight, and if the rain keeps up, they wouldn't be able to see us even if they did. We put the mountains of Rangitahua between them and us and go for it. We should be well over the horizon before morning. We won't put up any sails until we can't see any sign of Rangitahua, just to be sure."

Ray protested. "We should wait until it's safer. There's no one here to see our flares if we prang a rock."

"There is now," Ben grinned.

"Not once we're a day away there won't be!"

"It's our duty to take the news home," Hatoe insisted. "The People must know."

"We can't warn them if we're lost in a cyclone," Ray pointed out.

Hatoe was more concerned with keeping out of sight of the strangers than he was about the storm, now. "The cyclone's mostly gone. This is just the tail end."

"The seas in Boat Cove are worse than they were when we got here, and that was just the edge."

Hatoe could feel impatience with Ray rising inside him like a living thing. "Tell you what, then, we'll go down to Boat Cove and take a look. If we can't get to the Dolph, we make another plan."

"Right," Ben agreed.

"You want us to go down that trail and back up again right now?"

Hatoe gritted his teeth. "No, Ray, I don't. I want to have some tucker and head straight home. You're the one that's wingeing about it. Make up your mind what you want to do."

"I want to stay here."

The last thing Hatoe wanted in his life was to meet aliens face to face. "And if the people on the ship land?"

"Maybe they'll have fresh water that doesn't taste like rotten eggs."

"And maybe they'll hurt you, too."

"What? What do you mean?" Ray stopped cold.

Hatoe looked over his shoulder. "Don't you remember your school lessons? People used to kill each other. The whole of the ancestors' civilization collapsed because of the violence. That's why our people found a better way. We don't know what's on that ship, do we?"

Ray suddenly picked up speed, pushing on ahead of the other two, suggesting, "Why are we going to eat up here first? Everything tastes of sulphur here. We've got untainted water and food on the Dolph. Why don't we head straight down and eat after we get on board?"

Ben and Hatoe grinned at each other. Ben teased, "Hey, Ray, what's your hurry?"

"We should go as soon as. It's our duty. The People must know," Ray proclaimed. "And if they never see us, maybe they'll never find the other islands."

CHAPTER TWO

Johnny

"Quit flapping your gums and deal," Joe Mack demanded.

Vince returned, "You in that much of a hurry to lose your shirt?" He stopped his nervous chattering, but he kept right on shuffling.

Johnny looked up from his bible with a grin. He wasn't really reading, anyway – just sort of looking at it for comfort while the ship threw them around like they were on a riled-up green-broke colt.

"You tryin' to shuffle the spots off them cards?" Chuck challenged Vince. The three were sitting cross-legged on Vince's bunk trying to distract themselves from the storm by playing cards.

Johnny had a hard time keeping his mind on his Bible. His mind kept wandering. If he was honest with himself, he'd have to admit he was paying more attention to the card game than he was to the words on the pages. It might help him keep his mind on the holy book if only he could get dry, he thought. He estimated that he hadn't been dry or had a decent meal for a couple of days, now. Though it felt like more. The days since the Star of Galilee had run into the storm had not been pleasant. Though Johnny told himself firmly that they had absolutely no choice but to accept with good grace whatever the Good Lord sent their way, he couldn't help feeling exhausted, hungry, cold, and wet. There was no way out and no place to go if they wanted a break. The only hiding place was a cabin bunk and for the last day or so these had lurched about wildly and were difficult or impossible to sleep in. Their cabin had four bunks, and there were six explorers, so the bottom two bunks had been given over to the sickest, the rest of them making do as best they could. Trying to sleep on a chair or the floor was no less uncomfortable or impossible than a bunk, with or without someone else in it.

Johnny had just begun the thought that Vince looked a mite green when Vince shot backwards off the bunk and made a dive for the door across the bucking cabin floor, shouting, "Barf break!"

"Well, dadgum it," Joe Mack groused. "Now what are we gonna do?" They looked across at Johnny as if they thought he might fill in.

Gambling was too close to sin for Johnny to be able to join in their card games, though he kind of enjoyed their banter as they played. He didn't want to seem like a wet blanket by saying no, but he didn't know how to play cards.

From the bottom bunk across from Vince's a shaky voice suggested, "Deal him out."

Joe Mack rolled his eyes. "He's the dealer, Willie Jay. We cain't deal him out."

"Go back to pulin' and pukin' Willie Jay," Chuck advised.

Johnny thought that was a bit heartless. Chuck never seemed to get seasick, so he never had much sympathy for them what did get sick. Feeling for Willie Jay's misery, Johnny asked, "*¿Qué onda* **carnal**? How ya doin' son?"

It was true that at 22 Willie Jay was the youngest of the six explorers, but not enough younger to be anyone's son but Sam's. Even so, Johnny felt paternal towards Willie Jay because he was like that much younger brother that you always had to watch out for.

"Like the Good Lord done give up on me," Willie Jay moaned.

Johnny cajoled, "Oh, come on, Willie Jay, you know better than that." He knew he couldn't let the faith of the weaker ones falter. "The Good Lord don't never turn his back on no one."

Willie Jay's voice was plaintive. "You asked me how I feel. That's how I feel."

"Too honest for your own good," Chuck observed.

Joe Mack added, "Yeah, well, I feel a bit like that, too, and it ain't because I'm weak and sick like him 'cause I ain't seasick."

With each roll and thud anything loose in the boat got relocated, and with every shower of spray that whipped across the decks the salt water penetrated cracks and came inside as constant drips or occasional bucket sized drenchings. After days of this the cabin was a mess. They could of straightened things up some but doing anything that required moving in the bucking cabin seemed like a huge effort. Besides, the next wave threw things around again. It seemed to be pointless to make the effort. All they wanted to do was make time disappear and set foot on solid ground.

"The Will of God never takes you to where the Grace of God will not protect you," Johnny told him. He resented the way Joe Mack spoke. It was as if Joseph Machbanai Capernaum was doubting God. It would serve him right if . . . on cue the cabin tipped up as the ship climbed up a huge wave.

Everything that was not fastened down slid to the back of the cabin. Willie Jay moaned and dry-heaved. He didn't have anything left to puke with. Johnny was glad the cabin had no windows so that they couldn't see the heaving seas outside. Even his faith was tested when this happened. He didn't doubt God, or that God was great — just sometimes his faith that God intended to preserve their lives was in doubt.

The two on the bunk were no longer sitting casually cross-legged around the cards. They were gripping onto the underside of the top bunk, eyes wide, and teeth clenched.

The ship shook herself like a wet dog, then slid over the top. They could hear the scream of the engines as the screw left the water completely, then everything in the cabin slid the other way as the floor changed its tilt and they headed down the back side of the wave into the trough. They held on, tense and mute, waiting for the crash and shudder that told them they'd hit the water at the other side of the trough. The creaking and groaning of the ship as she headed back uphill again told them that she'd made it through, more or less.

"Big one," Joe Mack commented, unnecessarily. He might of claimed that he wasn't seasick, but he looked a tad unsteady to Johnny.

Chuck snorted. "Yeah, well, Sage says every seventh one is a big one."

"Who?" Johnny had no idea who Chuck was talking about.

"The head Weskie prisoner."

Joe Mack and Johnny looked at each other in surprise. "I thought his name was Shomer."

Chuck lowered his voice to a bare murmur. "That's the Christian name they give him when they baptised him, but his pagan name is Sage."

Johnny and Joe Mack looked around nervously.

Lowering his voice, Joe Mack warned Chuck, "Watch out they don't get the idea you're a pagan lover."

Chuck acknowledged that with a tilt of his head. "I'm careful. But the Weskies are here because they know the sea and we don't, so I like to learn what I can when I can. You never know when it might save your life. Sage says The Star of Galilee ain't built for this."

Johnny felt cold inside. "What does he mean, "It ain't built for this?" It's a ship. They're built to go on water, ain't they?"

"Yeah, but we're on the open ocean. The Star was built for rivers. You have to build them extra special strong for ocean storms."

"This is a freak storm," Johnny hastened to remind him.

"Sage says it ain't. If it is or not, the Star ain't built for it, so one of her plates could spring, and then we're done for."

"And you said Willie Jay was too honest for his own good!" Joe Mack exclaimed.

"Stupid idea to think something made of iron can float, anyway," Chuck groused.

Seeing despair coming and wanting to ward it off, Johnny, John Philip Balaam, reminded them that the iron ship had kept on floating for the whole six weeks since they'd left home, so however it worked, iron obviously did float.

"Yeah, but for how long?" Chuck muttered. "This is why no one's ever crossed the ocean and come back to tell us what's out there since Judgement Day."

Joe Mack shook his head. "Shomer's been bellyaching since before we left home that we shouldn't go because of all sorts of doom and gloom. This is just more of the same."

"I believe the Good Lord will see that the ship gets us back home again," Johnny was trying to reassure himself as much as the others. "It don't make no sense that the Good Lord would bring us out here to find out the truth and then not get us back home to tell the truth we found in His name."

It looked as if Chuck was about to argue, but they were interrupted by the return of Vince, grey faced and clutching the door frame. He was soaked to the skin, dripping and shaking with chill, so instead of arguing with Johnny, Joe Mack groused at Vince. "Shut the door. Was you born in a barn?"

Johnny jumped up to pull Vince into the cabin and shut the door behind him while Chuck gathered up the precious cards off from the bunk before Vince collapsed on top of them, and looked for another place for them to play, finally plumping himself down on the damp floor.

Joe Mack grabbed Vince before he fell and shoved him towards his bunk, telling him, "You should of used the bucket in here."

Between chattering teeth Vince stripped the wet clothing off, found something to rub himself down with, especially his hair, got into less wet clothes and tumbled into his bunk complaining, "Lost muh hat."

"Lucky you didn't go over the side like them other guys yesterday. You must of been hit square on," Joe Mack answered, throwing his own coat over the top of Vince's blanket.

Vince nodded, fighting to speak. "Wave right over me. Higher than a house."

Even after he rolled up in the blanket with the coat over him, he continued to shiver.

"He's got to get warm," Johnny was afraid that Vince would get pneumonia. He prayed, silently, "Lord, please, we need your help. Thy Will be done, but Lord God I beseech Thee to let us off this ship so the guys stop being sick before they starve and we can get dry before we catch our death of cold." Out loud he said, "If only we had something hot to give him."

"He can't keep nothing down," Chuck reminded them. "Willie Jay, move over. Let Vince bunk with you."

Simultaneously they both protested. "Aw, Chuck," said Willie Jay at the same time as Vince said, "*¡A la verga!* Shit!"

"Roll up in your blanket against the wall," Chuck ordered Willie Jay, paying no attention to the protests. "Back to back. Your heat will warm him."

Joe Mack and Chuck turned back to their card game while Johnny threw his coat over both of them, along with Joe Mack's coat.

"You'll get your coats puked on," Chuck warned.

"Thanks." Joe Mack snatched up a card from the floor, making Chuck yelp in protest. The sardonic sound in his voice was as much aimed at the warning about his coat as it was for the card.

"How did I get myself in this mess?" Chuck sighed, eyeing the cards in his hand and the ones on the table, sorrowfully.

"You come with us, to start with," Joe Mack grinned.

Chuck rolled his eyes. "Why'd you come?"

"I follow Sam."

Johnny nodded. "Me, too."

"Yeah," Willie Jay added from against the wall on the bunk.

Vince stayed silent, but Chuck included him by default. "I guess we all do. But why? For me it's because Sam's the only person I ever met that's got a vision like this."

Vince put in a bit sourly, "It's like he's charmed."

Joe Mack tossed a card down. "I thought he knew what he was doing."

Johnny felt horrified. "He does! He's doing the Lord's work!"

"You're sure of that?" Joe Mack waved his cards at Chuck to get him to make a move.

Johnny was confident of the answer. "Even if Sam don't know what he's doing, God knows what He's doing, and He's guiding us."

Chuck shook his head at Johnny, ignoring Joe Mack. "This storm ain't shook your faith none?"

"No. The only other people since Creation that were led by a column of smoke by day and fire by night were the Children of Israel when God led them out of Egypt to the Promised Land. 'And the Lord went before them by day in a pillar of a cloud, to lead them the way; and by night in a pillar of fire, to give them light; to go by day and night. Exodus 13:21.' The Good Lord himself was in the pillar of fire and smoke."

"Amen!" Willie Jay's voice was muffled by his blanket.

"Well, we can't see it now, can we?" Joe Mack snorted, glaring at Chuck.

"It's only because of the storm," Johnny assured him, feeling more confident as he heard himself say it. "Just when Major Temperance was turning back, the Good Lord showed us his column of smoke and fire to lead us on."

"I guess God's got a 'purpose' for the storm, too, huh?" Joe Mack sneered.

"To test our faith. We've got the Lord's Work ahead of us. We have to be faithful and strong in the Lord to see it through. If we're not worthy of the Truth we'll never find it."

"Leave him be," Chuck told Joe Mack, turning back to the cards. "Go back to your bible, Johnny. At least you'll go straight to heaven if we don't make it. Spare a prayer for us."

Johnny could tell that Chuck was only half kidding. He hastened to reassure him, "We wouldn't be here if it wasn't in God's plan, and He wouldn't of got us this far if He ain't got a Purpose. Let go and let God."

"This is God's plan?" Vince croaked from the bunk.

Joe Mack groaned. "Dang, Vince, go back to sleep. Let it alone."

Johnny answered anyway. "God didn't make you sick, if that's what you mean. That's just frail human nature."

Willie Jay turned in the bunk, making Vince grunt in protest, and raised himself up onto his elbows, wrapped in his blanket. "How can you be so sure it's God's plan that we're out here?"

Joe Mack slapped the back of his hand holding his cards into the palm of the other. "Shoot, Willie Jay, you don't understand nothing. Lay down and get some sleep."

"I just wondered why God would lead us like the Children of Israel is all," Willie Jay sulked. "We're not important like them."

As Willie Jay lowered himself back down on the bunk, Johnny made the decision that this was probably the best chance he was ever going to get to talk openly with the others. So many of the soldiers were seasick that they weren't being watched as much as usual. He went to the cabin door and opened it, intending to pretend to be shutting it properly if anyone was out there. The corridor was deserted. He closed the door firmly, turning to face the others who were staring at him. "The way I see it is the GR's gotten too far away from God's Purpose for His People." he was careful to keep his voice low just in case, and moved away from the door.

The others reacted in shock, with various shushings and warnings. "There ain't no one out there," he reassured them. "And with the racket," he waved his hand around his head encompassing the noise of the storm as well as the creaking and groaning of the ship, "ain't no one gonna hear us lest they's right on top of us." He sat on Vince's bunk, beckoning Joe Mack and Chuck to come closer. "The GR's getting too much like the Pharisees. I don't think we're the only people in God's creation to survive. I don't think Judgement Day was like Noah's flood. God promised He'd never do that again and gave us the rainbow to mark His promise."

Willie Jay raised himself back up on his elbows again, and shook his head. "He promised He'd never send another flood like that one, He never promised not to wipe everyone out again if the whole world turned away from Him."

"That's where you're wrong, Willie Jay." Johnny was sure Willie Jay's heart was pure, he just wasn't very bright, is all. "That's what He did promise. So, if I'm right, there are people out there, somewhere. I'm with Sam to find out. God will reveal His Truth and the Truth will make us free."

Joe Mack snorted. "Free from what? If you think finding a few survivors is going to stop the GR, you're pissin' into the wind."

For the sake of the others who seemed genuinely interested in what he had to say, Johnny carried on trying to explain himself, where he would normally have gone quiet. "It will make us free to know the Truth. Even if we only find one survivor, what will it do to the official line that we are the only ones God spared on Judgement Day?"

Chuck waved Joe Mack to silence. "I'm not saying you're wrong, Johnny. We all know someone or something is screwing with the government and the church. But do you really believe that coming out here will expose them?"

Johnny didn't know how to put into words what he really believed. He was sure this was the beginning of something, but he didn't know how to say it, especially not in the face of Joe Mack's blatant disbelief. All he could think of saying was, "That's not for me to say. God's Will will be done."

Chuck pursed his lips. "What if we don't find no one?"

Johnny felt a little bit more secure with that. He'd given it a lot of thought. "If we don't find land it don't change nothing. If we find land and there's no one alive, then the government will be able to say it proves they were right."

Chuck raised an eyebrow. "If we don't find land they'll say the whole world was destroyed on Judgement Day, won't they?"

"They sure will," Joe Mack nodded.

Johnny realised with a sinking heart that they were probably right. "You don't believe that, do you?"

"No. Do you?" The others all shook their heads.

Johnny told them, "Sam don't think it'll mean they're right if we don't find nothing. He says that just means we didn't find nothing, not that there's nothing there. He won't believe we're the only ones until someone's been able to search the whole world."

Joe Mack snickered. "Twice."

"What?" Johnny's rhythm was broken.

Chuck was chuckling. "Ain't it the truth! If we don't find nothing when the whole world's been searched, Sam will say we missed something and do it again."

Willie Jay sounded more cheerful when he chipped in, "Ain't nothing going to stop Sam. Every time the Major says it's over, Sam finds a way to keep him going."

That made Johnny feel better. "Yes, that's it. This is the first time anyone's tried this. We're just starting. We never even had a port until the Panhandle got pushed through. We've never even gone across the Ashlands, never mind the oceans."

Willie Jay put in, "Sam saved my life. I figured I owed it to him to help him make his dream come true."

Johnny nodded. "He's been working towards this since way before we had a port or any ships."

Joe Mack grinned a bit sheepishly. "I just got to see how something like that turns out."

Chuck grinned back at Joe Mack. "Me, too. Sam told me he's been saving up for this since he was just a kid. Then all of a sudden we've got a port and ships, and he gets his hands on one. Gotta go with faith like that."

Johnny beamed at them. "That's what I mean. If any man was ever touched by God, it's Sam. It's no working of man that we went from a small desert inland nation to having the Panhandle to the sea and ships. That's the Hand of God."

Vince stirred, raising his head and frowning. "So you do think the GR is the work of God?"

"No, I mean . . ." Johnny was appalled. That hadn't come out the way he meant it.

Vince cut him off, speaking with a bitterness that caught Johnny by surprise. "You think all those people were driven off their land by God?"

"No, no, that's not what I think. My people were conquered by the GR, too. What I meant to say is that it's time everyone in the GR, original GR and Conquered Peoples, learned the Truth, so God's making it possible."

"Your people are CP too?"

Vince seemed mollified. It was the first time he'd said anything about whether his family was old time GR or from the conquered peoples. Still,

Johnny couldn't help but wince at the derogatory term. "You call yourself a CP?" he asked.

Willie Jay spoke up. "It just means 'conquered people.' I bet everyone who questions the government comes from a CP family."

Chuck put in, "If you do the math three fourths of GR citizens got to be CP. Like you said, the GR started out as a small inland nation. There's no way on God's green earth that half of the people who claim to be original GR could be."

"That don't mean it's God's Will that we're out here, though," Joe Mack pointed out.

Johnny looked him right in the eye. "Can't be nothing else, there's too many coincidences. We just happened to reach the sea and start building ships. The military just happened to decommission a ship. Sam just happened to hear about it, and he just happened to have enough saved up to lease it and to hire the men to run it. His kids just happened to be old enough to take care of themselves for a while so that he could leave them, and he just happened to be able to convince the military to lease the ship to him. Come on, ain't it a bit too much to be just good luck? It's almost a miracle. Whoever heard of the military leasing top secret equipment to a civilian? And what about they go and rent us a whole detail to run it for us and keep the prisoners working? If you don't think the ship is a miracle, what else could that be?"

Joe Mack lowered his voice. "That could be the military getting us to do their dirty work for them on our dime."

Chuck, Chelubai Abijam Damascus, raised an eyebrow at Joe Mack. "You think so?"

Joe Mack leaned back on his hands. "Look at it this way," he kept his voice low. "They get to find out if anyone else survived Judgement Day and it don't cost them a wooden nickel. We pay them for this leaky old tub, and – get this, they must be laughing their asses off – we pay them to have their men with us, spying on us. Did they see us coming or what?"

Chuck pursed his lips. "I never did think about it like that." He glanced around and lowered his voice. "They take a decommissioned hulk that's built for rivers, not the ocean, and charge us to take it out on the ocean, and put spies and prisoners on it, and charge us to take them off their hands. If we don't make it back we're no loss, and if we do make it back they never had to risk good men or a good ship to find out if there's anyone out there. Pretty slick."

Johnny was appalled. "What d'you mean 'we're no loss'? There's a whole unit here!"

"You never served, huh, Johnny?"

"No. Flat feet and a squint. They sent me home before my year was up."

"If you knew what you was looking at, you'd know there ain't one of these guys that ain't pissed off a MP. They done stuck us with a bunch of shammers. Now that he said it out loud I can see Joe Mack's right. Ain't one guy on this ship they'd miss — not even the drunken Major — and we're paying them for the privilege of taking out their trash."

Johnny's heart sank. For a moment there he'd dared to hope he was starting to get through to them. "It's still a miracle," he insisted. "How else can you explain that God is leading us with His special sign? You can say anything you want about how we got the ship and the men to run it, but you can't deny that."

They didn't say anything more about it. Vince and Willie Jay lay back down on their bunk, Joe Mack and Chuck returned to the patch of floor where they could play cards. Johnny was always disappointed when seeing it right in front of their faces still didn't move their hearts, but he took his own advice to 'let go and let God' and went to return to reading his scriptures.

The door burst open a few minutes later and a breathless Sam stood there, shouting at them, "Land! They've seen land!"

There was a stunned moment when it seemed as if time hung suspended. Everyone stared at Sam, then glanced at Johnny. Chuck broke the spell by muttering, "You sure called that!"

Everyone who was able-bodied enough to do so scrambled to his feet and ran to the door, snatching the coats back up off Vince and Willie Jay without a glance at them, and ran after Sam up the narrow iron ladder to the deck above.

Spray was still being blown into their faces, the rain was still so intense they could barely see the ocean around them, the ship was still finding the waves heavy going, but it seemed to Johnny that it wasn't as bad as it had been. "How did they see land in this?" he shouted over the noise of the wind and waves.

"It's clearing up," Sam shouted back. "The Weskies say we caught the tail end of a hurricane. When there's a break in the rain we can see land."

The clouds shifted slightly, parting enough for them to see a red glow through them. "The column of fire!" Johnny shouted, delighted and reassured to see that the Hand of God was still with them. He prayed, giving thanks that his prayer for help had been answered so quickly.

He stood and waited, clinging for dear life to the rails, until the rain squall passed. "There it is!" someone yelled. Johnny looked at the others to see where they were looking, and tried to look in the same direction. He could see nothing at first, then there it was! Looming out of the gloom about ten miles away was a hillside. He got the impression of deep, dark greenness rising from white breakers. He looked down at the surface of the sea and realised there were many breakers between them and the shore. He watched one wave crash and splash high into the air. After it was gone the sea seemed to lower at that point before the next wave came and he could see just under the surface what was clearly rock.

He looked then at each of the other breakers between the ship and the shore. If they were all rocks, and there was no beach, only more rocks where the land met the sea, how were they going to get off the ship? As vision cleared in one spot, then another, he could see several little islands covered in greenery between them and the land.

The rain socked them in again, obliterating the view of the breakers, the red glow, and the islands. "Are we going to go over there?" he asked Sam.

Sam nodded. "We got to stay out here 'til the Weskies can see good enough to find a safe place to land. They say the waters are full of rocks just under the surface. Tomorrow is the Sabbath, but the Weskies say the storm will be gone after the Sabbath, so we get a day of rest and then it'll be safe to look for a place to land."

Johnny went back down to the cabin to tell Willie Jay and Vince, rejoicing inwardly at this further proof that God had them all in the palm of His hand. How else could it be that they hadn't hit any of the rocks they couldn't see? How else could it be that they had arrived where He had led them the day before the Sabbath? How else could it be that the weather would clear for them as soon as the Sabbath was over?

Ben

As three men took their shelter apart, Ben was careful to separate out the palm fronds that had been cut instead of pulled down. He shoved their ends into thick underbrush, so that the cuts weren't obvious. The ones that looked as if they could have come off naturally were left on the ground with the rest of the forest floor litter. He hoped that the driving rain would come back at least long enough to wash away their footprints, and that no one would notice that some parts didn't have the consistent coating of ash that the rest of the forest floor did.

Ray called to Ben, "Skipper wants us back at the hut."

Ben left the disassembled bivouac, glancing back to see if it was beginning to look as if no one had been there, and jogged into the open where the ruined hut lay. The rain was easing off, and the wind was in less sustained gusts. Hatoe was climbing into the wreckage. "Ray, you go to the fireplace. There was a heavy iron grate there. You should be able to make a bit off selling the metal from that." He paid no attention to Ray's wide-eyed surprise, telling Ben in the same, brisk tone, "Ben, give me a hand to get under here. They had metal cookware for cooking over the fire."

Ben was careful to recall where the pieces of corrugated iron he and Hatoe moved had been so that they could put it back looking as if it hadn't been disturbed. Hatoe was muttering to himself. "It should be right here."

"You okay, Skip?" Ray called out, grinning like a kid opening birthday presents, holding the black grate in both hands.

"Yep. We got our share, thanks." He handed several cast-iron pans, pots, and hooks to Ben, telling him, "Next time we come here we'd better strip this hut and not worry about the shipwrecks. Now that it's exposed to the elements the corrugated iron sheets will rust away in no time."

Ben stared at the treasures in disbelief as he picked his way out of the rubble to lay them down to leave his hands free so that he could help Hatoe restore the hut to an untouched look. "Our ancestors made pans out of iron?"

Hatoe raised his shoulders, his eyes twinkling, his mouth pulled back in a closed-lip grin. "Looks like they had so much metal that they used it for everything."

There was a sharp earth-tremor then, which shuffled and resettled the pieces of the hut. "Aue, Ruamoko!" Hatoe crowed, delightedly, getting back to his feet. "That saves us the effort of making it look like no one was here."

After trying a number of different ways, they finally found that the best way to take with them everything they'd carried up the hill was to lash the pieces of iron together so that Ben could carry them on his back, using one of the cushions to pad his back from the iron. Their own billy and other things were piled in the groundsheet that was then bundled up around them, tied into a swag, and heaved up onto Ray's back with another of the cushions. Hatoe had the last cushion and the hammock. He scouted around trying to make it look as if no one had been there, picking up the things that had been missed, and putting back the forest floor litter they'd cleared away from the base of their shelter.

They wore their survival suits without the ship shoes. They didn't want to risk wearing holes in the soles just in case they did end up in the water and needed water-tight suits for survival, so they left the soft shoes folded up and clipped to their kit belts.

At the beginning of the path down to the water they stopped and stared. The rain was pouring down again by then, making the steep path into a slippery waterfall. The bright orange guide rope they'd strung from tree to tree to help them climb up swung, showing how strong the wind was. The wind was now bringing the ash in their direction, making the path both more slippery and more abrasive at the same time.

Ben tried first, but it turned out to be impossible to carry the weight of the iron down the treacherous slope. Even with bare feet gripping at the stones and tree roots, and both hands holding tight to the guide rope, he lost traction, and fell, sliding down the path for a couple of metres before he could bring himself to a stop by snagging the grill on some bared tree roots.

"Stop and think," Hatoe called out.

All very well for you, Ben thought, sullenly, mentally checking where he hurt. It seemed as if he was only bruised. Nothing appeared to be broken. The tough fabric of the survival suit prevented anything from poking into him, as well as keeping him warm and dry, except for his feet. Too warm, in fact, and made it harder to move. He flopped over like a ragdoll where he'd come to rest, calling back up, "Right you are!"

"Why are you just lying there?" Ray's voice had the shrill edge of panic in it.

"Seems as good a place to lie around as any," Ben yelled back. Where he had landed was more exposed to the wind than they had been up at the top under thicker cover. The wind was coming over the island and down the cliffs into Boat Cove, hitting the trees and rocks then blowing upwards and outwards in every direction. The top of the path was not only protected by the thick forest, but it was also in the lea, away from the brunt of the wind-force. Although Ben was awarded some protection by the trees and palms around him, it was nowhere near the shelter of the thick forest at the top. By lying back, he kept out of the worst of it.

Hatoe called down, "Why aren't you getting up?"

Ben knew that his uncle was worried that he'd been injured by the fall, but he chose to deliberately misinterpret. "You told me to stop and think. So, I've stopped, and I think none of my getting up options is better than staying here."

The half-serious tone of Hatoe's voice told Ben that Hatoe knew he was playing. "Now I'm telling you to get up and get going."

Mock-grumbling, Ben started to his feet. "Stop start, start stop; how's a boy to know. . ." As if it had been waiting for him, the wind pounced, jerking Ben off balance and off the path, scrabbling wildly for the rope. He ended up clinging to the rope, both arms fully extended, his shoulders complaining about being yanked on. "All told, I think the option of staying down was a good one!" he shouted. Although he was only a couple of metres from the others, he had to yell as if they were far further apart.

He couldn't see the others at that moment, so he didn't know what Hatoe's reaction was, but he could hear Ray's high pitched, "How are we going to get down if we can't even keep our footing?"

Hatoe's voice came back steady and authoritative. "Put a lid on it, Ray. We'll do what we always do on a tricky slope. We'll lower the stuff by rope with a guy rope at the bottom."

Having managed to haul himself back under the guide rope to where he could once again lay back in the waterfall, Ben looked up. "I'll bet I'm elected fishy-at-the-bottom."

Hatoe grinned down at him. "What was your first clue, Sparky?"

"Oh, I don't know. A wild guess. Nothing to do with being the one that's already part way down."

"Yeah - nah," Hatoe agreed in mock seriousness. "Nothing to do with that. Can you get back up to where you can catch the ropes?"

"I'll give it a go," Ben hoped he sounded more confident than he felt. By remaining lying down he avoided the worst of the wind while he tied the iron to the guide rope, leaving the iron on the ground but making sure it wouldn't go anywhere. Then he climbed on all fours back up to the curve in the path a metre above him. "Ha!" he shouted in triumph, getting to his knees and raising one fist.

Hatoe tossed the ropes to him. "If they go astray, I'll haul them back up," Hatoe shouted. "Attach the bottom end of the one we've got to the iron, and one end of the loose one, then get yourself down with the free end of that one. We'll take up the slack and lower the iron first. Then we'll lower the rest of the stuff, then Ray. I'll come last bringing the guide rope with me."

That worried Ben. "She's right vicious, Skip. I don't like the odds of you climbing down with nothing to hold on to, eh?"

"Give me some credit!" Hatoe snapped.

Ben wished he hadn't said anything. He hadn't meant to imply that his uncle didn't know what he was doing. The old man had been so touchy since Aunty Annie'd died, he had to watch every word he said around him. One moment he'd be joking, and the next he'd bite your head off. As Ben slithered back to the iron with the ropes, he thought he didn't blame Hatoe. He couldn't imagine how he would keep going if ever he lost Miki. Hatoe was just hard to live with sometimes.

The wind suddenly dropped. Ben took instant advantage, untying the iron from the guide rope and scrambling as fast as he could down the trail carrying it.

Once he was out of the shelter of the path, minimal though it was, Ben was shocked by the power of the wind when it returned. It knocked the air out of him, and then took to knocking him over. He had to lie flat to lash the iron to the ropes, cursing himself for having not done it before. He could almost hear the wind-sprites snickering as he slipped and slid. Not liking the idea of a broken leg or worse, he lay flat when he was blown over yet again, bellowing up to the guardian of wind and storms, "Tawhiri! I could do with a bit of a break, here!"

After that it seemed he had better luck climbing down. Or at least he wasn't blown over so often. But down at the bottom worse awaited him. He clung to the guide rope staring in appalled disbelief. The storm surge had brought the ocean right up to the path, well above the spot where they'd spent the first night. And they'd been so sure that spot was higher than the ocean would ever reach.

All he could think at first was, "Thank goodness we didn't stay here! If that had come when we were asleep, we'd be goners." His second thought was, "How are we going to get out of here alive?"

Their belongings that had been carefully stashed down among the rocks were bobbing about. The dingy had moved down towards the Laughing Dolphin and was partly awash, despite the fact it was still full of rocks, and the Dolph herself looked as if she'd moved. Spray reached Ben, whipped up by gusts.

He flattened himself to give the wind as little purchase on him as possible and sealed his survival suit. Despite the fact that he couldn't dry his feet, he took his ship shoes from his belt-clip. "Well, this isn't the best, but it's better than nothing," he said aloud to hear his own voice, as he wiped away as much mud and other grime from his feet as he could with his hands. He glanced at the surf, looking to see whether or not there was a spot where he could wash his feet, but it was all too rough. He slipped the soft shoes on and sealed them to his survival suit, feeling the warmth at once. The spray was drenching his hair, so that he had to constantly brush it off his forehead with his arm so that he could see. He was concerned about getting wet ash into his eyes. That's what drove him to putting up the hood of his suit, unfolding the faceplate and settling it over his forehead and eyes. When he sealed the hood and faceplate he was surprised by the sudden drop in noise. The hood protected his ears from the battering winds. He could see, he was warm and dry, and his ears were no longer being assaulted. The result was a surge of confidence. He took his gloves from his belt clip and put them on as well, sealing them to the suit. The only parts of him exposed to the elements now were his mouth and nose. Taking care how he placed his feet so that he didn't slip on the unstable rocks, he manoeuvred into position to lower the iron.

First things first: get the others down so that they were all together, then figure out what they had to do from there, even if it was to go back up and wait for a better time.

The iron would not budge. Ray had to make his way down the hazardous path to dislodge it. Once it was free, Ben and Hatoe only moved it a metre or so before it snagged again. By the time the iron was at the bottom with Ben, Ray was most of the way down, too. Ben finger-spoke to him to finish climbing down, not go back up.

"Now how are we going to get the rest of our stuff down if there's no-one there to keep it moving?" Ray asked Ben in finger-speak as he sat down to put on his ship shoes.

They watched the rope eel its way back up as Hatoe pulled it to him once they'd given it a couple of sharp tugs to signal that it was free. "Blowed if I know," Ben admitted, his heart in his mouth because he couldn't see how his uncle could do it without getting hurt, and he couldn't begin to imagine what they'd do without him.

Unable to stand by helplessly, Ben set to work gathering up their scattered belongings, cursing the ones that had been moved as far as the surf. He slipped on the unstable rocks more than once. "I'm going to be right colourful after this," he muttered, thinking of the number of bruises he was covering himself with. He glanced back at Ray periodically, aware that he wouldn't hear if he were called. As the wind continued to push him over, he called to the guardian of the winds, "Aue Tawhirimatea! When I asked for a break I meant in the wind, not in my leg!" his hands were full, so he looked around for a place to put his salvage. Seeing where he'd left the iron gave him the bright idea of giving everything to Ray to take care of.

So, ggggggggg5t44444444444444444444444444444444444444444f he was right beside Ray when the swag bounced into view. Ben helped Ray climb back up the short stretch to retrieve it, then watched in admiration as Hatoe came into view. He'd made a kind of pulley for himself, looping the end of the rope tied to their belongings around a tree, lowering himself with it to the next knot of the guide rope, untying the guide rope, using it as a pulley to hold him while he loosened the lowering rope and pulled its loose end off the tree, then looped it around the next tree and loosened the guide rope, kicked the swag down as far as he could, pulled the loose end of the guide rope free, then lowered himself to the next knot of the guide rope and repeated the whole procedure. At all times he was supported by one of the ropes, sometimes by both, yet he managed to leave no rope above him.

"You're a genius!" Ben shouted in heart-felt praise as soon as Hatoe was in range.

Hatoe sat on the cement at the bottom of the path, catching his breath. He nodded to Ben and Ray, sizing them up. He took his cue from them, wiped his feet as dry and clean as he could, then donned and sealed his full survival suit. Now they were all in screaming colours; Hatoe in lurid lemon, Ray in putrid green, and Ben in eye-wounding orange, with the same swirling patterns on one shoulder of their suits in black as they had tattooed on their shoulders. No doubt they would be easy to find if they went overboard, but it was a bit much up close on land.

Hatoe looked at the Laughing Dolphin and said something that was too muffled by the survival suit for Ben to hear.

"Pardon?" Ben asked in finger-speak.

Hatoe signed back, "Didn't I tell her not to do anything stupid?"

Ben looked out at their boat. "Yes," he nodded, looking back at Hatoe to follow what he was saying.

"She's pulled her anchor. That's very stupid."

Ben nodded, smiling to show he appreciated the humour.

Hatoe gestured at the pile of things they'd collected and nodded approval. By finger-speak he directed Ray to continue gathering things up, and Ben to help him retrieve the dingy.

As Ben had suspected it would, it took all three of them fighting the wind to get the dingy back up a little way from the waves. They had no chance of taking it back to where they had originally left it. No matter what they did with it, gusts of wind would catch it and set it dancing, trying to fly. The only way they could keep it still was by filling it with rocks, and then it was useless. They gave up and concentrated on collecting everything from between the rocks and off the cement at the base of the trail; their iron and everything. They lashed it all into the bucking dingy, and then sealed the cover over it, so that even if it turned upside down nothing would fall out. They made a rhythm of removing a rock, pulling the cover, piling the rock on top again to hold it down.

Seeing how hard it was to control the dingy, Ben figured the only way they were going to board the Laughing Dolphin was by getting in the water. If someone had to do it, it might as well be him. He gestured to Hatoe, who nodded.

With Hatoe and Ray sitting on the dingy, Ben took his flippers from his belt clip, sealed them to his ship shoes, tied the orange rope that had been their guide rope around his waist, then made his way over to the mooring line they'd anchored with the huge rock. Instead of being taut like they'd left it, it sagged down to the water as waves came in, bringing the Laughing Dolphin closer, then pulled taut as the waves retreated and the winds blew the boat out as far as the mooring lines would allow.

Ben waited until the line slacked off, then made his way along it. He wasn't more than knee-deep before he could feel the power of the swell. He had to keep resisting the urge to throw the orange rope over the mooring line. The orange rope was so that Hatoe and Ray could pull him out of the drink if he got into trouble. If he tangled it in the mooring line and ended up under water, they wouldn't be able to pull him out. Just the same, all of his instincts told him to throw a loop of rope over the mooring line so that he wouldn't be swept out to sea.

The swell was not predictable, so he couldn't brace himself against the regular pulls in and out, it was just that the pull out was so strong he wasn't always sure he could keep a hold of the mooring line. He was pulled off his feet before he was waist-deep and never managed to get his feet on the bottom again. The sea pulled him this way and that so that he hung from the mooring line towards the ocean as the wave pulled out, then towards the shore as the next one came in, banging his knees painfully on the rocks below during the change-over. After a couple of tries he gave up on the idea of putting his feet down and turned upwards instead to hook them over the mooring line and crawl along it upside down.

That put his face under water a few times, but he made more progress. He put all his concentration into staying on the mooring line, praying that his gloves would keep their grip and not wear through. He knew they were tough, but he'd never done anything quite like this before. He was afraid of the abrasiveness of the volcanic ash. The wave action still pulled him from one side to the other, even though he presented a smaller purchase for it. He was just getting to the point where his head was always above water no matter how much it went up and down, and he was starting to wonder what he should do once he no longer had the water supporting most of his weight, when he felt something give.

Ben clung more tightly to the mooring line, alarm bells going off in his mind as he tried to figure out what was happening. The water was splashing into his face again, and it seemed easier to wrap himself around the mooring line. He clung like a barnacle as the next wave threw him towards shore, climbing frantically as the pull slackened, then gripping again as it pulled him towards the sea. Only this time it didn't stop. He kept on going with the water towards the deeps, even though he still had the mooring line. As his head went under water, he was aware that he'd somehow wrapped his arms and legs around the mooring line until he was virtually tangled in it. He felt no fear, only a vague puzzlement that if he still had the line how could he be heading out to sea?

Violently his ride jerked to a stop. The mooring line was taut. Ben slammed into something. He was tangled enough in the line that even the bang didn't shake him loose. It nearly knocked the air out of him though, which would have been bad, since he couldn't tell which way was up. He concentrated on figuring out which way to air, confused by bubbles all around him and the movement of the water. Then he realised what he'd hit was sloped. He felt a tug on the safety rope around his waist and gave two sharp jerks in reply. Leave me alone! The last thing he wanted right then was to be pulled along underwater.

Making sure the mooring line was wrapped around his arms; he felt the slope he was against. It was the Dolph! 'Dear old Dolphy, you've saved me,' he thought, feeling with his hands and kicking with his flippers. Although the waves did their best to drag him back in to shore underwater, Ben had caught on to which direction up was, from the shape of the hull. He shot to the surface, blew like a whale and sucked a lungful of air before his head was in the water again. He could see that, as he'd suspected, the mooring line had pulled free from the rocks. It was still attached to the Laughing Dolphin.

That split second above water was all he needed to orient himself. If he kept a hold of the mooring line, he would inevitably be washed along the boat by the wave action. If he got himself the right distance along the line, he would end up at the stern, so long as he didn't get sucked underneath the hull.

When the pull of the waves eased, Ben scrambled as far along the mooring line as he could until he felt the shift that meant the wave was flowing out again. Making sure the mooring line was firmly wound around his arms as well as held in his hands, Ben struck out for the Laughing Dolphin using the movement of the waves to his advantage.

All he really needed to do was aim himself at the Laughing Dolphin and let the retreating wave carry him to her. He swam strongly, using the flippers to advantage, fighting to go towards the east where he'd intersect the boat instead of south-west with the water heading back to sea. This time when he hit the side of the boat, he was ready for it. He brought his hands forward, keeping his grip on the mooring line, fended the hull off, allowed the wave to drag him along the boat until he reached the stern, and then triumphantly caught a hold of the handrails around the transom. The handrails were designed for people climbing onto the boat from the water, and he'd used them innumerable times in his life, so it was no challenge to him to climb up and sit on a step of the transom to rest and catch his breath before climbing the rest of the way up.

Then it was a matter of dealing with the awning in the wind, making his way to the bow, untying the safety rope from his waist and attaching it to a capstan so that Hatoe and Ray could use it to haul themselves and the dingy to the Laughing Dolphin.

Having lost one mooring line, she was now swinging a lot more, so, after coiling the mooring line where it belonged, Ben went to the wheel and started the motor to try to gain some semblance of control over the craft. He wasn't only concerned that she would be swinging too wildly for Hatoe and Ray to reach her easily as she was, but when they loosened the other mooring lines, he knew the swells would have even more effect on her.

Ben might as well have not bothered. The wind and waves had their way with the light craft as if she had no motor or steerage. It was hard work for Hatoe and Ray. Ray kept a tight hold of the rope that had been Ben's safety line. Hatoe untied the second mooring line from the tree and used it.

The moment that mooring line was untied the prevailing wind took the little craft to the south-west. Ben fought hard to stop her from being smashed into the rocks behind her in Boat Cove, then she was straining at her anchor out into the bay, facing away from Hatoe and Ray instead of towards them.

Ray and Hatoe had been pulled behind her on the life-raft. Between them and the two ropes they managed to make some headway against the surf, but despite their best efforts the dingy was flipped upside down, throwing both into the water. They had, however, tied both ropes to the dingy, and had both put their flippers on, and had both tied guide ropes to the dingy, so they were able to pull themselves to it, and it to them. When they both had caught the hand holds around the lifeboat, they climbed back on and started again, using the same methods, only with the dingy upside down.

The wind sprites weren't going to be defeated so easily, and simply flipped the boat again. And again. The dingy did not want to leave the surf.

Seeing the battle going on, Ben left the stern and went to the bow. In order to haul up their harvests of seaweed, the capstans could be used as winches. By that method he helped Hatoe and Ray to bring the dingy close enough to the stern that they could reach the rails and climb up. Then, between the three of them, they were able to drag the dingy up over the transom into the stern deck where they could deflate it and retrieve their belongings.

Exhausted, Hatoe and Ray remained in the stern while Ben popped quickly down into the galley to get refreshments. He knew, above all, they all wanted fresh water with no taint of sulphur. As well as that he heated some broth so at least they would have something hot and nourishing. Who knew how long it would be before anyone could go down below again once they started out into the big grey wobbly expanse out there.

They guzzled the water like men who'd been parched in a desert. The broth was wonderfully warming and welcome. Now that they felt relatively refreshed and content the wind eased off. 'Typical,' Ben thought. "Oh, very funny!" he called out to Tawhirimatea.

Their battle had taken all afternoon. The light was beginning to dim. "We'd better take advantage," Hatoe announced, returning the good fuel cell to its secret slot. "Up anchor."

"It's not dark," Ray squeaked.

"I want to go when there's still enough light to see the rocks under the surface." Hatoe stated. "If we can get out there when the light is tricky, they won't be sure of what they're seeing if they do catch sight of us – but I don't think they can. They're likely too far around the north to see us. Even if they have made it far enough along the east coast to catch sight of us, they won't be sure of what they saw in the poor light, at this distance, through the poor visibility. As long as we have no lights. Don't touch anything that might activate light until we're well over the horizon. Especially the eyes. They might not know what they saw if an unlit shape slips around the corner and vanishes, but everyone always sees eyes. We have to run like poachers. Move now. We have to be past the worst of it before the next band of wind."

Ben could see the sense in that and hurried to haul in the anchor. The Laughing Dolphin at once headed out into the bay. With the tide pulling to the south-west, it looked as if she was going to be blown into the rocks under the cliff on the west side of the bay.

"Come on, puddin'," Hatoe urged her, fighting to make headway against the swell.

Ray seemed to be frozen to the spot. "Why are we heading back into a storm we were sheltering from?"

'Bit late for that now,' Ben thought.

Once again Hatoe explained, "The storm is nearly over. The wind is coming in bands, now, instead of continually. It's not as hard or as strong. The rain is easing off. The storm is heading north. If we go due south, we'll soon be out of it. Then we can turn for home."

'I wouldn't have that much patience with him,' Ben mused.

There wasn't much they could do except watch as Hatoe managed to keep the little boat off the rocks, persuade her out to the open ocean. The swells rolled in at them, seeming to go on forever. The water would grow into a mountain, then a massive grey-green wall. They'd ride to the top, seeing the cliffs beside them as if they were riding on a glass-sided lift zipping them up. They got a magnificent view of the parts of Rangitahua that were close to them, then they'd slide down into the well of water surrounded by creaming foam.

What Ben was most afraid of was that they wouldn't see a subsurface rock and would hit it. Worse, perhaps, would be seeing one and not being able to avoid it. If there was a rock like that at the bottom of one of the troughs, there wouldn't be a single thing they could do to avoid landing on it.

But that never happened. Each swell took them further and further, the wind blowing them away from the island just as it had driven them away when they'd arrived. They didn't catch a glimpse of the alien ship, and soon lost sight of grey, rain-shrouded Rangitahua Island, volcano and all.

From then it was a matter of endurance in the most miserable, uncomfortable conditions that Ben could ever remember experiencing, until quite suddenly, as if they'd passed through a door, there were stars above them and around them a quiet sea.

Hatoe changed the heading to west.

Ray asked, preparing to put the sails up, asking, "Which ones do you want, Skip?"

"None of them," Hatoe shook his head. "We'll go flat out. We'll run the whole way on the fuel cell."

They both stared at him as if he'd grown a second head.

"The People must know," he proclaimed. "Don't look at me like that. There's no way out of coming back at this point no matter what we do. There'll be damage to the spinners to repair and who knows what else. The Dolph will have to have a complete check-up to make sure she's got no hidden cracks. If she's out of commission, we have to live on our savings until she's sea-worthy again or we rent a boat. It's all got to be paid for. Most important of all, we didn't tend the Pou Whenua. Refilling the fuel cells is the least of my concerns."

Ben was jolted. He'd forgotten the family touchstone. "We have to come back to do that," he agreed. "Where is it?"

"On the other side of the island from where we were. The north coast. The volcano might have eaten it or buried it."

"What form did it take?" Ray asked.

Hatoe told him, "A pole," adding, "Please don't say 'did.' Ruamoko might have spared it."

That was enough for Ben. "We have to come back and find out!"

Ray said quietly, "I'm not coming back."

Feeling the need for a change of subject Ben offered, "A proper meal?" loosening his survival suit.

"A proper meal," Hatoe agreed, with feeling. He warned Ben, "Don't get too relaxed. We can still run across bands of wind."

"Could I activate light in the galley?" Ben asked, resealing his suit.

"Yeah, no worries. We're well over the horizon from them now. Then you're in the bunk. We're back on our shifts."

It felt strange to Ben. Anti-climatic, somehow. After all they'd gone through, now they were back on their normal routine as if nothing had happened. He had to stop and think hard, conjuring up an image of the alien ship to be sure he really had seen it. They might as well have seen an ancestor risen from the dead, or a ship from outer space, he thought. What will happen, now? What will people do? Will anyone believe us?

CHAPTER FOUR

Chuck

After Johnny went back down to the cabin, Chuck stayed up on deck peering into the gloom, trying to catch another glimpse of the land. One part of him couldn't believe they'd finally found land. He felt mixed-up, as if it couldn't really be happening. He'd always known the GR twisted things, but to actually see with his own eyes that they'd been flat out wrong was too much to take in all at once.

The rain let up again. He peered out, straining to see, hardly noticing the movement of the ship until Sam's voice brought him back to reality.

"Don't lean out too far, Chuck."

He realised then that he was leaning over the rail, and pulled back. "It is real, huh, Sam?"

The red glow showed through the mists first. "Johnny's pillar of fire by night and cloud by day," Sam pointed. "Looks real to me."

"Maybe the little guy was right all along," Chuck suggested. All of a sudden he didn't know what he believed any more.

Like a veil being lifted the mists cleared, giving them a sudden clear view of several tiny islands to the west of them, between them and a land with its upper reaches shrouded in clouds. There were huge breakers around the islands, as well as over the rocks the Weskies had claimed were under the water where they couldn't see them. The red glow was revealed to be a river of red running into the sea, which it met with noisy explosions and gouts of steam that gleamed, pink-stained white against the glowing red. Above was the towering cloud that had guided them across the ocean. It had flashes of red in it, too, with occasional lightning. The tower of cloud vanished into the rain and storm clouds.

For a brief moment both the storm clouds and the boiling cloud were moved aside by the winds, and they could see the mainland itself. They looked out on a strange scene, in which natural beauty was scarred by sinister devastation. It revealed a brief peek at an angry black gash in the green land.

At the sight of that the Weskies set up a clamour for the ship to move south as fast as possible. Chuck couldn't make out what their excitement was about. "Why do they jabber like that?" he groused to Joe Mack.

"Yeah." Joe Mack glared at the Weskies.

The Major was too seasick for duty, his place taken by a grumbling first lieutenant who didn't want to change Major Temperance's orders without checking with him first. Sam had to leave the deck to go and remind him forcefully that the Weskies were there to keep them alive. Though none of them from the GR knew anything about volcanoes, the Weskies did, so they'd better do what the Weskies said, even if it made no sense to them.

Watching Sam head off, Chuck wondered about the word, 'volcano.' He'd never heard it before. Did Sam know what it meant, or was he just copying what the Weskies said?

Theoretically Sam was the boss, since he'd leased the ship and was paying the wages of everyone on board, but now that he was looking at it in a different light, Chuck could see that the military didn't see it that way at all. Everything pointed to Joe Mack being way more right than Chuck wanted him to be. The Major had a drinking problem, the lieutenant couldn't make a decision to save his life, and everyone under them had one problem or another that would have made them a misfit in a regular detail.

As he stood watching the islands after Sam left, Chuck's mind idled around the idea of who else might have been right all along. He glanced sideways at Joe Mack, the only one of the explorers still with him. Pitching his voice low to make sure the soldiers who were either throwing up over the side or looking at the land couldn't hear him, Chuck asked, "Do you think Johnny's right?"

"About what?" Joe Mack lowered his voice even before he looked around to make sure there was no one near enough to over-hear them. Seeing where the soldiers were, and what they were doing, he moved closer to Chuck to answer. "Religion? Hell, Chuck, Johnny's good folk, but he ain't of this world. His head is in the clouds. You can have faith, okay? But you've got to use the good sense God gave you!"

"*Agarrar la onda*. Right. Yeah." Chuck turned his full attention back over to looking at the land. They weren't moving forward much, even though he could hear and feel the engines pounding harder. The ship pitched up and down the mountainous waves, wallowing in between. The rain came and went, sometimes hiding the little islands, sometimes revealing them. "I still can't believe it's real."

Joe Mack grunted. "It's real. The folk on that land will be so grateful we rescued them that they'll pay us big time."

Chuck hadn't thought about that. "You mean take them with us? We don't know how many there are. There ain't a ton of room."

"That's the beauty of it. When they see we ain't got room they'll try to buy rescue like the poor bastards in that hurricane in the Panhandle, remember? They'd a give us their souls if it would a got them outta that hellhole."

"Right. Colonel Lewis let us help them. You think he made it look like we was helping them so they'd think the GR was gonna be good to them? They never defended their land after that. They just about begged us to take over."

"That's what I'm thinking. Same thing will happen here. They'll climb on top of each other to get rescued. There ain't a hope in hell for more than a handful of them. They see that, and they start to compete for the bunks. We'll make enough to pay for this whole thing, and if they got gold and shit, we won't just be out of debt, we'll be filthy rich!"

Chuck watched the land the whole time Joe Mack was talking. Discipline and routine might have gone out the window when too many officers got sick to stay on top of things, but that wouldn't stop some loser trying to get in good by reporting him if he looked like he might have unpatriotic attitudes. He was worried that the way he'd spoken about helping the hurricane victims could sound like he didn't think the Gethsemane Republic was God's Earthly home.

The ship was beginning to make headway towards the south. As he stared at the land, listening to Joe Mack, he could see more of the coast each time the rain let up. There were cliffs in some parts, in others the trees came right down to the water. Something about it struck him. "Are you sure there's more than a handful here? There's no sign of them."

"What?" Joe Mack turned his attention to the land. "What did you see?"

"Nothing, that's the point. De nada. No roads, no farms, no towns, no nothing."

"They just had a hell of a hurricane that ain't done yet. They're still under cover."

"Not them, their buildings. We couldn't see men from this far, but you can see towns and ranches for miles."

"I'm starving," Joe Mack said, abruptly turning away.

Chuck followed him, feeling the first smile on his face for days. "You know I'm right."

Joe Mack turned on him so suddenly that Chuck knew he'd got to him. He didn't care, he still felt like laughing, even when Joe Mack yelled at him, "You can't see them from here! It's too far and it's raining!"

"Yeah, right." Chuck stepped around Joe Mack and went on ahead.

Joe Mack pounded along at his heels, arguing the whole way. "It's got to be fifteen or twenty miles away! You can't tell me you can see clear that far!"

Mealtimes had changed since they'd into run into the storm. Once the ship had started rolling as well as pitching, even the Weskies who'd been doing all of the cooking were mostly missing. Those diners who were not seasick had the tables pretty much to themselves. What would be served to them was more of an adventure than a regular meal. Cloth was spread over the tables like tablecloths and kept wet to stop things sliding round, and everything was laid flat. Someone had nailed pieces of wood around the edges of the tables to stop everything being thrown off. Food had to be eaten with one hand while the other held the plate. Soup was a particular problem.

Seeing there was no one there but one hangdog Weskie, Joe Mack and Chuck continued to argue. "**¡Chale!** Give me a break! There ain't no way you can see that from here. No way, no how, no chance."

"I got better eyes than you, that's all."

"I ain't buying it." Joe Mack appealed to the Weskie, "You figure we're about twenty miles away from the coast?"

"About ten miles, Sir."

"There ain't no way to see clear over there, huh?"

The Weskie froze, eyes flicking nervously back and forth between them.

Chuck watched the Weskie for a moment, confused. Then he got it in a flash, and slugged Joe Mack in the shoulder. "Smooth move, asshole! You put him between a rock and a hard spot – he can't answer either way, and he can't not answer!"

While Joe Mack tried to figure it out, Chuck asked the Weskie, "What's your name?"

"Raamah, Sir."

"I don't mean your GR name, I mean your Weskie name."

The prisoner went right back to looking trapped and terrified.

"Don't scare the poor shit," Joe Mack turned the tables on Chuck with obvious pleasure.

Chuck felt bad. He'd meant to make Raamah relax so that they could talk to him, not make him afraid that he was being set up for one of the GR's cruel games that would end with him injured or worse. "It's just us here. You got nothing to worry about. Sage told me his name and nothing happened to him."

Raamah's eyes went wide, and he took a step back raising his head to look at Chuck in a whole new way, asking, "He told you that?"

Joe Mack, murmured, "Yeah, he did. But we get it if you don't want to."

Raamah nodded, looking at Chuck intently. "Rock," he muttered.

"What?" Chuck had barely heard him. Raamah had his head back down, his eyes lowered. It took Chuck a moment to piece it together. In the same soft undertone he confirmed, "Your name?" Rock nodded, so Chuck stuck his hand out. "Pleased ta meetcha, Rock. I'm Chelubai, but people call me Chuck."

Rock stared at the hand for a moment before giving it a quick shake, saying, "Rocky,"

Joe Mack stuck his hand out.

"Joe Mack, this is Rocky, baptised Raamah. Rock, meet Joseph."

"Call me Joe Mack when there ain't no ears. You don't mind none if I call you Raamah out there, huh? You know what would happen to us if we got called pagan lovers."

"Yeah." Rocky changed in front of their eyes, standing straighter, looking them in the eye.

"Got any grub?" Chuck asked, thinking that it was likely the GR had put the Weskies who were the most trouble on board.

"Nothing's ready." Rocky rushed to get something for them. "You're early."

"You mean we got to eat worms?" Chuck asked in a mock child's whine.

"Better than grubs," Joe Mack pointed out, with a laugh in his voice.

Rocky came back carrying two daily rations.

"No, it's not, it's D-rats," Chuck corrected Joe Mack.

"Made from real rats," Joe Mack added, pulling a face.

Rocky came close to giving them a grin.

Thinking that if Rocky didn't have anything ready, he wouldn't be able to talk to them, Chuck asked him, "You got a sec to tell me something?"

Rocky hesitated, glancing at the doors. "Don't know much."

"You know how far away we are," Joe Mack insisted. "Do you know if we could see people from here?"

Chuck quickly put in, "Or buildings or ranches?"

Rocky looked from one to the other. Carefully he said, "You'd see their boats and docks."

They stared at him. "What?"

"It's a coast. There'll be boats."

They stared at each other. "Yeah."

Joe Mack asked, "What about the smoke? Why did we have to move the ship? What's that all about?"

Rocky glanced over his shoulder towards the work he should have been doing.

"They'll flog you if there ain't nothing ready for them," Chuck realised. "We'll eat our rats and grubs 'till you got time."

By the time Rocky was free to answer their questions, there was another Weskie there and some of the tables had grumbling soldiers around them, picking at the food.

Chuck muttered, "No harm in talking about the smoke in public, huh?"

Joe Mack indicated the door with his head. "Ask him."

Chuck turned to look at the door. Sam was coming through, followed by Johnny and Vince. Putting up his arm to show Sam where they were, Chuck felt relieved. Sam would find out without causing any trouble. He waited impatiently for them to get their food. Before Sam had sat down Chuck asked, "Did anyone see any boats along that coast?"

"Good point," Sam nodded, his lips pursed in consideration. "It don't look like it. No one said nothing about it." He stared at his tray with undisguised revulsion. "God, I hope we fill the ship with fresh stuff. Potato, potato, potato. Every day, every meal. Dried onions don't fix it. Pickled cabbage, salt pork, beef jerky – if I'd known we were going to be tortured like this I might have not come out here."

The explorers grinned. "Yeah, right, Sam."

Vince looked nauseated. "I only came here to get something to drink. I'm so thirsty I could drink the ocean dry. Just don't talk about the food."

"It could have been worse, "Chuck told him. "We had D-rats."

Johnny looked up from his tray. "Why?"

Joe Mack told them, "We got here way early."

"Why did you stay?" Sam spoke slowly and quietly.

Joe Mack softly explained, "Waiting until the place was empty. We wanted to know why we had to move away from the smoke."

Sam chewed thoughtfully. "They said it's dangerous."

"Yeah, but why?"

Sam ate in silence, pondering.

"They're watching us," Joe Mack warned.

"Always are," Sam spoke without looking up. "Don't give them the feeling we're whispering together, guys."

Chuck decided that there was no problem with keeping to part of the subject. "We were twenty miles away from it," he stated, leaning back with his hands clasped behind his head, using a normal speaking voice. "Why were the Weskies so scared of it?"

"The Hand of God is in the Pillar of Fire by Night and Smoke by Day," Johnny reminded them. "Pagans fear the power of the Living God."

Chuck thought that was the right kind of thing to say out loud. He nodded to Johnny to encourage him, noting that Sam was doing the same thing, and loudly proclaimed, "Amen!" As Johnny launched into his favourite topic, Chuck used him as a cover to tell Sam, "The one with the long face is Raamah."

Sam looked over. The Weskies were already cleaning up. Very few had come in for the meal, so it was over way sooner than normal. Sam made a show of listening to Johnny, which slowed his eating to the point that they were still there when the soldiers were leaving.

Johnny, in full flow about the Greatness of God, wasn't eating. Joe Mack's eyes glazed over. Vince seemed to be paying rapt attention. Chuck leaned his elbows on the table, supporting his head with his fists to wait it out. A few soldiers stopped to listen and say, "Amen!" but with the majority of their unit seasick they were doing double and triple duty and had no time to stay.

As soon as the military left, Sam beckoned Rocky over and waved Johnny down. Talking over the top of Johnny's last few words he said, "Tell us about the smoke," when Rocky came within easy speaking distance.

Rocky eyed Sam uneasily.

Chuck tried to signal to him that everything was okay without attracting unwanted attention.

Rocky said, quietly, "Volcanoes don't just put out smoke, Sir."

"What did you say?" Chuck asked him. It was that word again. He was determined to find out what it meant, this time. "Is that a Weskie word?" He tried to sound non-threatening. "If that's what you call it in your language, what would you call it in ours?"

Rocky stuttered, "I – I – um – you . . ."

Chuck tried to put him at ease. "It don't matter if you know it or not."

They all agreed, at which Rocky's face cleared. Tentatively he asked, "You don't know what a volcano is?"

"No. Never heard of it," Johnny peered at him, bewilderment all over his face. Joe Mack looked like he'd been beaten with a stupid stick; his mouth hanging open, his eyes unfocused. Vince was staring at his beer.

It was Sam who surprised Chuck the most. "Tell me what it is." He lowered his voice, checking to make sure they were alone with the Weskies. "I think I heard about it once."

They all went quiet, including Rocky. After a moment of Sam looking at him expectantly, Rocky told them, "A volcano is where melted rocks come up out of the earth."

"What melts rocks?" Chuck had never heard of such a thing.

"The heat inside the earth."

Johnny's jaw dropped. "Do you mean to tell me that the Fires of Hell come to the surface here? That we've sailed to the very door of Satan himself?"

Chuck felt a shiver of fear. They all seemed as uneasy as he felt.

Rocky shook his head. "I don't know. We've got volcanoes and earthquakes where I come from. The Free West is more like heaven than the hell you people believe in."

Johnny rose to his feet, eyes flashing.

'Uh oh,' Chuck thought. 'Here comes a rant.'

"That can only mean that the Prince of Darkness is in your homeland!"

Chuck could see that Johnny was even more scared than Rocky, who stood with his arms dropped limply to his sides, staring at Johnny.

Sam's voice was kind. He put a hand on Johnny's arm, though he spoke to Rocky. "I'm betting you gotta get back to work mighty quick, huh?"

"Yes, Sir!" Rocky looked back. The other Weskie was wiping tables, watching them anxiously.

Sam turned, saw what Rocky was looking at, and beckoned the other man over, telling Johnny in the same kindly tone, "Sit down, son. We ain't never gonna find out God's Truth if we don't learn about new things when we see them."

Johnny slowly sank back down, still visibly upset. If he was honest with himself, Chuck would have to admit that the idea of setting foot on a place that opened to the Fires of Hell wasn't what he'd expected to find. It scared him, too. He took a deep breath, looking intensely at Johnny, willing him to look up, and making a mental note to talk to him later.

Sam checked with the Weskies, "It's a matter of life and death to stay away from that volcano, ain't it?"

"Yes, Sir!" Rocky was emphatic.

"Then it's as much your lives as ours."

They both nodded.

"To do this fast, tell me everything about the volcano, quick as you can. No one will interrupt. We're about fifteen miles away from shore. If that ain't far enough, why not? I got to know to make the Major listen to me."

They nearly fell over each other in their haste to explain, talking at the same time.

"It can reach a lot more than fifteen miles!"

"It ain't just smoke. It ain't like a forest fire."

"That's what you were following for the last two weeks. It had to go for hundreds of miles to lead you so far."

"The red stuff is melted rock. If any landed on the ship it would be worse than cannon fire."

"The hurricane blew it away from us, but now that it's dying we've really got to find shelter before the volcanic ash finds us. Really."

"The grey stuff is ash. If the ship gets too much of that it'll destroy the engines."

Sam held up his hand. "Hold it. I can't follow this. What're your names?"

Chuck saw his chance to show the Weskies how much the explorers sympathised with them. "Sam, this is Rocky, baptised Raamah. Rocky, this is Samuel Hiram Johnson." He turned to the other Weskie and apologised, "I'm sorry, I don't know your name."

Staring at him as if in a dream, the man said, "Cliff. Cain."

Sam nodded courteously to each of them, then asked, "Rocky, what kind of shelter are we looking for?"

"It looks like the mountains here are high enough to protect us from the ash, if the wind is in the other direction."

"So you're saying we got to keep going south along this coast."

Rocky nodded. "It's the best thing to do for now."

"For now! Then what?"

"Then try to get out of reach," Rocky said quite reasonably.

Chuck was just starting to think that it wasn't as bad as it sounded, when Cliff added, "If you can see a volcano it can get you. If the wind blows the smoke in our direction, it can pelt us with ash, pumice, and stones. The mountains are the only shelter we got out here."

They all grunted as if they'd been punched. The idea of taking off across the ocean died before Chuck had a chance to say it.

"How can ash wreck the engines?" Joe Mack demanded. "It's not like they're up on deck."

"Volcanic ash is not like wood ash," Rocky explained. "It's not soft. It's gritty, and so hard it grinds moving parts down, so powdery it gets into everything, so light it floats in the air, and so heavy that it brings down buildings if it makes a thick enough blanket."

Feeling too cold inside to be able to speak, Chuck was grateful to Vince for putting his whirling thoughts into words. "It can't be heavy and light at the same time."

Cliff didn't make Chuck feel any better by saying, "Its powdered rock. If it gets wet it goes back to solid rock, like cement."

Rocky added, "If you breathe it in, it makes cement inside you."

That was too much for Vince. "Pagan superstition!" he shouted. "Sam, be careful – this is how the Devil leads the Faithful astray."

Sam's tone made them all freeze. "Not so loud. We don't need help." He turned to the Weskies. "How do you know this?"

"We've got volcanoes on the Coast up north of the Free West."

"I've never heard nothing about shit like that."

The Weskies looked at one another. Cliff was trying to signal, "No," to Rocky with his eyes and minute shakes of his head.

Rocky saw that they'd noticed, faced Sam, swallowed, and said, "That's what the Ashlands are."

That caused a numb silence that was broken at last by Johnny pointing out, "The Ashlands ain't nowhere near the west coast. They're north of the GR, hundreds of miles away from the coast."

Chuck could feel something stirring in the back of his brain. "You never served," he reminded Johnny. "If you'd a done a stint on the northern border, you'd know that's what they're like."

"You never saw the Ashlands!" Johnny wasn't buying it. "The border's never been pushed that far north!" but he faltered when the others made, "Oh, yeah," kinds of noises.

Chuck wasn't surprised by Johnny's reaction. He had an answer ready. "Bounty hunters, recons, and captives all talked about it."

"Rumours and enemy propaganda."

"Why is it called the Ashlands, then, huh, Johnny? Is it because of rumours or because there's thousands of miles of nothing?"

Chuck thought he'd made a point no one could argue with, but he'd underestimated Vince, who quoted from the prophet Abraham Wright, "Lo, the Lord our God did bring down upon the sinners His righteous wrath and did smite them all with fire and brimstone."

Sam asked Rocky, "What do you say the Ashlands were caused by?"

Rocky sighed, looked into their faces and told them, "Your Judgement Day was the eruption of a volcano hundreds and hundreds of times bigger than this one."

Sam's hand was on Johnny's shoulder so fast the poor boy didn't have time to leap to his feet.

Vince, however, was not so constrained. He was on his feet, shouting, "Blasphemy! I can not stand by and hear the Word of God blasphemed!"

Sam got right into Vince's face. "Don't call every danged MP on the ship! They're seasick. That don't make them friendly." As Vince subsided, Sam prompted him more quietly, "Don't you think God could use a volcano if He wanted to?"

Vince reared right back up again. "It was not natural!" He bellowed. "It was the Hand of God!"

"Watch it, Vince! We don't need an audience. Who's to say the Hand of God wasn't in the volcano?" Sam took a deep breath and continued more conversationally, "If His Hand was in the column of fire and smoke that led us here, and it's a volcano, looks like He uses volcanoes when it's a big deal. That's your fire from the sky." Sam turned to the Weskies. "What about the brimstone?"

Cliff shrugged. "It's another word for sulphur. Volcanoes make huge piles of sulphur."

That seemed to satisfy everyone except Vince that Judgement Day was a volcano.

Chuck couldn't imagine how a column of smoke could devastate the continent, no matter how much fire and brimstone it carried. He asked Rocky, "How could something like that be so bad that it's called a Judgement Day? How could it make the Ashlands?"

"This one is a tiny little pimple of a thing next to that, and if this one was at Port Persistence it would bury the port, the shipyard, the railway, the barracks, the prison camp, the harbour, miles of the Panhandle, and square miles of real estate on both sides of it."

That made Chuck queasy in a way none of the gyrations of the ship had.

"And you call that small," Sam said.

"Yes," Cliff nodded. "This is a little volcano. It's a big eruption for a small volcano like this. It's been hurling ash into the sky for at least as long as we've been following it, if not longer, and its pouring lava into the sea." He picked up a scrap of food from the table-top and held it between his thumb and fore-finger, showing it to them all. "But to get an idea of what made your Judgement Day, think of this bit of potato as the little volcano out there and this whole ship as Yellowstone."

They all just stared, numbed, except for Sam, who seemed to know something and started to say, "Yellow. . ."

They were interrupted by a sneering voice from the door. "Well, ain't that grand. You girls look real cosy. I got me a mess of pagan lovers."

Chuck barely had enough time to glare at Invincible-faith Thomason for yelling so loud that a sergeant got nosy, when Sam gave the kind of roar that made anyone who had ever been in the military snap to rigid attention. "SERGEANT!"

Nose to nose Sam snapped at the stunned young man, "Name! Rank! Serial number!" then gave him no time to rattle them off, talking over him to say, "I am SAMuel HIram JOHNson, COLonel, reTIRed, Gethsemane Republic, Special Operations, called out of retirement for THIS mission. DO you understand?"

The sergeant answered in a quavering squeak, "GRSO?"

The explorers were reflexively at attention like the sergeant, but they didn't have Sam screaming in their faces, so they were able to look around as he roared, "That's 'GRSO, SIR!' And I do not believe I stuttered, Sergeant!"

"No, Sir!"

"WHAT?"

"I mean; yes, Sir, GRSO, Sir. No, Sir, you did not stutter, Sir!"

Hearing Sam tear into him, "Then clean out your ears!" Chuck realised Sam was giving them the chance to vanish. Chuck signalled to the Weskies to disappear in one direction while the explorers went in another.

"Yes, Sir! Thank you, Sir!"

"Anything you don't know about Special Ops you don't need to know. Do you hear me, Boy!"

"Yes, Sir. Thank you, sir."

Seeing the Weskies fade to the back, the explorers crept slowly to the door.

"On whose authority did you interrupt the interrogation of the only people who know how to stay alive out here?"

"Well, you see, sir. . ."

"No! I DOn't see!" Sam was shouting so loudly that they could still hear him when they were on the other side of the door.

Creeping away from the door, Johnny whispered, "Was Sam a Colonel?"

The others shook their heads or shrugged, motioning him to silence.

Neither Sam nor the sergeant could have heard them, because Sam was still bellowing, "At least now I can let Major Temperance know who is undermining the safety of this mission!"

Vince sped up at the sound of Sam's boot heels pounding towards them. Chuck was one who stopped and turned to face him. At the door

Sam roared back, "DIS-missed!" stepped through looking around, saw them and winked, and then strode off with his boot heels sounding like cannon fire on the metal decking.

Thinking that the first person that the poor, shell-shocked sergeant saw was going to suffer, Chuck raced to the cabin as quietly as possible, pleased to see the others had the same idea.

In the cabin they laughed out loud, exclaiming, "What the hell was that?"

"Did you see the look on that guy's face?"

"Sam about blew the hair off his head!"

Willie Jay raised himself to his elbows in his bunk, asking, "What's going on?"

Chuck asked him, "Willie Jay, was Sam ever a colonel?"

"No, why?"

The burst of laughter and excited talk this brought had Willie Jay sitting up straighter, repeating, "What's going on?"

Joe Mack didn't answer directly. "Are you sure?"

"Yes. He never had time to make rank and his folks had no money to buy him rank."

"That's right," Johnny nodded. "He told me he never went to the Academy."

Vince exclaimed, "You mean he lied?"

Willie Jay was outraged. "Sam would never lie!"

Vince sneered, "You can't have it both ways, Willie Jay. Either he lied to the sergeant that he was a colonel or he lied to us that he wasn't. So much for 'Straight-Shooting Sam'."

Willie Jay did that stammering and gulping thing he always did when he didn't know what to say. Normally it got on Chuck's nerves, but right then he was so fed up with Vince that he didn't notice. "You watch your mouth! The walls have ears." For effect he went to the door and checked outside the cabin. Turning back from the doorway he tore into Vince. "If Sam had to lie it was because YOU got to caterwauling and set the dogs on us!"

Willie Jay's jaw was slack and his eyes were wide. He sounded like a lost small boy when he asked, "Why would Sam tell a lie?"

Johnny told him kindly, "The sergeant said we were all pagan lovers. If the sergeant thought Sam was GRSO he'd forget all about what he thinks he saw."

"GRSO? Sam is Special Ops?"

The explorers groaned in exasperation.

There were times when Chuck didn't know why Sam had to bring someone so innocent. "No, Willie Jay, he said that to put the dog off the scent."

Joe Mack snorted. "That's one dog that ain't never gonna sniff around Sam again."

They laughed. Chuck almost felt sorry for the sergeant. "The poor shit."

Joe Mack snickered, "Finding out he'd got in the middle of Special Ops. On a scale of 1 to 10 that's a pucker factor of 86."

Even Vince snickered at that. "Yeah, and he ain't gonna get much sympathy from his friends."

The grin slid from Johnny's face. "You know . . ."

They stopped goofing around and stared at him.

"I just got it. We were with Sam. All of us 'interrogating the only people who know how to stay alive out here.' When word gets around, they won't only watch it with Sam, they'll be real careful around all of us."

It felt like a weight rolled off Chuck's shoulders.

"I'll be the first one to thank him if Sam's set it up that those good old boys ain't gonna throw one of us over the side before we get back home," Joe Mack said, with his voice lowered but his eyes intense.

"Our chances of surviving this just doubled," Chuck smiled, letting all of the air out of his chest in a huge sight of relief.

Vince snorted again.

Chuck wished he wouldn't do that. "What?" he snapped.

"Unless he is GRSO. Then we're screwed."

CHAPTER FIVE

Olarine

*H*aving lots of energy had always been something that people had envied about Olarine. Personally, she found it to be as much of a drawback as a benefit. For one thing it meant that she could never sit still and relax. Here she was, finally, able to linger in Abernaud's glass studio as she'd been dreaming about throughout the whole long session of her first government, and she couldn't keep still.

The main thing that was on her mind was their son's upcoming bonding day. She did her best to stay in the chair Abernaud had placed for her at a safe distance from the searing heat of the molten glass, but she kept remembering things they ought to do before the ceremony. She said these thoughts aloud until Abernaud complained. Not wanting to forget her ideas, Olarine jumped to her feet, crossed the studio to Abernaud's drafting table, and wrote notes to herself.

After several of these darts back and forth, Abernaud straightened his back, turned to Olarine and asked, "Can't keep still?" He wiped the sweat from his eyes with his forearm, turning her insides to jelly with a glimpse of his flat stomach when his shirt rode up.

"Sorry," she apologised. They used to argue about their differences when they were young. Now that they both had grey hair – if she was honest with herself, she had to admit that hers was white and his was grey – they had learned it was those differences which made their union work. His calmness kept her steady, and her restlessness kept him from slipping off into an artistic isolation.

"Can't you read or something?"

"Oh, uh, no, I'd rather not." Reading involved keeping her eyes off Abernaud. There was no point in that! Watching that man work was what she'd been dreaming of.

Thirty years of partnership, since that thin grey plait on the back of his neck was thick and auburn brown, and still the greatest pleasure of her life was watching the way the muscles moved under the smooth tanned skin of his back and arms as he turned the molten glass into beautiful art. The only thing that spoiled her enjoyment was her restlessness.

"I'll keep still," she promised.

"You've never managed it before, how are you going to do it now?"

"I really want to be here with you. I've been looking forward to it."

Abernaud perched one bum cheek on a corner of his drafting table. "Ol, you've finished your bonding gift for the kids. If I don't get this made now, they won't have it until afterwards."

"I had to draw the house plans months ago or their house couldn't be built!"

"And if I don't complete the stained-glass window, they'll have no front door for it, Pet."

"Oh, Bernie, I love watching you make it."

"And do you love watching me burn myself?"

"No! Of course not! I mean to sit still, really, I do."

"I know you do, Love, but I don't have the time left to take a break if you've reached your limit. I couldn't start the window until the door was finished so that I had exact measurements. You're an architect; you know how important precise measurements are."

"I know, I'm sorry, I keep thinking of things we need to do and I'm afraid I won't remember if I don't tell you or write it down. Old age is not doing a thing for my memory."

"It's not doing much for my concentration, either."

Olarine felt terrible. By this time of life, she had expected better self-control of herself. "I'm ruining everything, aren't I?" she sighed, picturing her son and daughter-in-law not able to move into their new house after their honeymoon because it had no front door.

"Not everything, Pet." He gave her a look of love and admiration that set her heart thumping. "The People made no mistake when they elected you First Servant. You're the best leader in these three thousand islands since the Freeze."

"You're prejudiced in my favour."

"So, strand me. It's still true that all we need to do is find a way for you to remember your ideas without breaking my concentration by jumping up and down all the time or suddenly saying something that's got nothing to do with what I'm doing or thinking." He handed her paper and a pencil.

Olarine took them, but she could feel the urge to move getting stronger. The image of Larry's new home not being ready for him because she had disturbed his father, or worse, Abernaud burned because she'd distracted him at a crucial moment, brought her to an abrupt decision. She got to her feet and kissed him. "Thank you, Sweetie. I think I'd better take a break and come back in little while. Would you like some tea?"

Abernaud had chilled water on tap in his studio. "No, thanks, but I'd love to see you in a bit to show you how it's coming along. It's one of the best things I've ever designed, if not <u>the</u> best." He went back to his worktable and picked up a piece of the glass that had started to cool while they'd been talking and held it up with his heat-proof gloves for her to see.

Olarine caught her breath. "Oh, Bernie, you've outdone yourself!" Even with his old gloves on either side of it holding it up instead of the lovely frame of the carved and polished multi-coloured wood of the door, she knew this was an award-winning piece of art. "You'll be the Premier Glass Master all over again. No-one can touch you."

"It's not for competition, Ollie. Do you think the kids will like it? Because it's for a door it's been treated to make it shatter-proof, so the colours might not be as intense."

They both nearly jumped out of their skins when the studio door crashed open and a frantic voice shrieked, "Madam First! Madam First!"

Abernaud dropped the piece of glass, which landed on one corner with a faint plink.

Olarine spun to face the door, sure there had been an earthquake or serious accident somewhere. "What is it?" Her heart was in her mouth.

"Madam First! They've seen a ship!"

She couldn't grasp what he'd said. "What? What do you mean? What does that mean?"

"One of the weedies. He saw an iron ship."

Her fright was turning to bewildered annoyance. All she could think of was Abernaud's hard work, his beautiful creation, broken for nothing, and now there was not enough time to make another one, so Larry wouldn't have a gift from his Dad on his bonding day. "An iron ship? What do you mean an iron ship? A metal hunter? Why frighten the life out of us for that?"

"No, Madam First, not one of our boats, a weird ship."

Olarine's mouth went dry. She could feel the blood drain from her face. This couldn't be true. She looked at her life partner for reassurance, only to see him frozen, bug-eyed, in the midst of picking up the brightly coloured glass with one bent corner and an unmistakable spider-webbing of cracks ruining it. "Y'wot?" Her brain was numb. She couldn't think. Those words, "Not one of our boats," echoed inside her head.

"An alien ship, Ms Eidola. The sea-weed grower and his crew came straight here to tell you. They're waiting to see you."

"An alien ship." She knew she was being incredibly thick, but she simply couldn't believe what she was hearing.

"Yes, Ma'am. What shall I tell them?"

"Tell them I'll be right there." That woke her brain up. "Where is it?"

"Out on the blue. They were blown way out by that storm that ate the Rangatira."

"It's too much to hope that this is the missing weedie crew turned up with a tale to tell?"

"No, I'm sorry, the one that's missing is the Rangatira from Te Whanganui a Tara; the crew who saw the iron ship sail the Laughing Dolphin from Matapihi."

They stared at one another for a moment, then he said, "I'll tell them you'll be along in a bit."

"Thank you." She turned to Abernaud and asked, "Optical illusion?"

"You're grasping at straws, Pet."

"This can't be happening."

He dropped the cracked glass into the recycle bin with a crash, slipped his heat-proof gloves off, then went to her and put his arms around her. "If it is there's no one better to pilot us through it."

"What on earth will I do if it is true?" she wailed, suddenly terrified by the responsibility.

"What do the Protocols say about it?"

"Nothing."

"Y'wot?" He stepped back and gaped at her. "The Protocols cover everything. Maybe you haven't . . ."

She cut him off. "Everything except what to do if we're contacted by strangers. It was one of the first things I was taught after the election. The Troggies couldn't predict what form the first contact would take or when it would be. There were too many variables, so they didn't leave any guidelines at all."

He blinked. "I suppose that makes sense," he said with such doubt in his voice that Olarine's apprehension overwhelmed her.

"It didn't matter then, because it was never going to happen in my lifetime, never mind in the five years I'll be in service. Who could have imagined it would be only a few weeks later? We're not even used to working together yet. I don't know what to do or where to start. How can I see those people when I'm clucking like an old hen? They'll need to see someone who knows what she's doing, not someone who obviously hasn't a clue!"

"They'll be pretty shocked, too, Pet. Whether or not they really saw anything, they believe they did, so their reality has been twisted even more than ours. They need to see the First Servant regardless of whether or not you have any idea of what to say or do."

His calm and steady manner took the edge off her rising fear. "What am I going to do?"

"I can't tell you that!"

"But you could give me some advice!"

"Look," he held up another cooled piece of the stained glass. "I melt sand. I add stuff to it to make it pretty colours or stop it shattering, and I shape it. That's what I know. That's all I've ever done. You're the one who learned about lots of different things and got involved in government as soon as the kids were old enough. There's a lifetime of know-how in that head of yours for you to draw on, Protocol or no Protocol."

Olarine threw up her hands. "And they had the same plus some! The people who put our society together were much closer to outsiders than we are. They were only separated by two or three generations; they had elders who had been overseas or had heard about it first hand. They weren't two hundred and fifty years away from it like we are. It was the heighth of irresponsibility for them to leave decisions that will affect generations to come in the hands of people with absolutely nothing to go on! They came up with the principle that the government exists to serve The People. The first requirement for service is adequate information."

Abernaud put his arms around her and kissed her. "You're good at that, you know. You should go into politics." He winked.

Caught by surprise, Olarine smiled despite her turmoil.

"That's better," he smiled back. "Where's all that confidence you showed during the elections?"

"I'm completely out of my depth. I can follow the Protocol, but I can't even begin to deal with something this enormous with no guidelines. Everything I've ever done has been following the way I was taught. I'm not an original thinker, that's your strength. I'm meticulous not inventive. And now I'm supposed to wing it with the most important event since we came out of the tunnels?" She could hear the rising hysteria in her voice, but she couldn't do a thing about it.

"Well, I can't give you any political advice. Here's what I would do in a situation like yours; firstly, I would talk to these weedies. Find out whether or not they really did see anything. If so, I'd call everyone back."

"Of course! It's not my decision to make. If there is anything there, the People have to decide what they want to do. But before we worry, we have to find out if there's anything to be worried about. It's so obvious. I don't understand why I couldn't figure it out for myself."

"A bit of shock, I think, and fear of the unknown. I've never known you to freeze up before, not in thirty years. But it matters so much to you to do the right thing for the People and the future that I can see where you could paralyze yourself when there's no right answer. That's why I never went into politics."

"I don't know what I'd do without you, you sweet man. Thank you. I'm sorry about your work. It truly was one of your best. And now it can't be ready for them in time."

Abernaud turned and went back behind his worktable. "Same thing would have happened if I'd dropped it on my own before it had cooled enough. When it's still flexible it's very fragile." As he was putting on his safety equipment, he said, "If the weedies really did see something, Larry's door is the least of our concerns."

As she walked through the studio door, Olarine looked at her back gardens thinking how strange it was that everything could look exactly the same when actually nothing was the same and never would be again. She closed the door behind her softly, but didn't lean against it so that Abernaud wouldn't see through the window in the door that she was hesitating after all of the effort he'd put into bolstering her up.

Because of the fire risk from the studio, it was a separate building. Olarine was thankful for the short walk to the house. She took full advantage of the moment of peace to compose herself.

For aesthetics she and Abernaud had surrounded the studio with a moat which was stocked with coloured fish and water lilies. It was fed by a soothing trickle burbling over artfully arranged stones and glass pebbles that caught the light. Stopping on the bridge over the moat, looking down at the lazy fish and the reflections of the trees and bushes overhead, she listened to the water and the birds, allowing the restful sounds to calm her, taking deep breaths of the flower-scented air. Abernaud had blown colourful glass balls to float on the moat, where they bobbed serenely, occasionally clinking together.

"Don't borrow trouble," she told herself firmly. "They probably saw the Rangatira and were confused by the storm. Even if our isolation is over, that doesn't mean anything will change. If there are people back on the oceans, they might be glad to learn a more civilized way of life from us." She strode along the stone-flagged path with her usual long-legged gait, planning, "Unless there's something really drastic, I'm not calling the Triune in from their break."

Sam

Too excited to sleep, Sam decided against sharing a bunk. Because Vince and Willie Jay were still seasick, each of them had a bunk to himself. Rather than try to bunk in with one of the others, Sam made do on the floor, despite the damp and stink. He'd started out balanced across two chairs, but the second time the ship threw him on the floor he gave up and stayed there. After very little sleep, he got up before dawn and went up on deck to make sure he wouldn't miss a thing.

Overnight the ocean had settled right down. The ship was barely moving with the waves, a gentle rocking that he'd found soothing when it had happened before the storm. This time he was too pent up to notice. All he could think of was that it was real. It was really happening. They'd found another land. It wasn't just foolish daydreams any longer.

Sam gripped the ship's rail tightly, staring out into the dark. The rail and the deck were covered with a fine, gritty powder. Although the storm had moved on and the sky was clearing to the south, where they were the clouds made a great black blot over the stars and the moon. Where there were breaks in the cloud cover, the stars were unfamiliar. Sam stared up at sky, marvelling that God could even change the stars above.

He could see a looming blackness where he knew the land was, but he couldn't make out the details. His eye was pulled to the glowing red river running down to the sea. It was behind them now, partially obscured, but still visible enough for him to know where it was. With the noise of the storm gone, the explosions drowned out every other sound except the hissing roar of the steam. Each time he looked away another explosion would boom across the ocean, drawing him back. The bursts of steam shot up like fountains, weirdly pink-stained by the shimmering red. Cliff had said that the river was molten rock, Sam remembered. He wasn't sure he believed everything the Weskies had told them, but he didn't disbelieve, either. It was all too magnificent and strange for him to know what he thought.

Back from the steam, inland from it, was Johnny's guiding tower of cloud. It shouldn't have been visible in the darkness, but it was lit from the inside by flashes of red and occasional lightning. As bizarre as that was, it was nothing next to the sight of it like a twister that wasn't twisting, seeming to boil instead.

Like Chuck and Joe Mack, Sam was more pragmatic about religion and God than either Johnny Balaam or Willie Jay Rimmon. Just the same he couldn't help wondering if he was seeing something evil, natural, or holy.

Sam knew there would be no question for Johnny; he would believe it was the Hand of God no matter what. Johnny's faith was so pure that he would believe God was guiding them unless God himself said he wasn't. In a way Sam envied Johnny his utter, child-like faith. Willie Jay had it, too, but then Willie Jay was child-like.

Sam sometimes wondered if it had been a good idea to take Willie Jay along on this exploratory journey. Who knew what dangers lay ahead, and who knew how much Willie Jay actually understood? He'd come up with last minute funds that Sam had desperately needed to get the expedition on its way. After that it didn't seem right to tell him that he couldn't come.

Sam's thoughts were disrupted by the ringing of the bell that summoned them to prayer. The first call to prayer on the Sabbath was always before dawn. Sighing, Sam left the deck to take part the in the day of prayer, fasting, services, sermons, readings, worship, and study.

It was not until after dark, after the day was over, that Sam was able to get anything to eat, or a chance to talk to his explorers. Because no one was allowed to work during the Sabbath, the ship had hardly moved during the day. Major Temperance's only response to the Weskie's frantic pleas to keep moving the ship further from the volcano was to say that the Gethsemane Republic military only worked on the Sabbath if they were in a fire fight.

Sam prayed long and hard that the winds wouldn't shift. He did not want to find out the hard way that the Weskies were right about the danger they were in. He was thankful that they'd moved as much as they had the night before Sabbath. A few times during the day he'd sneaked a quick look and had seen that the wind was blowing north-east again, now and then taking white steam or grey cloud right about where they used to be.

The glimpses Sam had caught during the day showed him the lushest land he'd ever seen. There wasn't one bare inch. It was filled with trees which were filled with birds. The birds could even be heard at night in between the explosions, and seen flying to and from the mainland and the forested humps of the little islands.

"It looks like we've found an arm of land sticking out like the one that shelters Port Persistence from the ocean," he told the others as they bedded down for the night. "Excepting this one ain't desert."

"Sage thinks it might be an island," Chuck said, lowering his voice when he said Sage's name in case the GR had started listening in on them again.

Sam felt a touch annoyed. He badly needed this to be what they'd been searching for. He didn't think he could make Major Temperance go any further if it wasn't, and if he went home empty handed there was no chance of pulling anything like this together ever again. "Just because someone said it don't make it so."

They all stopped what they were doing and stared at him.

"¡A poco! Look at who said it!" Chuck's amazement added doubt to Sam's irritation.

Joe Mack saved him the trouble of answering by snorting, "People think crap!"

"How come?" Chuck paused part way up the ladder to the bunk above Willie Jay's to turn to Joe Mack.

"Look at that sermon today teaching that God destroyed the world because His Children sinned, but the fact that they were destroyed proves that they were sinners all along and not true Children of God."

They all reacted at the same time, urgently motioning him to be quiet and pointing to their ears to remind him that the GR could be eavesdropping.

"We'll see if it's an island in the morning," Sam told them to stop any more talk.

He lay awake for a long time worrying about what he would do if all they had found was an uninhabited island. It couldn't be true. Surely God wouldn't have brought them so far, through so much, for nothing. 'Now I sound like Johnny,' he thought. 'There's no proof God's got anything to do with it. Right from the kick-off it could have been just Amos and me. I never bought into this idea that I'm doing God's work.'

He noticed that no one else was snoring, but said nothing. He didn't want them to start talking again. The last thing he wanted right then was to listen to Johnny and Willie Jay going on about how it was all God's plan, unless it was to hear Joe Mack and Chuck say it wasn't, while Vince never knew what he believed.

Sam had to use self-control to keep from sighing and starting the talk he didn't want as he finally admitted to himself that Vince wasn't as solid and dependable as he'd thought. Sam had originally believed that Willie Jay was the weakest link. Now, after living with them in close quarters for four weeks, Sam was getting the feeling that there was more to Willie Jay than met the eye, and less to Vince. Invincible-faith Thomason was sadly misnamed.

As he lay there, unable to sleep, Sam's mind took him back to when it had all started, before these five guys were born. He'd been ten years old, playing ball with his cousins and his brothers the day his life changed.

Sam's father and uncles had not been raised the Wright Way. Their nation had been conquered when they were old enough that the standard GR indoctrination of children hadn't fully worked on them. Needing the productive farms to feed its troops, the GR hadn't razed their area to the ground the way they did other places. Although Sam's father and uncles had grown up with troops constantly on the farm searching for indications of unpatriotic words, acts, or things, the Johnsons were not scattered and their homes were not destroyed, so they were able to hold on to some of their own ways, faith, and books. So, when the boys finished their chores before dark that day, a day when there happened to be no GR on the property, the men didn't force the boys to do extra work or study the wisdom of the Prophet Abraham Wright, they actually allowed idleness. As a reward for good work, they let the boys play until supper.

There was one ball left from the days before the defences fell, when Sam's Dad had been a boy. Sam's eldest cousin cradled it reverently as they all swore they'd stay in the back forty where they couldn't be seen from the houses or the road, post a look-out in case a patrol happened by, stay away from the hermit's farm, and be sure to be in before supper. They fervently promised not to be seen with, lose, or damage the ball, then they ran hard and fast, cheering and whooping, all the way to a scrubby wooded area with a clearing where they could play ball.

Sam was not the oldest or youngest, the tallest or shortest, the fastest or slowest; he was a middle boy, ordinary in every way. The others didn't bully him, they just didn't notice him. So, when they drew up sides for the game it was Sam who was not chosen for either team, and was sent to keep watch. He thought they would take turns, so he didn't sulk. It was after he thought someone else should take a turn that he got upset.

He was told, "No. Get back out there."

"But I want to play too."

It was the derisive laughter that really made him angry, even more than being told, "You can't run, you can't catch, and you throw worse than a girl."

His eight-year-old brother and nine year old cousin were playing, with allowances being made for their short-comings. "It's not fair!" he hollered. "They're worser than me!"

His fourteen-year-old cousin stamped his foot in Sam's direction as if he was going to chase him. Sam ran off, but he didn't stay away like he had at first. He hung around the edges, staying behind the trees, jealously watching the others play.

He saw his chance when the ball went off into the scrub. He'd seen exactly where it went, got to it first, and held it up to show them. He thought if they saw that he'd got it, they wouldn't think he was a loser anymore and would let him play.

His hopes were dashed when he was ordered, "Throw it here."

"I get a turn, now. I got the ball."

His twelve-year-old brother came out of the trees beside him and tried to snatch the ball, saying, "Don't be so stupid!"

But Sam had heard him coming, ducked his charge, and shoved him over, yelling at them all, "If I can't play, you can't play!"

Then they were all after him and he was running for his life, praying that the brother he'd pushed over would take a minute to get up. He could defend himself against any one of them, up to and including those who were two years older, but he had no chance against a pack. He heard someone promise, "I'll teach him!"

Fear lent wings to his feet. It wasn't until he put out a hand to steady himself as he whipped around a tree that he realised he still had the ball. If they got the ball back they might leave him alone. Without stopping, he chucked the ball as hard as he could back to them. Not even panic could improve his throw. The ball didn't go anywhere near the boys. It scudded between the trees and vanished into a huge hedge.

The hermit lived behind that hedge.

Without thinking, Sam threw himself after the ball.

Now he was in so much trouble he didn't care about the boys anymore. This was the kind of trouble that never went away. He'd done two forbidden things: he'd gone over by the hermit and he'd lost the ball. He hadn't meant to go near the hermit's property; he hadn't noticed where he was running. He would take a whupping for that without complaint. It was losing the ball that he couldn't bear. The last one. The only way to get a new one since the GR declared they were 'instruments of idleness,' was to risk the black market or make one. But if they made one it wouldn't be the one that came from his Dad's childhood, when the land was free. Sam would do anything to avoid the look of sadness the adults got whenever they lost one more thing from before the GR overran their homeland. He would do anything, risk anything, rather than cause that look in his Dad's eye.

Oblivious to the thorns, Sam flattened himself under the hermit's hedge where he thought the ball had gone. Rushing past, shouting threats, the boys didn't see him. He didn't care. He had to find the ball. Flat on his stomach in the narrow space under the hedge, feeling for the ball with his arms outstretched, he neither saw nor heard the dog until it was hauling him out from under the hedge by one leg.

Too shocked to scream or struggle, Sam was dragged into the hermit's yard. Once there, the dog let go and sat down to look at him. When it let him go, Sam rolled over and sat up to look at it. It was enormous. The biggest, meanest looking dog he'd ever seen. Any hope he had that the dog was just playing was blown to pieces when he tried to move away from it. The dog leaned forward so that its nose was nearly touching Sam's and gave the kind of snarling growl that made Sam think his arms were going to be pulled off, one at a time, like legs from a roast chicken.

Too panicky to know what he was doing, Sam started to scramble backwards. The dog barked in his face. It was so loud he couldn't hear himself whimpering.

A voice ordered, "Killer! Hold!" and then the huge mouth came down on his shoulder and pinned him there.

"Oh, God," he prayed "I'm got by a dog that's trained to kill. Please, God, please, please, I'll be good after this, for real, I promise."

The voice said, "It's just a kid!" and ordered Sam, "If I call Killer off, don't move, Boy!"

"Yes, Sir."

"He'll get you before you can get anywhere, and this time I'll let him do what he wants."

"Please don't let him eat me," Sam sobbed, staying rigidly still to convince the man that he wouldn't move if Killer let him go, keeping his eyes tight shut so that he couldn't see that jaws big enough to take his whole head off had him by the shoulder. He was terrified that he'd sealed his doom by forgetting to say, "Sir," and added it as an after-thought.

The man ordered Killer to sit and demanded, "Who do you work for, Boy?"

Sam was so taken by surprise that his eyes flew open, looking right into the hermit's stern ones, as he exclaimed, "I'm ten years old!"

"Don't mean you ain't gotta work to eat, same as the rest of us."

Having heard that those who don't work don't eat repeatedly throughout his life, Sam lowered his eyes and admitted, "My Dad. My Dad makes me work, Sir. And my uncles." He thought about his mother and aunts and the older kids, and figured he'd better tell the whole truth. "Everybody older than me makes me work, Sir." He heard an unexpected noise and looked up. The hermit's eyes didn't look so fierce anymore. Offended that he was being laughed at, Sam insisted, "Well, they do."

"You're one of them Johnson kids."

"Yes, Sir."

The eyes went hard and angry again. "What are you doing here?"

The injustice of it all got to Sam. "Warn't my idea. Killer drug me under the hedge."

"Killer can't fit under the hedge. And, I'd bet, nor can you."

Keeping a wary eye on the dog as he moved, Sam pointed to the place. "He cut me up some on it." The broken twigs, scuffed dirt, and pile of dead leaves and stuff clearly showed where something had been pulled out from under the hedge. The marks on Sam's clothes showed that 'something' had been him.

The hermit seemed to be unmoved by the sight. "Ain't no way Killer got through there and come got you. You had to be under there already."

Sam couldn't deny that. He was too scared to admit he had been under the hedge and anyway he couldn't think how he would explain it without mentioning the ball, and he couldn't lie. He no longer cared about being in trouble at home; that was nothing compared to this. He begged, "Please let me go home, Sir."

"Not until you tell me the truth."

"Oh, please, Sir, my Dad will wup me good."

"What did he send you here for?"

Sam stared, bewildered. "My Dad never sent me here. He don't know I'm here, Sir. He told us to stay away from here."

"He told you to stay away from here? What's the problem, then? You'll get a whipping for being here? How will they know you were here if you don't tell them?"

Sam couldn't take it anymore. He started to cry. "We promised we'd be back in time for supper."

"Then you better start talking, Boy."

Sam's mind went blank. He'd been told what to do his entire life. He'd never had to come up with answers on his own before, especially not such hard ones. It had been so drummed into the kids' heads not to tell family secrets to anyone outside the family that not even fear of Killer could make him say anything about the ball. In fact, he'd been so scared for so long that he didn't feel scared anymore, just numb and tired.

He didn't know how much trouble his parents would be in if anyone knew they encouraged idleness, but he was sure that if word of the ball got out there would be another search of the farm for outlawed items. If they found anything, Sam couldn't judge how bad the punishment would be. He tried to imagine his Dad, or his uncles being flogged, or their homes burnt down. It was more than the sadness in his Dad's eyes, he knew that now. With awful clarity he saw the full meaning of the threats that if anything was ever found again, the authorities would do whatever it took to make sure the children learned the Wright Way.

He understood, now, his mother crying at night, asking his father to give up so they didn't lose the children. What would they do if they lost their right of deferment, and all the boys had to leave on their thirteenth birthdays instead of waiting until they were sixteen — and what if they weren't given landsman's leave to come back and work the farm after basic training? No one over thirteen to help the men do the work, so the women would have to do men's work as well as their own. Too much work. Even with all of the little kids working as hard as they could, they wouldn't be able to get everything done. If they couldn't do all of the ploughing, or sowing, or weeding, or reaping, then they were going to be hungry. Especially if the government upped the amount they took as taxes again.

Sam had been angry with his mother when he'd heard her say that, lying in bed with his sleeping brothers, his fists clenched because she'd said, "Give up."

At the time his father had disappointed him by not telling her they were no quitters, but now his father's reply came back to him forcibly, "We're doing it for them and their children and grandchildren. Someone's got to keep the faith and the knowledge for future generations. If we give up it's gone forever. When the GR're gone how'll truth and freedom and true Christianity spread again if no one preserves them?"

It all came to Sam in a flash; the memory of the search and the threats when he was younger, overlain by the whispered conversation between his parents, and comments by the older boys about going hungry and farm boys' deferment.

And it was all his fault. He, stupid little Sam, had lost the ball where someone might find it and blame his family. He'd gone where he'd been told not to go. He looked at Killer. The dog was quite happy, sitting at semi-alert watching his master's face, and Sam knew without a doubt that Killer would do anything he was told quickly and enthusiastically. There was no way out. He could not run or get through the hedge before Killer would have him.

"I'm waiting, Boy."

Sam just wanted the nightmare to end. He could think of no way that wouldn't bring the law down on his family. "Mister, you better just tell Killer to eat me 'cos I ain't talking." Then he shut his eyes tight and turned his head away so he couldn't see it coming. In the silence that followed he tried not to think of Mom so that he wouldn't cry, and prayed for forgiveness for breaking his promise and for courage.

Finally, he heard, "Right. Let's see. If I believe you weren't sent under the hedge because only a skinny kid can fit under it, then the way I see it, it's one of three things; you were playing, hiding from someone, or looking for something."

Sam opened his eyes and stared at the hermit in bewilderment.

The hermit no longer seemed angry or suspicious. "You ain't talking, and I can't find out about two of them if you don't, but I can try something with the other one. Killer. Seek." He pointed to the hedge, down past where Sam had been dragged through. The huge dog bounded off joyfully, and was soon as snuffling and snorting under the hedge.

At first Sam wasn't concerned because the dog hadn't been given instructions on what to find and was nowhere near where he'd thrown the ball, but as Killer worked his way along the hedge, he sneaked a peek at the hermit. The man was watching him so intently that Sam jumped.

"So, there is something."

The hermit sounded so pleased with himself that all Sam could do was pray the hardest he'd ever prayed in his life that God would keep Killer from finding the ball. He squeezed his eyes tight shut to pray, and was embarrassed by tears sneaking out under his eyelashes.

"Better move back a bit so the dog don't stand on you."

Sam just lay there. He'd been so afraid to move that now he couldn't.

"What's your name, Boy?"

"Sam."

"Well, Samuel Johnson, can't you get up?" The hermit picked Sam up and carried him to the side of the house, put him down on the grass, squatted beside him and said, "Let's see where old Killer cut you up."

Sam could have handled anything but kindness. It was too confusing. He struggled manfully against the tears, but they wouldn't stop.

The hermit paid no attention. He asked, "How did he pull you through the hedge?"

Miserably, despising himself for crying like a baby, Sam pointed a shaking finger at his right leg.

The hermit rolled up the leg of Sam's pants. He let out a low whistle. "You must of kept real still – he never hardly broke the skin." Sam felt that there was something admiring in his eyes and his voice when he asked, "You're being pulled along by a dog with his teeth in your leg, and you don't kick or scream? How come?"

"I know dogs, Sir."

"Don't that beat all? Let's take a look at that shoulder, now."

Because his pants had been handed down from an older boy, they were too big for him and nearly threadbare, so they had folded back easily. The shirt, on the other hand, although it was handed down too, was tight. Sam had almost grown out of it and yelped when the hermit went to uncover his shoulder. Until that moment he'd hardly felt anything. Now he hurt all over. He hurt so bad that he lost track of the dog and didn't notice a change in its snuffling.

When the man stopped paying attention to him, rose to his feet, and encouraged Killer, "That's the boy! Good boy! Get it! Bring it here!" Sam knew he was done for. He'd been abandoned by God, even after he'd prayed his hardest.

Killer forced his way into the hedge, whining a bit as thorns and twigs jabbed him, got the ball and took it to his master.

After praising the dog, the man turned back to Sam. "So, this is what it's all about. You were playing, the ball went into the hedge, you tried to get it back, Killer caught you, and you couldn't say nothing because your folks have been searched before. How'm I doing so far?"

Sam stared at him. "You know about that?"

"These are sad times."

"Can I go home, now, Sir, please?"

"Not just yet." He scooped Sam up and carried him into the house. "I'm Amos. Before you try to walk on that leg, I'd better look at it."

Sam was in despair. Grown ups always did this to kids. They'd say you had to do something because of one thing, then, when you did it there'd be something else no one had ever mentioned. He was too scared to jump down and run with the dog right there. All he could think to do was beg and plead.

Begging and pleading didn't help. All Amos did was shake his head. "Look, son, we don't know if you can walk all the way home on that leg. My dog bit it; it's my duty to see to it." He made the dog stay outside, kicked the door shut and sat Sam on a chair beside a table covered with stuff like an untidy work bench. "Quit your blubbering and roll up that pant leg."

Sam felt comforted. Amos was talking like he was mean, but he was being as gentle as Mom. No longer afraid he'd never see his home again, he said, "Yes, Sir," wiped his eyes on his shirt, and bent down to hike up the pants leg. To cover up that his shoulder hurt when he reached down, he complained, "I promised I'd be home for supper. Now I won't get none." The good smells coming from the pot bubbling on the wood stove made his mouth water and his stomach rumble.

"You'll eat here." Amos crouched down beside the chair with a rag in one hand and a bottle of spirits in the other.

Sam got no further than, "But . . ."

Amos tossed the ball to him, "Play with this to keep your hands busy. Bite it if you want to. This is going to hurt."

And hurt it did. It hurt so much that Sam reacted without thinking when Amos put the point of the knife into the shirt and tore off a strip.

"My Mom made that!" The effort to not cry out like a baby as raw alcohol was dabbed onto every break in his skin had driven everything else out of his mind.

"The dog already ripped it." Unconcerned, he ripped another strip.

"She could've mended it!"

"You don't like that shirt, do you?"

"Oh, no, I – Sir – Amos, I . . ."

"It's too small for you. You got to mop up that blood with something, and if it's not something you got with you, where did it come from?"

Sam bit his lip to keep from saying anything else stupid while Amos finished reducing the shirt to bandages, except for the top part with both sleeves and the collar attached. Holding up the bandages, Sam said, "Bind up your leg with these and make a sling out of the sleeves. I'll show you how, but you've got to do it so it'll look like you did it."

Busy wrapping up every part of him that was bleeding, Sam forgot about not staying for supper until Amos told him to shift himself, spooned stew into a bowl and tore off a chunk of bread for himself.

"Your arm ain't so busted up that you got to be waited on like the President." Amos sounded angry, but Sam noticed he didn't act the way he spoke. "Sit."

"Yes, Sir, Mister Amos."

As Amos plunked the bowl of stew and chunk of bread in front of Sam, he said, "That's just Amos."

Sam didn't know what to do or say. No adult had ever before told him to use just his Christian name. He was even more confused when Amos sat on a chair with his back to the table and his elbows on his knees ready to eat like that. "Do you want me to take the stuff off the table?"

"Nah, son, eat your stew."

"We don't got to sit up at the table?"

"Why would we have to do that?"

"My Mom makes us. She says we got to keep up our standards."

"Ain't no women here to tell me what standards to keep up. We do things my way, here."

Sam was delighted. "When I grow up I'm going to eat how I want like you." He had a sudden twinge of doubt. "Do you say a blessing?"

"Sure. Between the lips and over the gums; look out stomach, here it comes!"

Caught off guard, Sam let out a shout of laughter. Nervously watching Amos, Sam reigned his laughter in. But Amos wasn't angry with Sam for laughing at him. To Sam's amazement, he winked. Then Sam had more understanding of why no one had any contact with the hermit: Amos was not only fiercely protective of his privacy; he was a very bad influence. Quietly Sam said grace to himself, then tucked into the thick and delicious venison stew. He knew he should disapprove, but he couldn't keep a grin from tugging at the corners of his mouth. He sneaked a peek at Amos and was startled to see a twinkle in his eye.

"That's better."

Sam looked Amos right in the eye. He wasn't the least bit scared of him anymore. "It's okay for you – you're not going to get the hide tanned right off your back."

"Not today, but I've had my share. Why are they so mad at you?"

With Amos acting more like a bratty kid than a grown up, Sam felt like confiding in him. "I took the ball and I run off with it and I missed supper."

Amos kept on eating, pushing the bread into the stew and scooping up meat, vegetables, and gravy that he bit off and ate with a slurp. When he finished his piece of bread he tore off another chunk and carried on.

Sam copied him, finding food slurped up from a bowl held on his knees tastier than supper at the table with everyone minding their manners and paying attention to the lessons. Because the Johnsons wanted their children to be what they called 'well educated' the table became a schoolroom every time there were no GR around to punish them for 'teaching lies.' Sam discovered that food was a whole nuther thing when he could eat without thinking about anything else.

As they ate in companionable silence, Sam glanced around the room. It was a big front room lit by a candle hanging over the table, and light from the fire in the huge stone fireplace that filled the wall opposite the front door. The room had obviously been the entire house at one point, with cooking done in the fireplace and sleeping done in a narrow loft up under the roof. There were only three windows: a tiny one the size of a gun barrel beside the front door; a small square one with a felted wool blanket nailed over it in the wall across from the table; and a larger one with a wide sill above the table. The window next to Sam was also covered with a blanket, but this blanket was only nailed along the top and down the left side where there was a dangling string to tie it back and let some daylight in. There was no glass in the big window. Drafts sneaked in between the slats of the closed wooden shutters, making the candle dance. It had been a snug one room log cabin before the kitchen was added. There was just room on the right of the fireplace for a stairway going down, and on the left for the narrow kitchen.

Amos had given Sam more for supper than he got at home, so Sam was surprised to be asked, "Want some more?"

"Really?"

"I don't say things just to hear my own voice."

"Yes, yes please. Thank you."

"You're welcome." Amos refilled Sam's bowl and gave it back to him, asking, "How come you run off with the ball?"

"Thanks." Sam tore off a hunk of bread and poked it into the stew before answering, "They wouldn't let me play." He figured since Amos knew about the ball there was no point in denying that they'd been playing.

"If they wouldn't let you play, they couldn't have the ball."

Sam nodded without looking up from his stew.

"Why run here?"

"They were chasing me. I didn't watch where I was going."

"How did the ball end up in the hedge?"

"I thought if I gave it back, they'd let me go."

"What happened?"

"My aim ain't so hot."

Amos gave a bark of laughter. "Were they anywhere near where you threw it?"

Sam looked up from his stew. He was disgusted with himself and annoyed that Amos was so amused. "Not even close."

Beaming, Amos took the remains of the loaf of bread and tore it into chunks, saying, "Let's get this straight: the kids were chasing you and they don't know where you went."

"No, they don't. They thought I cut over to the crick. I was under the hedge, and they ran right past saying how they were going to dunk me in the crick when they got me."

"There's your answer." Amos dumped the bread on the table and took a piece which he poked into his stew.

Sam watched him for a moment, trying to figure it out, then gave up and asked, "What?"

"Bigger kids were after you, right?"

"Big ones and little ones."

"It's the big ones that'll take the fall. Little ones are useful because they always tell." He took a bite and continued with his mouth full, "Look at it this way: they chased you and now you're missing."

"I'm dead." Sam felt so despairing that the stew that had been so appetizing lost all flavour for him.

"Yeah, that's the point. You stay out past where they're mad at you to where to they're scared for you. Then they'll be mad at the bigger kids for chasing you off. Then when you show up, they'll be glad you're okay instead of mad at you."

Sam had never heard of thinking like that. He couldn't believe what he'd just heard. "Just stay out?"

"You want to go home right now?"

"Oh – um – it'd be okay to wait a bit."

"Figured as much. Eat your supper and then you can help me clean up."

"Clean up? Ain't that women's work?"

Amos fixed Sam with a look that made him hang his head. "No women and it don't do itself. You eat here you clean."

"Yes, Sir." Sam was afraid he'd spoiled the comfortable feeling he'd had with Amos. To make amends he offered, "It was a real good supper. Thank you."

"Never let it sound like anyone's cooking is better than your Mom's, even if it is."

Sam stared, dismayed.

Amos winked and grinned. "Guys' survival tactic."

Sam was lost. He didn't know what to do or say. He finished his stew silently, then got up to do his share of the chores. Without warning his leg collapsed beneath him, pitching him forward onto his face. He lay there, confused, watching the bowl clatter across the floor. It flickered through his mind that it was a good thing it was a wooden bowl or else he'd be in trouble for breaking it.

"What happened?"

"I don't know."

"Looks like that leg ain't gonna hold you. Can you get back on the chair?" Amos scooped up the bowl.

Sam was glad he hadn't fallen at home where the older kids would have called him a clumsy ox. Before he tried to answer, he tried to get up to see if he could. By getting up on one leg he managed to get to his feet.

His hurt leg felt like it wasn't going to support him, so he hopped back to the chair. "Does this mean I have to stay here forever?"

"I ain't feeding you." Amos picked up the dish pan with all the dirty dishes in it and carried it out the back door.

Sam was more comforted by Amos's brief answer than he would have been by any amount of reassurance. He figured Amos had a pump or a well out back. His Mom would have made one of the girls carry a bucket of water in and heat it to wash dishes, but he thought that might be just girls being too sissy to put their hands in cold water.

Amos burst back in through the kitchen door with a straight branch in one hand. "Can you whittle?"

"Yes, Sir." Sam thought that was a stupid question. Everyone had to know how to fix things and make things.

"Then whittle a crutch out of this."

When Sam's mother sewed pants, she always made pouches that hung from the belt on the inside of the pants. Sam slipped his fingers under his belt and pulled out his whittling knife before Amos had a chance to ask him if he had one.

"Right. That'll keep you busy while I tend the critters."

"But I don't . . ."

Amos didn't hear him. He'd already gone.

Sullenly, Sam looked at the branch. "I don't need a crutch," he muttered. "My leg's not broke. I'm only gonna do it 'coz you said." To prove his point, he stood up. The bruises and punctures on his shin and calf throbbed but they didn't hurt as much as the pulled muscles in his groin and hip. He could stand still, but he knew taking a step meant putting all his weight, however briefly, on the injured leg. He was afraid it would pitch him onto his nose again.

He sat back down on the chair and took a serious look at the branch. Amos had chosen well. He'd broken off a piece close to the right height to fit under Sam's arm. It had grown at almost right angles to its parent branch. Amos had broken both ends of that off, too. He hadn't cut any of the ends, but had broken them all, leaving jagged slivers.

Sam knew that the first thing to do was trim the ends so that he didn't get a splinter. He set to work quickly, repeating to himself the mantra his uncle had taught him so that he wouldn't cut too deeply. In a short time, he had tapered ends and no slivers on all three broken stubs. All that remained was to remove the bark from the piece that went under his arm. That was easier than Sam had dared to hope. The bark peeled off exposing creamy smooth wood with no sharp points.

Because he didn't need to do any work on the arm piece, the crutch was finished in no time. Not having anything else to do, he decided to try it out. Before he'd taken two steps the tip slipped on the wooden floor, and he was flat on his face on the floor again.

From that angle he saw two things: the pile of wood chips he'd made on the floor and the clever carpentry attaching the kitchen to the log cabin. Being fascinated by how things were put together and how they worked, Sam took a close look at the way the joins were made so that he could tell his Dad. Remembering that his mother was not pleased when they whittled in the house without first putting something down to catch the shavings, even if they were making something for her, he figured it would be smart to clean up after himself before Amos came back.

He got up the way he did before, balancing on one leg. He looked around for a broom. There was a straw broom leaning against the wall by the kitchen door, which was the whole length of the room away from him.

Being very careful, Sam made his way along the kitchen, holding on to the counter in case his leg gave out. By the time he reached the door he'd found a way to balance his weight so briefly on the sore leg while he moved the good one that the pulled hip didn't have time to throw him on the floor.

At the kitchen door he stopped to look for something to pick up the sweepings with. The woodstove stood at the entrance to the kitchen, spilling its warmth into the cabin. From the door Sam could see that it was backed against the side of the fireplace and shared the chimney. He thought that was clever. Beside the stove was a table with cut firewood stacked under it and tools on one side of it. What surprised Sam was another door into the kitchen beside the table.

He stared at the door, wondering, and then thought if Amos didn't sleep in the loft, then a room that had the back of the chimney against one wall and the back of the stove at the corner would be a nice warm place to sleep. He figured he'd better not open that door, but he did want to see outside. He cracked the door to the outside open a slit and peeked out. It was too dark to see past the steps. He could see one of the bowls on its side. Something large was slurping in the other. Fear of the dog had him pull the door shut.

In the kitchen beside him was a work surface, then a clay sink, then, across from the stove, shelves and hooks bearing items for cooking and eating. There was a window over the sink covered by a wooden shutter. Nowhere did he see anything to sweep the wood scraps onto.

Using the broom as a walking stick, Sam made his way to the wood shavings. He swept them over to the hearth, taking care to balance on his unhurt leg. Reaching the hearth, he sat down on one corner of it, and picked up the scraps with his fingers, putting them with the kindling at the side of the hearth.

Looking at the chairs and the table from there, Sam could see how rough they really were. They could not have been made by the same person who had done the very clever carpentry in the kitchen. There was still bark on them, the pieces were big and chunky, mis-matched, ill-fitted, uneven, and badly finished. They were held together by big ugly wooden pegs of every shape. Some were properly turned and rounded, others were squared off, then there were some wedge-shaped that looked as if they'd been hammered in, and some that were so poorly trimmed that they were neither one thing nor the other.

Sam's Dad would never have put up with such shoddy workmanship. Curious, Sam bent down to look at the underside of the chair seats. They were rougher than he'd expected. The wood on the bottom was as raw as the day it was sawn, and probably full of splinters. Not only that, but there were big globs of glue around the bases of the pegs. He sat back up to compare the tops of the seats with their underneaths. The seats had been sanded and rubbed until there was a smooth surface to sit on, but not all of the pegs were flush with it. Nearly all of the pegs at the rear stuck up a bit, and the odd one or two poked up more than that. On the sides they were flush and level, so Sam figured Amos knew how to do it, he was just lazy.

Using the broom, he got up and hobbled back to the crutch, and practiced with it to put the broom away and get back to his chair to sit and wait for Amos. He wriggled and fidgeted as he perched there, staring around the room at the gun racks and antlers on the wall, the ladder up to the loft, and the dark well of the stairs. It all looked friendly in the firelight and candlelight, but Sam felt uneasy. He'd started to like Amos and to trust what he said. Now it was starting to look as if he was one of the worst kinds of people who were not GR: the kind who drove people off their land then said it was theirs. One thing was sure; whoever made the furniture didn't have the skill or care of whoever made the cabin and added the kitchen. He knew from working with the other boys and men in his family that some had more talent in woodwork than others, and he was real sure no one who did such beautiful work as the cabin and kitchen showed could put up with the laziness of the unfinished furniture.

Disgusted, Sam examined the chair Amos had sat in, thinking how easy it would be to whittle the pegs flat. Even he could do at least one piece each evening. He could see where some of the pegs had been worked on a bit but not finished. He fiddled with the ones on the chair he was sitting on, wondering what he could or should do. There was no point in making a run for it. But what else could he do?

Frustrated and scared, he yanked on the pegs of his chair.

One of them moved.

Sam's scorn for Amos reached a new high. Dollops of resin and he still couldn't seat a peg properly. Sam examined the peg that he thought had moved. It was one of the ones that stuck up quite far. There had been a half-hearted attempt made to whittle it down, leaving a flat spot. This couldn't be the one he'd felt shift, it had a ring of glue all the way around it. He tried the others the whole way around the chair and back to that one again. Thinking he must have imagined it, Sam fingered it, muttering, "Stupid thing."

His surly tugging on the peg moved it again.

Sam slid off the chair to have better leverage. By working at it, he managed to turn it. Once he'd figured out that it turned, resin or no resin, he was able to keep turning it. It was stiff and took all of his strength and both hands, but he'd soon turned it enough to see that under the flat whittled piece at the top it was a round threaded wooden screw, and the glue was attached only to it, not to the chair seat.

While he struggled, Sam tried to figure out why expert woodworking like a threaded screw would be hidden in the ugly chairs. But nothing prepared him for the sight of a cavity where the peg had been. The peg didn't go all the way through. It wasn't holding anything together. He checked underneath. It was a spike at the bottom. He took another look at the peg. That wasn't a sloppy attempt to whittle the peg down, it was a brilliant way to disguise that it was a screw not a spike. Unless you sat still for a long time, as Sam had, and manipulated it, he thought, you'd never see that there was a round peg there.

He peered into the hole, trying to see if the slat that the peg was supposedly holding went through since the peg didn't. There was a curled-up piece of paper in the way, so he pulled it out and felt around with his fingertips. The slat was right there. The cavity had been whittled right through it.

Sam's view of things shifted so suddenly that it he felt it like a physical shake. Catching a hold of the chair, he took another look at it, its companion and the table. What if they weren't sloppy at all? What if they were made like that so the GR would think they were junk?

Trembling, he opened the piece of paper.

It was a list. Sam read no further than; "sulfur, lead, coil of copper wire . . ."

Terrified, he replaced the piece of paper as close to the way it was as he could and screwed the peg back into place. The peg went in sweetly and turned easily at first, but it got harder and harder, until he was sweating and panting, straining with all his might to get it back down to where the resin touched the chair seat, making it look like it was glued in. No matter how hard he tried, he could not get it all the way down, not even when he used the crutch as a lever.

Defeated, Sam retreated to the fireplace where he sat down on the hearth and stared out into the room. Nothing that he had thought before was right. The furniture was every bit as well made as the building, if not more so because it was designed to look like garbage when it was really a hiding place for the same kinds of things that his family hid. He looked at the furniture in a whole new light. The heavy pieces of wood could have any number of small hiding places carved into them, and those huge pegs made ideal ways to get into them without giving away that there was anything there.

Once he had caught his breath and stopped shaking, Sam again felt positive towards Amos. Now he admired him for his smarts as well as his skill. Just as he thought how much his Dad would love to know about the things he'd learned from Amos, he remembered how much trouble he'd be in if his Dad found he'd disobeyed and had gone on to the hermit's property. He couldn't tell anyone what he'd seen or where he'd seen it, and he couldn't tell Amos what he'd seen, either.

What if Amos didn't notice the peg, and there was a raid? If Amos was caught it would be Sam's fault. He had to 'fess up. Nervous about what Amos would do when he found out Sam had discovered his secret, Sam turned to tend the fire.

He was putting a log on the flame when he heard the thump of a door and Amos's voice call, "Sam?"

"Here." Before Sam had a chance to think of what to say or how to say it, Amos was behind him, talking.

"That's right," he approved Sam's fire tending skills, not giving Sam time to respond before saying, "Let's see how you're doing with your crutch. Oh, you've finished it. I didn't think I was gone long enough." He quickly turned the crutch over and around, examining it from every angle as he spoke, then put it down against the hearth and took the poker from Sam, telling him, "I'll do that while you square off that end. Don't want the fire too high while I'm out of the house."

The moment Sam sat down to do as he was told, Amos changed his mind. "No, maybe not. The point you put on it will work better in the dirt. Did you tend the wood stove, too?"

"No, sir."

"I'll do it."

Sam looked at the pointed end of the crutch, picturing it sticking into the dirt as he walked along the road or across the fields. He wanted to tell Amos that the point of the crutch slipped on the floor, but Amos seemed to be in a hurry. He was already finished with the fires and was kneeling in front of Sam rolling his pant leg up saying, "How's the leg?"

He checked it over, letting out a whistle. "You're getting a bruise that'll impress the kids and convince your mother you've been attacked by wild dogs or wolves."

"I don't like to lie to my Mom."

"You don't have to. You can tell them anything you want. If you want to tell them you were here you can, but if we set it up right you don't have to say a word. They'll do it all."

Sam remembered that he hadn't gone home for supper and didn't know what to say.

Amos fixed the shirt sleeves into a sling for Sam's arm, showing Sam how to do it for himself, handed him his crutch, and said, "You'll be cold with a bare chest. Wait here." He went out through the kitchen.

Sam heard the kitchen door open then close, the rattle of the wooden bowls being set down, and then the other door opening and closing. It hit him that the other door had a different sound from the kitchen door, and that was the sound he'd heard when Amos came in. That meant the door Sam had thought led to Amos's room had to have access to the outside. Sam went to the entrance to the kitchen to try to figure it out.

He was standing by the wood stove when Amos came back. "Cold, huh? This'll keep you warm until you're nearly home." Draping a sweater around Sam, he continued, "I can't take you all the way. Before your dogs raise the alarm, I have to turn back. It'll be chilly for the last bit without my sweater, but that'll help your cause. You want more to eat before we go?"

"What? No. No, thank you, I'm still stuffed." Sam felt confused all over again. But they were, honestly, on their way. The fear that had been nibbling at the back of his mind that he would never get away was gone, leaving him dizzy with relief.

"That's okay. It'll help your cause if you got no appetite."

"Okay." It was the second time Amos had said that and Sam still had no idea what it meant.

"Got your ball?"

Sam turned to pick it up from the table, but his crutch slipped. Amos caught him before he hit the floor. "Thank you, Amos. It always does that."

"You're welcome. I thought it might do that. You'll be okay when we get outside."

Sam let Amos carry the ball, following him to the front door happily except for one thing. "What about Killer?"

"He'll whine his fool head off when he finds out he ain't coming."

Amos was right about that the way he was right about everything else.

When Sam arrived home all the men and older boys were out searching for him while the women and children waited fearfully, taking care of the little ones and calling for him every now and then. The outcry when he answered their calls made him feel that maybe he wasn't just stupid Sam to them after all.

The girls came running to meet him. They cried out at the sight of him, some racing back to say he was hurt, some trying to help him without hurting him. Just as Amos had said they would, the adults assumed he'd been attacked by wolves or wild dogs without asking him, showing each other that the bites were too big to be from a coyote.

He felt guilty when they praised him for the way he'd bound up his wounds, whittled his crutch, and got himself home, so he tried to explain, but they weren't listening. Rather than force them all to listen and start a whole mess of trouble, Sam went quiet and let them think whatever they wanted to.

By the time the news reached the search parties, and they'd come in, Sam had been cleaned up and all of the strips of shirt removed. Amos had got him to roll in the dirt on the road, plus he'd fallen once, so his mother tenderly cleaned him, and picked the bits of grit out from his knees and the palms of his hands. She was doing that when the search party arrived. Sam jumped when he saw his father standing in the doorway. His mother thought she'd hurt him, so she started telling him she was nearly done and how brave he was. The only thing Sam could think of to say to his father was, "I didn't lose the ball, Dad."

He was confused and dismayed when the women all started crying. He was sure, certain sure, that the whole truth would come out then. After that, no one would ever believe anything he said for the whole of the rest of his life.

But they didn't make him tell them exactly what had happened. His father swallowed hard, picked up the crutch, and said in an odd voice, "That's good thinking to put a point on this, Son, for going along outside. I'll put a flat tip on it for you for inside the house." Then he was gone.

Sam could only stare at his father; he couldn't talk because the look in his father's eyes knocked the words right out of his head.

"Your Dad's very proud of you," his mother explained.

That was the look Sam had seen. Respect. But he didn't deserve it. "But Mom . . .""Now, Sammy, I don't want you to worry. Your job now is to take it easy and get better."

Confused and guilty, Sam did as he was told. Amos was right; the older boys were punished for chasing him off. The younger ones ratted on them. What Sam didn't expect was all the boys coming to him to tell him how sorry they were for chasing him away. They were so genuinely upset that Sam was too embarrassed to know what to say. But it seemed like the more he blushed and mumbled, the worse they felt and the sooner his mother shooed them away to let him rest.

As much as Sam needed to talk to someone about it all, he never got the chance to speak to anyone alone. His mother made a bed in front of the fire so that he wouldn't get chilled during the night and wouldn't have to share a bed with his brothers until he'd healed some. That was okay except that it meant he was in the middle of everything. No matter how much his mother made everyone hush and stay away from him so he could rest, he could hear them whispering to each other, trying to figure out how he'd gotten away from a pack of dogs. The more Sam heard that the worse he felt, until, when his father sat down beside him to wish him good night, and added, "How did you do it?" Sam was so overcome with guilt and shame that he burst into tears.

"Raphael! Really!" Mother scolded. "Can't you see he's still in shock? Leave the poor kid in peace until he can bear to talk about it."

"I didn't . . . how was I to know . . ."

"It's obvious! He ain't breathed a word, he can't eat a bite."

"But that don't mean . . ."

"When was the last time you saw a kid miss supper and not want nothing before bed?"

To Sam's horror his father backed down. "I'm sorry, Dad." He fought as hard as he could against the tears, but he seemed to be too tired to stop them. "I'll tell you."

"No, son, Mama's right. You're not yourself. No one will ask you nothing until you want to talk about it. I trimmed the end of this for you, and put a leather patch on it so's it won't slip on the floor." He ruffled Sam's hair and left.

Exhausted, unable to see how to straighten it all out, Sam turned on his mother. "You didn't have to do that, Mom."

"Do what?"

Instead of giving him comfort, the gentle patience in her voice made him feel even worse. "Get mad at Dad." Sam wasn't used to being noticed by his father and treated respectfully by the others. He couldn't handle it. His father was his hero, the person Sam wanted to be like more than anyone else in the world. Seeing his dad look shame-faced because of him gave Sam new levels of feeling low that he didn't know existed.

"Don't worry about your Dad, Sammy, he's a big boy, he can take it. The only thing for you to think about is getting better."

Sam hurt so much that he was glad there was no one else in the bed with him. His leg throbbed where Killer had grasped him, his groin burned where it was pulled, his shoulder ached where Killer had held him, his armpit hurt where the crutch had rubbed against it, his knees and hands stung from the fall on the road, and various parts of his body were sore from falls and other bumps and bangs and the thorns in the hedge. He did his best to make no sound when trying to move sent red-hot stabs of pain through him, but his mother always seemed to know and came to him as quiet as a ghost with cool, damp cloths, soothing hands, and a soft voice. She wrapped the sore spots in willow bark and made some into a tea, which he did drink even though it tasted like dried out old bark.

The nightmares started two nights later, when Sam's aches and pains had settled down enough for him to be able to sleep properly. His dreams kept going back to the horrifying moment when Killer had him by the shoulder, leaving him drenched with sweat and shaking.

His mother woke him by gently shaking his unhurt shoulder and sat up with him until he'd calmed down enough to sleep. Once it was his father doing the duty, telling Sam, "You're okay, Son, you got away. They ain't gonna eat you now."

"What?" Sam was groggy, still in the dream with the feel of the teeth in his shoulder.

"You were shouting something about, "Don't let them eat me." Ain't nothing gonna eat you here."

"He's gonna pull my arms off!"

"Sam. Samuel, son, wake up. You're having a bad dream. You're safe, now."

Sam woke up enough to realise that he was alone with his dad. He sat up and looked around, listening to see if anyone else was awake. "Dad,

Dad," he whispered. "I have to tell you. It wasn't a pack, it was my fault, you see, I . . ."

"Are you telling me those kids didn't chase you? They were all lying to me, every last one?"

"Well, no, sir, but . . ."

"Sam, I want you to listen to me good. You had a bad dream. What you saw ain't real, son. I seen it in the military; guys'd dream things that never happened, and they'd believe them more than what was real, and no one could tell them different. It's like you seen combat. I'm gonna get you some of the potion your Mama made for you. I want you to go back to sleep after you drink it, then I don't want to hear no more about it."

Sam lay there confused, trying to sort out in his mind what was real and what was dream. His dad couldn't be wrong, so he had to be. The image of Killer ripping his arms out of their sockets was very real. He could see it, smell the blood, feel the terror, both shoulders hurt, but he knew his arms were both still there. In the unfamiliar surroundings of waking up in front of the fire instead of in the bed he shared with his brothers, and the spookiness of the dark house lit only by flickering orange-red firelight, Sam wasn't sure what was real and what was a dream.

He accepted the tea from his dad, drinking it gratefully despite the nasty taste. His dad had also warmed up some milk. "If you still ain't hungry, it's okay, but if you can get it down and keep it down, warm milk will help you sleep and hold the dreams off."

"My arms are both here," Sam said, looking at them, "But I felt him pull them off. I saw it and I smelled it and it hurt worse'n fire." He reached for the mug of milk and to give the tea mug back to his dad, watching his arm move. "But I still got them."

"That's a bad one. Don't think about it. Don't talk about it. Put it behind you. You're a man, now, and a man don't yap on and on like a little kid."

If his dad had meant to make him feel better by saying that, it hadn't worked. All Sam really felt was more confused than ever. Not wanting to argue with his dad, or to point out that he was only ten and couldn't possibly do a man's work in a day, Sam used the only authority he knew of that his dad might listen to. "Mom says I'm just a little boy."

"Women do that. They never want their babies to grow up. Nothing she can do about it. You've been in battle and you've got battle fatigue. Whether she likes it or not, you've grown up."

Satisfied that Sam was okay, his dad left him. Sam lay awake for a long time. Fortunately, his mother thought he needed to sleep in the afternoon until he was stronger. The fact that he hadn't wanted anything to eat when he got home had her more upset than anything else. Not only did she make special things for him to tempt his appetite, but so did all of the aunts, despite the fact that he was eating as usual on the first morning.

Eating the feast that was left after Sam had eaten everything he could a few days later, one of the older boys suggested, appreciatively, "Could you do it again, Sam?"

Caught off guard, Sam nearly choked. No matter how much the poor unfortunate explained that he was kidding, no matter how much Sam pleaded on his behalf, the sinner was marched off to the woodshed. Distressed that people were getting into trouble because of him, Sam asked to be excused from the table and went off by himself. He could hear them whispering, "He's not the same."

It was some time before he was able to sleep with his brothers again, but even when he was fully recovered no one ever called him 'Stupid Sam' again. No one ever questioned him about exactly how he'd escaped from a pack of wolves. Over the years it ceased to be 'either dogs or wolves' and was only mentioned as 'a whole pack of wolves when he was only ten. Yes – and he can't talk about it to this day. He's never been the same, you know.'

He heard the whispers all of his life. In his mind he wasn't 'the same' because he was no longer 'Stupid Sam,' but he saw the story of his life remade until he'd been the fastest, smartest, best-looking kid there before that day. He wondered sometimes why none of the kids reminded the adults that he'd been hopeless at running, throwing, catching, roping, and too puny to be as much use as everyone else was at ten.

It was forty years since Sam was ten. As a parent himself, he understood more of his parents' point of view. The child he'd lost was the dearest girl – though he sometimes wondered if he'd felt that way about her when she was just one of the crowd. Perhaps he and his wife, Mercy had revised history just as his parents had. He couldn't be sure. He couldn't talk it over with Mercy because it would have upset her too much. Since he'd grown up keeping what mattered the most to him from those who mattered the most to him, he fell into the habit naturally in his marriage. He also couldn't check with his parents because he had never spoken to them about the way he'd gone from the kid no one noticed who wasn't good at anything to the most talented boy the world had ever seen.

He'd always intended to tell his parents what had really happened. As a child he hadn't known how, and as time went on it became more and more impossible. As a grown man with a family of his own, he was determined to clear it all up once and for all. Each time he went to say something about it, there was a reason to think that it would be better to leave it until tomorrow. Eventually his parents ran out of tomorrows. Of all the things Sam regretted in his life, not telling his parents the truth before they died topped the list.

The only one who'd ever known everything Sam thought, felt, or believed was Amos. Because Amos did know the whole truth Sam had gravitated towards him. Lying there in his bunk on the Star of Galilee, listening to the explorers sleeping, Sam realised he hadn't thought about that day for years. He could tell Mercy that they'd discovered a strange land, of course, but it wouldn't be the same as sharing the wonder with Amos, who had spent his life saving for this and planning it.

Unable to sleep, Sam crept from the cabin up to the deserted deck. The ship had moved far enough that he could no longer see any sign of the river of molten rock. He could hear the explosions, but they were muffled now, coming from north side of the mountain ridge they'd sailed past.

By the direction of the sound of the breakers against the rocks Sam could tell they'd gone past the spit of land. He strained to see or hear any sign that there was more land to the west. He didn't think he could hold his head up if it turned out to be an uninhabited island. As his eyes got used to peering through the darkness, he understood that the pale line he was looking at were the breakers throwing themselves on the rocks. He was encouraged by the sound of more breakers in the distance. There was more land. This really was just a spit.

Staring into the night, Sam had to admit there was no sign of life except the birds. But still, if it was a large place the people might have moved away from the volcano. Come to think of it, if it was an island, the people could have sailed away from the volcano. All he had to do was find their buildings and that would prove that the GR was wrong.

His spirits high, he watched the land come into view as the day dawned. The view from the south was very different from the view from north. Not only was there no black gash in the green hillsides or towering column of smoke and cloud, not to mention no boiling rocks pouring into the ocean with great explosions of steam, but the land was steeper. The mountains cut the volcano off from their view. Sam only caught sight of the plume of smoke way up in the sky to the north.

Instead of tree covered slopes, the southern coast was mostly cliffs. There was a bay about two miles across at the far eastern edge of the south coast. It looked sheltered. Sam thought it would make a safe harbour for them while they explored the land. He ran inside so excited that he didn't even notice that he'd had hardly any sleep.

The first thing Sam wanted was for Vince to make sketches before the ship changed course. The main reason Vince had been included as one of the six explorers was his ability to draw the things he saw quickly and accurately. The sketches he'd made of the pillar of fire, before the storm hit them and made him too sick to do anything, were impressively exact.

As soon as the morning prayers were finished, Sam went to have breakfast with Major Temperance, sending the explorers to go up on deck after breakfast to make sketches and take notes. He hoped the Major wouldn't be too drunk or hung-over to talk to, and was disappointed to see that he had the kind of bear-like antagonism that meant he was part-way sober and craving a drink. Steeling himself for a hard time of negotiating, Sam tried to start on a low-key, friendly note, but the Major would have nothing to do with the idea of having a Weskie prisoner in the room while they ate, even if he didn't eat with them, so Sam had to spend a frustrating half hour making tentative plans when neither of them knew enough about what they were looking at to make a decision. Sam thought it was a complete waste of time. He was impatient to see Sage and hear his assessment, reminding himself not to use the man's name when he spoke to him, in case he forgot and used the wrong one in front of the Major.

Eagerly, he leaped to his feet as Sage was frog-marched into the Major's Ready Room, blurting out, "Did you look outside this morning?"

"I'm sorry, Sir."

Sam turned to the Major, doing his best to look confused as he asked, "How can we fix that?"

"Take him up on deck, of course."

Sam noticed that the Major spoke as if he thought Sam was an idiot, but he didn't care. At least they were going to take a look with someone who had a better idea of what they were looking at than they did. "Wouldn't we get a better vantage point from the Command Tower?"

Major Temperance was outraged by the mere suggestion. "You don't let the enemy see your Headquarters!"

"They built it."

"Are you trying to sabotage this whole mission?"

Sam realised he'd gone too far. He had to remind the Major that this was not a military mission, and that he was paying the Major's wages. "Not at all. I put my life's savings into it. This mission's got to succeed for us to get back home and get paid for it."

"What do you mean? You said you paid for it."

"I didn't bring the money with me. It's waiting at home for me to get there and get it so you all get paid."

The Major had that flicker of doubt that told Sam he had a chance of making his point this time if he was careful. Looking the Major right in the eye, Sam told him, "They took full payment for all of the equipment and supplies. They said they'd settle up with me for scrip that was issued during the mission, along with repairs and collateral expenses after we get back."

There was a silence while the Major digested this. Sam knew there was no need to spell out to him that the Brass didn't expect them to return to claim their wages.

As his expression changed, Sam sensed that the Major was figuring out that the military could add in enough 'collateral' expenses to keep Sam in debt for the rest of his life if he did get back, or to break his family if he didn't. He judged then that the time was right to tell him, "I used all my life's savings. I'm cleaned out. But I'm not the only one who believes in this mission. I have support my family knows nothing about. I must get back or there ain't gonna be no collateral nothing paid. My wife don't know from insurance, huh?"

The Major shrugged. "Think that'll stop them?"

"She can't tell them what she don't know. What do you think is the best move we can make to get us all home and paid?"

"Turn the ship for home."

"Without taking on fresh food and water?"

"Yes, well," the Major glared at Sage. "What could you see from the Command Tower that you couldn't see from the deck?"

"The bridge is higher, Sir . . ."

"Command Tower! Do <u>not</u> use pagan names on my ship!"

"Yes, Sir. I'm sorry, Major Temperance, Sir."

"You'll be flogged if it ever happens again."

"Yes, Sir."

The Major turned to Sam. "You see how impossible it is to train pagans. The only thing they understand is the business end of a lash."

With the Major looking right at him and the security detail in the ready room with them to make sure the prisoner didn't 'try anything', Sam couldn't signal Sage in any way. All he could do was distract Major Temperance by talking about the benefits of a higher vantage point.

Up in the Command Tower at last, they stood together, gazing intently at stretches of rugged headlands and wind-swept cliffs dropping straight down to the breakers below the thickly forested land.

"Are you sure it's an island?" Sam asked Sage. "If we turn west and sail past those cliffs what's to say there's not a whole lot of land on the other side?"

Watching the Major carefully, Sage answered Sam, "The main thing is that it looks like there's nothing but ocean on the other side of those cliffs."

Major Temperance snorted. "You can see around corners now, can you? Through solid rock?"

Sam didn't want their time wasted trying to prove that Sage didn't know what he was talking about. He wanted to figure out what their best options were before they made a move. "Whether it's an island or not, there's no one there, is there?"

"No, Sir, not likely. If we were going to find any boats, that would be the place." He pointed to the wide bay in front of them.

Sam could see the sense in that. "It's protected from the volcano on the other side by those mountains, and there ain't none of the little islands in the way. Do you think we should go in there?"

Sage pointed at the cliffs. "It don't look like there's any place to land. If we turned to the west we could see if it's safe to go in."

Major Temperance demanded, "What d'you mean, Boy? This here's a goldurned GR iron ship, the strongest thing on the ocean. It ain't one of them panty-waist wooden crates your people use, and don't you never forget it!"

"No, Sir. I'm sorry, Major Temperance, Sir."

In an effort to distract the Major, Sam pointed to breakers he could see near the shore about halfway along the bay. "It looks like some rocks under the water there like there was to the north."

Finally convinced, the Major ordered the ship to be turned south-westward to go across the bay without turning all the way into it. They could all soon see that the waves were breaking against a group of islets and rocks. When Sage suggested that they stayed at least a mile offshore, the Major gave the order without comment.

"Look at how the land sort of curls around on the east side of the bay," Sam thought out loud. "It's kind of a bay within a bay."

Sage nodded. "If you were looking for a sheltered place to anchor, that's the kind of thing you're looking for. If we're going to find any docks they'll be in there."

"No sign anything was ever built there." Sam sighed. He hadn't really expected anything else, but it was disappointing, just the same.

Major Temperance knew exactly why. "No one would ever put a port there. Those rocks are in the way." He was pointing to the islets.

Sam stole a quick glance at Sage's eyes and knew from his expression that there was a way. Curious, he dared irritating the Major by asking Sage, "Would you build a port in a place like that where you come from?"

Sage nodded. "It would depend on the tides. Do you see how the wind's heading north-east?"

Sam nodded, interested in learning sea-lore from the Weskies. "You can't see the cloud from the volcano."

Sage flicked a nervous glance at the disapproving Major before explaining, "It went in the same direction for a week or more before the storm blew it all over, then it went in the same direction again. That could mean it's a prevailing wind, which . . ."

"What's that got to do with if we can park there or not?"

At the Major's bark, Sage jumped, then answered carefully, "You need a smaller, more manoeuvrable ship to get around those islets and rocks into and out of the cove, Sir, and the prevailing winds could make strong swells that could push a ship like this up onto the rocks."

"Yes or no is all I want to hear from you, Boy. I can see for my own self ain't no ship that can get through there, so don't you even try that 'ship like this' crap with me! This here ship is the Star of Galilee, built by the Gethsemane Republic. The GR don't build no crap, and don't you forget it!"

"Yes, Sir, Major Temperance, Sir."

Sam felt as if he spent more time placating the Major than anything else. "There's nothing wrong with the Star of Galilee, Major," he lied. "It's like the difference between a bicycle and a tank. You use one to go through narrow spaces, and the other one to . . ."

"I know how to handle a tank, thank you! Which is more than you know, ain't it? Bet you never got further than buck private, did you?"

Sam thought it might not be a bad idea to remind Temperance about the rumour that he was Special Ops. "I had land deferment," he spoke quietly, then looked Temperance in the eye and winked. "You know how that works – you do your one year of basic, then it's back to the farm, out of sight, never heard from again and no questions asked."

The Major went pale and mumbled something Sam didn't catch.

Sam wasn't interested in what he'd said. All he wanted was to know whether or not there were any structures hidden in the back of the cove. "Can you see anything back there?" he asked Sage.

"No, Sir, I don't think so, unless that's something square at the foot of that landslide."

Sam thought he could see what Sage was talking about, but it didn't help. "I can't tell if it's really something or not. If it is, it could have been there for two hundred and fifty years, so it's not worth risking the Star against those rocks and mini-islands to find out. We are going to find a better spot than this, aren't we?" He raised one eyebrow at Sage. "One where we won't need mountain climbers to get up those cliffs."

"You're right, Sir," Sage answered solemnly. "Even if we found an anchorage here, we still couldn't go ashore." He gestured to the high rocky cliffs they were approaching. "If my people had built a port in that cove, we would have built a road down that hillside to it."

Sam could only nod sadly. Whether or not they had seen something square, it was obvious there was no way to carry goods up and down that steep hillside.

On the western side of the bay were about two miles of cliffs hundreds of feet high with vegetation growing on what looked like bare rock. Sam couldn't believe the way this place could grow greenery. "Look at that," he said, pointing. "How can they grow there like that? There can't be any soil there."

Neither the Major nor Sage was interested. They were watching a valley about half-way along the cliffs. It didn't look like there were rocks under the surface where the valley came down to the sea. "What do you think?" Sam asked Sage, seeing what they were looking at.

"I think the water is too deep to anchor right up to the shore there, and we don't know if there are deeper rocks that we might hit. I'd rather see if we can find a real beach."

The Major didn't answer. He turned his attention to the massive cliffs that they could see as the ship angled out to go along the south coast, keeping a mile away from it as ordered. Sage was watching the water at the base of the cliffs. He pointed out a rock that actually poked right up through the surface, and breakers at another spot.

"What is it?" Sam stared at the base of the cliffs himself trying to figure out what had Sage's attention.

"Can you see where there are breakers in the sea where we can't see anything for them to break against?"

"Yes, I think so."

"That means there are rocks just under the surface. This whole place is one big booby trap."

"What?!" The Major jerked to full alertness, staring around intensely. "Can you see them?"

Sam and Sage glanced at each other, trying to figure out what had upset him. It dawned on Sam that the Major hadn't caught exactly what Sage had said, he'd only heard 'booby trap.' "No, we can't see rocks that are under the sea, Major, that's the problem."

Backing down while trying to save face, the Major muttered, "How did they get there?"

Sam could only shrug and look to Sage, who took a breath and explained, "It's a volcano. Volcanoes throw rocks. If the blast had come this way instead of that way, the lava would be pouring into here instead of there."

"What's that got to do with hidden rocks?"

"Well, you see, Major Temperance, Sir, lava is melted rock. When it cools down, it turns back into hard rock. When it hits the sea like it is on the north coast, it gets blown apart by the explosions, and that makes piles of rocks under water, as well as the rocks that fall down from the volcanic cloud and in the land slides."

Sam and the Major both looked back at the rockslide in the cove. It was behind them now as the ship chugged across the bay, turning towards the south to give the south coast a wide berth. They were all silent for the rest of the time it took to leave the bay.

As they passed the end of the bay and the south coast came into view, they could see it was about two more miles of cliffs just as steep, if not steeper than the ones in the bay, and about a thousand feet high. This time there was no valley.

Sam was disappointed that the coast was so short. That made it so much more likely that Sage was right and they'd found an island that he couldn't stand it. "Thank you for your hospitality, Major. I need to go down on deck, now, and see my men."

Security marched Sage off back to whatever work he had to do as a prisoner, as Sam strode away.

The explorers were all in the bow of the ship, even Willie Jay. Vince was sketching like a man possessed, with the others holding the paper for him against the wind, and taking the ones he'd done as he finished them. Willie Jay was so awe-struck it was as if he'd forgotten to be sea-sick. Vince was sketching everything, not just the land, but also the weird birds and plants.

"You did it, Sam," Joe Mack greeted him with a twinkle in his eye and his hand out-stretched. As Joe Mack pumped his hand and slapped his shoulder, the others crowded around to thump him on the back.

"Give it a rest," he pushed them away. "You've been looking at this island for two days, now. There's nobody here."

Vince went back to sketching.

Willie Jay implored him, "There's more around the corner, ain't there, Sam? There might be people there, huh, Sam?"

"We'd better get used to the idea that we're going to come up short in proving our point."

Johnny stepped forward. "Sam, you're doing the Lord's work. Keep your faith and the Good Lord will make your way clear."

"Right, then. The first thing we got to do is figure out how in the world we're going to get off this ship if the only part that's not cliffs has got rocks and islands in the way."

While they talked it over, Vince continued his sketching and Sam looked for the first excuse he could come up with for having Sage and Rocky brought to him. Even with the inevitable security standing around glowering at them, he was able to let them know if there was ever anything he could do for them, he would.

They had not reached any kind of conclusion about how to set foot on the island when Chuck whooped, "He was right! By all that's holy, Willie Jay was right for once!"

As the ship neared the end of the cliffs, where a mountainous headland jutted out preventing them from seeing around to the west until they were about to clear it, Chuck spotted breakers about four miles further on. Everyone stood quietly watching to see what would appear.

Slowly it became clear that it was not a bunch of rocks and islets, but a long arm of land that rose up from the familiar cliffs and bluffs to high forest covered ridges. A hillside jutted out towards them, then, as the ship moved further the edge of that hillside was seen to be sheltering a beach from the sea. "That changes everything." Sam felt almost tearful with relief.

The beach was partially hidden behind a bare black rocky island with surf pounding against it. The Weskies sighed nostalgically over the surf on the beach, trying without success to explain surfing. Before the ship made the turn the Weskies changed their tune, crying out in horror and demanding so forcefully of Sam that the ship must not turn, that Security stepped forward, menacingly.

"Back off," Sam frowned at Security. "What's going on?" He asked Sage. "Calm down. You can't just freak out like this."

"Can't you see the steam coming from that black island? This is another volcano! We can't turn in there!"

Sam studied the black mass of rock poking up out of the water about a mile from the beach. As soon as he took a closer look Sam could see what Sage was talking about. The rocks were hot enough for the sea water that splashed onto them to hiss with steam. "Come with me," he told Sage and Rocky. "It's going to take all of us to explain this to the Major."

Just as Sam was turning to the security team to convince them to let the Weskies go with him, there was a cry of such horror from Vince that they all spun to look at him, then at where he was pointing.

"A wrecked ship!" Vince choked.

Poking out from behind the black island was a rusted hulk on the beach. It was mostly buried in the sand, but Sam could tell it had been bigger than the Star of Galilee. He pointed it out to the security team, exclaiming, "We have to get to the Command Tower right now and make sure that don't happen to us."

Instantly, one started escorting Sam, Sage, and Rocky, while hurrying his companion, who was hesitating.

As they ran towards the bridge as fast as they could go, one of the security said, "You know, the south of this island reminds me of an anvil."

"Yeah?" Sam hadn't thought about it, he'd been too caught up in worrying what he was going to do if they couldn't find any evidence that anyone outside the GR had survived Judgement Day.

"Yeah. The square end of the south coast is like the base of an anvil, and the way the north curves down to become the west, then curls under is like the club end. Where that long spit sticks out to the east it's like the spike end."

"I guess," Sam sort of agreed.

They waited outside the door, catching their breath while one of the security team tried to persuade the officer on duty that there was an emergency. He returned with a worried frown saying, "Major Temperance ain't there. You can bet your bottom dollar that not a one of those guys'll change his order or listen to your reasons."

"I'll bet you're right," Sam nodded in disgust. "I don't mind risking my life for the mission, but I'll be hanged if I'll lose it because no one would listen." He took a chance and looked the security guard in the eye. "How about you?"

He shook his head. "No way. What can you do?"

"I got to get the Major to change his order so we can all get back home."

"I'm all over that!" the one guard exclaimed.

For the first time his companion spoke up. "What's he got to do?"

Sam looked at Sage, who said, "Turn the ship around and get as far away from the volcano as we can, as fast as we can."

Sam hadn't intended for Sage to talk about turning back without landing, but having both of the guards agreeing that they had to disturb the Major in his quarters was too valuable to side-track by worrying about details. Such things as persuading the Major to set foot on the island could be sorted out later, once they were away from this deadly looking bay.

Sam was actually a lot more nervous than he let on. There was no way of knowing what the Major's mood would be. On top of that, security could just as easily be setting them up. Hard on the heels of that thought was the knowledge that if the meeting with the Major went sour, security would sell Sam and the Weskies down the river to save their own skins. His heart was in his mouth when the guard knocked on the Major's door.

The harried looking adjutant was not impressed by the motley looking group, and was sending them away when Sam stepped up and raised his voice. "We've never seen anything like this before. The Major is the only one with the guts to face it head on. You know this is a one-way mission. But the Brass was wrong about him, and when he pulls us out of this they'll know they underestimated him. They'll name the island after him. Come on, we've got to let the Old Man in on this."

They were all staring at him as if he'd grown another head. "That ain't going to help," the adjutant murmured.

Before anyone could say anything else, Major Temperance called, "Let them in, Corporal. Don't keep them at the door."

Sam could see instantly why the adjutant wanted to keep the Major out of sight. He'd suspected as much at the sound of his voice. The Major was in the stage of inebriation where he was everybody's friend. "Come in. Come in. Sit down. Sit down. Have a drink?"

"I'd love to, Sir, but it don't agree with me."

"Can't hold your liquor, huh? That ain't good in a man."

"I really came to see you, Sir, because there's a pretty bad problem. It's your leadership skills that will get us out alive." Even while he was hoping he wasn't pouring it on too thick, Sam could see from the expressions on the faces of everyone else there that they thought he was.

The Major acted as if boot licking and slavish adoration was his due. "What seems to be the problem, son?"

It took all of Sam's self-discipline to maintain a stone face, made all the harder by the glint of wicked enjoyment in the eyes of the security men at Sam, who was older than the Major, being called 'son' by him. "There's a wrecked ship on the beach."

"A ship!" He looked at the Weskies. "One of yours?"

"No, Sir," they chorused.

Sam continued, "It's an iron ship bigger than the Star of Galilee."

There was silence as the implications of this sank in.

Sam added, "It's half buried in the sand. We don't want that to happen to us, but how can we sail safely to find a place to go ashore when there's an island in the way that . . ." lost for a way to describe the steaming island, Sam glanced at the Weskies for inspiration.

Sage took that as an invitation to speak. "It's another volcano, Major Temperance, Sir. If we sail anywhere near it we are in danger."

Temperance smiled at them all. "Don't park near the volcano or the wreck."

Sam tried again. "For safety, Major, how can we sail across the bay with the volcano right there?"

The Major took a drink and complained fuzzily to Sam, "It's terrible that you won't drink with me. Even Special Ops got to relax some time."

"I'm sorry, Major. What are your orders regarding the bay?"

He looked at them all, one after another, smiling genially. "Don't look so worried. You've got nothing to worry about. We should be able to go ashore from a beach. Then we'll get fresh meat and fresh water and everybody will be happy."

Sam tried again. "That's what we came to see you about, Major. There's no one but you who can figure out how we can get past the volcano in the bay."

The Major hesitated. "Where is it?"

Sage told him, "It's in the middle of the bay, Sir, about a mile offshore."

Major Temperance laughed out loud. "Did you all hear that? Shoot, the pagans think you can have fire on water, now! What next?"

"Well, you see, Major, it's not exactly on the water. It's got its own little island between us and the beach."

"You said it was on the island," Temperance frowned at Sam.

Not wanting to spoil the Major's mood, Sam tried to keep him on topic without arguing with him. "I apologise for the confusion, Major. You're the one with the real skill at this. The island with the second volcano on it is between us and the beach. If we try to go around it to the east we've only got a bit over a mile's clearance between the island that's on fire and the coast of the big island. How are we going to do that?" He kept hoping Temperance would pick up the reins and say something useable before he got p'd off with them or reached the belligerent phase of his cycle, but that hope was fading.

"Same as we did it before," Temperance shrugged, taking another swig. He grinned his "friends with everyone" expression around to all of them, adding when he looked at Sage, "That worked last time, huh?"

"Major Temperance, Sir, we got to turn back," Sage pleaded in desperation.

Temperance chuckled, winking to Sam. "Nah, we don't gotta do that. We can go the other way around it."

Sam smiled back at him, delighted. This he could use. In a quick aside he asked the adjutant for a pen and paper, and then beamed at Temperance. "That's brilliant, Major. We can go the other way around it and go past it the same way we got past the other one." He accepted the pen and paper and immediately started writing, saying, "That's a good idea, Corporal. The Major's got too much to do to have to go back to the Command Tower when he's off duty." He knew the last thing the adjutant wanted was the men seeing the Major in that condition. He didn't want it, either. It made the Major look dangerously weak. No one on that ship was there for good behaviour, so Sam wouldn't put it past them to stage a mutiny if they realised that the Major had a weakness they could exploit. The chaos that could arise from a mutiny could destroy their chances of getting the ship back home. Still scribbling, he asked, "Major, how's about I take your orders in writing to the Command Tower? You have your men so well trained that they'll never take orders from anyone but you, and there's no reason for you to have to go back there when you've just gone off duty. You have so much to do without adding extra things like this. I'd be honoured to do this small service for you. Tell me what you think of that. Is it what you'd want to say?"

Preening, the Major was too busy bragging about his prowess as a leader to pay much attention to the note. As they waited for him to run out of exaggerations to tell them, Sam comforted himself that at least no one was laughing or gagging at the Major's patently ridiculous boasts. Finally, he was able to get the Major to put his seal on the note and set about extricating them from his quarters without setting him off and before they were hit by anything from the volcano.

Sam didn't relax until the ship was headed for the horizon away from the deadly bay. Then he went back on deck with the Weskies to join the explorers.

Vince was sketching the changing views as they chugged away from the island. Willie Jay was holding a fat roll of finished sketches. Chuck and Joe Mack were helping Vince keep his paper from fluttering in the sea breeze.

"Where's Johnny?"

"Gone to get more paper," Chuck supplied, adding, "Say, Sam, what are we doing?"

"Getting fifteen miles away from that volcano just like we did from the other one."

"D'you think this one's got melted rock and ash, too?" Joe Mack asked.

Sam shook his head. "Can't hear no explosions." He raised an eyebrow at Sage, who replied, "This don't look like its doing the same thing, but that don't make it safer. There's no way to know what it might do or when. If that thing blew it could take us out from further away than fifteen miles! There's nothing between us and it. We got to get back behind the cliffs." He pointed back to the bluff of the south coast.

Sam looked back. If they turned around now he knew there was very little chance of setting foot on a strange land. They would be facing towards home, and he didn't think it would be possible to get the ship turned around again. The idea of trying to get the Star of Galilee into that little cove they'd seen made him shudder, but they hadn't seen any other part of the island that wasn't steep cliffs that went straight into deep water with hidden hazards; cliffs that no one could climb even if they had been able to find anchorage near them. He had to find out if there was a more approachable area on the north coast. He ran the risks through his mind, but decided again that there was no chance of getting to the north coast by going back the way they'd come, since it wouldn't be possible to go back past the first volcano. It was now or never. "Sorry," he almost called the man by his proper name right in front of security. Binging himself under control, he continued, "I know what you're saying, and I believe you, but we just got to pray God'll see fit to let us pass."

Sage went silent, watching the steaming black rocks with an expression somewhere between fear and resignation. "Look at that," he said, pointing to the cliffs behind the flat area above the beach. Dense clouds of steam rose from fissures in the cliffs.

The further they got from the islands, the more clearly they could see how steep the beach was, how heavy the surf was, and how much bigger than their ship the wreck had been. When they had sailed around the corner from the south coast, the wreck was partially obscured by the steaming black island, but once they had put a few miles between themselves and the bay, their perspective changed and Sam could see the full length of the partially buried ship. He didn't need to measure it to know it was at least twice as long as the Star of Galilee.

Instead of leaning over the side to look back, the explorers, along with the Weskies and their guards, moved to the back of the ship to look from there. The wind subsided to a pleasant breeze, and the thunder of surf came as no more than a distant echo across the sea. The sea broke in a single toppling wave of sapphire blue on the beach of coarse sand. From the strip of foreshore, an encircling wall of cliffs rose straight up to a height of nearly a thousand feet. Cresting the island was a jagged line of peaks and pinnacles which Sage insisted were all volcanic. Deep ravines and razor-back ridges showed dark blue, purple-shadowed, among the green forest that clothed the entire island. High above all, crowned with a filmy wreath of mist, rose the peak of the highest mountain, which they collectively estimated was well over 1,500 feet high. They didn't see the smoke again over the mountains until they were more than ten miles from the island, then they saw it boiling away from them beside the tallest peak. A scene of sub-tropical beauty, thought Sam, leaning over the rail, lovelier than anything northern lands could produce until that showed up.

Except for breaks for meals and things like that, they stayed where they were until the ship passed the spit of land at the westernmost point of the big island and the north coast was revealed to them.

They were interrupted only once by Rocky shouting, "Sharks! Look, look! They're following us!"

Startled, they all looked down and saw a pack of ten or twelve cruising just beneath the surface of the water, their sharp dorsal fins cutting it as they kept pace with the ship. After the first moment of fright, however, the explorers took no further notice of them. They had eyes only for the scene which was unfolding as the ship drew nearer to the north coast.

As the ship turned back towards the island and its menacing shore, the explorers stared in forlorn bewilderment and disappointment. There was still nothing to be seen but sweeping terraces of brown sand hills, rocky cliffs and beach, and in the background dark, forest-clad mountains. Sage and Rocky eyed the white line of surf thundering down on a wide-sweeping beach with misgiving, muttering to each other in their own language until Security ordered them to speak GR.

"The approach from the north doesn't look any better," Sage said, obediently.

"There are beaches on this side," Sam objected. "Even from fifteen miles away I could see the difference." He sent a message to Major Temperance, "Make a landing on the north coast if you can."

As the Star crept cautiously onward, the sight of the towering glass-green rollers upset the Weskies. "The surf is nearly as heavy there as it was in the bay on the south side."

But the sight of a beach, however small, was enough for the Major. He ordered the ship to cruise as close to the shore as it could, taking soundings and looking for a place to set the anchors.

Sam was watching for a place with no high cliffs to climb, no steep dark grey beaches with huge surf and wrecked ships. However, when a sandy slope was found on the sea floor where all four anchors could get good purchase, he was well content to let the Major order the ship to heave to for the night, despite Sage's anxious reminders that the volcanoes were just over those hills, and big surf like that could pull them up onto the rocks. Why the sea floor sloped, instead of the steep drops of the other coasts no one could say. How there could be so much difference in such a short distance, Sam couldn't imagine, but he was thankful that they were able to find a secure anchorage where, barring storms, they could stay for days.

The quiet that descended when the huge engines were shut down was unnerving. The bird calls came across the water, and the ripples lapping against the sides of the ship made a calming background music.

He felt guilty for avoiding Sage for the rest of the evening so that he didn't have to listen to the cautions. He knew he was being irresponsible, that he had encouraged Sage to speak up to keep them all alive, but at that moment he wanted to get off the ship so badly that he couldn't bear to hear anything against it.

During the day Major Temperance had gone through his cycle from 'friend of everyone;' to suspicious and belligerent; to enraged that his orders had been changed, and claiming the orders Sam had put in writing were a forgery when they were shown to him; to trying to drum up a witch-hunt to find out who was plotting against him. Sam had been called away from his observations a couple of times to calm the Major down. Not even the Major's most loyal supporters wanted to see any more men thrown over the side only to have the Major wonder where they were in a day or two.

Yet, when Sam sat down with him to eat their evening meal, Temperance seemed perfectly rational. "Looks like there could be good places to put small boats on the beaches," Sam started, not wanting to leave any room for doubt about whether or not they were going to set foot on the island.

Instead of the argument Sam expected, Temperance only said, "We can put out a hunt and get us some meat."

"Yeah!" Sam was elated. "I can search for any sign of that there were people here once, and we can take on fresh water."

Temperance nodded. "The Weskies want to clean the ship and move the rest of the fuel closer to the fire boxes."

"That's a huge job. There are tons of coal. We could be here for a week."

"Thought you'd like that."

"Oh, I do! And I like the idea of the ship getting a real good cleaning and drying out. With the boys puking in all the cabins and nothing but sea water to swamp them out with, it stinks like an out house. But I'm surprised they want to stay here to do it with the volcanoes so close."

"They say we'll all get sick if it's not done and there's no other source of fresh water."

"This is true."

"And you'll have time to search every inch and put an end to this blasphemy that someone out here survived Judgement Day once and for all."

Sam grinned at him. The Major thought he was being so wily. Little did he know Sam had already come to terms with the fact that if there had ever been people here, they were long gone, and was making strategies in his head to convince everyone to keep going.

The morning dawned as perfect as could be. The clouds had lifted from the high peaks and shafts of sunbeams poured down into the shadows of the ravines, lighting up the deep greenness of the groves of foreign looking trees, highlighting the colours of the flowers that seemed to be everywhere, even on the trees themselves, and shimmering off the blue waters of the ocean. The surf had been reduced to gentle, peaceful ripples that kissed the rocks and sand like playful lovers.

After what they'd seen this looked like paradise, even with the column of smoke boiling up from the other side of ridges about nine miles away. It looked to Sam as if there were spaces wide enough for the ship's boat to get through between the rocks protecting the shore. If they could reach the steeply sloping beach across the clear blue water, they would be facing a tree covered slope that led by stages to the mountain ridges that had presented such steep faces on the east, south, and west sides of the island. He found himself thinking of it as 'Anvil Island' because of its shape, even though he knew Temperance would want to name it Temperance Island. There were cliffs on this side; some coming down to the sea, some above beaches, but he could see a spot where there seemed to be a break in the rocky barrier leading to a beach with no cliff behind it. That's the spot he asked the GR to aim for.

Lowering the rowboat made clangs that were heard throughout the ship in the silence of the idle engines. Frightened as they were of falling into the ocean, the men were only too pleased to get into the rowboat with its promise of time off the ship. All at once the sharks were very much in the forefront of everyone's mind, even though they hadn't been seen again. The hunters went first, made it between the rocks, and waved triumphantly from the beach as the boat came back for the next group. The hunters were followed by the explorers. The first thing Sam noticed as they left the ship was the smell; salty and clean. Looking at the forest on the hillsides, the palm trees coming all the way down to the beaches, he couldn't help saying, "I wonder if Eden was like this?"

Johnny immediately launched into explanations of why a seashore could not be described as 'like Eden.' Joe Mack's and Chuck's irritation with Johnny distracted all of them from the fear of being rowed from the ship to the island across deep shark filled water, so Sam let them squabble.

The pleasure of hearing and feeling the boat touch solid land came perilously close to bringing tears to Sam's eyes, made Joe Mack and Chuck cheer, and caused an outbreak of ecstatic prayers from Johnny, Willie Jay, and Vince. Jumping out of the boat to wade ashore was no hardship, but discovering that the land felt as if it was rolling just like the ship had was almost more than they could bear. The soldiers of the hunting party were equally dismayed by the swaying ground. They were having trouble walking in a straight line, reeling about like drunks, so they hadn't set off yet. Some thought the island was bewitched, others were afraid it wasn't solid ground at all, but a floating rock that could roll over.

The Corporal leading the hunting party, having never experienced anything like that before, had no idea what to think, except to get out of sight of the ship so that Major Temperance couldn't see that they weren't doing what they were supposed to. It wasn't until the first Weskies were dropped off to do the slave labour of collecting fresh water in buckets and carrying it back to the ship that they found out there was nothing wrong with the island, it was them. After weeks at sea, it was normal for everything to appear to undulate for the first little while.

Disgusted, the hunters left to look for game trails in the forest, while the Weskies searched for lakes or rivers, and the explorers went along the beach to make sure they weren't where the hunters could mistake them for deer in the thick forest. As each group headed in the direction they intended to go, the ground shook them all off their feet.

In shock, Sam shouted back to the Weskies, "The ship never did that!"

When they could get back on their feet again, Sam thought he recognised one of the Weskies and asked Chuck, "Isn't that Rocky?"

"Yes, I think so."

"What's his GR name?"

"Raamah."

Sam hurried back to the Weskies, telling their guards, "I just need a word with Raamah." He challenged Rocky, "You're not going to tell us that was just our heads getting used to being off the ship, are you?"

Seeing Sam, the Corporal left his hunting party and hurried to join with Sam.

"No, Sir. That was an earthquake."

Sam had heard of earthquakes. "The earth shakes where you come from, don't it?"

"Yes, Sir."

"Why would it do that here?"

Rocky pointed to the volcanic smoke. "Volcanoes always shake the ground when they erupt no matter where they are."

"How much of that shit are we going to have to put up with?" the Corporal demanded, shrilly.

"There's no way to know for sure, Sir," Rocky told him. "There are two volcanoes here, one about five miles south of us on the other side of the hills we're going to climb, and the other one about ten miles east of us. They're both erupting. Either one or both could shake the ground at any time."

The Corporal bellowed at the hunting party, "Get your fat asses in gear! The faster we get us some deer, the faster we get our asses off this hell hole. Move it! Move it! Move it!"

That brought the Sergeant in charge of the guards to life. "That goes for you, too, you God-forsaken pagans! The sooner we get that water, the sooner we leave this dog turd of a place behind us. Get moving or I'll flog the hide right off your backs!"

Sam made his way back down to the beach. It dawned on him as he was repeating to the explorers the explanation about earthquakes that this was the first time the six of them had been alone with no GR around, so he could speak his mind. "I wish there was some way to get those guys out."

Vince gaped at him, "You kidding, Sam? They're the enemy."

Sam couldn't believe what he'd just heard. "You're CP, I'm CP – all of us know what it's like to be conquered by the GR. the only difference between us and them is they ain't conquered."

Vince spluttered, "They were captured on our land!"

"Yeah, in the Panhandle, which, until a couple of years ago, was theirs and the Southies' and a few other smaller desert nations. Some of these guys were prisoners of war, some were saboteurs, but you know what? They were fighting to hold on to their land and then get it back, just like your people did and mine."

There was silence for a short time, then Joe Mack asked, "What's your plan, Sam?"

"I ain't got one."

"How're you going to set them free with no plan?"

"I never said I was, I said I wished I could. You know what would happen to me if I tried something like that."

Chuck nodded. "If you were real lucky and got off easy you'd just be executed."

Johnny was sure that since Sam was doing the Lord's work, God would protect him.

Not even Willie Jay went along with that, reminding Johnny how often God's people were martyred. Sam had to bring them back to the point of exploring the island to find out whether or not there had ever been people living there, not only to stop the squabbling, but also to put an end to speculation about what could happen to him if the GR ever found out what his beliefs really were. To distract them he pointed out how tame the birds were. It was as if they were all pets. They didn't move out of the way, even when they were shooed.

A half a mile along the beach they found a small run-off creak burbling down from the slope and vanishing into the sand before it reached the sea. They climbed up the slope until they reached a point where they could drink from the stream. The cool, clear, clean water was more delicious than wine after weeks of stagnant ship water. Sam warned them not to drink too much so that they wouldn't get sick. "We'll have some here, and more at the next crick." A few yards further on was another run-off stream where they did the same thing, and after a couple of hundred yards they found a third. At each creek their spirits lifted more. After about a mile the beach came to an end. The cliff they were facing wasn't anywhere near as high as some of the others they'd seen, but above it was a bigger one. "We can get up to the top of the beach cliff in that gap there," Sam suggested, pointing to what looked like a pass between the top of one cliff and the base of the other.

No one had a better plan, so they all started to climb up off the beach. In no time they were all complaining, and all except Willie Jay and Johnny were cursing, even Sam. The land was steep, the footing was slippery, and the foliage was dense. The palm trees had shed their gigantic fronds all over the forest floor. They didn't crackle under foot like normal dried leaves, they slid. Some of the trees shed bark when grabbed for balance, meaning their hands slid off them. They fell repeatedly, having nothing charitable to say about the island that had seemed so close to paradise before the climb.

At last they were on top of the sea cliffs, looking out over the glassy blue ocean at the other side of the small islands that they'd seen through the heavy rains of the storm. The closest ones were about nine or ten miles east of them. They could see that the barrier rocks came to an end a few yards from where they stood, but it didn't look as if there was any more beach. They continued climbing along the top of the cliff towards the east hoping to see if there was beach around every bend.

They'd only gone about a half a mile before they discovered that they had to climb down the side of a steep ravine.

"This place gives you no breaks at all," Joe Mack grumbled.

"I'm not ready to turn back yet," Sam declared.

"When we do get down this, we'll only have to climb up the other side," Chuck pointed out, looking across the narrow chasm.

"It's not that far, or that high," Sam encouraged them.

So they fought their way down and back up again through dense forest undergrowth, tripped by tangled creepers and vines which caught their shirts, pulled off their hats, and stuck down their necks under their collars.

"We're spending more time pulling these blamed vines off us than anything else," Vince complained.

It was easier going back up on top of the cliff again, because they only had a strip of forest to fight through, then they were on open land. They happily surged forward, only to find another ravine after less than half a mile. Still, it appeared to be smaller than the one they'd already crossed, so, muttering, they fought their way down it and back up. This time their persistence was rewarded. They found themselves on a flat area with a lovely beach at the bottom of the cliff. They ran down to the beach, whooping like children.

They watched the straight lines of low swells forming out at sea and rolling in towards them to break at their feet in chuckling ripples, sliding back out again leaving the sand glistening brown in the sunshine. The clean sea air caressed their faces, the salt tang cleared their breathing passages, and the endless birds swirled around them making strange alien cries unlike any bird calls they'd ever heard before. They took off their shirts to pull the last of the twigs and leaves and burrs out of their collars and hats, then made their way back up onto the terrace to see if they could find anything worth finding there.

The grass was waist high. They waded through it more than walked. They were completely alone in the world, no sight or sound of another human being, not even the hunting party. The rolling feeling of being on the ship was leaving their legs. In sheer high spirits they chased each other through the terrace, whooping and laughing.

Johnny warned them, "Don't get separated too far. You don't want to be picked off by a cougar."

Vince snorted. "You seen any sign of cougar, there, Johnny?"

"No," Johnny had to admit.

"Ain't no sign of nothing," Willie Jay added.

"Ain't it the truth. There ain't no game scat or tracks here," Chuck added, looking around.

Willie Jay commented, "I don't figure there's much in the way of deer living here in this."

Vince joined in, "Shoot, if anything ever tried to walk through this, some of it would be broke down some."

Joe Mack agreed with him. "No deer grazed on this. Ain't one clear inch been munched on."

Chuck snorted, "Graze? Ain't nothing could've walked through this before us. No sign of nothing, and where you got no grazing animals you got no bear, no cougar, not even a wolf pack."

Sam started to feel uneasy. It wasn't as if the game had left when the volcano erupted, unless it had been going on for many years, because it would take a long time for so much growth that there wasn't even a sign of any kind of path. "It's not possible that there are only birds here, is it?"

"Well, if we've got to eat birds, they're going to be easy to catch," was Chuck's comment.

"Sam! Sam! Sam!" Willie Jay shouted, bringing them all at the run.

He'd found a piece of wreckage.

"There were people here," Sam said in great satisfaction. "This used to be a building."

"Not for a really long time, Sammy boy," Joe Mack pointed out.

"I know. Ain't no way to prove it's been here since Judgement Day, but it still shows that there were people here once. We could go back down to the beach and get around that bend."

"That's getting close to the volcano," Chuck objected.

Sam stood on the grey sand staring out at the little islands to the northeast. "You know," he spoke slowly, trying to form his thoughts as he talked. "We knew this was dangerous before we left home. We all knew we could only get back alive through the Grace of God. Remember when we saw those when we first got here?" He pointed to the islands. "We saw them from the other side, between us and the steam explosions. The volcano was supposed to get us, but it didn't. Before that the storm was supposed to get us, and after that the other volcano was supposed to, but neither of them finished us off. I'm not saying we should tempt fate, but it looks to me like we could have a bit of faith. I'm not asking anyone to come with me, but I'm going to find out what's on the other side of that hill." He started to climb up the slope away from the beach, but quickly found that the dense entanglement of trees, branches, vines, and leaves made it impossible.

Back down on the beach again, the explorers saw that the promontory was the open end of another ravine, but this one was easy to cross because it opened to the sea on a wide flat expanse of sand. The barrier rocks began again right there, as well. They could see where water had run across the sand, so they clambered into the ravine until they came to running water. Drinking deeply, Johnny murmured in satisfaction. Sam laughed at him.

Johnny grinned. "Dunno why this is the best tasting water I ever had."

"Maybe 'cos there ain't nothing fouling it up," Joe Mack suggested. "No people, no animals, no nothing."

Sam thought he was probably right, but he didn't want that to be the case. Feeling worried that this was all he was ever going to see of the rest of the world, he made his way back to the beach in silence, and stubbornly continued towards the east, volcano or no volcano. At that point he didn't much care whether the explorers followed him or not. If there really was nothing on this island, then there was no reason a man couldn't go off by himself in perfect safety.

Around the corner the steam explosions were louder. The explorers reacted with various degrees of horror and disbelief that he would consider going any closer to the volcano. "Look," he told them, gesturing to the ravine they'd just left. "If it's green the volcano ain't killed it, so it should be okay for us to take a quick look."

Reluctantly they followed him along the beach for a few yards, which brought them to the opening of yet another ravine. The explorers insisted on wandering up this one as well. Sam figured they were just stalling, but he went along with them for curiosity as much as for peace. There was no running water at the beach, so Sam figured this one was dry. He was saying as much when they heard the burble of flowing water.

Forcing their way through the lush growth they found a spring bubbling up from the ground in a shadowed hollow. The ground was carpeted with mosses and ferns, lit with dappled sunlight that filtered down through a lacy canopy. The greenery was garlanded with a profusion of flowers, the like of which none of them had ever seen. Aside from the brightly coloured blooms growing on flowering plants and shrubs, there were slender ivory trumpets falling in shining cascades from the trees, catching the sprinkles of sunshine and lighting up the hollow like fairy lights. They gave off a sweet perfume that made the men stop and sniff in appreciation.

"I don't know that I've ever seen a place so lovely," Sam breathed softly. "I'd give anything to be able to bring Mercy here."

Johnny led them in a prayer of thanks for the beauty of God's creation, and a request for God to find a way that they could all show this magical place to their loved ones one day.

They drank from this spring, too, even though none of them was thirsty any longer.

"Oh, now, lookee here," Joe Mack crowed after he'd drunk his fill. "Watch your footing, you don't want to fall into it."

Cautiously they made their way over to the spot he'd retreated to drain his bladder. He'd narrowly avoided falling into a huge reservoir. "I'm betting that thing would have held fifteen thousand gallons, give or take a thousand or two. What do you say?"

"I wouldn't argue with that," Sam grinned. "It's too overgrown to be able to get a closer guess or measurement. "There's no mistaking it now. Someone lived here long enough to build big things."

"Can we follow the pipes?" Willie Jay suggested.

"Good idea, except they're buried so deep after two hundred and fifty years that we'll spend weeks digging down to them, and the trees are just as thick on that hillside as they were on the others."

They looked at the tangle resentfully. "What's with the forty-foot-tall ferns, anyway?" Chuck muttered, "Ain't no way that's natural."

By unspoken agreement they retraced their steps to the beach and continued from there. But they were faced at once by another cliff. Up they climbed, ignoring the roaring from the volcano, looking around at the masses of greenery to keep up their nerve. Over the hump they could see another beach and another flat area, this one barely above sea level.

Vince, sketching as always, pointed to a discolouration in the sea water off the beach a few yards ahead of them. "What's that?" It looked as if the sand of the beach was steaming.

Crowding over to take a closer look, they speculated. Willie Jay asked, "Do you think it's a fresh water source that the Weskies could use?"

"Not mixed with salt water, it ain't." Joe Mack put a snappy end to that.

They made their way to the beach and ran along until they came to the anomaly.

"It's hot!" Johnny yelped.

They all stuck their fingers in the sand. They had to be careful not to burn themselves, it was that hot. Sam beamed at them. "It's fresh."

Chuck shrugged. "What good is it full of sand?"

"Boiling hot freshwater seeping through sand? I don't know – what could we use hot water for?"

Then they got it. "Baths! Washing clothes!"

Greatly cheered, they looked beamed at each other. "Looks like it's time to go back and tell the others what we've found," Sam suggested.

Chuck grumbled. "I ain't looking forward to getting through that blamed forest again."

"It'll be easier going now that we've broken our way through it," Sam reminded him.

When they reached the boat pulled up on the beach, they followed the footprints in the sand until they reached the hills, then they followed the trail of the others until they found them hunkered down behind a dip in the land to eat their lunch where they couldn't be seen from the ship.

"Let's see what Rocky's got to say," Sam suggested.

"Raamah," Joe Mack corrected as they jogged along to rejoin the others.

"What did you find?" Sam panted.

The Corporal gestured up the hill. "There ain't no way to get good hunting when we can't even walk. Not one track. Nothing. And I got me a jones on for real meat like you ain't never seen before."

"We couldn't get through it, either," Sam confessed, looking over at the Sergeant guarding the Weskies.

"We got some water back to the ship, but only from piddling little cricks. No decent rivers anywheres."

Sam asked Rocky, "You ever see anything like this before?"

"No, Sir."

"We'll have to get axes and chop our way through," Sam felt annoyed with God. Enough with the challenges already! Hadn't they proved themselves yet?

"A good burn would clear it quicker and flush the deer at the same time," the Lieutenant pointed out.

Sam didn't need to see the Weskies' expressions to know what their objections were. "That's going to get ash and soot and crap in the cricks." He turned to Rocky. "There ain't no point in hunting over the other side for rivers, right?"

Diplomatically he answered, "You might be right, Sir. I never saw any big waterfalls on the cliffs, and I can't see no streams running across the beach."

It seemed to Sam that had never occurred to anyone else. They all stared up and down the beach.

Rocky added, "If there's running water only when it rains, that'd mean no one could live here, even without the volcano."

That was a thought that had never struck any of them. "Someone did, though. We found a spring in a gully over yonder that had a cistern that held thousands of gallons. It's full to overflowing."

The Sergeant beamed. "Praise the Lord!"

"You can't carry the water from there to here. Too many ravines to cross and too much tough terrain. We'll have to get the Major to move the ship."

They looked at one another.

"He ain't going to do that so easy. The ship's shut down. Lay off on telling him about that until we can get him to move the Star. I don't fancy climbing up and down ravines covered with this shit all day every day."

The Weskies looked very relieved when they all agreed. Sam asked them, "How could the place be so green, then? There's got to be lots of water."

"Lots of rain," Rocky suggested. That made sense to Sam. When he nodded, Rocky suggested, "If that's what it is, it'll be too wet to burn."

Coming from arid lands, the idea of a forest being too wet to burn was impossible for them to grasp. Those who had lived in tree covered areas had grown up under constant threat of forest fires, and were no more able to picture it than the boys from the deserts were. The GR were jeering. Sam held his hand up to stop them so that he could hear Rocky. "Have you ever seen it too wet to burn? Any of you?"

A number of the Weskies nodded. Rocky spoke for them. "We get dry years when the Santa Ana winds come over the mountains bringing fires higher than these hills, and all we can do is go down to the ocean and pray. Other years it rains so much the hillsides slide into the ocean and nothing will make the trees burn. You can't even get enough dry wood to make a fire to cook on."

"What makes you think this is like that?" Sam asked respectfully, ignoring the hoots of derision from the GR.

"Well, Sir, the first thing is, there's a volcano erupting in the middle of this island and it's still green. You'd think the whole place ought to be as black and bare as that little island we just saw."

There was silence after that, until Joe Mack thought to let everyone know, "We found hot fresh water on the beach, seeping through the sand into the sea."

The GR stared at him, disbelievingly.

Sam backed his man up. "It's really hot. Hot enough to raise blisters, but I thought if we dug in the sand back from it a ways we could make bath tubs and wash tubs."

Rocky beamed at him. "If the water's clean and don't taste too bad we could collect from there."

The Sergeant was all over that idea as if he'd thought of it himself.

"There's no need to go that far," Sam told him. "We found more than one crick between here and there."

The Weskies made another foray for water. When they returned to the ship with it, the hunters and the explorers asked them to bring back as many axes as they could get to hack their way through the jungle. The hunting party was determined to try again, despite the explorers and the Weskies pointing out that if there were any animals on the island, there would be trails for them to walk along. The explorers also told them about the grass, but nothing could dissuade the hunters.

Once they had axes in their hands the explorers headed back towards the east listening every once in a while to make sure the hunters were heading west, away from them. Vince stopped now and then to sketch, then hurried to catch back up.

They struck inland at the hot water, clambering over sand dunes. They didn't go any further along the beach to see how far it went because they could see the familiar formation of cliffs not far away, and the area they were on was fairly flat. Besides, they were getting close to the volcano, and didn't want to be any nearer than they were. The noise of the volcano was like standing beside a locomotive. The regular explosions were loud enough that they couldn't hear each other or anything else when they happened. The ground trembled constantly as if a train was going by right beside them.

There was ash on the ground, but it had obviously been washed off the leaves and grass by the rain. Despite the wind blowing all of the smoke away from them, there was a strong smell of sulphur.

"Rotten eggs," Vince exclaimed in disgust, his nose screwed up.

'Brimstone,' Sam thought to himself, without saying anything.

They made their way inland over the sand dunes across the flat area, moving away from the volcano, back towards the west. There was scrub to get through, but not the fierce tangles of the other forests, so they made good time. At the end of the flat land was a rise which they didn't hesitate to climb up so that they could look around. The bursts of steam were easily seen shooting up from the other side of the cliffs when they looked back.

Willie Jay got further onto the higher land than the others, continuing to poke around while they stood and looked back at the volcano. "Sam! Sam!" he yelled, getting them all spinning to face him.

"What?" Sam shouted, running in the direction of Willie Jay's voice.

"There's buildings over there!"

"Where?" Sam couldn't believe his ears.

They rushed as quickly as the thick undergrowth would let them. The remains of a few buildings could be made out. They hacked the greenery off them to try to figure out how old they were. Most had collapsed, all were overgrown, some were partially buried. Pulling the plants off some made them disappear. All that was left of them was the shape of a building in the greenery, and when they cut it away there was nothing standing left.

"People lived here, once," Sam said.

"They've been gone a long time, Sam," Joe Mack sighed.

"Two hundred and fifty years," Sam agreed, sadly. "Let's call it a day."

As they made their way across the barer patches of the higher land towards the beautiful gully with the big cistern in it, they found more signs that there had once been dwellings there. Once they realised what they were looking at, they could make out the trees that had been planted in straight rows.

"Bet there were gardens there, too," Joe Mack said.

"We'll look for signs of that tomorrow," Sam promised. All he wanted at that moment was to have time to himself to figure out how to get Major Temperance to carry on. It looked like fresh water and birds were all they were going to get from this place.

"Maybe we could get something to eat," Chuck suggested.

They stopped and looked around, but didn't find anything that they recognised, and carried on empty handed.

After all the reports had been given, and the disappointment of a meal of fish, and birds that tasted like fish, had been endured, plus Major Temperance's inebriated sneering had been tolerated that anyone who thought there could have been survivors of Judgement Day were too stupid to live, Sam lay awake in the bunk he shared with Willie Jay. He decided to camp on the island for the rest of their stay.

At first all he was thinking about was keeping away from the Major, but as he started imagining being on a strange land hearing the strange birds and smelling the strange plants, he wished again that Amos could have seen the marvel of an alien land for himself. Not only did Sam miss the old curmudgeon, but Amos knew more banned information than Sam did. Amos might have known about volcanoes. Sam was sure he'd said something about a place called Yellowstone. It was ringing a bell in the back of his brain but he could not connect it.

Sam didn't ask the explorers to sleep on the island with him, and none of them volunteered, so he had unnerving sensation of being the only person on the land. "This must be how Adam felt before Eve was created. No wonder he told God he needed a companion."

The spookiness made it impossible for him to get to sleep, though he knew there were no dangerous animals, there didn't seem to be any snakes, or even many bugs. There was nothing to keep him awake except for the eeriness of being completely on his own.

Instead of staying where he'd built his camp, he got up and wandered in the cool evening, using the moonlight to see. He made his way along the path they'd cut, back to the ravine that had the flowers that looked like lilies hanging down like a curtain from the trees. As lovely as the scent had been during the day, at night it was such a beautiful, exotic fragrance that Sam drank it in with huge, slow, deep breaths that soon filled him with a peaceful drowsiness. Despite the coolness and dewiness of the shady hollow at night, not to mention the rumbling and trembling of the ground, Sam had the deepest, most refreshing sleep he'd had in years.

The pre-dawn chorus of unfamiliar bird songs woke him. He felt more rested than he had ever felt after a night on board. He woke up not only refreshed, but feeling young again and full of enthusiasm. The sky was starting to pale. Too energetic to lie on his back and watch little triangles of sky through the fluttering leaves, he made his way carefully to the spot where the delicious water bubbled up out of the ground, drank his fill, and washed the sleep out of his eyes. The easiest way out of the tree-lily ravine was along the path they'd hacked out. Although he wanted to see something new, in the dim light it made the most sense to take the safest route.

Despite the volcano roaring away right there, he had a feeling of complete freedom that he had never known in his life before. It filled him with a reckless joy. He looked up the slope towards the volcano. There was no one there to stop him. Who knew if he'd ever have another chance? If he made good time he could take a look over the edge and get back down to the beach before anyone from the ship came to join him.

Now that he was totally alone, he was going to do exactly what he wanted to do. The thrill that gave him brought back memories of returning to Amos's house when he was ten, after the pulled muscle in his groin had recovered, and although the last thing Amos had said to him was, "Don't ever come back."

For ten-year-old Sam the allure of the fascinating things he'd seen in Amos's house were irresistible. They'd never been out of his mind from the moment he'd wrestled the peg back into its hole in the chair. He'd never forgotten the items on the list. When he was able to walk around on uneven ground again, but not yet back to man's work, he asked his mother if he could strengthen his muscles by taking walks on the uneven ground without his walking stick. His mother encouraged him to walk around the house, and to help as much as he could with the barnyard around the house. He didn't mind feeding the chickens and ducks, because it fit into his plans. Soon he was able to go off by himself under the guise of searching for eggs. He stayed out longer and longer until he was able to go all the way to some old ruins to see if he could find some copper wire for Amos.

The buildings made before Judgement Day were strange compared with the good, strong houses his family built. Instead of thick adobe walls to keep the cold out in winter and the heat out in summer, the ancient ruins had thin walls and huge windows. The walls were mostly cement, coloured and shaped to look like adobe, but thinner. Sam had no idea how the unbelievers had kept warm on cold nights, or kept cool on hot days with thin walls and big windows. All of the glass was long gone, either taken out and used in new buildings or just smashed, leaving the ruins with an empty eye-socket look like skulls.

Ten-year-old Sam had shivered as he got close to them, unnerved by the ghostliness. When he was with the other boys they had dared each other to go into the ruins, something strictly forbidden because fugitives, bears, cougars, wolves, or snakes could be hidden there. The ruins were frightening enough when the boys were together, but facing them alone made him more afraid than anything in his life except Killer. He had to stop to catch his breath and build up his courage before he could make himself go into the ghost town. There was a place where someone had dug into the walls sometime in the past. Some people told stories and legends that the unbelievers had some kind of power inside their walls that made light without candles and kept their houses warm in the cold and cool in the heat. They'd never found anything but a bunch of useless wires. They weren't thick enough to be used for fences, and there wasn't enough metal in them to melt down for ploughs or cooking pots, so the ruins were left to their spooky selves.

Sam hoped that if he found that spot he could find copper wire to use as a peace offering to Amos. His joy was so great when he did find copper wire, and was able to pull enough out of the wall to wrap around his waist and hips under his pants, that he cried like a girl. Taking care to arrive home with some eggs in hand, he planned to set off to see Amos the first chance he got.

It was no easy trick to keep the wire out of sight until he got a chance to go back to Amos's house, but Sam managed it. When Killer heard him coming and set up a blood-curdling barking, growling, and snarling,

Sam stood completely still on the other side of the hedge until he heard Amos. Then he called, "Amos, it's me, Sam."

In the blink of an eye Amos's angry face appeared, scolding in a furious hiss, "What the hell do you think you're doing, you stupid assed kid? If they're watching you've done us both in!"

"I got something for you." Sam dropped his voice in case someone was listening.

Amos hesitated for a moment, then called the dogs back and let Sam in, scolding, "I thought I told you never to come back."

"Yessir."

"Don't you obey no-one? Your Daddy tells you to stay away from here, but you come here anyways. I tell you not to come back, but here you are when you ain't hardly healed up yet. You need a good whopping."

"Yessir." Sam felt reassured by Amos's gruffness. It felt right. He understood it. Once they were inside the house where they couldn't be seen or heard, he took off his shirt to reveal the wire. He'd wound it around his chest this time.

Amos went silent, watching Sam with a stony expression.

Sam unwrapped the wire and held it out in one hand, where it dangled down both sides, and pointed to the chair with the other. "That's the illegalist thing I ever saw."

Amos reeled back. His eyes were popping out of his head, his cheeks were so white that the black hairs of his beard stood out as if they'd been painted on. "How did you find that, you sneaking little worm?"

Sam lost his bravado. He could barely speak around the lump that suddenly filled his throat. "I never meant to. I'm sorry I did, too. I can't stop thinking about it, and I'm scared if the GR ever do question me now I really do know something and they'll know I do, and I can't tell no-one nothing, not even my Dad."

"Not your Dad more than anyone else." Amos glared, then the hardness went out of his eyes and he said in a pleading tone, "Look, boy, I got to know how you found it. I thought it was invisible. If you can find it any search party can too."

"I fell down again, and I was mad, and I sat on the chair to wait for you, and I kind of fiddled with the pegs and one of them moved, so I twisted it and it moved some more."

"Where did you get that?" Amos pointed to the wire, still making no attempt to touch it.

"There's some ruins from before Judgement Day on our land. I pulled it out of the walls."

"Probably broke it," Amos muttered, grudgingly taking the wire. "If you knew I wanted it from looking in the chair; that means you can read."

"Yessir."

"You know not to let the GR find out you can read, don't you, boy?"

"Yessir, I sure do."

"It ain't for farmers like you and me to know about reading and writing."

Sam looked at Amos carefully. "Can you tell me why my brother said guys got flogged for reading and their families got searched?"

"Don't you know what tree we learn of in Genesis?"

"The Tree of Knowledge."

"Right first time. The Church tells us what we should know. If we find out anything we want to, it will put a coyote in the chicken coop."

Sam didn't know what to say to that. He thought his parents didn't believe it because they kept saying how important education was, but watching Amos brought a whole new idea to his mind: what if Amos did believe it and wanted to cause trouble? He was afraid to ask. To change the subject he returned to the chair. "You know what? Maybe no one else can find your hiding places cuz maybe no-one else is gonna sit still and pull on those old pegs til one of them moves."

"By God, I think you're on to something there, son. Kids don't see things the same way men do. Kids see things men don't, and men see things kids don't. Maybe the raiders won't find it even if you did."

"Except I couldn't get the peg all the way back down. They can see the threads if they look close."

Amos snatched the chair up and checked it out. "Okay," he said as he tightened the screw.

Sam's relief spilled over in nervous chatter. "I'm sorry, Amos, I tried my hardest but I really couldn't get it down. I used the walking stick to force it and everything."

"Okay," Amos repeated.

Sam heard the 'shut up' tone in his voice, but he couldn't stop himself. "I thought about it all the time. If the raiders come back on you and catch you it's my doing for touching something that ain't mine and not putting it back the way I found it and not letting you know right away and . . ."

"I said okay!" Amos barked so sharply that Sam nearly jumped out of his skin and Killer growled at the door.

But words were still bubbling up inside Sam. In desperation he blurted out, "Why did you make hiding places in chairs, anyhow?"

Amos glared at him, then explained, "I was cleaning up after a search one day when I got that I always clean up the same things. They break the backs off of all the furniture that ain't built in looking for false backs, and punch the bottoms and backs out off all the drawers for the same reason. And they dig all the caulking out of the walls and pry up every loose floorboard. When I had good chairs they smashed them, so I built rough ones. They made fun of me but the chairs didn't break easily, and they never once chopped them up to see if there was anything in them."

The words stopped churning inside Sam. All of sudden he couldn't think of a thing to say. He thought Amos was the smartest man he'd ever seen. Maybe even smarter than his Dad – but he couldn't say that. All he could do was gaze at Amos in admiration.

Amos looked back, blinked, then asked in a kinder tone of voice, "Do your folks know you're here?"

"No, sir."

"Didn't you hear me tell you not to ever come back here again?"

"Yes, sir, I did."

"You don't even care if Killer rips you up again?"

"Yes, sir, I was real scared."

Amos stared for a bit. "You come all this way just to tell me that?"

"Yes, sir. I couldn't take it thinking you might get caught on a search. And I brung that for you." He pointed at the wire.

"Do you know what it's for?"

"No Sir, I don't, I'm sorry, it's just that you wanted them, and I knew where they were."

From that point on Amos became Sam's mentor. For the rest of his childhood he slipped out to visit Amos every chance he got. When he was caught he refused to take his punishment, telling his father that he would leave home and live with Amos before he'd stop visiting him. That completed the estrangement between Sam and his family.

After Amos was the first person Sam saw on his release from the military, he did end up living there.

Sam was thinking so much about his childhood that he was back on the beach of Anvil Island without remembering picking his way along the gully.

Without another thought he climbed up from the beach and headed off uphill, taking care to leave an easily followed trail for the explorers. It took the best part of the morning to make his way across the flat area to the hillside and then climb up to the top. The gritty powder that the Weskies had called 'ash' was not only covering the ground like cement, but every time he moved branches aside it fell off the leaves, showering him until he looked like he'd been out in some kind of clumpy snow. He pulled his hat down over his eyes to make sure none of that stuff got in his eyes. It was bad enough when some got in his mouth. He pulled his bandana up over his nose to make sure he didn't breathe any of it in. That helped with the stink of the sulphur, too. Because the wind was blowing the smoke to the north-east, Sam climbed to the south. It was a longer climb, but he thought he shouldn't ignore everything the Weskies had said, even if he was ignoring some of it.

Despite the dense foliage, he could tell the moment he reached the lip of the crater because the land abruptly fell away in front of him. Lying on his stomach, Sam peered through the greenery over the edge and down. He'd never seen or dreamed of anything remotely like it. Jets of steam squirted from the torn, blackened cliffs on the other side of the chasm. At the bottom it looked like a giant pot of boiling burned chilli. Black, charred bits floated on top of searingly hot red stuff that burped and hissed as it flowed to the sea. The air over it was so overheated that it was like trying to see through water.

To rest his straining eyes, Sam looked away, across the massive bowl. From what he could make out around the smoke and steam, he guessed it was a mile or more north to south and over half a mile east to west. The activity was concentrated in the north-east corner of the bowl, leaving the rest eerily untouched when compared with the devastation around the eruption. Near the eruption the sides of the crater were lined with shattered and ripped up trees and palms that looked like boiled soup-bones. Every trace of bark and greenery had been seared off. Bare trunks stood up stark and white; the ghostly skeletons of a forest, limbs uplifted as if pleading for help that never came. Like offerings to God broken branches held up great lumps of dried mud.

Sam looked to see where the mud had come from. On the southern edge of the eruption was boiling mud. If he used his imagination, Sam could picture that the area that blew up had been a lake. There was more boiling mud in a steaming hollow further south. The bloop bloop of the mud was mesmerizing. One pot of badly burned chilli and one of brown porridge that smelled like rotten eggs.

One big, long lake had filled the bowl – he stopped himself to reconsider, studying the wreckage of a hump of dried mud and shattered rock that covered the few hundred yards between the boiling mud in the hollow to the south and that at the edge of the boiling rock. Two small lakes, he corrected himself – as long as the water wasn't deep enough to submerge the hill in the middle. He couldn't see how there could have been lakes there, no matter how small, because there was no sign of any rivers.

What he couldn't get over was that right beside the army of tree skeletons on the roasted, scorched cliffs to the north, all of the encircling cliffs to the south were untouched. There was almost a line between the barren rock and the verdant forest. It had obviously been too wet to burn. The edges were crispy, that's all. Other than that, the southern slopes rose almost vertically to a height of five hundred feet or more still clothed in their dense greenery as if nothing had happened. The blast had apparently come from the north end and towards the north, leaving the south end surprisingly unscathed.

Leaning out to try to see what had happened on his side, Sam figured out that he could move along the rim to the bare area where he might be able to see more. If it turned out to be hot he could always move back to a cooler spot. The rotten egg smell and the noise of the volcano got so strong when he reached the clear space that he at once retreated to the shelter of the trees. He noticed some small yellow berry-like fruit and absent-mindedly picked some, dusted the ash off and popped them into his mouth. They didn't have much favour, but they did a surprisingly good job of getting rid of his thirst. By the time he realised what he'd done and worried about whether they were poisonous or not it was too late to worry about it. Besides, he reassured himself, if they were going to poison him, he would have felt something by then.

To put the nagging worry out of his mind, he turned his attention to something new – peering past the writhing twister-that-didn't-twist to see if he could find out what had happened to the north. The winds pushed the smoke this way and that, always heading north-east away from him, but sometimes billowing more north or west than others, plus the smoke moved of its own accord, so he'd catch sight of things for a split second, only to lose them again before he could be sure what he'd seen. He lost all track of time, becoming absorbed in the challenge, his eyes watering in the fumes so that he wasn't sure what he'd seen when the wind gusted due east, leaving a clear view of the sea for a split second. It had almost looked like a big chunk of black metal sticking straight up from the rocks. He couldn't tell if it was metal or rock. All he knew was if it wasn't his imagination, it was huge.

If only he could catch another glimpse of it. The image of a massive black triangle was burned into his mind's eye. That couldn't be right. Nothing in nature was that shape. If it existed, it had to be man made. The touch on his shoulder nearly catapulted him right up and over the crater rim.

Joe Mack's, "What the hell are you doing?" was met by his own forceful, "What the fuck!?"

"Sorry, Sam. You mean you really didn't know I was there?"

"Do I look like I knew you were there?" Sam knew he was screaming at Joe Mack, but he'd had such a fright he couldn't pull in the rage without showing his fear.

"That's not keeping your guard up, Buddy."

"There ain't nothing here to keep your guard up against. No critters, no enemies – not even bugs." So, what if it was lame? It was the truth.

Joe Mack looked away. "You left a big, wide trail."

"I thought you guys'd join me here."

"What for? Willie Jay's gone and found something that's got Johnny's briefs in such a bunch he's gone back to the ship to fetch the pastor."

Intrigued in spite of himself, Sam started back down the mountainside with Joe Mack.

"What'd he find?"

"Some kind of pagan idol."

"Sheee-it. How much do you want to bet the stupid ass will want to destroy it?"

"You don't want him to?"

"Hell no! If we can take a good look at it without getting all hysterical we maybe could get a clue from it how long ago these people were here and where they went."

"Look, there's a fire over there now. I guess they burned it up already."

Sam peered through the leaves of the trees on the slope over the plain below. He easily spotted the thin whisp of smoke rising up from higher area at the other side of the flats. He cursed under his breath and kicked at the leaf litter on the forest floor. "No point in hurrying now!"

Joe Mack asked, tentatively, "What's the matter, Sam?"

That exasperated Sam. Of all the explorers, he had thought Joe Mack was the most sensible. He crashed along the trail he'd cut, shouting over his shoulder, "Don't you get it? None of you? We ain't here to burn their stuff, we're here to find out if anyone but us made it, and where they got to. We can't find out nothing if we burn every fucking thing we see before we find out what it is and where it came from and how old it is."

"How can you get all that from a pole?"

"Maybe we can and maybe we can't, but we sure as hell can't after it's a pile of ash, can we?"

"Don't yell at me, I never burned the blamed thing."

Sam felt bad for taking it out on Joe Mack, though he still felt disappointed that Joe Mack didn't get it the way he'd thought he did. "What's everyone else doing?"

"Vince is in a panic over the pagan idol."

"I just bet he is."

"Chuck's down on the beach with the Weskies taking a bath."

"Our idea with the hot water worked, huh?"

"Like a hot damn! You gotta do it, Sam. I never felt so good as I did after."

"Yeah, I'm heading down there now."

"What're you gonna do after?"

"Have a word with Johnny and Vince about not damn burning the stuff we came to find, then keep on trying to find something that'll tell us if these guys were here less than two hundred and fifty years ago. And if we do find something, trying to figure out how to get old Temperance to keep on instead of turning back."

Joe Mack gave a snort.

Sam glanced at him in surprise. Seeing the wicked twinkle in Joe Mack's eyes he asked, "What?"

"The Major running low on booze?"

"I dunno. He's got to have less than he started with, why?"

"Tell him we found a still."

All of a sudden, the bad mood that had descended on Sam when Joe Mack startled him evaporated. "That'd work," he grinned. "Man, I feel lousy," he admitted.

"No sleep?"

"Great sleep! Best sleep I've had in years. We got to spend every night in that gully, it's a little piece of heaven. Nothing to eat or drink and breathing in them God-forsaken fumes is what did it."

He stopped talking as they reached the beach. All of the tubs that had been dug out of the sand were filled with GR. Sam decided he'd put his bath off until they were all gone. Chuck came towards them all smiles.

"I never knew how itchy I was until I wasn't any more."

"I'd settle for a drink of clean water."

One of the Weskies stepped over to him with a pitcher of water and a dipper. Quietly, so that none of the nearby GR could hear him he thanked the Weskie and then drained two full dippers.

"Easy, Sam, you don't want to over-do it," Chuck cautioned him.

"Yeah, I know, but I was sure thirsty."

"What were you doing?"

"I looked over the edge." He pointed up to the rim of the crater.

"Are you nuts?!"

"Yeah, but I saw something incredible." He stalled, looking at the end of the beach. "And I saw something else, too. I don't know what it was. It was just on the other side of that hill."

Chuck looked out at the little islands. "There's something on one of them?"

"No." Sam shook his head, trying to keep his patience. He knew he was being short tempered because he hadn't had anything to eat, but he still had to struggle to keep a lid on it. "On this island. On the rocks just around this bend right here." He started walking towards the end of the beach.

"Sam! What are you doing, man? The volcano is right fucking there!" Joe Mack leaped towards Sam, grabbing to catch his shirt sleeve and missing it.

Sam glared at him. "Yeah, I know. I spent the whole morning watching it. I know exactly what's there and where it is."

They all tried to convince him not to climb over the rocks at the end of the beach and go around the corner; Chuck, Joe Mack, the Weskies and the GR. The more pressure they put on him, the more stubborn Sam got. "I just got to find out what I saw," he insisted, marching doggedly on. The Weskies and most of the GR dropped back, one of the soldiers calling after him, "Go on, then. Kill yourself, you dumb ass."

Sam glanced back to see if Chuck and Joe Mack were with him. When he saw them, he slowed down to mutter to them, "He only wants to get rid of me so that he can go home."

They grinned back, though Joe Mack muttered in reply, "He's got a point."

"Good God Almighty!" Sam stopped in his tracks. Only part way around the comer and he knew what he'd seen. He was looking at the back of a massive iron ship, completely up on the rocks out of the water. Its anchors were still up, so it hadn't been anchored when it had been wrecked. The massive brass propeller was resting on the rocks, shining golden in the sunlight. Everything else was black. It looked like iron that a blacksmith was working. It had that same kind of blackness that hot iron gets when it's plunged into cold water. Sam crept slowly over the rocks, staring at the apparition. He was only vaguely aware of the mumble of voices behind him as the others commented on the sight.

The ship was lying on its side, a burnt hulk. There was nothing but metal left of it. Everything else, even the paint, had been burned away. What he had seen, silhouetted against the ocean, was the triangular point of the bow sticking out from behind the cliff-side. As he got closer Sam could see where the molten rock had come up against the side of the ship and had melted it.

"God Almighty," one of the GR breathed. "Is that what the Weskies said would happen to us if that stuff had a got us?"

At that Sam straightened up and looked around at the others. He could feel his head clearing as the stunned shock gave way to acceptance. "What could put a whole ship up on the rocks like that?" he asked the explorers.

"The rudder's gone."

Sam jumped, startled to hear a Weskie accent. He thought they'd all stayed on the beach. There was one there, shirtless and shoeless, with his pants rolled up to his knees, scars from a flogging laced across his back. He pulled back from the edge, sheltering from the noise of the explosions of steam where the lava hit the sea so that he could hear better. "How could that get it way up there?"

"You get a big enough storm, and hit one of the hidden rocks out there, and it snaps your rudder off, then you can't steer, and the storm can do anything it wants to with your ship. It would be a real big swell to throw it right out of the water like that, but a big storm-surge could do it."

"And it's kind of melted. It's sort of folded over."

"That's how hot lava is."

Eyes wide with horror at the idea, most of the GR made their way back to the beach, bursting with news.

"Do you know why it would reach the ship then stop?"

"Lava flows downhill like water. If there's something in its way it goes where it's easier going." The Weskie moved forward and looked, then pulled back. "Looks to me like there was a big flow that's settled down some. It's just going into the sea at the lowest point, now. Looks like there used to be a land bridge here that this eruption has blown it away. There's lots of rubble and it looks like the hillside was torn away. I think it didn't used to reach the sea here. The land might have risen up. If the ship was on the beach and the land was pushed up it'd lift the ship with it."

Sam just stared at him, trying to understand what he'd just heard.

"Get back to work!" one of the GR bellowed.

Sam didn't stop the Weskie from racing back to the laundry. He leaned on the cliff-side, staring at the end of the ship. Joe Mack and Chuck ventured further around the corner, and then pulled back beside Sam.

"There's two shipwrecks on this one island, and it's not very big," Chuck pointed out, unnecessarily.

Sam nodded. "And no way to tell how long either one has been here."

Joe Mack stated at the wreck. "I'd bet if this one was here two hundred and fifty years it would've rusted more than that."

Sam stared at it again, noticing something he hadn't seen before. Parts of the propeller were missing. It wasn't melted at all. It was as if someone had cut pieces from it. He stared at the straight edges for a moment, then shook himself and said, "Let's get over to the pagan idol and see what those guys are up to."

I wasn't difficult to find the others, because all they had to do was aim towards the smoke from the little fire. Sam said nothing until he was sure they were well away from any soldiers. "What chance do you think there is that the ship's been there less than two hundred and fifty years?"

Joe Mack glanced around, and then shrugged. "Ain't no way iron can last that long in the wet. In the desert maybe, but this ain't no desert. It oughta be rusted to rat shit."

Sam looked at Chuck, who raised both hands in submission. "I ain't never seen a ship rust away, but I know when we served in the Panhandle stuff rusted more near the coast than it did in the desert. We got lots of cars and stuff from before Judgement Day at home."

Sam nodded, mulling it all over in his mind, not wanting to say anything about the straight lines that looked as if someone had been cutting pieces off the propeller if no one else had seen them.

A tantalizing smell drove everything out of his mind as the wind blew the smoke towards them just as they climbed to the top of the steep escarpment at the end of the small plain. "They're not just burning the idol, they're cooking something!" Sam exclaimed. His empty stomach reacted so strongly to the smell that it hurt.

They could see Willie Jay before they'd gone very far from the top of the escarpment. He was tending a fire surrounded by appreciative GR. Chuck ran on ahead, shouting, "What're you doing there, Willie Jay?"

Willie Jay turned with a big grin. "I got us a mess of vittles."

Sam felt faint with the clawing of his stomach for good food. "You got some good water there?" he asked, finding a spot to sit down.

Joe Mack brought him a tin cup of the delicious water from the streams in the gully. Willie Jay had found outlines that looked like gardens, so he had dug around searching for potatoes. He didn't find any regular potatoes, but he did dig up sweet potato tubers which he lit a fire to roast. He'd found a spot that had obviously been a barbeque spot, though there were no racks. He'd lit the fire in the pit to roast the sweet potatoes while soldiers had killed, plucked, and gutted birds. They'd kept the feathers to make themselves new pillows, and had flayed the birds open, roasting them over the fire on three pronged sticks. Even without salt Sam devoured the fresh food as if it was the best thing he'd ever eaten in his life.

Willie Jay looked like a new man, cleaned and shaved, with clean, mended clothes. "If Willie Jay can look that good, I gotta clean me up, too," Sam joked.

"Yeah," Joe Mack agreed with a grin. "I never thought about getting shaved and prettied up. Better get right on that. Can't have Willie Jay getting all the girls when we get there."

Chuck choked on his mouthful. "No, man, that just ain't right."

"Where's Johnny?" Now that he'd eaten and his mood had improved, Sam had to get on with business.

They had to ask around to find out the pagan idol was on the other side of some scrubby bushes and ferns nearby. Sam got up and went over there. Johnny, Vince, and the pastor were praying up a storm, begging God to protect them all from the evil of the pole. He stood watching them, surprised by a slight fear hovering in his chest, making his heart pound, at the idea of actually seeing a real pagan artifact. But when he really looked at it, it was only a pole sticking up out of the ground. A wooden pole, gleaming faintly in the sunlight from some kind of coating. Not a paint, and not really a stain, either. He couldn't be sure just what it was. It looked as if the wood itself had that odd greenish-brown colour, rather than a stain.

The pole was decorated with carving and shining white spots that spiralled down it in a pattern.

He knew without a shadow of a doubt that pole had not stood untended for two hundred and fifty years. There was no way it would have looked like that. It would have been cracked and worn, colourless, if not rotted clean away in that time. Besides, it should have been over-grown.

Sam looked around at the clearing as that thought occurred to him. That grass had not grown untended for long. A year's growth, perhaps, if things grew very fast here, and it looked as if they did. On the edges of the clearing, where the trees and bushes started, he noticed obvious signs that they'd been cut back. Recently. Some cut ends of branches were grown over and grey, others had bright pale surfaces as if they'd been cut not too long ago. A year at the most, he had to admit.

Raising his head from his prayer, Vince noticed Sam, leaped to his feet and rushed up to him, eyes wide with fear. "Sam! Sam!"

The other two looked around at Vince's cry. Johnny immediately got up and walked over, the pastor followed more slowly.

"Hi, Vince."

"We're in the presence of evil here, Sam."

"It's a wooden pole, Vince."

"It's pagan! It should be thrown in the fiery furnace!"

With a jarring shock Sam realised he had to preserve the pole. If they burned it he'd never get a chance to look at it more closely to try to figure out how long ago people had been here. All his years of living a double life kicked in, providing him with a way to convince them not to destroy the pole. "Are you sure you want to touch it?" he asked.

All three of them recoiled in the same way.

He pressed his advantage before any of them had a chance to think about it. "What if it's cursed?"

The pastor blanched and decided it was time to return to the ship.

"Do you really think it's cursed?" Johnny asked.

Sam could never look into those honest blue eyes and play his games. "Even if it is, I believe God is all powerful. I believe there is one God. If those poor souls don't, that doesn't affect God's power. It all depends on whether we have faith in Him or not."

"What if this is one of their gods?" Vince sounded desperately frightened.

"It's a piece of wood, Vince. If you think it's stronger than the living God, then you've got problems. It changes nothing for me."

Vince went quiet, though his Adam's apple bobbed up and down in this throat.

Johnny asked in a completely different tone, "What do you think it is, Sam?"

"It could be a grave marker, like a tombstone, or it could be a kids' thing. It could point north. Who knows? I'd like to find out."

Sam walked closer to the pole, looking all around. The shiny spots were pieces of shell, beautiful with rainbows of colours in them, like the rainbows in oil on water, but cleaner. They were artfully shaped into ovals with pointed ends, and set into the wood. Whoever had done that was highly skilled.

He noticed a white stone in the grass and went over to it, to see another one further on. By walking from one to another he realised that there was a circle of white painted stones, most of them hidden by the grass. It was like a line around the clearing. Some of the stones were white, others were painted white. Then he saw a larger stone, mostly overgrown. When he looked closely at it, he realised there was a plaque attached to it on the outside of the circle. Standing in front of the plaque, pulling the vines, ferns, and grass back from it so that he could read it, he discovered he'd wasted his time. It made no sense whatsoever. "This Po Whenua was erected by the Ngāti Kurī 2006."

Johnny ran around the circle to the other side, and started clearing greenery away from a matching larger stone.

Vince and Sam ran over to see if there was another plaque. There was. This one read: "In memory of Mark Kearney, a Department of Conservation observer, who was killed by the eruption of Green Lake, 17 March 2006."

"It's a memorial," Sam declared, snorting in disgust, "Pagan idol! You've been reading too many comics. You were going to burn these poor guys' memorial."

"Whoever heard of a wooden memorial?" Vince yelped. "It don't look like no Christian memorial I ever seen! And what's with all the pagan markings?"

"Maybe the poor guy had kids."

They were both silent and shame faced at that. Sam changed the subject. "Am I imagining things, or do you think someone's been here recently?"

Johnny and Vince stared around, not speaking until Sam said, "Vince, go get the others. Tell Willie Jay to leave his cooking to one of the GR. Joe Mack and Chuck are over by the fire with him."

While he waited, he told Johnny about the ship up on the rocks, and that the Weskie had said sometimes the land rises.

Johnny couldn't believe that, but when Sam told him about the ship being partially melted, he went dumb.

As the four others approached, Joe Mack called out, "Do you really think this thing's important, Sam?"

He shook his head. "It's some kind of memorial. There's a plaque over there listing people who've been killed by that thing." He pointed to the volcano. "What I want is for all of you guys to take a good look at this clearing and tell me how long you think it's been since the last time someone cut the grass or trimmed the trees."

He watched them, turning things over in his mind.

Joe Mack was the first one to come back to him. "What are you thinking?" he asked.

"No, I want to hear from all of you, first."

"Well, I'm thinking this grass has been cut inside of a year. There ain't no old dried stuff from the winter, just fresh green. And I'm thinking the trees have been cut back over and over again. There's some rotted stumps and some fresh."

Sam nodded. "Some branches were cut back years ago, and some were cut back recently."

"Are you thinking what I'm thinking?" Joe Mack asked as the others gathered around them. "These folks come and go to tend the graves, but they don't live here because of the volcano."

Sam raised his hands. "I'm thinking someone survived Judgement Day."

Chuck nodded. "No doubt about that. That pole's been cleaned inside of a year. Ain't no creepers growing over it, and they're growing over purty near everything else."

Willie Jay added, "Ain't never seen words carved in a rock like that. Ain't no chisel marks. It's like they're cut out of paper."

Sam had been too busy thinking of other things to notice that. He blinked in surprise.

Joe Mack conceded, "He's right. The paint ain't weathered at all, by wind or rain. Paint can't stand up to rain worth a hill of beans at the coast in the Panhandle, and its way drier there than here."

Chuck added, "And there ain't no way those bits of shell would stay stuck to the wood for even one year."

"They creep me out," Vince complained. "They look like eyes."

"I think some of them are supposed to be eyes," Johnny said, looking back at the pole.

Vince shuddered.

"So, they took care of that, but they let the houses fall down," Sam muttered, trying to make sense of it all. "I wonder if both those ships came from these guys coming here to do this?" He looked over towards the fire, watching the smoke curling lazily up to where the wind caught it and whipped it away. "Where did they stay when there were here? Or are they close enough that they could come here and go back in one day?"

Willie Jay suddenly had an intense expression.

"What?" Sam demanded.

"I think maybe they stayed near the gardens," Willie Jay ventured.

Sam started walking back towards the gardens, asking, "What makes you say that?"

"Just a hunch. I can't rightly say. I'll have to show you."

Sam nodded. He couldn't believe what was unfolding. Could it really happen? Something was bound to go wrong. "Not that it'll do us any good," he grumbled. "I'm never going to be able to get Temperance to keep on going."

"The guys found a still," Joe Mack told him.

"I know I said that was a good line, but now I don't think it's such a good idea."

"No, Sam, listen. The guys found a still."

"What?" Sam stopped and stared at him.

"Well, they figure it was a still, anyway. There ain't no metal, just glass."

"What's with these guys?" Sam muttered, but didn't say anything more. He figured he'd best keep his observations for when the GR couldn't hear them.

"See, look at this, Sam," Willie Jay said, leading the explorers to the area he'd dug up the sweet potatoes.

Sam stared at the mounds. Even covered with grass and weeds, he had the impression that someone had dug in that area a while ago. Like maybe about a year ago. "I see what you mean," he told Willie Jay.

Thoughtfully they all trooped behind Joe Mack. "Where's the still I heard the guys talking about?" he asked a soldier.

"Ain't no gin."

"We know that," Joe Mack said. "I want to show my buddies what you found. They're good guys. They won't say nothing to no one."

Grudgingly the soldier took them to the partially collapsed building where they'd found what they took to be a still. "Might not be a still," the soldier admitted. "Ain't nothing left but the glass and some weird kind of tubing, but if it had copper tubing and a good cooker it'd be a still. If we're gonna be here a week or so, we're gonna get some bits and pieces from the ship and find something to make a mash and make us some moonshine. We can't get glass like that, but we can get us some pots and pipes to put with it."

Sam stood and stared at the glass. "I think you're right," he told the soldier. "I think they were brewing beer here, and it won't take much to turn this into a still. Good luck with it." He beckoned to the explorers to leave with him. He had something he wanted to talk over with them in private.

But before they could get out of earshot of the GR, one of them came running over, calling, "Say, have you guys seen this?"

So, they followed him to find out what 'this' was.

It was a large house with a porch all across the front, facing the gardens. This building had not disintegrated the way the others had. Sam could see why, too. Repairs had been made at different times. "I guess this is where they stay," he muttered.

"I would, too!" Chuck exclaimed. "Look at that view!"

Sam stood on the porch looking out over the gardens to the peak on the other side of the volcano. It was handsomely cone-shaped, more than five hundred feet high, and deeply green with its dense forest cover. When the gardens had been cultivated they must have been lovely, and they were big enough to keep several people fed. Beyond them was the drop off to the low flat-land, which reached to the steep rim of the volcano in front of him, but to the left stretched out to the sand dunes that edged the beach. Beyond the shore were the little islets, coming and going into and out of view as the steam obscuring them was blown about by the sea breezes. When the wind blew the sulphur smell the other way the air was fresh and clean, scented with greenery and ocean. "I would, too. What I don't get is why they don't stay here." He looked at the smoking menace of the volcano. "Except for that, I mean."

"That and there ain't nothing to eat," Joe Mack reminded him.

Sam thought briefly about what it would take to bring cattle and pigs over the ocean to this remote place and turned to take a look inside without comment.

Their boots echoed on the wooden floors. It was dry inside, but they could see stains where the roof had leaked, and where it had been mended. There was still glass in the windows, affording a view of the thick covering of vines and ferns that had overgrown the building. The light that came through was dappled by the leaves covering every window.

There were ashes in the fireplace and hammocks strung in two of the rooms. "That makes sense," Sam noted. "You'd have a comfortable place to sleep, but no mattress to get rotted."

He inspected the hammocks. They were strung between built-in wooden bedframes. There was evidence that once upon a time there had been iron bedsteads there, which had been replaced by the wooden beds. There was something else, too. He went from room to room. Yep, in every room of the house all of the wiring had been stripped from inside the walls. Sam knew exactly what he was looking at, even when the walls had been patched afterwards, since he'd done the same thing himself as a child. He went into the kitchen out of curiosity. If the house was used on a regular basis, they had to leave the kitchen intact, didn't they? But no, it was the same there. Every piece of metal had been stripped from the house. Much more expensive stuff was left, like big glass windows, while cheap junk like iron bedframes had been taken. What did these guys cook on, then?

He called the explorers together. "Come on, let's look around," he said. "And I got to get me a bath and some clean clothes, too."

They followed him in silence back towards the ship. "What's up?" Joe Mack asked after they'd passed the night-flower gully without going in.

"We got to get a close look at that other wreck."

"Are you nuts?" Chuck objected.

"Yeah, but we still got to do it."

"Why?" Joe Mack didn't sound argumentative, just curious.

"Notice a pattern here? All the metal was gone from the still and out of the house, but the real expensive stuff was left behind. And I saw something else, too. Someone's been cutting pieces off the melted wreck."

"What do you mean, 'cutting pieces off'?"

"Just that. Big brass propeller sitting up there on the rocks with straight cuts on it, like slices taken off."

"I want to go back and take another look at that," Joe Mack told them.

"Yeah, but not just now. First, I want to see if the first wreck we saw's got the same thing."

"Why would they go to the trouble of cutting pieces off the propeller? Why not just take the whole thing?" Vince wondered.

"Good question," Sam nodded at him. "Whoever these cats are, they've got their priorities backwards."

"Pagans would, wouldn't they?" Johnny suggested.

"You can't prove they're pagans, man," Sam shook his head. "Just because they put up a wooden memorial instead of a stone one."

Johnny's eyes went wide.

'Ha!' Sam thought. 'He's been so busy thinking they were pagans that he's never considered anything else.'

They made their way with difficulty through the tall grass, entangling vines, jungly stands of bushes and trees, until they came to the top of the hills overlooking the big bay on the south side of the island. Then they stopped in dismay. It was a sheer drop of at least four hundred feet down to the beach where the ship lay in the sand.

"Oh, man, there's no way," Joe Mack declared.

Sam looked everywhere for a sign of a way down, and couldn't see one. "We'll have to go around." He pointed to the spit of land reaching over a mile away from them.

"We can't get there and back today," Chuck said flatly.

Sam conceded. "No, maybe not today. I'll take care of the bath and all that, and make my respects to Major Temperance. Then we'll spend the night here and find a way to get down there in the morning."

"What are we going to eat?" Willie Jay asked.

"You figure something out, son," Sam suggested, turning to make his way back down the long climb to the boat that would take him back to the ship.

By the time the explorers set off the next morning, Chuck and Joe Mack had found a steep gully where it was possible, if very difficult for them, to make their way down through the forest growth to the sandy beach. There were plenty of foolish birds for them to catch to roast over a fire to eat for lunch once they'd finally made it all the way down.

"Did you notice these cats never left any iron in the fire pit we ate at yesterday," Joe Mack asked.

"Yeah," Sam nodded, remembering now that he'd been reminded. "It's like these guys are collecting all of the metal, even the cheap stuff."

"Weird," Willie Jay commented.

It was easy to get to this wreck. It was mostly buried in the sand. It didn't take much to hack down some smaller saplings and branches and build a ladder so that they could climb up onto it.

"Hey, Sam," Vince called. "I bet I know why this one didn't rust away."

"Why?"

"It's coated with something. Not exactly a paint. Some kind of glaze."

Sam took a closer look.

"You're on to something."

When he wasn't needed to build the ladder, Sam spent the time while it was being built studying the outside of the wreck. The screw on this one had been cut completely away above the sand. Sam dug down into the sand with his hands, and discovered that the cuts were below the level of the sand, as well. So, they'd dug the sand away to get at the brass, had they?

He dug deeper, curious to see how far they'd gone. Something sharp pricked his finger. With a curse he sucked the blood, then dug carefully to see what had jabbed him. It was shiny, silvery, and as he carefully brought it to the surface it reflected the light like a jewel. Sam went down to the water to rinse it off and see what he'd found. It was a broken piece of blade, the extremely sharp business end glittering. Carefully he put the dangerous little thing in his pocket without saying anything to anyone.

He walked across the beach to the edge of the forest, hoping it looked as if he wanted to relieve himself. When he was out of sight, he took the blade out of his pocket and examined it, then he wrapped it in leaves to protect his pocket, and slid it out of sight. That's what they were cutting the ships up with, he was sure. A diamond studded blade. There was no way that blade had been there for two hundred and fifty years. There was almost no tarnish on it. It wasn't steel, then. He didn't know what it was, but if they could afford diamond blades, why on earth were they bothering with brass and copper and iron?

He rejoined the others and climbed up the ladder onto the ship. They could go inside it without any trouble. For access inside there were ladders made of some kind of brightly coloured rope that not one of them could identify. Inside there was no doubt that people had come often to cut pieces of metal, and at each cut they had painted the edges with their glaze which prevented rust.

"There is no way to deny that someone's survived Judgement Day," Sam announced. "There is land to the west, I know there is. I'm going to work on Temperance to keep going until we find it. Telling him they make beer might help, but I'm going to have a shot at telling him they make bourbon."

"Do you think they'll be good Christians, Sam?" Vince asked.

"God didn't spare no one else," Johnny assured him.

"Think we'll be able to pay for this expedition by rescuing them?" Joe Mack put in.

"Everything we've seen so far is so strange that I'm betting we won't know what we're going to find until we find it," Sam told them.

"Let's get started on climbing back up that God-forsaken cliff before it's too late in the day for us to make it all the way up today," Joe Mack said in a resigned voice.

They climbed back up the weirdly coloured rope ladders into the sunshine. Sam stood for a moment, staring out to sea wondering, "Who are you? Where are you?" He thought of Amos again, and how much he would have loved this. They for sure weren't going to come back down here again, so they really ought to look around while they were here. Amos would have. He watched the steam rising from the black cinder islet, and the sheer rock walls of the cliffs behind it. "Let's just take a quick look around first," he suggested.

They spread out in all directions along the beach and the gentle land between it and the forest covered cliffs behind them. Parts of the cliffs on their side were sheer vertical rock like the ones on adjoining side, but most of the ones facing south were sloped enough for the forest to cover it. There was a swampy looking area, which Johnny had run towards. He called back that there was a lovely lagoon there. They all joined him, stripping off to swim in the warm, clean, fresh water. It was as good to drink as it was to play in. Chuck found the remains of a hut, which they all looked at, deciding that it hadn't been used as much as the bigger house, but it had been repaired enough to be used as a shelter.

It was Willie Jay who found the graves. There were several of them, mostly mounds that had been decently tended at some time in the not-too-distant past, with crosses stuck into the earth, some with names, some without, but one startled them all to silence. It had a large copper plaque streaked with green. The plaque read: "SACRED To the Memory of Fleetwood James Denham, the dearly beloved son of Henry Mangles Denham, Captain of Her Britannic Majesty's ship HERALD, and Isabella Denham. He died aboard the Herald at this Island on the 8th day of July, 1854, aged 16 years, leaving an afflicted parent to mourn his loss here, and many at home who dearly loved him. This tablet is erected by his bereaved father and shipmates, as a last testimony of their esteem. SUNDAY ISLAND South Pacific July 9, 1854."

They said prayers for the repose of the souls who'd died and been buried on the island, then, feeling greatly comforted that the people they were setting out to find were good Christians who would be thankful to be delivered by God into their hands, they climbed back up the exhausting, grinding slope to spread their good news among the GR and to convince Major Temperance that it was his duty to continue until they found them.

CHAPTER SEVEN

Glen

*H*atoe lived less than five hundred kilometres south of Olarine on the east coast of the same island, Te Ika a Maui. A thousand kilometres further south of Hatoe, on a paddle-shaped peninsula thrust out into the ocean on the east coast of another island, Te Waipounamu, lived the Third Servant, Glendritz Tomptell.

Glen was tall and gangly, soft spoken and slow moving, with thinned hair that had greyed past the pepper and salt stage, and the slightly hunched posture of someone who had spent his entire life curled up with books. Although his parents had both been outgoing and energetic, they had fondly let their only child stay indoors playing his violin and reading, instead of making him play outside with other children. They had raised him amid music, books, and meaningful discussions. He had devoured every book he could get his hands on from the moment he first could read.

Now, at fifty-two, Glen gave a genteel atmosphere to a room when he entered it. His steady blue eyes were kind and gentle. He had a graceful dignity in his manner, and people called him 'wise.'

People outside his home, that is.

Early in the morning of the day Hatoe told Olarine that he'd seen an iron ship, Glen dabbed his mouth delicately with his serviette. "Thank you, my dear, that was splendid," he told Istellona, his partner of twenty-two years, as he rose from the table.

"It was only breakfast," his mother-in-law, Ilona, sniffed, as if he'd said something ridiculous.

Glen didn't pay much attention to Ilona anymore. Her disparaging comments had become of no more consequence than the faint whirr of the spinners on every outside wall of his house. "And a first-rate breakfast it was, too," he smiled at Istell as he took his dishes from the table. He carried them into the kitchen where he put them carefully in the sink, placing the cutlery in its holder and stacking the plates precisely.

When he didn't return to the dining room after he'd taken care of his dishes, Glen heard Ilona's petulant protest behind him, "Surely you're not leaving the room before we've finished!"

Glen reversed his direction from going to his room. He walked back down the hallway and poked his head back into the dining room, to say courteously, "Please excuse me, I need to get ready for the hearing."

Ilona was indignant. "You're leaving without doing the dishes? Isn't it your turn?"

"I'll take a double turn next time. I can't be late."

"There's no reason for you to attend these things. You're retired."

"I didn't retire because of age or ill health; I retired because I was elected." Glen was annoyed with himself for being caught yet again in the endless loop of these arguments with Ilona. Whether her understanding was beginning to slip, or she honestly thought he did nothing useful, he couldn't tell. What he knew was that his explanations had made no difference the last hundred times he'd made them, and likely would make no difference this time, either. "I'm sorry, Ilona," he spoke quietly, but turned to go so that his words were stronger than they sounded. "I must not keep the Conclave waiting."

"You don't have to work. You're retired. You can ring them and tell them it's inconvenient. They can start without you. It's not as if you're arbitrating the hearing, you're just an observer."

He spoke patiently. "There is a difference between being a consultant and being an observer. I gave my word. They're expecting me." He strode off down the hallway too quickly for Ilona's answer to reach him. If he heard her his innate courtesy would prevent him from walking off without answering.

When she'd first moved in with Glen and Istell, Ilona had been able to keep him spinning endlessly on the spot, but as time went on, he was getting better at escaping from her.

The theory had been that Ilona would live her own life in her own flat. The reality, however, was that she spent very little time in her flat, didn't make friends in their neighbourhood, and didn't travel back to her old neighbourhood to visit with her old friends. She had all of her meals with Glen and Istell and was with them enough to criticize both of them all day every day. Glen had quickly learned to tune her out, though he did gain an insight into why Istell was such a perfectionist. Nothing Istell ever did was good enough for her mother.

Nothing he did was ever good enough, either, come to that. Ilona hadn't even been proud of him when he'd been elected to the Triune. All she had said about that was to sniff disparagingly and comment, "What a shame you couldn't do any better than third. Still, I suppose you need to be outgoing and charismatic to do well in something like that."

Glen knew that any other mother-in-law would have been either surprised or proud that her son-in-law was one of the three people leading the island government, but he held no grudge. There were priorities in his life. He could live with this irritation. His mind on the hearing, he didn't give Ilona another thought as he changed into his formal clothes for the Conclave.

He was dressed and was combing his remaining hair in the mirror when Istell arrived in their room. Automatically brushing invisible specks off his shoulders, she said with gentle reproach, "Mother's upset that you walked out on her like that."

"Pardon?" Blinking, Glen struggled to haul his thoughts back home, and to sort what Istell was saying.

"Mother was saying that we expect you here just as much as they expect you there when she realised you weren't there anymore. Do you have to walk off on her like that? You know how it upsets her."

"I'm sorry, pet. I didn't hear her say that. You know I can't be late."

"That's all very well, but Mother won't understand if you go without doing your share. It's your turn to clean the kitchen, I cooked."

Gently Glen told her, "How we organise our housekeeping is between the two of us, Pet. Your mother is welcome to have her breakfast with us any time that she doesn't want to cook for herself. Your mother is welcome to spend as much time as she wants to in our home if she feels lonely in her flat. What your mother is not welcome to do is to tell us how to run our house."

Istell gasped, "I can't say that to my mother!" Nervously she adjusted the way his sash hung across his tunic.

He picked up his satchel and opened it to check that he had replaced all of his notes after reading them the previous night, as he said, "We've been through this before. If Ilona needs help to understand we can talk to a behaviourist."

"She doesn't need to see a doctor," Istell said too quickly, picking up a cloth and reaching over to dust the outside of the satchel.

Glen waved her off. "You do need to think about it, Pet. When your father passed away, we created the suite for her in our house so that she could live with us, but we could still have our own home and our privacy. This is what she agreed to but look at what's actually happening here. She has almost all of her meals with us and has no concept of privacy."

Brushed off from her efforts to attain perfection in Glen's appearance, Istell turned to straightening and adjusting their room which had nothing out of place. Defensively she claimed, "Mother doesn't like to eat alone."

"She makes no attempt to go out for meals or to have friends over to eat with."

With a slight frown she argued, "She doesn't know anyone here."

With only half of his mind on their conversation, and the rest on the contents of his satchel, Glen didn't notice her discomfort. "She makes no attempt to get to know anyone here, or to go back and visit her old friends and neighbours. She spends all of her time in our place. The reason your mother is upset all of the time is that she's got nothing fulfilling in her life."

Her thin fingers restlessly tidying things that were tidy, and straightening things that were straight, Istell protested, "How would you like it if it was your mother?"

"Stel, Sweetie, my mother is widowed too, and she's ten years older than Ilona, but she doesn't seem to have any problems staying in her own home or eating on her own, or keeping in touch with friends and relatives, or making new friends, or getting involved in new interests."

"She's in better health."

"The reason for that is that Mum keeps herself busy, and Ilona doesn't. I was a behaviourist before I became a mediator, remember. I can arrange for us to see the most talented behaviourist on the islands."

"Think how embarrassed Mother would be if we hauled her off to see one of your friends!"

Glen shut his satchel with a snap. "We couldn't see one of my friends, protocol doesn't allow it. Do think about it, Pet, I've been working in behaviour for over thirty years, I don't say these things lightly."

"And I suppose just because I'm an accountant and not a behaviourist I don't know anything about my own mother! All she needs is a little bit of time to adjust to losing Daddy. After all your years of training, you should understand that."

Glen slung his satchel over his shoulder, considering explaining about depression and loneliness in the elderly, but he remembered such explanations had never made any difference before and would likely make no difference now, plus he had to hurry up or he'd be late. He decided against it.

As he turned to leave, Istell hurried across the room to catch him at the door. "Mother says you're only doing this to get out of the house."

Glen stopped and looked Istell in the eye. "If that were true, I wouldn't come home for lunch. I'm doing this because I was asked to. I'm not consulted on challenging cases just to annoy Ilona. It's my duty."

Istell adjusted the satchel on Glen's back. "That's as may be, but do you have to jump up and run every time they flick their fingers? They should learn to come to their own resolutions."

Glen sighed patiently. "I only choose the most interesting or the most important ones, it's not as if I accept every request. It's one of the things that happens when you have years of experience and a reputation for good outcomes. I sought help from senior arbiters when I was a mediator, and when I was an arbitrator after that, and a moderator after that. You know this. How many times did we host meetings and consultations before Ilona arrived?"

Istell's shoulders rose, miserably. She checked that each button of his quilted tunic sat properly and reached up to make sure the round neck of his shirt sat smoothly against his neck and didn't roll down, and the tiki around his neck was perfectly centred on the snowy white shirt.

Glen brushed her cheek tenderly with the backs of his fingers. "I know your mother can't see why they come to me. Neither of us can tell her. She'll have to hear it from them. It's because they respect my judgement, unbelievable though that might be to her. But then she doesn't understand why you need to close your office door to do your work, either, does she?"

Istell sighed, and they walked together to the front door. On his way Glen took a moment to poke his head into the kitchen and say, cheerfully, "I'll see you at lunch time, Ilona," to his mother-in-law who was slaving away cleaning the kitchen alone in full martyr mode, to which he did not react.

He went to the front door and sat on the stool beside it to put on his shoes before he went outside. Te Waipounamu had a cooler climate than Te Ika a Maui. Glen didn't walk barefoot outside the way Olarine and Hatoe did.

He picked up his black cape from the hanger by the door and gave Istell a chaste peck on the cheek before he opened the door because Istell would never have accepted a show of affection in public. Glen thought of how deeply he loved Istell as he bent to kiss her. His look brought out a smile in her eyes which warmed his heart.

When he reached out for the doorknob, Istell pulled Glen's hood up over his thin hair to keep his head warm, saying softly, "I'll see you at lunch time."

Feeling loved and cared for, Glen set off for his day with a light, quick step. His long legs took him across their veranda in two strides, and down the steps to the paved path in a blur of black-clad legs.

The branches of the trees lining the foot path drooped over his head, making the shady path almost into a green tunnel. The 'just washed' smell was no longer lingering from the rainstorm a few days previously, but he still filled his lungs appreciatively with the scents of greenery and flowers.

Most of the verandas held flowerpots or boxes, or had hanging baskets of herbs and flowers, which Glen sniffed and looked at without noticing what he was doing. His mind was on the details of the hearing he was to attend. When he'd offered his services as a consultant, Glen had been sent a list of hearings where the moderators or judges wanted him to sit in. He'd chosen the child custody hearing, not because he liked them – he didn't – but because he considered taking care of the children to be the most important of his duties. He was soon so deep in thought that he didn't realise he'd slowed his pace or slipped the hood of his fleece-lined black cape back off his head.

The foot path he was walking along was divided from the bike track by trees planted between the two. Mostly there were only the trunks of the trees in his view, the branches and leaves being over his head. He could see people going by on their bicycles. Pre-occupied, Glen didn't acknowledge anyone he knew on either the foot path or the bike track unless they called him by name. Then he wished them good morning, courteously, nodding his head politely, though he couldn't have told anyone a moment later who it was he'd spoken to.

Interspersed in the line of trees as well as on either side of the foot path and the bike track, the huge decorated wooden beams of the train trestle rose far above him. The interlocked beams reached up into the treetops. A metre over Glen's head the branches were trimmed back so that they wouldn't interfere with the three tracks at that height: the two rails for private vehicles on either side, and the one for emergency vehicles in the middle. Above them were the rails for the islands' main mode of transportation, the fast, light, electric, fibreglass train nick-named the "Flying Fish" because its skin of small solar panels looked like fish scales.

The faint whine of the Flying Fish whipping back and forth over his head was enough of a familiar constant that Glen didn't really hear it anymore. It wasn't loud, just a soft background noise that didn't even drown out the liquid notes of the birdsong all around him.

His thoughts were still on the hearing. His long legs swung in great strides that covered the short distance between his home and the meeting house in less time than it would have taken most people at a jog, his soft shoes making almost no sound on the ceramic pavement.

The only time he was distracted from his musings was when a neighbour walking in the same direction caught up to him and commented on the news that the small seaweed collecting boat was still missing with three men on board. Glen nodded, absently, glancing between the tree trunks at small glimpses of the local harbour that spread out below them, the sandbars in the middle gleaming wetly in the rising sun. "It doesn't seem like that was enough of a storm for a boat to go missing," he said.

"Apparently it picked up strength up north."

"Ah."

"Looks like you've got a lot on your mind, Mr Third," his neighbour excused himself, politely. "Sorry to have troubled you. Have a good day."

"Oh. Oh, I'm sorry, I didn't . . ."

"No worries, Mr Third. I'll leave you to it. Don't work too hard, now."

Vaguely troubled that he'd been inadvertently rude to his neighbour, and not sure how to react to his new title being used instead of his name, Glen turned at the Y-shaped intersection to walk the final stretch to the meeting house. He could have ridden the Fish, but he preferred a nice brisk walk in the fresh morning air. It kept his old legs limber, and got the blood flowing, which made him more alert all day long. Glen wished he'd watched the news that morning to find out whether any sign of the little boat or her crew had been found. That stray thought made him glance briefly between the tree trunks at the view of the harbour spread out below him with the morning sun glowing off its mud banks. Ilona would really have something to complain about if he made his living going out to sea for days at a time. Dismissing her from his mind and going back to his work of that morning, he resumed his fast pace.

He realised he was walking alongside other people who worked at the meeting hall when he was greeted, "Good morning, Mr Third." He nodded greetings in return, pleased when he heard the occasional, "Good morning, Morena, Judge Tomptell." He liked that better. It was familiar and gave him the comforting feeling of being back home.

Over his head there were stations every second or third intersection. The north-south rails ran one and a half or two floors up, the east-west rails three or four floors up. At the last station before the meeting house, he could hear the sounds of many feet on the wooden platform and stairs, plus the rattle and squeak of the lifts and the rhythmic chugging of the moving stairs.

Down the stairs and out of the lift and off the moving stairs came more people who worked at the meeting house. They joined the ones walking past, greeting their friends. Glen recognised some secretaries, a reporter or two, counsellors, calmers, behaviourists, mediators, moderators, arbitrators, arbiters; the usual crowd who dealt with conflicts when Islanders were unable to settle them without professional help.

"Kia ora," one of the other judges, Frank, greeted him just as they reached the ornately carved gate before the meeting house. As they crowded to a stop at the gateway, and the murmuring of conversation died down, he added, in a low voice, "Really glad to have you give us your time during the government break, Glen. Missed you."

Glen only had a chance to smile in return before the ritual call, the karanga, rang out from the steps of the whare nui, the largest meeting house, the one that was closest to the gate. In the shuffle of people, it suddenly hit Glen that he was left alone in front, just behind the eldest women who were giving the answering call to the woman standing on the front porch of the whare nui. Even Frank was standing back, courteously just far enough behind Glen's shoulder that he wasn't standing beside him.

It wasn't Glen's white hair they were respecting; he knew. He'd been white haired before he'd retired, and no one had ever left him uncomfortably right out in front. He'd been standing near the front for a while, of course, as a judge and an elder, but not by himself like this with even his friends no longer beside him. It unnerved him to the point that he hesitated when the karanga came to an end. In that momentary hesitation the deference they all felt for him now became unmistakably clear to him. No one moved until he did, not even his friend. Then they all filed in through the gate after him, going their separate ways to the various buildings.

Glen and Frank went straight into the judges' lounge in the whare kai, the eating house. In contrast to the rigid tidiness and cleanness of his home, the lounge had a comfortable lived-in look about it. Glen looked around at the coloured walls with their decorations and plaques with the huge relief of feeling that he was back where he belonged. He hadn't realised until that moment what a strain it had been to be in Tāmaki-makaurau while the government was sitting.

A third judge, Meg, was already in the lounge, comfortably ensconced in one of half a dozen brown plush armchairs, documents on the table beside her and on her lap, the reading lamp over her head giving her a halo of light. She looked up over her glasses. "Hey! Morena! Good to see you back in this neck of the woods, Mr Third. Kia ora, Frank. Tea's on."

"Thanks, Meg," Frank said, standing back so that Glen could be first at the wardrobe.

"Please call me Glen," Glen said, hanging up his warm black cape and taking out a light one for indoor use.

"It's still an honour to have a member of the Triune as a consultant." Meg took a sip of her tea, her grey curls bobbing forward as she bent her head to her cup.

"I'm Third Servant. We're the Servants of the People, you shouldn't treat us like stars," Glen complained, sitting down to slip off his outdoor shoes.

Frank laughed. "I didn't see any screaming teenagers mobbing you."

Glen blushed and hastily went to the tea pot, took a cup from the cupboard and poured himself a cup of hot manuka tea. All they had in the lounge was a tiny sink, a mini fridge, a hot water dispenser that kept water ready to make tea in the tea pot, and cupboards above and below the sink to keep cups and a few odds and ends in. It wasn't a kitchen, they couldn't cook there, but they could have something to drink without having to go to the cafeteria.

Frank grinned good naturedly, kicking his shoes off. They knocked Glen's tidy pair askew, but he shut the wardrobe door without noticing, and asked Meg, "What time did you get here? We're early, and you're already hard at work."

She grimaced. "I've been here a couple of hours. I'm trying to get a handle on this one."

Frank nodded as he followed Glen to pour himself a cup of tea, "Oh, you've got that violence appeal, haven't you?"

Meg nodded, asking Glen, "Do you know about this one, Glen? A young man who was sent to a secure mod vil for violence. He's claiming he's been treated unfairly, and his parents are petitioning to have him brought back home for treatment."

Glen stood, leaning on the counter, "The situation rings a bell. I think it was one of the ones I was sent. They sent me a list, with just the briefest of explanations of what each case was about. No details. Where do they want him brought back from?"

"Kamautaurua Island."

"So far away?" Frank turned, crossly. "No wonder his parents are petitioning. How can they ever see him down there? How can a person heal if he's cut off from his family?"

Meg nodded again, "That's their point, you see. The mod vil has medical experts to explain why he's not ready to be returned to a less secure mod vil, and the parents have medical experts to explain why he can't become ready where he is."

"That's a stickler," Glen felt sympathy for the family, and for Meg needing to make a decision about it. "I'm assuming they've tried to move him to a local mod vil before."

"Yes, they did, and he escaped, so they had to put him in one where they could keep him until he's ready to keep himself where he's supposed to be."

Frank carried his tea over to a small table beside a chair across from Meg, saying, "It's not good enough, you know. We need a secure behaviour modification village right here. It isn't right that families who have someone who needs time in a secure mod vil have to either move down there or be cut off. How many people like this bloke would get better faster if they were near home and family?"

Glen took his tea to a chair, and set it on the table there, touching the smoked glass shade of the reading lamp over his chair so that a warm light shone down where he would hold his files to read them. "It's an old argument, Frank. Everyone knows the problems, but there just aren't any suitable islands any closer."

Frank left his tea at the table he'd chosen and went to a file cabinet where he looked through file folders, saying, "There's got to be a way of making a secure mod vil without needing to put it on an islet."

"That would mean building some kind of wall to keep people in who won't voluntarily stay for treatment, and you know would be even worse for mental health than being away from their homes and families. Apparently, this fellow escaped from a less secure mod vil. If he doesn't do better than that, he can't be sent home. How long has he been there?"

Meg checked her files. "Years. He was in secondary school when he started a fight. He's been in treatment ever since. Apparently, he won't take responsibility for his behaviour, and still reacts aggressively to anything he doesn't like, so he's too much of a danger of re-offending to risk another escape."

Going over to join Frank at the file cabinets, Glen said, "There," thinking that settled it.

Frank carried several folders to his table. "Who's to say he wouldn't have been able to take responsibility by now if he could have been treated closer to home?"

"I think there's something profoundly wrong with this boy, Frank," Meg put in. "Reading the file, it seems to me there's more going on here than just a need for behaviour modification. I'll need to have a behaviourist explain some of it to me, but that's what I'm picking up."

"We shouldn't deal with this kind of thing at all," Frank declared, settling into his chair. "This kind of thing is for doctors, not judges."

Glen looked through the file cabinets to find the files that had been put there for him. He picked them up and took them to an empty chair to read through and familiarize himself further with the case he'd agreed to sit in on. "We were all behaviourists before we went into mediation, Frank."

"Yes, but we're not doctors. This kind of thing needs specialized medical training, not negotiation skills."

Meg put the files on her lap on top of the pile on her table and got up, stretching. "The People need to have some kind of court of appeal. If not us, then who? Granted we're not medical experts, but we can call the medical experts in and listen to both sides. What if the people at the mod vil are missing something? I have no problem with the idea that people can appeal to us for that kind of thing. Someone who is not a doctor has to watch the doctors, just as we're watched by the Ministry who are not mediators. There's always got to be someone watching the watchers, someone guarding the guards. No system functions without corruption if it's only subject to internal investigations."

Both Glen and Frank had opened the files on their laps. Glen asked Meg, "Have you made any plans about what you're going to do?"

Meg walked over to refill her teacup. "Listen and learn. Study precedents. I'll probably have to consult with everyone who has rendered judgement on similar cases and look at the results of their decisions to see what succeeded and what failed. I wish you'd agreed to sit in on mine."

"A situation like yours is terrible, but if something like this custody is mishandled, the outcome can cause situations like that one. Children must be nurtured carefully when the parenting bond dissolves, or else they have all sorts of problems. When I was given the cases that would have liked a consultant, I chose it because I thought it was the most important."

Frank told Glen, "I'd love to have you with me, but I didn't think I needed a consultant when we were asked. I've got two families who are each petitioning to make the other family move. They're neighbours. It all started with a dispute over a fence, and all the behaviourists in the world haven't been able to prevent it from escalating to this point."

Glen shook his head. "Something so minor going to this level?"

"It's been going on for a while now. They've gone up each level, unable to get satisfaction from any of the mediators. They appealed arbitration. After I've decided the recompense for property damage, I'm going to order full family counselling to get them to find a way to accept what compromise means and order the behaviourists to find out which members of the families are keeping the others from accepting solutions. Those ones will need extra counselling, and if necessary, time in a mod vil. Preferably the same one, so that they learn how to work with one another. This should have been done long ago. There's no reason for it to have reached a judge."

"It's the little things that drive you mad," Meg commented

"But still." Frank slapped the file on his lap. "You'd think they'd be embarrassed to take something so petty so far."

"If you think small things don't matter, try to sleep with a mosquito in the room," Meg quoted an old saying, returning to her chair. "You chose that deadlocked custody negotiation?"

Glen sighed. "Yeah."

"It never fails to amaze me when parents can't work it out for their children's sakes," Frank muttered. "If they can't put their kids' needs ahead of their own, how did they get their parenting certificates in the first place? Do the tests need to be reviewed?"

Glen thumbed through the file in his lap. "I don't think so, Frank. This is the kind I hate the most. There's nothing to make a judgement on with these two."

"No?" Meg returned to her chair with her tea, her eyebrows raised in surprise. "Why can't they compromise, then? It's normally pretty easy to sort out which one's holding things up."

"This situation's not like that. Neither parent is from Te Waipounamu. They both came here when they finished school to take apprenticeships away from their home islands. The mother is from Rakiura Island, the father is from Aotea Island. They wanted to strike out on their own, away from their parents. They met at work, partnered, and passed their parenting certificates, and had their child here. Now the bond has dissolved, and each wants to take the child back to their parents where he'll grow up near his grandparents."

"Oh, man, that's – what? – three, four thousand kilometres apart?" Frank asked.

"Right. Too far for frequent visits. They might not even travel that distance once a year with a small child."

Meg asked, "One parent's not better at parenting than the other?"

"Not that shows up. Each of them even says the other is a good parent."

"So, it's not rancour?"

"Doesn't look like it. Each really wants to have their child with them, to raise it near their parents in their home town."

"What about the grandparents?" Frank asked.

"As near as I can tell from what I've read, both families will provide good extended families for the child. I'll know better after I've seen them in action, but so far, I can't see any reason for making a preference."

"What about the parent better able to provide for the child?"

"Their job prospects look pretty close to the same. Similar, anyway. They apprenticed at the same place, same trade, and both sets of grandparents assured the mediator that there are jobs for them at their respective hometowns."

"Do you have any idea what you're going to advise the mediator?"

"Mediation failed. It's in arbitration."

"Who's leading the arbitration panel?"

"Erana."

"She's good."

"No amount of talent is going to rescue this one, I'm afraid."

"Any idea what you're going to tell her?"

"Not at this point. After I've observed this morning, I'll spend the lunch recess going through the precedents, if nothing has come up that offers a solution. Ether way, it looks to me as if there's no satisfactory solution to this one. If custody is awarded to one parent, the child is cut of from half of his heritage, and from a parent who would be a huge loss to him. If the parent moves to be with the child, then that parent loses his or her home base, and the child still is without half of his extended family. I'm afraid no matter what is decided that the decision will be appealed."

Silence followed this. They looked at each other for a moment, then dropped their heads and each concentrated in silence on their files. The only sounds in the room were the turning of pages or the faint scraping of pens until Meg's secretary tapped on the door and poked her head around.

Before her secretary spoke, Meg got up. "Excuse me, gentlemen, I have arranged for a discussion before the hearing." She and her secretary gathered up all of her files and notes, put them in file folders and left, taking the files and notes with them.

Glen got to his feet, as well. "I'll leave you, too, Frank. I want to talk to Erana and her panel before the hearing." He put his files and notes in a file folder and left. When he'd chosen which hearing he would sit in, he'd been told which hearing room Erana had been assigned.

In the hallway the man who had been his assistant greeted Glen with a wide smile. "Good morning, Mr Third! We've missed you!"

Glen's pleasure at seeing Manu again wavered. "Morena, Manu. Please call me by name."

Manu's black eyes widened in surprise. "But Mr Third, it's a great honour to . . ."

"Please. It was hard enough to get used to in Tāmaki-makaurau, but it was fitting there. Now that I'm home it just feels awkward, especially coming from someone like you who's known me for years."

"I – I," Manu stuttered awkwardly, then changed the subject. "Did you hear that one of the seaweed collecting boats is overdue in that storm we had?"

"Yes. They haven't found anything yet?" Glen was glad of the change of topic. "I didn't have time to look at the news this morning."

"No, nothing so far. Everyone's glad to see you back. I thought you'd be on holiday."

"No. No, it's not a holiday. We have work to do in our home districts when the government's not in session, so I thought I'd volunteer my time. To keep my hand in, you know, so that I can slip right back into place when my time is up."

"So much for retirement, eh? You'll only serve one term?"

"One is more than enough for me. What have you been up to since I've been gone?"

"I got a position in admin." Manu led the way to an office that had his name on the door, past empty desks. "No one's here yet," he explained unnecessarily. "I came in early because I reckoned you'd be here early."

"Thank you," Glen looked around Manu's little corner. "I thought you'd be a moderator. You would have made a good one."

"Thank you, Mr – er – Ju . . . I like administration better."

Glen left Manu's office to walk to the arbiters' lounge, saying, "Look, Manu, we worked together for years. You always called me by name then. I'm still Glen."

Manu followed. "I'm sorry, Glen. I can't get used to it. I've never known a Public Servant personally before."

"It's a job. It's a duty. I'm not a hero."

"I remember the day you were elected. We were all so excited. It's not very often there's a Public Servant from Te Wai Pounamu, we have so much less population than Te Ika a Maui, and from a little place like Ōtautahi! We were jumping up and down and screaming, and you didn't look pleased at all."

"I wasn't. I was dismayed. I was quite comfortable as arbiter in Ōtautahi and Minister of Forestry and being a judge. I was persuaded it was my duty to accept the nomination of the Ministers to stand for election as Public Servant because we didn't have the required seven candidates. It never occurred to me that anyone would vote for me. No one outside of Ōtautahi knows me. I did nothing to get elected."

"You didn't even tell us you were on the ballot. We found out about it on the news. I don't think you ever realised what a widely respected arbiter you are. You're known more widely than you know."

Glen smiled, stopping at the door. "That's generous of you, but I think it was one of those odd things where people weren't entirely happy with the ballot, so they voted for the unknown name."

Manu shook his head, as he walked away.

"Kia ora," Glen said, stepping into the arbiters' lounge.

"Really glad to have you give us your time during the government break, Mr Third," a dark eyed woman with caramel coloured hair greeted him. "We were delighted to receive your offer to be a consultant."

With a sigh Glen answered, "Kia ora, Erana. Please call me Glen."

In the hearing Glen sat behind the parents so that he wouldn't distract them as they each explained their points of view to the arbitration panel. With his unassuming manner, and by putting himself out of their line of sight, he was able to have the parents soon forget he was there and continue their debate unaffected by his presence. The three arbitrators and the moderator could see him behind the parents, taking his notes. They ceased to glance over at him before the morning was over.

When Erana called for a two-hour midday recess with nothing decided, Glen quickly and quietly packed all of his notes into the file folder and slipped out without a word to anyone. He thought over what he had heard and seen as he put his outdoor clothes back on, in the judges' lounge, put the file folder back in the drawer he'd taken it from, took his notes with him, and took the fifteen-minute walk back home.

It was the kind of hearing that he'd hated the most when he had been a mediator, and when he had been an arbitrator. The parents were immovably entrenched in their positions, each utterly convinced that his or her decision was best for their child, neither one at fault in anything they were proposing, so that there was nothing to choose between them, but their desires were diametrically opposed and could not both stand. One or the other would have to give in, and if neither would, whatever the panel decided would be appealed. When he had been an arbiter, Glen had hated having to deal with this kind of appeal. There was no right or wrong answer, and the child was too young to be included in the decision.

As he walked to his own home, mulling it all over, Glen replayed the words and actions of the parents and the arbitration panel in his mind. He searched the experience of a lifetime for a recommendation that he could make to the panel for a way they could assist this young couple to come to a decision that would aid their child to grow up without being cut off from one parent and half of his heritage.

If only he could find some kind of compromise. Nothing seemed likely. He planned to look through the library of precedents for some clue of how to find a satisfactory solution after he'd eaten his midday meal, before he headed back to the hearing. Whether Ilona understood or approved or not, once he'd shut his office door, she would leave him in peace in his office.

It was times like these that he was immeasurably grateful to Istellona for who she was and how she did things. It had been a sorrow to them that they had been unable to have children, but that had freed him to pursue a distinguished career as a behaviourist, then in turn, a mediator, an arbitrator, a moderator, an arbiter, and finally a judge. At the same time he had been elected to local politics as a Speaker, then had been elected by the Speakers to represent them, then by the Representatives to the Ministry, and now that he had been elected by the whole populace as a member of the Triune governing all of the islands, he'd had to resign his post as judge and arbiter to devote all of his time to serving all of the islands. Only when the Triune was not in session could he spend time as an advisor and consultant.

Istellona might have been a bit too prim and proper for Glen's parents' taste, but he had learned how to live with her rigid attitude. Not only did he love her dearly, and see the good, kind, gentle person underneath the perfectionistic fussing and fretting, but he had to admit he appreciated having his home so flawless at all times. It had stood him in good stead throughout his careers to always know that no matter what was asked of him, the house would always be ready to accommodate any kind of meeting with persons of any rank from the King or the Triune all the way down to neighbours asking for informal help to sort out disagreements or talking about local politics and needs.

He expected, as he sat down in the entranceway to take off his shoes and put on his slippers, that his midday meal would be ready and Istell and Ilona would be waiting for him. Istell did most of her work from their house, just as Glen did when the Triune was not in session.

Once he had put on his slippers like a good boy, and had set his shoes neatly into their shoe box with the inlaid wood lid, and had hung his satchel on its hook with the tasteful drape that matched the entranceway drapes to cover it so that it wouldn't look messy, Glen stepped into the kitchen expecting to be either greeted by a formal peck on the cheek, or to be scolded for being late if he was so much as a half a second past the time they had decided to put the meal on the table.

He stood, nonplussed and numb with bewilderment, when both women nattered at him excitedly. Such a thing had never happened in twenty-two years of partnership, not even when his father had died nor when Istell's father had died.

Istell's irritated, "Right now!" penetrated his confusion.

Ilona was simultaneously scolding, "They rang here, and Istell told them where you were, but you must have already left when they rang there, so they rang back here."

His garbled mind sorted out that he had to ring the First Public Servant. Something monumental had occurred in the few minutes it had taken him to walk from the hearing to his home: something so monumental that Istell and her mother were expecting him to ring back right that moment even though the meal was on the table. Moving like a puppet, Glen went to the wall unit and pressed the buttons. "Glendritz Tomptell," he introduced himself to the voice at the other end.

"I'll put you through right now, Mr. Tertiary, Madam First is expecting you."

Before Glen could say, "Thank you," the First Public Servant was saying, "Glen!" in his ear.

"Olarine, what on earth has happened?"

"There's a strange ship heading towards us."

Glen stood in silent bewilderment.

Olarine continued, "I've recalled Pita, too. If we're being contacted, we have to get together and decide how to deal with the strangers."

"Strangers?" It was the last thing Glen had expected to hear. It had always been his theory that when contact had been lost with the rest of the world two hundred and fifty years previously, there had not been any survivors of the violence in other places. He felt as disoriented and uncomprehending as he would have if he'd been told that aliens had landed from outer space.

"We're the Triune, Glen, it's our duty. I've been looking up the protocol that the Troggies laid down, and it says nothing at all about contact from the outside. It's up to us."

A generation after contact had been lost with the outside world, there had been what had been termed a 'Mini Ice Age' which the islanders had dubbed the 'Big Freeze.' To survive, the islanders of two hundred and fifty years ago had moved underground where they could keep warm and were protected from the icy winds of the surface. During that time of desperate endurance, the new, non-violent society had been designed as a means for the population to survive in cramped, dark, unbearable conditions. Those who had lived in the tunnels, which they casually referred to as 'dug-outs' as if they were canoes, had called themselves 'Troglodytes' which had been shortened to 'Troggies' – an attempt to make light of an appalling experience, which had become a term of reverence and admiration over the generations that had followed.

The Troggies had written a comprehensive protocol, governing all aspects of island society. It came as an incomprehensible blow to Glen that the protocol had not covered contact with the outside world. "What do you mean it doesn't?" he stammered, unable to imagine that it didn't, when it covered everything else. "It's up to us?" he squeaked. He heard the falsetto in his own voice and was annoyed with himself. Not once in his gentle rearing or properly ordered adulthood had he come across a situation that had shaken him like this did. And he was expected to make decisions about it that would affect the lives of his people for generations to come?

"Who else?" Olarine sounded so calm that Glen felt foolish. "I must call for an emergency meeting of the Triune so we can work something out before the ship reaches us."

Glen realised there was nothing he could do about his voice squeaking. He felt lightheaded, he could feel the flush rushing over his face, and if he didn't find a way to excuse himself very soon, he was going to do something he hadn't done since he was two years old.

"Do you need me there right away?" he asked somewhat desperately. "We were just about to sit down to lunch."

"It's not a level one emergency, Glen. No volcanoes are erupting. Have your lunch."

Glen felt like a fool.

Olarine continued, "Pita should be here tonight. The two of us will put our heads together tonight. It's going to take you until tomorrow to get here at the earliest, anyway, since you have to take the interisland ferry. The strange ship is slow moving, and it's a good ways out. There's no guarantee it knows we're here. Even if it heads this way right now, it'll take a few days to get here."

"Oh, then it might be a false alarm," Glen's voice and heart settled down. "I'm in the middle of a hearing, so I'll need to see it through, then I'll get there as soon as I'm free and go through the protocols to see if I can find something for you."

"Thanks," Olarine said in a wry voice.

Glen hadn't meant to make it sound as if Olarine didn't know what she was doing, but she was an architect, her training was not in the extensive use of government documents the way his was.

Before he could find words to explain his meaning, Olarine continued, "Even if they don't know we're here and don't find us, it's not a false alarm. It means someone else definitely survived. Someone is back on the oceans again in iron ships. We still have to get together and form a protocol. Even if they come directly towards us, if you catch the ferry tonight you should beat them here by enough time for us to have a meeting before we have anyone to talk to."

"I'll extricate myself from the hearing," Glen said, hardly above a whisper.

When Olarine broke the ringer link Glen rushed to the toilet room, then returned and stared at the perfectly set table without seeing it.

"What is it?" Istell asked in alarm.

"There's a . . ." he shifted his focus to her face and swallowed. "There's an iron ship."

Ilona spoke up sharply. "So much fuss over a metal hunter finding a wreck?"

"No. No, Ilona, this one is not wrecked. This one is sailing."

There was complete and utter silence in the room. Ilona didn't even notice that the meal was getting cold. Istell reached out to hold Glen's hand.

CHAPTER EIGHT

Joe Mack

Joseph Machbanai Capernaum had no idea what had changed Sam. He'd been different somehow since they'd climbed inside the wreck in the sand on the south beach. Sam was quieter, as if he had the answer he'd been looking for. He no longer asked anyone if they thought someone had been there recently. It was as if he knew. Somehow, he knew from then on as surely as if he'd seen them with his own eyes.

So, it was no surprise when the announcement was made that evening that the Star of Galilee would search for one more week before going home. The complaints from the soldiers that they could search for the rest of their lives, they'd still never see a living soul meant nothing next to Sam's confidence that one week was all he needed. Joe Mack didn't know how Sam had persuaded Major Temperance to continue with their quest, but he'd never been in any doubt that he would. Sam could persuade birds to swim and fish to fly. Maybe he'd told Temperance there'd be booze, maybe not. Joe Mack wasn't going to ask. "No one can say, "No," to Sam when he's like that," Joe Mack commented to Chuck.

"You got that right!" Chuck agreed. "It ain't a bad call for us to a stay off the ship for the next few nights."

"I ain't crazy about it," Joe Mack admitted. "I done my share of sleeping on the cold, hard ground. And there was no volcano there, the ground didn't shake, and the birds didn't scream all night long."

"It ain't such a bad idea to be out of reach of Temperance tonight is all."

"Which is worse; Temperance exploding or the volcano exploding?"

Outwardly Joe Mack grinned, but inwardly he was not thrilled. It didn't take long before he reconsidered and viewed it as a good thing. They collected grass and ferns to make the most comfortable beds any of them ever remembered sleeping on. There was as much of the cold, clean water as they wanted. "We'll never taste water like this again," he sighed.

"It's what the ship's tanks got refilled with," Vince pointed out.

"Yeah, and as soon as this pure water's poured into those stinking tanks, it'll be tainted by them. What do you bet it already tastes stale?"

Chuck sighed, sadly, "No matter what, it won't be the same as scooped straight out of the stream."

After two of the soldiers had died from eating poison berries while the explorers were on the south coast in the second wreck, all fruit from the island was banned. By themselves, with no one to see what they did or didn't eat, the explorers were free to cook and eat anything they wanted to. All they figured they had to do was stay away from things they didn't recognise. Hot food from Willie Jay's grill, fresh clean water, and comfortable beds was their idea of heaven.

"I guess this is as close to Paradise as I'm ever likely to get," Joe Mack supposed in deep satisfaction, eating a nicely roasted bird with crispy skin and moist, juicy meat.

"Ain't heaven to me without no beef," Vince argued.

Joe Mack grinned to himself, going ahead of the others towards the gully so that they couldn't see his face. "Hey, Johnny," he called back, "Tell us what it says about the lion lying down with the lamb in

Paradise. Don't that mean ain't no one going to eat no meat? How can it be Paradise if you ain't got no meat?"

"We will be transformed," Johnny explained. "We'll be freed from the demands of the flesh." The thought of Paradise to come prompted Johnny, Vince, and Willie Jay to give thanks for it, which led to a prayer for their safe return home. Joe Mack hadn't gone far enough away to pretend he hadn't heard them, so, with a sigh, he turned back to join in enough to avoid suspicion. As soon as they could get away with it, Joe Mack, Chuck, and Sam said, "Amen."

"Let's get some wood and make a fire in the gully," Joe Mack suggested.

"Why?" Vince wanted to know. "It ain't cold, and there ain't no animals."

"Because we can," Joe Mack said over his shoulder, walking away from the others to put an end to the argument, raising his eyebrows at Chuck, who joined him.

"What are you up to?" he asked when they were out of earshot.

"I want a fire," Joe Mack told him. In a fit of deviltry, he added quietly, "Ain't my idea of heaven without meat."

Chuck grinned. "If I cain't eat, I ain't goin'.'"

Joe Mack laughed out loud. It felt good to be able to just throw back his head and laugh without worrying about having to explain himself. In the dusk after the sun had gone down behind the mountains, they found dry grass and twigs for kindling, plus some fallen wood that they dragged along the ground behind them. "Hey, you guys," they called out as they returned to the spot in the gully where they'd made their beds, "Go and get some more wood before it gets too dark. It's as easy to find as the birds are to catch."

There was something so pleasant and relaxing about lying in comfort around a fire, knowing there was no one there to overhear them, no predators of either the two or the four-legged kind, surrounded by the heavenly scent of the tree-lilies, that the constant noise of the volcano no longer bothered them. They paid no more attention to the shuddering of the ground than they did to the rolling of the ship. Joe Mack couldn't resist the urge to stir up trouble. "This is like heaven, isn't it?" he started.

"Sure is," Sam answered.

"And the GR were so sure it was the gateway to hell! It's more like the gateway to heaven to my way of thinking."

He heard Chuck trying to muffle a snigger.

Johnny was not at all pleased, warning Joe Mack to be careful.

"They get everything else wrong, why not that?" All at once he didn't feel mischievous anymore. Knowing that no one could hear them or sneak up on them without making a noise in the dark jungle, Joe Mack was overwhelmed by the need to talk about things that he'd kept bottled up his whole life. "They tried to fight their way to a coast for a hundred years – or to hear them tell it, two hundred years. That's the kind of thing that first started me wondering. You're supposed to just not remember what was drummed your head as Truth from God when they change something. If it was Truth from God, how come it changed? They never explained nothing, no reason how come God's Truth could suddenly be different that day from what it had been the day before. And you didn't dare talk about it or ask anyone, or you could be hauled off for being unpatriotic. Now I got to tell you something; ain't no one in my family ever been unpatriotic. We're old time GR. From before the first expansion."

"How come you say 'them,' instead of 'us,' then?" Vince wanted to know.

Joe Mack was annoyed. Trust Vince to miss the point. "Because somehow something's gone off track from what the Gethsemane Republic was all about."

"What do you mean?" Chuck asked.

Joe Mack never minded questions from Chuck, because he knew Chuck wasn't putting him down. "You know how Johnny said they're too much like the Pharisees these days? Well, that's part of it. But it's more than that. The GR's not what it was in the beginning."

Sam's voice came quietly out of the darkness. "What are you calling the beginning? How far back does your family go?"

Joe Mack was startled to silence. It should have been obvious what he meant. "The beginning is the beginning, isn't it? You can't have more than one beginning."

"Well, now, that depends. Are you talking about the beginning of the Gethsemane Republic, as in when it was named, or as in when it started its mission, or as it was before its name was changed?"

After hearing Sam ask that, Joe Mack was too stunned to speak. The other explorers must have been going through something like that, too, because he didn't hear a peep out of them, not even Vince. Desperate to put an end to the nerve-wracking silence, Joe Mack suggested, "Best thing'd be to start as far back as you can go."

That seemed to jar Vince back to life. "But what do you mean, "Its name was changed?" The Gethsemane Republic never had a different name! The Lord God spared it because the GR were the only true Children of God – the only ones walking in true righteousness – the only ones in the whole world! That's why all the people that used to live here got killed. You've seen it with your own eyes!"

At first Joe Mack was nervous that Vince's hysteria would be the end of their cosy fire-side talk, but Sam's calm voice brought them all back to earth. "Vince. Can it. It's all right. God ain't gonna strike us dead. The GR ain't gonna arrest us for blasphemy. This is the one time we can speak freely. We don't gotta be scared."

"I ain't scared," Vince sounded to Joe Mack like a six-year-old, but he knew Sam would be able to say his piece, now.

Johnny spoke up, his face orange in the firelight. "I never heard nothing different either, Vince, but I want to hear what Sam found out. It shocked me, too, you know, but some things just don't make sense no matter how you play them."

If Johnny, the most deeply religious one, felt that way about it, then the rest of them had no hesitation.

"Yeah," there was something Joe Mack had wanted to get off his chest for a long time. "What gets to me is when they rewrite history to make it fit whatever'll make the government look good when something new happens. God changes His mind, does he? Or do they get it wrong and then fix it?"

"Yeah," Chuck agreed. "If you wonder what's going on your blaspheming. But they can't have it both ways. If they're really giving the Word of God it wouldn't change."

They all looked towards Sam, even though he was hard to see in the darkness away from the fire. "Before Judgement Day the whole land was one nation, all the way to the coast, and further north than the GR ever got, all the way to the other side of the Ashlands, and further west than the GR ever got, way past the Mississippi, and all the way south to the Gulf Coast. You know how the Weskies said Judgement Day was a volcano thousands of times bigger than this one?"

There was a general sort of muttering. Some sounds of disbelief, and some of agreement.

"Think about it. If this ash here on the plants and things was hundreds of feet deep instead of inches. If the land was dry and burned instead of damp like this. If the crater was bigger than this whole island and it was dumping rocks and ash on land instead of into the ocean, so people got buried, and their houses and cities, and dams got bust and flooded downstream taking out the next dam and the next one after that, flooding cities and washing people and towns away. If the farms got covered in ash and the crops and cattle got killed so there weren't nothing for the survivors to eat, and people got hungry and the guns came out to get food and shelter. It ain't pretty, and when it settled down anyone alive had a hard way to make a living. Hunting what's left of the game and trying to grow crops.

Just about all that was left of the great nation was little groups of people who got together to help each other out. One bunch of people did okay. They had fresh water, farmland, hunting, and an iron mine right near oil wells. They kept the knowledge alive of how to do it, and after two or three generations they started to smelt iron again and tried to refine oil. They traded with the descendants of the survivors of the military who called themselves the White Sands Army. The two groups merged and named themselves the Rio Grande Republic.

Between them the two groups made a thriving, strong community. The military had a very strong ethic of service. As things got better for the Rio Grande Republic they reached out to other bands nearby, offering protection and expertise. The Rio Grande Republic grew from people asking if they could be part of it. It got the nickname of the Grand Republic, and that got shortened to the GR.

It's a good history, something to be proud of, and they shouldn't of hid it."

"Why hide it?" Joe Mack asked. "That don't make no sense."

"If something makes no sense on the surface there's something happening underneath that you don't know about."

"Like what?" The fire was dying down and Joe Mack couldn't see Chuck, but he knew him well enough to be able to imagine his expression: partly curious and partly cynical. Joe Mack felt divided in two, himself. In one way he hoped that it was true that what Sam was saying was true, which would mean that the GR had made up their version, but in another way he couldn't see how Sam could possibly know.

He lay quietly in his bed as Sam answered Chuck. "Like what really happened don't make it look like you were chosen by God near as much as your version does."

"I can see that," Joe Mack was almost convinced by that one idea alone. "But what I don't get is how you could know about it."

"Let's just say what happens leaves traces that people can find no matter what stories are told or what's done to hide what went on."

Vince sounded pleased. "You're not two-hundred-and fifty-years old Sam. You weren't there. How do you know what happened was different from what we been taught?"

All at once Joe Mack didn't want to know. There was always the risk that the GR would get suspicious of the explorers and want to question them. He hadn't actually taken part in any interrogations, but he'd seen and heard enough to want to have as little as possible to hide. He told Vince, "All of us know something the government don't want us to know."

Chuck's voice came out of the darkness. "Yeah, and even if we don't, all of us explorers think things they don't want us to think."

It had become dark quickly in the gully when the sun went down, and with the fire dying down there wasn't enough light to see anyone anymore. Still, it was good to hear in his buddy's voice that he'd picked up on what Joe Mack had said and backed him up.

"Are you telling me you don't want to hear any more?" Sam asked.

"No, I'm not. I want to hear it all," Joe Mack answered.

"Me, too," Chuck agreed.

"Yeah," from Vince.

"I got to hear it to know what I got to pray about," Johnny declared.

After a few moments of silence Willie Jay realised they were waiting for him, and he started to stutter, "W – w – w – w – w . . ."

"Just yes or no, Willie Jay. You don't got to make no big speech," Chuck told him.

Joe Mack could hear Willie Jay's gulp clear over on the other side of the fire. "Maybe I did oughta hear it so I know if it's true or not, but – but if it's sinful talk I didn't ought to hear it, but Sam don't make no sinful talk, so that's good, but I ain't never done nothing like this and if it's against the Word of God then . . ."

Realising he could go on all night like that, Joe Mack stopped him with, "You're out-voted five to one, Willie Jay. If you don't want to hear it, you got to move your bed to where you can't hear us."

Willie Jay stammered, "I – I never – Joe Mack, I did – Sam, I never said I don't want you to tell it."

"Okay, then. No matter what Judgement Day was, the Rio Grande Republic grew into a stable nation. They defended themselves so well against the Raiders that other groups of people living nearby wanted to join them. They grew slowly but steadily from others merging with them, and after two or three generations they were prosperous, they had an elected government, towns, a capital city, and a population that felt safe enough to have festivals and parades. Those were the original GR.

It was about that time, about a hundred years after Judgement Day that a man who called himself Abraham Wright appeared."

There were gasps when Sam said that. He snickered. "Yeah, I thought that'd get you. I know you was taught he was original GR, but the older stories have him coming from the East Coast way north and east of the GR. The man was a genius, there's no question about that. He invented the process of getting rubber from guayule which gave us tires and rubber hoses and waterproof boots and tarps, and he solved problems in refining oil, so it ran engines better. Without his genius there's no doubt we wouldn't be where we are in making and using vehicles. It seems as if he was very popular. He was acclaimed President, and re-elected three times, so he was in power for sixteen years – the longest ever. If you're a genius and charismatic you can do just about anything."

Vince sounded offended when he said, "You sound as if you don't like him! He's the greatest man that ever lived!"

Johnny objected to that. "The Son of God is the greatest man that ever lived."

"Except for him," Vince allowed.

"I'm not saying he wasn't a genius, and it's obvious he was a first-rate leader. Even if he had books that would be banned today, it's still an achievement no one will ever match to be able to take the information and not only figure out how to put it into practice, but persuade everyone to follow his lead, and to keep his popularity while he did it. There's no getting away from how prosperous the Rio Grande Republic was because of him. My problem with him is that under his Presidency the GR started to attack instead of only defending itself."

There was a few moments of silence as they all lay in the dark, digesting that, until Johnny spoke. "He was called by God."

Sam sighed. "Look at it this way. Every time there was a change of government the Raiders attacked. You can see from a military point of view that they were taking a chance that there could be confusion then. When Abraham Wright was elected the citizens celebrated. Maybe they let their guard down too much, maybe it was a bigger raid than usual, maybe what was written about it at the time was exaggerated, but it seems that more damage was done than usual. President Wright decided that the best way to make sure that never happened again was to go on the offensive, to 'teach the Raiders a lesson they'll never forget;' to hit their homes. You know Raiders. They haven't changed between then and now. They don't live anywhere. They're always on the move. So, you can figure out what happened – the GR military hit people who'd had nothing to do with the raid. But they never said they'd made a mistake, they only promised to do it again if anyone ever raided them again. Anyone they thought might be 'harbouring' Raiders was fair game. So, it wasn't long before the Raiders were making small raids, then, when the military went out to retaliate, made bigger raids while the military was gone, and then raided the places the GR had hit before they could get their strength back. So, alliances started to form against the GR. People didn't only want to protect themselves against the GR, they wanted to retaliate for the attacks the GR had made on them."

"You make it sound like it was all our fault!" Vince sounded indignant.

"There's a difference between thinking you're lucky and God has spared you because he loves you, and thinking God singled you out because you're better than all the others. One leads you to help others in the name of God, the second leads you to dominate. The Rio Grande Republic had been a peaceful nation which others depended on and wanted to join. Up until they started attacking others it looked as if they would have ended up reuniting the whole continent under one government, given enough time. Once they had started that, and refused to admit it had been a mistake, they started down the route of being feared and hated, and others not only didn't want to join them, but also those who had joined started to want to leave. The Wright government couldn't allow that. If the GR got smaller it would get weaker. So, the troops went into the streets to protect the nation from the unpatriotic."

Joe Mack shifted uncomfortably on his bed. This was a different angle on what he'd been taught, where Abraham Wright had been original GR and had led the nation out of confusion to the Wright Way, the way chosen for them by God.

He was thankful that Johnny asked, "How do you know what was written back then? All of that was lost on Judgement Day except for what God preserved for our teaching. Are you sure you weren't led astray by the trickery of the devil?"

"Pretty sure, son. It's true that all of the stuff in the north was destroyed. There's near to nothing in the Ashlands, but south of that there was plenty of knowledge for a long time after Judgement Day until it was lost in purification purges. Inside the GR ain't nothing left, no one can read, and no one asks questions. The Conquered Peoples are different. Lots of them still have books, can read, and grew up asking questions. Burning their books, taking their children away to be trained in the Wright Way, and hauling off anyone who asks questions don't erase their memories. Sometimes it don't even stop them from handing their knowledge down, and sometimes it don't get all the books or stop kids from learning how to read them. You can't stop ideas with guns."

Sam got up and walked off into the woods for a bit. When he came back, he stirred the fire up, put more wood on it, had a drink of water, and looked around at them all, just dark humps around the fire. "You want to go to sleep now?"

Joe Mack didn't want the story to stop there. "I'd like to know how Wright went from that to being taken up by God in a flash of light."

"It's a long and winding tale," Sam answered, getting back into his bed.

"I'd like to hear it," Chuck said, getting up. "In a minute."

"Pee break," Joe Mack announced, getting up to follow Chuck. One by one the others did the same. "You think any of this is true?" Joe Mack murmured in Chuck's ear.

"It's got more of a ring of truth to it than any of the stuff we've been told before. And it answers a lot of questions that nothing else ever has."

Joe Mack could feel the truth of that deep in his heart. All he could manage in response was a grunt, but he got himself a drink of water and headed back to his bed feeling as if he was at last hearing the answers to things he always wondered about. "No wonder no one's allowed to talk the way we are," he said to Sam as he crawled back into his bed.

"For sure, Sam agreed. "If you're trying to rewrite history, as Joe Mack put it, you can't let people get together and talk about what they remember. Someone will know one thing, someone will know something else, and the next thing you know no one's buying your stories. They take the kids away young, teach them only what they want them to know, get the parents too scared to set the kids straight, teach the kids it's their sacred duty to inform on parents who try to anyway, and in a generation, you have a nation that knows nothing but what you want them to know. Only problem with that is there's always someone, somewhere, who finds out what really happened. The truth is the truth whether we believe it or not. It stays the same, and someone always finds it, no matter what you do about it."

"So how did he go from being President to being Prophet?" Chuck prompted.

"After he was President a longer time than anyone before or after him, he was called by God to spread the Word of God the length and breadth of the continent. No one will ever know what led to that. We can believe the official story, or not. The problem is no one knows anything else. There's only speculation. Was his popularity slipping? Were the people starting to doubt he was really appointed by God? Was someone else pressing for power and getting so that he could take over, so it was better to go while the going was good? Like I said, the man was a genius. You'll never find another case of someone who had all the power and gave it away without a fight. So, either he was smart and made his move for his own reasons, or there was a fight we never saw and will never know about.

Another thing you can never deny — he was the first person since Judgement Day to travel from one coast to the other, to cross the rivers, and to travel as far into the Ashlands as people have settled, and as far south as the Gulf Coast. It's also true he had followers who went with him, took care of him, and protected him. The story that he was surrounded by the Shield of God came from them telling how he was shot at and never hit. The stories of his miracles came back from them. They sent messengers home regularly to bring news, and people set out regularly to join the crusade. Some of them were never heard from again, others came back talking about signs and wonders. As to him being snatched up by the Lord in a flash of light: in the Ashlands they say he was shot for trespassing. Not bullet-proof at all. Some of his disciples were disillusioned and settled where they were. Some continued the crusade, which went on for the rest of their lives, with stories of signs and wonders reaching back home just like before. Some came back home to tell of miracles. One of them, Adam Witness, was a fire and brimstone preacher who had a clear vision that the GR was chosen by God to reunite the continent under God's Law."

"President Witness," Chuck muttered.

"What?" Vince asked.

"My Grandpappy said President Witness changed everything."

"My Grandpa said the first time the GR came close to our homeland was under President Witness. He used to call him President Witless."

Sam snickered. "Yeah, my folks called him things like that, too, until the GR conquered us. Then they just stopped talking. Under Witness the GR got the name the Gethsemane Republic to note how we were surrounded by the enemies of Christ. That's also when the aggressive expansions started, when every boy no matter what his mental or physical ability had to learn how to defend the GR – that means is taken into the military at thirteen and growing up in uniform away from his parents, with GR doctrine pounded into his skull all day every day. From then on you could tell who was GR and who was CP by their names. GR names were Biblical and nothing else, CP names could be anything."

"My family was CP," Johnny confessed. "I heard some of these things from the older people who didn't want the truth to die. I wasn't fit for service. I got beat up a lot and sent home as a reject in a year. I dedicated my life to God. I heard him calling me. My Grandma told me the truest gold is tried by the hottest fire. I can read, so I read the Bible for myself, and I found out quick that half of what they claim God said ain't in the Bible at all. At all."

"Yeah, I know what you mean," Vince chimed in. My family's CP. We were over-run after President Witness got shot. They said the assassin came from our area. Nearly everyone my Grandma knew was wiped out in the clean up and the nation was razed to the ground. We only survived because my Grandma's mother knew something bad was going to happen and put her kids up on the horse, took what food they could carry and got out of there right before the invasion. They could see the red glow of the fires on the horizon behind them at night. But they had nowhere to go and nothing to eat, so they ended up going to the GR as refugees. They always had to keep secret where they'd come from, change their names, and make like it was a revelation from God that had led them to the GR. I've lived a lie my whole life. All I ever wanted to do was draw, but that's a sissy job. My Grandma said it was a God-given gift, but it's been more like a curse. Don't none of you never say nothing about what I told you."

Sam reassured him, "None of us can tell anyone about what we've said and heard here, Vince. What happened on Sunday Island's got to stay on Sunday Island."

"Amen," said Johnny, followed quickly by all of them.

"I know what you mean, Vince. I've lived a lie my whole life, too," Sam added.

"I never thought of it that way," Joe Mack said. "I just figured half of the stuff didn't add up."

Willie Jay finally joined in. "I figured it was me always getting things wrong. They booted me out of the military when I was sixteen for being a screw-up. I never did all that good at home, so I figured I'd make a career of the military, but they wouldn't take my re-up."

"Are you GR or CP?" Vince asked.

"I dunno. They always said we were original GR, but if what you say is right and three fourths of the people who think they're original GR ain't, then maybe we ain't neither and don't know it."

Lying on his back, staring up at the stars that peeked now and then between the leaves of the trees overhead, thinking about everything he'd heard, Joe Mack was unaware he'd fallen asleep until he woke up to a fresh breeze softly caressing his cheek. He'd hardly ever in his life felt so comfortable. He was on a comfortable surface, he wasn't involved in a military action, he didn't have to worry about a police raid, he wasn't hungry or wet or cold, and the scent of the tree-lilies surrounded him.

He got up, relieved himself, had a drink of the lovely water that he knew he was going to remember fondly for the rest of his life no matter how long it was, then made his way along the gully towards the beach. Part way Chuck caught up with him. "Wotcha doin'?"

"Going to have me a hot bath to start the day."

"I had the same idea."

As they came around the corner of the side of the gully, both looked up towards the highest peak. It was shrouded in mists against the blue skies with high, thin mare's tails of clouds pink with dawn. At the hot stream the Weskies had left soap ready for today's work. The two men dug out comfortable tubs in the sand and lay back in them after liberally soaping themselves. Ripples sometimes came up the beach and invaded their tubs, but they were welcome to ease the heat off a bit before it got to be too much.

"Tell me something," Joe Mack started.

"Tell me what it is, first."

"Is it my imagination or is that volcano quieter?"

"I was just thinking there's not so much lava hitting the sea."

"I thought the steam wasn't exploding like it did. Not so loud and not so much."

"And the island's not shaking like it was."

"And maybe not so much smoke."

"Either we're imagining it or it's not so loud."

"Or we got used to it."

"Want to poke around some today?"

"Yeah. Let's get the grill going and roast us some of them sweet potatoes and get ourselves lost."

They jumped up with a will, air dried by dancing around on the beach, pulled their clothes and boots back on and ran up to the buildings. They had their breakfast nicely grilling when they saw the first sleepy heads of the others down on the beach heading for the hot stream. Grabbing some large leaves of some nearby plants they tossed their breakfast into them to carry them and struck off into the bush. Plodding along, snickering like two small boys, they were in no hurry. As the sweet potatoes cooled enough to be tackled they started to nibble on them as they went, complaining about burnt lips.

By taking it slowly they were able to thread their way between trees, palms, and ferns without making a trail that anyone could follow. The footing was mostly soft forest floor covered with leaves and fronds that had not been trampled down by anything, so when they came to something hard it was noticeable. To test it, Joe Mack stamped his foot. It made an unmistakeable thud. "What the hell?"

They sat down with their backs against a tree at the edge of the hard stuff to finish their breakfast. Then Chuck started to dig into the leaves and fronds, pulling the dry ones aside, and using the ends of sturdy ones to dig out the muckiness of the ones underneath that had rotted down. "There ain't any big ones here," Joe Mack realised as he looked around.

There was a completely square area that had only smaller ferns, no trees, like a fern covered clearing.

"No wonder," Chuck grunted. "It's cement."

"What?" Joe Mack broke a branch off a tree and used the end to dig and push the rotten leaves and fronds off the cement. "Well, would you look at that!"

They looked around. "What's it for?"

"Floor?"

But as they dug along the edges they came across no sign that there had ever been walls or anything attached to the cement. They uncovered the edge all the way around, then stood back to look at it.

"It's big enough to be a shed or a room," Joe Mack figured, watching Chuck to see what he thought.

"What for? It's not near the other buildings, there's no sign it was a barn or a house. Let's see if there's anything in the middle."

"Like what?"

"If there used to be walls here they'd have holes in the cement to seat the studs."

"Right."

Although they hadn't found any sign of studs along the edges, they pulled aside the little ferns that were growing in the leaf litter to see if they could uncover any sign that there had been roof joists or wall studs. Joe Mack pulled up a handful of ferns and froze. There was something under them. "Hey, Chuck?"

Together they pulled everything off, uncovering a large oval bowl almost knee high. "What is it?"

They walked around it, studying it, noting the bolt holes in the top part, and the bits of rust that showed there had been bolts in the holes in the base, though why they'd been needed Joe Mack couldn't imagine, since it was set into the cement.

"Let's get Sam. If anyone can guess what this is, he can."

"Right."

For a while Sam was as baffled as they were. "If you put an oval shaped cover on there, and put a water tank back here where those bolt holes are, I'd say it was like the toilets I've seen in the ruins of pre-Judgement Day buildings. But it can't be that because there's no drainage. There's no water pipes coming in to it, and there's no way to drain it, it's set right into the cement. I don't know. But it should keep the best of the military engineers busy. Let's tell them we found it, and we don't have the slightest idea what it is. That's should keep them out of our hair for the rest of the time we're here." He grinned, wickedly.

On their way back to the ship to report their finding, Joe Mack asked him, "What do you really think it is?"

"I'd say it's a toilet, but it couldn't be. No one would make a big slab of cement and put a toilet in the middle of it with no water to it and no drainage and no walls. It makes no sense. It looks like a toilet, but it couldn't be."

The engineers decided it was a pagan version of a baptismal font. None of the explorers bought that, though they had no better ideas.

"Do you think it was a joke?" Joe Mack wondered.

"I don't get it," was Sam's only response to that.

To keep his mind off the things they'd talked about on the island, and to distract himself from the discomfort of being back on the ship travelling on across the ocean, Joe Mack spent his time wondering why a toilet had been put in the middle of a slab of cement out in the middle of nowhere.

Although the Weskies had cleaned, aired, painted, scrubbed and washed every inch of the ship, including cleaning everyone's clothes and bedding, it was still a hard adjustment back to shipboard life after the days on the island. Even with all of the mattresses re-stuffed with fresh straw from the island, with fragrant pine added, the bunks weren't as comfortable as the beds of grass, and the cabin didn't smell as sweet as the tree-lilies in the gully. And the water was no joy to drink. They reverted to drinking beer and coffee, and not touching plain water, remembering the streams on the island as if they'd been a dream.

"You're sure we'll find someone?" Joe Mack muttered to Sam as they passed a series of tiny, uninhabited islands on the first day.

"I'm sure," Sam nodded, adding in a normal speaking voice, "We left at the right time, look."

Behind them the island they'd called home for a week had vanished over the horizon, but the blue skies they'd enjoyed were being covered by grey. "Holy cow! Just in time, huh?"

"Almost like someone was watching out for us," Sam grinned.

"How do you know which way to go?" Joe Mack muttered under his breath.

"Same way I knew other things," Sam returned low, then turned to look out across the broad blue sea in front of them. "Let's hope the bad weather stays behind us," he said loudly.

Joe Mack laughed. "The only other guy I ever knew with gold horseshoes up his ass like you was Major Jaakobah Lycus."

A soldier near them suddenly came alert. "You served with Old Jack?"

"Sure did. I was with him in the Panhandle when they pulled him out and sent him to the South. I upped to go with him, but they sent me to the Ashlands instead."

"Me, too. Only I never got sent to the Ashlands. I went AWOL when I found out I was going to have to stay there without Old Jack. Spent time breaking rocks after they caught me, then got posted here."

Joe Mack nodded, moving away so that he and the soldier couldn't be accused of fraternizing. "That's rough, man."

Ahnya

As the Flying Fish pulled into the station, Ahnya was surprised and pleased to see empty seats. Oh, to sit down!! She thought for a moment that some youngsters were going to beat her to the seat she was aiming for, but at the last moment they changed their minds and flocked to the front of the carriage, the sound of their laughter and chatter reminding Ahnya of magpies.

In relief Ahnya sank into the seat and put her briefcase under her feet as a footstool. All of the windows were darkened to keep out the brilliance of the day's sun, which made the carriage feel like a dimmer, cooler, refuge. It was the end of the day now, no longer so hot and bright, so she touched her fingertips to the glass. It was instantly transparent, and she could see the sunset. Watching it, she leaned her cheek against the window. The coolness of the glass windowpane, and its smoothness against her cheek, were just what she needed. Because she was short her head only just came in contact with the window, and she had to cushion her chin from the ledge with her cape. It was too warm to wear the cape, anyway.

The Flying Fish started off so smoothly that she didn't feel it moving, it was a change in the tone of the faint whine of the electric motors that told her she was on her way home at last. It was getting dark. Soon the solar panels wouldn't have enough light. She realised that instead of dozing off, she was listening for the familiar faint click of the switch-over to battery, so she gave up trying to get some rest.

When she got home, she would be able to rest. The meeting had gone on so long that Donstan would have the children fed and bathed by the time she arrived, so she'd be able to sit down and talk it all over with him. She found herself longing for his common sense and calm rationality as if they'd been apart for weeks instead of hours. She tried to think over the various important points of the meeting, but the image of Donstan's long, lean frame kept coming into her mind and interrupting her train of thought. He was 1.86 metres tall; her head didn't reach his shoulder. That's where she wanted her head to be – against his chest, not against this unloving windowpane. There was no point in going over it in her head, she couldn't concentrate, so she gave up trying to do that, too. She opened her eyes, sat up straight and instantly regretted it.

"Tough meeting, Substitute Speaker," the middle-aged man across from her said before she had a chance to get more than the merest glance of the tree tops whipping by the carriage window.

"Err . . . yes, Baraham, it was." She focussed on him. It was one of her Hundred. He'd been sitting in the meeting, about four rows back from the front, when he wasn't jumping up to shout out his opinions. "Tough meeting."

"I could see it took it out of you, the way you had your eyes closed, there. Headache?"

He sounded so kind, so sympathetic, she simply couldn't howl at him, "Be quiet and leave me alone!" the way she wanted to. Besides, if she started acting like that she would be voted out as Substitute Speaker before she could blink, and rightly so. "No, not a headache," she said mildly. "Just thinking."

"Not much to think about if you ask me. We've done well enough on our own for two hundred and fifty years, we don't need to change it now."

Ahnya nodded, noncommittally. Of all the people to want to talk to her on the train, why did it have to be a reactionary type? There was no point in saying any of the things on her mind; it would only get the entire argument started again, to no avail. She unbunched the cape from being a pillow, smoothed it, and folded it into a square in her lap to give herself something to do other than look at Baraham. She didn't want to give him any encouragement. She watched the door idly as the Flying Fish stopped at a station, and the doors automatically slid back with a swishing sound, acting as if she were interested in the people getting on and off, hoping he'd take the hint.

No such luck. "Glad to see you agree with me. Sounded almost like you didn't when you were up there."

Now she had to look him right in the eye. "Baraham, I nodded that I know what your opinion is. I don't give my opinion. While our Speaker is ill, I'm the Speaker. I Speak for the Hundred, not for myself."

"But you've got to see we can't have anything to do with the strangers if they find us. They'll bring back to us all the problems from before the Dark Days. That's why we stayed to ourselves in the first place."

Ahnya was vastly relieved that the ladies seated behind her spoke up so she could answer them instead of Baraham. "Has your Hundred just had your meeting?"

"Yes," she turned to smile at them. "We're on our way home from it now."

"Which one are you?"

"Red Seven."

"We're Red Two Twenty-Nine. We're meeting tomorrow. What happened at yours?"

"A lot of fools blathering on about things they know nothing about!" Baraham exclaimed, forcefully, causing the women to exchange glances.

"Don't go giving 'looks' like that! Young people these days get their voting rights far too easily. In my day we had to sit a hard test and pass the whole thing before we got to vote. It's letting standards slip like that that's led to things like this."

Ahnya could see from the expression in the women's eyes that they knew as well as she did that the Citizenship Test hadn't changed since Baraham was a boy. The Flying Fish was slowing down for her stop. "The one thing I noticed," she told the women as she got to her feet, "Is that every single one of my Hundred was there. The entire Hundred for once, and every one of them had a different opinion on what we should do. I don't have a clear vote to report to the Representative."

"Just tell him we can't have anything to do with it!"

She didn't bother answering Baraham, he knew, or should know, she couldn't do that. As she stepped onto the platform she called to the women, "Be prepared for a wide range of opinions and a long meeting to argue them out."

She could hear Baraham holding forth as she took the wooden stairs down from the platform. It was a relief to have his voice cut off by the door closing, though she spared a flash of sympathy for the women trapped in there with him, as she walked along the walkway under the rails for private vehicles. The evening birdsong rose above the whine of the Flying Fish starting up again. She could see the last fading colours of the sunset through the wooden beams of the trestle. Another set of wooden stairs took her down right to the wooden gate to the entrance on the second floor of her house. She shook her thick, short, dark hair back, feeling the fresh evening air on her face, grateful she had the corner house and didn't have to walk even as much as one house length to get home. She was glad she had been able to slip away by herself while the members of her Hundred were standing around the Marae talking after the meeting. She hadn't wanted to discuss it all the way home. The longing for Donstan's arms around her was almost like a physical pain, it was becoming so intense.

Like a soap bubble her feeling of relief at being home popped and was gone as she let herself into the house and the sounds of howling children assailed her. Oh, no. Not tonight.

Conquering the urge to flee to the hills, Ahnya steeled herself to approach the cacophony. Even the caged birds were shrieking instead of singing. Donstan had one year old Donya howling on his hip, holding her with one arm, jiggling her in a vain attempt to soothe her while he stirred dinner on the stove with the other hand. He looked absolutely haggard.

Four-year-old Ahnstan was racing madly about the house shouting at the top of his lungs, "I'm the Flying Man! I'm the Flying Man!" Occasionally leaping off the stairs or chairs with thunderous crashes that sent the birds flying hysterically about their enclosure, squawking. Three-year-old Wynson sat miserably in a huddled heap behind the table, using it as a shield to protect himself from his brother, while keeping up a muted whine, "I'm hungry, Daddy." Donstan was simultaneously trying to murmur comforting words to their daughter, assure their adopted son that it would be 'just a moment' and bellow at their first born to stop that racket and get ready for dinner, all while trying to cook one handed and ensure the sobbing baby on his hip didn't get burned by the pots bubbling on the stove.

Ahnya caught Ahnstan, told him to stop shouting and sent him to wash his hands and face for dinner. Then she went to Donstan and gave him a peck on the cheek. He just looked at her, his blue-grey eyes weary beyond description. Donya reached for her mother. Ahnya took her, wiped the little red and swollen face with a cool cloth, while checking on Ahnstan, which made Donya cry all the more, then returned to the kitchen, sat on one of the kitchen chairs, sat Donya on her lap, and opened her shirt so that her daughter could occupy herself in finding her own way to a breast which quieted the sobs instantly, except for the occasional whoop or sniffle.

"I'm hungry, Mummy," Wynson whined, sidling around the table to her.

She put out her free arm and he snuggled up under it. "Daddy will have dinner on the table as fast as he can, Sweetie, don't you worry."

"What took you so long?" Donstan asked wearily, shaking out the arm that had been holding the baby.

"Tough meeting."

"Yeah, well, it would be, wouldn't it? Did you have to stay to the bitter end?"

"I didn't, really. They voted me Substitute Speaker while Olwyn's sick. I got out of there as soon as I could. They were still talking in the courtyard when I left."

"They did? And you with little ones? Good for you!" He looked at Donya sitting contentedly on Ahnya's lap, suckling, with only the occasional hard caught breath to show how hard she'd been sobbing. "I can't tell you how glad I am you're home, though."

"She wouldn't take the bottle?"

"You'd think I'd tried to poison it." He corralled Ahnstan who was racing in from the bathroom, dripping water everywhere. He appeared to have tried a submerse-and-shake ablution technique. "Now, you sit there, son, and no more running about."

Ahnstan wriggled in protest.

"Flying men sit still at the table," Ahnya informed him. His big grey-blue eyes were reproachful, but he did settle down, at least enough that his father could towel off the excess. Ahnya felt too weary to try to deal with a family meal. "Let's just feed them and get them into bed, then we can eat in peace and talk," she suggested to Donstan as he set the table. He nodded.

Finally, they were able to sit on their veranda and watch the stars through the trees, eating their dinner in bowls on their laps, sitting side by side in blissful silence. Thank goodness they didn't often both have a bad day at the same time.

It had taken so long to get the children settled, that by the time Ahnya and Donstan sat down, she was too tired to notice what she was eating, or to care. A soft breeze floated by carrying with it the scents of evening flowers. Ahnya sighed involuntarily.

"What?" Donstan asked.

His voice sounded as if it came from miles away. Ahnya murmured back, "We missed the sunset."

"Mmm." He closed his eyes and leaned his head back against the faux wallboards of the house, but Ahnya watched the bugs flying in circles in the column of light glowing down from the light paint on the tree trunk in front of their house. Their mindless circuits were oddly comforting. Would contact with the outside world mean the peacefulness of their world would change, now? In a way she hoped the will of the people would be to tell the strangers to leave them alone. Their ancestors had worked so hard to create a peaceful, ecologically stable society in the Rebuilding, she couldn't bear to have any of the horrors she'd been taught about the Old Times come back. As Speaker, even temporarily, she had a secret vote, but she wasn't to try to lead opinion. Her responsibility was to report opinion, not to influence it. She wished she could speak up the way the citizens could at the meeting. Perhaps she should try to hold a position like Speaker when her children were old enough for her to stand for election.

Donstan belonged to a different Hundred from Ahnya's. They'd planned that when they'd first decided to have children, so that they could go to meetings on different nights. Different Hundreds sometimes saw things in different ways, so it gave them more to talk about. Plus, it meant they didn't need to find someone to watch their children on meeting nights.

"Do you want me to step down as Substitute Speaker before Olwyn gets back?" Ahnya put the question very quietly.

"Don't you think you can handle it?"

"Well, yes, but you had a pretty rough day."

"It got away from me," Donstan was defensive. "I've seen it get away from you sometimes."

"I know, I was only checking. You know, when they're older . . ."

"I'll tell you if I can't handle it."

"Okay."

"Tough meeting, you said?"

"Oh, you don't know how much I was looking forward to coming home and talking to you about it!"

"Ahoy, the veranda!" a cheerful voice rang out.

Ahnya winced. Was nothing going to go her way today?

Donstan hushed their visitor, "Not so loud, we've just managed to get the kids down."

"Oh, right. Sorry." It was Carlton, the Speaker of Donstan's Hundred. He lowered his voice. "Do you have a minute? I was wondering how it went for you tonight."

Ahnya shrugged. "Come in," she said getting to her feet. "Our voices will carry from here. We'll sit in the lounge and that way we won't wake the kids up."

Ahnya and Donstan didn't even bother to exchange a look as they got to their feet. They'd rather have been alone, but if they had to have someone there, it might as well be Carlton. He and Ahnya could talk, Speaker to Speaker, and he and Donstan could discuss all the angles before they had to attend their own meeting.

"I don't have a clear vote from my Hundred, you know," she told both Carlton and Donstan as they went into the house and closed the door behind them. "It's almost evenly split between the ones who think we shouldn't have any contact under any circumstances; those who think we should proceed cautiously and reserve the right to cut contact again if any trouble comes up; those who think once we've been found we can't be isolated again, so we'd better find a way of living with it; those who think it'll open up new doors for us and we should embrace it whole heartedly; those who believe now that we've been found we have the opportunity to show the world real civilization; and those who say we don't have enough information to make a decision. Then they all argued their points. It was the most crowded, the most stressful, the most emotional meeting I've ever seen from the time I first got my Citizenship Certificate when I left school. I've certainly never had to chair anything like that before."

"That's what I'm afraid of," Carlton nodded.

"Tea?" Donstan offered.

"Ta, mate," Carlton answered.

"Thanks, Honey," Ahnya told Donstan, saying to Carlton, "It's the first time I've ever seen all Hundred there in any Hundred I've ever belonged to."

"Shows how seriously everyone's taking this."

"They're taking it seriously, all right. I've never seen people so emotional about a vote before. I wish there was something in the protocol about it. It's hard to make the laws ourselves."

Donstan rejoined them. "I'm with the ones who say we can't do anything about it, so we'd better learn to live with it."

Both Speakers looked at him.

He shrugged. "Look, when the Dark Days came and our ancestors lost contact with each other no one could have contacted us, even if they'd wanted to. Then there was the Freeze on top of that. It's taken two hundred and fifty years for someone to get back to building ocean-going ships again, but now that they have, we can't turn back time. We don't have to like it, but we do have to face reality."

Ahnya got up to answer the kettle, to give herself a moment to think. She had so looked forward to talking it over with her partner, but she hadn't wanted to hear this. She could hear the men talking behind her as she put the tea set on the tray, warmed the pot and put the manuka leaves into steep.

She carried the tea tray into the living room. The men were talking about the wisdom of exchanging a few people with the strangers so that they could learn about each other. "What about the violence?" she asked.

"What violence?" Donstan looked startled.

"The world was awash with violence. Terrible things. People killing each other, blowing things up, wars. That's what caused the Dark Days. We can't go back to that."

"Who says we must? We have a peaceful society, what's to say they haven't done the same thing? After all, the break-down was worse on the big continents than it was in the islands, if what our ancestors heard before contact was lost is anything to go by. They'll have adjusted just like we did."

"I don't know. People don't always do the same things. Look how different opinions are from person to person, Hundred to Hundred. Imagine differences like that between nations that have been cut off from each other for two hundred and fifty years. They might be very different from us. I can't remember my history lessons about what was happening when the last contact was made. I'll have to look it up. But I just don't want the children to grow up in . . ." She couldn't say it.

They all stared at one another.

"Unimaginable," Carlton said. "People killing one another. They can't still be living like that, or they wouldn't be there."

"We still have no choice but to talk to them, even if they are," Donstan said quietly. "If they find us, they'll talk to us. So, we might as well talk on our terms."

Ahnya felt her insides go cold with foreboding.

CHAPTER TEN

Vince

Vince was mad with himself for saying the things he'd said to the other explorers on the island. At the time it had been a relief to spill his guts – like a giant weight off his shoulders. No one had ever known how he felt before. He'd even been surprised to hear it himself. He'd never put it into words, never admitted it to himself.

Now that they'd left the island behind its magic had been left behind as well. The first misgivings had occurred as he watched the island shrinking behind them. By the time he couldn't even see the tall mountains anymore, his spirits had sunk. He had watched the island until it had all been reduced to a brown smudge on the horizon, and even the column of smoke that had drawn them to it was swallowed up by the clouds moving in over the blue sky they'd enjoyed so much. Who could have imagined, seeing that cloudy dark lump, how much peace and beauty could be in one place? He beat on himself for the things he'd said, being afraid that the others would take advantage of him.

As rested and relaxed as he had been when they'd all had to go back on board, the shipboard routine was already establishing itself, bringing the heavy weight back down on his neck. The GR were punishing the Weskies in case any of them had enjoyed themselves. Not that he'd ever cared before about what happened to Godless pagans, but it was getting under his skin now. The problem was it wasn't only pagans who were treated like that in the GR. Anyone who was low status enough to be slave labour went through the same mill. That meant the same thing could have happened to the members of his family that no one had heard from since they were invaded. It was something he'd refused to think about before, but now he couldn't get it out of his mind. There were rumours that people who were picked up for heresy, or blasphemy, or un-Republican activities, or for being unpatriotic, were worked to death. Now that he'd been so stupid as to tell the explorers how he really felt, any one of them could turn him in and he'd be facing the same thing himself.

What was worse, he couldn't even save his own skin by turning them in, because it would still come back around to him. It was small comfort that they were all in it together. If he had never said anything then no one would have anything on him while he had something on all of them. He kicked himself for not thinking about that at the time. **¡Chale!** He never did, that's the trouble. 'You moron,' he blasted himself, mentally. 'If you don't get your act together, you're going down.'

He wished he'd never become an explorer. He'd been carried away by Sam's vision. He'd really believed Sam would find the answers to what was eating him. Now he wasn't so sure. He was beginning to doubt that Sam knew what he was doing. They seemed to be going on forever for no reason. **Chingadazos.** It was all more of the same, grey seas, grey skies, confined to this God-forsaken ship with someone listening in all the time, trying to catch them out.

It hurt Vince to think about how lovely the island had been before they left; a beautiful dewy morning, the tall mountain peaks shrouded in mists under blue skies. It felt as if the weather had changed the moment he'd set foot on this floating prison. Joe Mack had been right, curse it all, the water was tainted as soon as it was put into the storage tank.

Compared to the way it tasted in his hands straight from the stream, the water on board was undrinkable.

Another thing that made him feel that God was mistreating him was that the addition of fresh vegetables, fish, and birds had not stopped the food on board from being horrible any more than the work done in the cabin had made it comfortable. It was misery to him to share a bunk after sleeping undisturbed on a mattress of fresh grass and ferns that he could make as big as he wanted to, sleeping as long as he wanted to, under the stars and fragrant pines in the tree-lily gully. Much as he'd longed for a good steak to barbeque on the grill when he had been on the island, he now looked back on the food they'd had there as if it had been nectar of the gods. And who knew the next time he'd have the chance to soak in a hot bath any time he wanted to, as deep as he wanted, for as long as he wanted?

The more he thought about it, the more fed-up he felt. It wasn't fair. Why did God have to give him a **chingadazos** life like this?

On the second day out from the island, not only did Vince feel no better, but he was also jarred to see a massive rock sticking straight up out of the sea like a gigantic finger.

"It's God beckoning us on," Johnny said with his usual optimistic faith.

Vince said nothing, thinking to himself what a **culo** Johnny was. No matter what happened, Johnny was always sure God was taking good care of them. Vince was no longer even sure there was a God. If there was one, then the finger rock looked more like God was giving them the finger than beckoning them on. If they did find something, and Vince was pretty sure they wouldn't, it would only be another deserted island like the one they'd already found.

For another two days they sailed on, nothing ahead of them, nothing on either side of them, nothing behind them but endless grey sea under grey sky. It was just like it had been when they'd started, except it was worse now. They'd been at sea for weeks. Oh, sure they'd found a strange land, but there was no one alive, so Vince was having doubts that Sam knew what he was talking about.

Sam had been so sure, so confident that people had survived Judgement Day that Vince hadn't questioned it. But when they'd found nothing, Sam had carried on being just as certain. Vince couldn't help wondering if Sam wasn't loco. Just his luck to put all his life's savings, not to mention his life itself into a damned-fool scheme led by an idiot. He should have known better than to trust anyone. He thought Sam was special. But Sam had turned out to be yet another disappointment. 'Why does this always happen to me?'

For the whole four days it took the Star of Galilee to chug laboriously across the ocean, Vince's mind went in circles over the same thoughts again and again. What bad luck he'd had all his life, what an idiot he'd been to trust Sam, what an idiot he'd been to open up to the explorers, what an idiot he was to have put all of his savings into this hopeless adventure and leave himself nothing to fall back on for the rest of his life. His life was ruined. He had no future, nothing to go back to. These idiots – all the explorers were loco for being taken in by Sam, and Sam was the biggest idiot of them all – had put everything they had into something that had sucked their futures down a black well. And none of them had the smarts to figure out what idiots they'd been.

He was angry, sometimes, when he wasn't too miserable to feel anything but fear of the future and sadness. When he was angry, he swayed between anger with himself, anger with Sam and all of the explorers, and anger with God. He'd trusted God, he'd believed God's promises, and now he was literally at sea.

At the same time as he was scornful of Johnny Balaam and Willie Jay Rimmon for their unwavering faith, he envied them. If only he could be sure like that. But how could he? They could only believe they way they did by ignoring everything they saw all around them. He wasn't that blind or gullible. If there was a God, he sure as hell didn't answer the prayers of Invincible-faith Thomason! In fact, Vince noted, resentfully, an awful lot of people were never answered. What about his family's desperate prayers when the GR over-ran their homeland? What about everyone else the GR had conquered, taken prisoner, or enslaved? God hadn't answered any of their prayers, either, had he?

Over the dreary time spent sailing to nowhere, with steadily increasing fear that they'd never see their homes again, the GR soldiers became more and more resentful and superstitious. Their mutterings and grumblings affected Vince, making him bluer than ever, as well as convincing him once and for all that there was no God.

He was lying on his bunk, brooding, when sounds of unusual activity caught his ear. There were boots pounding past the cabin door, and there was talking in a tone of enough intensity to penetrate his funk. He listened until he couldn't stand it anymore and got up to see what was going on. "What is it?" he yelled at the first man he saw.

"Birds."

"Birds? Birds! What the ..." He stomped up on deck in a rage, striding up and down the length and breadth of the ship until he found the explorers. "Why make all this fuss over a measly bird?"

"You never see land birds out over the ocean," Sam explained in his maddeningly patient way. "Birds that are not albatrosses mean land. The Weskies are figuring out where it is from here by watching the birds."

That was about the stupidest thing Vince had ever heard. As if you could figure out what direction to go by watching birds flying in circles! He stood back to watch the stupidity play itself out. Of course, Johnny and Willie Jay were praising God. Sam looked so pleased with himself Vince wanted to strangle him. Joe Mack and Chuck were congratulating

Sam as if he'd accomplished something. If Vince wasn't so terrified of the deep water, he would have thrown himself overboard right then. It was all so pointless and dumb.

They turned in the direction the Weskies chose. In a few hours men were jumping up and down sure that there was land on the horizon. Vince could see clouds along the horizon, but no land. He was surprised by how much it pleased him that Johnny said all he could see was clouds, too. At least he wasn't completely alone in everything.

It wasn't until they were quite a bit closer that both Vince and Johnny suddenly saw that it wasn't clouds at all. It was land. Not a small island, but a long expanse of land that went for hundreds of miles.

"Better," Sam grinned. "There's no column of smoke."

"There ain't no people, neither," Vince muttered.

Chuck looked at him with contempt. "Give it up, Vince."

Vince didn't bother answering. They'd find out soon enough. He was staring at the land slowly coming into focus, thinking how good real meat was going to taste, when someone yelled, "What's that?"

Everyone strained to see what he was talking about, saying there was nothing there. Then the light caught it as it moved and there was a chorus of, "Sail!!"

Vince went completely numb. He couldn't speak, he couldn't move, he couldn't think, he couldn't feel. All he could do was stare at the sail speeding towards them as if he was in a dream where he was stuck up to his knees in tar.

Soon they could see dozens of sails speeding to meet them on tiny little boats. Major Temperance gave the order to prepare to defend themselves. Sam laughed at him. "Oh, like they're coming to attack us in those silly little things! Don't you know a hero's welcome when you see one? They're beside themselves with relief that we've finally found them!"

Temperance shot Sam a look of pure loathing. "Hold your fire until we see their weapons."

But as the boats got close enough to see the people in them it was obvious Sam had been right again. The people in the boats, both men and women, were singing and chanting. Vince stared in numb disbelief. There really were people, lots of them, who had survived Judgement Day. The GR had that totally wrong. He could not snap himself out of the dream-like state. This could not be real. If this was real, how much else had the GR got wrong? Had Sam got it right after all?

The strangers had done more than just survive – they looked healthier than most of the public citizens of the Gethsemane Republic. Standing up in their boats, waving, singing, chanting, they all looked happy, strong, healthy. They weren't wearing shoes or boots, some of the men seemed to be wearing something like a towel wrapped around their hips. Big, strong, grown men wearing skirts with feathers in their hair?

"Depravity!" someone shouted.

That startled Vince back to his senses. Could it be God didn't save only the True Children of God? Vince started to laugh, struggling to find something to say.

Before he could, one of the men noticed that some of the women's breasts weren't covered and let out a whoop and a cheer. The cheer was answered joyfully by the people in the boats, and a game broke out of shouting back and forth, each side matching the shouts of the other.

What caught all the ones paying attention by surprise was the way the tiny vessels moved. They swooped in circles as they reached the ship, danced across its wake, and some circled around the entire ship, looping it as if it was standing still. Vince stared in amazement. The boats made hardly any engine noise, put out no smoke, were small, brightly painted, and shiny. As they arranged themselves alongside the Star of Galilee they adjusted their sails. It was a heart-stopping sight, to be escorted by dozens of boats. They formed an orderly flotilla, always shifting places so that all of them had a turn right beside the ship. The singing never seemed to stop.

"They got to have done this lots," Sam figured. "Ain't no way to get organised like that without lots of practice."

Vince was staring at something that was making him very uncomfortable. "Sam."

"What?"

"All them boats got eyes."

Everyone noticed it, then. It was the weirdest, spookiest thing Vince had ever seen. It creeped him right out to see the boats all looking back at him, as if they were watching him. "What did they have to do that for?" he asked the others.

"Witchcraft," Johnny suggested.

Vince pulled back from the rail. The nightmare was more real and more horrible than he could ever have imagined.

Looking down onto the boats everyone tried to figure out what they were made of. At first, they'd all assumed it was wood, but when they saw them up close it wasn't like wood or iron. Plus, they had tiny windmills spinning on every part that wouldn't be walked on or snag lines, and they all had pictures painted on the sides. Some of the pictures were clever, like a hawk done in such a way that it seemed to fly along the water, and dolphins that seemed to leap in and out of the waves with the movement of the vessel. The names were on both sides of the fronts as well as across the backs of the boats, though it took a while for anyone to realise that's what they were looking at because the words were so strange.

What sort of name for a boat was 'The Greedy Gull' or 'The Laughing Dolphin?' and what was 'Hoiho' or 'Te Mokihi' supposed to mean? Plus, under the name at the back there was another word that made no sense. 'Hauraki' 'Matapihi' 'Tauranga.' One thing they knew for sure, they weren't Christian words.

Their escort was guiding them towards the north. As they got closer the blur of land sorted itself out into small islands in front of a massive island. From far out it had become obvious that there were two big islands, and they were heading for the northern one. The southern one stretched away into the cloudy distance over the curve of the earth.

As they drew closer more and more boats joined them. There was something creepy about that, too. If some new kind of people arrived where Vince came from, he was more likely to hear about it afterwards. Everyone seemed to be really enjoying the welcome, but Vince was getting more and more uneasy. "How did they all know we were coming?"

Joe Mack stopped dead. "Good question," he said, making his way over to Sam.

Vince muttered to Willie Jay, "I don't like this at all. How do we know we're not being led over the Precipice?"

If he'd expected Willie Jay to get rattled, he was sadly disappointed. Willie Jay beamed at him like he didn't have a brain in his head. "Relax, Vince, God's got us in the palm of his hand."

"What if they're pagans?"

"That's why God led us here. So we could save them."

Vince felt disgusted. Willie Jay was scared of his own shadow most of the time, but now, when there was something he should be terrified of, the stupid ass was quite happy. "Retard," Vince hissed to himself. He felt a rush of jealousy that he couldn't have faith like that, swept away almost at once by scorn that anyone could put all his trust in something that didn't exist.

All at once it hit him, if God didn't exist, neither did heaven or hell. He went back to the rail to stare at the pagans in a new way. When he wasn't scared of them he noticed something about them he'd missed before. They looked freer and happier than people did at home. "What difference does it make if they worship something that doesn't exist?" he mumbled, watching the unflagging joyfulness below him. He caught his breath in shock as one of them, showing off by balancing on the outer edge of the deck fell off his boat as it bounced on the waves. Vince was sorry to see one of these laughing people drown. He was disgusted to see the islanders laughing at the poor soul in the water. To the amazement of everyone, the young guy popped up through the surface. He didn't just bob back up, he actually came up out of the water past his shoulders, shaking his hair out of his eyes and laughing. The boats coming up on him swerved around him, none of them stopping to try to rescue him.

"That's what happens when you don't follow the true God," Johnny commented. "You don't have proper human compassion. You can watch your buddy drown and laugh about it."

But the guy in the water wasn't trying to be rescued, he was swimming around, laughing and answering the other islanders who were calling to him. Finally, the boat he'd fallen out of made its way back around to him. Vince caught his breath in admiration to see how the islander got back on board. The boat hardly slowed down. As it went past him, he caught something on the other side of the boat, out of Vince's sight, and just seemed to vault out of the water up onto the deck, landing on his stomach with one leg along the deck, with two other people catching him. From there it was only a second or so before he was standing on the deck bowing to the GR who were cheering, and the islanders who were hooting.

Vince was stunned. "He didn't drown," he said, stating the obvious, but unable to believe it any other way.

"Looks like it's nothing to them to fall in the water," Chuck mused.

"How deep is it here?" Johnny wondered.

"Too deep for us," Vince answered, thinking, 'The devil looks after his own.'

They were close enough to see the white surf line around the islands, and to distinguish between rocks and trees. They couldn't see any cities, but piers and jetties poked out here and there. There were still more boats coming out to join them, and flocks of birds. Three massive canoes came towards them, powered by rows of men and women with white tipped black oars. The canoes were bigger than the boats. They had high carved panels in front, and poles at the back with streamers that floated in the wind right down to the water. Standing upright in front of each one was a big man, arms crossed, looking powerful.

"How do they balance?" Willie Jay wondered.

As the canoes drew closer, they could hear another chant keeping the paddlers in time. All of the people in the boats picked up the chant. It sounded to Vince like, "Oh! Oh! Oh ay ah. Oh! Oh! Oh ay ah." All of the little boats stopped whipping around and formed v's, dropping back from the ship. It was impressive to watch, like precision drills, only on water.

Major Temperance gave the order for all the Weskies to be locked in the brig, and the troops to stand at attention. Vince was surprised to see that he was recognising that the islanders were trying to be formal. He swelled with pride at the sight of the soldiers in formation, at attention. 'We're not perfect,' he thought, 'but we can still show these savages civilization.'

"What the hell do they think they're doing?" Chuck exclaimed.

Vince couldn't see what he was talking about for a moment, then realised that the three canoes were turning, one on either side of the ship, and one right in front of it. "We'll run the stupid ass over! The Star can't spin on a dime like those little toys of theirs!"

But to their very great astonishment, the canoes on either side of the ship kept pace with it, and one in front finished its turn and took the lead before the ship reached it.

"Holy Hannah, those guys can really row!" Willie Jay breathed, looking for all the world as if the savages were heroes.

Before Vince had a chance to straighten Willie Jay out, Sam said "Look at the size of that guy!"

Double checking the men standing up in the front of the canoes, Vince was dumbfounded to realise one of them was a brown woman. The biggest woman he had ever seen. She was taller than most men in the GR, with a bull neck, powerfully muscled arms, and a stony expression. He nudged Joe Mack. "There's one for Temperance," he murmured, then watched in satisfaction as Joe Mack nearly hurt himself trying not to laugh in a way that would have to be explained. He knew from the reactions of the others that Joe Mack was passing the quip along.

"At least she'd keep him in line," Sam murmured in Vince's ear.

Picturing that formidable woman ordering Temperance around gave Vince a problem of not being able to look at Temperance, chest puffed out, without snickering. Temperance was standing on a box to look taller than his men, his face florid from whiskey. Much as he hated to admit it, Temperance compared badly with the islanders when it came to stone faces. He looked like a purple bullfrog in a major's uniform.

Not wanting to be caught laughing at the major, Vince looked away. "That guy there," Willie Jay urged him.

He looked, started, and looked again. If he thought the woman was big . . . she was at least six foot two, possibly six-three. He, however, had to be more than six foot seven – and he was no skinny bean pole. Not an ounce of fat on him, but muscles where there didn't ought to be bulging muscles. The same bull neck, but a bare brown chest the width of two normal men's chests, arms about the size of Vince's chest, and a bush of black curly hair caught into a braid at the nape of his broad neck. The expression on his face was dignity itself, despite the fact that all he wore was a sash across his chest from one shoulder to the opposite hip, a short red skirt under a skirt that ended just above his knees and looked like it was made of long oval brown and black beads, a head-band and feathers sticking up at the back of his head. Same family, Vince guessed. You wouldn't get two like that. Some kind of freaks being paraded as, "Look how big we can grow them."

In the front canoe the man standing up was a really old guy. He still stood straight, and you could see he'd once been a powerful man, but now he was white haired, and his skin hung loosely. They all wore the same outfit, except for the woman's strapless top, but the old man had more feathers in his hair and a cape that was covered in feathers around his shoulders. It was then, noticing that he couldn't see the old man's shoulders, that Vince realised most of the islanders had tattoos on their shoulders. Everything seemed to be decorated: the boats, the canoes, the sails, the people themselves.

The guys in the canoes beside the ship were shouting something. "They want us to do something," Sam figured out, but no one could understand them

No one could make any sense of their gestures, either. Finally, one of the men in the woman's canoe threw a light line up to the ship.

"Do they want to come on board?" Temperance asked.

Sam tried to convey the question by gestures because the islanders seemed to have no more luck understanding the GR than the GR had understanding them. Apparently, they didn't want to come on board, they wanted the line attached between the ship and the canoe. Sam tried to indicate this, and got an enthusiastic acceptance.

"Oh, I get it," Temperance was pleased with himself. "They're plum tuckered out. They want us to tow them."

Sam didn't argue with the Major, but he mumbled to the explorers, "Not with this light rope they don't, and not from the front of the ship." But he tied the rope on to keep everyone happy and went over to the other side to see if they wanted the same thing. They did, tossing him a line that he caught after a few tries and tied in the same way.

Then the islanders did something no one expected – the canoes at the sides sped up, caught the one in front, handed the lines over, then dropped back to row alongside the ship. "They're making it look like they're towing us!" Temperance exclaimed in surprise and annoyance.

"Maybe we should slow down a bit," Sam suggested. "Ain't no way they can keep up this pace."

"Why the Sam Hill should we make it easy for them?" Temperance snarled.

"Hey," Sam raised his hands. "I don't care. Just if they're happy they might share more of their goodies with us."

"What makes you think those savages got anything to share?"

"Dunno, Major, but they did have a still on that island. Maybe they don't know what a man oughta wear, but they know how to brew beer. I would love me a big feed of steak right about now."

Temperance didn't reply, but the explorers noticed the ship slowing down a few minutes later.

Vince stood quietly, watching as the land grew closer and closer. The escort of small boats was still in v formations as precise as an army drill. He couldn't see how they kept discipline like that without any sergeants shouting orders. As they started to thread their way between small islands, all sorts of pleasure craft joined in, from canoes and rowboats to rafts and tiny little one-person sail boats. All slipped into the formations as if they'd had years of practice drills. Vince was impressed until he noticed something that disgusted him. All small children were on leashes like dogs. They wore bulky jackets with something that looked like a handle sticking up above their heads from the collar, and with straps that went down between their legs, and a ring on the back that clipped to a leash on a line that ran the length of the boats. No doubt about it, these savages needed civilizing.

"They're sure happy we got here to rescue them," Joe Mack was saying. "We'll be able to make back everything this trip cost us, plus some."

Vince instantly felt better. If these people would hand over cash or valuable goods for being rescued, his greatest fear would be taken care of.

Rounding the last corner was another surprise. There was still no sign of cities or farms or roads, but there was a large wharf, with a big ship that had obviously been anchored back from it to make room for them. On the wharf, and on the banks above it, were cheering crowds that picked up the chant from the canoes as they came into earshot. Threads of songs in women's voices floated across the water, to be drowned out by deep men's voices in throbbing chants.

The canoes peeled away to either side as the Star of Galilee approached the wharf, the leading canoe tossing the lines to the wharf, then turning aside out of the way. The ship slid gently alongside the wharf, bumping only once, and eager hands took mooring lines tossed to them, eagerly tying the ship up. It was the strangest, unreal feeling; to be tied up to a wharf in another nation on the other side of the world when he'd spent his whole life being taught that nothing existed.

The people from the canoes were on the wharf at the head of the crowd. Vince had no idea how they'd managed that. It seemed incredible that the old guy could have moved that fast. The singing had changed. None of the soldiers had moved a muscle because Temperance hadn't given the order. He seemed frozen. The old guy was calling out by himself, being answered by the men. They were stamping on the wharf, using it like a drum. The drumbeat was like a heartbeat. Vince could feel his heart synching up with it. Ba-dump, ba-dump, ba-dump, ba-dump.

The old guy leaped high in the air, his feet tucked right up to his butt, and landed, lightly as a cat, then danced, running zigzag across the wharf, approaching the ramp put down for them to get off the ship. The old guy had a wooden staff, as long as he was tall, that he swung around as he danced. Never in his life had Vince seen someone that old able to move like that. The skin under his arms waggled like wings, but his arms were still able to flip that staff around like a feather. The beads of his skirt clacked together as he danced. There was no music playing, just the deep voices of the men chorusing the chanting answers to the old leader's calls.

Then the old guy laid some leaves at the foot of the ramp and danced back from it. Vince stared at it. What the . . . ? He watched the old man. He was grimacing, dancing in the bouncing way he had. Really, the faces the island men were pulling were insane. Frightening, if Vince had to be honest. Rolling eyes, tongues poking out, eyes bugging out – normal, sober, sane men didn't act like that.

"I think that means something," Sam said, slowly, looking at the twig of leaves.

"So what?" Temperance didn't look the least bit happy.

"They seem to be waiting for us to do something."

"Why don't they just say so, then?" Temperance didn't move.

Sam watched the islanders. The old guy danced forward towards the leaves and back again.

"I think we're supposed to pick that up."

Temperance was emphatic. "I ain't taking part in no pagan rituals."

"I'll give it a shot and see what happens," Sam said. "What's the worst that can happen? These guys ain't armed."

With a jolt Vince realised not one islander that he'd seen so far had a sidearm. There weren't even gun-racks in the boats. That was not a bandolier across the big guy's chest; it was just a band, like a beauty pageant winner. Watching Sam walk down the ramp, Vince started to feel different about the whole thing. If he was the only guy here that was armed, he'd be more powerful than the President, he'd be like a conqueror. If he stayed here, he wouldn't have to worry about anything any more, ever again. To prevent others guessing he was planning something, Vince worked hard to keep a smile off his face.

Sam went slowly down the ramp. The islanders ramped up their chanting and actions as Sam got closer to the twig. Although they were unarmed, the rhythmic chanting and stamping was unnerving.

Temperance gave the 'at ease' order. Glancing at him, Vince noticed a calculating look in his eye. 'Two-faced bastard,' he thought. 'He thinks Sam's going to be killed.' It was as clear to Vince as the smell of the salt sea air: if the Special Ops guy was gone, Temperance would be free to do whatever he wanted to do and claim whatever he wanted to claim had happened on the voyage, including that anyone who looked like they might say something might not make it home. He made up his mind then and there that if he couldn't pull off his plan of being ruler of this place he'd go home and make sure the right people knew Temperance was a screw-up.

Sam hesitated, watched the dancers thoughtfully for a moment, then took the last few steps, keeping his eye on them, then bent and picked up the twig when he reached it. Immediately the chanting changed to a celebratory sound.

Vince breathed a sigh of relief. It surprised him to hear similar exhalations around him. He glanced at the other explorers. Chuck and Joe Mack both had grim sets to their jaws. Johnny and Willie Jay both had the vacant expressions of idiots who had faith God would take care of them no matter what. Vince clenched his teeth to stop himself yelling at them. Sam was the one who'd been right, not the GR and the GR religion. He felt one with Chuck and Joe Mack, superior to the other two. Between them they'd see to Major damned Temperance!

The old man stopped his chanting and dancing, and an old woman started a sing-song chant. Behind Sam the big woman from the canoes started the same kind of chant. It was almost like a chanted conversation, the voices rising and falling, now and then joining, but in counterpoint, not chorus. During the performance Sam stayed where he was, looking around as if he had no idea what to do.

When the women stopped there was a silence as if the islanders expected something. Sam looked around. The soldiers stayed where they were, glaring suspiciously, but the explorers ran down the plank to stand beside Sam. No matter what came next, they were going down together. Vince drew his sidearm, but Sam snapped at him, "Put that back unless we need it!"

Vince slipped it back into his holster, feeling embarrassed and resentful.

The big woman came up to them and said something in a soft, but deep and melodic voice. They all stared at her, bewildered that they couldn't understand a single word that she said. "Sorry, Ma'am, I didn't catch that," Sam told her courteously.

She blinked, took a step back, and spoke again, more slowly, but no more successfully.

"Sorry, Ma'am," Sam shook his head and raised his shoulders and hands in an 'I give up' gesture.

She turned towards the old guy and gabbled some pagan nonsense worse than when the Weskies talk to each other. Then she turned back to Sam, smiled at him, pointed to her imposing chest and said, "Wineera Rangituri."

They looked at each other. "What the hell does that mean?" Chuck snorted.

"Don't curse in front of a lady," Johnny scolded.

"Guys!" Sam pulled them in. "I got no clue what it means, but let's try telling her our names. If we start somewhere, maybe we can work from there." He turned back to her. "Sam," he said, pointing to himself.

She beamed at him, nodding, and reaching out to take his hand. "Wineera," she pointed to herself. "Sam," she pointed to him. Then she pointed to each of the others. They said their names as she came to each one, and she repeated them in the weirdest accent.

"That was her name," Joe Mack muttered. "What a weird name!"

Wineera indicated that she wanted them to go with her.

Sam nodded, telling the explorers, "Here we go, guys. It's all been for this moment."

"I still want to see her with Temperance," Chuck muttered.

Try as they might, they couldn't hold back the grins or even a bit of a snicker. The effect was electric. The moment they saw the explorers' lips twitch, the islanders surged forwards, hands outstretched, huge beaming smiles. The crowd started singing again, accompanying the people who were bearing the explorers off, giving the explorers flowers. That was embarrassing. Men in this place wore skirts and gave other men flowers? That's just not right! Vince had the uncomfortable feeling if they changed their minds about going with these sissies it wouldn't make a lick of difference. No one would understand them.

They were taken to what looked like a hunting camp, no roads, just paths under trees to wooden houses built in a circle, overgrown by the same kind of jungly vines, ferns, palms, and trees that they'd found on the volcanic island. In the centre of the circle of houses there were long tables of food and drink.

"Not a steak in sight, Sam," Joe Mack whined.

"No smell of it, either," Sam sighed.

"Bullshit! ¡**Chingadazos!**" Chuck snapped at both of them. "There ain't no way on God's green earth those guys got that big without no red meat!"

They had to give him that one.

Concerned about Chuck's tone, the islanders crowded over making worried sounds. Sam did his best to at convince them that there was no problem. Unfortunately, from then on the islanders looked at them warily.

"What's with these guys?" Chuck whispered. "You'd think I threatened their old aunt Fanny."

Various people were trying to talk to them, looking for words they had in common. Sam hissed, "Just cool it, okay?"

None of the others responded. Only Willie Jay said, "Okay."

Immediately one of the islanders got excited. "Okay!" he said with a huge smile. "Okay, okay," only he said it 'okeye.'

"Okay," the explorers nodded and smiled.

They were taken to the tables and told by gesture to help themselves to food. "Weird kind of welcoming feast," Vince grumbled. "At home someone coming from someplace new gets taken to see the President and waited on. They don't got to get their own food and eat outside."

"Go with it," Sam murmured. "Let's just see what happens."

They looked over the enormous spread. Not a piece of meat to be seen. 'All vegetables,' Vince thought at first. It took him a moment to notice the fish and egg dishes on different tables, then he got it. "They got vegetables and fruit here, eggs there, fish and crap there, and drinks on that one."

"Looks like this island is like Sunday Island: no animals," Joe Mack suggested.

They sighed and tried to find things to eat that they could recognise or at least figure they could swallow without disgracing themselves in front of their hosts.

"We can't understand a thing these guys say," Sam said as they sat down at one of the tables where their hosts indicated. "But we could read some of the writing at Sunday Island."

"Yeah," they nodded enthusiastically.

"Yeah," grinned the old guy, who was seated at the head of the table with Sam at his right hand. "Yeah, yes, okay."

They nodded and smiled, repeating after him, "Yeah, yes, okay."

They had each grabbed something to drink, copying the islanders, who had clipped their cups to their plates with a flexible clip for ease in carrying food and drink. The flatware could also be clipped to the plate with a differently shaped clip. "This is ingenious," Sam said, examining his. "What's it made of?"

"Blessed if I know," Chuck shrugged.

"My bet is this is how they always do things here," Sam mused, watching the islanders in orderly lines collecting their food in a steady low hum of chatter and laughter.

"Uncivilized!" Vince sniffed, thinking one of the first things that would change if he could take over was that he would be waited on like a President.

"It's kinda friendly," Willie Jay smiled in what Vince thought was one of the stupidest comments he'd ever heard, and considering how lame-brained Willie Jay could be, that was going some.

It disgusted him to no end that Johnny said, "You've got a point, there."

None of them had touched their food, waiting to bless it first. Vince was convinced the islanders were pagans and would never give thanks before eating, so it came as somewhat of a shock to him when the last explorer sat down and the old guy got to his feet and started a sing-song chant that had all of the islanders stop what they were doing, catch their children, and stand in silence except for answering. Their answers were not proper 'Amen,' but sounded a lot like the rowing chant, only instead of, 'Oh ay' they seemed to be saying, 'Ow ay.' Johnny bowed his head and quietly said a proper blessing.

'What the hell,' Vince thought. 'One imaginary god is the same as another,' and did his best to copy the "Ow ay," though he had no chance of saying whatever it was they said next. It was too long and impossible to twist a normal tongue around.

When the old guy quit, the islanders went back to getting their food, chasing after their kids, sitting down at the tables or plunking themselves down on the grass under the trees. Vince refrained from saying how uncivilized it was to sit on the ground, or even to have kids at a diplomatic meal, if that's what this was. It was a strain to keep from saying anything, but he managed it, if only because he knew Sam would be mad at him if he didn't.

Sam leaned forward and said quietly, "My guess is I'm sitting by the leader."

Vince took another look at the old guy. No way. He gave his head the slightest shake, mumbling, "How could a leader be that old?" He looked down the table, but that wasn't the leader down there, either. It had to be the old guy's wife, a tall skinny old broad with white hair in a long braid down her back. She was wearing a loose, long gown like a night dress. 'Shows you where we rate,' he thought. 'They can't even be bothered getting dressed and doing their hair to eat with us.'

Sam was trying to find words both he and the old guy understood, but wasn't having any luck past, "Yeah, yes, okay." Sam mimed writing on the table. The old guy said something to his wife, and she spoke to one of the islanders who vanished into one of the buildings and returned with a pad of paper and a pencil, which he gave to Sam.

As soon as Sam started writing words down, and he and the old guy read them to each other, Vince saw what the problem was: the islanders couldn't talk properly. No matter what word they said, they said it so wrong that you couldn't recognise it. The most irritating part of it all was that Willie Jay caught on faster than anyone else. He not only started repeating words back to the islanders close enough to their mangled way of saying things that they could understand him, but he started picking out what they were saying while it was still gabble to everyone else.

"Good, Willie Jay. Looks like you got a gift for this," Sam beamed.

Willie Jay blushed. "Gawsh, Sam. I ain't never been good at nothing before."

Vince thought he was going to puke. And not because of the weird food, either. Some of the food wasn't as bad as it looked. And some of it was worse than he could have believed.

Willie Jay had picked beer from the beverages offered. He now took a sip of it, in his full 'aw shucks' manner. He stopped, his eyes wide, and asked, "You guys try this?"

They shook their heads. Vince had stayed with water, hoping what they had here would be close to what they'd found on Sunday Island, too uneasy to try anything he didn't recognise. Joe Mack had picked what he'd thought was coffee, but it didn't taste like any coffee he'd ever drunk in his life. Chuck had gone with juice, which he claimed was excellent. Sam had picked a different coloured juice which he refused to comment on but was not drinking. Johnny had picked something hot from an urn like the 'coffee' and had no idea what it was but liked it.

"You gotta try this," Willie Jay insisted.

One after another they took sips. "Oh, I gotta get me some of that!" Sam exclaimed.

"Better not tell in-Temperance about this, Sam, he'll never want to go home," Joe Mack quipped.

Sam chuckled, then turned to Willie Jay. "Willie Jay, tell these guys that's the best beer we ever had, and we all want some."

Willie Jay gabbled to the old guy, who smiled vacantly and said something down the table to his wife. The old broad smiled and nodded and gabbled at Willie Jay. He turned to her and gabbled back. She started laughing, gabbled loudly enough that everyone at their table and the two tables near them heard what she said, laughed and some of them got up and went over to the drinks table, coming back with foaming mugs for all of the explorers.

They laughed and thanked the islanders, but Sam held up his beer mug saying, "Look at this, you guys."

The islanders enthusiastically held up their mugs, shouting something no one could understand, clinked mugs with each other and took hearty swigs. The explorers did the same. As soon as he could be heard, Sam told them, "I was trying to say look at the mugs. Have you ever seen glasswork like that in your lives?"

Vince took a closer look at his. It was beautiful. It had swirling colours in the glass, and it looked like bubbles rising up the sides. Every mug was different, and all of them would be worth a fortune at home, if you could even find anything like that anywhere. Vince tapped his with his spoon to see what kind of ring he'd get. The sound startled him so that he took a closer look.

"No metal," Sam pointed out.

Vince took a closer look at the flatware. Even the knife wasn't metal, yet it cut like it was very sharp.

"What's it made of?" Joe Mack asked.

Sam wrote the question on paper for the old guy.

"Ceramics," he wrote back. "The First Servant's partner is a glass master."

"What in Sam Hill does that mean?" Joe Mack exclaimed.

Sam pointed to the words 'First Servant,' and asked, "Who is this?"

The old guy gestured to the old broad down the end of the table and said something that sounded like, "Ollyreen eye-dole-ah."

"That's her name," Sam shook his head. "I remember they said that before, but who could guess that's somebody's name?"

"What do they mean, 'First Servant'?" Joe Mack wondered.

"It's probably the servant their President trusts the most or something like that," Sam guessed. "I wonder how we can get to see the President?"

"We're not doing real well so far," Vince groused. "They've stuck us out here with the servants."

Sam looked around. "Yeah. Olarine is the First Servant, which I guess is like the President's housekeeper, and I guess he's like the butler or something. He's too old to be the Chief of Staff or Vice-President. I can't get his name."

Chuck shook his head. "No chance. I never heard such a long name."

Vince demanded of Sam, "Are we just going sit here and take it?"

"Yeah, Vince, cool it. They're being nice and friendly now. Let's not piss them off. We're way out numbered."

Vince patted his holster. "Betsy here says we ain't as out numbered as we look."

Olarine asked what it was that Vince had on his belt. She pronounced his name, 'Veence.' She spoke to Willie Jay as well as writing it down.

Seeing his chance to impress the islanders and get them to either fear or respect him, he didn't care which, Vince stood up and walked over to Olarine, taking his side-arm out of its holster so that she could see it and touch it. The islanders stared at it in such a way that Vince knew for sure they'd never seen a gun before. Drunk with the idea that all he had to do was stay behind when the ship left and he'd be like a god to these ignorant savages, Vince showed off how he could handle his gun, take it apart, load and unload it, twirl it, whip it out almost faster than you could see, and toss it from hand to hand. He was too wrapped up in his vision to be able to hear Sam's warnings to take it easy. He beckoned the islanders to come and see what else he could do with it. He pointed to a bird sitting on a branch, singing, showed his gun in its holster, showed his hands palm up, empty, then in a fraction of a second had whipped the gun out and shot the twig out from under the bird.

He stood there, grinning, proud of himself, for only a few seconds. The outcry was utterly bewildering. They weren't impressed, or scared, or anything he could have expected or understood. Instead, they were outraged. They raced to the tree, the happy music stopped, and a chant started, and before he could catch his breath two large men were either side of him.

He woke up in his bunk with all the explorers furious with him. "What the hell?" was all he could say.

"What the hell did you do that for?" Joe Mack demanded.

"Do what?" Everything was foggy to him. He had a metallic taste in his mouth and a raging thirst.

"Fire your weapon."

Vince blinked, then got a vague memory of shooting a twig out from under a bird without hitting the bird. "I never hit the bird. I saw it fly away. You try to hit a twig and not the bird on it." He straightened his shoulders, proud of his marksmanship.

Even Willie Jay shook his head, which deflated Vince's pride. "You discharged a firearm on private property without permission of the hosts," Willie Jay said, sadly.

Chuck made it clearer with an angry snort. "We were guests. We're representing the Gethsemane Republic to another nation. We came here to find things out, to explore, not to go to war."

Vince got angry with them. They were being ridiculous. "Oh, **chingadazos**! Nobody went to war! The sissies here wanted to know what a gun was. I showed them. I never even shot the God-damned bird!"

Johnny spoke up. "Blasphemy's never necessary, Vince. Even if they did freak out more than anyone could have figured they would, you still just about blew the whole deal. Sam told you not to, and you wouldn't stop."

It just wasn't fair. No matter what, they always blamed him. "I never heard Sam tell me not to. How did I get here? I don't remember leaving."

"We never saw you leave," Joe Mack told him. "When we got back here you were on the bunk out cold. The guys said two big guys carried you to the ship and handed you over."

That gave Vince the shakes. He had a blurry image of two big guys either side of him, but he didn't remember anything after that. They didn't touch him, but he ended up back here. All he really remembered was the out-cry. All of the islanders rushing to the tree he'd shot.

"I got to have something to drink. My mouth feels like I sucked a gun-barrel," he said, getting up and wobbling slightly.

The others were still glaring at him. "Sam's trying to calm Temperance down," Chuck told him.

Vince stopped and looked at them all. That seemed significant, somehow, though he couldn't see what it had to do with him.

Joe Mack explained, "They won't let us set foot on their land if we're packing."

"What?!" Vince couldn't get his head around it.

"Major Temperance is so mad that his guys can't carry weapons that he wants to go back home right now," Chuck glared at Vince.

"Well, shoot, that's just plumb crazy. Ain't no one going to go with nothing! You can't blame me for that!"

"We were doing okay. We were going to get food and water and fuel. They never even knew we had weapons until you had to go and show off!"

Knowing that showing off was exactly what he was doing, Vince stalled. He concentrated on getting something to drink. There was nothing in the cabin, so he started for the door.

"Where are you going?" Joe Mack stood in his way.

"I got to get something to drink. My tongue is sticking to the roof of my mouth."

"It's not a good idea for you to be seen right now. All the guys are blaming you that they don't get no shore leave."

Vince stared. "You can't be serious!"

"Listen, *Naco*, you screwed up big time. And screwed all of us. **De la fregada.**"

Vince went back to the bunk and sat back down, feeling sorry for himself and angry with the islanders. He tried to lick his lips and swallow, but he couldn't get rid of the metalic taste in his mouth.

"I'll see if I can get you something," Willie Jay told him, leaving the room.

"Thanks," Vince called after him.

"Not that you deserve it," Chuck frowned at him.

"Shit!" Vince was getting fed up with all of it. "They wanted to know what the gun was, so I showed them. What was I supposed to do as a good guest? Tell them no? How was I supposed to know they'd freak right the hell out? Why didn't they do what any normal man would do and want one for themselves? Then we could have made some money to live on when we get home."

There was silence then.

Johnny was the first one to speak. "It was like you shot their god."

"What?" Vince stared at him. "I never shot the damned bird. It flew away."

"No. The tree."

"The tree?!" They all stared at him.

Joe Mack yelped, "You think these weirdos worship that tree?"

"Maybe not that one. Just think about what they did. They ran to the tree, and got all upset that it was damaged, and then they were asking God for forgiveness."

"No way!" Vince couldn't buy that.

Johnny looked at Joe Mack and Chuck. "They rushed the tree, right?"

"Yeah. I saw some of them hugging it and stroking it and talking to it."

"You're kidding!" Vince gaped.

"You never saw that?" Chuck peered closely, as if he didn't believe Vince.

"No. I don't remember nothing between everyone jumping up from their seats and running around yelling and waking up here. Nothing. There were two big guys, but they never touched me."

Willie Jay came back with a beer for Vince who was very thankful. "Oh, man, my mouth is so dry, and I got the worst taste. What did we eat, anyway?" He downed the beer, thankful that it scoured out the metallic taste.

"Weird." Chuck commented. "Two big guys brought him back to the ship."

"So what?" Joe Mack didn't make anything out of that. "All we had to eat was the same shit we had on Sunday Island, only no birds. These islands are the same. No animals."

Chuck objected. "You can't have a place this big with no critters."

"You see or hear a dog? No meat to eat, no pets. I wouldn't have thought of it either if we hadn't just been to an island with nothing but birds and fish to eat."

"How can those guys be so big with no meat? It ain't possible," Chuck shook his head.

Johnny turned to Willie Jay. "Could you make out what they were saying? Did they beg God for forgiveness?"

Willie Jay stared for a bit, then started to stutter, "Th – th – th . . ."

Vince was sick of Willie Jay stuttering and stammering every time everyone was looking at him. He was a nice enough guy, but pathetic.

Finally, Willie Jay managed to spit out, "There were lots of words that didn't make no sense, but if I think about they were sorry to God, then I can make sense of some things that I couldn't work out before. They were sorry, maybe, that they didn't have permission to take wood off the tree."

Joe Mack shot Johnny a disgusted look. "So, they didn't worship the tree."

Willie Jay stuttered again for a bit.

Not having the patience to wait until Willie Jay had sorted himself out, Vince interrupted, "It makes no sense that they asked God's permission to cut wood. They had wood everywhere."

Sam burst back into the cabin in a bad mood. "I can't get anywhere with Major Temperance," He said loudly, then mouthed at them silently, "The damned fool."

"We're going straight home without fresh supplies?" Vince asked.

"Not quite. He wants to go to another island where he figures they won't have heard of us and start over."

"That's not a bad idea," Joe Mack put his head on one side, looking Sam in the eye.

"I'm not so sure. How did so many of them come to meet us? How did they know we were coming?"

The explorers all glanced at one another. It was Joe Mack who asked Sam, "What are you getting at?"

"These guys have got to have some way of watching what's happening over the horizon, and of spreading the news. The first sail we saw didn't turn around to go and get the others; they were already with him. The same with those canoes; they were on their way to meet us before anyone went on ahead to tell them we were there."

Chuck shrugged. "We were close by then. They could have seen us coming."

Sam gave Chuck a look that Vince was very glad was not aimed at him. "Not and get all those guys in them and organized. Not enough time. And they had that ship moved back out of our way before we came around the corner. And someone had time to put on a feast for us that would have taken the best part of a week to get together."

Vince knew what Sam was getting at, but it was too fantastic to take seriously. "Don't worry, Sam, if we leave right now there's no way the other islands will hear about us before we get there. And what if they do? It's not like these guys can control all the islands around here. There are dozens of them, miles apart."

Sam gave a half-smile that made Vince doubt himself almost before he'd stopped talking. "On second thought, I'd kind of like to go to another island just to see what happens when we get there."

CHAPTER ELEVEN

Calline

Three hundred and fifty kilometres southwest of Ahnya's town, Wairoa, Calline Digan, a thin, timid, little blonde med school student walked around the cases in the student cafeteria, putting the dishes that appealed to her on her tray. Part of her mind was on what she was doing, part of it was on the news. Her friends were all around her, picking out their food, greeting one another. "Hey, Kiri! Did you go?"

Kiritoe Amaru, a larger-than-life brown skinned youth with unruly black bushy hair boomed back in his deep voice, "Oh, yeah, eh! I wouldn't have missed that for the world! It's history, man! It's the biggest event in all time since the Freeze."

Calline was shyer than the others. She looked up as each one came in, but she hadn't said a word.

"Lina?" Kiritoe prompted her. "Did you go?"

"No." The idea of travelling all day just to look at an iron ship, then rushing back again, was more than her reticent nature could bear to face.

"How could you bear to miss it?"

"I watched the news on the wallie."

"Oh, like that's the same!" they were laughing at her, she knew, but it was easier to take that than to take speeding off and speeding back and all those crowds.

A political science student, Talford, pressed Kiri eagerly. "Did you see one of them?"

"Yeah - nah. I saw the ship, but I couldn't see them."

"I thought you'd be able to see over the crowds."

"Couldn't get a good spot."

Calline had everything on her tray that she wanted for lunch. She had her blond hair in a plait over her shoulder with her beads looped around the end for easy access. She went to the cashier, took off enough beads to pay for her lunch, put the rest and the change back on the thread and tied it back around her plait again, while looking around for a table big enough that they could all crowd around it.

A girl with bright red hair beckoned to her. "Lina! Over here!"

"Oh, Tui, thanks." Gratefully Calline carried her tray to the table Tui had saved for them.

"I think we can all fit around this one," Tui beamed triumphantly. By that she meant they could pack more than ten around a table meant for four.

"Did you go?" Kiri asked Tui, joining them as Calline sat down.

"Oh, nah – yeah, eh? Everyone in psych went. We're getting credit for our observations. It's considered field work."

"Lucky duck!" Talford exclaimed, arriving behind Kiri. "It should have been for Poli-sci. I'm going to bring that up in the next lecture."

"Not that it had much to do with politics," said an awkward looking boy with hair over his forehead and powerful glasses.

"Come on, Brain, use some of that famous IQ," Kiri scolded. "What's more political than being contacted by another nation?"

Fedrack blinked at him, owlishly, flicked the hair out of his eyes, and complained, "You're always trying to make everything political. I saw an ugly, stinking iron ship and some weird looking men, then they left. What's political about that?"

"Well, they didn't go far, if they thought that was leaving!" Tui exclaimed. "They went to Motu Aotea. That's what – a hundred klicks away from Tāmaki-makaurau? Not my idea of leaving."

Jo, a lithe young woman with light brown hair, attached at the hip to Talford, laughed. "Did you hear that they thought no one on another island would know they'd been forbidden to bring their weapons ashore? How stupid can you get? Why wouldn't they know?"

Tui offered, "It could only mean that no one would have known where they're from."

Everyone ate silently for a bit.

Calline had been horrified and frightened by the news that the strangers had injured a tree for no reason and had been incredulous at the idea that they were not to have weapons with them at all times. In a voice made soft by emotion, she asked Tui, "Does your psych training tell you why these people want to have something with them at all times that's only to cause damage?"

Tui shook her head. "I'm planning to ask about that among other things when classes resume."

"You're not going to watch them and get credit for a trip to Motu Aotea or Te Waipounamu?" Talford teased.

"You're just jealous because we got credits and you didn't," Tui teased back.

"Too right!" Talford exclaimed around a mouthful.

Calline admired the way Tui met everything head on. Everything about Tui was sparkling, from her cheery mop of hair with her beads scattered through it like haphazardly tossed baubles, her clear alabaster skin, her shining brown eyes, her chirpy voice, the bright colours of her clothes, to the radiance of her smile and the infectiousness of her laugh. The glowing red hair was an indication of the personality, Calline thought, just as her own mousy non-descript not-quite-blond, not-quite-brown was an indication of how boring she was. She wished she could be more like Tui. It was no surprise that Tui always had male companionship. It lightened your day to be with her.

They squeezed up to make room for another couple. The young man, Sonny, was a med student with Calline. His girlfriend, Fern, sat on his lap to be able to reach the table.

Calline smiled at both of them. Sonny had been her boyfriend a year ago, and she still had good feelings for him, even if she didn't want to be with him anymore. She was not really paying attention to them, what she still couldn't understand was why Kiri seemed immune to Tui. All the other boys were besotted with her. She bet Sonny would drop Fern like a hot rock if Tui gave him any encouragement.

"They're going to get a shock," Kiri was saying, "If they think no one on Te Waipounamu will know what they did in Tāmaki-makaurau."

Sonny chuckled, "You don't think they'll catch a clue when they're met by the Third Servant?"

Everyone but Fedrack and Calline laughed. Fedrack usually missed subtleties, and Calline doubted the premise. "That won't surprise the strangers, will it? They must expect that a senior government official would be there to welcome them to his island. I expect they'll be pleased to see Judge Tomptell."

Sonny shook his head. "Lina, Lina, you're missing the point. Those blokes tried to go to Motu Aotea where they thought no one would know they carried weapons with them all the time. When that didn't work, they moved on again. It's obvious they're trying it again."

Lina had no trouble arguing with him. She didn't feel shy with him, after he'd been her first boyfriend when they'd both arrived at the Turitea campus, both overwhelmed by their first foray away from home. "It's not obvious to everyone. They tried it; it didn't work, so now they're going where they can get coal. They use coal as fuel to drive the engines of their ship, and they need to refuel to go home. Te Waipounamu is the best place to get coal, that's why they're going there."

Kiri's deep voice prevented a squabble from breaking out. "You could be right, Lina. Only time will tell."

Jo snickered. "Did you see on the wallie where they nearly came unglued when they were invited into the tub by the Representative of Motu Aotea?"

"Yeah, I saw that," a number of them nodded at nearly the same time.

Talford added, "What was it that upset them like that?"

Lina supplied, "The news said in their society people don't appear in public without clothes."

They stared at her. "That can't be right," Tui objected. "Everyone's got a body. How could that possibly be upsetting?"

Talford shrugged. "Something else to ask your psych prof when you see him."

Calline watched them all in a detached way as they argued about the strangeness of the aliens. Despite being with Fern, Sonny was all eyes for Tui, just like Talford. Fedrack didn't seem to notice her, but then Fedrack didn't seem to notice much but mathematics. A good person, probably the truest friend you could ever have, but weird somehow.

Calline remembered how pleased her parents had been when she'd taken Sonny home with her for them to meet him. They'd rushed off in directions Calline and Sonny hadn't even thought of, planning that when they'd both finished med school they could go into practice together. It had been embarrassing. She'd even taken Tui with her so that they'd realise she and Sonny weren't serious. Tui had been with Talford back then. Her mother had not been impressed by Tui, saying she was 'a bit much,' though her father had called Tui, 'bewitching.'

She and Sonny had broken up that weekend. Not because of her parents, but because Sonny had fallen for Tui. They'd been getting ready to go back to school after the long weekend spent in Taupo with Calline's parents. Calline was oblivious to the fact that Sonny had fallen for Tui until Tui had looked at her with those wide, flashing brown eyes with a peculiar expression. All at once it was clear to Calline that Sonny was dancing attendance on Tui and Tui felt guilty about it. All Calline had felt as she realised it was relief. She raised her hands, palm up, in a 'so what?' gesture and turned away. From that moment until the next one swept her off her feet, Tui and Sonny were a couple.

Fond as she had been of Sonny, Calline had found the demands of the relationship distracted her from her studies. Strong emotions made her uncomfortable, and she really wanted to do well in her studies. She had liked knowing she was capable of being part of a couple, and had found Sonny an exciting lover, but had intended the relationship to be more along the lines of friendship and companionship than planning a life together, and was quite happy to have the tricky business of getting out of something she didn't know how to control taken care of without needing to say anything that might hurt Sonny's feelings. She liked him, she didn't want to hurt him, but she didn't want it to get so intense.

Talford, who'd been devastaed to lose Tui, had gravitated to Calline, assuming she was heartbroken and promising to comfort her. In fact, he'd wept on her shoulder. Somehow, she wasn't quite sure how, she and Talford became a couple until he met Jo. Then he was off in a flurry of apologies.

Calline wasn't sorry about any of it. Talford had been comfortable and comforting in bed, but they never had been truly involved with each other. She was relieved when it was over and was quite happy to stay on her own from then on. Relationships with men were intimidating to her. Besides, she was happier observing. She didn't hang around with many med students. Their wildness made her uncomfortable. She preferred this group of all different disciplines.

So, she was content with the way things were, and Tui – she looked at her – Tui was moving the foundations of the planet to get Kiri's attention. Every other man fell at Tui's feet. Why didn't he? Calline felt sorry for Tui, loving someone who didn't notice her. She'd never experienced unrequited love herself, but she knew it had to be painful.

Calline watched Kiri to see if she could see something that she might use to give Tui some advice with him. He seemed like a nice enough bloke, but she didn't really see the attraction. He was smart, but big and sort of clumsy. She didn't think he and Tui would be well suited, but she was very fond of Tui, and didn't want to see her hurt.

The sense that if you put yourself out there like Tui did you ran the risk of being left hanging made Calline suddenly withdraw internally. Head down, she glanced around the table. And caught Fedrack staring at her in open adoration.

Oh, no! Not Fedrack! I mean, he's nice and everything, but no! Wrong! Wrong! What could she do?

In abrupt and complete sympathy with Kiri she looked at him to see how he was handling Tui's advances. Mostly he just seemed oblivious to them. Okay, that's what she would do, then. Pay no attention. She tuned back in to the conversation.

"Did they say what it is?" Kiri was asking.

Not wanting anyone to see that she'd lost the thread of the conversation, Calline didn't ask what they were talking about, she waited, hoping it would become clear.

Sonny said, "It seems to be a new kind of virus. The symptoms are like a cold in most people, and flu-like in others."

"Probably a mutation," she put in. "Cold and flu viruses are constantly mutating."

They nodded. Sonny told her everyone knew that.

Kiri dismissed the topic by saying, "What's the big deal about people catching cold? We've got more important things we should be thinking about."

"Yeah, like classes are resuming this afternoon, and now we have to make up for getting a day off to go and see the alien ship," Talford sighed.

"No, I had in mind something that affects our futures, and the future of all Aotearoa."

"What are you going on about?" Jo put her knife and fork on her empty plate and picked up her juice to sip it.

"Have you thought about sitting for your Citizenship Tests?"

There were immediate howls of protest.

"What do you want to go and bring that up for?" Fedrack complained.

"We've got time yet. We don't have to start going to meetings yet," Jo put her glass back down.

"Oh, come on let's not go and talk politics again!" Sonny protested.

"What do you think, Lina?" Tui asked.

"I've started studying for it," she admitted quietly.

The herd howled again.

"What do you want to go and do that for?" Talford looked quite disgusted with her.

"That's torn it!" Fern glared at Calline.

"I'm sick to death of politics! It's all we ever talk about these days! What about the boat races?" Sonny got up from the table.

Calline felt her cheeks blushing bright red and lowered her head.

"How are you doing so far?" Kiritoe murmured to her but was drowned out by an interruption from another table.

"Forget sports! You wanker, this is the Big Fish!"

"Even if it's the fish of Maui himself, we can't do anything about it. They're already here. They've found us, our isolation is over whether we like it or not, so we can just stop squawking about it all the time!" Talford turned to try to see who he was arguing with, and half-stood in his seat to peer over the heads around him.

Before an argument could change the subject, Kiritoe continued, his deep voice drowning the others out. "Well, that's why I was thinking about sitting for my Citizenship, so that I <u>can</u> take part."

There was a mumbling sort of quiet punctuated with the sounds of eating.

Calline had seen many times that everyone tended to give way to Kiritoe because he was so big. With his bull neck that was almost no neck, broad shoulders, powerful bulging brown muscles, and commanding height, everyone tended to dismiss him as brawn. They did as he said because he was huge and intimidating, but they didn't really listen to him. Even his friends expected he'd be a sportsman while he was in school, then a fisherman like his Dad, Hatoe. But Kiritoe wasn't in tertiary school to put off the day he had to start work; he was there because he had a passion for history and had begged his father to let him study. He was majoring in history at the University, with a minor in marine biology to salute his Dad, and a love of music. If he wasn't going to teach history when he finished his degree, then he'd be more likely to be a musician like his mother, Anakiri, and his brother, Anatoe, than he was to be a fisherman. And not just in honour of his mother's memory, either. His love of music was second only to his fascination with history.

To break the silence Fedrack said, "But look, we're still in school. There's no pressure on us to join a Hundred before we graduate."

Kiritoe shrugged. He pushed the salad around his plate with his fork. "The way I look at it is, this is going to affect my life, my future, any kids I have. I want a say in it."

"He's right, you know," Tui muttered, with an edge of surprise in her voice.

Kiritoe took heart. "Well, it's that the Public Servants can't make this decision for us. There's nothing in the Protocol to cover it, so the People have to decide what we want to do. I want to be a voter so that I can be one of the ones making that decision."

"You're behind-hand. It's already happened. Trying to decide now whether or not we want to have anything to do with these aliens is like securing the mooring after the boat has sunk," Sonny declared, still on his feet, but still beside their table.

"I don't see why there isn't anything in the Protocol to cover it," Fedrack grumbled.

"Good one, Brain." Talford nodded at Fedrack, then turned to the others to explain his point. "Everyone's always talked about, "Someone's going to find us one day." If they knew it was going to happen, why didn't they prepare for it?"

"Yeah, you'd think since they knew this was going to happen, they'd have been ready for it, eh? Then we wouldn't be stuck like this." Tui sounded sullen, her full lips pushing out in a pout. When Kiritoe looked at her she tossed her hair over her shoulder with a flick of her head that exposed the curve of her white neck.

Jo gave Tui a fierce glance. She sounded so bitter she was almost spitting. "We've heard our whole lives how wonderful the Troggies were. How could they be that great and miss something so important?"

Kiritoe spoke as if he'd given this some serious thought. "I think what it was, was that even though everybody knew someone would contact us eventually, the ancestors couldn't predict what form the contact would take, so they couldn't make any rules about it for us. We're the ones who're here; we know what our situation is, so we have to come up with our own answers, just like they had to come up with their answers when the Dark Days hit them, and then the Freeze."

"What do you think we should do?" Fedrack asked.

"You should do what's right for you to do. Don't copy me."

"I want to take part, too," Calline ventured. It annoyed her that her voice barely came out above a whisper. Embarrassed, she kept her head down. "That's why I've been studying for the test. But I don't want to join a different Hundred from my parents. If I go to meetings here, won't I have to join a Hundred here?"

"While you're here you will." Kiritoe sounded sure of that. "You can't go all the way up to Taupo every time there's a meeting. Especially while this is going on and all sorts of special meetings are being called. When we graduate, we'll all be looking for space in Hundreds near where we live."

"Is it hard?" Fedrack wanted to know.

"What?"

"The citizenship test."

Kiritoe grinned. "Depends if you paid any attention in the right classes in secondary school."

"It's all very well for you, you love history," Fedrack grumbled.

Kiritoe shrugged. "You're taking maths, and that's one that leaves me cold. I'll help you with history, if you'll help me with maths."

"Done," Fedrack held out his hand across the table to Kiritoe. "What else do we need?" he asked Calline as he shook hands with Kiritoe, his skinny pale hand swallowed up by Kiri's broad brown one.

She ticked them off on her fingers. "History, geography, economics, critical thinking, and societal studies."

There was a collective groan around the table. "It's a wonder anyone ever gets to vote at all," Fedrack grumbled.

"Well, I'm not doing it, for one," Talford declared.

"Oh, come on, Tally, old son," Sonny teased him. "It doesn't mean you can't watch the races, you know."

"Sonny! What a terrible thing to say!"

Tui sounded outraged, but Kiri just looked sad when he asked, "How can you joke about something like that when those seaweed farmers haven't been found yet!"

Calline reminded Sonny, "His Dad is a seaweed farmer."

Sonny went beet red. "Oh, hey, I'm sorry, mate, I forgot. Did you know those blokes?"

Kiri shook his head. "Anyone heard the news? Anything on them yet?"

Jo licked her lips, nervously. "They've found some pieces of wreckage. They're finding out if it came from the Rangatira."

"Like it came from anything else," Talford muttered.

"What a way to make a living!" Tui exclaimed. "You're not going to work with your Dad after you graduate, are you, Kiri?"

He shook his head again. "No, I'm useless on a boat. No instinct for it. No love of it."

Fern asked Sonny, "You're taking geology, aren't you?"

"Yep."

"Can you tell us why Raukawa Moana is so treacherous?"

"No. I don't know. We haven't covered that. We're dealing with mineral deposits."

Kiri spread his hands wide on the tabletop. "It has to do with the direction of the currents on the west coast and the shape of the strait. The currents flow north, the strait slopes south-east. That makes turbulence as the water changes direction. Then, before it calms down it runs into the water flowing in the opposite direction from the east coast. On top of that there are faults that make the seafloor very uneven there, adding to the turbulence. And then, as if that wasn't enough, there are hot spots. When the heat comes up it also makes currents, which gives us the 'washing machine' effect. Add a storm to that, and you'd be nuts to take a boat out in it and expect to get back in one piece."

Sonny gaped at him. "Great leaping sharks! No wonder it's illegal to operate a ferry service straight across!"

Tui's eyelashes batted at Kiritoe. "You know so much about so many things," she murmured.

Kiri shrugged. "I grew up on the sea. Boaties know the sea."

Fedrack grumbled, "Well, I wish these blighters from the Gethsemane Republic had never come here."

"So do we all, but they did come, so that's what we've got to deal with."

"You lot just go right ahead and deal with it then," Talford pushed his chair back. "I'm off to the library. Got a test." He made his way through the crowd to the door with Jo in tow. Sonny and Fern followed in their wake.

"That doesn't solve anything," Kiritoe said quietly. "I don't like it either but pretending it hasn't happened can't stop it from happening."

"What's _really_ happening, after all?" Tui wriggled her way into the space Talford had left, her slim hips sliding around chairs and people with hardly a ripple. Her full name was Tuitaerua, but everyone knew her as Tui.

"Haven't you heard the latest?" Fedrack was surprised.

"Yeah Brain, but you know how it is when everybody's talking about something – it shifts a bit every time it's told."

"Too true," Kiritoe nodded. "This much I know. A ship sailed into Hauraki. It wasn't under sail power; it was driven by huge engines. There were only men on it. They were all wearing weird clothes. They said they came from the Gethsemane Republic. They think they have things we want and need and say that we can trade with them. They say they'll bring civilization back to us and re-establish communications with the outside world."

"What makes me so mad," Tui interrupted, "Is that sounds like we aren't civilized. They wanted to talk to our 'president,' and when they found out we didn't know what they meant, they acted like we need them to govern us."

Kiritoe shook his head. "Let's not get carried away, we weren't there, we don't know if that's what happened for sure."

"It's pretty sure, eh? Everyone's saying it."

"Just the same," Kiritoe was firm. "I want to stick to things I know for certain. The First Servant said she'd have to ask her People what we wanted to do. They told her to hurry up about it, because they don't have long."

That made Calline uneasy. She spoke softly. "I heard that they said they could wait a week for our answer, but, you know, when you put it that way, I get a creepy feeling it doesn't matter what we want, they're going to do what they want."

"Oh, come on!" Tui was impatient. "They're civilized, they have democracy, they know that the majority vote is the answer. If we tell them the majority isn't ready for contact yet, they'll go back home and not contact us again. Don't you even know the basics of how voting works?"

Calline felt foolish. She lowered her head to hide the flush she could feel sweeping over her cheeks.

Kiritoe frowned. "Enough, Tui."

Not wanting the others to think badly of her, Calline tried to explain, "I just have a feeling," but her throat was tight with embarrassment, so her voice was hardly above a whisper.

"I have a bad feeling about this, too," Kiritoe nodded. "The more I hear about them, the more I don't like their attitude. They aren't any better than us, maybe not as good in some ways. They're boasting about the way they conquered the weaker states around them, as if violence is something to be proud of."

"You know this for sure? You heard them say it?" Fedrack challenged him.

"No," Kiritoe admitted. "I didn't hear it straight from them. But people in Tāmaki-makaurau and on Motu Aotea heard them talk. They don't even talk properly, you know, you can't understand them until you learn how, and they won't learn how to talk our way, because they say <u>we</u> aren't speaking properly."

"Lingual shifts," Tui said.

"Pardon?"

"In etymology . . ."

"What's that?"

"The history of language."

"What about it?"

Tui said patiently, "Before the Dark Days the most widely spoken language in the world was called English. Where they came from always did have a different form of English from us, because when people are separated the language they speak shifts over time. Now that we've been cut off completely for more than ten generations, our language will have shifted in a different way from the way their language shifted."

"That doesn't make any sense. You should stick to psych. We talk exactly the same way our parents did, and their parents did."

"Drop it, Brain, that's not the point."

"What is the point?"

"The point is their attitude. They act as if we need their help and they're doing us a favour by coming here. They said they came to restore contact, but they're acting as if we're children who need help and they're the grown-ups, when actually they're more like children who need to spend some time in behaviour modification."

"Grown men acting like that?" Calline's head came right up, and she looked Kiritoe straight in the eye. "Are you talking about them injuring the tree for fun, and refusing to go anywhere without weapons?"

"Yes, that, too. Should we trade with these people or not?"

"What do they have that we want?" Tui leaned forward, her brown eyes intent on Kiritoe.

"What do we have that they want in return?" Kiritoe answered.

"More to the point, what do they have that we don't want? The only reason we shouldn't trade with them is if that will bring us things we don't want." Fedrack declared.

"Very good, Brain. That's it, exactly. We don't want violence back. We don't want to change our way of life."

"What do you mean, 'change our way of life?' This is the way we live. How could we change that? Why would we? You go too far with things sometimes, Kiri. Ever since your Mum died you've been seeing doom and gloom in everything that happens. They want to trade with us. What's the difference between that and trading with Te Waipounamu?"

"Oh, subtle, Brain! Very sensitive!" Tui reared back from the table. There was a collective groan from everyone within earshot. Calline reached out a tentative hand to Kiritoe, but he stood up and marched with quiet dignity out of the cafeteria. The group cleared the table, stacked the dishes and trays, put the food scraps in the re-cycle bin, then trailed behind him, Fedrack blustered the whole time, trying to explain what he'd meant, beet red with embarrassment and getting no sympathy from his friends.

CHAPTER TWELVE

Willie Jay

Willie Jay had been wrong about pretty near everything his whole life. His Daddy was ashamed of him. Sometimes Daddy got so frustrated he yelled, "You can not be the fruit of my loins! I'm gonna give your Mama such a smack!"

Even as a grown man Willie Jay didn't catch what his Dad meant, or that he wasn't serious, and unfailingly begged, "No, Daddy, don't smack Mama. It ain't her fault."

And never understood why his Dad stalked off muttering, "Well you sure ain't my fault!"

So, when the explorers said he got things wrong, Willie Jay wasn't surprised or upset. The only person in his whole life who had listened to him and thought he had something to say was Samuel Jonson. His Mama had loved him, but she shook her head over him and told people how much she worried about him. He'd even overheard his mother fretting to his grandmother, "That boy just ain't right, and I don't know what to do with him."

Vince was the hardest on him. Joe Mack and Chuck weren't as bad, they but gave him no credit, so he was grateful to Johnny Balaam for accepting him unconditionally as a Child of God. Willie Jay liked Johnny and looked up to him as a role model of how to walk in faith. He knew

Sam didn't have the strength of faith that Johnny had, but he admired Sam so much that he overlooked any sign that Sam might not be perfect. After all, he'd been quite happy to defy his father and go to the far ends of the earth just on Sam's say so.

Because Sam believed people had survived in other parts of the world, Willie Jay believed it, too. For the first time, his parents ordering him to stay away from someone who would fill his fool head with such nonsense had no affect. Until he met Sam's son, Rubin, and became one of Sam's followers, Willie Jay had always been utterly obedient. Sam taught him something brand new – to think for himself. Not only that, but he also had a right to use the mind God gave him. He went on hanging around with Rubin and listening to Sam.

Enos Rimmon's admonitions that Willie Jay wasn't bright enough to know when someone was blowing smoke up his ass, so he'd better move back home where they could keep an eye on him, backfired. Willie Jay found being treated as someone who could think for himself so enticing that he wasn't about to give it up and go back to being the family embarrassment. He reminded his astonished father that he'd been sent to the city to earn a living because they thought he couldn't do it at home, then he left before the bewildered man had the time to react.

From then on Willie Jay was estranged from his family. He became part of Sam's family to the point of being introduced to reading, writing, and the shadowy world of illicit knowledge. Antique books had been kept hidden during the periodic book burnings during the Purifications of the Liberty Wars during the Redemption period.

He wasn't shown, and didn't want to know, where such things were hidden, just in case the Morality Squad did a raid while he was around and questioned him. He was terrified that he knew anything he shouldn't know.

Most people had never heard of the things Sam knew, and Willie Jay didn't dare ask how he'd found them out. You never knew what might set off another wave of Purification. After one of his parents' friends had vanished one night during a Purification Willie Jay had lived very vigilantly. His parents had managed to stay un-noticed, though they never heard from their friend again. They were proud of the fact that they had no books, so there was no question of whether or not they had any banned books. If he thought about it, Willie Jay assumed Sam must have read things he shouldn't have. Mostly Willie Jay was careful not to think about it.

Unbelievable as it was, he was, at last, there: anchored off the coast of a land in the South Pacific. It was bigger than he thought it would be, with dozens of small islands all around the big ones. He had, somehow, always assumed that if they did find anyone alive, they would be seen as heroes, long awaited rescuers. Nothing in his wildest imagination had prepared him for a society that had to vote on whether or not it wanted to be contacted.

He could see that Sam felt insulted, offended, and bewildered by the way he ran his hand through his greying hair, looking helplessly at the men in front of him as he joined them in the meeting he'd called. "Hey, Guys. Where're the others?"

Vince answered, "Johnny and Chuck got that flu thing that's been going around."

"How many did it get, does anyone know?"

"Doc said pretty near everyone that goes ashore comes down with it."

"Is it really a flu, Sam?" Willie Jay trembled with anxiety. "I've been ashore a time or two myself, y'know. I don't want to come down with nothing."

Sam looked a mite queasy himself, when it came right down to it. "Doc Hosannah said it's something to do with local bugs. The locals are used to 'em, but we ain't. It really is a kind of flu."

"The Major ain't going to make us pull out, is he?" Joe Mack pushed his hat back on his head and mopped his forehead and neck with his kerchief.

"I don't reckon we should waste any time. If we keep getting sick and the crew catch it from us, he might."

"D'ya think that might happen?" Joe Mack leaned forward, anxiously.

"I can't rightly say. So far, it's only the guys who went ashore that got it. Doc says it shouldn't get any worse than a mild flu. He thinks it's because bugs change fast, so if people are apart for two hundred and fifty years, they toughen up to their local bugs, but there ain't no way to toughen up to bugs they ain't never come across."

Vince's eyebrows rose. "You mean the pagans'd get sick if they came to the Gethsemane Republic?"

"Sounds like it, Vince. In fact, they might get sick just from coming on board."

"Ah. Something to keep in mind," Vince nodded.

"We should toughen up pretty fast, huh?" Joe Mack asked.

Sam shrugged. "I ain't no doctor. I'll ask Dr. Hosannah some more questions. Now, what've we found out about these people that we can tell the folks back home?"

"Not much," Joe Mack answered.

"Spooked the crap out of me when that old guy was waiting for us when we got down here," Vince complained. "How did they do that?"

Sam explained, patiently, "You saw how fast their boats are."

Vince frowned. "You ain't sayin' the heathen got better boats than us!"

Willie Jay caught his breath, scared that the GR was listening, and would burst in if anyone gave any kind of answer that could be twisted to sound unpatriotic. He was relieved to see both Sam and Joe Mack motioning with him for Vince to be careful of what he said.

Sam said in a seemingly normal tone, "The Gethsemane Republic is the greatest nation in the world, so of course we got the best."

They all controlled their faces so that no one could catch them acting like they didn't believe it.

Joe Mack was the first one to get his voice under control. Willie Jay was thankful that Joe Mack changed the subject. "Did you talk to their old Servant woman, Sam?"

"Yes, I got a shot when she got down here. She seems like a nice enough old crow, but she just won't tell me who their decision maker is. Johnny Balaam was trying to find out."

Willie Jay figured that was his cue. Holding up some sheets of paper from the pile in front of him, he spoke up. "Johnny gave me his notes when he got too sick to do any more. The only answer he got was that the citizens make the decisions."

"It won't be good if the Major wants to pull out now, before we have something to give the folks back home." Vince pursed his thin lips. "We've got to have a story to sell if we're going to make any money back from this here venture."

Joe Mack nodded, "If we could find out where their capital city is, we could sail there and find out for ourselves."

Willie Jay sighed, "You know, Sam, I can't find nothing about it in Johnny's notes. It's like they don't got one."

"Don't be ridiculous, they must have one. Where is their capitol building?"

"Reckon they don't got one."

"What do you mean, "They don't got one?" Where do they fly their flag, then?"

"Well, Sammy, it looks like they don't got no national flag, neither."

Sam raised his eyebrows. "What do you mean, "They don't got a national flag?" I saw flags all over the place."

"Well, in Johnny's notes, every island, township and sports team got a flag, but it don't look like they got one for the whole country."

"That just don't make sense. Every nation's got a flag!"

Joe Mack shrugged. "Look at it this way, Sammy boy. Who are they going to show their flag to? They ain't seen nor heard from no-one in two hundred and fifty years."

"We kept our traditions alive, why wouldn't they keep theirs? Aw hell," he grumbled, shaking his head, "this is getting too weird for me. I knew it would be different, but not this different. I got to find out where their capital is. We can't make no progress until we got that. How are we going to get it if they won't tell us? Why won't they just tell us?"

"That's more than one question, Sam. You only get one question a turn," Joe Mack grinned.

There were grins around the table.

Sam frowned. "No, seriously, you guys. What else've you found out about them?"

Vince offered, "These guys are real weird."

Willie Jay shrugged. "In Johnny's notes here, it says the citizens meet regularly in groups of one hundred to vote. These voting groups are called Hundreds. They're numbered. That seems to be their idea of local government. There are 20,104 of the 'Hundreds,' which gives a voting population of 2,010,400 and change. Each Hundred's got a Speaker."

Joe Mack interrupted, "I guess that's like a Speaker of the House."

Willie Jay looked up at them, working his way around the table from one face to another to see who thought that made sense and who didn't. He shrugged, unable to figure it out from the bewildered faces in front of him, so he looked back down at the notes, turned over a page and said, "Don't say nothing about that here."

Vince said, "So there must be Mayors and stuff like that."

"Johnny don't say nothing about Mayors in his notes. The notes say the Speakers, and I didn't hear nothing about Mayors when I was ashore. It says the Speakers report to a Representative."

Vince insisted, "It must be the Mayors that report the votes to a Representative."

Joe Mack nodded, "So they got like a House of Representatives, even if they don't say that." He turned to Sam and complained, "They made a mess out of government. Mayors don't report to the House of Representatives. What about Governors? They made a mess out of the language, too. You can't understand a blamed thing they say. They don't speak real English, and some of ain't English at all, and it sure ain't Spanish! They just don't get what we're asking them."

Vince asked, "Is it that they really don't get it, or are they trying to hide something?"

Sam pursed his lips, thoughtfully. "They seem to be a very open people. Naïve and innocent in the way they go about things. When they know what we want, they just give it to us."

Vince asked with some irritation, "¡A la verga! Then why won't they tell us who their President is and where we can find him?"

Willie Jay shrugged again. "I don't know. It don't say nothing about that here, it says there's one Representative for every fifty Speakers."

Vince frowned. "You don't have fifty Speakers; you have one Speaker of the House. What a mess. Why'd Johnny give that to you, Willie Jay? You never get things right."

Sam looked at Vince for a minute, then said, "I guess you're right, it's Mayors or Governors that they're calling Speakers." He turned back to Willie Jay. "Do the Speakers or Mayors meet, or see the Representatives separately, or have meetings, or what?"

Willie Jay held the sheaf of notes towards Sam. "Here, look for yourself. All Johnny says about it is there's 403 Representatives."

"You couldn't find out where these Representatives meet?"

"Not so far. The Representatives report to Ministers in the same way the Mayors report to the Representatives. There are twenty-one

Ministers. If they all get together in one place like a Senate or a House, or send messages, there ain't one word about it in Johnny's notes. They just don't get what we're asking them."

"And you're truly sure that's what it is? Why wouldn't they understand, "Who is your leader? Where is your capitol?" Are you sure they ain't trying to hide something?"

There was a suppressed snicker behind him.

Sam turned, frustrated. "What now, Vince?"

Vince crowed, "Maybe their leader wears skirts like those guys we saw, right Joe Mack? With feathers in their hair? If their leader was one of them, I just bet they'd want to hide him from us!" He laughed, looking around expectantly for the others to all laugh with him.

"Well, we are here to bring civilization back to these people, aren't we? Anything else?"

Willie Jay thought Sam wanted him to continue, so he read, "The Ministers report to a Triune, whatever that is." He was disappointed when no one seemed interested in what he had to say any longer.

Joe Mack ventured, "That old Ollyreen broad is called the First Servant, but the two men are Second and Third."

"That ain't right!" Vince's fists were clenched. "It's against the Wright Way to raise a woman above a man. That's the kind of thing that brought on Judgement Day."

Sam smiled, indulgently. "They're only servants. What difference can it make what the servants are called?"

Joe Mack raised an eyebrow. "Well, Sammy, we couldn't see no churches anywhere."

There was a stunned silence.

Sam murmured, "Now that you mention it . . ."

Joe Mack joked, "Well, you can see Abraham Wright never made it this far."

"If ever a people needed a prophet and an evangelist, these people are it," Vince's voice was hushed. "Who'd've thought that a people could lose its way so completely in a mere two hundred and fifty years?"

Sam spoke quietly, "I'm not a religious man myself, but for a whole country to have no churches – that's unbelievable. What did these poor people lose? Their faith and their language."

Joe Mack cocked his head to one side, "And all industry. There ain't a building over three floors high anywhere that I've seen. Not a smokestack, no roads, no traffic, no farms, and that damned jungle has penetrated even those shabby little towns of theirs, and they don't have the get up and go to clear it out. That child's toy they took us in to see their Third Servant ain't no way to transport goods for heavy industry."

"They call it the 'Flying Fish,' Sam. It does seem to be their only transportation," said Willie Jay. "It does look kind of like a fish on its side, all shiny silvery and blue, and flat front and back."

Vince sneered, "A flimsy railcar, running along on a wooden trestle, about three floors up? It can't be the only transportation there is in the whole country."

"We ain't actually seen the whole country," Joe Mack pointed out. "We ain't even sailed along the coast. We've only seen three spots so far. Maybe this is the poor section. That fish-train is a rickety looking thing, for sure. I can't tell what powers it, but it's real quiet. When I rode in it this morning, all I could hear was a hum, and no exhaust. I couldn't see no sign of private vehicles. There ain't no roads, just paths between the houses, and no blocks. When you get up in the Flying Fish you can see the houses all crowded together in circles. The town I saw was like cadet camp. Not a straight road anywhere. Like a ghetto only cleaner and quieter."

Willie Jay shook his head. "Can I tell you something, Sam? The way they live is right restful, like going on a holiday in a cabin in the woods.

Put me in mind of going hunting with my daddy. First thing I'm going to do when we get home is call my daddy about going out and getting us some deer. And you know something else? That train up on logs overhead and no cars means that there's no traffic. It ain't noisy down on the ground like at home, and I ain't never smelled that fresh green camping smell in any of our cities, no Sir, and you can take <u>that</u> to the bank. Even when it runs by right over your head, that train of theirs is quiet, anyway. It sure was real nice in their towns. You could hear the kids playing and laughing, and people whistling and singing, and talking to each other. All of the houses have them porches in front with chairs and hammocks and porch swings, and people sit on them and talk to their neighbours. It's right neighbourly. All the buildings I saw are made of wood, and they blend right in with the trees and stuff."

Vince Thomason rounded on Willie Jay. "Blend in with the trees? They got panels on every roof, and windmills on all the gutters and walls. Little spinning windmills like kid's toys on every goldurn building, leaves and flowers and birds and butterflies all shiny and glittering and spinning in the wind. How can you say that 'blends in' with anything?"

"Yeah, okay, their decorations are a bit silly, but they ain't so bright as them police crowd control lights at home. There ain't no bright lights anywhere here, no signs, no traffic lights, not even their streetlights are bright."

"They got no streets."

"I know, but even the lamps that they hang in the trees only give enough light for you to walk on the paths at night, they don't light up the city."

Vince persisted. "They ain't lamps. These cats ain't even got real lanterns, just some kind of stupid paint stuff."

Willie Jay knew Vince was impatient with him, but he wanted Sam to know what he'd seen, anyway. Stubbornly, he insisted, "I like the way it's safe to walk on the paths at night, even in the towns. Even in the middle of the biggest town I was in you could see the stars and hear the frogs at night, and there's no traffic noise, no car horns, no sirens. It's like a little bit of paradise."

Vince snorted. "The only godless 'paradise' I ever heard of! And all those little kids will grow up heathen, with no hope. What future have they got with no industry? They need teachers, missionaries, developers, and who knows what else!"

Joe Mack sniggered. "Tailors. They ain't got no decent clothes."

Willie Jay felt defensive of the islanders. "Those two islands we were at up north they weren't wearing much, but on this one where it's colder they got more clothes."

Vince looked down his nose. "And that's another thing that's ungodly. Bad enough the stars are wrong, but its colder south instead of warmer, and warmer north instead of colder."

Willie Jay was grateful to Joe Mack for steering the conversation back to his point with, "And cooks. Y'all can't eat what they got here."

They all rolled their eyes at the thought of the food they'd been offered.

"Are you sure that's not what's making everyone sick, Sam?" Vince repeated.

Sam shook his head. "I know there's plants, and herbs, and spices that I've never tasted before, but you know, I've heard that vegetarian diets are better for you, so actually their diet should have made us feel better, not made us sick."

Joe Mack snorted. "You're kidding. An old carnivore like you believing that load of mierda?"

"No, give me a good steak any day. I'm just saying that's what I heard. Beef fat's not all that good for you. These guys eat some fish and some eggs with their vegetables and fruit; and look how healthy they all are."

Vince sneered, "If you can call being skinny as a beanpole 'healthy'."

Sam shook his head. "There's not a one of them in the lot that's overweight, not that I've seen anyways, and not a one that looks starved, either. Look how long they live. Did you ever see so many old folks looking so fit and happy?"

"If you like skinny, flat-chested chicks," Vince muttered.

Jo Mack groaned. "All I knows is when I get back on board, I'm ready to eat anything that's dead or seriously slowed down."

They all laughed and agreed.

"Did you draw much, Vince?"

"Yeah, Sam." He took out a sketch pad. "I used up all the paper we had, and they gave me more. Look at this stuff." The paper was different from theirs. It was both lighter and stronger at the same time. There were sketches of beaches, houses covered in vines, trees loaded with fruit, jungle-like forests full of ferns of every size, bare breasted women, naked children on the beach, and brooks with clear running water.

"Did you get some pictures, Willie Jay?"

"I got them developed by that guy on board like you said. I got them right here." He pulled out an envelope and shared photos of many of the same things as Vince had sketched, with the addition of children digging in the beach sand.

"You got pictures of kids playing?"

"No, I don't think they were playing. It was on that smaller island we stopped at. They were digging up shellfish they call pippies and putting them in those baskets, then they ran off saying it was for kai."

"What's kye?" Sam asked, fascinated by the photos.

Willie Jay shrugged. "Supper, maybe?"

Vince snorted in disgust. "Now, see, that's just not an English word at all. Even when they're digging for clams they say 'pippies.' They didn't only make a mess of English, they ain't even speaking it half that time."

Willie Jay nodded. "I'd say it *is* about half the time. It's like they've put two languages together. Half the names are sort of real sounding, half are real weird. That Servant lady's name is Olarine. Nice name. Never heard it before, but it's a nice name. The girl who's helping her's name is Ricky. Nothing wrong with that, except they go and spell it 'Riki.' You could get used to that if they did it with everything, but no! That Second Servant guy, his name is Peter Metty My-tie. What sort of a name is Metty? Only then they go and spell it 'Pitamete,' like they spell pippy 'pipi,' and they spell his last name 'Meithei.' It just ain't English. It's like they pronounce every letter. Then I got them to write Olarine's name for me, and I asked them why they said it Olareen and not Olarinny like the way they say Pitamete, and they said it's because they got two traditions woven together. So I says, "How can you tell which is which?" and they just said they know. How in Sam Hill are we ever going to make head or tail of that?"

"You can talk to those guys?" Sam was impressed.

"Not really. Sort of pointing and shrugging and rolling my eyes and that kind of thing."

"But you figured out their names a bit."

"Well, not really, Sam. Just wait, there's more. Sometimes their names are a bit of one kind and a bit of the other just sort of tacked together. There ain't no way to keep track of it."

"I just realised something."

They all turned to look at Joe Mack. He was holding up some of the pictures. "There ain't no farms around the towns. No cattle. Come to think of it, no animals of any kind. Just birds."

Vince shrugged. "Yeah, we already knew that. It's like that Sunday Island. Nothing there but birds and fish, and fruit that kills people."

"Then they need them some beeves, too," Joe Mack grinned.

"No, listen," Sam was suddenly very serious. "The folks here are fixing to vote against any more contact with us. We might not agree with it, but if it's a majority vote, we must respect it. That's what democracy is all about."

Vince shrugged. "Votes schmotes. They don't even got a proper head of state."

"Maybe they do and maybe they don't. We just ain't found him yet. A vote is still a vote."

Vince fixed Sam with a level stare. "We ain't bound by no one else's votes. What I want to know is, how are we going to make back the cost of this here expedition? I hate to bring this up, but we got to pay off our debt. We ain't going to find no riches here. There ain't nothing here. Not even jewellery or gold. We have to sell a story back home, and it's got to be a good one to sell books and make us back the money we owe. What would make the best story? That this is a paradise, or that it's a heathen wasteland?"

Joe Mack shook his head. "The heathen wasteland ain't going to sell. No one's shot at us, no one got mugged. The people are polite and gentle and kind . . ."

Vince stuck his chin out, stubbornly. "Bunch of pantywaists, you mean."

"So, you see why the 'it was hell over there' won't sell? Ain't nothing bad happened here."

Sam shook his head. "Half the crew is sick, a third of our own group, and I don't feel that hot myself."

"Sam, that's just it," Joe Mack insisted. "The worst thing that happened is a bunch of us ate a bad wiener. It's just not enough even for 'trouble in paradise.' I'd leave it right out of the story, myself. We went to the other side of the world and found paradise. The Islanders survived the Mini Ice Age, or maybe it never hit here, and they've made a new nation where they live like they's on summer vacation all year round. They have a democratic society in a clean and peaceful land, but there ain't nothing there for us, not enough to trade to make it worth while shipping all this distance. Both men and women walk around without shirts. There, think that will sell?"

Vince snorted. "I thought when we got here, we'd find nobody survived, and we'd be able to get treasure from the abandoned cities. But there ain't no sign of any kind of city anywhere. The skinny broads they've got here are all too small breasted to sell stories back home about them going topless. We'll have to make the naked natives busty to sell that story, it's got to be a real good story to make the money we would've got from treasure."

Sam shrugged. He ran his hand through his hair again. "I don't want to make things up just to sell stories, even if we do have a godawful debt to pay off. I wish I knew more about their government. All we've talked to so far are Servants. I don't want to deal with any secretary or assistant or old auntie. I have to talk to the head man. There's got to be a ruler, dictator, president, general, something. Can't you get on that tomorrow, Willie Jay? Find me their leader and where he's at?"

"I'll do what I can, Sam. You know, you don't look that great. Maybe you should go see Doc Hosannah."

Pete

Back up north after the explorers had left for their home across the ocean, Secondary Public Servant, Pitamete Meithei, was welcomed by the First Public Servant, Olarine Eidola into her office, which was built off her living room. Along with the Tertiary Public Servant, Glendritz Tomptell, the three of them were the Triune, the head of the island's government.

"How are you?" Pete asked as he and Olarine hugged.

"I wish I'd never won the election. Not even a lifetime as an architect, raising my children, nor all my time in public service after the children grew up; nothing prepared me for this," she sighed as she turned from him to her desk. "I was only elected at the beginning of the last session, but it feels more like ten years. If you'd got just a few more votes you would have been first instead of second and all of this would be your headache."

Pete reached across her desk to stroke her arm. "Right, Ol, and if Glen had got more than either of us, he'd be First."

Olarine gave him a wan smile. "I know, I know. You asked how I am – that's how. Sad, tired, scared for the People, and afraid I'm not up to it."

There was a chime at the second-floor door, followed immediately by the sound of feet running down the stairs. "That'll be Glen," Pita commented.

He looked Olarine over, using his training as a Calmer to see if she was just feeling a bit overwhelmed, or if she was beginning a serious downward slide. In the months the three of them had been working together, they had become close. She looked tired and worried as she welcomed Glen into the room. As far as Pete could see her blue mood was nothing worse than a normal reaction to stress.

He stood up to greet Glen, who Pita thought also looked tired and stressed.

Olarine's adult daughter served them all tea and biscuits, then left the room. In keeping with the island ways, they relaxed together drinking tea before they got down to work.

They each had a Recorder with them to record the meeting. Protocol dictated that the words of the Public Servants had to be written down by independent witnesses as well as recorded by any recording device. Apparently, there had been times in the past when crucial parts of recordings had been deleted, so the Troggies had tried to design a system that would make it as difficult as possible for any public person to cover his or her tracks in case of ethical questions.

Pitamete sat back in a big rattan chair that was on the edge of not being quite big enough for him. He took a deep, appreciative breath of the cooling breezes from the veranda. Olarine had slid the glass doors back along the walls to let in the fresh air, scented by the hibiscus she'd grown over the doors. She flicked her grey braid over one shoulder so that she wouldn't sit on the end of it. Pete caught the movement of it out of the corner of his eye and saw that he could see them all in the reflection of the glass doors against the wall.

Olarine was behind her white desk in a long soft blue caftan. She had slipped her sandals off and put the soles of her bare feet thankfully on the coolness of the stone tiles of the floor. There was a hibiscus blossom behind her left ear.

Glendritz sat to her left hand, peering over his half-glasses, and clearing his throat unnecessarily. He was dressed in the heavier clothes of the south, which were evidently becoming uncomfortable, because he was wriggling as if he couldn't relax. Glen was thinner than Pita, milder, and more nervous.

Pita sat to Olarine's right hand, wearing a bright red patterned shirt with the top few buttons open. He was unconcerned to notice a few white hairs coming in among the black fur of his chest. His knees were wide apart, his big brown arms resting on the chair arms, his hair in a great woolly mop, his full lips in a contented grin.

The three Recorders sat beside the person they recorded, sipping tea and relaxing with them.

Pete might look younger than the other two, but they were all three much the same age, early to mid fifties. Olarine was quite grey, and Glen had lost his hair, but Pita wasn't any younger than they were. In fact, at fifty-two, Glen was the youngest of the three.

"I heard your Abernaud won an award for the door he made for your son's house," Glen said to Olarine in his courteous way.

"Yes. It's a beautiful thing. I'll show it to you when we've finished the business. The kids delayed their bonding ceremony until after the GR left."

"One more thing they disrupted," Pete observed. "Still, now that they're gone, we can go back to normal."

Olarine looked at him. "As a Behaviourist, do you really think we'll ever be the same as we were?"

"In some ways, no. In some ways everything's changed. In the basics of everyday life, yes. People will carry on with familiar routines and the visit will fade into a story."

Olarine took a deep breath. She straightened her back, which made her look more professional, and less thin and worn. "We might as well get down to business." She looked around at the three Recorders. "Are you all ready?"

They set up their encoders and took out their pads and pens. Riki wrote on one side of Olarine's desk with her encoder beside her. Pita's Recorder had a small portable desk that sat on the arms of his chair with an encoder on it. Glen's Recorder sat further apart from the rest of them, with an encoder on a small desk to one side.

When all of them had answered, "Yes, Madam First," Olarine intoned the formal introduction of date and time and who was present, including the three Recorders. Her voice was low and melodic, not blocking out the bird song from outside, or the quiet tapping of the keys as the Recorders typed in her every word.

After Olarine had put on record why the extraordinary meeting of the Triune had been called, she went on, "The first item of business is, of course, the strangers. Have you had a chance to read over the reports from the Speakers yet?"

Pita shrugged. "All the indications I've had so far are that the Islands are evenly split in about four or five different ways. I looked through the Representative's reports, too. What the Speakers reported to them, and the Speakers' own input is all across the board."

Glen agreed. "Same here, I'm sorry to say, Ms. First. If any one group is pulling ahead according to the Ministers, it's the one that says once contact has been made it can't be unmade, so we have to find a way to deal with it."

The First Public Servant nodded. "I'm afraid that's the reality of the situation, even if I haven't the slightest idea what 'dealing with it' can be."

"The best possible scenario is if they never come back again," Pita muttered.

"I wish it hadn't come in my term," Olarine sighed. "If wishes were fishes, we'd all have full dishes. What recommendation should we make regarding going out ourselves to make contact under our terms?"

"I think it's foolhardy," Glen exclaimed with surprising force. "If we run into more people like those ones, we don't want to attract them back here. I found it frustrating and a bit insulting that the strangers continually demanded to see our decision maker, regardless of what we told them."

Pita tried to soothe them both by saying, "The best translations we could manage gave me the impression that they were expecting to be taken to some important building, and it insulted them that we brought them into the commons of Olarine's hex, and then into Glen's home."

"Insulted?!" Olarine and Glen shouted as one, startling Pita so much that he slopped his tea.

His Recorder jumped up and ran out to get help while the others mopped Pita's lap with their serviettes. Olarine's daughter arrived back with the Recorder, both carrying paper towels to mop up.

"Are you burned, Pete?" Olarine asked.

"More embarrassed than anything," he said, looking ruefully at the mess he'd caused.

"Good thing it's a stone floor," Olarine said, her good-natured tanned face splitting in a wide grin that showed her large white teeth. "It'll mop up in no time. Abeline, dear, see if any of your father's lava-lavas will fit the Second Servant, his is soaked through."

Olarine's daughter smiled at Pita. "It won't take a second for me to rinse that out for you and hang it on the line. It'll be dry by the time you're ready to go home."

In the hot weather, most men wore a short wrap, tied with a knot over one hip, almost like a short sarong. They were made of the local linen, and formed a light, cool garment in summer that was easily cleaned and lasted a long time. They were worn with linen shirts or bare chests, and sandals or bare feet. Women wore much the same, or caftans, in summer for every-day dress.

They quickly re-assembled, Pita wearing two lava-lavas tied together to make up for the difference between his size and that of Abernaud.

After the formal notes on what the interruption had been about in order to have the written record agree with the taped record, Olarine started with, "Where were we?"

A momentary flash of humour flickered across Pita's mind, with punch lines about him with a lap full of hot tea, before the gravity of their situation reasserted itself and wiped the grin off his face.

Glen reminded him, "You were telling us that our 'guests' felt insulted to be taken to our homes. How could they take insult that we showed them such honour?"

Pita couldn't imagine. He shook his head. "I don't know. I really don't know. It's much harder to deal with strangers than I ever imagined it could be. The wonder to me now is not that our ancestors ran into insurmountable trouble, but that they managed to avoid it for so long. I've been giving it a great deal of thought. All I can think of is that the way they do things is so different from the way we do things that we can't understand each other. The behaviour is as different as the language is."

Olarine sighed. "I think we're going to have to have a proper counted vote on this, since it looks like no clear answer is going to come from discussions and meetings."

Pita and Glen turned to their Recorders, making sure the record showed that Ms. First had called for a counted vote and had been seconded by both of them.

"We need to call the Ministers in, then, for a special sitting of the House. They're expecting it. A number of Ministers and Representatives have made it clear to me that a full-scale plebiscite is the only way – and it's likely to be so close that there'll be at least one recount." She turned to her Recorder. "Please book the Marae for a full meeting of the House."

Riki nodded, making a note, "Yes, Ms. First."

Glen glanced quickly at Pete, then assured Olarine, "You're right, Madam First: the Ministers have been expecting to be called. I've heard from the People of all walks of life saying the same thing, no matter what they think the outcome should be."

Pete was taken by surprise by the firmness in that brief glance from Glen. He was so used to those grey-blue eyes having a mild expression that he wasn't prepared for anything else. It gave him an abrupt, clear image of how this gentle, non-challenging man could have been a successful judge for so long. He added his tuppence worth of opinion to Glen's. "This is a once in a life-time experience. We all knew it would have the highest priority, one way or another."

Olarine rolled her eyes. "One way or another is it. No one could have predicted what form first contact would take, but I had never imagined it would be so bewildering. I had always imagined it would have been an exciting, glorious time, not this feeling of being wrong-footed all the time."

"Do you want me to record that, Ms. First?"

Olarine looked at her Recorder, considering.

Pita nodded at her that he thought it was a good idea.

She looked at him for a moment, and then turned back to her Recorder. "Yes, Riki, put it down. People in the future might want to know how we felt and what we based our decisions on." She poured herself another cup of tea, waiting until all of the Recorders were poised, ready for her to continue. "Now, gentlemen, we need to try to understand why the gentlemen from the Gethsemane Republic needed to leave before we could have our plebiscite, just in case they or someone else comes to see us again so that we know what it is they want from us."

Glen suggested, "I think they left because people were getting sick. It seemed to really frighten them."

Olarine shook her head. "We have people getting sick, too. Princess Wineera has taken to her bed, and that's rare for her."

Glen nodded. "Just the same, it seemed to frighten them in a way it doesn't frighten us."

"Does that mean they don't have colds and flu where they come from?"

"I don't think so. I don't know. We're speculating."

Pita put his cup down. "I still don't understand what they meant by wanting to see our president. I've asked historians to search the archives and see what meaning the word used to have. We only use it for sports clubs and businesses, but they seemed to have a different meaning for it. No one has yet translated their word 'Leye-dah' but from the context it seems clear they meant 'leader' but they were never satisfied with talking to any of us. We were not what they were looking for."

Olarine got up and walked to the doors to look out over her garden. "Do you think they want to talk to the King?"

Glen raised his hands, helplessly. "I was coming to the conclusion that they might have been looking for the King, but they were insisting on wanting to know about our government."

Olarine shook her head. "What would they want to bother poor old Uetaoroa with government matters for? They saw him at the Hui. They sat right next to him and didn't say a word about it."

The wall unit chimed, interrupting them.

They all looked at it, Pete asking, "Abernaud calling home?"

Olarine got to her feet saying, "Adjourn the meeting while I answer this. It's not the personal line. It's official. Take a break, everyone."

The two female Recorders immediately left the room. Pete murmured to Glen, "It can't be us, we're here."

Glen had the ghost of a smile. "It can't be a Minister; they all know there's an extraordinary meeting."

Pita realised that meant it could only be the King and lost all feelings of playfulness just as Olarine answered, "Olarine Eidola."

She was answered by the King's voice, sounding very tired. "Madam First, Uetaoroa Turiahi." He stopped for a moment to clear his throat, then continued in a ragged voice as if he was fighting a sore throat to get the words out, "I'm very sorry to have to tell you that the pieces of wreckage found in Raukawa Moana have been positively identified as the Rangatira from Te Whanganui a Tara."

"Oh, no! I can't believe they took a little light boat like that out into the Washing Machine in a cyclone."

Hearing the tone in Olarine's voice, Pita got up and put a hand on her shoulder.

"There is no proof they went into the strait. They probably tried to sail away from it and were caught on the rocks. The currents and storm surge took the pieces into the strait afterwards." The King broke off to cough. "Sorry," he said, fighting to have enough voice to continue. "Search and Rescue just left. Excuse me."

They waited in silence as he sipped something brought to him by someone who spoke to him in intense, concerned tones, but so softly that they couldn't make out what was said.

When the King spoke again, he said, "Sorry. I have to get this out before I lose my voice completely. They found one of the crew up on the rocks. No sign of the other three. When Search and Rescue have made sure the kirituhi match the designs on the survival suit they'll notify the next-of-kin."

"He was wearing a survival suit, and he still didn't survive?"

Between coughs the King told Olarine, "I don't know if they found a man or a woman. I have to tell the People before I lose my voice."

"Can't someone else do it? You're really not well."

"I've just got that bug that's going around. I can manage one small message. No sense making the People think it's worse than it is."

They looked at each other in silence after the ringer link was broken. "Let's leave the meeting adjourned until after we've seen the announcement," Glendritz suggested.

"Good idea," Olarine nodded, turning on the screen and flopping into her chair to watch it.

"I don't like the idea of the King catching this bug. It's spreading everywhere," Pita fretted.

"I have a bit of a fever myself," Glen confessed.

Pita suddenly realised what he'd been seeing. "You do? I saw you fidgeting. I thought your clothes were too heavy."

"They are, a bit, but if I put on something lighter, I feel chilled."

Olarine shook her head. "I'm fighting off a scratchy throat, too, and I feel a bit light-headed."

Right then the chimes sounded that there was going to be an official broadcast cutting through the programme. They turned to the door as the Recorders returned and held their fingers to their lips. They watched the King tell the islands what he'd just told them, only in a more complete and formal way.

"Oh, he looks so ill and tired!" Olarine exclaimed.

"Do you think King Uetaoroa will retire soon?" Glen asked. "He's becoming frail. He looked exhausted after the haka, and that was before he came down with this bug."

Olarine nodded. "I would bet leading the haka when the GR arrived was nearly too much for him, especially since dealing with them wasn't easy, and now this. I should think he'll realise he can't keep up anymore. The People will sympathize with him. He'll get full support when he asks leave to retire."

Pita nodded. "The dear old man. Grandfather of the islands. While we're speculating privately, who do you guess will win the election for the next King or Queen?"

Glendritz said, "Oh, I think his son, Ngaronoa, will walk away with it."

Pita was surprised to hear that. "Not Wineera?"

"She might, she's very popular, but she doesn't have the presence that Ngaronoa has. He was so comforting when Tarawera erupted, and worked his heart out in the rescue efforts, risking his life to get people out, and hardly ever resting. People remember things like that. Besides, he's one of the few three voters we have on the islands. That's what we need in a King more than anything else, someone who makes us all feel better when times are tough, and who leads the cheers when times are good."

Pita defended Wineera. "The Princess was just as heroic diving into the water over and over again when the bridge was swept away with a train on it. They had to sit on her to stop her going back in after she was exhausted."

"Yes, we know she's as much of a hero as he is, but is she as suited to be Queen? Ngaronoa was a Calmer before he became a boat builder, so he's got years of training in human behaviour. They're both good candidates, but I think he edges her out, there."

Glen watched Pita closely. "I take it you'd vote for Wineera. She's got her second vote for outstanding service to the community, but Ngaronoa has that as well as his training. She was in the train that went into the river, so she might have been in shock when she was so heroic – he was safe at home and went to the eruption of Tarawera to rescue people. That's a different level of bravery."

Pita shrugged, giving in to the inevitable. "I wasn't surprised he did that. We grew up together. I went to school with Ron, and I was on the life-saving team with him. One of the finest captains we ever had."

Olarine shook her head, and said into her tea, "Only a man would think being a good team captain would make a man a good king."

Pita protested, "It means he's a good organiser, and a good leader. People look up to him. Besides, you said it yourself, there's a lot more to him than that. He and I were both Calmers for a while after we left school, before I started growing fruit."

When Glen chuckled, Pita realised he was being teased, and he'd risen to Olarine's bait. He subsided with a quiet, "He might even be able to give us some advice in dealing with the GR."

Olarine glared. "Royalty is not permitted to have anything to do with politics."

Pita threw his hands up. "I didn't mean like that. I meant King Uetaoroa has seen so many governments come and go, he's seen it all, and he can give words of wisdom to newly elected Servants. Ngaronoa might be his son, but he is our age, he's a grandfather, so he has seen a lot, and he's been at his father's side while the old King's been getting frailer. I just thought he might have that touch of wisdom, too. After all, what is royalty for, if not to give stability and continuity?"

Glen eyed Pita shrewdly. "You're fond of them, aren't you?"

'Oh, here it comes,' he thought. "Ron's my best friend. We've been inseparable since we were seven. His dad has been like a second dad to me since I was knee high to a duck."

But no one acted as if he was name-dropping. They looked a little surprised, but other than that, there was no reaction.

Glen nodded. "I can see why you would want Princess Wineera to win the election when Grandfather King retires. You'll have to be careful to avoid the appearance of impropriety if Prince Ngaronoa wins."

Pita took a deep breath. He'd been avoiding thinking about that. "Only if King Uetaoroa retires while I'm still a Public Servant."

Olarine sighed. "Back to work." She glanced at the Recorders to make sure they were all ready, gave the intro, and then continued after explaining that they'd been interrupted by the King's broadcast, "In conclusion, a special meeting of the House will be set up with all of the Ministers so that the Triune can recommend a universal plebiscite on whether or not to have contact with the rest of the world, and if so, what form it will take. More work needs to be put into translating the language of the GR. Have I covered all points?"

Pita had an idea flash into his mind as he pictured the assembly. Instead of concurring, he spoke up. "What if this was a filmed assembly?"

Olarine blinked in surprise. "We couldn't hold it in the whare nui, then. No cameras in the Marae."

"How hard is it to hold it somewhere else? If the People could see the decisions being made the government wouldn't have to explain how they came to their decisions about the plebiscite later."

"Good point, Mr Second," Glen leaned forward in his chair. "This is one of the most momentous decisions in history. It needs to be transparent."

Olarine bit her lip, then said, "I concur." She turned back to her Recorder. "Riki, would you be so kind as to find out where the Ministry could meet with cameras and recording equipment allowed, please?"

"Yes, Ms. First. If I might make a suggestion?"

"Of course."

"I think the sports arena might be a good place to start."

Pita was enthused. "Good suggestion! It's already set up for recording and cameras; it's big enough for all twenty-one Ministers, plus the three of us, all the Recorders and recording machines and reporters, and an audience besides. I motion we try to get a sports arena."

Glen looked doubtful. "I don't know if that'll fly. Aren't they usually booked up?"

"We need to find out," Pita agreed.

"I second the motion, on the understanding that if they're all booked up, we'll need to look elsewhere."

"Then I concur," Glen sat back. "If we've finished with that item of business, Ms. First?"

"Yes, I think so. Mr. Second?"

"Yes, Ms. First, I concur."

Glen smiled in a way that had Olarine and Pita look at him in surprise, then glance at each other, questions in their eyes. He ended the suspense quickly by saying, "I have an item I need to bring to you both. My partner is expecting."

"Oh, congratulations! This is a surprise!" Both Pita and Olarine got to their feet to shake his hand.

"Yes, it is."

"You have to be so careful with older mothers like that. Oh, off the record, off the record, this is private."

"Which part, Ms. First?"

"My remark. That's personal opinion."

"Yes, Ms. First."

"Right, right." Olarine leaned forward and took Glen's hands in hers. "It gets more risky the further past forty the mother is."

"Yes, it is. We'll do everything, of course. Um – but this part is business, now." They all sat back up. "I will have to tender my resignation as Tertiary Servant in order to be with my partner."

"Of course," Olarine said in her formal voice. "Effective at what time?"

"This is what I need to bring to you both. If I resign there will be an election. It'll have to be after the plebiscite, won't it?"

They looked at each other. "Should we suspend our normal business because of it?" Pita asked. "The GR ship is gone."

"I just don't think that it's right to dump dealing with all of this and the plebiscite in the lap of anyone new."

"I propose that we accept Mr. Tertiary's resignation effective at the counting of the plebiscite. Agreed?"

"Agreed. I second the motion."

"I agree depending on the health of my partner. I reserve the right to resign effective immediately if anything changes."

"Do you agree to Mr Tertiary's condition, Mr. Second?"

"I agree."

"Carried, with Mr. Tertiary's conditions noted. Any other business?"

"Not from me."

"I move to conclude this Extraordinary Meeting of the Triune, and to make it wholly public."

"I second both motions."

"Concluded." She waited until all of the Recorders put their pens down and turned the encoders off. "Riki, could you get Abeline to come back in here, please?" She turned back to Glen. "When did you first hear?"

"A few weeks ago. We didn't want to say anything until we were sure it was going to happen."

Pita grinned. "You sly old bat. You sat through the whole meeting not saying a word."

Glen lowered his eyes. "I didn't want to interrupt other business. I thought it might distract you, considering it means another election. I decided before we started that it had to be the last item as we were concluding."

Olarine nodded. "That's smart. And you were smart to wait before you made it public, too. It would be hard enough if anything went wrong, but to deal with that after a public announcement . . . oh, I can't imagine. How is she?"

"She was doing well, but she's been getting tired lately. The GR were an awful strain on her, and she's terrified of getting this new flu bug. We had our plugs removed as soon as we'd passed our Parenting Certificate twenty-five years ago, but it never happened for us. I've been able to devote my life to public service because we had no children. But now, at last, long after we'd stopped thinking about it, it's happened."

Thrilled for him, Pita beamed at him. "Say goodbye to a good night's sleep."

Olarine hugged Glen. "We will have to have that election as soon as we can so you can stay home with Istell." She sat back down. "You know, usually there's a full counted vote once every four or five years. Now we'll have two, or three depending on the King, within a few weeks, and it's only a few months since the last election."

"You're right. The plebiscite as soon as we can organise it, the government election, and the royal election can't be far off. I don't know of any time in history when something like this has happened, do you?"

"No, nothing like this has happened for two hundred and fifty years." Pita grinned, feeling cheeky.

Olarine rolled her eyes at him. "I didn't mean that, you clown. I mean three major votes inside of a month. Ah, there you are, dear. You remember my daughter Abeline? She agreed to stop by to help me today, because Abernaud is over on the other coast on business. They're experimenting with those hang-gliders, you know, and the winds are just right for them off Mount Taranaki."

"How are they doing with that? It's exciting, isn't it?"

Abeline spoke up, her voice bursting with pride in her father. "Oh, yes. Our ancestors had air travel, you know. We've just managed to perfect a kind of fibre-glass fabric that's light and strong enough for the wings, and a light frame that's strong enough to bear the strain. Everything else that's been tried was either too heavy or too brittle."

"You were part of the development?"

"I was one of the chemists."

"And you didn't get to go?"

"We couldn't all go. Besides, the strangers arrived, and I wanted to see them. That's the bigger news."

Glen rolled his eyes. "Actually, it's more anti-climactic, really. I don't know what I expected, but this wasn't it. These fellahs are just not very bright, eh?"

Pita thought about that for a moment. "I don't know. We need to know more about them before we can be of any use to them in teaching them more civilized ways. To change the subject, I should get going right away. I should be at home for this shipwreck. There are three more bodies to find. It's my jurisdiction."

Olarine was about to protest, but Glen stopped her with a look. "I'm sorry, Ol, I really should get home, too, before this bug gets a hold of me. I'm feeling worse all the time."

She sighed. "I don't know if your lava lava will be dry, Pete. Why don't you wear Abernaud's home and send them back later. I don't feel the full bead myself. If you both have to go, I'll send the minutes of the meeting to the Ministry and go to bed."

CHAPTER FOURTEEN

Rocky

*R*ocky shuffled towards the galley of the Star of Galilee. The raw patches around his ankles were at last starting to heal, now that the shackles had been removed. The Weskies had been kept under lock and key the whole time the ship was near the inhabited islands. Whenever they had to be let out to work, they were chained and shackled. Most of them had spots that had been rubbed raw by the cuffs or shackles. Rocky didn't need to shuffle any more. It had become habit. Besides, all of the Weskies had discovered that the more broken down and defeated they appeared to be, the less the GR tried to break them down.

The Weskies were supposed to be under guard when they worked, but now that the GR were laid low by the flu, the Weskies were frequently unsupervised again just as when the GR were down with seasickness. The greatest freedom for them was being able to talk to each other.

Quietly, just in case there was a GR in earshot, Rocky greeted Cliff, "Ho."

Cliff nodded, looking around.

They said nothing further until they'd checked every nook and cranny for GR while making breakfast. Once they were sure the coast was clear, Cliff dared to ask, "What're the chances of this tub making it all the way back?"

"If it can be done, Skipper is the guy that can pull it off."

"Yeah, he was a first-class seaman before the GR captured him," Rocky nodded, remembering how Skipper had been forced to show the GR how to build and sail ships.

"Not that it makes any difference to us," Cliff muttered under his breath.

Rocky spun to look at Cliff, startled to hear how despondent he sounded. Scared that someone might overhear them, he looked around carefully, and then murmured into Cliff's ear, "Don't give up, now. Things're going to be different."

Cliff looked as if he pitied Rocky as a poor sap for clinging to hope. "How?"

Rocky was feeling real low himself, until he heard it in Cliff's voice. Then he was annoyed to think that the GR were destroying the Weskie's hearts and souls. It was bad enough to enslave them. He wasn't going to let the GR take any more from them if he could help it. Something hardened inside Rocky at that moment – a resistance for resistance sake. "These guys found a whole bunch of people that didn't get wiped out. They aren't the only ones their God saved any more."

"Two things," Cliff dumped the powdered eggs and powdered milk into the four-gallon cook-pot, nodding towards the water can. Loudly, he ordered Rocky, "Pour slow so there ain't no lumps." As Rocky carefully poured the water into the pot, Cliff leaned close as he stirred so he could say right into Rocky's ear, "First off, they never were the only ones: they always knew about us, and the Southies, the Ashlanders, the Swampies, and the Eastern nations. We never stopped them from being the Chosen Ones, so what makes you think one more will?" He changed from stirring to beating the mixture noisily so only Rocky could make out what he said. "And second, if they do, do you think there's a hope in hell anybody on this ship will live to tell the tale?"

Rocky didn't answer right then because they heard someone come in.

Thinking about that short exchange as he went through his exhausting daily work, Rocky started to fight his way out of the numb depression of losing the war, failing to drive the GR back by guerrilla warfare and sabotage after the war, then being captured and enslaved. He wasn't human anymore; he was a work unit without human needs or considerations. He knew they didn't care if he was worked to death. His life had no value to them.

Instead of despairing any longer, giving in to the hopelessness, Rocky began to wonder what he could do within that framework. The first place his mind went was what the GR had taken from them: their freedom, human dignity, religion, name – and as he went through the list, he fought back against the overwhelming despair by asking himself, "What's left?"

All he could think of was their will to survive, their innermost thoughts, the basics of who they were. He had no clue how they could use that against the GR without getting themselves killed. As he thought it over, he reluctantly concluded that they didn't know enough to screw with the GR without making things worse for themselves. All he could do right then was watch and learn.

Taking advantage of the diminished supervision while the flu worked its way around the ship, Rocky managed to talk to the other Weskies a few words at a time scattered throughout the days and nights. He took great care to always look as dull and defeated as he used to feel so that there wouldn't be any change in him to attract attention. The GR paid no mind, other than the usual ordering him around like a dog and threatening him. In fact, Rocky had an easier time of it than usual because the GR who weren't too sick to be on duty were too over-worked to notice anything subtle.

Rocky started to think he was cleverly keeping his new watchfulness hidden, but then he got the creepy feeling that the guy who had hired the ship, Sam, was watching him. He never could catch him at it, but he was sure he wasn't imagining it. At first Rocky was so freaked out that he was twice as careful to look stupid and slavish. After a day or two he remembered that Sam had always seemed to be on the side of the Weskies. Just in case Sam's sympathy was a set up, Rocky became so aware of him it was almost like ESP. He soon knew for sure that Sam had seen through him. His fear eased off some when he realised Sam had known about him for a week or more and had said nothing to the GR. There was no choice, he had to talk to that man. It didn't seem remotely possible. Rocky was hoping for a chance to catch the explorers alone in the mess so that he could let Sam know he wanted to talk to him. He saw an opportunity when the ship stopped at the volcanic island again.

While he was cleaning the tables, Rocky stole glances at the explorers. He was startled to see Sam looking right at him. The first time it shook him so much that he instantly dropped his eyes. It took him a moment to work up the courage to raise his eyes again. When he did, he was unnerved to seen Sam looking him in the eye again. That was more than spooky. It had been impossible to catch Sam watching him, and now, the moment he was ready to show his hand he couldn't avoid it. 'If I'm going to do this, it's now or never,' he told himself firmly, refusing to listen to the little voice in the back of his head that wondered if the explorers could read minds. Picking up a pile of trash from the tables he'd cleaned, Rocky turned as if he was going in the direction of the explorers next, looking Sam in the eye for a split second, desperately trying to convey, "I want to talk to you," in that short time, without speaking or making any gesture that would attract the GR's attention.

Instantly, as Rocky turned to the table beside him, Sam announced, "My men and I will live on the island again while the Star of Galilee is anchored here."

The officers looked as if they'd like to say something.

Sam saved them the trouble by continuing, "The column of smoke and ash is just puffs of steam, now. It don't look like the ground is shaking near as much, and the lava has stopped flowing into the sea. It's safer this time than it was before. I need a worker. That one with the long face will do. He don't got no particular talent."

Rocky was so startled he had to put the plates down quickly so that he wouldn't drop them. It was as if all the air had been knocked out of him. The GR immediately hounded him for insubordination, ordering him to get a rowboat ready on the double, promising to teach him proper obedience when he got back. The next thing Rocky knew, he was rowing the explorers ashore. The weather was over-cast but calm.

On the way across Sam murmured to him, "Don't say a word until we're out of sight." Then the explorers chattered loudly about where they were going to sleep, what they were going to eat, and what parts of the islands they were going to explore.

As if he was dreaming, Rocky put his back into rowing, thinking, "What the hell just happened?" To keep his mind off the torture that awaited him after this excursion was over, he tried to figure out how Sam was reading his thoughts.

Under the cover of the other voices he heard Sam murmur, "Carry our stuff like its real heavy."

He could only assume that was meant for him. He didn't dare look to see who Sam was talking to, or ask Sam what he meant, because he couldn't give any indications that messages were going back and forth. The GR had a policy of keeping the Weskies in line by punishing their friends. He wasn't afraid for the explorers if a watching soldier saw something that made him suspicious that the explorers were too friendly with him. After the bawling out the sergeant got for calling them pagan lovers during the storm, it wasn't likely that the explorers would be spoken to about it. The Weskies on the other hand, would take the hit in proportion to how mad the GR were that they didn't dare go after the explorers.

As the boat grounded on the shore Sam murmured, "Don't take this personal," then yelled at him to jump out and pull the boat up the beach, help them out of it, unload all their bundles, haul the boat right out of the water, and carry most of their stuff.

Although they hefted their bundles high on his back, Rocky quickly noticed that the load wasn't near as heavy as they made it look. He struggled along behind the explorers with his back bent as if under a great weight until Willie Jay said, "We're out of sight now."

Rocky straightened up and looked around. He was in a gully off the beach.

Speaking quietly, Sam advised, "Act like a slave until they've all gone back to the ship for the night."

Rocky did his best to suffer from being in a peaceful, lush, scented gully cutting grass and ferns to make big, soft, sweet-smelling beds, one of which would be his, but it was difficult. He was in real danger that a GR might see him being far too happy to be left unpunished.

Once the camp was ready, the explorers decided to find their way over to the south shore. They didn't want to go to the beach on the west of the island, where they had examined the shipwreck in the black sand behind the smoking cinder islet, but on the east where they had seen a bay that the unwieldy Star of Galilee couldn't navigate. Because Johnny was not completely over his bout of the flu, and Vince was starting to cough, the two of them were left at the campsite.

The rest of the explorers and Rocky went south by climbing up the steep mountain side where the gully began instead of going down to the beach where they might run into GR. Once they'd fought their way to the top, they argued about whether they would be smarter to go down into the next gully or carry on along the crest of the ridge. What struck

Rocky about the argument was that it was like the discussions at home where people gave their reasons for their points of view, listened to each other and came to a consensus. It was a relief after the GR who took any difference of opinion as an insult.

The decision was to stay on the ridge, which soon connected with the edge of the crater. Skirting around the crater meant hours of fighting and hacking their way through dense jungle. As they passed the mid-point the going became easier because the land sloped down for a while. They laughed and danced, because they could. Rocky dared to let himself smile, then came close to tears when they grinned at him instead of punishing him. The rejoicing came to a quick end when they had to climb again, but then they were on the summit of the ridge looking across the south end of the crater at the tallest peak shrouded in clouds. They could see far out to sea between the branches of the trees and had a good view of the island. "Too bad Vince isn't here to sketch it for us," Sam sighed.

Joe Mack shrugged. "Maybe we can take a shot at it when we get back."

Chuck grinned. "If we ever get there and back."

Sam frowned. "We'll never get anywhere by standing around!"

Grinning, they toiled on down to the east. It was way past lunchtime when they finally reached the bay on the eastern edge of the southern coast. It had taken half the day to go a couple of miles.

The bay they wanted to explore turned out to be a sheltered curve with high cliffs on the western side blocking the wind, and the steep forested slopes on the east side curling back towards the west, making a protected anchorage. Sam leaned against a tree, beaming. "Sage told us this would be the place to put a harbour. I wanted to have a good look at it."

Rocky could barely keep his feet, it hit him so hard that the explorers listened to his people, remembered what they said, and took it seriously. That was the moment he knew in his heart that learning their real names and using them was not a trap or an affectation on the part of the explorers. The idea that he honestly could trust someone knocked the breath out of him.

They were on a steep slope above the cove. "It's not a cliff," Joe Mack decided.

Chuck snorted. "Near enough as makes no never mind!"

Sam ordered, "Fan out along the edge. If you find a way down, whistle and we'll come and see if we can use it."

It was Willie Jay who whistled. His path was steep but usable, so they headed down single file, grabbing the tree trunks to stay upright.

Rocky could see that water had run down where they were trying to walk, though the stony ruts were dry. In fact, that had been the only flaw Rocky had seen in Sam's plan: they hadn't found any drinking water. He was wondering if it could be that a lush place like this could possibly have running water only when it rained, when he was distracted by the sight of the clear blue depths of the cove.

Enchanted, Rocky asked Sam, "Do you want me to catch fish for your lunch?"

"If you can, that would be great," Sam beamed. "Not just for us, for you, too. We'll make the fire while you're fishing."

Joe Mack raised an eyebrow, "How're you going to catch fish with no net and no line?"

Chuck winked, "Put a spell on them so they jump out of the water and into the fire?"

Rocky had a mad urge to laugh but wasn't sure if he dared.

Sam asked, "What's your plan, Rock?"

Rocky did his level best to keep his voice steady. "When we were fishing on the north side when we were here before, the fish came right up to us. I figured if the fish in this cove are like that, I can flip them out of the water, and you guys can kill them."

They all laughed at that. Rocky stripped down and dove into the clean, clear, refreshing water, taking care to miss the rocks that he could see scattered all around. He popped back to the surface, feeling insanely happy. Fishing in the clear water around the island for fish he knew he would be able to eat was closer to being back home than he'd ever thought he could be again. Knowing he wouldn't be beaten while he was with the explorers gave Rocky the first feelings of safety that he'd had since the GR had captured him.

Shaking water out of his eyes, he called up to them, "Looks like a lot of land slides dumped rocks down here." He could tell by the looks on their faces that they didn't really get the idea of land slides, even though it was explained to them before. Where they came from, the land was dry and flat with no steep mountains and no earthquakes. He'd learned from the GR how limited some people's imagination could be, but he couldn't help feeling a bit disappointed in the explorers. He'd thought they'd have more imagination than that.

Part way along the east side of the bay was a square shape among the rocks. It was obvious to Rocky that it had to be man-made. He swam towards it, calling to the explorers, "I'll throw the fish up there, okay?"

They immediately started to scramble towards the cement square. Rocky took a lungful of air and dove under the sunlit surface looking for fish that would let him touch them. After a few false starts he came across one that was big enough and passive enough that he could hook two fingers in its gills and swim to the surface with one hand holding the fish trapped on the other. In two kicks he burst through, arms high, flipping the fish up out of the sea to sail in an arc, glittering in the sun, to the top of the cement pad.

Flicking the water out of his eyes, Rocky snickered at the explorers' frantic efforts to catch the flopping fish before it escaped back to the sea. He swam down for the next one before they saw his grin. It was all too lovely to risk by laughing at his superiors. By the time he'd caught what he thought was enough for them to all eat their fill, a fire was lit on the cement and the first fish were cooking over it.

Rocky climbed up diffidently, not sure of what to do or say.

He needn't have worried. Sam reached out a hand to help him up. "Good work."

Willie Jay beamed at him, holding out a roasted fish splayed out over three sticks fanned out the way Cliff did it when they were cooking fish on this island the first time. Rocky would have taken over the cooking, but they waved him off. Thanking Willie Jay, he lay back against the sun-warmed stones to eat, letting the warm sun dry his bare skin. Lying above the water like that, eating fresh food cooked outside in the clean air, he could have been at home except for the weird sounding birds.

He remembered the first time he'd been away from home without his parents. It had started like this; lying in the sun eating fish he'd just caught. The difference was he'd been fifteen then, full of energy, and confidence, convinced that he would live out his life quarrying limestone like the rest of his family; and he'd been lying with his five brothers above the river that flowed past their home.

They lived in a small commune, so all of the children were considered siblings because most of them probably were related in one way or another. There were other communes in the near vicinity, but to avoid the horrors of inbreeding, everyone was urged to look further afield for sweethearts. Rocky's twenty-year-old brother was talking about how tired he was of not being able to find anyone.

At that age Rocky was a raging, walking hormone himself. "Don't you go over to Peace Promise?" he asked, sure River visited the fun-loving young women there as often as he did.

His brother, River, gave him a withering look. "I'm not talking about boys' games. I'm talking about having kids that don't turn out like Roadapple."

They all stared at him.

Moss, who was sixteen, asked, "You're not thinking about moving out, are you, Riv? The old lady'll melt down!"

"Nah, nah, nah, man. What I mean is, we don't go far enough to meet girls that we're not related to. Every fair we go to someone met someone there once."

Rocky was both amused and intrigued. "What about Beltane?" he challenged. "People travel all up and down the coast, from the mountains to the shore, to celebrate Beltane."

To his surprise, instead of squashing him, River pointed at him triumphantly. "That's what I'm talking about! For Beltane this year we got to go further than we've ever gone before. We got to add a little cleaner to our gene pool or we'll all be having kids like Roadapple."

The boys all talked at once: "How are you going to get the elders to go to a new place where they don't know anyone?"

"When you say, 'we,' you don't mean us, do you?"

"You can't go by yourself!"

"Where you going to go?"

Rocky couldn't make out the rest because they were all talking at the same time. He sat up straight, watching River closely.

"I don't know, man, I don't think the parents are going to go where they don't know anyone," Moss insisted.

"The whole point of Beltane is for the <u>young</u> people to affirm the fertility of the world. The parents had their day."

"They have to be at home to renew the hearth fire from the May Fire, anyway." Rocky's brother, Hawk, was nineteen.

"You're going by yourself?" Moss sounded appalled.

"I'm not as stupid as you look." River got to his feet. "Who's coming with me? One of us might get lucky enough to be Jack in the Green."

Their little sister, Butterfly, appeared on the rock ledge above them. They knew she'd been sent to get them, but she didn't call them or look at them. She stood on the far edge, her arms outstretched, her face raised to the sun, her hair blowing in the wind.

River couldn't bear it. "Buffy! Get back from the edge!" he roared, complaining, "I never knew a kid with a better name. She's got butterflies for brains."

Rocky watched Butterfly with a secret envy of her free spirit. He decided then that if there was a trek at Beltane, he would be part of it.

In the end three of them went on the long journey up the coast. They found a place called Mars, River was Jack in the Green for the Beltane rituals, and they did meet the perfect girl. She was not just beautiful, she was nice, and smart as well. All three of them were in love with her. To this day, so many years later, she was still Rocky's ideal woman.

He sat up and stared across the bay at the cliffs on the other side. Try as he might, he could not remember her name. Because they had called her Cleaner, she had refused to have anything to do with any of them. They were all crushed. Even though his brothers said he had no chance with her because he was too young, Rocky was so upset by her rejection that he was in tears. A sadder and wiser group of boys turned south to head home.

"What's that sigh for?"

Rocky jumped and looked around. The explorers were all staring at him. That snapped him back to reality.

"Sorry," he mumbled.

"You were smiling and sighing at the same time," Willie Jay's open, honest expression invited Rocky to spill it all, but he knew he couldn't tell them about pagan festivals and expect to keep their support.

Scrambling to edit the story so that he could tell it to them, Rocky was encouraged by Sam saying, kindly, "You were miles away, Son. Good memories?"

In spite of his memories, Rocky relaxed. "This place – being with you guys – eating fish like this – reminded me of the spring I was fifteen. First time I fell in love."

He had their full attention. As he watched their expressions of recognition and nostalgia, he felt fully that they were all the same.

Chuck had a far-off look in his eye. "She was beautiful, huh?"

"She was the most beautiful girl I ever saw in my whole life."

Joe Mack's voice was soft with sympathy. "You left her behind when you went to war."

"No, no, no, man. It's cool. My brothers were after her too, but we kept calling her 'Cleaner' so she wouldn't give the time of day to any of us."

They nodded and grunted in sympathy, some of them talking about the mistakes they'd made with girls, Willie Jay asked, "Why did you call her that?" and Sam told them it was time to get going.

"It took us all morning to get here. We want to be back at camp before dark."

Obediently they got up and started packing up to leave. Rocky tried to keep his distance from Willie Jay so that he didn't have to try to explain 'gene-pool' to someone who had never been introduced to the concept of genetics.

Sam came up to him while he was throwing the remains of their meal into the water, except for the pieces wrapped in leaves that they were taking back for Vince and Johnny. "Sage said this bay would be the place the islanders would have an anchorage if they had one."

Rocky straightened up and looked around. "I think they did at one time, sir." The cracked cement they were standing on was being split apart by tree roots. He could see where various bolts and things had been attached to the structure. "This was a landing stage of some kind."

"Do you think they tied their ships up here? It don't look big enough."

"It had stuff built on it. We can't tell how big it was two hundred years ago, but the water's deep enough for ships bigger than the Star of Galilee. There've been land slides all over the place here. This could have been a flat area where they could have built a wharf that got buried by a land slide."

"Yes, I can see that." Sam looked all around. "There's no sign of buildings here, but you can see where iron was cut through right down to the cement. They took every scrap of iron from here, too. I guess they can't use this bay now."

Rocky looked at Sam's face carefully to be sure he wanted him to answer. "If I wanted to moor a boat in here," he started glancing around for a good place to tie a mooring line, "I'd go for a tree like that one there . . ." he stalled, unable to believe his eyes.

"What is it?" Sam stared in the same direction.

"On that tree there's a rope burn exactly where you'd put a mooring line."

They went together to take a closer look. The wound was so fresh that the sap was still pooling where the bark had been abraded away.

"You think they tied up here?" Sam asked.

"Yes, sir."

Rocky watched Sam pull something out of his pocket. It didn't occur to him that anything was going on until Chuck asked, "What have you got there, Sammy boy?"

Sam opened the package to show them a silvery piece of metal glinting in the sun like a bright jewel. "It's the piece of saw blade I found in the sand when we climbed over that wrecked ship. This is what led us to them. When I saw this, I knew for sure someone was out here. If I'd seen this, I would've been even surer. It's only a few weeks since this was done, at the most. Metal seems to mean more to these folk than it does to us. They've stripped every bit that they could get at from every corner of this island, and it looks like they come back here to cut pieces off the ships. That's a hell of a long way to come for a chunk of iron. Can you imagine sawing through that ship with this flimsy thing?"

They all looked at the blade, shaking their heads.

"It's a keepsake to me, but it might be a big deal to them, so I'm fixing to leave it here where they can find it. They'll know it was over the other side of those cliffs. That way they'll know that we were here." He jammed the blade under a peeling shred of bark, carefully so that the wickedly sharp edge wouldn't cut his fingers. "Let's go."

From that moment they put everything they had into getting back to the north coast faster than they'd gone south. They made good time, arriving in time to check on Vince and Johnny, as well as catching birds for supper before the sun started to go down.

As evening fell, the GR, who were in the tubs dug into the sand, started to make their way back to the ship for the night.

"Incoming!" Joe Mack called.

Sam told Rocky, "They're checking up on you. Get over there and start digging a latrine."

Rocky looked around wildly. "What with?" he squeaked.

"Why do I care?" Sam returned. "Find a bent stick. Use your hands. Use your teeth."

The GR came into view shortly after Rocky started digging on his hands and knees.

In a panic Rocky leaned forward until his head was nearly in the hole and dug into the earth as if his life depended on it.

They told Sam, "We can take the Waster off your hands, sir."

Rocky continued to dig frantically. He was terrified that he was going to be marched back to the ship right then.

"That's okay, Sergeant, he's kind of useful."

"Yes, Sir. Want me to detail some guys to ride herd on the Weskie, Sir? That's the only thing these Wasters understand."

"Thank you, Sergeant." Sam's voice was cold and hard. "I know how to ride herd."

"Yes, Sir. Of course, Sir."

Rocky couldn't believe it when the GR left without him. Just in case it was all a trick he kept on digging until Sam told him to stop.

"Okay, quit that now. Time to eat."

Rocky got up, covered in dirt, wondering if he was going to be treated like a slave after all.

Sam grinned at him. "God, you look like a mutt that rolled in the dirt."

Still shaken by the visit from the GR, Rocky wasn't sure whether Sam was jeering at him or not, especially when the explorers laughed.

Johnny protested Sam using the Lord's name in vain, then told Rocky kindly, "Its okay, Rock. They're gone. They won't be back tonight."

Sam assured him, "You're okay, Rock. You're with friends now; at least until morning."

Vince's short bark of a laugh turned into a cough that wouldn't stop.

They all looked at him and at one another, worried. Some of the men who got the island flu were really sick. Right in front of their eyes Vince started shivering.

"Better get in your bed," Sam told him. "We'll make supper and eat it in the tree-lily gully." He turned to Willie Jay. "You ain't too sick to fix us some eats, are you, Boy?"

"No, Sir. I got it first. T'weren't hardly nothing."

Chuck shook his head. "Don't that beat all? He was the sickest one in the storm, but this time he don't hardly sniffle when bigger guys're flat on their backs."

Rocky helped Willie Jay to build the fire. While it burned down to coals, he and Willie Jay looked for more sweet potatoes.

"You dug up a whole mess," Willie Jay grinned.

Astonished, Rocky exclaimed, "I never saw them."

"Betcha that's why Sam got you to dig here; to save us work later. He's smart that way."

Rocky couldn't see any of the others. While he and Willie Jay had been busy, Chuck, Joe Mack and Sam had moved around the hill to pluck the birds that had been caught earlier, so that the loose feathers would blow away from them. Rocky and Willie Jay worked the fire to create a good layer of coals for roasting the birds. Rocky showed Willie Jay how to make large leaves into pouches to carry the hot food in after it was cooked.

Willie Jay was fascinated. "How'd you learn to do that?"

"We do it where I grew up."

"We don't got that kind of leaves where I come from," Willie Jay told him. "We carry things in leather sacks."

Rocky nodded. "We all come from different places with different stuff."

Willie Jay poked at the coals to settle them into an even shimmering layer. "If the GR thought different about things, we could all trade with one another, and we'd all get all that different stuff."

Rocky stared at him. He'd always thought Willie Jay was a bit touched in the head – not only because of the way the explorers treated him, but also because of his stammer and the slightly lost look in his eyes, yet he made more sense than the smart ones. Before Rocky could think of an answer the others arrived back and he was too busy cooking.

Vince ate very little, coughed a lot, and soon fell asleep. He slept fitfully, frequently coughing himself awake.

While the rest of them ate around the fire in the darkening gully, Rocky took the chance to ask, "What were the people like on the islands?"

Willie Jay commented sympathetically, "Yeah, I guess you never got a look at them, huh?"

"Nah. They kept us locked up."

Joe Mack's voice was sneering, but somehow Rocky knew from his tone that he was scornful of the GR, not of him. "Yeah, scared you'd escape."

"Would you?" Willie Jay asked, apparently sincerely.

Rocky stared at him for a moment. "Hell, yeah!"

Johnny protested the use of the word, "Hell."

Willie Jay spluttered, "B-but then you'd never be able to go home."

Rocky thought, 'I was right the first time. This guy's as dumb as a brick.' Out loud he said, "Do you think I got any chance of going home from the GR? Ever? Alive or dead?"

Sam quickly answered Rocky's original question. "The islanders ain't like anyone I ever met before."

"You got that right!" Chuck agreed forcefully. "They never let us see their President. They never even took us to their capital."

Joe Mack sounded equally exasperated. "You'd think they'd be happy to be rescued after all this time. But no! They took a vote on if they wanted to know us or not! Can you believe that?!"

Rocky couldn't stop his lips from twitching. "Yeah, as matter of fact I can. If a vote would make any difference, I bet the Free West would vote against knowing the GR."

The explorers snickered.

"Yeah, no doubt," Sam nodded. "My people voted the best they could with guns and explosives. If that didn't stop the GR, a paper vote's going to do even less. If the oilionaires want something the islanders got they'll get to know them, vote or no vote."

Rocky was surprised. "You don't know how they voted?"

They shook their heads. "Nah."

Joe Mack explained, "Major Temperance figured the islanders were the devil's own. He already wouldn't let his men go ashore without arms, even if they would have gone, which they wouldn't, but after guys got sick he made it a direct order that no one was to set foot on devil's land – and that included us. We couldn't stay as long as we needed to because Temperance insisted on bugging out as soon as he got sick."

Rocky stared. "What? What do you mean 'without arms'?"

It was their turn to stare at him.

"You mean you never heard about that?" Chuck shook his head in disbelief. "Everyone was talking about it all over the ship. I figured for sure you heard about the ace shot there taking on a tree." He gestured to the snoring lump in the shadows back from the fire.

"Yeah, we heard Vince shot a tree that the islanders worshiped, and they were so mad they drugged Vince and carried him back to the ship unconscious."

There was silence for several moments, with the explorers staring at one another and at the fire. Rocky started to worry that he'd said something wrong.

Sam broke the tension by saying, "The one part I know for sure you got wrong is the islanders worshiping trees. They don't. They got a God they got to ask permission from before they cut wood."

Rocky thought about that. "So, it's true that they're Pagan." He felt strangely comforted by the news that there really were other nations aside from his that lived outside of the GR religion.

"Yeah, that part's true," Johnny leaned forwards. "God brought us here to save their souls."

Joe Mack leaned back, propping himself up on his elbows and stretching his feet out towards the fire. "Shoot, Johnny, I thought you said God done got us all the way out here so's His Truth'd be known."

Rocky could tell this was an old pattern between those two. It sounded exactly two brothers bringing up an age-old irritation. One part of him was reassured by the normalcy of it, while another part stayed tense in case it erupted.

True to the nature of such things, Johnny started to wind up. Equally true to form, Sam cut them off. "What we meant by, 'without arms' is after the gun was fired the islanders didn't want no one on their land that packed."

That astonished Rocky so much that all he could do was stare. His mind went blank as he grappled with the image. "If they got no weapons, what were they going to do if you paid them no mind?"

Sam said quietly, "At that time we figured they couldn't do nothing. I was respecting their wishes so we could find out about them, but now I want to know why you said Vince was drugged."

Vince snarled from his bed, "How many times do I got to hear about that?!" He subsided into a fit of coughing.

"Let's leave him to get his rest," Sam suggested, getting to his feet. "The GR can't see the tubs from the ship. We can spend all the time we want in the tubs and talk there."

Willingly they got up and left Vince to his misery, made their way along the gulley to the beach, then along the beach to the hot seepage. Rocky was surprised by how much light was left in the sky when they were out from under the thick foliage of the gully, where it was pitch-black. It was dusk outside, but not the deep night he'd expected. They enlarged the tubs until they had three which were each big enough for two men to sit comfortably in the warmth.

"Now, then, first," Sam started when they were all comfortable, "Spill the beans on this story that the islanders drugged Vince."

Rocky was still trying to come to terms with being safe, well fed, and on an equal footing with his companions. He stammered, "It was – um – it's just – he was out cold, and he wasn't drunk or sick, and he wasn't hit on the head – not that we heard about, anyway."

Joe Mack gave a gusty sigh. "I hate to admit it, but with everything else going on I never gave much thought to Vince's state."

"You ain't the only one," Chuck shook his head.

Sam added, "I was so busy looking out at all the weird things out there, I missed what was right under my nose."

Willie Jay asked, "Do you think it's true, Sam?"

"Of course it is, son. There ain't nothing else it can be."

"But, Sam, Vince said the islanders never touched him."

"I don't know how they did it, but it's got to be them. Ain't nothing else it can be. That answers your question, Rocky. We don't know what they would have done, but we know we wouldn't have got away with it."

Rocky had learned from watching and listening to the explorers that Sam was like the Dad more than the leader of a unit, Joe Mack and Chuck were like the big brothers, Johnny and Willie Jay were like the little brothers, and Vince was like the annoying middle brother that's barely tolerated by the rest of the group, not really fitting in with either the older ones or the younger ones. "What made you do this?" he asked them all, generally.

"We follow Sam," Joe Mack murmured, sliding down into the warm water until all that could be seen of him was his hat tipped over his eyes, hiding his face, the back of the hat brim resting on the sand behind his head.

"I had hoped you had some curiosity of your own," Sam reproached him gently.

"I do, I want to know what's out there," Willie Jay sounded like an eager child. He reminded Rocky of a puppy wagging its tail hopefully.

"I want to know the truth," Johnny stated firmly.

Chuck grinned, his teeth shining in the moonlight. "How do you like it so far?"

"What?"

"Your 'God's own truth.' How do you like what you've seen of it?"

"I don't know what's true and what's not," Johnny sighed.

Rocky looked at him with new respect. Until that moment he'd had no respect for anyone who followed the GR religion. This was the first time he'd heard any GR admit that he didn't know something, never mind something about religion.

Feeling safe with his companions, he dared to tell them, "I'm really glad I don't have to start tomorrow by swearing allegiance the flag, prayer, church services, bible studies, listening to teachings from The Wright Way and The Wisdom of Abraham Wright, and fasting until it's all over."

He half expected his idyll to end abruptly after that, but Sam commented, "One of the first hints I had that the GR was going in the wrong direction is that swearing allegiance the flag comes first, before prayer. No matter how much you love the flag, prayer should come first. By putting allegiance to the flag first they're looking in the wrong place for guidance."

"That's the whole point, Sam," Johnny said with feeling. "If you put the wrong things first you leave yourself open to sin."

Chuck answered dryly, "Thanks, Johnny, we got it."

Sam continued as if they hadn't spoken, "Before my homeland was conquered my people knew a lot of things that the GR call, 'Propaganda of the Devil.' There was a man by the name of Thor Hyerdahl who had crossed the ocean in a boat of reeds and found islands. When I was a kid, I had a teacher that I thought I could ask about stuff like that. He told me stories like that were unscriptural fantasy, like flying to the moon or reptiles the size of houses, or that the world is round, and that believing in ungodly stories was one of the sins that had brought about Judgement Day. He gave me three stripes to make sure I never strayed into wrongful thoughts again and told my father I had got into sinful misinformation."

"What did your Dad do?" Chuck asked.

Willie Jay's eyes bugged out. "My Daddy would've whopped the hide right off my back."

Sam sighed. "My Dad was always disappointed in me. He thumped me pretty good for putting the whole family in danger. What if the teacher had reported it to the authorities? What if they'd figured I'd got the stupid ideas from my family and searched the place? What if they took me away from my parents to 'protect me from their wrongful influence'? It was a big lesson learned that day to keep my mouth shut."

"But it never taught you to stop believing, huh, Sam?" Joe Mack asked from under his hat.

"No, I knew it was the truth. The GR needs to keep the citizens ignorant so that they won't know enough to be able to tell when they're being snowed. Put patriotism, religion, and allegiance in place of thought and knowledge and you got folk that don't kick near as much." Sam sighed. "There's no way to know if it was planned that way or just sort of happened. The only thing that's sure is that's what they're doing now. Instead of wanting to know what's out there they want to control what's right under their noses and ignore everything else."

Joe Mack raised his hat slightly to peer out from under the brim, "If you've got the right answer, you don't need to look for answers no more."

"There's more to it than that," Sam insisted. "Sure, there are lots of citizens that feel that way, but more and more these days I get the feeling that the way people believe is not natural somehow."

Chuck slid down until the warm water was up over his shoulders. "You getting to be a conspiracy theorist, Sammy boy?"

"I don't think so. I don't know if it's a 'conspiracy' or not. What it looks like is: it matters enough to someone to stop us questioning anything and everything that he or she or it or they are willing to go to a lot of trouble to make sure that thinking and asking anything at any time is anti-social, unpatriotic, and sinful. It's overkill. So why is it that important to them, and who are they?"

Willie Jay stared. "What do you mean, Sam?"

Joe Mack sat up. "You don't think it's the religion?"

"No, I don't. I think the religion is being used. Oh, sure there are people who truly believe, but their faith is being used against them. Who's doing it and why?"

"If you're right," Johnny said, slowly, "Then it would be working for the Lord to work against them."

"Slow down, Johnny," Sam sounded alarmed. "Think about what you're saying."

Johnny took a deep breath and said, "If they're misusing the Word of God I can't just stand by."

"No matter what?" Chuck asked.

"No matter what."

Johnny's voice was barely above a whisper, but Rocky could feel his sincerity. The leap of hope in his heart quickly died as the thought jumped unbidden into his mind, 'What can one man do?'

Joe Mack shook his head. "Give your head a shake, Johnny boy. What good will it do for you to get yourself killed?"

"I don't know. All I know is I can't do nothing."

"Even if we all got in it with you, what do you think six guys can do against the GR Military and all the citizens who think you're going against God's Word?"

Sam nodded. "That's my point that someone's using religion to control the nation."

"More to the point," Joe Mack continued, "Do you really think Vince would be part of it?"

All heads turned to look back towards the tree-lily gully.

"I bet he'd figure we're anti-Wright," Chuck muttered.

Willie Jay spoke up, "No, he's one of us! He'd stick with us."

"I doubt it," Chuck pursed his lips. "What we're talking about is insurrection. That's suicide. I don't think Vince believes in anything enough to put his life on the line for it."

"All we got to do is tell him about it! He's not here. You're not being fair to him!"

Sam's calm voice settled them all down. "You're a good boy, Willie Jay, as loyal as the day is long. Not everyone is as loyal as you. You don't get that yet, and I hate to be the one to break it to you. I'm sorry to say, I think Chuck's right. Vince don't believe in nothing enough to risk his life for it. What we're talking about here is an underground. Open rebellion ain't going to get us nothing but shot." He turned to Rocky. "I'd sure like to free you guys, but I don't see how we can. Don't wait for us. If we can do something we will, but more like you got to save your own selves. We can't even keep in touch with you. There ain't no way to get messages to you. We can't even take the ship away from those guys, so there ain't no way we can break you guys out of Port Persistence."

Joe Mack spluttered, "Take the ship away from them? Are you out of your mind?"

"No, I'm just saying what we can't do. What good would it do us if we did take control? Even if it was all six of us, and the Weskies didn't get thrown in the brig before they had a chance to help us, what next? Where are the survivors going to go?" He turned to Rocky. "What would be the chances of your people welcoming this ship?"

Rocky could see it in his mind's eye. The Star of Galilee with assembled banners of the Free West sailing towards the harbour. He knew they'd think it was a GR trick. With a heavy heart he told them, "There's no way to make them believe we're the good guys, they'd think it was a GR trick. They'd sink us first and find out who we were later."

"How could they sink the ship?" Willie Jay yelped.

Rocky felt unutterably sad. "It wouldn't take much to sink this tub. As it is, we'll be lucky if she makes it home. The GR pushing through to the coast is a disaster to everyone on the Coast, not just the Free West. Everybody's watching and waiting for them figure out how to use the port to come at us from the sea. That's why so many of us risked everything to stop them getting through, and then to push them back. I'd give my life over again if I thought it would stop them taking our kids' freedom."

"It was Colonel Lycus. The damned guy is a genius. Someone in the brass has it in for him. Don't know why, but it's just as well they do. If they used him properly it'd be all over. He's like a snake – sits and watches until he's sussed the enemy out. Ain't never seen no military commander work like him." Joe Mack looked over at Chuck as he finished.

Chuck agreed. "If the brass ever figures out what they got there, everything'll change. I figure they got it in for him on account he don't do things their way."

"Yeah, well, let's just be glad we're not going up against Old Jack. Last I heard he was trying to push the southern border south," Sam said. "He's not what we're worried about. We're not going to start no military campaigns; we're going to start an underground. What we got to figure out is how in God's name to do that, where we're going to do it, and what we're going to use it for. Don't say a word to Vince until I give the say so. I'll suss him out and see if he'll be part of it or not. Meantime you all think real careful about what you're getting into. It's deadly dangerous – not only to us, but to everyone we know and love. Don't come in with me if you're not sure."

"I'm sure," Johnny said promptly. "I got to do this, no matter what."

The others, even Willie Jay, were quieter about it.

"The main problem as I see it, is that the oilionaires control all the fuel and iron. Ain't nothing happens that they don't get a profit from.

Like exploring. They couldn't see that it was profitable, and it posed threat to security, so they didn't rate it as essential."

"But once they got the port, they figured you could test it out, huh, Sam?" Joe Mack grinned, a dark, unfunny grin.

Sam shrugged. "There was no other way to do it. I don't care what their reasons were for letting us do it, I was just glad to get the chance."

Chuck and Joe Mack glanced at each other. Quietly, Chuck warned, "Their reasons for letting us do this can come back and bite us."

Johnny piped up, enthusiastically, "That don't matter. We know for sure someone in the rest of the world survived Judgement Day. God wanted us to know the truth, and now that we know it, He will use it according to His Will. 'Ye shall know the Truth and the Truth shall set ye free'."

Joe Mack laughed softly. "Ye shall know the Truth and the Truth shall make ye freak."

Johnny refused to be tamped down. "We will tell our stories when we get home. All of us. There's no way they can stop the truth. 'All things work together for good for those who love the Lord'."

As the explorers argued, Rocky day dreamed. His mind wandered back to his home every time he had a chance to think, as if his subconscience couldn't face where he was or what had happened to him.

After Rocky and his brothers had returned from their failed quest, the oldest one, River, claimed that he'd seen girls flocking around guys in uniform. He was going to hike south to the Free West and join the resistance against the GR. Remembering it, Rocky would have laughed at their naïveté if he hadn't been so close to tears.

In considering their aim to become heroes in uniforms without too much risk, they decided against the closest battle-site, on the other side of the mountains. The GR fought hard there, and often advanced, being beaten back by super-human efforts by the legendary mountain men. There would be plenty of glory if they fought over there, but, although they wanted to protect their homeland from the GR, River's plan was for them to live to come home and get the girls. The younger boys were all for that, so they headed off to the coast with the intention of making their way south to the exciting nation of the Free West.

All the way down the coast to the Free West, the people had treated them like heroes. They'd been willing to work for food and shelter, but as soon as they said they were on their way to join the army to fight the GR, they were fed, clothed, housed, and praised. Toasts were drunk to their bravery, speeches made about the future depending on young people like them, and local kids were asked why they weren't as brave as the strangers. At every place the brothers stopped, a young man or woman joined in their trek.

Everyone wanted to see the Free West at least once in their lives. It was known as the last hope of civilisation, because everyone knew if the GR ever managed to fight their way across the desert, the only thing that would stand between freedom and military occupation was the bravery and fighting spirit of the Free West.

It was an exhilarating place to be. Men and women in uniform on the streets, big vehicles in camouflage paint rumbled along carrying either troops or weaponry, filling the air with the scent of hot vegetable oil. None of the young people had ever seen anything so busy in their lives. It got the boys' blood pumping, stuffing their heads with visions of how the girls would flock to them once they were part of it all.

Because of the way the coastal nations had treated them when they said they wanted to fight the GR, they all assumed that they would be welcomed with open arms by the Free West. It was a rude shock to discover that 'hicks' weren't prized recruits.

"More trouble than you're worth," the recruiting officer grumbled.

River was indignant. "We walked for weeks to help in the fight to keep our freedom."

"Your kind always does. You come here with no discipline; you have no clue what it means to go to war; the first time you have to do something you don't like you run home crying for Mommy."

A few of their new friends went back right then. Boot camp was a nasty shock for the ones who stayed. More dropped out at each stage, until, by the time Rocky saw combat, there was only a handful left of the merry band who'd arrived.

After the first shock of actual combat, most of the fighting blurred into one long nightmare that went on for years. His teens, his youth, slipped away and still the war went on. The confidence they'd had when Rocky was green bled slowly away as the GR gradually began to advance. In the days when they could still send word home, he lost his brother, River. Pulled to the Medic by his sergeant, Rocky sat with River throughout his last hours.

"We should've gone to the mountains," River said with an attempt at a grin.

In an effort to be light-hearted, Rocky returned, "This was supposed to be the easier one, with the Southies here to hit them from the other side. It was supposed to be better than taking on the GR by ourselves like the mountain men do."

River winced. "It was, too, before they got that new guy."

"Yeah. We can blame the mountain men for that, too. If they hadn't killed so many GR and their colonel, the GR wouldn't have sent so many good troops from here."

That got the reaction Rocky was looking for. River stared, confused. "Are you serious? If they'd sent all the good troops to the Sierras, we would have had it easy."

"Yeah, but then they wouldn't have sent the new guy here." Rocky was grasping at straws, desperate to distract his brother. He had no idea if it was the right thing to do or not, but he couldn't think of anything else.

"What's with that guy, any way?" River sounded fretful, not amused as he'd hoped.

He decided to give up trying to be goofy and answered thoughtfully, "He's like a vulture circling overhead while you walk across the desert. You think it's nothing, but when you wake up in the morning it's sitting a hundred feet away looking at you. If you try to drive it away, you just waste energy. It just hops out of reach and then circles over you all day again. And when you wake up the next morning it's sitting and waiting, looking at you. Only this time he's fifty feet away and you get scared that he knows something you don't. From then on you know you're his next meal and there's nothing you can do about it."

River nodded. "You've got it. No matter what we do, we can't drive that guy back to the GR. He keeps on gaining ground. We've got to stop him, no matter what it takes."

Distressed by River's intensity, Rocky soothed him, "You don't have to worry about that. That's Sarge's job. Your job is to get better so you're in shape for all those girls we're going to meet when we get home."

River shook his head. "I'm not getting home." He held up a finger to cut off Rocky's protest. "This is about way more than girls, man."

Rocky knew that. He'd known it for some time, but he wasn't able to talk about it right then when he was facing losing his brother. All he could do was shake his head, swallow hard, and blink.

"No, man, come on, Rock, we don't have a lot of time. Find me something to write on." Tears blinding him, Rocky ran from the tent. With superhuman speed he found paper and pencil and sprinted back with them.

River was visibly weaker in that short time. A nurse was wiping his forehead. She wanted to show Rocky how to do it, but River waved her away. "I want to be alone with my brother."

He wrote as much as he could before his strength faded. Then Rocky took the letter and wrote as River dictated to him. He said nothing when he ran out of paper, but kept on making the sounds of writing hoping, that River wouldn't notice. There would be plenty of time afterwards to find another piece of paper and write the rest down. He knew he would never forget River's last words.

It wasn't long before Rocky wasn't even pretending to write. River was no longer dictating; he'd drifted into a rambling kind of reminiscence of their childhood. His eyes were shut, his voice was faint, and Rocky didn't need the nurse to tell him it wouldn't be long now.

River asked, "Do you remember that day we decided to go up north to meet girls?"

Rocky did his best to laugh. "I sure do! We found a beautiful girl, but she wouldn't go with any of us because we called her 'Cleaner.'"

He was rewarded by a faint smile. "Yeah, we sure messed that up, didn't we? We thought we were It."

Rocky felt his heart drop with sadness for the innocence and faith that was gone forever. "Yeah, we sure did. Then we came here so the girls would like us. Mussed that up, too, huh?"

"No, no, no, man. Don't you get that it's not about girls now? How many times have I got to say it? It's all about stopping that vulture. I'm not going to be around. **Estoy jodido.** You got to do my share. ¿Aggaraste la onda?"

Rocky was appalled. He had been trying to be cheerful so that River wouldn't think he was dying and give up. He clung to the desperate hope that if River believed he would live, he would keep on fighting. "Don't say that!" he choked.

River sighed with a sadness that made Rocky guilty. "Out of everyone I thought I could tell you the truth."

Rocky gulped. "No, no, River, we can tell the truth to each other. It's – it's just hard for me to hear it."

"I don't have time to wait for you to get used to it, I'm feeling cold already."

Rocky felt his insides knot up. Climbing to his feet he choked out, "Can I get the medic?"

River caught his arm in a surprisingly strong grip. "No. Listen to me. Now that it's all over for me I see things I never saw before. This guy is a real vulture. He'll pick our eyes out while we're still alive, and we can't do a thing about it. Promise me you'll never stop fighting against him. I can't rest easy thinking you're going to give up and go home."

"I won't quit, River, I promise."

River let out a deep sigh and relaxed. "Do you remember how Buffy used to dance in the long grass?"

"Yeah, I sure do. You always got mad at her. You said she was a butterfly-brain."

"I didn't know then how important feeling free is. She's the freest person I ever met in my life. I want her to stay that way."

"She won't be a little girl anymore."

"No, no, we missed that, didn't we, Bro? All the kids grew up. I'm sorry I never got to see them again. If you get home again, you'll tell them how much I love them, won't you, Rock? And tell Buffy I'm sorry I was impatient with her. She's the special one, you know. She's the one I dream about."

Delighted that he wasn't the only one who did that, Rocky told River with genuine enthusiasm, "Me, too! I dream about her laugh. You know how she used to play tricks on us and give herself away by giggling? I had a dream about that, and when I woke up, I was smiling. I got to fight against the vulture, no matter what, so that people stay free like that. You know what they say it's like for women and children in the GR – no play. I couldn't bear to see a happy soul like our little Butterfly go under the heel of that, even if she's a big girl now."

River didn't answer.

Rocky looked more closely. He couldn't believe it. He shook River and shouted at him, but he didn't respond. All that happened was the nurse came running and covered River's face. Rocky shouted at her, too. "I was talking to him! I was holding his hand! I would have heard or felt something!"

But she reminded him that there were other wounded there, and his yelling was disturbing them.

After all this time his brother's death still unnerved Rocky. He still couldn't accept that you could be alive one second and dead the next and someone looking at you, talking to you, and holding your hand wouldn't notice. One part of him still blamed himself, while another part was thankful that he'd been there, and that it had been peaceful enough that he hadn't made a sound.

Not wanting anyone to see him with tears in his eyes, Rocky dipped both of his hands in the water and splashed his face as if he was washing it. As he wiped the water from his eyes, he realized that there wasn't enough light for them to see details like tears. He lay back again, listening. They were arguing, in very low tones, how an underground could be run. Amazed, he recognised that they really were planning to work against the GR. Not only that, but they were in no doubt that it was life-threatening to do so.

He sighed in relief. These guys were for real. He could depend on them. They might not be able to do anything, but if it was at all possible, he knew without a shadow of doubt that these guys would pull it off. Meantime, he could let the other Weskies know that not all of the GR were the same. He'd stay alert for any chance that they could do something for themselves. "For you, Bro," he whispered. Looking up the dark, rocky slope outlined in the moonlight against the star-filled sky, he could almost see Butterfly standing right out on the far edge, her arms outstretched, face tipped up, and hair blowing in the wind. "For you, too, Sis."

He reaffirmed to himself that he would do it all again, even though Major Lycus had defeated the combined forces of the Free West and the Yucatan Junta and pushed a Panhandle through from the GR to the coast. The colonel who took over was the one in charge when Rocky's unit was captured, but Lycus was still the one he feared. That slow, unstoppable advance was the stuff of nightmares.

No longer thinking of himself as a loser for getting caught, Rocky relaxed while he had the chance. He wasn't even afraid of what lay ahead of him when he got back on board. It was something he had to go through, something he could go through, for his people and for his family. He stared up the rocky slope again, willing the vision of Butterfly to come back to him. She was eight years old to him, always, with the wind in her hair, standing way too close to the edge. He refused to think about the years that had passed since then. That image was what he was fighting for; that freedom, that confidence, that love of life, that innocence. If he'd had the wherewithal to build an altar, he would have sent an invocation to the Goddess to shore him up.

Remembering that for the last few years he had felt that the Goddess had abandoned him, Rocky had a strong urge to make his apologies for his loss of faith. He wondered if Sam would understand. As soon as he thought of that he knew he couldn't say anything like that in front of Johnny. He was going to have to give it a miss.

But Johnny fell ill during the night. The explorers tended to him, worried.

"He already had the flu, Sam," Chuck fretted.

"What'll happen to him if he gets it twice?" Willie Jay asked.

"Pray for him," Sam advised.

"Dumb ass shouldn't have got in the water if he was still sick," Joe Mack grumbled.

They took turns sitting up with Johnny. In the silence while Sam was on watch, Rocky approached him about making an invocation to the Goddess.

"You can't wake the guys up," Sam shook his head.

Rocky murmured, "If I had a piece of paper and a pencil, I wouldn't make any noise at all."

"We don't have anything for you to sacrifice."

"We don't do anything like that. That's a GR lie."

Sam's voice had a completely different tone. "You don't say!" He got up. "No one's going to hear you?"

Rocky was anxious to reassure him. "No one will hear a thing, and I'll make sure Johnny, Willie Jay, and Vince don't see a thing."

With a grunt, Sam turned and went to his bed roll, returning with a pencil and paper which he dropped into Rocky's lap. "I'm real tired," he said and turned away.

"Get some sleep,' Rocky advised him. "I should take a turn with Johnny like everyone else."

Sam paused, and then muttered, "I was going to call Joe Mack in two hours."

Rocky felt truly one of the explorers at that moment. He hunkered down beside Johnny, at the edge of the fire pit to write out his invocation, thinking about the trust that had been put in him by leaving their most helpless member in his unsupervised care.

It suddenly hit him. The Goddess hadn't abandoned him. She'd been taking care of him all along, even after he turned his back on her. It was obvious to him, now that his head was clear, that she had put him in this place with these people. He took deep breaths, filling his lungs with the scent of the tree-lilies. He was convinced beyond a shadow of doubt that the Goddess was in the gully. It was too beautiful and smelled too sweet to be natural. So, she had given him this rest, with these men who accepted him as one of them, and now he knew that there were men in the GR who sympathised with the Weskies and would help them if they could. That, by itself, changed everything.

Rocky reached carefully into the cool outside edges of the fire pit, scooping up ashes. He walked clockwise around the fire letting a thin trickle of ash spill from his fingers until he had created a circle around the whole fire, with enough room near Johnny that he could sit inside the circle without getting burnt, and stay right by Johnny. With his ashy fingers he drew symbols on his bare skin. Staring up at the dark canopy overhead, he wished he could see the stars. Watching the smoke and sparks float up until they vanished into the jungle, he moved his lips, soundlessly asking the four quarters to watch over his invocation and make sure it caused no harm. Then he thanked the Goddess for continuing to love him even after he'd lost faith. He told her how sorry he was that he'd given up on her. Then he pleaded with her to keep his family safe, to help her people escape the GR, and drive the GR back from the coast.

Mindful that he was telling the Goddess how to do it when she knew more than a mortal ever could about what was going on and how to fix it, he stopped himself. He had to wait for the tears to clear before he could see to write on his piece of paper. Then he wrote, 'I seek the greatest good for the greatest number of people. So mote it be.'

His tears dripped onto the paper as he tried to read it over to make sure it said what he wanted to say and saw his family in his mind's eye. Leaning over the heat of the fire to get enough light to read brought beads of sweat to his forehead. Feeling them, he pressed the paper against his brow to add his sweat to it. Next, he picked at scratches on his arms from pushing through the jungle until they bled so that he could add his blood to the paper as well.

Just as he was reaching out to hold it over the embers, intending to watch it burn and float up into the night, Johnny's ragged breathing changed. He gave the kind of rattling cough that Rocky had heard from those expiring on the battlefield.

In a split second he had dropped the paper the flames, hastily murmuring, "East, West, North, South, thank you," and to the Goddess, "Thank you for listening to me." All while he leapt to his feet and brushed the side of his left foot across the ash, opening the circle counterclockwise as he left it.

Kneeling beside Johnny, he whispered, "Are you okay, Man?" Getting no response, he shook Johnny's shoulder, calling him, "John! Johnny! Wake up, Man!" He was rewarded by a hacking cough as Johnny woke up, coughing so hard that he couldn't catch his breath.

Rocky helped Johnny to sit up, and then left him to sprint around the fire to shake Joe Mack. "Hey, wake up! Johnny's in rough shape."

He ran back to Johnny hoping he would be able to erase the ash circle before Joe Mack saw it. Kicking the ash every time he passed any part of the circle was the best he could do. He hoped that was enough to make it unrecognisable before anyone saw it. "How are you?" he asked.

Johnny was still coughing and gasping for air.

Joe Mack came galloping up. "Where's Sam?"

"Sleeping. He let me take a watch."

"You're a good guy." Joe Mack leaned down to see how Johnny was.

Pleased as he was with the kind words, Rocky didn't think it was the right time for him to get attention. "If we prop up his head he can lay back and still breathe."

"Yeah, with what?"

"My bed." Rocky ran to his bed, pulled his blanket off and scooped up an armful of the ferns and sweet-smelling greenery.

"What're you going to sleep on?" Joe Mack whispered.

As he stuffed the plants under one end of Johnny's bed, Rocky murmured, "I can make what's left into a bed."

"Bullshit! ¡**Chingadazos!**" Joe Mack kept his voice hushed even though he spoke forcefully enough to make Rocky jump.

"Don't," Johnny gasped, putting his hand on Joe Mack's arm.

"You don't get it, Johnny. This guy gave his bed to you. Ain't no way in . . . ain't no way he's going to sleep on the damp ground."

Johnny tried to shake his head, but that set off another round of coughing.

"You take my bed while I sit up with Johnny," Joe Mack ordered Rocky. "I'll take Willie Jay's bed when he takes his watch."

"Thank you," Rocky said, getting back up. "I might as well get the rest of it, then. Can you support Johnny so I can make it even for him?"

So, Joe Mack helped Johnny to his feet and held him there so that Rocky could pack all of his mattress under one end of Johnny's, making a raised pillow so that Johnny could sleep semi-upright, with his head and shoulders supported.

As Johnny got into his bed and Joe Mack tended the fire, Rocky made his way to the water tank with a cup and brought back cool water to soothe Johnny's throat.

When he got back and gave the water to Johnny, Joe Mack turned from the fire, sitting on his haunches with his arms on his knees. Rocky made sure Johnny was comfortable, and then went to Joe Mack to see what he wanted.

"We got water," Joe Mack pointed out when Rocky was close enough for them to talk without waking the others up.

"It's not cold."

"Right." Joe Mack looked over towards the water they had scooped up to have handy. Even though they'd put it back from the heat of the fire, there was no way it would be as cool as the tank water. He turned back to Rocky, saying, "You think of everything, don't you?" Then he noticed the soot and ash all over Rocky's arms, chest, and face. "What the hell?"

Rocky regretted getting close enough to the fire for the marks to be seen before he had a chance to wash it off. The thought of washing brought to mind how clean he'd been when they'd got out of the tubs, simultaneously giving him an idea of why Joe Mack was so surprised, and how to explain it away. "I don't want to look so clean that they think I had it easy."

Understanding dawned in Joe Mack's eyes. "Don't worry, Buddy, we'll kick you around so bad they won't punish you for having a good time."

Rocky got up to head off to Joe Mack's bed. "Oh, thanks, man." He couldn't keep the wry tone out of his voice.

"Now you're just being picky."

Rocky had to fight the urge to laugh aloud.

They returned to the ship in the morning with two sick men. Vince recovered in the average amount of time, but Johnny was frighteningly ill and wasn't fully recovered by the end of the trip.

Rocky didn't tell the other Weskies about his conversation with the explorers. Not only was he afraid of being overheard, but he was also afraid if any of them were tortured they might let it slip, and he wanted it to succeed. He felt very close to the explorers from that time on, even though he knew they couldn't do anything for him directly. He worried with them as Johnny's health declined until he was so ill that they were all afraid he wouldn't survive, and then rejoiced with them as Johnny pulled through.

It was a thin and frail Johnny who joined the rest of them at the rails as they turned around the bottom of the long spit of land and sailed up the inside towards Port Persistence. Despite his weakness, he was excited at the sight of the port, taking the fact that they'd made it against all odds as proof that God's Will would be done.

The sight of the explorers clapped into irons and hauled away in prison vans as soon as they set foot on land struck Rocky like a physical blow. He went numb and cold all through, watching his last hope evaporate. Besides, they were good guys, even Vince, and Rocky seriously doubted any of them would ever be free again.

He was pleased, though it wasn't enough to lift his spirits, to see the MPs swarm over the ship questioning the soldiers and screaming at Major Temperance. Fortunately, a number of the men had boasted that the Weskies had been locked in the brig the whole time they'd been at the foreign islands, so the Weskies weren't interrogated the way the GR were about what they'd seen. They were simply ordered to have seen nothing, then questioned closely about how to handle the ship. While they were giving as little useful information as they could manage, they made sure to let it drop that military property had been damaged by the Major's orders, both military and prisoners being thrown overboard as a punishment.

Assembled on deck in preparation for being marched back to the slave quarters, the Weskies were left untended for a few moments after they were yoked together and shackled. There was the briefest chance to speak to each other, and they used it to tell one another that they'd got back at the Major. It was difficult to keep from grinning when they found out that most of them had the same idea, and, even better, several of them got a chance to say it. They had no way of knowing if the seeds they planted had any effect, but it was a comfort just the same to hope that maybe they had.

Teeth clenched against smiling, Rocky distracted himself by looking north. He wasn't aware that he'd sighed until his yokemate, Cliff, murmured, "What?"

"Home," he breathed, his throat tight.

It was as if the air had been let out of them. There was a collective sigh, and all of their shoulders slumped. Staring north towards the home he knew he'd never see again, the only positive thought he could come up with was that when the GR got their detail together to march them off, they would all look like they were miserable enough not to need much in the way of beating down.

To keep his mind off what lay ahead of him, and what might be happening to the explorers, Rocky cast his thoughts back to his youth; back to trying to remember what Cleaner's real name was. He couldn't think of it, but he wished her well and hoped she was safe, mentally telling her, "It's all for you, too."

That brought him his usual memory of his little sister, Butterfly. "And for you," he vowed, feeling slightly disloyal.

He pictured all his family, wondering what they were doing at that moment on the other side of those mountains. There would be kids he hadn't met, and the ones he did know would be grown. Even Roadapple. It was the boys who'd nicknamed their slow-witted brother, 'Roadapple' and now Rocky couldn't remember his real name any more than he could remember Cleaner's real name. "We were such rotten little shits," he thought, wondering why they'd never realised it. It was up to him to make up for it with Roadapple. He was the only one left now.

The detail arrived, screaming at them, and they shuffled off. Rocky kept his head down, eyes lowered, shoulders slumped, feet shuffling with the others so that he seemed the same. But he was completely different inside. "Where there's life there's hope," he told himself, thinking of Sam. Somehow, he would let the other Weskies know that there were people in the GR who were actively involved in resistance. Perhaps they would find a way to escape, perhaps not. Rocky didn't know. He only knew he would never again give up.

CHAPTER FIFTEEN

Ray

It was the end of a long, hard week. Actually, it was a short week, but it had been such a grind that it felt as if it had lasted twice as long as it really had. Staying close to shore going over areas that had been picked clean generations ago, out and back to the same islands over the same seafloor day after day after day, never finding a thing, was tedious. There was nothing there, they knew there was nothing there, but Bram insisted that they had to keep to the course no matter how fruitless it was.

Because Mere had been born early, when Hine reached the latter half of this pregnancy, Bram only worked three days a week, and no overnights so that he would be there when she went into labour. He didn't even work the three days in a row. He went out on Moonday, stayed home on Mercuryday, went out again on Venusday, stayed home on Terraday, went out on Marsday, then stayed home both Saturnday and Sunday. He would be fretting about missing the birth of his son within an hour of leaving the dock.

And he was no picnic to be with, either. His mother, Beth, one of the Kaumoana's ten regular crew, pointed out, "Everything close to shore has been combed and re-combed for two hundred years, ever since our great-great grandparents first started hunting for metal under water."

Bram snapped at her, "Who's the Skipper here? Do you want to take over?"

Beth didn't say anything at the time, but she didn't go out with them anymore, claiming she was needed to help Hine's mother take care of Hine and Mere.

While Hine and Beth were staying ashore Bram filled the spaces in his crew by hiring Dailies like Ray and Ted. Glad as he was for the steady work, Ray still took work from other boat owners like Sue and Keisha. Partly he did it to fill in the extra days when Bram stayed ashore, and partly it was to avoid going out with Bram to take a break from the tension aboard the Kaumoana.

He didn't work on the Laughing Dolphin, however. Even though he knew Hatoe and Ben needed an extra hand with Miki staying home because of her pregnancy, and Nat going off to be a musician, he had avoided them ever since the trip to Rangitahua. He didn't know why he'd come apart out on the deep blue. He was embarrassed that he had, and ashamed that Ben and Hatoe had seen him in that condition. Even though neither of them had mentioned it to him or anyone else, talking to them or being near them reminded him of his humiliation, so he kept away from them as much as he could.

As the Kaumoana drew into dock, Bram made a running jump off the side of the boat onto the pier, landing in a scramble for footing, and racing to the ringer link.

"Damn fool's going to go in the water one of these times," Ted muttered, tossing a mooring line over the capstan on the pier to pull the boat gently up to the dock.

"Might cool him off a bit if he does," Ray muttered back, tossing the next line over the next capstan. "His Dad'd tell him first thing if anything happened. He's the Harbour Master, after all."

They had the ship moored and were washing her down when Bram came swaggering back to pay them. "I can't wait until this boy is born," he told them as he counted out the beads for Ray's and Ted's wages.

"You're not the only one!" his sister, Poma, exclaimed with great feeling.

Bram blinked at her in surprise. "It's not so bad for you. You don't have to live with Hine."

"No," Poma sounded as if she was agreeing until she added, "It's worse for us. We have to put up with you."

The ten people who usually crewed the Kaumoana were: Bram; Hine; Bram's mother, Beth; Poma; Poma's partner, Drew; Drew's parents and brother; and Hine's brother and sister-in-law.

Bram looked genuinely taken aback. "What do you mean?"

"Look at the way you spoke to Mum for starters."

"When?" he motioned to her not to air family laundry in public, "She hasn't sailed for a week."

Poma rejected his concerns with a dismissive wave. "Never mind about them. They've had to put up with you as much or more than we have." Then she fixed him with a stern look. "Why do you think Mum's keeping her distance?"

"She's got to help Hine."

"It's not Hine's first baby. She doesn't need that many people around. She's got her own Mum, Miki, all of the women of Matapihi, and the whole medical establishment of Te Ika a Maui. Not to mention the midwife."

The whole crew was gathered on the foredeck by that time, showing their agreement with Poma by the expressions on their faces, nods and small sounds. Bram looked from one face to another. "You're my family! I thought you'd understand how worried I am!"

His sister was relentless. "We do. But there's a limit. Dad would get word to you if you were needed. No matter how much stress you're under, a Skipper can't take it out on his crew."

Bram started to deny it, "But I don't!" then he gave in to the frowns on all the faces around him and appealed to them. "It's not really that bad, is it?"

Ray reckoned this was his one chance to speak up. "You know when I'm too busy to work for you sometimes? I do that to take a break."

Poma pressed the advantage. "I've been leaving Elly with Dad or Miki so she's not exposed to your temper, but if you can't find another way to deal with your worries, I'll stay home with her. It's not fair to expect Dad to take care of her while he's working. He has a lot of responsibility as Harbour Master, and don't forget Miki's pregnant, too."

Ray wasn't at all sorry to see the bravado knocked right out of Bram for once. He didn't feel the least bit sympathetic as Bram scrambled to explain, "It's not the same with Miki as it is with Hine. Mere was born way before now, so Hine's never been pregnant like this. She's huge, she's uncomfortable all the time, and depressed, and Mere's running her ragged, and the baby could come any minute. He's wearing her right out."

"There's no guarantee it's a boy," Ray muttered.

Unfortunately, Bram heard him. "Much you know!" he flared. "You're not a family man!"

"I've got a daughter," Ray defended himself.

"He's right," Drew's mother, Lia, put in. "You never can tell until you hold them in your arms."

"She's enormous, Lia, and there's only one baby. There's no way this is a girl. It's going to be big for a boy in our family."

Drew teased, "A big girl."

Bram was not amused. "There are no Wineeras in our family!"

"I was joking," Drew said in a flat voice.

"If you're finished with me, I'd like to go and grab a bite," Ray said, turning towards the side, badly wanting to get off the ship and away from all of them.

"Oh. Look, I'm sorry. Maybe I am a bit touchy. Can I take everyone out for tea to make it up to you? I'll go and get Hine and Mere and meet you at the Sea, Soy and Soda. It'll do her the world of good to get out of the house. Then we can all relax together and bury the hatchet."

That wasn't at all what Ray'd had in mind. Sea, Soy and Soda was a small, quiet tea shop that catered to a younger crowd and didn't serve alcohol. The live music was mostly kids singing about teen angst and young love. It was the ideal place for Bram to take his young family for their evening meal, but what Ray really wanted was to get away from the crew of the Kaumoana and have a lot of beer. "Oh, hey, ta, Bram. That's big of you, mate, but Sea, Soy and Soda is not where my taste buds were leading me. I'll catch you later."

"Where were you heading?" Bram asked.

"I don't know. Mean Eddies, probably."

"That's a really good idea!" Ted exclaimed.

"Yeah, I'm with you," Drew's father, Barry, joined in.

Before Ray knew what was happening, they were all agreeing to meet at Mean Eddies, and Bram had given in and agreed to go to Mean Eddies instead of Sea, Soy and Soda. That wasn't what Ray had planned, either. As he strode along the pier towards the ramp up the bank, he toyed with the idea of going to The Brown Jug without saying anything to any of them, but he thought better of it. It would look as if he was trying to avoid them, and though he was, he didn't want to make his relationship with them any more strained than it was. Bram had accepted their protest with surprisingly good grace. Ray didn't want to seem as ill-spirited about is as he felt.

Besides, The Brown Jug was a bar, not a restaurant, and he had his mouth set for the food at Mean Eddies. He resigned himself, telling himself that it wouldn't hurt him to be polite to Bram and Hine and the rest of the crew for a few minutes. Then he could retreat to the back room, work his way through a pitcher or two of beer and maybe gamble a little bit.

Mean Eddies was a boatie's hang out. It was the best place to come across boat owners looking for dailies to hire, and to hear what was going on in the boating communities. On top of all that, Mean Eddies made flat pies with crispy crusts that they baked on concrete slabs over gas fires. He had it all planned: he'd start with a big pitcher of beer and two pies to himself at a small back table; the salty fish pie called a 'Backwater' and the screaming hot 'Lava Flow.' If the Backwater was especially salty, he might even need a third pitcher of beer before staggering home and sleep it off. Maybe he wouldn't feel nearly as fed up tomorrow.

Ray walked in through Mean Eddies' front door of plain glass with the menu and operating hours painted on it, which put him inside a glassed in area facing another front door of round stained-glass panels that looked like the bottoms of many different colours of bottles. That arrangement kept out the worst of the cold wind in winter, and the blasts of heat in the summer.

To the right of the second door as he entered was an open, glassed in kitchen so that the customers could watch the cooks at work. There was a bench along the wall under the glass. It had probably been put there for people to sit on to wait for their food if they were taking it home, but the bench was always filled with children standing on it watching through the windows into the kitchen. The cooks always hammed it up to the kids, letting them see their food being made, letting them indicate through the window if they wanted this or that. The kids loved it, it kept them occupied, and it added to the friendly, cheerful atmosphere in the place.

At the end of the bench was the order counter. Ray ordered a mini backwater pie, making sure he included salt preserved fish, and a mini lava flow pie with extra horopito leaves to make sure it was hot enough to warrant the extra pitcher he'd talked himself into.

Hine's brother, Renny, was already there, calling to him from a table near the open wall to the beer garden. Renny and his partner, Gay, had a little boy. Often on board the Kaumoana there were three children all about the same age. Poma and Drew's Elly was a little bit older than Mere, and Renny and Gay's Ian was a little bit younger than Mere. Lately, since Hine had been staying home, and Bram had been increasingly hard to get along with, the children had been left ashore with grandparents or neighbours. Ray didn't miss the little children. It was a bit of relief to have a child-free ship to work on.

It's not that he didn't like kids, it's that he preferred to limit his interactions with them. It wasn't a thrill for him when little Ian darted across the restaurant shrieking, "Uncle Ray! Uncle Ray!"

"I'm not your uncle, kid," he muttered under his breath, automatically putting his hand on the boy's shoulder and patting him. "Let's go and see your Daddy and Mummy."

Renny reached out his arms for his son as they came up to his table. "Have you heard the latest?" he asked Ray.

Ray felt defensive. "I only just got here," he protested.

"They found another body from the Rangatira."

Ray was appalled. "Tangaroa of the sea!" He sank into a chair beside Renny. "How unspeakable for the family. They've already buried their child. Now they've got to go through it all again."

"It's better than never finding him, though, isn't it? All they could bury was his fingernails and hair clippings. Now they have his whole body."

"Her," Gay corrected him, making her way back to him from the direction of the women's toilet.

Realizing he was in Gay's chair, Ray got back to his feet and moved to the side, holding the chair for her.

"I thought it was one of men they found," Renny protested.

"Ta," Gay thanked Ray. "No, it was a just on the wallie in the back room."

Renny looked amazed. "You were in the back room? I thought you went to the women's."

Gay explained, patiently, "I did. Keisha's here. She told me."

Handing Ian over to his mother, Renny looked around asking, "Where is she?"

"In the back room," Gay said, absent-mindedly, her attention on her son.

Ray thought that much was obvious, but Renny protested, "What's she doing back there? Why didn't you ask her to join us? The more the merrier!"

Ray was about to break it to Renny and Gay that there wasn't any way he was going to try to eat in the beer garden with dozens of kids running around, shrieking, when the front door opened and in came Bram and Hine with Mere, followed by Ben and Miki. Bram had been right about one thing: Hine was enormous, waddling along with one hand pressed against the small of her back. She was barely recognisable as the slender and vibrant Hine she had been until a few weeks ago. The men and Miki were trying to keep Mere under control since it was obviously physically impossible for Hine to chase after her. Ray thought Mere was the most stubborn kid he'd ever met.

Everything about the evening so far made Ray so uncomfortable that all he wanted to do was run. It was not easy to avoid Ben when his partner was Hine's best friend. It was hard enough to duck Hatoe and Ben with the Laughing Dolphin moored directly opposite the Kaumoana across a pier only three metres wide without Miki showing up everywhere Hine went. He wanted to take off so that he wouldn't have to talk to Ben. He didn't know how to talk to Hine without looking at her, and the sight of her made him panic, she looked so miss-shapen and uncomfortable.

The last straw was Ian and Mere shrieking at the top of their lungs their delight at finding each other, and Ian shrieking, "Aunty Hinny!" in exaggerated joy as if he hadn't seen her for months instead of a few days. Ray didn't know how the adults could bear the high-pitched squeals. If either of those children had been his, he would have told it to keep its voice down. Instead of trying to quieten their kids, they were beaming, saying how cute it was, while to him it was like having nails driven into his head.

When his number was called, he escaped with all haste and no intention of rejoining them, ignoring Bram's protest, "You ordered yours already? I thought we'd order together and eat together."

Ray hadn't even reached the counter when the noise behind him reached painful new levels as Elly reacted to hearing her cousins and joined them from the beer garden, screeching with excitement.

Bram called out, "We'll be in the beer garden with Poma and Drew!"

Ray half turned and waved so that Bram would know he'd heard and wouldn't chase him. Then he flipped a bead-chain over his head and unhooked the beads to pay for the pies, carried one pie in each hand the couple of steps from the order counter to the end of the bar beside it, and ordered a four-litre pitcher of beer for the back room. He slid his hands from under the flat ceramic plates to pay for the beer right there so he wouldn't have to think about it later when he might not be able to.

His movement prompted the bartender to tell him, "I can get someone to carry that for you, sir."

"Thanks." Ray picked up the salty pie and wandered the length of the six-metre bar feeling free as the air and twice as light. Without looking, he knew the children had been taken outside from the drop in ear-splitting shrieks. To make sure he didn't see any of his crewmates beckoning to him, Ray kept his head turned the other way, watching the activity behind the bar.

At the end of the bar a waitress was emptying a stack of plates by scraping paper into what he supposed was a recycle bin out of his sight under the bar, food scraps beside the paper, stray beads rattling into something glass, then, without looking, the plates were flicked with a graceful turn of the wrist to fly across the space between the back of the bar and the wall to scuff through a slot not much bigger than the largest plate and clatter down into some kind of container on the other side of the wall. Ray was fascinated by her. She was so fast, never once looked at the slot, and never once missed it.

The bartender paid no attention to her, scooping empty glasses and mugs off the bar and down out of sight, where he washed them with quick thrusts of his arms up and down below the bar and the splooshing sound of hot, soapy water followed by the clink of glasses being dropped into a sink full of clean water.

Ray was so taken by their dance-like actions that he forgot for a moment to keep watch in the reflective coating over the lip of the bar. It was the colour of brass, but he knew from touching it that it was synthetic, held in place with wooden pegs painted to look like metal studs. It was more reflective than polished brass, which Ray used to his advantage by glancing at the mirror-like surface every now and then to make sure none of the crew was heading towards him. Hastily glancing into the faux-brass façade, Ray satisfied himself that no one in the main dining room was walking around. The diners were all at their tables, eating with their fingers, filling the room with a pleasant hum of conversation. The shrill voices of two- and three-year-olds drifted in from the beer garden over enough distance that it sounded pleasant to Ray. That was the way Ray liked children: at a distance.

What he wanted to do at that point was to be deep into his beer quickly so that if Bram came to talk him into joining the crew he'd be in no fit state to do so. There was no point in hanging around the bar watching them work. He had some serious drinking to do! With a bang one of the swinging doors beside the plate slot bounced open, just as Ray decided to get going. A young man burst through carrying a stack of clean plates of different sizes, the largest on the bottom, tapering in a tower to the smallest on top.

As quickly as the boy was on them, the girl was faster, leaping back from behind the edge of the bar at the sound of the bang, before the door had time to swing open. With a cheeky flip of her hips, that Ray was sure was meant for him, she sashayed around him and off across the floor. At the same time the bar tender scrunched himself into the sink so that the boy careened behind him without losing any momentum and continued down the whole length of the bar and on into the kitchen past the waiter at the other end who was pouring beer from the tap into a four-litre pitcher. Ray saw his lava flow pie sitting on a tray on the counter beside the waiter, reckoned the beer was for him and he'd better get a move on.

As he passed the swinging doors, they opened again, much less violently, to let out a pimply faced young man who was not wearing an apron. Everyone who worked at Mean Eddies wore a red shirt, black pants, black shoes, and a white apron. No bare toes or bare legs. Surprised to see someone there without an apron, as he crossed the open area between the end of the bar and the folding wall, Ray watched the youth.

They walked almost parallel to each other. The swinging doors had a sign announcing, 'Scullery' in cursive script on the right side, and round windows made to look like port holes in both doors. On one side of the doors was the plate chute, on the other was a triangle shaped stage filling the corner between the doors and the folding walls that Ray was heading for. There was a stone fireplace in the middle of the room, with the folding walls reached out to it from the men's toilet on the left side and the stage on the right.

The youth ignored the stair up to the stage and stepped straight up from the floor, sat down on the stool in front of an ancient white upright piano, and began to jangle the tinkly antique keys as Ray reached the fireplace. Pulling the wall back to get around it into the back room, Ray sorted it out. 'He's not wearing an apron because he's not handling food,' he thought, pulling the wall closed behind him to shut out the sound of the piano.

The back room was a contrast with the front room. Where the front was full of light and activity, surrounded with windows and light colours, the back had no windows at all. The ceiling beams were dark, the walls were panelled with wood alternated with red wallpaper, and it was quiet. The only light came from candles in small glasses on the occupied tables and fibre optic lamps over them. They were mostly set low, giving just enough reddish light to show the food or cards. There was a billiards table in one corner and a wall unit showing sports in another.

Ray's favourite table was clear; the first one behind the folding wall, against the red wallpaper on the right. It wasn't right up against the folding wall because there was a door to the scullery in the corner. Unlike the double doors in the front room, this door had no window in it. Instead of letting him see the clouds of steam, the activity and bright lights in the scullery, this one was comfortingly thick, heavy, and dark, blocking everything, leaving his table peaceful. He slid onto the bench, looking around in relief and satisfaction.

From his position Ray could watch what was happening around the back room. By looking over the fireplace he could see part of the front room as well. He put his shoulders against the wall, setting his pie down and reaching up to touch the glass shade of the lamp over his table, barely brushing it with a fingertip to set it to the lowest level. A warm glow enveloped him and his pie. He picked up a wedge-shaped slice, noting that it was hot enough that he had to be careful when he bit it, and turned his head to see who was there as he nibbled cautiously.

The folding walls slid back to admit the waiter carrying a tray bearing his lava flow pie, four litres of beer, and, to Ray's surprise, four chilled mugs. He thanked the waiter, not commenting on the extra mugs. Evidently four litres of beer meant four people.

Watching the waiter leave after he'd lit the candle on Ray's table, Ray noticed some young people had started dancing to the piano music in the open area on the other side of the folding walls. It irritated Ray that the waiter didn't close the wall all the way up to the fireplace, letting in some of the noise and light from the front.

He turned to the table beside him to make sure it was empty, put three of the mugs on it, then filled the fourth, emptied it in one long chug, refilled it, and turned his attention to his pies. A comforting buzz soon started in his brain, at first dampening the restless, anxious feelings. After quickly chugging down another two full mugs of beer the dampened distress was gone completely.

He was deeply involved in puzzling out whether he would be better to take one bite of each pie or eat all of one kind and then all of the other, punctuating each thought with another generous quaff of beer, when Keisha plunked herself down at his table. "G'day."

Ray blinked at her, feeling that she'd interrupted something important, but not sure what.

"Are you available for tomorrow?"

Ray shook his head.

Keisha's eyes widened in surprise.

It dawned on Ray's buzzing brain that she knew Bram was only sailing on alternate days, and Ray wasn't sailing with Hatoe anymore. Everyone knew everything in a small, one-industry community. To stall for time while he tried to straighten his thoughts out, he asked, "Who else are you hiring?"

Coyly she smiled at him. "No one."

Ray felt trapped. He wished she'd approached him before he'd started to drink, when he'd been in a better condition to cope with tricky spots like this. He hadn't seen her come into the back. No one could get past the folding doors or the scullery door without him seeing them. That meant she must have been in the back room all the time. Oh, right. Someone had said Keisha was in the back. That made him resentful. He pictured Keisha over in the far corner by the wallie where he wouldn't see her unless he went over there, watching him drinking, and then making her move. Well, he wasn't that easy. He drew himself up and said with great care, "I've had a lot to drink, and I plan to have a lot more. I won't be in shape to two up a boat. Sorry, Skip. If you were running three up, I might be able to sleep it off by the night shift."

She shook her head at him. "They'll cut you off."

He indicated the three empty mugs on the table beside him and grinned up at her as she stood up. "They think I'm four people."

She looked at the three empty mugs. "Careful you don't end up with a drinking problem, Ray."

Thinking, 'I don't have a problem with drinking, I have a problem with people talking to me about it,' he looked towards the front room she was about to walk into. The kids were still dancing. The tune was catchy. "Do you know what that is?" he asked her. "I've never heard it before."

"It's a new one by Nat."

"Nat?" he couldn't make out who she meant.

"Hatoe's Nat. Anatoe Amaru."

The penny dropped. "Our Nat? From here? But that's good!"

Keisha laughed. "Don't sound so surprised. People from here can do good things other than work the boats."

"But we're a bunch of boaties!"

"That doesn't mean we can never do anything else! The trouble with you, Ray, is the world is full of possibilities, and you can't see that."

She flounced off to the front room, hips swinging provocatively.

Ray refilled his beer mug, munching on a slice of pie, trying to remember what it was he'd been doing when she'd interrupted. He wasn't sure what she'd meant by her comment, but he resented it just the same.

Ted came through where Keisha had just left.

"Close it properly!" Ray snapped at him.

"Cor, man, what's up?" Ted pulled the wall right to the fireplace, saying, "Keisha just came out of here looking like she just found out someone's been poaching her weed, and here you are as cranky as Bram. You two have words?"

"Nah. I'm fed up with people leaving the wall open, so the racket comes through, and she's looking for crew for tomorrow."

Ted sat down at Ray's table. "You're not going with her?"

"No."

"Why not? Bram's not going out tomorrow – oh, by the way, Bram wants you to join us – are you making enough to live on in three days a week?"

"No, of course not. That's why I'm sitting here trying to work out what I'm going to do. It's all right for Mr Mighty Bramaroiti Heteraki. He has his own boat and his whole family behind him – one of the wealthiest families in these three thousand islands, I might add. He doesn't know what its like to try to cover costs on a Daily's wages. I'm not coming."

"Tangaroa on the Sea! If you're not getting enough work, why are you turning down good work?"

"I have my reasons for not sailing on the Laughing Dolphin anymore."

"More fool you! I've picked up good work from Hatoe and Ben. Why won't you go with the Wild Woman, then?"

"Because she is a wild woman. She scares the living day lights out of me the risks she takes." He took a swig, then muttered, "And she wants to go out two up tomorrow."

"What's wrong with that?"

"She bangs like a dunny door in a strong wind."

Ted stood up, looking in the direction Keisha had gone. "Fair dinkum?" Then he frowned, turning back to Ray. "Why would any man say no to that?"

Ray picked up the pitcher, looking deeply into the bubbles floating upwards through the dark golden liquid, and sighed. "Ah, mate, I'm not going to be able to do anything two up tomorrow."

"I should find her. I haven't had any in a while, and I'm not hired for tomorrow. Yes, I know, I know," he said over his shoulder at the fireplace, "Don't leave the wall open." Pulling the wall tight to the fireplace behind him, he was gone.

Ray noticed with sorrow that his pies seemed to have disappeared. All he was left with was the beer, and it was nearly gone. He blamed Ted. Somehow, without Ray seeing him, and without marking a mug, he'd helped himself to a lot of Ray's beer. Sneaky sod. "Won't do you any good to chase Keisha," Ray mumbled. "There's no guarantee she'll hire you, and if she does there's no guarantee she'll want to swing the hammock with you. There's a reason you're on your own so much." He discovered he was getting up. It was funny how badly he needed the men's room considering he hadn't drunk all that much.

He was surprised by how much further away the men's room was than he'd remembered. "You should have gone around the other side of the fireplace, you silly sod. It's not so far that way," he scolded himself. He fought with the door, wondering why it was stuck until he realised he was trying to push it open instead of pulling it.

He chose the urinal at the end so that he could lean on the wall beside it. His concentration on hitting the bug painted in the middle of the drain was interrupted by a couple of men bursting in, loudly. He looked up, partly curious, partly annoyed.

"Hey! It's Ray! Where'd you get to, mate?" Renny and Drew were laughing.

"Funniest thing you've ever seen!" Renny exclaimed.

"Ted's gone off the deep end," Drew explained. "Keisha wants to go out alone tomorrow, and Ted's acting like she's insulting him! They've had a bit of a barney about it and the manager asked them to leave."

They laughed again.

Ray wasn't amused. It was all his fault. He'd caused that.

Renny noticed and asked, "Hey, Ray, what's the matter, mate? Why the long face? What a dag! Ted just made a bigger no-hoper out of himself than you ever would have guessed!"

Drew was paying more attention. He told Renny, "He's half-cut."

"No," Ray shook his head, needing to catch hold of the wall as he did so that he wouldn't lose his balance.

Renny argued with him. "Nah, yeah, you are, mate. You're deep in your cups."

Ray wanted them to understand. "No, listen. It's my fault. They wouldn't have blown up at each other if I hadn't told Ted that Keisha was looking for someone to go out two up. He's stroppy because he knows she'd rather go alone than go with him."

"Ooo." They shook their heads. "Ouch."

"Well," Renny changed back to cheerfulness. "You're not completely off your face, then, if you can figure that out. And Ted's still a doze. Bram sent him to tell you to come out to the beer garden, and he couldn't even get a simple message like that right. Silly bugger's as unreliable as."

"He did tell me," Ray defended Ted.

What Ray was really saying dawned in their eyes at the same time.

Renny blustered, "Come on, mate. Muck in with us. The whole idea was that we would all eat together and have a good time. It's only going to work if we're all there."

Ray headed for the sink to wash his hands. "It's a family thing."

"You're like family," Renny protested. "You're crew."

Drew spoke up on Ray's behalf. "You know what Bram's like, Renny. He goes too far sometimes. Always has."

Ray leaned his elbows on the counter around the sink. "I just need a break, that's all." He did his best to explain without saying anything bad about the children. "I'm not going out with anyone tomorrow. Keisha's been voted 'most likely to prang' more than once, so I turned her down. I just want some peace and quiet."

"Better give us your beads, then," Drew said dryly. "That way you'll still have some the morning after."

"There's no need for that." It annoyed Ray that Drew would say something like that.

"Suit yourself, mate, but that's the only reason you had anything left of your big win that time."

Renny hastily put in as Ray turned to leave the men's, "We'll tell Bram not to wait any longer for you. We'll tell him you're three sheets to the wind, so there's no point expecting you. He'll get over it."

"Ta."

Drew added, "Come on, Ray, cheer up. It's not all your fault Keisha and Ted had a go at each other. He has to try all over the place to get work because skippers would rather have a short crew than put up with Ted's nonsense. He only does a half-pai job unless you're right on top of him. A few more scenes like that one with Keisha and no one around here will hire him at all anymore."

Ray leaned on the wall beside the door. "Ted's not from here, eh?"

"Well, we know that!" Renny exclaimed.

Ray told him, "I flatted with him once. He's a pain in the neck. He's always treated badly, everything's always somebody else's fault. He works in a place until no one will hire him anymore, then he moves on. He's had partners, but he can never pass the parenting certificate."

"You'd think he'd learn," Renny said, unsympathetically.

Drew shrugged. "You're sure we can't persuade you to join us in the beer garden, Ray? Bram's buying."

"No. Ta very much. I've got my own."

"We'd better go back to Bram," Renny told Drew.

Ray pushed the door open and stood still, staring. He let the door swing behind him, forgetting about the other two.

"Hey, what's that for?" Drew came out of the men's, protesting about the door swinging into his face.

Renny was right behind him. "Great Tane, what's this?"

Ray was confused to see the folding walls thrown wide open so that the restaurant looked like one big room. The fireplace had been reduced to a square stone pillar in the middle, its flames hardly noticeable in the bright light. The light bewildered and distressed him more than anything else. Ever since he'd first come to Mean Eddies the back room had been dark and restful. Now the familiar dark beams were shining brilliant white, making the back as bright as the front. The wallie that was usually only loud enough for people who were close to it was turned right up so that it could be heard over the noise of the crowd. Crowd. That's the other thing that was wrong. Everyone from inside and outside the restaurant, including the staff, was surging into the back room. Anxious about his beer, Ray made his way through, cutting across the flow, back to his table.

Disoriented, Ray kept his head down, concentrating on his beer, unable to make head nor tail of the comments he heard about the results of the plebiscite. He was vaguely aware that the Triune and the King were all talking to the People, but he couldn't follow it. Having the wallie loud didn't make the words clearer to him, it made him more befuddled. His sanctuary, where he went to lick his wounds, had been blasted out of existence by light, noise, and crowds. It was so bad that the door beside him was open letting the glare from the scullery assault his eyes. Two people stood in the doorway, partially blocking the dazzling effect of the shiny white walls and gleaming work surfaces.

He wished he'd gone home. If he'd gone anywhere else, it would have amounted to the same thing. Everyone wanted to know the plebiscite results, except for Ray who just wanted quiet. He was sure someone had been at his beer; the pitcher was down to its last dregs. He was sure there had been more left of it than that, and he knew he couldn't get any more while everyone who worked there was glued to the stupid wall unit. Why couldn't they give the results some other time?

People were talking about what was being said, others were shushing them so that they could hear. All Ray was concerned about was more beer. He refilled his mug and took a slurp. It wasn't cold anymore. He was slowing down. He didn't feel like pouring it down his throat anymore.

The crowd made a collective noise, like a moan, and shifted. Ray put his legs along the bench and leaned his back against the wall, squinting against the light to peer into the backs of the people nearest him. He couldn't see the wall unit because of the people standing between it and him, and couldn't make sense of what he could hear, but he was sure something important had just happened. Something was expected of him. He tried to sort out what that was. A sudden silence fell, except for small children who were too young to realise something was happening that would change their lives. That's what it was. He was supposed to care about this. Funny how he didn't. He wondered if that made him a bad person.

The old King's wavery old voice came through the hush. "By the narrowest of margins, the Decision of the People is to keep to ourselves and wait to see whether or not this visit from the Gethsemane Republic is an anomaly."

There was an outburst of muttering from those who disagreed, along with pleased exclamations from those who agreed, and shushing from those who still wanted to hear. Movement started as some made their way out. Ray caught words as people moved past him. "Stupid." "Recount." "Not a majority."

The voices were like an annoying hum surrounding him. Someone was pulling the walls back across to divide the front room from the back room. He twisted on the bench, searching for the touch panel that would lower the light. The light was beginning to dim, though Ray couldn't see how. The relief was enormous when the scullery door was shut. The glare had left spots in front of his eyes. The wallie was turned down to its normal level where it wouldn't distract people playing cards or billiards.

Ray closed his eyes, leaning back against the wall, striving to get the relaxation he'd been searching for since he'd got off the boat.

Bram's voice cut right through. "What did you think of that?"

Ray opened his eyes. Not only was Bram standing in front of him, but he was also with Drew, Renny, Lia, Ben, Barry, Beth, and Bram's Dad, Poko.

Feeling skewered by his unworthy thoughts about the children, Ray stumbled around inside his quagmire of a brain searching for an acceptable answer.

Bram plopped himself down on the bench across the table from Ray, not seeming to notice Ray's confusion, continuing, "In a vote with five different choices that came in that close, there isn't any way a majority of the People want us to sit on our hands."

Ray's head reeled. What was he talking about?

Drew's dad, Barry, plunked himself down beside Ray, arguing, "Maybe not, Bram, but that is the decision."

Bram's head seemed to rise on his neck like a cock bird with its hackles up. "It's not my decision! It's not a majority decision! The rest of us have as much say as they do!"

Drew lowered himself down onto the bench beside Bram, saying soothingly, "Now don't go off with your sails half set. Let's talk this over sensibly." He reached a handout to Barry, who reached back to the table beside them, picked up the three empty mugs and set them down in the middle of the table. To Ray's dismay, the three of them shared out the few drops he had left of his beer.

"We need more beer," came out of his mouth before he could stop it.

"Here, give me your beads, mate," Barry said, standing up, reaching over and lifting Ray's bead-chains over his head. He walked off with them.

Ray watched him go, struggling to work out what had just happened. He knew Barry and Drew had pulled something on him, he'd seen them look at each other, but he couldn't place it. He couldn't get past the part where they had taken his beer and were getting him to pay for the next round.

More people were joining them, standing around the table, or pulling other tables closer, arguing furiously. Ray wondered why. He'd missed something. He knew he had.

"More people want to wait and see what happens first, before we do anything else, than any of the other alternatives," Poko re-iterated.

"There's no sense in that!" Bram raged. "We can't just sit here like sleeping ducks on a pond with a hawk overhead. Those blokes have got no respect, they kill and eat living creatures, and they skite about the way no other nation can stand up to them. We can't do any more about them than sleeping ducks can do about a hawk, but we don't have to sleep!"

"You're right," Renny put in. "We can't do anything about them."

Bram carried on as if no one had said anything. "We can let others know they're out there! If we survived and they survived, then someone else did, too. We should find them and tell them."

Beth frowned. "You're asking us to change who we are."

"Our world has changed. We have to keep pace with the changes just like our ancestors did."

Poko looked furious. "You don't have the right to make that decision for everyone else."

"It's reality, Dad. We have to be realistic."

Renny shook his head. "Your reality is not everybody's reality. You can't impose your will on the rest of us."

Barry rejoined them, followed by waiters bearing two pitchers of beer and enough mugs for everyone. Ray forgot about whether he was paying for it all or not in the sheer joy of a mug full of ice-cold beer with a lovely foaming head.

Bram's urgent, vehement statements no longer hurt Ray's head when he insisted, "Don't you understand it's already happened? We've lost our isolation. The Troggie's protocol is now invalid. The only choice we've got left now is whether we go and meet it on our terms or sit here and wait until it comes to us on its terms."

"The choice has been made, Bram," Lia told him.

Bram threw his hands up in disgust, causing several people to grab anxiously for the pitcher and mugs near him. "I don't know how the Troggies got all of the People to change from the way they'd always done things to seeing a whole new way to live. Obviously, our ancestors were a lot smarter than people are today."

Barry glared at him. "They held a vote just like we did, except that they went with the majority decision."

"You can't tell me they all thought the same thing! There's always someone who thinks differently."

"You can't have it both ways, Bram," Ben said. "The majority voted for us to keep to ourselves. The minority went along with it whether they agreed or not because that's how a democracy works. Our ancestors knew what they were doing when they decided we should keep to ourselves."

"Yeah," Renny agreed. "You can see the trouble we've avoided by doing that. If we'd kept in touch, we might have had to cope with people like the GR."

"It's who we are, it's what we do," Drew nodded.

Bram snorted. "We're not on our own anymore whether we like it or not. We've lost our isolation. We have to learn about these other people because they've found us. We need to be the first to find others before they do so that we can pool our resources and band together to convince the GR that we don't want anything to do with their ways."

Poko was just about the only one who could stop Bram mid-rant. "Now just you listen for a moment, my boy! There are two points here. One: it's the Will of the People, and we must abide by it whether we like it or not. Two: there's nothing to say that anyone we contact will be any better than the fellows who've just left. Give it a rest. Put your energy and attention into your family and let cooler heads prevail."

"It's because of my family that this matters so much!" Bram persisted.

Barry declared, "If you felt this strongly about it you should have spoken up before the vote."

"I did," Bram growled, disgustedly.

Ray closed his mouth, aware that it had been hanging open in apprehension. He tried to focus on them and follow the squabble, but they were paying no attention to him.

Ted must have talked his way back into the restaurant because he returned, telling them with a smile, "I bought another four-el."

They were all pleased with him for that. For a brief moment Ray thought he might like Ted a little bit after all.

Then Bram's answer to Barry saying, "You can't do anything about it," cut right through the fog in Ray's head.

"I can take the Kaumoana across the Ditch to the West Isle."

The image of the deep blue appeared before Ray's eyes. He felt cold inside. His head was abruptly completely clear. He could see and hear everything around him. The fog was gone, and it was all in sharp focus, as if he'd had nothing to drink. He needed the men's room very badly — almost as much as he needed to escape from the arguing. He got up and fled, clearing the fireplace without thinking about it.

Before he ventured back out into the cruel world he washed his face with cold water, telling himself, "He can't mean it." Feeling as if he was in a dream, and badly wanting to wake up, he went back to his table again. Empty pitchers had been cleared away, and a new frosty one sat in the middle of the table. Ray thought sadly of his, thinking it had been a waste of good beads, since the shock of hearing what Bram wanted to do had sobered him right up. He considered ducking out and going to the Brown Jug to start all over again, but right on the heels of that thought came the resentful feeling that they owed him this beer since they'd drunk his, and he wasn't going to let them chase him away from it.

Looking around at Ray as he made his way back to his spot, Bram told him, "As soon as the baby's born I'm off. Hine won't be able to work so soon after having the baby, so I'll need you . . ."

"No," Ray blurted out before Bram finished.

"I don't mean tomorrow. Even if the baby's born tonight I'm not leaving tomorrow." The others were all arguing with him at once, but Bram just raised his voice to make himself heard over their objections. "You wouldn't know what it's like to have a family. I want to see what my boy's like, and make sure Hine's okay before I leave. I reckon it'll take us a few days to get there, then we have to give the Aussies time to get over their shock. They might not even believe us at first, so we might have to put in a bit of time to persuade them, then a few days to get back home. I reckon it'll be a couple of weeks, tops."

"No," said Ray.

There was no chance for Bram to hear him, everyone was shouting so loudly at Bram, all trying to make themselves heard over everyone else, all appalled by what he was saying and trying to make him understand that it was out of the question.

Ray couldn't sort out who said what with them all talking at once, and so upset that they didn't sound like themselves. "I'm with Ray," someone called out. "There's nothing to say those blokes will ever come back, and then you've stirred up a wasp's nest for nothing."

"What if the people you find are just as bad as, or worse than, the GR? Then you've made it twice as bad."

Ray couldn't make the rest out, in the confusion of raised voices. No one convinced anyone else to change their point of view. Each was as entrenched as they had been when the argument started. Finally, the management of the restaurant asked the whole crowd of them to move the argument out of the building. Grumbling they all moved back to their original places; the crew of the Kaumoana went back out to the beer garden and others went back to their cards or left to go home.

Bram was in trouble with Hine for taking so long. Rightly so, Ray thought, settling down alone again surrounded by empty beer mugs and pitchers. He thought sourly of what a beautiful woman Hine was, and that Bram didn't pay her nearly enough of the right kind of attention. Self-centred, self-absorbed, selfish, and with an ego as big as the whole ocean, was what Ray thought of Bram. In some ways maybe he wasn't that bad of a bloke, but this business of always being right was wearing thin. He didn't deserve a woman as good as Hine.

It wasn't fair, really, when Ray thought about it. How did a cocky skite like Bram attract a girl like Hine, never mind keep her around for years when Ray couldn't find anyone?

He looked sullenly at the dregs of the pitchers to see if there was enough beer to fill his mug. He fingered his beads to see if he had enough to buy another pitcher, astonished to realise that he had only one bead-chain. What had happened to the others? It was just like last time. Beads just slipped through his fingers, and he had no idea how.

He looked over at the card games, now underway again, and at the billiard table. Cards were the better bet. He could win enough to pick up at least one pitcher. You never know, though, he might just make a heap like he did when he turned in the metal, he brought back from the trip to Rangitahua.

While the three of them had been in the big smoke trying to convince the First Servant that they really had seen a foreign ship, Ray had taken his precious piece of iron to the metal merchant. He'd been a bit nervous about the checks to make sure it wasn't stolen, but the experts had identified it as an antique fire grate and congratulated Ray on finding an ancient house with anything left in it. They thought for sure everything like that had been picked clean generations ago, but didn't ask Ray where he'd found it. Nearly everyone who found metal, legal or otherwise, kept their source secret, so there was no point in asking. Ray was hugely relieved by that. He'd had no idea how he was going to account for it if someone had asked.

With the beads from that and his pay from the trip, Ray arrived back in Matapihi with the most money he'd ever had at one time in his whole life. He went to the bank to convert all the small denomination beads into bigger ones, but he didn't want to leave them in the bank. He wanted to see them and marvel at them. He bought necklace bead-chains instead of keeping them in his hair or in a pocket, so that he could wear them around his neck. He liked the feel of them around his neck, he liked the look of them in the mirror, and he liked unclipping a bead to pay for something and seeing how much he had left.

He'd never done anything like that before. It gave him pleasure which almost, though not quite, made up for the trauma of that trip.

He sat cross-legged on his bed clipping the beads into place, seeing how the bead-chains were graduated so that you clipped different values in sequence and same values together. He'd never had a golden kiwi before. He had to get a special bead-chain to hold it. He held his bead-chains up in the sunshine to admire them. A golden kiwi, worth ten silver kiwis, or a hundred bronze kiwis. Four silver kiwis, two either side of the golden kiwi, and four bronze kiwis, two either side of the silver kiwis. He had three bead-chains of lesser values, with half bronze kiwis, quarter bronze kiwis called tuawha, gold ferns, half gold ferns, quarter gold ferns called quarters, silver ferns called quids, half silver ferns, quarter silver ferns called thripence, bronze ferns called tuppence, half bronze ferns called ha-bonnies, and quarter bronze ferns called farthings. When he put them all around his neck, they gave him a feeling that he'd never had before. A sort of confidence, as if he was going to be all right after all.

Knowing that everyone in the boating community went to Mean Eddies sooner or later, Ray wore his beads over there so that he could show them to everyone. The inevitable card game was under way in the back corner. After a few beers he couldn't see any reason not to join it. He played like he'd never played before. For one thing it didn't matter to him what cards he had in his hands, he knew he was okay, so he didn't get tense, and no one could guess whether he had a good hand or a bad one. He also took risks that he normally would never have taken. The end result was that he'd more than doubled his beads by the time the game broke up. He went to the bank the next day to exchange the ferns for kiwis again and had to buy another bead chain for his extra kiwis.

The man who'd never owned a golden kiwi in his life now had two of them.

He sat on his bed again clipping them into place and holding them up to watch the sunshine catch them as the chains spun in his fingers.

"This is the beginning of a whole new life for you, Raethew Perenara," he announced to his reflection in the mirror.

He wrapped his bead-chains in a towel and slept with them, waking periodically in the night to feel them and assure himself they were real, and he hadn't imagined the whole thing. He felt like a small boy on midsummer morning waking up to see if Santa had come in the night and left his heart's desire in a pillowcase on the foot of his bed. He dreamed of being a small boy again, eating fish and chips on the beach, wanting to take all of his new toys to the beach and arguing with his mother who said he would lose them. His father wasn't there.

In the morning, he remembered his dream and thought of his daughter, Raewyn. He wasn't there for her, either. He decided he had to see Raewyn, so he took the early Fish to Tauranga and caught the ferry over to Matakana Island. It wasn't until he was on the Flying Fish on Matakana that he wondered if he should have rung Raewyn's mother, Bronwyn, first. What if they weren't there? What if they didn't want to see him?

He got off the Fish and walked along the path between the trees, trying to decide whether to carry on regardless or go back home, when he saw Raewyn. There she was on her push-bike. He stood still, watching her, marvelling at her beauty, wondering how she could have grown so much in such a short time. He couldn't understand how a life as messed up as his had produced this perfect, lovely creature. She stood up on the pedals, speeding away from him, her shoulder-length brown hair flying in the wind.

He sighed with deep love and satisfaction, walked to the house and stood uneasily on the veranda wondering what to do next. A goose hissed angrily at him, making him jump and yelp with surprise. Bronwyn was at the door in a trice.

"Ray! What are you doing here?"

So much for all the clever opening remarks he'd planned to say. "I – I come into some big bickies." He lifted the bead-chains to show her. "And I kind of thought you and Raewyn – you know – maybe you could use some, eh?"

"She's not here. She's got a school trip today."

"I know. I saw her."

"Come in, don't just stand there looking like a wet hen. I'm on my way out the door to work. Did you talk to her?"

Ray stopped just inside the door, feeling foolish. "No, she didn't see me."

Bronwyn paused for a second, glanced at him, then threw her wrap around her shoulders. "Come on, I can't be late."

"I'll get out of your way, then."

"Oh, no you don't! You'll vanish again and Raewyn will break her heart if she knew you were here and she didn't see you. You'll walk to work with me and have a bite to eat."

Following obediently, he protested, "I've already had breakfast."

"Where are you staying?"

"I just got here."

"Splif will put you up. You can play darts. That way I'll know where to find you when Raewyn comes home this afternoon. You didn't even say hello?"

Ray was almost trotting to keep up with Bronwyn's stride. "No, I just watched her."

"You're amazing."

"Well, I just – she's so beautiful. I didn't know if she'd want to see me, eh? She looked very happy."

"Of course she'd be pleased to see you, you nong! That girl worships the ground you walk on. She lives to see you! Why can't you ever see that?"

"Well, she – I don't know why."

"I don't know why, either. But there it is. And it tears her heart out when you don't show up or write to her or even ring up once in a while. I could strand you for hurting her."

"But I – well, I – I just never know what to say."

"'Hello' would be nice." She came to a stop in front of a pub that hadn't been there when Ray was growing up there.

"You work here?" he asked her, in surprise.

"No, I work in the snack shop in the station."

"You work on land? You left the boats?"

"I'm a single parent. Your Mum and my parents are all on the boats. Someone's got to be on land in case Raewyn gets sick or hurt at school."

Ray was so shocked by the idea that Bronwyn, who loved to sea more than he ever had, was stranded ashore. Guilt hit him so hard all he could think to say was, "She gets hurt?"

Giving him a pitying look, Bronwyn didn't answer. Instead, she pointed at the pub. "That's Splif's place. Go in there and have fun. Be there when Raewyn gets here just after 3. Don't gamble away all of your beads, and don't you dare take off or py korry I'll hunt you down."

"I won't gamble them all away! That's how I got this much!"

But she didn't look pleased to hear that. She muttered, "Fancy that," and walked on down the path to the snack shop at the Flying Fish station.

Obediently he stepped into the place Bronwyn had sent him. All the feelings of responsibility and failure that he'd been trying to avoid clouded over him. What he really wanted to do was run. Bronwyn wasn't like this when they'd been partnered. He couldn't understand the change in her. If that was how she was going to turn out, it was just as well he'd left. He could never have lived with a woman who spoke to him like that. She was worse than his mother had been.

What had attracted him to her, aside from her beauty and her skill as a sea woman, had been how organised she was. He'd thought having someone around who could keep things organised would make his life easier, less confusing. But not long after their bonding ceremony, after they'd passed their parenting certificate, he'd started to feel inadequate. Once Bronwyn was pregnant his life had fallen apart. Not only was she no longer taking care of him, but she also expected him to take care of her. It was overwhelming. He started accepting long voyages, staying out at sea, using the excuse of needing to earn more for the baby, especially once Bronwyn couldn't work. She wasn't one of those women who worked until she was actually in labour, she'd been sick and had to stay ashore. By the time Raewyn was born Ray had moved to Matapihi. Technically, they had never broken up or separated, but in reality, he had never lived with Raewyn. He kept expecting Bronwyn to dissolve their partnership, but she'd never mentioned it.

He looked around inside 'Splif's' and saw a comfortable place, just the style he liked. Comfort food, sea men and loggers playing darts and cards and billiards, a small wall unit in the corner showing sports. How well Bronwyn knew him! He thought it wouldn't hurt if he had a game of darts before he took off. One thing led to another and before he knew it Bronwyn and Raewyn were in the doorway.

Raewyn raced over to him calling, "Daddy! Daddy!" and flung herself at him.

He caught her, embarrassed by the noise when blokes were concentrating on their games. Hastily, he went outside with them, standing on the veranda beside Bronwyn with Raewyn in his arms. By that time, he'd won a few games, lost a few games, had a few beer, eaten a few snacks, and still managed to leave with more beads than he'd gone in with. He felt expansive. "Want to go over to the Mainland to grab a bite?" he asked.

"Oooo, rather!" Raewyn sounded ecstatic.

"What did you have in mind?" Bronwyn didn't sound angry, just guarded.

"I thought you should have some of this." He put Raewyn down and fingered the bead-chains. He sent something every month to support his child, but this was different. This was a windfall, and he wanted Raewyn to have some of it. "And is there anything she needs?"

"Well," Bronwyn hesitated. "She's growing out of her clothes."

"New clothes, then."

Raewyn jumped up and down, tugging at him. "Daddy, Daddy, can I have red rain boots, please?"

"Red rain boots."

"And a raincoat to match? And a new satchel?"

"Raincoat, satchel." He grinned at Bronwyn.

"How far are you going to go with this?" she asked with a smile.

He pulled Raewyn's hands off him and picked up one of the kiwi bead-chains. He lifted it carefully, disentangling it from the others until he could lift it over his head. He put it over Bronwyn's head, letting it drop to her shoulders.

She stood still, shocked.

He smiled at her, happy that his plan was working out after all. "That's yours, and we'll kit the kid out for the year, and maybe something special, too."

She stared at him for a moment, then led the way down the steps from the veranda saying, "I'll just run over and tell them that I can't come in to work tomorrow."

Ray and Raewyn trailed after her, hand in hand, watching her finger the bead-chain, murmuring to herself, "A golden kiwi, silver kiwis, bronze kiwis . . ."

Raewyn whispered, "Daddy, can you get a seal pup for me? I've always wanted a seal for a pet."

That snapped Bronwyn out of her shock. She spun on the spot, saying sternly, "Raethew Perenara, don't you dare buy that child a baby seal! I can't possibly take care of it!"

Ray had no idea how he could have found one, anyway. This way he didn't have to say no. "Yeah, nah, Ma'am," he said like a good boy, hoping Raewyn didn't see how relieved he was.

"What did you do?" Bronwyn demanded. "Find a shipwreck?"

"Kind of. I came across some metal, then doubled my take at . . ."

"Never mind. I see."

"What, Mummy?"

"You take Daddy home and change into a nice dress to wear out to tea in Tauranga. I'll meet you there in a few minutes."

Raewyn shrugged. Ray could tell she knew there was no point in pursuing it. "Come on, Daddy, I can show you my new push-bike. It's an old bike, really. Jini Hawkins got too big for it, but it's new to me."

By the end of the evening Raewyn had more clothes than they could carry home, so they had to arrange for delivery, along with a new push-bike with a bell and a basket and streamers from the handlebars. Raewyn also had a new hair style and a promise from her Daddy that he wouldn't be away for so long this time.

Ray also paid for Bronwyn to have her hair done so that the two of them could sit beside each other and giggle like two children while Ray took a break from all the femininity and popped into a bar for a moment.

Not only did he get a surprising amount of pleasure out of seeing the two of them enjoying themselves, but he really needed a break, and he hoped Bronwyn would look more kindly upon him than she had when she'd hissed, "For goodness sake don't make promises to that girl unless you're going to keep them."

They laughed together, had a wonderful meal in an expensive restaurant with a stunning view of Mauao, went to a show, and rode the

Fish back to the ferry with Raewyn's sleeping form bundled up against him. He felt truly happy for the first time in years, thinking that it would always be like this.

But as they waited for the little ferry that plied the strait between Te Ika a Maui and Matakana, he visualised being in Bronwyn's house, panicked and bought only two tickets. Raewyn, half asleep, missed it until he gave the tickets to her mother. "Where's yours, Daddy?"

"I'm not coming, sweetheart."

She started to cry. "I'll never see you again."

"Yes, you will. But I have to be at work in the morning."

"You can work here."

They all knew that was true. "I have a job. I told them I'd be there. They're expecting me."

She clung to him.

Bronwyn hissed, "When will you learn buying things doesn't replace being with her? It's <u>you</u> she misses."

Those words rang in his head the whole way back to Matapihi. He stared, unseeing, out of the window of the Flying Fish, the smooth, quiet passage through the dark tree-tops flashing by as if in a dream while his mind roiled over and around the idea that a person, that beautiful, sweet child, loved him.

She was wrong. He wasn't that hero she thought he was. He conceded that he was a better Dad than his father had been, but he didn't deserve this open-hearted admiration. He felt angry with her that she expected so much from him. He resented that she had never blamed him for leaving her. What was the matter with her? He'd resented his Dad when he'd been her age.

What kept his mind churning was the circle from resenting Raewyn's unrealistic expectations to loving her and being grateful for such unconditional love, to knowing he didn't deserve it, and back to resenting that he was expected to.

Sitting at the table at Mean Eddies, remembering the visit to his daughter, Ray slouched over the dregs of beer with tears in his eyes. If only he could stop beads from slipping through his fingers, he could take proper care of her. He was thankful that he'd given the bead-chain to Bronwyn. She would make it last far longer than he ever could.

He looked over at the card game, but he was no longer in the mood. He knew he was starting another downward slide, so his luck would all be bad from now on. He decided the best thing he could do was take what was left of his beads home while he still had them. Even though he'd had hardly anything to drink, and had sobered up from that, finding his flat was hard. It was as if the path was moving, trying to throw him into the tree trunks.

When he got home, he fell face down on his bed, holding the one remaining bead chain in his hands, crying himself to sleep, wondering how his life could have turned out so badly.

A few days later, Ray was working on Sue's boat when Hine finally gave birth to her over-due baby. Sue was laughing as she told him, "Hine and Bram had a girl."

He couldn't help snickering. It struck him as the funniest thing he'd heard in a long time. "For once Bram didn't get what he wanted, eh?"

Sue was even more wicked. She fluttered her eyelashes at Ray. "Bram couldn't have been . . . um . . . wrong . . . could he?"

For the first time in a week Ray laughed out loud. "Must be a big girl."

Sue chuckled. "Would it be considered unkind to call her 'Wineera'?"

Ray laughed until he couldn't stand up straight. "Yeah," he finally gasped out. "It wouldn't be fair to the poor kid."

"I suppose you're right," Sue sighed in mock disappointment. In her normal voice she told Ray, "I'm going to visit Hine as soon as we get back to port. I'll tell you what the baby looks like tomorrow."

Ray was happy with that because it meant Sue wanted to hire him for the next day. He was starting to feel that the pickings were getting shallower. Bram was staying in port while the baby was new, Ray didn't want to face Hatoe and Ben, and Keisha wasn't talking to him since her blow up with Ted. Nearly all the other boats in Matapihi belonged to families who had enough sailing relatives not to need to hire outside the family. He was starting to go to the Mount and Tauranga to find work.

Ray couldn't understand why things were going wrong for him lately. It wasn't as if he was like Ted. Until this last little while Ray had been the one who'd been in high demand, and Ted had needed to take the Fish to other towns to find work. Now Ted was working more than Ray was.

"I'm doing something wrong," Ray said to himself. It couldn't possibly be that Ted was a better worker than Ray. What could it be, then? If they went out two up again tomorrow, he would swallow his pride and ask Sue. He'd have to be sure he wanted to know, though, Ray reminded himself, because if he asked Sue, she'd tell him.

But the next morning when Ray got up there was a package on his kitchen table with a note from Drew saying, "I thought I should give these back to you in case you need them before I get back." Inside the package were all of Ray's missing bead chains. He sat at the table staring at them. Something stirred in the back of his brain. A fluttery scrap of memory that he couldn't quite pin down. Drew and Renny saying something to him in a men's room. Drew and Barry giving each other a look that irritated him. He didn't know how he knew, but Ray knew Drew, Barry, and Renny had taken his beads from him. He remembered something else, too. When he'd had all that money after the trip to Rangitahua he'd done a lot of heavy drinking for a long time before he'd finally been able to drown of the sound of Bronwyn's voice telling him Raewyn missed him. He didn't know what had happened to all of those beads, but it seemed Drew always had some of his every time he ran low.

He resented that Drew, Barry, and Renny took it upon themselves to supervise his finances. He jumped up and ran all the way to Drew's house to have it out with him, but there was no one home. They must have gone down to the marina awfully early. Come to think of it, Drew must have dropped the beads off in the middle of the night if Ray hadn't heard a thing. He hadn't been drinking after work, so he wouldn't have been sleeping very heavily. He would have heard someone opening his door if it had been morning.

With an uneasy feeling Ray raced all the way to the Marina without stopping to have breakfast. Where the Kaumoana moored was an empty space. Ray came to a stop in front of it, staring at the water where the biggest boat should have been.

Hatoe was normally on his boat before Ray got to the marina in the morning, but the Laughing Dolphin was still dark as Hatoe stood on the pier staring at the space across from his boat. "I've got a bad feeling about this, Ray," he said.

The flatness in Hatoe's tone scared Ray. He blurted out, "He wouldn't have gone across the Ditch. His Dad would never accept the course."

"Across the Ditch?" Hatoe's startled eyes gleamed eerily in the greenish light from the dock light-paint.

Ray mumbled, "Bram talked about sailing to the West Isle after the baby was born."

"Not even Bram would be that stupid! No, I take that back. He's arrogant enough . . ."

"But the Harbour Master . . ."

Hatoe sighed, turning away and heading towards the Laughing Dolphin. "It's quite possible to file a course with Poko and go somewhere else."

That's what he'd done when they went to Rangitahua, Ray remembered. Without another word he spun on his heel and jogged the length of the pier to Sue's boat. She wasn't there yet, so Ray went aboard the Karoro and started to set her up for the day's work.

When Sue arrived, he asked her, "Why do you think the Kaumoana left in the middle of the night?"

She stopped in her tracks. "He didn't, did he?"

Ray nodded.

"The only reason for that would be so none of us could talk him out of it." Head down, shoulders slumped, she boarded her boat and ran through the checks before casting off.

Ray went through his part of the routine until the little weed collector was backing gently and quietly away from the pier. Sue was at the wheel. Ray went to stand beside her. "You don't think he really did it, do you?"

She looked as glum as he'd ever seen her. "He filed a course to Tuhua Island. Poko gave him a good growling over talking about sailing the Ditch. He was upset enough to threaten to lock the Kaumoana down, so Bram promised to give over. But look who's gone."

"Drew," Ray said quickly.

Sue nodded. "Drew and Poma left Elly with Poko and Beth last night. Supposedly she wanted to sleep over with her grandparents."

"How could he get Drew and Poma to go with him? They were dead set against it. And even if they did, that's not enough crew for a boat that size."

"I can see Drew going along to keep Bram out of trouble," Sue mused, turning the Karoro and heading out of Matapihi Harbour under the bridge into Tauranga Harbour. "Notice anything?" she asked, pointing back at the marina.

Ray turned to look back. Other boats were getting underway, their eyes gleaming in the pre-dawn light. Only one thing looked out of place: Keisha was almost always the first one away, but that morning the Sea Hawk was still dark. He stared at it, bewildered. "Where's Keisha?"

"My guess is she's gone with Bram."

"No! Why would she go with him? She's got a boat of her own, she doesn't need to work as a Daily."

"Maybe not, but you refused to go, he needed an extra hand, and you know what a jump-off-the-cliff personality she's got. There's no chance she'd turn down an adventure like that."

"How do you know all this?"

"Bram kept talking, just quietly, after he'd promised his Dad he wouldn't. He kept away from me after I told him I'd dob him in for it."

"He never said another word to me after the night the results came out."

"Yeah, nah, he wouldn't. You're too much of a stand-up straight sort of bloke. He'd keep it on the down low from you, but I heard enough before he gave up on me to put it all together now. I wish I'd put it together then; I might have been able to stop him."

"Who would go with him? His family told him not to be so full of himself."

"Fret not, Ray, I could be wrong."

"Have you got a patch of weed out near Tuhua?"

"No, why?"

"We could go there and see if he's around."

"Too right! So, we could! We'll take the scenic route. If we see them, no worries."

But there was no sign of the Kaumoana.

The Kaumoana wasn't back in port that night, but the boaties told each other that she was doing an overnight trip to bring up metal. It stood to reason that Bram couldn't continue to make the pointless day trips over sea floor that had been picked clean. No one could keep on running up operating bills and not bringing anything in to pay them.

High seas on the north-west coast of Te Ika a Maui told of a storm to the west, but no sign of it appeared on the horizon, so most people paid no attention to it. Ray had nightmares about it, recalling how he'd felt to be in a cyclone out on the open ocean, out of reach of help.

In the morning, shaken by his nightmares, Ray sought Hatoe and Ben out, contrary to the way he had felt about talking to them for the last little while. "Do you think its true Bram went to Australia?"

"Poko says there's no chance Bram would leave his new baby, and no chance he'd lie to his Dad like that," Hatoe answered.

"Do you think Poko's right?"

Hatoe looked unutterably sad. "No, Ray. I'm afraid he's not right."

"How could he get people to go with him? They were, all of them, against it." He turned to Ben in desperation. "You were there, you heard them."

Ben raised his hands in submission. "I was. I did. Bram could talk the hind leg off a duck while it was still using it. Who knows how he did it?"

"The Kaumoana would be okay if she was in that storm, wouldn't she? We were in a whole cyclone in the Dolph and we did okay."

They both looked at him. "She'll be jake, Ray," Hatoe assured him. "Bram might be an arrogant sod, but he's one of the best skippers I've ever seen."

Ben assured him, "It wasn't a real storm. Nothing like a cyclone. It didn't even peek over the horizon. Bram's taken the Kaumoana through much worse than that."

Ray had to be contented with that. "If they did go that way, chances are he was already there before the storm went through, eh?" He tried to reassure himself. "There's nothing to say he did go that way. If he had a big strike, he wouldn't let anyone know where he went. I've been with him when he's been out for a whole week. He's got the best people with him, eh?"

Hatoe and Ben agreed with such vigour that Ray got the creepy feeling they were trying to convince themselves as much as he was trying to convince himself.

As he walked home, he looked at all of the closed houses, listing in his mind who was missing: Hine's brother, Renny; Renny's partner, Gay; and their little boy, Ian; Bram's sister, Poma; Poma's partner, Drew; Drew's parents, Barry and Lia; Drew's brother, Andy; plus Ted and Keisha. Ten crew and a child. No wonder the township felt empty. Despite the brave words he'd said to Hatoe and Ben, Ray couldn't shake the feeling that Bram had gone due west. He couldn't imagine how Bram had persuaded some of them, like his sister, to go with him, but he told himself he'd find out when they came home.

The best he could hope for was that the Aussies hadn't already been taken over by the GR or someone like them, and people like that wouldn't follow the Kaumoana back home.

When there was no sign of the Kaumoana after a week, people started to pressure Poko to accept that Bram had slipped off in the middle of the night to go against them all. Finally, Poko had to file a missing boat report. Coastal Rescue wasn't worried about a missing metal hunter. Metal hunters were notorious for not filing accurate courses. There had been no big storms around the coast. It was assumed the Kaumoana had made a big strike. Bulletins were broadcast in case anyone had seen the boat, but no questions were asked and Poko offered no extra information, other than the boat had not been seen around Tuhua Island, her filed course, and was later back than intended.

The reports of a boat answering that description being seen heading north past Te Hiku o te Ika, the northernmost tip of Te Ika a Maui, brought most of the community into Mean Eddies. They were a bedraggled group, hushed and bewildered looking. It took very little discussion for the consensus to be that Bram had gone across the Ditch. They argued quietly whether or not they should report it to the authorities.

"You want me to dob in my own son?" Poko asked. He seemed to have lost his leadership abilities.

Hatoe stood up and told everyone, "None of us wants to see Beth and Poko hurt, and we don't want to buy trouble for Bram and his crew, but if they really have contacted another nation in direct opposition to the Will of the People, it's our duty to let the People know."

"The People must know," Sue agreed.

"Couldn't we wait a bit longer?" Beth pleaded.

Ben said, "The People must be warned in case someone follows the Kaumoana home so that we can prepare ourselves."

The woman who moored her boat beside the Laughing Dolphin asked, "Prepare ourselves for what?"

There was a confused and distressed silence. No one knew what might happen. After the experience of meeting the GR, no one was excited about the prospect.

Spontaneous chants broke out, invoking the gods to protect their lands and people.

With sorrow, and no little fear that he would be found negligent of his duty and relieved of his position of Harbour Master, Poko contacted the authorities and let them know that the local gossip was that the Kaumoana, with a crew of ten and a child, had gone against the vote and crossed Te Tai o Rēhua to see if anyone in Australia had survived the Dark Days and the Big Freeze, and to warn them that someone uncivilized was back on the High Seas.

It was as if the islands had turned into a wasp's nest that had been kicked. Watching the uproar, so like confused and angry buzzing, on the wall unit, Ray felt ashamed to be part of the community that had unleashed this. He made up his mind to have a few strong words with Bram himself when the Kaumoana got back home.

While Ted was away Ray found himself in high demand among the boaties who needed to hire help. It was a relief to him, not only financially, but it kept him too busy to think or drink, and it meant he didn't have to leave Matapihi to find work. He was only too pleased to stay inside his own small community and not face the questions and recriminations of outsiders wanting to know what sort of people lived in Matapihi that they could take it upon themselves to defy the Will of the People and, possibly, put all of the islanders at risk.

A week later west coast boaties reported seeing wreckage on the ocean.

In all of the islands, the only boat reported missing was the Kaumoana.

A black pall hung over the village of Matapihi, despite the fact that the Coastal Rescue reports were that the pieces of wreckage didn't have easily identified markings on them.

When Coastal Rescue asked if someone from Matapihi could travel up north to try to identify the wreckage, Poko was unable to do it. He seemed to be paralyzed with grief and guilt. He blamed himself, saying he should have taken Bram seriously and stopped him. Locked the boat down, if necessary.

Hatoe stepped into the breach, offering to go in Poko and Beth's place. They had to stay with their grand-daughter, Elly, but he was free to go, and after all, he knew the boat as well as anyone. Ben couldn't go with him because Miki went into labour.

Ray felt as of he was in a dream. Nothing looked or felt real. Barely aware of what he was doing, he went to Hatoe. He'd seen that Hatoe was living on the Laughing Dolphin, no longer going to his house. Much as he didn't want to set foot on the Dolph and bring back bad memories, he felt compelled to step down onto the familiar white transom.

He'd hardly stepped over from the transom into the shining clean back deck when Hatoe appeared at the companionway door. "Ray?"

Ray had no idea what it was he wanted to say, so he blurted out, "Going by yourself?"

Hatoe looked haggard. "I've got to go, Ray. I know what it is to lose someone you love."

"You saved my life," Ray told him. "I owe you."

"How do you reckon that?"

"I never had any idea I would come unglued on the deep blue until I went with you and Ben. Because I went with you two, I didn't go with Bram."

"I thought you didn't go with Bram because what he was doing was illegal."

"I know. Everyone assumed that, so I let them, but really I was too scared to go."

"I appreciate that you've chosen to tell me the real truth." Hatoe stood looking at Ray as if he didn't know what Ray expected of him.

Ray didn't know how to put it into words. He mumbled, "I've never been up north."

Hatoe nodded. "Glad to have you. I've got to go home and pack. I'll meet you at your place."

"Right-o." Ray hesitated. Nothing made sense to him anywhere in the world anymore. He felt as if he just had to understand at least one thing. He asked Hatoe, "Why are you living in the Dolph?"

Hatoe looked at him with such sadness Ray wished he hadn't said anything. "I couldn't bear the house. Thinking that they were lost made the loss of Annie feel like it had happened only yesterday. It brought it all back to me like it was brand new all over again. The house was too big and empty."

Ray couldn't think of anything to say. He just nodded and walked away.

They took the local Flying Fish inland to the Matamata Hub saying hardly a word to each other. Ray couldn't shake the unreal feeling, and Hatoe seemed to be sunk too far into misery for Ray to know what to say to him. Ray had never been in a Hub before, but the multiple levels of Flying Fish coming and going in different directions didn't spark his interest. He felt made of wood. He also hadn't been on the Long Haul Fish before, but he barely took in the differences between it and the smaller local carriages. They got off at Remuera where Nat was supposed to meet them.

Ray was glad to get off and stretch his legs. He had a faint buzzing sound in his head, which he assumed came from hours of sitting in the carriage with the whine of the electric motor. Hatoe wanted to sit inside a restaurant to wait for Nat, but Ray preferred to sit outside in the fresh air and let the breeze blow the cobwebs out of his head.

"Hey." Nat greeted them, hugging his Dad and nodding to Ray. "Tough one, eh?"

"Bloody oath," said Hatoe, softly.

"The dozy bugger wasn't really going to cross Te Tai-o-Rēhua, was he?"

Ray raised his hands. "Yeah, he really was."

"Doesn't he know that's one of the roughest patches of water on the face of the planet?"

"He thought the Kaumoana could take it."

They caught the next Long Haul to the north while they were talking. Ray took the chance to bring up something that had been bothering him all along. "You don't really think this wreckage is the Kaumoana, do you?"

"We won't know until we see it," Hatoe told him, seeming to feel better now that he had his son with him.

"I don't see how it could be," Ray felt better now that he was finally putting it into words. "First, Bram is one of the best sailors around. Second, we got caught in a cyclone in the Dolph and we got back home, and the Kaumoana is way bigger and stronger than the Dolph. Third that storm wasn't much."

Hatoe nodded. "I know. But there are other points you haven't taken into account. First, Bram isn't invincible, and what's the most dangerous is he thinks he is. Second the Dolph being light means she floats no matter what. Plus, she's completely sealable. We could make her watertight, baring something holing her. The Kaumoana is heavier. She's got iron davits. There's always a chance that a really vicious storm could rip the davits off, and that would hole her. If she took on water, she could go down where the Dolph wouldn't. Third, we don't know how big that storm was."

Ray didn't want to talk about it anymore. It didn't make him feel better, now, it made him want to get horribly drunk.

Nat tried to talk about the adventures he'd had playing music in the northlands, but Ray curled up, staring out the window, not seeing the unfamiliar landscape. His head was filled with images of the boat caught in a terrible storm, the crew not able to stop the boat from breaking up, and too far from help for anyone to be able to save them. "Maybe they were already there when the storm hit," he said.

"Maybe," Hatoe responded, but Ray could tell he didn't believe it.

The Main Trunk Line headed west for a while before turning north again. At Whangarei, the furthest north any of them had ever been, they got off the Main Trunk Line and onto a more familiar local type of Flying Fish for the short hop to the west coast. There they were met by a couple of members of the local detachment of Coastal Rescue and taken to a tiny place called Rehutai where an emergency shelter had been set up to house the salvaged pieces of wreckage.

There was no question any longer in any of their minds as to why the wreckage hadn't been identified. "It's just fragments!" Ray exclaimed, his hands going to his face. He looked at the others. Hatoe had his hands over his mouth, his eyes bulging over them. Nat had his hands over his whole face.

"It is your boat, then?"

Hatoe glared at the man. "Who could possibly tell? Whatever boat this was, it's been smashed to pieces. There's no piece of the hull big enough for us to be able to be sure of the design."

"We have counsellors on hand if you need to talk to them," the Coastie offered in a gentler tone.

They shrugged him off, then, but later, after picking through the bits and pieces, they all agreed to sit down with a professional and talk about their overwhelming feelings.

Ray really needed to numb the pain, but he didn't dare start drinking because he was afraid he wouldn't stop and he had to do this.

They were put up in the one Coastie's house. He and his partner were a couple about Hatoe's age with two grown daughters who had left home. In deference to his age, Hatoe was automatically granted one of the girls' beds. Nat was set to flip a bead with Ray for the other one, but Ray bowed out. He let father and son share the room while he crashed on the sofa in the lounge.

Next day they went out with the Coasties, joining the flotilla of local boats looking for more pieces floating on the ocean. Ray didn't mention to anyone that he was scared. He didn't want them to know that he couldn't stand to be out of sight of land. Floating on the surface, aside from pieces of fibre-glass hull, bits of wood, a floatation cushion, and a lidded cup, there was something flat that moved gracefully, almost like a giant jellyfish. Ray got the boat he was on to head over towards the boat that was pulling it up.

Ray went cold inside as he saw it pulled out of the water. It was a square of cloth with the exact same pattern as one of the tablecloths Hine put on the table in the Kaumoana to 'make it look nice.' "I have to see that," he told the Coastie. They went alongside the local boat so that the cloth could be handed over.

As Ray searched along the edges of the cloth tears started to pour down his cheeks. There, in one corner, was a mend. Ray remembered that mend. One of the children had torn the corner, and Hine had mended it. Choking, he asked for the Coasties to find the boat Nat was on. Nat had apprenticed with Bram. He might remember the cloth.

He did.

The trip home was even harder than the trip up north had been. All those people. Ten adults, and one child from a community of less than three hundred adults. "I have to tell her myself," Hatoe said.

"Who?"

"Hine. The poor girl has a brand-new baby, and she's lost her love. I know what it is to lose your love. Imagine losing a personality like Bram. No one else could ever fill his place. He might have got on our nerves, but he was a huge personality. He'll leave a huge gap."

"And Keisha," Ray added. "She was so alive. She was so very alive."

"Whole families were lost," Nat mourned. "Hine lost more than Bram, she lost her brother and sister-in-law and her nephew. Her parents lost their son, daughter-in-law and grandson as well as their son-in-law. There are families who will never recover from this."

Hatoe took in a deep shuddering sigh. "Considering I haven't found a way to recover from the loss of one when I have all of the rest of my family intact, I can't imagine how they'll get through. Poko and Beth lost both of their kids, Bram and Poma, as well as their son-in-law. All they have left is their granddaughter. If Elly hadn't wanted to stay with her grandparents they would have lost her, too."

"Elly didn't only lose her Dad, she also lost her other grandparents and her uncle," Nat pointed out. "That's another whole family wiped out. Barry and Lia and both of their sons."

"How can we tell them?" Ray couldn't imagine giving news this bad to his friends, people he'd worked with and lived with for years.

"We don't," Hatoe said. "Even though nothing has been said publicly about what we found, or that we found anything, the Coasties will have told the behaviourists at home. There'll be a full contingent on hand to deal with every family."

"That'll let them know right off," Nat pointed out.

Ray couldn't think about it. "I wonder if anyone was able to find out where Ted was from to let his family know."

"We don't even know his real name, much less where he was from," Nat said, "But I'm sure they know how to deal with that sort of thing."

"You think he didn't give his real name?" Ray was amazed.

"All I know," Hatoe answered, "Is that some of his stories didn't hang together."

"How do you cope?" Ray blurted out, feeling angry with Hatoe and Nat for having gone though so much and still remaining functional.

Hatoe sighed. "Sometimes you don't. You just keep on putting one foot in front of the other. You don't get over things like this; you learn how to live with them. You can't do that by blotting them out or running away from them, but by facing them. Sometimes that's too hard to do, but you never stop trying. What would help you the most would be going to see your daughter. Give her an extra hug because you still have her."

Ray withdrew into himself. It was all very well for Hatoe to say things like that. He didn't know what it was like to have a daughter who thought you could walk on water. He wished now that he had spent that last day on the Sea Hawk with Keisha. He wondered why on earth he hadn't wanted to. He kept remembering her, full of life and daring, taking risks and laughing about them, daring death to come and get her. And now it had. She was somewhere under tons of water on the ocean floor, and all her family had to bury was the little pouch of fingernail and hair clippings that all boaties left at home 'just in case.'

He slept on the train, curled up on the seat, pulled in on himself like an anemone at low tide, beset by dreams of Keisha being rolled over and over along the silty sea bottom by the mean eddies of the ocean floor, her glossy brown hair floating upwards like seaweed, and mud in her livid throat.

CHAPTER SIXTEEN

Rubin

When word came that his father had been released from prison after two years hard labour for keeping banned books and being a bad influence on impressionable minds, Rubin just had to go and find the old man. He would have gone even if his wife had objected, but he was lucky that Dixie Rae was an understanding kind of woman. Her given names were Dariah Rachel, but she'd always been Dixie Rae to him – the more so when she let him set off like this without raising a fuss.

Rubin had a car, but with the recent increases in sabotage and insurrection there was no guarantee that he would be able to get gasoline in some of the smaller, isolated places, so he decided to take the horse and buggy. That required delicate negotiations with Dixie Rae because she needed the horse and buggy nearly every day. She listened to his reasons, sighed and said, "I can manage if you don't take too long. No visiting. Just get Sam and come back as fast as you can."

"Yes'm." It was with love and gratitude that he kissed her goodbye. His Dad was important enough to him that not even a row could have stopped him, but it made life so much happier this way.

His thoughts about how lucky he was with Dixie Rae naturally turned to comparisons with his parents' marriage. That pretty near choked him right up. His whole life, until she had turned him in, he had loved and admired his mother. He had also believed in his parents' marriage so much that he patterned his on theirs. Nothing could ease the shock of the news that his mother had turned against his Dad while Sam was away on his ship. How in God's Name was he going to tell his Dad that?

He had to tell him, there was no getting out of it. There was no way in hell he could let Sam come home to an empty house without warning.

Sam might not have realised that Mercy had left him, even after he hadn't heard from her for the whole two years of his incarceration, because the GR made it a habit to 'lose' the mail of anyone they wanted to lean on. Rubin prayed that his Dad suspected something was up; otherwise breaking the news was going to be nearly impossible. As it was, it was the hardest thing he'd ever had to do in his life, and he wished with every fibre of his being that he didn't have to do it.

The journey by horse and buggy was long and slow, needing less of Rubin's attention than driving would have. There was nothing to occupy his mind except facing his father with his mother's betrayal. The whole way he wrestled with his memories trying to reconcile the brave woman who had raised him with this new Mercy who had taken the children away from their father and their home, leaving the man she'd professed to love and who she'd vowed to love, honour, and obey for the rest of her life. He could not, for the life of him, understand what had changed her.

When he reached the prison town, it took Rubin longer than he'd expected to find Sam. it seemed logical to ask at the prison until he tried it. The staff was less than helpful. Not only did they not know what happened to people after the door shut behind them, they didn't care. Laughing, they advised Rubin to wait because his Dad was sure to be back in a day or two. "His sort always is."

Rubin knew they were playing him and refused to rise to their bait. One of the hardest things he'd ever had to do was walk calmly away in the face of their jeering laughter.

Driving around the prison town Rubin saw that its name was no exaggeration. It was a one industry town. Everyone who lived there worked in the prison or for it or supported those who did. There were homeless people in the streets. There was a mercy kitchen on one corner. Rubin went there to see the good people trying to feed the homeless, hoping they might be able to give him an idea of where he might look for his Dad. He was sure the prison just put Sam through the door with no money or food, so it made sense that Sam would've gone to the mercy kitchen at least once.

What he didn't expect was a dirty, ragged, gaunt man to shuffle forward from the back as he was talking to the lady at the front door and ask, "Rube?"

"Dad?" Rubin wouldn't have known him if he'd seen him on the street.

"What are you doing here?"

"I came to bring you home. What did they do to you?"

"They let me out alive."

Rubin had no answer to that. Not only was it true, but he could also see that it would be a bad idea to say anything negative about the GR. "Come on, Dad."

"What?"

It bothered Rubin that Sam seemed confused. He'd thought it was obvious that they should get going as quickly as possible. "I came to take you home, Dad. Old Blaze is outside with the buggy."

Sam frowned. "I can't walk out on these guys right this second."

Rubin was afraid that Sam had lost his mind. He tried to be reassuring. "I'm glad you were able to get something to eat when you needed to, but you don't need this place anymore. Dixie Rae packed sandwiches and chicken for us. We can buy more on the way home, if you want."

It caught him off guard when Sam glared at him. "If that's all you think of me, you can just go on home without me. I've got work to do." He turned on his heel and shuffled back the way he'd come.

Rubin stared after him, bewildered. "*¡Chale!* What just happened?"

"Your Dad is a proud man. He don't take kindly to being spoke to like a retard."

Horrified, Rubin ran after Sam without even glancing at the woman. He found Sam stirring a steaming pot. "Dad? I – "

"I'm no beggar! I work here! If you think I'm just a bum, you get on back to your wife. Go on, get out of here!"

"No, Dad, I never thought you were a bum. I was in a hurry. I've got the buggy. Dixie Rae needs it."

Still furious, Sam yelled at him, "I ain't about to walk out on these poor shits right before lunch! They depend on us. This is the only food they can get. If we don't feed them, they'll starve or get arrested or shot for stealing food. You've got no clue. You've never been that hungry."

Rubin was shaken up. He'd never seen his father like this – teetering on the edge of irrational. Afraid he wouldn't be able to find Sam again if he lost sight of him, Rubin said, "I'll help."

"You don't get it. These guys have been tortured. They can't go home. They've been changed."

Rubin looked at the wild-eyed, unkempt man who used to be his strong, calm father and knew he was talking about himself whether he would admit it or not. "I said I'd help. What do you want me to do?"

Once everyone had been fed, Rubin enlisted the help of the woman who ran the place to persuade Sam that it was a good time for him to leave. Listening to Sam rant on and on about what a bad idea it was for him to leave, and how she hadn't meant it at all when she'd said it was okay, and how no one but him knew what the ex-prisoners were going through, Rubin despaired of ever having a rational enough conversation with him to be able to tell him about Mercy. He did his best to understand that anyone who had survived what Sam went through would be changed, but he still had no idea how to handle it.

Finally, they were both in the cart and headed home – way later than Rubin meant to, and with Sam anxiously nattering on and on about the men who had needed him and now he'd run out on them.

At times the endless chatter got on his nerves so much that he wanted to shout, "Shut up!" Immediately he felt guilty. He had to look at Sam to be sure that's really who it was, because this pointless fretting and the whiny voice were so unlike the father he knew.

No matter how hard he tried, Rubin could not understand how Sam could bear to be dirty. His Dad had always had personal pride. Too embarrassed to say anything outright, Rubin waited until they came to a stream. "Blaze needs a drink," he said, pulling the cart off the road. He eased the cart behind some scrub until it was out of sight from the road. Then he jumped down and let the horse loose, ignoring Sam's fussing that the GR could see them.

When the horse was happily slurping, he finally thought of something to say. "That's why I hid it, Dad. Why don't you go up on the road and see if they'll be able to spot it?"

To his horror, Sam started to tremble. "If they're watching, they'll see me."

Shocked, Rubin assured him, "That's okay, Dad. I'll check." He ran up to the road, and then took his time walking past them and back again so that he could have a moment to think. It was as if his once calm and rational father was shattered. On top of the weirdness of not getting the obvious that if the GR were watching, they already knew where he was and what he was doing, Sam seemed disconnected from what was going on around him. Then there were the frayed nerves.

After a little time to pull himself together, Rubin ran back down to the water's edge. "No sign of anyone and you can't see the cart from there." It was an exaggeration to call the track they were now on a 'road' – once they left the town it quickly deteriorated to a rutted track along an ancient roadbed. The horse was rolling in the dirt, watched in a dazed sort of way by Sam. Rubin saw a way of getting Sam cleaned up. "I'm going to take a swim and rub Blaze down to get the sweat off his back."

"I guess I should wash up some for your Mama."

Sam got up and stripped off, giving Rubin another awful decision to make: should he use the mention of his mother as an opening, or should he wait until they were closer to home in case the news drove him right over the edge? Too unsure of Sam to be able to guess which course of action to take, Rubin let the moment pass.

As he led Blaze back into the water, Rubin asked, "Can you get some straw for me to rub him down with?"

"Yeah." but as he handed the straw to Rubin, Sam got resentful. "You're doing it by yourself? You don't trust me! I taught you everything you know about horses, Boy! Or did you forget that?"

"No, Dad, it's not like that. One of us has got to rub Blaze down and one of us has got to wash our clothes. I don't care who does what. You choose."

It had been made up on the spot, out of sheer desperation, but it seemed to work. Sam's indignation evaporated. "Oh, yeah. I never – the thing of it is . . . I don't know what's wrong with me."

Rubin's confusion and fear went up another notch. His Dad knew he was being weird but couldn't stop it. That was worse, somehow, than when he'd thought Sam didn't know. The words sticking in his throat, Rubin struggled to say something that wouldn't make it worse. "You just got out of the joint, Dad. Everyone's got a bit of joint jitters at first, like those poor bastards we fed." Seeing that Sam looked upset by that, Rubin hastily added, "You're in better shape than those guys. You're going to be okay. Give yourself some time."

"You think I lost my nerve!"

"No, no, no. You know everyone who gets out alive's in rough shape. How many have you sorted out over the years?" Rubin was about ready to give up at that point. "Are you going to wash Blaze or the clothes? We can't stay here all day."

"Right. Sorry." Sam looked around, and then asked, "Is it okay if I do the clothes?"

"Yeah, sure." Rubin stopped himself from saying anything about his Dad asking permission. He reminded himself that everyone who had been in prison asked permission before they did anything, even going to the bathroom. This was what he'd wanted. Washing their clothes in the river would clean his Dad up quite a lot without him needing to do anything else. To help his plans along, as he groomed the horse, he asked, "Would you give me a hand to trim my hair when we've finished this?"

He was hoping he could turn that into trimming his Dad's hair in return, but Sam caught him by surprise by saying, "Oh, sure! I got to clean up, too, for my Mercy."

Caught off-guard, Rubin let out a grunt before he could stop himself.

Sam was right on it. "What? Is your Mom okay? She isn't sick, is she?" When Rubin shook his head, Sam got more upset. "She didn't die, did she? Tell me she didn't get sick and die while I couldn't be with her! It's all my fault! I never should have left her. It was all a big waste of time, anyway. All that for nothing."

"Dad! Dad, Mom's okay!"

"Oh, thank God! I couldn't bear it if anything happened to Mercy. They used to try to get to us by saying things about our families, like 'your son turned you in' and 'your wife left you.' It tore some guys apart, but I knew they were lying. They told one guy his wife was fooling around on him when she was dead, but they didn't know that. So, it was all lies. I don't know what I would've done if I couldn't count on my family. It would be the nearest thing to hell. I've kept myself going by thinking of your Mom, my Mercy, waiting at home. "

Rubin couldn't stand it anymore. "Dad." He ducked his head down behind the horse so that he couldn't see Sam's expression and to hide his face. "I'm sorry, Dad, that time they weren't lying."

"One of you boys ratted me out? That makes no sense. Why did they pick up my whole team?"

"No, Dad, not us. Mom."

"Are you trying to tell me Mercy ratted me out? I don't believe you! She wouldn't . . . How dare you talk about your mother like that!"

Hearing Sam slosh towards him, Rubin quickly looked up over Blaze's back, afraid he'd tipped his father over the edge. "No, Dad, no. Mom didn't finger you and your team." He sent the horse out of the river and busied himself gathering up their clothes that Sam had left before they floated away downstream.

Sam was still angry, though he didn't attack. He turned, confused, as Rubin passed him. Seeing what Rubin was doing, Sam hurried to grab the floating clothes, shouting, "There's a special place in Hell for boys who dishonour their mothers! 'Honour thy father and thy mother!' It's a God-dammed Commandment, you ungrateful little shit! ¡Eres tan pendejo!"

Rubin thought, 'So's taking the Lord's name in vain.' In his entire life his Dad had never abused him like that. It was as if it wasn't Sam at all. He looked at Sam closely. That was definitely his Dad. A strange and unpleasant Dad, but Dad none-the-less. Ignoring Sam's shouting, Rubin carried their clothes up the bank, hobbled the horse so that it could graze without wandering off, then started to spread their clothes along the bank to dry. His upbringing kept him from getting into it with his father, so all he could think of was keeping busy.

As soon as he could get a word in edgeways, Rubin suggested that they could eat while their clothes dried. Sam was instantly distracted.

In a moment he was raging about food being taken from the hungry. "We should have left this for them, it's better than anything they've got a chance to get their hands on. We'll get something to eat when we get back home, but those guys got nothing. They can't even get out of town and hunt."

Rubin noted that Sam's objections didn't affect his appetite.

As Sam ranted about the way the GR subdued independent thought by destroying people, he made short work of his chicken.

"I sure hope there's no GR close enough to hear you say that, Dad." Rubin kept his voice soft.

Sam leaped to his feet, all thought of food forgotten. Scrambling to put on his wet clothes, he hissed at Rubin, "We got to get out of here!"

Not wanting Sam to touch the horse and spook it when he was so tense, Rubin rushed to put on his own wet things, telling Sam, "I'll get Blaze; you make sure we don't leave anything behind." He hitched Blaze up, thankful that the day was warm enough that they wouldn't catch their death of cold from racing along in wet clothes. He was so sure Sam needed to get away in a hurry that he put Blaze to a trot, knowing that if they were being watched any speed would be seen as suspicious. Once they were under way, he suggested, "We should give Blaze a break. He can't keep up this pace the whole way home."

"We got to get away!"

"We can't out-run them, Dad. If they want to catch us, they've got way better horses than we can afford. Even a second-rate nag can beat an old guy hitched to a cart."

Sam looked stricken. His hands trembling, he licked his lips and said hoarsely, "If they get me again, they'll finish me."

"They ain't on our tail now, so like as not they ain't here. Best we slow down before someone wonders why we're in so much hurry."

He started to ease Blaze back even before Sam began to freak, "Why did you go so fast, you fool? Are you trying to get us killed?"

Rubin was beginning to see a pattern to Sam's reactions. It hurt him to see his father like this, but now that the first shock was over, he was sorting out in his mind what was going on and how to handle it. "I thought you wanted to move." He thought Sam might not be quite as close to total breakdown as he'd feared. "If they were watching and listening to us, we were done, anyway. If not, it wouldn't hurt to trot a little bit."

Sam opened his mouth to answer, raising one hand to gesture, and then stopped. For a moment he stared at the way his hand trembled, and then pressed one hand hard on his leg, rubbing it slowly. "It's like it's not me. Is this what all those guys with the JJs felt like? Like they've been possessed? I never knew."

"Looking at those guys you showed me, I'd say you're right. But now that you do know you'll be able to help anyone with the JJs better than anyone who'd never been through it." Rubin wasn't totally sure, but he was encouraged enough to say it in the hope it would become a self-fulfilling prophesy.

Sam was quiet for a few seconds. "I hate to think of myself as a basket case, but at least I know what it is and what to do."

"You're not a basket case, Dad. These things take time."

"The only thing that's keeping me going is my home and my family."

Not wanting to risk talking about his Mother again at that point, Rubin changed the subject. "As soon as we find a town, we'll have to buy you some new clothes and boots." He looked Sam over. "And a hat. Do you want a hair cut or to tie your hair back?"

"No, I don't want a hair cut."

"That's good. I can go into the shop, and you can make sure no one takes our cart." To forestall a protest, he added, "What happened to your clothes?"

"They never meant for any of us to survive."

"They took your clothes and left you to die?" Rubin was confused.

Sam frowned. "No. You're not listening."

"Tell me what happened, Dad." Not only did he want to know, but he hoped that talking about it might help Sam.

Sam shuddered and sighed. He sat with his eyes closed for a bit, then said in a raspy voice, "They arrested us for un-Christian activities the moment we set foot off the ship."

Rubin didn't answer. He concentrated on keeping Blaze at a steady pace so that nothing would distract Sam.

After a pause, Sam took a deep breath, and continued, "They taught us that we never saw what we saw."

"What did they say you saw?"

"Nothing. No one survived Judgement Day outside of this continent."

"Do you remember what you saw before they said you never saw it?"

"Sure do!"

Rubin was pleased to see a flash of the old indomitable Sam in the defiance of that declaration. "How did you do that? They're real good at brain-washing."

"I gave in. I let them think they broke me before they did."

A dozen different answers to that flickered through Rubin's mind, all the way from wondering how it was done to doubting it was possible. None of them seemed like the right thing to say, so he just sat there wishing he could come up with something clever.

"They never made me believe I never saw what I saw. It's there. It's real if they like it or not."

"What's there?"

"The Islands and the Islanders. I saw them, I talked to them, and I ate their food. Weirdest cats I ever saw in my whole life, but they're as real as you and me, and there ain't nothing the GR can do about it even if they torture me and all my explorers to death."

Not wanting to think about what really happened to his father, Rubin kept on the topic of the islands. "What were they like for real? Is it true they worship trees?" Sam jumped as if he'd been shot. He glared at Rubin so intently that it felt like his eyes were boring holes in his skull. It took all of Rubin's willpower to act as if nothing was going on. "When you said they were weird, did you mean they're godless heathens?"

"What the hell is this?!"

It was Rubin's turn to jump out of his skin. "What do you mean?" He had no idea what had enraged Sam.

"Very clever. Two years of beating and burning, water-torture and starvation couldn't break me, so you get my own son to trick me. Well done. You've got me dead in your sights." He looked at Rubin with immeasurable sadness. "You got no guilt at all about doing your old man in, huh? Think you're doing the right thing, do you?"

Rubin was bewildered. "Dad! What's the matter? I'll never do you in. I'm not trying to trick you; I'm trying to get you back home."

"How did they get to you? I'm done for – it can't hurt to let me know."

"Dad! No one got to me! You're not done for; you're on your way home. It's hard for you to believe after everything you've gone through, but if you can hold on a bit longer, you'll see for yourself that we're heading home."

As hard as Rubin was trying, he didn't seem to be able to stop making it worse. In disgust, Sam growled, "Bad enough you've betrayed your own father, but don't act like I'm stupid on top of it. Maybe I can't kill you with my bare hands and get away like I could have once, but that don't make me stupid, that makes me old and tired and too smart to fall into that trap."

Appalled, Rubin asked, "What trap?"

"Oh, give me some credit! You think I don't know they're out there, watching us, and the moment I try anything I'm a dead man." He looked at Rubin with a mixture of sorrow and disgust that made Rubin flinch and look away. "At least you still got the decency to feel guilty. I ain't going to take it out on you. I figured you for the one to stand up to them. I was wrong. Naturally, I'm disappointed, but I won't do anything to you. I'd have to kill you, and I can't kill my own son. I got no fight left in me. Chances are they're holding your kids, so you had no choice. All that's keeping me going is knowing Mercy will be there, waiting for me when I get home."

Rubin felt so sorry for his Dad he couldn't stand it. Not only was the poor old guy too tired and worn out to defend himself, but he also wasn't making any sense. The way Sam was repeating himself reminded Rubin of the stories he'd heard about folks getting released from prison with joint jitters, or men discharged from the military with shot shock. The story was, once people started to say things over and over like old people, they never got better. He couldn't bear the idea that his smart, dependable, cunning father was gone and all he had left was this nasty old goat who accused him of things he'd never do. He felt as if he'd lost both of his parents. No matter what Sam said, Rubin couldn't leave him with the belief that Mercy was faithfully waiting for him. "Um – Dad?"

Sam went very still, his eyes fixed on Rubin's face. "They're holding your Mom to force you to bring me in."

"No, Dad, they're not."

"Then she's safe at home."

"No, Dad, she's not. I'm sorry."

"She passed away? My poor Mercy. My poor baby. I never should have left her all on her own."

"Dad! Dad, Mom's not dead. She's alive and well and living in 'The Blessings of Righteousness Compound'."

"What's she doing over there?"

"She's left you, Dad. I'm sorry."

"Mercy would never abandon the kids."

"No, she took the kids. The house is empty, Dad, that's what I've been trying to tell you."

Sam sat quietly for a while.

They were coming to a small town. To break the silence, Rubin told him cheerfully, "When we get in the town, I'll buy you some clothes."

He jumped and the horse flicked its ear when Sam suddenly shouted, "I don't believe you! You never said how you knew about the islands."

Rubin stared at him, utterly lost.

"Pretty slick the way you changed the subject there, but it won't work."

"I wasn't trying to pull anything. There's no secret. Everyone knows about the islands."

Sam snorted. "I told you not to act like I'm stupid. No one knows about the islands except the guys who were there. They nabbed us before we could say a word and tried to brain-wash us that we saw nothing. Not even the guys working on us knew what we found. So don't try to tell me everyone knows. No one knows. Never try to kid a kidder."

It all sounded so strange to Rubin that he didn't know what to make of it. "I don't get it. If they don't want anyone to know about the islands, why are they letting people publish and sell comics about them?"

"What?" Sam stared at him.

"Everything I know about the islands I saw in a comic."

"I don't believe you."

"Tell you what, when I'm in this town getting clothes for you, I'll get a comic too. That way you'll see for yourself." Pleased to see that he'd finally managed to say something that stopped his Dad's attacks, Rubin said nothing to spoil the blessed silence. He drove into the town without speaking until he stopped the cart. "How about you see if you can find some water for Blaze while I go into the store?" It was a relief when Sam got down quietly. Rubin didn't know whether it was a good sign or not, he was just glad he'd got a break before he lost his temper with his father and broke the Commandment: 'Honour thy father and thy mother.'

Rubin was aiming to have them settled before it was too dark to see the drawings in the comic book.

Sam didn't speak until they'd left the town behind. He grunted when Rubin pointed out a place to stop for the night. He got down without a sound when Rubin suggested it was a good time for him to clean himself up and put on his new clothes. Although he looked pained, he said nothing when Rubin took his rags and buried them. All through the work of making camp Sam stayed quiet. Pleased with himself for getting everything done while there was still light in the sky, Rubin grinned. "Let's look at the comic."

He no sooner had it open than Sam muttered, "Vince."

"What?"

"One of my explorers: Invincible-faith Thomason. We called him Vince. I'd know his style anywhere." Sam had a deep frown. As he turned the pages, he got more upset. "This is a pack of lies!"

"But you do see now that I told you the truth."

"Yes. I'm sorry. I never imagined this." He looked up. "What are they doing? Why go to all the trouble of brainwashing us to forget what we saw if they were going to put it all in comics? Look at this – there are no words. It's meant to reach people who can't read."

Rubin took the comic, looked it over in a whole new way, and then handed it back. "You're right. I never thought about that before." He puzzled it over, saying, "They didn't want you to say anything, but at the same time they're talking about it."

"They were after more than that. I got severely corrected for promising I wouldn't talk. The only thing they'd accept was we saw nothing."

Rubin considered that. "You knew what really happened, but they want to wipe that out. This is a pack of lies, but it's okay to spread them all over."

They looked at each other. "They're okay with the baloney but not the truth," Sam said, a light in his eyes at long last.

"What are they trying to hide?"

Sam flipped the pages over. "We ain't going to find out from this."

Rubin was so relieved to see a spark of the old Sam that he nearly couldn't control himself. "What's different in there from what you would have told everyone?"

"Everything."

"Not everything. Those are islands, right? And you found islands, didn't you?"

"Yeah!"

Rubin didn't want to make Sam withdraw again, so he avoided eye contact by staring into the fire and talking to himself. "I can't stop wondering what they're not saying."

Sam went very still. "Have something in mind?"

"Not past knowing they're pulling something over on all of us poor saps." He snapped some dry twigs with his fingers, tossing the fragments into the fire and watching them flare up on the hot embers. "I don't know what it is; I just know it's there."

After a pause, Sam said, "The day we nail that is the day we take over."

Rubin snickered. "Let's work on that." He was almost brought to tears by a twitch of Sam's lips. It wasn't a smile, but Rubin was sure that he had found the way to reach his Dad. His whole life Sam had been driven by the need to know. The first sign that he wasn't completely broken came from the challenge of trying to figure something out. Rubin saw that keeping Sam's need to know stoked was the key to getting him back. He got up and went to the buggy to get their meagre supper, saying, "What would we figure out by seeing what's true, what's not, and what's twisted?"

"I told you it's all crap."

"So, you never did find any people? The GR were right after all, were they? No one survived Judgment Day off this continent."

"You know there were islanders. I already talked about them."

Rubin was determined to keep the momentum going. He handed Sam the last of the stale sandwiches, and squatted on his haunches across the fire, saying, "There are islands, and there are islanders. That's two truths in the comics, which raises two questions: first, is anything else true? And second, why is it okay for us to read about someone else being spared on Judgment Day when it's been Blasphemy to say it?"

Sam nodded, taking another pass through the pages with more concentration. "We never saw countryside like that. Vince made that up." He showed Rubin the pictures. But this is right – hardly any of them wore shoes, and there were giants there."

"Giants? Like Goliath?"

"Well, I don't know about that, but this guy – man! He had to be more than six and a half feet tall, biggest damned head I ever saw, bull neck, and the shoulders on him! Holy Hannah! Rube, he couldn't have got through a regular doorway without ducking his head and turning his shoulders sideways. In his bare feet his shoulders are higher than my head and I'm no midget, plus I was wearing my boots. He was the biggest one I saw, but there were lots of big guys there, and women bigger than a normal man. Those two guys that took Vince…"

"They took Vince?" Rubin tapped the comic. "This same Vince?"

"Yeah. He shot a tree. It made them nuts. See, this here is wrong – he's got them worshiping trees like they're God, but that's not how it was. They had a God of the trees that they had to ask permission before they did anything to a tree."

"So, it's true they've got false Gods?"

"Oh, for sure!"

"So that's another thing that's true."

"Kinda, but it's – well – twisted, I guess is the best way to put it."

"How did you get Vince back?"

"They took him back to the ship. They …" Sam held his head in both hands. "It's giving me a headache. Can we talk about something else?"

Rubin figured that must have been one of the things his father had been taught didn't happen. "What do you want to talk about?"

"All I want to think about is home. Did you boys get the irrigation to the west corner so we can put fruit trees in?"

"Dad, things have changed since you left."

"You never did a thing while I was gone, did you?"

"It's not that. The farm's just fine. I got some apple seedlings started. It's just …"

"You weren't raided, were you?"

"Not really, but I had to let the sacrificial books go to save the others. I'm sorry."

Sam sat up straight. "Had to … then you were raided!"

"Not exactly. You see, Mom …"

"Don't you dare say anything against your mother again!"

The sudden nightfall of the desert was upon them. The moon wasn't up yet, and the starlight wasn't making any headway, but enough of the daylight had leaked away that the firelight was all Rubin could use to see his Dad. Sam appeared reddened and gaunt in the glow of the fire, but his expression couldn't be seen under the shadow of his new hat. Just as well, Rubin thought. It makes it easier to tell him when I can't see the look in his eye. "I got to, Dad. I can't let you go home to an empty house with no warning. I'm sorry."

Sam seemed to shrink. "Empty house?" His voice broke. "You were telling the truth?"

Rubin moved closer, not knowing how to deal with the pain in his Dad's voice.

"All my kids."

"Mom took them with her."

"Where did you say?"

"Blessings of Righteousness."

"What's she doing there?"

"Having babies with her new husband."

Sam sat bolt upright. "What?! How . . . Did she think she was a widow?"

"No."

"She must have. Otherwise she'd be a bigamist."

"Or a divorced woman."

Sam folded over, his head in both hands. "You better tell me everything."

"Do you remember right before you left Elder Benedict's wife died? Well, not long after that he started coming around looking for you, only you were off on your 'hunting trip' and we couldn't tell him when you'd be home. After that he kept coming around 'helping' Mom 'discipline' the boys. Then Mom started to say things like you'd abandoned us."

"I never did! I was only going to be away for three or four months. You older boys are full grown; you should've been able to handle it."

"Yes, we did. The kids didn't need his idea of discipline. It was all going real good until he helped out. Mom got a divorce on the grounds that you wasted the family legacy on non-Christian activities."

"What?! She couldn't do that! The only grounds for divorce are adultery and abandonment."

"Unless a Church Elder wants to marry your wife. Then, it seems any grounds will do. Besides, they had 'abandoned' pretty much covered."

"Oh, God! How did it come to this? Mercy and I planned this since we were kids. She knew I hadn't abandoned her. Look, you've got to know; I never used anything that you kids had a right to. Do you remember old Amos?"

"I remember you talking about him. He left his house to you. Our home."

"Right. He saved up his whole life to find out if anyone survived in the rest of the world. That's what I used: Amos's life savings. He didn't leave it to my family, he entrusted it to me to carry on his life's work."

"Thanks, Dad. I knew you would never do anything like that. But it's good to hear you say it. The way I look at it is our legacy is knowledge, not money."

Sam caught his breath. "That's it! I was raised to believe that the knowledge will outlast governments, so we have to keep it for the future. We're being lied to by the GR, so it was important for us to find out for ourselves."

"Dad, Mom told them about our forbidden books."

"She couldn't have. If she had they'd know where everything was."

"They did."

"I would have been executed if they'd found some of that stuff!"

"I know. That's why I moved most of them and sacrificed some so they'd think they'd found them and stop looking."

"Thank you, son. You've done your bit for the future. It might not be your kids or their kids that benefit from what we're doing, but the day will come when people want to know what our ancestors knew."

"I don't understand how Mom could have done it. She knew that, so how could she just hand it over? Doesn't she care about the future of her kids and grandkids?"

Rubin was surprised by how distraught Sam sounded. He had assumed that when his Dad heard what his Mom had done he'd be so mad at her that there wouldn't be any more tears. Instead, Sam burst out with, "Poor little Mercy! The pressure they put on her had to be unbearable. She would only do something like that to protect the kids."

Rubin wanted to yell at him, "She didn't protect them! She turned their legacy over to the people we were trying to hide it from!" But he couldn't talk like that to his Dad about his Mom. Hoping Sam would figure it out for himself, he gritted his teeth and said, "They kept on at us that they knew there was more, but I moved everything by myself at night when everyone else was asleep, so Beulah and Bart had no clue. I made out I had no idea what they were talking about, and, of course, the younger kids knew nothing."

"I knew I could count on you."

Knowing he sounded bitter, but not able to soften it for his Dad's sake, Rubin growled, "Yeah, well, it didn't do any good, did it? Once they found one banned book that was hidden, Elder Benedict had all he needed to be named the kids' Protector. Mom went for a divorce and didn't even try to stop them rounding all the kids up and hauling them off to save their souls and keep them from wrongful thought."

"You can't blame your mother, son. She probably thought they'd be taken from her if she didn't make it look like she was going along with it."

Rubin couldn't understand Sam's reaction. Not only had Mercy run off with another man, but she had taken all the kids into a hellish life and had turned her back on everything they had worked for and believed in through their lifetime together. Anyone else would have been hurt and angry, but Sam kept on making excuses for her. It was starting to get on Rubin's nerves. "She did more than make it look like she was going along with it: she went with them."

"At least the kids are together, and she found a way to stay with them."

"They tried to make us all go. They didn't care if the stock and crops had no one to tend them."

"Don't kid yourself. They had someone picked out to profit from our hard work."

"Mom knew I'd be homeless if I got booted off our land and didn't go with them, but she never said a word."

"Your mother couldn't help you there without risking the younger kids. She just had to hope and pray you pulled it off."

"I had to fight in court to keep the farm."

"How did you do that?"

"I went the moment I heard them talking to each other about running me off. I had my court documents in my hand before they even got started. I took the paperwork to prove that the farm was left to you by a neighbour who'd been in trouble with the law and lost his kids, so maybe the books they found came from him, which is why we didn't know anything about them. I got the preacher to say we are a hard-working family, and none of the kids said things they didn't ought to say. And I got Uncle Kenaz to say our land used to belong to a neighbour us kids had to stay away from because of wrongful thought, and when he died, he left his place to the bordering farmer because he couldn't find his kids, and our folks had lots of kids. He figured you got it because you were younger, but it could have been any of them, or the farms could have been combined, or his sons could have showed up, then some other guy would be chased off for something he didn't know about that was there before he was."

"That's not quite how I got Amos's farm, but okay, if that story did the trick. Ken never really knew how I got Amos's land. You're lucky to find a judge who was willing to buck the Church. The Elders won't like that."

"I kind of didn't make it clear that it was a Church Elder who was after me. He might have got the idea it was the military."

Sam whistled. "That'll mark you for retribution."

"I'm being watched."

"They watched Amos all the time, too. Mercy and I kept our heads down." Rubin heard the catch in his voice and expected him to stop, but Sam continued, "You better not take me home. I'll be dangerous for you."

Rubin was thrown by that. His mind was still set on the image of everything being back to normal when Sam was home. Even as he spoke, he knew it would never be. "One night can't hurt."

"Yes, it can. You don't want them taking your kids and putting you in the situation I put your Mom in."

"It's not your fault, Dad. She's the one who . . ."

"I should never have left her. I thought you'd all be okay for a few months. No different from a long hunting trip. Men leave their families all the time to hunt or go on pilgrimages. My own stupid pride. I planned this my whole life. Amos planned it his whole life, too. It was our dream, Mercy's and mine, to find out. It was our thanks to Amos for everything he did for us. I never thought anything would happen to her with you grown boys there to look out for her. Poor little Mercy. She's right. I did abandon her."

"No, Dad, you didn't. We were taking care of Mom, the farm, the kids, and everything. Only thing we couldn't do was stop the Church. I guess you're right. It's not Mom's fault. She couldn't stop them, either.

Once she wouldn't listen to us there was nothing we could do. I'm sorry. I'm sorrier than I can say."

Sam sat silently for a long time, and then said, quietly, "I don't blame you."

Taking some comfort in that, Rubin moved closer. "Thanks, Dad. Bart and Beulah went with them to see what was going on, then escaped. He's looking after things while I'm away. Beulah's in hiding. They're looking for her. Elder Benedict's got a husband for her to train her in the Wright Way."

"The hell he does!"

"Bart got her out just in time. But he ain't there to get the other girls out before they get married off."

"What about Cyrus?"

"We lost our land deferment. All the boys over thirteen are doing their time. Good thing about that is their stepfather can't stop us from writing to each other when they're not in his house. But it still hurts, you know. When I think about those poor little kids..."

"Don't!" Sam drew a deep, shuddering breath.

Rubin looked away from him, staring into the darkness past the campfire towards the sound of Blaze cropping grass at the edge of the river. It took a moment for his eyes to adjust from the brightness of the fire so that he could make out the horse's shape. He didn't know what to do for his father except give him privacy. If he'd been with a female he would have patted her hand, but a man didn't touch another man in that way.

Eventually Sam pulled himself together enough to speak. "They'll be alright once I've seen them."

Rubin's heart sank. "They're not going to let you or me anywhere near them."

Sam's voice shook. "They can't stop me from seeing my kids! I'm their father! Mercy wouldn't . . ." His voice trailed off.

Staring at the ghostly shape of the horse, Rubin explained, "The kids were 'rescued' to 'save their souls.' They're being raised in the Wright Way. Bart ain't cut off yet. He got Beulah out. He'll get the others out as he can. Cyrus will repatriate home, so he'll be able to help. They've got to have some place to go, so you and I must be careful we don't get arrested."

"Our farm is the first place they'll look."

"True. And while they're looking there it gives the kids more time to get somewhere else."

Sam grunted with the most positive sound Rubin had heard from him yet. It seemed to be the best time to call it a day. He rolled under the cart where he wasn't easy to see but could defend in any direction against all comers from big cats after the horse to robbers trying to roll them while they slept.

Sam started off to the side where anyone disturbing them would be caught in the crossfire. Rubin tactfully didn't hear the sounds of grief coming from the direction of his father. Sam moved several times, finally spending the night curled up against the belly of the sleeping horse.

Setting out before dawn, they ate dried meat and hard tack on the road. "I was thinking," Rubin said the first words of the day. "I've heard about a guy who lost his family like us. I don't know who did what, but the old guy is trying to run his farm on his own."

"Can you find out about him?"

"Yes."

"If he checks out, I could go there and take the heat off you. That's what you want isn't it?"

Rubin felt defeated. Every time he thought his father was okay, Sam would say something so unlike the Sam Rubin knew that he had to glance over to make sure he really was sitting next to the right man. In as even a tone as he could manage, Rubin answered, "What I want is for you to be back home. I was trying to find someone you might get along with, seeing he lost all his kids and his wife."

"And you still blame your mother, even when you know this is what they do to folks that think."

"You never saw her with him." Instead of flipping out, Sam was suddenly calmer. His unpredictability was the hardest part for Rubin to cope with. He got upset over things Rubin figured were fine, then he'd be okay with things that Rubin expected would put him right over the top.

"We'll never know what your Mother went through now that we can't talk to her. But I know my Mercy. We've been together since we were young teens. She always agreed with me about how important it is to keep our heritage alive. That was one of the things that attracted us to each other in the first place. She was one of the few people in my life that I was ever open with, and that was because we shared the same outlook. The only reason for Mercy to go against her beliefs is to save the kids." Rubin opened his mouth to point out that the kids had not been saved, but Sam cut him off. "What would you do to protect your kids? If the GR'd been there while you were picking me up, what would you do if they said you'd never see your kids again unless you proved you followed the Wright Way? Think about it seriously. How far would you go?"

Rubin was unable to form the words to make an answer. Chaotic images filled his mind: his home without his kids; Dixie Rae frantically doing whatever it took to be with her babies. Like his mother. Even then he felt angry with Mercy. There was no reason for her to be so friendly with Elder Benedict. Or was there? Could she have done it any other way? Still, she'd had no right to tell him about the books.

Sam's voice cut through his swirling thoughts. "That's why the knowledge is passed down to only the ones who can handle it. Amos chose me over any of his own kids, and my parents picked me out of their kids."

"Grandma and Grandpa were part of this?"

"Now you know it wasn't all Amos. My parents and Amos both grew up in Logan where the knowledge of the ancients was revered, not destroyed. They both hid as much as they could, believing that the GR would be defeated, and they'd be free to rebuild Logan. Now it's your turn. Bart doesn't know as much as you do, and Beulah knows very little, unless your Mom filled her in, but you can likely trust both of them if you can't hand it on to your kids. What you have to watch for is who they marry. It's hard enough for a man to keep stuff like that secret from his wife if she's not into it, but it's just about impossible for a woman to keep it secret from her husband. We never let you in on all of it until Mercy and I were sure Dixie Rae believed like us. You've got to be just as careful with Bart and Beulah, and with deciding what to tell Cyrus."

"You're talking like you ain't here!"

"I might not be. We don't know if they're lying in wait or if we gave them the slip or if they'll raid later. If I'm there it makes you a target. You must protect your kids."

"Dixie Rae's waiting for us. Like yesterday. We got to show up. Where will you go if you don't come home?"

"Into hiding."

"I figure we gave them the slip. Come home and let me find out about the place I told you about."

"How will you do that?"

Not wanting to say too much, Rubin muttered, "I know people who know people."

Sam looked at him so sharply that he made Rubin feel uncomfortable. "That sounds like an underground."

"It's not like that . . ." Rubin would have explained, but Sam cut him off.

"Don't tell me. If I end up back in the jar they can't get what I don't know. I got my reasons for being interested in an underground. I've got a lot to tell you about what I learned. Not about the islands, but the Weskies."

"Who?"

"The Westers. They were slaves on the ship. They came from dozens of little nations all along the West Coast. They had different names like we used to be Loganites before the GR over-ran us. The GR called them Wasters, which I guess came from Westers. Plus, they thought the Weskies were a waste of skin. If any of the Weskies won't get baptised the GR shoot them. So, the others put up with it to stay alive. Christian names were put on them, but they were still pagans inside."

Rubin was surprised. "You made friends with pagans?"

"I got to tell you, I saw more bravery, honesty, and loyalty from the pagans than I did from the GR, one true God or not."

That reminded Rubin of something he'd heard. "One of the things that happened while you were in the joint was a big attack on Port Persistence that freed a lot of slaves."

"Good. That's good. I hope and pray the guys I got to know got away. How did you hear that?"

"I know people who know people."

Sam's grin at that lifted Rubin's spirits like nothing else had. "It's good you can get news the GR don't want you to hear. Communication is the key. We can't touch them for weapons or fighting strength. None of the small nations they've over-run can touch them that way, but it's what all of us try first. That's how they get us in so deep. It's like fighting quick sand. The more you struggle, the deeper you go. They're stronger than everyone else with their iron and oil and organisation. Where they're weak is knowledge, understanding, and communication. That's where to hit them."

Rubin was impressed. "This is new. What happened to: 'no organised army ever beat a guerrilla army'? Are you saying the resistance ain't doing no good?"

"Oh, they're doing some good alright, but they can't defeat the GR by themselves. The GR weakness is in their belief that God chose them to reunite the whole continent into one huge nation. Because they're 'doing God's work' they're right and anyone who asks questions is sinning. It's because of that attitude that they think book learning leads to sin and is what brought about Judgment Day. So, the true GR have had generations with no learning outside of the Church and the military. They know so little that they don't know that they don't know. If we can find out and spread the truth of what they're doing, folks will lose faith in them. If what we find out is bad enough folks will rebel against them."

"A full insurrection, Dad? Hundreds will be killed!"

"Hundreds are being killed now. That's one of the things we must spread the word about."

The concern that Sam had lost his mind pricked Rubin again. Not wanting to start a useless argument he made what he hoped was a neutral answer. "Did you learn this on your trip?"

"I learned a lot on the ship. I don't just mean about the islands and the people there. I mean my own guys, the Weskies, and the GR. Like you, the only time I was away from home was when I did my year of basic, when I was sixteen. That time I was a kid who paid no mind outside of my sergeant and how to get home alive as fast as possible. This time I was grown, so I understood more, watched more, there was more to see, I could talk it over with my guys until we were arrested, and then I had two years with nothing else I wanted to think about but what makes the GR tick. It kept my mind off what they wanted me to fear to think about; like what I'd seen and heard."

"Now you're talking! My Dad's back!" Hugely relieved, Rubin whooped. His Dad was still in there. He was battered, and fractured around the edges, but still Sam after all. Rubin thought he had the answer: the closer he got to home, the more like his old self Sam was. The fear Rubin'd had that he'd lost both of his parents was replaced by admiration for the old man.

Sam blinked and gave Rubin a curious look. "Question is, how do we spread the word without getting people killed? I know how to make a radio."

"How did you learn that?"

"Amos."

"Figures."

"When I was ten, I got copper wire for him from a pre-Judgment house ruin. We made a set, but we never heard a thing."

"Nobody else knew how to make one."

"Or they couldn't get the parts."

"Or they heard you and couldn't answer."

"Or they answered, and we couldn't hear them. What we got to do is make two and make sure we can hear each other. Then we can teach people what radios do, what they need to make them, how to make them, and how to use them."

Rubin realized he'd been holding his breath when he let it out to protest, "That will make sure the Purificators come sniffing around!"

"We'll only tell the underground. It's a kick-ass way to spread news. That's why it's better if I do it someplace away from you."

"Okay, I get that, now."

"Another thing an underground can do is find out what happened to my guys: if any of them survived. They're like family to me. They paid a big chunk of the costs of my trip. I never saw any of them again after we were arrested. I know Vince is alive and drawing picture books, but what about Joe Mack, Chuck, Johnny, and Willie Jay?"

That triggered Rubin's memory. "Is Willie Jay's name B. J. Rimmon?"

"Yes. How do you know?"

"A letter came for you from him about a year ago."

"Thank God! That's great news, son! He's alive!"

"Well, he was a year ago."

"You don't get it: Willie Jay is the one I worried about the most."

"I didn't want to send it in case it was a problem, and every time I tried to visit you, I was put off by a different story: like you weren't in custody, then that you'd died, and then, a month after they said you were dead, they said you'd been moved."

"You never posted it?"

"And I didn't bring it with me in case I was searched."

"Good thinking. Was he out of jail?"

"I never opened it. I hid it so if you ever showed up it would be there for you."

"I can't thank you enough for that."

Sam's voice was cracked with emotion, but he was sitting straighter with more energy than Rubin had seen yet. Rubin was sure he'd seen the last of Sam's freaky behaviour. "No point in letting it fall into GR hands."

"Very true. You never know what Willie Jay'll say. He's an innocent, huh? When I get settled in my new place, I'll answer Willie Jay and see if he's got any idea what happened to Joe Mack, Chuck, and Johnny. Good thing we taught that boy to read and write."

They talked about the explorers all the rest of the way home.

At first Rubin thought he was imagining things, but soon he couldn't deny it: Sam was unravelling again. Rubin couldn't understand it. Sam was getting better the closer they got to home, and suddenly he was getting worse when they were nearly there. To distract Sam, Rubin asked questions about the explorers. Talking about them had perked Sam up more than anything else. Now not even that helped. By the time the first farm dog came into sight joyfully barking welcome, Sam's hands were shaking, his shoulders were hunched, and he had the same gaunt, hollow-eyed, whipped-dog look that he'd had in the beginning. He hardly reacted when Fred, whining with pleasure at recognising him, jumped up onto the cart and tried to lick his face.

Trying to buck him up, Rubin assured him, "Not long, now."

Sam jumped, then snarled with such force that Fred yipped in surprise and jumped down, "Can't wait to spring the trap, can you?"

Too late Rubin realized Sam was seriously worried that they were walking into an ambush. Personally, he thought it was joint jitters more than a real threat, but he didn't want to cause another out-burst, so he said nothing until Dixie Rae, Bart, and the kids and dogs came running to meet them with open arms.

"No company?" he asked as he jumped down.

Bart clapped Sam on the shoulder, pulling back when Sam flinched. "Nope," he said, leading the horse away, saying over his shoulder, "Good to see you, Dad."

Rubin shook his head at the others from behind Sam's back, kissed his wife and scooped up his kids.

Dixie Rae said nothing about Sam's appearance, telling him in a cheerful way, "Rubin and me are in the big room, now. You okay with that?"

He didn't answer. He followed her into the house looking dazed.

Rubin sighed and went in behind them with a kid on each hip.

During the time since they'd inherited their house from Amos, Sam and Mercy had expanded it to fit their growing family. When there were too many kids for the lofts on either side of the room, girls on the right, boys on the left, bedrooms were built for the over-flow. A floor was built across the height of Sam and Mercy's room to make a girls' room up under the eaves. A room for the boys was added on to the back of the house. Without a word to a soul, Sam walked right through the house to that room.

Rubin and Dixie Rae fetched up in the kitchen, looking at each other in confusion. Rubin was embarrassed. "He's got a bad case of joint jitters," he explained, setting the kids down.

Dixie Rae gave him a pitying look. "He's just got home to an empty house. That's going to take a while. Give him a chance." Disentangling the two-year-old boy from her skirts, she headed off to the fussing baby in their room.

"Quiet!" Rubin called uselessly to their five-year-old daughter romping noisily with the dogs in the great room. Picking his son up again, he soothed him, "Shush. Mommy will be back in a minute," as he stepped back into the great room to send the dogs outside. Shutting the door between Candace and her playmates caused an immediate howl of protest. The only quiet kid was the nursing baby.

Dixie Rae joined them in the great room, holding the baby to the breast with one arm, while she corralled little Sammy with the other one, sat down and sent Candace running to find something, all at the same time.

Ignoring the absurdity of calling a house filled with so much life and activity, 'empty,' Rubin defended himself, "I warned Dad that Mom was gone."

That earned him another pitying look. "So, if you lost all of us, you'd be okay with it if someone told you about it?"

"No, no, no, I didn't mean that. What I mean is he's acting weird, not just sad."

"On top of seeing his home for the first time without his wife and kids here, he can't even go into his own bed."

That hit Rubin. "Maybe we should move."

"We can't. There are too many of us for our cabin, now." When Rubin decided to propose, he got his brothers to help him build a one room cabin for them to start in. The plan was to add to it as their family grew.

"Little Sammy wasn't born when your Dad left. Now there's another one as well. If your brothers were still here to help you build, we could, but with only you and Bart to do everything, it's never going to happen. Candy and little Sammy are too young to be in a loft by themselves, and I can't be up and down ladders with the baby. That rules out the girls' room, too. Besides, you'd hit your head on the rafters up there. The only room big enough for us with three kids is your parents' room."

Rubin was sure they could have worked something out, but he knew better than to argue with Dixie Rae when she was set on something. "Where's Bart going to sleep?"

"He can have our cabin, if he wants."

At that he decided it was time to get back to work and talk to Bart.

The brothers expected their Dad to be his old self now that he was home and safe, but Sam continued to walk around in a daze, unable to concentrate, jumpy as a turkey before Thanksgiving. Taking him to his childhood home next door, where Beulah was hidden as a male hired hand, made very little difference. Their Uncle Ken, Sam's older brother, told Rubin, "It looks like shot shock."

Rubin sighed. "I thought it was joint jitters."

"Same thing. You get one in action and one in prison is all."

So that they wouldn't attract the attention of any watching GR, the different branches of the Johnson family had little contact with each other. Rubin had taken the risk of arranging the visit, and of taking Sam over there, because he believed it would help Sam to see his daughter. Making his way back home knowing they might have led the GR to his sister for nothing; Rubin had his lowest moments since the whole nightmare began. No matter how much he believed that Sam needed to be in his own home, Rubin finally had to face the fact that the only choice left was to find out if the other old man who'd lost his family was willing to take Sam in and pray that a new start would do the trick.

He sent the message out at his first opportunity and settled down to wait.

Before first light, a few days later, the dogs sparked. There were several ways out of the house. They depended on the dogs raising the alarm before the house could be surrounded. Rubin had his boots on and was slinking out of the bedroom window like a cat, weapon ready, before he woke up.

Bart had elected to sleep in the boys' loft, which left him with no easy way out. Going purely on instinct, he slid through the front door, knowing it could easily be seen by anyone watching the house. He crept away to draw whoever was out there away from the family.

On the other side of the house, screened by the hedge, Rubin sorted out what was going on. The dogs were focusing on one person who was standing still and silent on the other side of the gate. Seeing he had respect; Rubin whistled the dogs to quiet.

No one moved for a moment, and then Bart strode back, weapon at the ready, demanding, "State your business."

The dogs growled. The person didn't move or make a sound. The word, 'decoy,' flashed through Rubin's mind, but he knew that they had no chance against anyone who really wanted to take them down, so he decided to play it straight. He whistled the dogs again, which had the effect of stopping Bart as well as them. Taking advantage of the stillness, Rubin asked, softly, "Can we help you?"

To his enormous relief a woman's voice said, "I got a message."

In excited relief after she'd gone, Rubin burst in the front door and strode right through the length of the house without taking his boots off. He hadn't seen or heard Sam outside, so he assumed he'd either slept through the whole thing, or he was still out there, undetectable because of his superior tracking skills.

"Hey, Dad!" he threw the door open to find Sam cowering down on the floor in the far corner. "What are you doing?"

Sam stared at him as if he didn't recognise him. They stayed there, frozen, for a moment, then Sam's eyes cleared. He shook his head, glanced around, and claimed, "My boots were over here."

Rubin didn't believe a word of it. Deeply shaken by the manic look in Sam's eye, he said with a lot less enthusiasm than he'd felt a minute ago. "You're welcome at the farm of the guy I told you about. I'll take you over there in the next day or so if you still want to go."

A change came over Sam. Right before Rubin's eyes the haunted creature in front of him turned back into his Dad. "No, it's best if I get there by myself. Tell me where it is, and I'll go without involving you."

Rubin had no confidence that Sam could take care of himself. "I can't get away today, Dad, I've got too much to do, and Dixie Rae needs her cart. You'll get there faster and safer if I drive you."

"Don't be an ass. They're likely watching you, and they're for sure watching me. They're just waiting for you to do something like this. Even if they don't bust you for aiding a criminal, we'd lead them straight to that poor old guy. Tell me where it is, and I'll find it. Let him know I'm gonna be a while. I'll take a butterfly route so if they're following me, they'll think I found it by accident. It's important that you can honestly say you have no idea where I am if they come looking for me. Make sure they can't find any connection between you and him or whatever his family did."

Rubin could see there was no point in arguing. Sam was decisive like he had been when he was planning his trip. He'd been impossible to stop then, too. "I want to know that you're okay."

"Let me know how to contact your people who know people. They can get the message to you."

Rubin knew he'd have to be content with that.

CHAPTER SEVENTEEN

Nat

*N*at strolled slowly along the path, letting the dark eyed toddler take her own sweet time. The sunshine was warm on his face; the smell of the sea invited him to a luxuriant laziness. The beauty of it was, while he was indulging himself, everyone thought he was wonderful. He beamed down at the shining mop of black curls beside him thinking, 'Could life be any better than this?'

Tia pointed her fat little brown finger at everything, demanding, "Zat?"

Peaceably naming each item, Nat wondered why people got impatient with the insatiable curiosity of a two-year-old. To him it was a small price to pay for lovely, lazy mornings like this. With one plump fist holding one of his fingers, sturdy little legs pattering along beside him in total trust, Tia felt to Nat like his own daughter. He couldn't have loved her more if she had been. He was the one who had been with her every day of her life since she was about a month old. Nat could not understand how Bram could have left Hine and Mere as soon as Tia was born. No matter what he wanted to do, there's no way Nat could have gone away from those little faces at a time like that . . . never mind leaving Hine alone with a newborn and the world's most stubborn three-year-old. He had never said it out loud, not even to the grief counsellors, but Nat thought Bram hadn't deserved Hine. He couldn't understand what she'd seen in him.

There were times when Nat was angry with Bram for the heartbreak he'd caused, and other times when he was almost grateful to him for magical moments like this. As many times as he'd walked along that path to the marina in his life, Nat had never seen the magic in the trees, plants, birds, the stones of the path, people's front gardens, and the carvings on the railings, until he saw it all through Tia's eyes.

As Tia ran her hands over the carvings on the posts down at her level, Nat averted his eyes from the marina so that he wouldn't see the space where the Kaumoana should have been. The piers were all empty: every boat was out, but the only gap he could see was where the metal hunter used to be. Looking to the side to avoid seeing the gap, he saw someone lying on the bench beside the stairs from the ramp to the beach.

Concerned that the man on the bench might be ill, Nat took Tia's hands off the carvings, picked her up, and carried her as he ran down the stairs to the beach. Part way he realised the man was Ray. "Gidday, Ray," Nat greeted him. "Are you okay?"

Ray grunted, looking around blearily.

Tia froze, fingers in her mouth.

Nat saw that Ray was more inebriated than ill. "Not feeling good, mate?"

Ray lurched upright on the bench, blinking and shading his eyes with one hand while holding on to the back of the bench as if it were moving.

Tia buried her face in Nat's neck.

Ray wasn't even hung-over, he was falling-down drunk, and it was before ten o'clock in the morning. Nat checked in his head, since he wasn't wearing a watch. That was about right: he'd taken Mere to school by nine and he was sure that was less than an hour ago. That scared him. Ray was in far worse shape than anyone had suspected. Because Tia seemed scared of Ray, Nat didn't offer to help him make his way home. He suggested, "Maybe you should go home and sleep it off."

Ray flared like a lit match. "Maybe you should go soak your head!"

Nat caught his breath in amazement. "I'm sorry I can't take you home, but I've got Hine's girls today."

"I don't need your help! You just spend all day baby-sitting the girls so their Mum can take a whole day's pay away from hard working seamen just so she can snare a Daddy for her kids."

"Ben was on board," burst out before he realised how lame it sounded.

"All very well for you," Ray grumbled. "You're not sick."

"You wouldn't be, either, if you didn't drink so much."

"I wouldn't be either if you didn't natter so much."

So, he wouldn't say anything to embarrass himself any further, Nat walked away along the beach, past the Harbour Master's hut. Well out of earshot from Ray, he tried to put Tia down to play, but she clung to him. He straightened up and snuggled her close, wrapping his arms around her and burying his nose in her fragrant curls, murmuring songs until she started to wriggle and giggle. He reckoned she could sense he was seething with rage with that uncanny instinct small children have, so he focused on calming himself down and reassuring her.

"Hey, Anatoe!"

The cheerful voice interrupted him. He looked over Tia's head to see the Harbour Master, his grandfather, Hatoe's father, coming towards him. Kahutoe was seventy-nine years old and as agile and energetic as men one third his age. "How's my little princess?" he asked Tia.

Instead of greeting him with joy as she usually did, Tia hid her face in Nat's neck.

Kahutoe stopped in surprise. "She's not going shy on us, is she?"

"Ray scared her."

"For real?" Kahu played peek-a-boo with Tia, circling Nat so that he was facing her no matter how she twisted and turned, until she was giggling. "That's better. You don't want to hide from old grandfather Kahu, do you?"

"No!" Tia shouted, then, surprised by her own daring, she gave a deep, throaty laugh.

Nat and Kahu laughed out loud.

"Who would have thought a laugh like that could come from a wee wahine like you," Kahu grinned.

"She's not …"

Kahu waved Nat to silence. "You're as pretty as a parti-coloured poppy, aren't you?" he tickled her tummy until she wriggled down from Nat's arms. They pretended to chase her for a bit, leaving her to play as soon as something caught her attention.

Then they moved back out of earshot. "Never let her hear you say she's not a little girl."

Nat was taken aback. "But she's not."

"Never let her hear you say that. Too many people are calling her the new Wineera. She's not Wineera. She's Roitihia. Princess Wineera has never been known for her beauty. She's known for bravery and service to the people. If that's what Tia wants to do with her life, good on her. More power to her. But it's got to be her decision. It can't be because she thinks she's expected to. All the boys in our family were expected to work the boats. Look how that's turned out."

Nat couldn't deny that. "Neither Kiri nor I will earn a living from the Laughing Dolphin. Kiri hasn't made up his mind what he wants to do yet."

Kahu gave a slightly sad smile. "That boy's drifting through life. He hasn't made up his mind about anything. Annie always said he'd be a late bloomer, but if he loved the sea, he'd know it, and you've got to love this to do it for a living, as you well know. That's exactly what I mean. The life of service that the Princess lives is all-encompassing. That sort of thing has to come from within or it's destructive."

Nat shook his head. "Granddad, no one is telling Tia she has to do what Wineera does. She's a big girl like Wineera is, that's all."

Kahu shook his head. "That's not what people are saying. They're saying she is the next Wineera. Children take that kind of thing to heart. Tia is a very feminine little girl. Look at the way she plays, the things she likes to wear, and the way she looks at you through her lashes. She'll be beautiful if she believes she is. With everyone else in her life saying she's the size of a barge, it's vital that you remind her and them how pretty she really is."

Nat felt a weight of responsibility pressing down on his shoulders. "Why me?"

"Because of your relationship with her. You are the closest she can come to having a father. You're with her every day and you take care of her while her mother goes to work. Whether you like it or not, she'll see what she's going to be like as a woman reflected in how you speak to her, treat her, and talk about her."

The difference between the way Ray referred to Hine going out on the boat, and the way Kahu said it, struck Nat so hard that he glanced down the beach towards Ray.

"I'll get to him," Kahu followed Nat's eyes, "But this is important. Tia is a delicate flower petal soul living in the body of a forester. It's up to you to make sure she doesn't get a negative image of herself."

Nat watched the innocent toddler's play for only a moment before he could see something he'd never noticed before: she was playing in a completely feminine way. Busily trundling around, she was collecting fragments of seaweed that had washed up on the beach and was placing them on pebbles and shells with infinite care, patting them into place, standing back to admire her handiwork, then adjusting as she thought necessary before busily trotting off to find the next piece. She was talking non-stop, but he couldn't hear a word she said. He finger-spoke, "Pretty," to her. His suspicions were confirmed when she lit up with a beaming smile, holding up a muddy, tattered piece of seaweed to show him. He nodded and smiled, finger-speaking, "Good girl," to Tia while saying, "You're right," to Kahu.

Nodding, Kahu observed, "She's pretending the seaweed is flowers, and she's decorating with it. You'd better get her cleaned up before her mother sees her."

"Miki's invited us for lunch. She'll clean everyone up."

Kahu laughed. "Cheat!"

Nat laughed, and then asked, "How do you know about raising girls? Our family only has boys."

"You see and hear a lot of things when you live as long as I have." He sighed. "And one of the things I've learned is that it does no good to put things off." He turned around to face the way they'd come. "And I've put off dealing with him longer than I should have."

Nat saw where he was looking. "Ray?"

"Yes. Not that I have the slightest idea what to say or how to say it. Poko is much better at this sort of thing than I am."

The sadness in his voice brought a mental image of Bram's grieving father to Nat. "He's not the Harbour Master anymore."

"That doesn't help."

"I suppose not. I'm sorry. I don't think he'll be able to help you, either. He's that wiped out by the loss of the Kaumoana on his watch he can't bear to come down here and see the space where she used to moor."

"We're all still cut up by it. It takes years to come back from a loss like that, if you ever can. Some people never do. That's what's wrong with Ray."

Nat felt impatient. "Ray didn't lose any family in it. Poko and Beth lost both of their children and their son-in-law. All they have left are their three granddaughters: these two of Bram's, and Poma's Elly. Not to mention that Poko blames himself for not stopping Bram. And just think what Hine has gone through these last two years losing her partner, both parents, brother, sister-in-law, and her nephew right after she had her baby – but you don't see her asleep on a bench at ten o'clock in the morning, do you?"

"We've all suffered. This is harder in some ways than the eruption of Tarawera wiping out whole families. At least that was a natural event. This was done to us by one of our own. All the Behaviourists in these three thousand islands talking at once can't do anything about that. People wouldn't have guilt on top of their loss if they could never have done anything to stop it. Well, except for Ray, of course. If it had been a volcano, Poko and Hine wouldn't be tearing their own hearts out for not stopping Bram, but Ray would still have crippling survivor guilt."

"Crawling inside the bottle doesn't help that."

"Doesn't help anything. Never does, never will. But people who can't find relief any other way will still fall into the bottle like they always have. The rest of us are supported by our friends and families, even Hine, who lost nearly all of hers. Ray didn't have strong coping skills to start with, on top of which he has no friends or family here."

Nat objected to that. "Everybody likes Ray!"

"Who's his best mate?"

Nat had no answer. He stood beside Kahu facing down the beach watching Tia, while Kahu faced up the beach watching Ray.

Kahu sighed. "That's what I was afraid of. He only has superficial relationships. I don't know what to do to help him."

Nat froze. He didn't want to think that his grandfather was asking him for advice. He stared at Tia, half of his mind pulling back from saying anything about how to help Ray, the other half picturing taking Tia to Mauao where she could play on a white sand beach. The expectant silence made him so uncomfortable that he finally gave in and tried to think of something to say. "You could tell him that no one will hire him in that condition."

"I think he already knows that, since he never shows up for work drunk."

"What?" Nat was amazed to hear that when he could see the evidence to the contrary with his own eyes.

"Sometimes he's hung-over. In fact, he might have been sliding down hill and we didn't notice, now that I think about it, because he'll only go out when he can work a later shift. I thought he liked late shifts, but what if he's always got to sleep it off these days?"

Nat didn't believe a word of it. "What happened today?"

"He was working fit until he found out Hatoe was taking Hine out today. Sue wasn't looking for a Daily today, and for some reason he didn't head out to look for work. He came up to my hut to look at the job board, complained about it and then walked away. I thought he'd gone to work until I saw him on the bench. It's the first time he's done this."

"If he usually goes home to hit the turps we'd never know."

"Tangaroa on the sea! You're right. This means he brought it with him today. He can't be carrying plonk on board like that. It's my responsibility to see to safety. I don't want to dob him in, eh? I thought I could substitute for his family, but I think he might need professional help."

"We've lost too many to take any chances." Nat didn't want to hurt Ray, but he couldn't bear the idea of Ray being drunk at the helm of the Laughing Dolphin with his Dad asleep in the hammock. "I'm going to tell Dad, you know. I don't need to see the Dolph in pieces like the Kaumoana."

"No more do I. I'll talk to him right now. It might not be that bad."

Nat walked away so that he wouldn't say anything else. He was so angry that Ray had shown up to go out with Hatoe that morning with enough alcohol to be right out of it, that he knew if he started, he wouldn't be able to stop.

As Nat strode angrily towards Tia, Kahu walked slowly in the opposite direction.

"He saw the wreckage! He knows what can happen!" Nat growled out loud. Seeing Tia look up at him, her big brown eyes wide with apprehension, he forced himself to calm down and smile, saying in a high-pitched, encouraging voice, "What have you got to show me?"

She ran to him. He squatted down on his heels so that he could give her a big hug, nuzzle her hair, and blow bubbles into her neck until she squealed and wriggled free. He sat on his heels in the brown mud, pretending that the battered pieces of seaweed were beautiful flowers, singing her baby songs with her, and allowing himself to let go of adulthood and slide back into the purity of childhood.

His pleasant little holiday from reality was interrupted by a call. He looked up to see the skinny shape of a musician he knew coming towards him. He stood up to greet Iggy. As he stood there, he got a whiff of a smell that caught his full attention. Someone who didn't know what it was might have called it a stink, but for Nat the fond memories it brought of fun with his Mum and Dad made it a sweet scent on the morning breeze.

Iggy hugged Nat. "Gidday mate."

"Good to see you." Nat put his hand on Iggy's shoulder.

Iggy sniffed. "Cor! What's that pong?"

"The tide's extra low today so the mud flats in the middle of the harbour are at the surface."

"How can you breathe?"

Nat laughed at Iggy's expression of disgust. "We're used to it. Great flatfish fishing when the tide comes in."

Iggy, who was a vegan, wrinkled his nose again. "I don't know how you could live in a place like this after you were in the big smoke."

Nat looked around at the brown mud beach, the three piers of the small marina, and he could see where it might not impress someone used to a big town, white sand beaches, and big marinas. His heart swelled with love for his home, smells and all. "I don't know how you live in a big place like Tāmaki-makaurau."

"You're joking!"

"Not a bit of it." He squatted on his heels to be on Tia's eye level. "Come on, Poppet, we have to go to Miki's for lunch."

In the best of traditional form for two-year-olds, Tia shouted, "No!"

"I'm hungry," Nat coaxed. "Aren't you hungry?"

"No!"

"Tickle monster's coming to get you!" Nat got between Tia and the sea, crouched down, and went towards her with his arms outstretched, his fingers making tickling movements.

She tried to resist, but when his fingers nearly touched her tummy, she couldn't help backing away, squealing, "No, no!"

"Once you've got them moving, you're half-way there."

Iggy watched him herding Tia along the beach, laughing with them. "She's not yours, is she?"

"No, I'm watching her and her sister so their Mum can work."

"Your nieces?"

"No. They lost their Dad in the loss of the metal hunter when this one was born. I don't know if you remember the news of two years ago."

"Yeah, I do. That's when you left us."

"Right. That's the one." Putting his head down as he pretended, he was going to catch Tia and tickle her, so that he didn't look at the gap, he waved his hand towards it. "She used to moor right there."

"It doesn't look like your marina does much business."

Nat looked around to figure out what Iggy meant. To him it looked like a busy day because every boat was out except the official ones. When he pictured bigger marinas, he realised what was missing. "We don't have any pleasure craft here. It's purely a working marina. Fishing boats at the north pier, weed collectors in the middle, and official craft at the south end: search and rescue, harbour patrol, harbour master, water taxi, and water ambulance."

He no longer had his full attention on Tia, which was all it took for her to realise she was being taken further and further away from her play. With a shout of, "No!" she made a break for it. Alerted by her shout, Nat flicked out a hand and caught her, which brought on a scream of pure rage.

She went limp to slip from his grasp, but he was ready for that and caught one hand, telling Iggy, "Grab her other hand. We'll swing her." He called out, "One, two, three, whee!" On each number they paced forward and on 'whee' they swung her high into the air between them. They did that the rest of the way to the stairs, by which time she'd stopped roaring and was laughing again. Averting his eyes from the gap on their right, Nat was relieved to see that Ray and Kahu were gone. Snickering at Tia's squeals, he said, "She's so easy to redirect that she's a joy. The other one, Mere, is the most stubborn child in these three thousand islands."

Tia pulled at their hands, demanding, "More! More!"

"Can you manage it up the steps?" Nat could see that Iggy wasn't having as much fun as he was, but he didn't care. It was easier to deal with a happy toddler than one that was screaming and fighting.

"I reckon." As they swung Tia up the steps and then on up the ramp to the path, Iggy asked, "This is your life, now? Nursemaid to a neighbour's children?"

That hit Nat hard. Until then he'd believed that he'd made a useful, fulfilled life for himself. "There's a little more to it than that."

Iggy must have realized he'd touched a nerve, because he said a heartfelt, "I'm sorry, mate." Then he spoiled the effect by adding, "I couldn't believe it when you walked away from your career."

On the path Nat hid his expression by bending over Tia. He explained, "I just had to come home," then coaxed Tia to run to Mere's school.

"But you never came back."

Nat straightened up, but he still couldn't let Iggy see his face because he wasn't sure he could control it. Paying way more attention to the trees and bushes lining the path than they deserved, he muttered, "I couldn't."

"But, man, your career was just taking off. You were getting island-wide exposure playing at the glass championships. You were becoming a household name. I thought you'd have a music studio here, but when I asked at the canteen, they said you were down at the beach."

"I was."

"I was sure you'd be making music on the beach, not baby-sitting!"

Picking up the pace so that Tia didn't get too far ahead, Nat struggled to find the words to make Iggy understand. "Iggy, mate, you have no idea what it was like. Whole families were gone. There are fewer than three hundred people in Matapihi, and we lost ten of them. Do the arithmetic. You have more than fifteen hundred people in Tāmaki-makaurau. You'd have to lose fifty adults and five children to have a similar blow, plus they'd have to all be friends, relatives, and neighbours: no strangers. On top of that, you'd have to lose a major industry that affected the entire city. We had one big boat. One. And she's gone. No one even wants to use her mooring. It hurts that much."

"I can't imagine."

"Nearly all of us apprenticed to Bram or his Dad, Poko."

"You can't seriously want to be a fisherman! With your talents?"

"I apprenticed when I was sixteen. My family cultivates and harvests seaweed for plastics, medicine, and food."

"This is how you're spending the rest of your life? Diving to hack off arms full of seaweed? With the gifts you've been given? It's a criminal waste!"

Nat ran ahead, calling to Tia not to get too far ahead. When Iggy caught up, Nat muttered, "I had to be with my Dad. My Mum died when I was in Secondary School. This opened up old wounds. That's the end of it. I can't talk about it anymore." He indicated the garden gate that Tia was trying to open. "I have to get the girls."

"Girls? I thought Tia had only one sister."

Nat opened the child-proof latch, letting Tia enter, saying over his shoulder, "There's also their cousin, Elly. She was orphaned." He charged along the path and took the stairs two at a time. The teacher, a cousin of Hine's, met him at the door. She managed to greet Nat, chivvy the girls into collecting all of their belongings and hurrying up, look curious about Iggy hanging back at the gate, ask after Miki, and prevent Tia running into her house: all at the same time, and without appearing to do anything.

Nat, on the other hand, felt pulled in all directions as he turned to face Iggy again at the same time as Mere wrinkled her nose and told Tia, "Pooh! You stink."

Tia immediately howled in protest. "No!"

Elly backed Mere up. "Yes, you do. You were in the mud at low tide."

Nat did his best to defuse the situation, wishing the girls had been sweet so that Iggy could have seen what a pleasure they were and understood his point of view. "Now, girls, be nice. We're going to Miki's. She'll clean Tia up."

Clearly jealous, Mere thrust her artwork at Nat to carry for her, shrilling, "I'm not getting in the tub with her!"

"You probably won't be allowed in if you talk like that," he chided, taking Elly's artwork as well, to protect it.

"Can we run, please?" Elly asked.

In an instant they were off, hair flying, Tia trailing behind, calling, "Wait! Wait!"

Nat broke into a jog to stay with her, telling Iggy, "After I leave the girls with Miki, we can have lunch."

Warned by the girls, Miki met Nat at her front door. "Oh, Nat, did you have to?"

"She had a choice time. She made gardens with the seaweed."

Miki held Tia back from going into the house. "I don't suppose you brought a change of clothes for her?"

"Um – no, sorry." seeing that Tia was starting to fuss over being kept out, Nat quickly told Miki, "These are what the girls did this morning. Their names are on them. Let me introduce you to my friend, Iggy. Ig, this is Mikitonia Westimaru, my cousin, Benatoe's partner, and that's their son, Mikitoe."

Iggy mounted the steps and took Miki's hand, pressing it and placing his nose gently against hers so that they could share a breath.

"You're welcome to join us for lunch, Iggy, but it's going to be a few minutes while I take care of stinky-winky, here."

"Thank you, but we didn't mean to land on you."

She started to say it was no trouble, but Tia made a dart into the kitchen. Nat caught her by whipping out one long arm. He stepped in to bring the shrieking toddler back out, saying, "Iggy's a musician from Tāmaki-makaurau."

Miki started stripping the clothes from Tia, coaxing her into being excited about going into the tub, around saying, "I'm glad you're seeing your musical friends again. It'll do you a world of good."

"We'll be at Sea, Soy, and Soda if you need me."

"Ta, but she'll be jake. By the time I've walked the girls back to school the little ones will be ready to sleep, and then they can play in the commons. Fret not, if you're not back, Poko and Beth can walk Mere home with Elly."

"You're a legend, Mick!" Nat jumped down from the veranda like a ten-year-old let out of school. "We have the whole afternoon," he beamed.

Iggy jogged to keep up with him. "Look, man, if you're that pleased to get away from it, why are you doing it?"

The joy slumped out of Nat. He came to a stop, then walked slowly on, wondering why it mattered so much to him that Iggy understood. "I don't know how to tell you what it means to me. Tia is the light of my life. Just being with her makes it feel as if my life has meaning. I'm needed here."

"Are you involved with the mother?"

"No one is. She's gone through so much . . ."

"I know, you told me. So, you plan to be stepdad to these girls when their Mum's ready?"

"I don't know if she'd have me. She's six years older, and Bram was a powerful, muscular sort of man. She won't want a weedy little runt like me if he's her type."

"Great Tane, Nat! You've got no self confidence. If you're in love with the woman six years is nothing. Don't even try to compete with a dead man. She has to love you for who you are. Does she even know who you are? Does she know you're a brilliant interpreter of music?"

Nat was both taken aback and embarrassed by that. "I wouldn't go that far," he muttered, striding quickly the rest of the way to the restaurant.

Iggy said only, "I would, and I know what I'm talking about," then he was quiet until they saw it. "That's the place where I asked how to find you."

Not wanting Iggy to get so fed up that he left before they'd had a chance to sit down and have an uninterrupted conversation, Nat grinned, turning his head to make sure Iggy saw his expression. "They're good people. True blue. Look, I can't go in there with these stinky feet. You go in and grab a table for us while I find a way to get the mud off." He bounded up the steps and across the wide, wooden veranda, leaned in the doorway and called, "G'day, Bruce!"

"G'day, Nat." The restaurateur sauntered over to the door. "What's rattling your cage?" He spotted Iggy behind Nat and nodded, "I see you found each other."

Iggy grinned. "Yeah. Chur bro."

"No worries." Bruce looked around all of the empty tables on the veranda, and asked, "Lose the nippers?"

Nat explained, "Miki's got them, eh?"

"Oh, she'll love that! Little girls to dress up."

"Nah, yeah, well, I was down on the mud flats,eh? Do you have anything to clean this pong off my feet before I come in?" He held up one mud caked foot.

"You never cleaned up before you gave the girls to Miki? That'll get you in the cactus, mate!"

Although it wouldn't have worked to walk Tia back to his home to wash up, then to the school, then all the way to Ben and Miki's home, he couldn't help feeling a bit foolish that he hadn't come up with a better plan. Taken the train, perhaps. "She wasn't too mad about it," he defended himself. "It was just Tia. She had a blast playing with the seaweed."

He was none too pleased to see Bruce wink at Iggy. "It gets better all the time, doesn't it?"

It didn't help that Iggy snorted with laughter and chortled, "You should have seen her! Covered in it."

Bruce looked at Iggy's sandals. "Were you in the muck with them?"

"Not like they were. Maybe I can just slip these off." When he did so, not only did some mud drop onto the veranda, but a smell wafted up from them. "Or not."

"There's a hose on the side of the house. I'll chuck ya a brush."

Nat leaped over the railing on the side of the veranda, followed by Iggy carrying his sandals. They found the hose and were rinsing their feet, Nat's lower legs, and Iggy's sandals when Bruce called, "Heads up!" and threw a scrub brush to them from the veranda along the side of the house.

"Ta!" Nat shouted, ignoring the people seated around the tables on that veranda, eating their lunch and enjoying the side-show he was providing. He resisted the urge to respond to the friendly teasing.

"Find any good weed down there?"

"Going to start a business in mud?"

"Hey, Nat, who's your friend?"

"Hey, cobber, watch out or Nat'll get you covered in muck."

That one made Iggy snicker. Pleased that his friend was enjoying the warmth and humour of his neighbours, Nat asked, "Do you have a bunch of jokers like this?"

"Oh, yes. Not the whole ruddy town, mind you, but when I go back to my home hex it's just like this."

Thinking he was at last getting through, Nat pressed his point. "You see how everyone here watches over everyone else?"

"I certainly do. There's no need for you to sacrifice your life. There are plenty of others who could and would take care of the orphans."

Exasperated, Nat threw the brush down. Lowering his voice so that their audience wouldn't hear him, he growled, "Why do you keep harping on that?"

"Because you keep justifying it. Even your cousin's partner thinks it's a good idea for you to take a break."

Nat picked the brush up and went back to scrubbing his feet, saying, "Ig, you've never gone through anything like this, so you can't imagine what it's like. I can't just turn my back on them in the hope someone will step in. They depend on me, and they've already lost . . ."

"Yes, so you keep saying. You're always talking about them and what happened to them. You never mention what you went through."

Nat felt cold inside. He knew Iggy was right. He rinsed his feet and legs without a word, and then offered the hose.

Iggy shook his head. "When I first met you, I met this musician who was on the way to meet his destiny even though it upset his Dad. Where is that Nat? That's who I came to see. What have you done with him? Where's Anatoe Amaru?"

Caught off guard, Nat couldn't answer. He shut the hose off, rolled it up, made a play of bowing to the audience, and then stepped away to a dry patch of grass. As he dried his feet by wiping them on the grass, he muttered, "I'll tell you when we're sitting across a table."

Iggy nodded and said no more. He stopped before the steps up to the front veranda to prop his sandals up against the veranda posts to drain. Arriving inside first, Nat stood reading the offerings of the day on the chalkboard up on the wall behind the counter, waiting for Iggy. Most of the tables inside were empty. Only the side veranda was crowded. "Quiet lunch?" he asked.

"Dead," was Bruce's response as he carried a tray of lunches out to the veranda, followed by a teenaged girl with another tray.

Nat turned his attention to the contents of the glass display case as Iggy appeared and the woman behind the counter gushed, "It's so good of you to take care of Hine's girls so that she can go back to work. Do her the world of good, it will, and a perfect day for it, too. I've been talking to Tawhiri all day to have the ideal winds for her to have a lovely day for her first day back on the water."

A middle-aged man sitting alone at one of the inside tables put in, "Not that it'll be any comfort to the poor girl to be a Daily on a little weedie after being First Mate on a metal hunter."

Nat didn't want to think about that, so he turned back to the counter and asked, "What's the soup today?"

"Mushroom."

He asked Iggy, "Do you like mushrooms?" When he nodded, Nat ordered two bowls. Then he asked, "Did you want anything else?"

"You go ahead. I'll get it."

"No, mate, it's my shout. You're my visitor."

"No. I've got it. You're broke."

"Is that what you think?" Nat felt annoyed. "I've got enough beads to cover this." He told the woman, "Don't take his beads."

Iggy looked him up and down, from his thin and stringy hair that would never hold beads, to his neck bare of a bead chain, his wrists bare of bead chains, his see-through white singlet that obviously had no pockets or sleeves, and his tight little red short shorts that also had no pockets. "You keeping beads somewhere I don't want to know about?"

The woman behind the counter laughed, then waggled one eyebrow, saying cheekily, "I know where he keeps his beads. I'll be over to collect them later, toots."

Iggy froze for a moment, then doubled over laughing.

Looking up at the board, Nat changed the subject abruptly by asking, "What do you mean: 'the biggest plate mushies you've ever seen'? Plate mushrooms are as big as a plate, that's why they're called that."

Bruce came back with empty trays. "These are monster. They're bigger than your head."

Everyone within earshot started to argue the point. Nat took the chance to find out what Iggy wanted, order their meals and drinks from the woman and ask her, "Is the back veranda open?"

"Yeah, nah, Love, just the north side."

"Mind if we sit there?"

"We don't have enough staff on to serve two verandas and inside."

"Fret not, we'll serve ourselves."

She hesitated, looking at Bruce, but he was too busy arguing about the size of the mushrooms to notice.

Nat didn't want any of his neighbours to hear what he said. He thought if he explained himself, she would give in, so he told her, "This is my mate, Iggy, from Tāmaki-makaurau. I haven't seen him since I came home. We'd be truly grateful to be able to talk privately."

To his dismay she let out a wail that got Bruce's attention, and everyone else's. "You're not thinking of going back there, are you? Don't you know how much it matters to Hatoe to have you here? How could you leave him again? They all depend on you . . . not only Hatoe, but also Kahu, Poko and Beth, Ben and Miki, Hine and all of the children, eh?"

"I'm not leaving. I just want to have a chin wag in the back room with my cuzzie, eh?"

Bruce frowned at his staff. "A man's got to live his own life." He nodded to Nat, "Go ahead and open the back. I'll serve you myself."

"Chur bro." Nat carried the tea he'd ordered for himself, his bare feet making no sound on the smooth stone tiles of what had been the living and dining rooms of Bruce's family home. Iggy followed with his mug of steaming dark brown liquid of roasted, ground, and boiled dandelion roots, which was called 'coffee.' The blinds were all down in the unused part of the room, so it was dark and cool. When Nat opened the door, he let in light and sea breezes.

"This breeze is going to be a pain," Iggy grumbled.

"She'll be jake." Nat put his tea on the table in the northernmost corner of the wooden veranda. There were thick clear plastic blinds rolled up all along the sides. Nat unrolled the one at the end, tying it down firmly at the bottom, and then sealing the sides by pressing a tongue of fabric on the edge of the blinds into a groove on the post. Seeing how he did it, Iggy lowered and sealed the first two of the long side. That was all it took to create a pocket of calm, protected from the breezes, but still able to see the harbour where it showed through the trees.

Now that he had promised to tell, Nat was anxious to unburden himself. Iggy might not understand or be sympathetic, but he was not a local dealing with his own loss, and he wasn't a counsellor. The need to talk to someone unconnected with it was almost overwhelming. "You wanted to know . . . well . . . here it is . . . we identified the pieces of wreckage. My Dad, me, and one other bloke named Ray."

Iggy peered at him. "Your music will help you with that."

"Not this time. Dad is just starting to be a bit more like himself. Ray has crawled right inside the bottle. If someone doesn't reach him very soon, he'll die there." As he said it, Nat realised that was the truth. Distressed by the insight, he stalled, turned his head to look at the harbour. Idly he watched a father teaching his son how to handle a canoe.

Iggy didn't let him drop the subject. "Don't you people have counsellors? They said on the news that the very best were sent here."

"They were. Counsellors can't work magic. There's only so much they can do." Sadly, he turned back to face Iggy. "If these last two years taught me anything, it's that there's no magic."

"But still . . . "

"If I lost my leg, no matter how much counselling I had, it would still be gone. All a counsellor could do is help me to learn to live without my leg. And they can only do that if I'm willing. If I had been a dancer, I would have lost more than my leg. I would have lost my livelihood and my self-image. It takes more than counselling then; it takes some kind of inner drive to go on. My Dad only now wants to go on. After two years. Ray isn't doing as well."

"You're still not talking about yourself."

Nat realised the truth in that. As much as he wanted the release, the habit of pushing his feelings aside was too deeply ingrained. He nodded, and took a large swig of his tea, trying to find the words.

He was hugely relieved that Bruce arrived with their soup right then, though Iggy's grunt of irritation raised Bruce's eyebrows. "Y'know, Nat, if you are planning to go back to music, take it from me that Hatoe and all of the others will be alright. Don't hold back. We'll all pitch in."

"Chur bro." Nat smiled at him, touched by the support, even though it had been prompted by a miss-reading of the reaction.

Smiling in return, Bruce offered, "What if I bring the rest in fifteen or twenty minutes? With all the blinds down, I can't see when you're ready, and if I raise them other customers will see you and come out here." He nodded to Iggy apologetically, "That way I won't need to interrupt again."

Nat waved off Iggy's attempt to explain, saying, "Ta very muchly. Please give us twenty minutes."

"Good oh!"

Nat took a mouthful of the warm, creamy, comforting soup, then took his wavering courage in both hands and launched into it. "For nearly two years I couldn't play a note."

His spoon poised in mid-air, Iggy peered at Nat with an expression of more confusion than concern or sympathy.

"Don't look at me like that. It was like my arms had been ripped out of their sockets without anaesthetic and I was just left to bleed. A major part of me was gone and not a soul in the world understood it."

"What did the counsellors say?"

"That my creativity would return. That trauma makes some people more creative and others less so. I am starting to play a little now, but it's not the same as it was. It used to be how I coped with life. It was how I expressed myself. It just flowed. Now it's a slog."

Iggy stared into his soup. "You need to get away from here."

"To go where? To do what? This is my home. This is where I belong."

"It doesn't matter where. To have a break from this all-encompassing sadness. To get a new perspective. To heal yourself so that you can come back and be more help to the others."

Nat was surprised and touched. "I thought you were going to say I had to go with you."

"I did come here to make a proposition to you, but I can see that it's not going to happen."

Relieved, Nat confessed, "I don't think I'm cut out to be a soloist. I can't write original lyrics, for one thing."

"Yes, I can see that. It wasn't actually about you playing solo."

"No? What was it about?"

"Well, you are . . . were the best interpreter I've ever seen. When you were playing for the glass championships you took old favourites and woke them up. You have a brilliant way of building a crescendo that gets the whole crowd on its feet. We wanted to work on something with you."

"Adapting something or a new piece?"

"New."

Nat was disappointed. For a moment there he'd felt the old juices start to flow again, then he realised Iggy wasn't listening. "No, I'm serious. I cannot write."

"Yeah, nah, but I can, eh? What I need help with is the arrangement. I've been working with a composer, but we can't get it right. What we need is someone who can take a good piece and make it great. So, I thought of you."

"Really?"

"You're the first choice."

"Really! Can I see it without going to Tāmaki-makaurau?"

"You mean you'd be interested after all?"

"I won't know 'till I've seen it."

"Here, then."

When Bruce came back, they had the whole table covered with sheet music and were deep in conversation, their soup forgotten. He moved another table over beside them, set their lunches on it, and left without a word.

They didn't notice time passing until Bruce interrupted their discussion to ask them if they wanted to order tea. Astonished, Nat looked around. "It is teatime! Hine said she'd be back to give the girls their tea. I have to go." He ran down the veranda and leaned over to see if the Laughing Dolphin was at the dock. "They're not in sight yet. I might have time to get them on the pier to meet their mother."

Iggy looked uncertain. "What about this?"

Nat walked back to the table, looking at the music. He hadn't felt so alive since that day. He didn't want to lose that feeling now that he'd found it again. He looked through the clear blinds, trying to find the canoe. He finally saw it being carried up the beach on the man's head. Suddenly he knew what he had to do. He'd take Ray out to the mud flats in his canoe, and then he'd be free. He would visit Tāmaki-makaurau. He turned to face Iggy with a broad smile. "There's something I have to do tonight. Give me your ringer number and I'll meet you in Tāmaki-makaurau tomorrow."

"You're coming on board?"

"We'll set it up tomorrow. I've got to run."

"Give me your number."

"I didn't bring any cards," Nat confessed, tucking Iggy's card into the waistband of his shorts.

"Left them with your beads, I suppose," Iggy teased, handing Nat a pen.

"Yep. I wasn't going to need either today," Nat grinned, writing his number on the top of the sheet music. He decided he could take another minute before running full out all the way to Miki's house. "I'll show you how to get to the station from here," he said, helping reorganise the sheets of paper.

"Ta. Don't you have to run?"

"She'll be jake."

Iggy turned to Bruce. "He's true blue, this one."

Bruce smiled. "You're welcome here any time. I don't know what you did to Nat, but he's like a whole new man."

"Feel like it, too," Nat nodded to Bruce, striding off through the front of the restaurant. "You were right, you Maui," he muttered as Iggy sat down to put his sandals on.

"Hey, hey! I didn't trick you into anything!"

"Much." He walked off as if he was annoyed so that Iggy had to jog to catch up.

"Silly bugger," Iggy said, shoving Nat's shoulders when he caught up.

Nat chuckled, saying, "I'm sure music will help me deal with things now. The key is to work with others, not by myself."

"Do you mean you'd do this as a steady gig, not just a one off?"

Because the restaurant had started its life as a house, not as a business, it was not directly under the station for deliveries, but a short walk. They ambled along, taking their time, focused on formulating plans to work together, until they reached the Flying Fish station. Coming towards them down the station stairs was a vibrant young woman wearing a rucksack over a short orange dress that showed her legs to advantage. The straps of the rucksack on her back pulled the fabric tight across her chest. She paid no attention to them. All her focus was on a piece of paper in her hand, and on checking what was written on it with what she saw.

"Hmm, hmm," Iggy murmured.

Nat was never sure when their discussion died, but at the point when she passed them, they weren't speaking, just watching her move. As she passed, their heads turned in one smooth, synchronised movement to see if she was as good from the back as she was from the front. She was.

"Relative of yours?" Iggy mumbled.

"Never saw her before. Bruce hires secondary school graduates on their gap year. Maybe she's headed there. Since his kids left, he's got a couple of spare rooms . . ."

Iggy held up one finger to stop Nat's chatter. "Do you mind?"

"Yeah, nah, I've got to go. Catch you tomorrow."

"Spotcha."

Nat strode off towards Miki's house, While Iggy went back the way they'd come. At the corner Nat turned to look back. Iggy was walking beside the girl, carrying her rucksack for her, engaged in what was evidently a happy conversation. He ran the whole way across the town, his thoughts cycling through being amused by Iggy, to being resentful that he didn't have Iggy's skill with women.

Collecting the girls, he raced back to the marina. He could see the Laughing Dolphin sailing under the Flying Fish Bridge and wanted to be on the dock when she arrived. He scooped Tia up and challenged Mere, "Let's run."

Mere announced, "I don't have to."

Oh, no! Why did she always have to make everything so difficult? "No, you don't have to," he agreed. "Tia and I will. We want to be there when Mummy comes. You can come when you're ready."

He started running, but stopped at the sound of Mere's panic stricken, "No!"

He looked back but made no move towards her. "Come on, then." He waited only a moment before continuing. "Hurry up if you want to come with us."

Crying in frustration, Mere stumbled along behind him, frequently pretending to fall. "Don't go so fast!"

He continued until he was sure she could find her own way, then stopped to challenge her, "Okay, if you can't keep up, we'll come back and get you after Tia and I have tied the Dolphy up and told Mummy about your painting. Wait here.""

"No!" this time it was pure rage. Mere ran off, flying along the paths and down the ramp to be the first one on the pier, triumphantly crowing, "You can't catch me!"

For Nat the triumph was being on the spot to catch the mooring lines when Ben tossed them to him. With the girls clamouring for their mother, Nat stepped aboard to leave Hine free to tend to them. "Good day?" he asked, noting the amount of mess on the shiny white deck.

"You should see this girl swim!" Hatoe beamed. "She should have been named Hinemoa: I'm in no doubt she could swim Lake Rotorua."

Hine was hooking the freshwater line up to the coupling on the boat. She looked embarrassed, taking the beads from Hatoe without a word to put into the slots so that they could spray fresh water over the heaps of seaweed in the holds to wash it off and make it look its best. The boat was washed down with seawater, taken from what were called 'tanks' under the wharf. They were actually made of very fine mesh that filtered out all sand and creatures so that the water used to wash the boats was as clean as possible. The fresh water was used only for human consumption and for rinsing seaweed harvests.

Nat had no response to Hatoe's admiring comment. He looked up from his scrubbing to see what his cousin, Ben thought of it, but Ben was busy categorising the harvest. Thinking it would give him a chance to be alone with Hatoe before they went home, Nat offered, "I'll take the weed in, you go to Miki. She's had a day of it."

"What happened?"

"She had all the kids."

They laughed at him, then. "Couldn't do it, eh?"

Seeing that Hine looked a bit concerned, because she needed someone to take care of the girls if she was going to work, he explained, "We were doing well until my friend, Iggy, showed up. It was Miki's idea for me to leave the girls with her." He didn't say who Iggy was because he didn't want to go into it until he'd talked to his Dad.

To his relief there was a distraction right then.

"Would you look at that!"

They all looked at the harbour entrance where Ben was looking.

"Sue!" Hatoe exclaimed. "I wonder why she's coming in early?"

"And who is that with her?" Hine added.

"Has she picked up a new Daily from somewhere?" Nat guessed.

"I don't think so," Hine said, thoughtfully. "He ducked out of sight when they saw us watching."

Hatoe shook his head. "Well, well. Bang goes the theory that everybody in a small town knows everything everyone else is doing."

"We can soon fix that!" Ben exclaimed.

He and Nat laughed, but Hatoe went back to work saying, "Yeah, nah, let them have what little privacy they can get, eh?"

"Oh, poor Ray." All at once Nat had more insight into what had tipped Ray over the edge.

"Why? Was he sweet on Sue?" Ben sounded surprised.

"Yeah, nah, it's the work. He was upset that you didn't need him today, and Sue didn't need him, either."

"That's reality for a Daily." Hatoe didn't sound as if he gave Nat's theory any credence.

"I think he's worried that he might have lost both permanently."

"Silly bugger, why would he think that?"

"Between Ben, Hine, and me, you're not going to need a Daily, and if Sue's found someone she won't, either."

They all looked along the empty pier to Sue's mooring. They were tying the Karoro up, which gave a clear view of the muscles rippling under the tanned skin of a broad, bare, male torso.

"Hum, hum," Hine purred.

"Really?" The three men looked at her, and then looked at Sue's crew again.

"Good on Sue!" Hine smiled.

"If you say so." Hatoe turned away, so they all went back to work.

Nat was deep in thought as he worked, mulling over whether or not it was time, now that she was showing an interest in men again, to say something to Hine about getting together with him. Self-doubts assailed him. He couldn't strike up easy, relaxed conversations with women like Iggy. And he wouldn't be her type, anyway. If what she liked were well toned muscles like that bloke of Sue's with his hairy chest, or Bram with his bronzed skin and powerful personality, there wasn't any chance she would be attracted to a sorry specimen like him with his stringy hair, sallow skin, and hairless chest.

His thoughts were interrupted by Hatoe saying, "Thanks for saying you'd take care of the delivery."

"Glad to," Nat smiled. "Ben can have an early day for once and the girls need their Mum."

"Chur bro," Ben beamed, picking up his kit and jumping from the boat to land beside Hine.

To Nat's surprise, Hatoe did the same thing. He watched, struck dumb, as his chance to have a man-to-man talk evaporated. A sudden image of his Dad waiting for him to come home after delivering the harvest made him call out, "Don't make tea for me tonight, Dad, I'm going to be Ray's best mate."

Ben handed his kit to Hine. Lifting Tia up on to his shoulders, he snickered, "Good luck with that!"

Mere set up a wail that it wasn't fair that Tia could sit on Ben's shoulders.

"He needs a mate," Nat explained.

Hatoe nodded. "Yes, he does." He handed his kit to Hine so that he could pick Mere up, saying, "But he won't be back until night fall. We have time to have tea."

Hine looked over at Nat, "Come to my place. I'll fix you both a big feed."

"Thanks, Hine, but he didn't go out today. The reality of being a Daily eeled up and bit him."

"Silly twit," Ben spun around to make Tia laugh. "Why doesn't he go home, then, and work on his parents' boat? Then he wouldn't be a Daily, he'd be family."

Nat had no answer for that. "I reckon I'll have tea with him."

"Better get him out of Mean Eddies before he's past the point of eating," Ben advised.

"I know."

Hatoe went very still. "Do you really think he'll drink that much tonight?"

Feeling as if he was betraying a friend, Nat nodded, "Yes, I do, if he hasn't passed out. He's been drinking all day. If he doesn't get off the sauce, he'll end up in a mod vil."

"Probably the best thing for him at this stage," Hatoe sighed.

They released the mooring lines and uncoupled the fresh water, then left Nat to deal with the delivery by himself. "How could it be that I somehow always manage to get the wrong end of the oar?" he muttered to the boat as he fired her up and eased her away from the pier. He kept glancing back, watching the three of them, trying to figure out why his Dad left early with the others. Somehow Hatoe had Mere laughing. He'd have to take lessons from his Dad if he was going to be a successful step-father to that one.

There was something different about Hatoe. It wasn't until they were out of sight and Nat was concentrating on clearing the north pier so that he could get to the delivery dock north of it that it dawned on him what it was: Hatoe's head was held high, and he had a touch of swagger that Nat hadn't seen in years. In fact, his Dad's shoulders had been slumped ever since his Mum was diagnosed with liver cancer.

Nat went through the routine of handing over the manifest, having the weed hauled up out of the holds and weighed, and collecting the payment, on automatic. He barely noticed any of it, his mind was so focused on how great it was that his Dad was coming back to life at the same time as he, too, was starting to feel like himself again.

With an enthusiasm and energy that he hadn't had since he was in school, Nat started to make plans. If Hine would have him, he'd work with his father to have a steady income to support his family. Hine deserved a partner who put their family first. He could still have his music if it was a hobby. If he didn't go to Tāmaki-makaurau often, or for long, he might be able to bring home a bit extra to supplement a weedie's income. Iggy and the others would have to understand that he was based in Matapihi or get someone else.

Humming, Nat had completed the sale, motored back to the pier, rinsed away the drips from the seaweed being hoisted out of the hold, secured the boat for the night, and was lacing up the awning with the bag of beads held in his teeth when he became aware of everything he'd done. Disconcerted, he stood on the pier trying to remember what he'd done to work out whether he'd forgotten anything or not. He'd been so preoccupied by his daydreams and plans that he couldn't remember doing any of it, much less if he'd missed a step.

He waved to Sue on her way to the delivery dock. She waved back, looking none too pleased. Nat guessed that she'd come in early to be finished and out of sight by the time anyone else came in. Knowing how much he wanted to keep his intended relationship to himself, especially during the first, fragile stages, he could sympathise. Let Sue keep her secret. He waved again, then finger-spoke, "I'll keep my mouth shut."

She saluted him.

Tossing the bag of beads in the air and catching it with one hand, Nat decided to leave well enough alone. If he was good enough to do the job with his mind on something else, he was good enough to do it thoroughly. Sheer high spirits prompted him to jog all the way back home to drop off the bag of beads and change into clothes a little more suitable for being on the water after the sun had gone down.

Hatoe wasn't there, yet, but Nat didn't expect him to be. He knew his Dad: after taking Mere and Tia all the way to the door for Hine, he would have visited Ben and Miki for a bit, then, knowing Nat wouldn't be home for tea, he would be more be likely to eat with them, or his brother, Rota, Ben's father, or his father, Kahu, than he would be to go home to face an empty house. Nat hoped Hatoe did go to see Kahu and Haro. He hoped news about Ray would be spread that way and news about Sue wouldn't.

The low tide in the morning had been somewhere around ten o'clock, so the next low tide would be somewhere around ten o'clock that night. He didn't bother to check. All he needed was a rough guess. He didn't even bother with what time it was then. All he knew was that it was probably going to take quite a while to find Ray, and to get him moving, and that he had plenty of time before low tide to achieve both.

He checked Ray's flat first. No sign of him. Nat took that as a good thing, meaning Ray wasn't passed out on his bed or drinking alone. The next guess was the Brown Jug, but they said they hadn't seen him. That left Mean Eddies, and Sea, Soy, and Soda. Thinking Mean Eddies was more likely, he tried there first and found Ray in the back room at a card table trying to win enough to buy a pitcher of beer.

Nat's self-confidence was so high that he was able to roust Ray from his dark cave, assisted by the staff of Mean Eddies suggesting that it was time. Nat persuaded him to choose something to take with them to eat in the canoe, and even to choose some non-alcoholic drinks for them. Nat was so chuffed by the last accomplishment that he whistled all the way back to Ray's flat. Having no alcohol on the canoe was huge. It meant his plans were going to work. It meant Ray wasn't a full-on drunk, he just needed a mate. The fact that Ray couldn't walk a straight line made no difference to Nat, he was sure that would wear off in time.

The whole day had lifted Nat's spirits so much that not even Ray's bellyaching could lower them.

"Knock it off!"

"What?"

"Do you have to keep chirping like a freaking bird?"

Assuming Ray wasn't serious, Nat laughed. "I've had such a good day I can't help it."

"Oh, like you've got something to be happy about?"

"Well . . ."

"Your life's the pits. What've you got to be happy about?"

"I had a few things happen today that I thought you might be able to help me with."

"I'm helping you with your flaming canoe, aren't I? You've got nothing to be that chirpy about."

Nat grinned, thinking Ray meant to be funny.

When they stopped at Ray's place so that he could change clothes, Nat ignored Ray's fretting that they shouldn't go out on the water during earth tremors, because there weren't any. It wasn't the earth that was making it hard for Ray to walk.

Once Ray had finally found shoes, long pants, a long-sleeved shirt, and a jumper, they headed off to Hatoe's house with Ray grumbling the entire way about Nat's cheerful whistling.

When he touched the light paint so that they could see inside the shed, the whistling stopped of its own accord as the neglected piles of junk were revealed.

Nat left Ray trying to wrestle the canoe out of the shed while he popped into the house to get sealable, waterproof lunch boxes so that if their food fell over-board, they would still be able to eat it. Back outside he helped Ray, who was sweating profusely and swearing a blue streak. Between them they got the canoe disentangled from all of the bike tires, garden tools, outgrown toys, and sports equipment that was piled in, on, and around it.

"First chance I get I'm cleaning that shed out," Nat muttered, turning the canoe onto its side to hose out several years of spider webs and other crawlies.

"Not that it needs it," Ray teased, brushing himself off.

"Hasn't been touched since Mum last made us do it. I reckon Dad didn't have the heart and it's not the sort of thing teens think of by themselves. Here, give me a hand to turn Bessie upside down so's she can drain."

"Yeah, it's going to be a fun night in boat full of water."

Nat chuckled, heading back into the shed. "Think my Dad will admit I'm an adult if I clean the shed up?"

"You're not doing it right now, are you?" Ray sounded panicked.

Nat laughed. "No, you doze, there are some lamps we need, and flat-fish spears. Give me a hand to dig them out."

"You spear them?"

"Yep. Only way to get them." Nat had a moment of hesitation. "You're not a vegan, are you?"

"No. I've just never speared anything before." He stalled, peering into the shed. "You're not paying me enough to go back in there."

"Okay, then, I'll double it." That was an easy promise to make, since Nat wasn't paying him.

"Yeah, you're just saying that," Ray grinned, following Nat.

Encouraged by the first sign of fun from Ray, Nat retorted, "Hey, it's as good as the paper it's written on."

"Your Dad is never going to see you as a grown man no matter what you do."

Concentrating on digging the lamps, Nat tossed back, "I'll do it when he's on an over-nighter, repaint it as well as sorting it out and cleaning it, and I'll tell him, "Today I am a man!" Ah, there they are."

"As if that'll do any good! My Dad still thinks I'm four years old."

Picturing Hatoe's laughter at his posing, Nat worked one lamp free, being thankful that the old, good natured Hatoe seemed to be coming back. He held the lamp out to Ray, saw the look of pain on his face, and went after the other lamp biting his lips to stop himself from saying that Ray was probably treated like a child because of the way he behaved. Nat didn't want to say anything like that to Ray. He wanted to be a source of comfort and support to him, not criticism. He handed the second lamp to Ray, saying, "Put these next to Bessie. All we've got left to do now is check the lamps to make sure they work and get the spears loose from the octopodes in here."

Ray looked back into the shed. "If I haven't heard from you in a week, I'll send in a search party."

"Cheers." Nat's voice was flat as part of the game, but inwardly he was elated that Ray was coming out of his drunken negativity and starting to joke around.

Once they had everything Nat thought they needed, including the right kind of long-handled paddles, they turned Bessie back over and filled her with all of it, and struggled to carry her down to the slip. It was much harder to transport the canoe upright, loaded with stuff than it would have been to portage an empty canoe upside down over their heads. None of their efforts were helped in the slightest by Ray's state of inebriation.

Nat didn't care. They had more than enough time, since there was no point in being there before the tide had come in again, so he let it take as long as it took willingly resting every time Ray wanted to stop. Besides, in the three hours or so since he'd pulled Ray away from his card game, Ray had sobered up quite a bit. He was walking straighter, was easier to understand, and was no longer convinced that the earth was moving.

By the time they reached the marina, all the boats were bobbing quietly in their appointed places, their eyes gleaming silver in the moonlight. Most were dark, closed down for the night, but a few were still lit up and occupied.

The slip was between the north pier and the delivery dock. Ray complained, "Why are we hauling this thing so far? Bung her in the water here."

"You're out of your mind, mate! We can't jump off the wall into a canoe . . . she'll roll over as soon as look at you."

"Oh, nice piece of junk."

"Oi! This is my Dad's canoe that he's had since he was eight. She's a corker, so don't you go disparaging my Dad's favourite canoe. We had a lot of good times in her before my Mum got sick."

"That's why you chose this one . . . because its Hatoe's favourite. Bet the others are better."

"This is the only one."

"You're trying to drown me in a leaky old tub."

"Am not. She doesn't leak. And anyway, you swim like a fish."

"Yeah. Whatever you say. Who cares? That's a fit end to a rotten day like this."

Not even Nat could make that bleak tone into an attempt to be funny. He was very glad that they had reached the slip, so that, without appearing to change or avoid the subject, he could concentrate on not tipping the canoe and dumping their stuff into the harbour as they lowered it from their shoulders. They kept their hands on it, wading out, down the slip, until Bess was in water deep enough that she wouldn't bottom out when they climbed aboard. It was that strange time of day when the same water that had felt too cool to let Tia swim in it now felt warmer than the air. It was refreshing to his legs and feet. He stretched his toes on the concrete slip to make sure his footing was secure. One of the daily duties of the Harbour Master was to clean the slick mud off the slip at low tide so that it wouldn't build up.

Nat and Ray each reached into Bess, from opposite sides. Just as Nat moved the tridents out of the way, Ray reached for a paddle and yelped, "Hey! Watch it! You could put someone's eye out with those things!"

"Sorry, mate. They're fish spears . . . tridents."

"It's a lethal weapon, mate!"

'It's working!' Nat thought, delighted that Ray had called him, 'mate.' Happily, he whistled through his teeth as they moved everything off the seats.

Ray still wasn't happy about the tridents. "If you have to kill fish, why don't you use a normal harpoon?" He gestured for Nat to get in first.

Taking care not to slop any seawater into Bess, Nat got in, explaining, "These are flat fish, eh?"

"So what?" Ray wasn't as expert at canoeing as Nat, which had Nat wishing he'd gone second so that could have held Bess steady for Ray. "We never had anything like that at Matakana."

"You don't have mudflats at Matakana," Nat said, steadying the canoe until Ray was settled in his seat, then reaching for the paddles.

Touching the paddles shifted the tridents, which made Ray yelp again, "Careful! These bamboo points are dangerous. They could hole my leg."

Handing a paddle to Ray, Nat grinned, "Keep your legs away from the business end. They're perfectly safe where they are."

Ray took the paddle and immediately put it in the water. "Could have fooled me! Why are they crooked like that? They're busted."

As they paddled gently away from the slip, Nat explained, "They're not busted. The prongs are in a triangle instead of a row because that increases your chances of getting a flat fish. They flip away in any direction." He forestalled Ray's next negative comment by changing the subject. "We're a bit early. The mud flats are too near the surface. We need to wait until the tide has covered them enough for us to row over the top of them."

They shipped the paddles and drifted with the current.

Nat asked, "Do you know how to scull a paddle so that it doesn't break the surface?"

Ray's savage sarcasm caught Nat off-guard. "No, I was brought up in the ruddy desert and I've never been on the water in my life."

Thankful that Ray was sitting behind him and couldn't see his face, Nat swallowed his irritated retort and said, mildly, "Lots of people are good rowers but don't know how to move a canoe without making a splash or a drip. We can't let them know we're there. We make no sound that they'll recognise as a predator." He gestured to the seagulls noisily squabbling in the water over the mud. "Not even a drop of water hitting the surface when we get close." He picked the lamps up, handing one to Ray. "We hang these off either side." He hung his off the clip near him. "If you angle them right, they put the light down into the water and not up into our eyes."

Ray watched how it was done, found the clip near him and copied Nat. "There's a real science to this. Special long-handled paddles, special spears, special lights." He listened with rapt attention to Nat's instructions.

"When we're over the mud we turn the lamps on. The flatties take off to get away from the light. We see the puffs of silt and get them. If they know we're here, they're gone before we have a chance to see them."

Ray nodded. "So, it has to be fully dark for the lights to scare them."

"Yes. Plus, we need to have the spears poised and ready before we switch the lights on, because they're tricky . . . you can never tell which way they'll go, they're fast, and the water kind of warps what you see from where they really are."

"Can't you tell from the puffs of silt?"

"The currents spread the mud they kick up so quickly that you can't tell where it came from if you don't see it happen."

"Yeah, yeah, right, right."

Ray's obvious interest made Nat feel relaxed enough to say, "I'm really glad you came with me tonight. I need to talk to you."

The venomous look that earned him was so powerful that not even he could mistake it for anything but rage as Ray spat, "Oh, no! Not you, too!"

"What?"

"Don't even try that! As if you didn't know."

"But if I knew I wouldn't need to talk to anyone about it."

Ray pulled his paddle out. "I'm going back right now. You and your grandfather can just shove it."

That's what it took for Nat to catch on that Ray thought Nat had got him alone to talk to him about his drinking. "Hold up, there, Ray. My granddad has no idea I'm here with you. I have problems of my own. What I want to talk to you about is personal. I've never mentioned this to Granddad or anybody else, but I can always trust you to keep a confidence."

Ray slowed down, though he didn't put the paddle back. "You know what he said to me? That I had booze with me this morning! I never touched a drop after I went to bed last night. I had to work this morning, I wouldn't . . ."

Nat listened to the indignation, watching Ray's face closely. It was obvious that Ray was sincere. He meant what he said, he was genuinely outraged and insulted that Kahu would say he would drink before work. Nat was convinced Ray wasn't trying to hoodwink him, which meant to Nat that either Ray was having problems with his memory, or he was deluded, because he didn't think it was possible for anyone to be as drunk as Ray had been that morning without adding more alcohol.

". . . All I had this morning was the coffee <u>he</u> gave me in his ruddy hut. There was something wrong with it. It made me woozy. So, I sat on the bench for just a moment before I took the Fish to look for work, and the next thing I know he's giving me an ear-bashing!"

Evidently, Ray had forgotten that he'd seen and talked to Nat before Kahu went to see him. Nat thought it best not to remind Ray of that right then, but he seriously doubted that Kahu would have been as harsh as Ray was saying. It was more likely Kahu had been courteous and concerned, but Ray's own conscience made him feel scolded.

Not knowing how to answer Ray without spoiling the atmosphere of trust he was trying to develop, Nat changed the subject by suggesting that they paddle over to the warning buoys at the edges of the shallow water, tie up to a buoy and have something to eat while they waited. "It's nearly there, eh?" he said in satisfaction as he turned on his seat so that he could face Ray. They sorted out whose lunch kit was whose and settled down to enjoy their food. Nat chugged a large swig of his bottle of water, coming up for air to see Ray carefully adding something to his juice from a flask.

He stared, stunned. Everything changed. Ray didn't need a friend; he needed professional treatment. In that instant Nat saw several truths at once: Ray had agreed to have no alcohol on the canoe and had brought some with him anyway; it was obviously not beer in the flask, so Ray drank more than just beer; and Ray did carry concealed alcohol after all. Nat was sure of those facts. What he couldn't figure out was when Ray had filled the flask and how he'd hidden it. He'd had to help Ray walk from Mean Eddies to his flat, so he was sure Ray hadn't had the flask then, which meant he had to have got it when he was changing clothes. That stumped Nat. He'd been with Ray the whole time, needing to lend him a hand now and then. He couldn't see how in the world Ray had done it right under his nose. Plus, Ray had to have done it after he had agreed to bring no alcohol.

"What are you staring at?" Ray challenged him.

Nat sealed the lid of his water bottle and bent over to put it down by his feet. Knowing that nothing he said would make any difference, and having no back-up plan, he was tongue-tied.

"Didn't you bring any?"

Caught even more of guard, Nat could only blink, wondering if it could be possible that Ray had forgotten that the whole point had been to <u>not</u> bring any. "No," he mumbled.

"Want some?" When his head jerked up to see if Ray was serious, Ray continued, "Don't take too much. It's all I've got with me. It's got to last me until I get home."

"Thanks." Nat had an impulsive thought that if he drank some there would be less for Ray. He picked up his juice, drank some to make room, and held the container out so Ray could add a slug to it himself. That way, Nat reasoned, Ray would control how much Nat had and would trust that Nat was not trying to take his booze. Getting his juice back from Ray, he sniffed it to find out what had been put into it. It was a fruit liqueur, he guessed. He had to admit it tasted great. His nod made Ray perk up like a child on his birthday morning.

A wave of sadness washed over Nat. Ray must have chosen it to go with the juice. There were no chances left for Ray. He'd trusted Nat enough to reveal his secrets. Even if one part of him wanted to be caught, most of him, and Nat for that matter, just wanted to have a good time with a friend he could trust. Now, no matter what Nat would rather do, he had to make sure Ray didn't go out on any of the boats. He wasn't safe. He had to go away for treatment. Well, Nat would just make sure he had a good time first. If he knew he had a friend to come back to when he was sober, he'd have a starting point. "When we get the flatties we can build a fire on the beach and roast them. Totally delicious."

"We're going to eat them tonight?"

"Yeah, mate. They're fighting fresh, and we don't have people freaking at us for eating flesh."

Ray held up his fish pie, laughing. "Right oh! Where?"

"Top of the slip on the concrete. Plenty of driftwood to make a fire. Capstans to sit on. It's hidden from view under the trees there."

Ray looked back at the slip, exclaiming, "This is corker!"

The sound of Ray's laughter, and the child-like delight in his voice, made it all worthwhile for Nat. "Nothing like fire-roasted flatties by moonlight," he mused, smiling with fond memories. "Can I talk to you about the girl now?"

"What girl?"

"It's what I wanted to talk to you about. There's this girl . . ."

"Why would you want to talk to me about women?"

"You've had more experience than I have."

"I'm not exactly a roaring success!"

"I'd be too scared to talk to you if you had crowds of them following you around, eh?"

"You're in sad shape, mate!"

"That's it, you see. Girls don't like me."

Ray took a sharp look into Nat's eyes and asked quietly, "What makes you say that?"

"I'm funny looking. I have this hawk-beak nose. My hair's not the sort they want to run their fingers through. I'm skinny . . ."

"So's your Dad. And his brother and father. And your cousin, Ben."

"I'm not lean and strong like them. They look like boatmen. I look like . . ." Words failed him.

Ray surprised him with, "A musician."

His heart leaped. "Yes?"

"True. Tried standing up straight? Cutting your hair or tying it back?"

"Makes my nose stick out."

"Don't worry about it. Women like musicians."

"Really? Are you sure? I haven't seen that."

"You had hardly started when . . ."

"True." Not wanting to talk about the Kaumoana, Nat hastily cut him off. "There's this one woman . . ." Then he couldn't think of a way to talk about Hine without giving away who she was.

Gently, Ray asked, "Does she like you?"

"I don't know."

"Have you talked to her?"

"Not about . . . I thought you'd . . . um . . ."

"You're up the Boohai without a paddle, mate! It's the women who chose. You've got to let her know that you're interested."

The very idea terrified Nat. "What if she laughs at me?"

"I know that's what stops me, too. But you've got more oars in the water than I do. You know, some women do go for looks, but not all of them. Keisha could have any man she wanted, but we had a good time and I'm no prize."

Nat was surprised to hear Ray admit to his relationship with Keisha. Ray was one of those men who normally never spoke about their private lives. "Did you love her?" he could have bitten his tongue out as soon as he said it.

Ray turned his head and looked down the length of the north pier to where the Sea Hawk moored. Inherited by Keisha's cousin, she still moored in the same spot, her eyes gleaming in the moonlight. He turned back, head low, and reached for the flask, saying quietly, "No. I've never loved anyone but Bronwyn. Keisha was too wild for me. Exciting as a volcano to be around. I was more alive when I was with her than I've ever been any other time. The most electric lover I've ever known . . . made you feel like a god. I wish I'd gone with her that last day."

Nat's heart caught in his throat. "You can't blame yourself."

"For Keisha? No, I don't. Not for her. I never could have stopped her from doing anything she wanted to do. No one could. It's that if I'd gone at least one of them would still be here. They might have left the boy at home. Better people than me died and I didn't. That's not right."

Not wanting to get caught up in an argument about who might have survived if things had been different, Nat changed the subject back to Keisha. "You don't think you could have talked her out of going?"

"Not a chance, mate. She lived on the edge of the precipice. She loved it there. Terrifying. I would never want to live with someone so hectic. That's the point, you see."

"What is?"

"Women want us for different reasons. Keisha liked me because I never wanted to move in with her, and never wanted to make her pull her wings in. Someone will want something about you that you don't see as a plus, and she won't even see the things you're worried about."

"Thanks, mate, you're a legend."

Nat was genuinely grateful, but Ray barely acknowledged his thanks with a nod. "Is this girl of yours with anyone?"

"No, it's nothing like that. She's been on her own for a while."

"Let her know you're interested."

"I'm more than interest, I want . . ."

"Don't go too fast, or she'll flee for the hills, screaming."

Nat laughed. "You're a good bloke. True blue. Let's see if we can catch a feast." He turned around so that they could paddle gently to the centre of the mud flat, sliding the paddles along under the water, and then turning them on the backstroke instead of lifting them, so that they made no splashes or drips. "This is why the handles needed to be so long." When Nat judged they were in a good place to start, he told Ray, "When I say, "Now!" turn your lamp full on." He turned back to face Ray so that Ray could watch what he did. As he did, he noticed Ray putting the flask back down. With his trident at the ready, he said, "Now!" and ran his finger up the lamp frame. Instantly, both lamps shone bright white light down through the murky water to the silty bottom less than a metre below. There were puffs of silt as the creatures under it flipped away in all directions. Nat went for the closest, but it was too far away, and he missed it. "Get the idea? Think you can do it?"

"Yes, and yes."

"These ones know we're here. Let's move further along." They turned the lamps off.

Ray said, "I'll bet the moon is bright enough for us to see the bottom so we can figure out where they are and get right over them."

"Could be," Nat smiled, pleased that Ray was so enthused. He knew that they wouldn't be able to see anything under the silt unless it moved, but he didn't want to dampen Ray's eagerness, so he said nothing.

Ray peered over the side with rapt attention. Since Ray had added more to his juice from the flask while Nat set up, Nat though it was only fair if he had some from the flask while Ray set up. His thinking was that there would be less for Ray if he drank some. He was encouraged by Ray absentmindedly handing the flask over when he reached for it. Watching Ray, Nat could see that he was so absorbed in staring at the harbour floor that he was paying no attention to what Nat was doing.

Nat got the idea that if he poured his sip of the liqueur into the harbour, neither of them would drink it. Keeping a close eye on Ray, Nat carefully tipped the contents of the flask onto the handle of the paddle so that they ran down into the water without a drip or a splash to give him away. He painstakingly made sure that he didn't tip out enough to make Ray suspicious, resealed the flask and put it back where Ray had it.

"Here," Ray whispered.

Nat put his hand on the lamp so that when Ray said, "Now!" both lamps would go on at the same time.

"Now!" yelled Ray, hurling the trident with such force that the canoe rocked alarmingly. He brought the trident back up with a small flat fish struggling on one tine. It was only caught by one fin, so it was able to free itself before Ray could get it into the canoe.

"Well done!" Nat congratulated him, as they moved the canoe again. "Hardly anyone gets anything their first time. Want to go again?"

"It's your turn."

"She'll be jake. I've been doing this since I was knee high to a duck. You should get the first one."

"Cor! Ta very muchly. We already gave the first one back to Tangaroa, eh?"

Nat snickered. "Doesn't count, mate. We didn't give it back, it got away."

"Oh, too bad."

"And watch when you spear them. We don't want to end up in the drink, here. That mud stinks like nobody's business."

"Right-o, then!" happily, Ray bent over the side, all his concentration on the harbour floor.

Seeing how absorbed he was, Nat thought he might as well take the opportunity to get rid of more of the booze.

He was focused on pouring just the right amount, not too much or too little, on the handle of his paddle when he was startled nearly out of his skin by Ray's bellow, "What do you think you're doing!?"

All he could think of saying was, "Offering to Tangaroa?"

"Crab crap! You were pouring . . . you're one of . . . you never meant any of . . . and your granddad . . ." He picked up the tridents and threw them out of the canoe.

"Hey! Those are my Dad's!"

"You throw my stuff . . . I'll show you . . ." Ray was spluttering with rage. The lamps, Nat's clothes, and the lunch kits joined the tridents.

"Don't take it out on my Dad!" Nat stretched as far as he could to retrieve a lamp that was bobbing just out of reach.

"How do you like it?" Ray took a firm grip on both sides of the canoe and rocked it violently, throwing Nat overboard.

He came to the surface to see Ray paddling hard for the closest pier. "Ray!" he shouted but got no response. "I didn't try to trick you! I did mean it!" All he got from that effort was a stream of obscenities.

So that his feet didn't sink so deeply that he was stuck, he folded his legs and sat on the mud in water up to his neck. He watched Ray go, saying to himself, "Well, that went well. He's bound to have real trust in me now."

Fighting to free his feet would only sink them further, so he did as he'd been taught and leaned back along the top of the water, letting the current pull him away from his feet, so that he could gently and slowly work them free, then swam around to collect the tridents, clothes, and lunch kits before they floated too far away. If the bottom had been firmer, he would have waded.

Wondering how to collect everything, he spotted the buoys and had an idea. The largest buoy had a platform on it and a ladder from under the water to the platform. That buoy was intended to be more than a warning of shallow water, it was intended to be a place that boaties who got stuck on the mud flat could get out of the water and wait for rescue. He put the items he had saved up on the platform and swam off to fetch the rest. The lamps, which had sunk, were in less danger of being swept away by the tide, so he left them to last, only to discover that it was hard to find them by moonlight.

Eventually, he had both up on the platform. By that time there was no sign of Ray. With a heavy sigh, Nat swam for the closest set of stairs down from the north pier. Nothing would have convinced him to call for help. It was far and away too embarrassing. Friends and family would tell the story and laugh for the rest of his life if he did.

The nice surprise was that Bessie was tied up to the stairs, her paddles shipped properly. Apparently, no matter what Ray's condition, his seaman's training held sway. Thanking Ray and feeling terrible that he now had no choice but to tell the Harbour Master that Ray carried around a hidden flask of hard liquor, Nat paddled back to the buoy, retrieved everything, then paddled to the slip. He used one of the capstans there to haul Bess up out of the water, but it was beyond him to carry her home by himself.

Nat took a while to sort out how he could carry all the bits and pieces in one trip. He turned the canoe upside down and left her with the sodden clothes draped over her. Then he threaded the handles of the lunch kits and lamps over the tines of the tridents and shouldered the tridents and the paddles to carry them home in one bundle.

All the way home he muttered about what a stupid clot Ray was, and what a doze he'd been to overplay his hand with Ray.

He couldn't smell the stink of the mud flats anymore, but he knew from previous experience that was because he was so covered in it that his nose was not registering it anymore. Swimming wasn't enough to get rid of the smell; that took scented soap, hot water, and a brush.

He put everything in the shed except for the lunch kits, which he put down on the back lawn. Hoping to get any remaining mud, and the worst of the smell off, he hosed the lunch kits and himself down thoroughly, gasping as the cold water hit him, and then he carried the kits into the kitchen and dropped them softly into the sink. When he'd left the house that morning to go to Hine's house to take care of Mere and Tia for the day, Nat had left his teacup in the sink. He couldn't understand why his Dad hadn't cleaned up before he went to bed. There were only the two of then in the house. If they didn't make an effort to keep it tidy it would be a magpie's nest in no time. He would have cleaned it and put it away if he'd been the first one home and it had been Hatoe's cup.

Because Hatoe had to get up so early to take the Laughing Dolphin out to the weed patches, Nat didn't turn on any lights, tip toeing silently on his bare feet to the bathroom. There he closed the door and turned up the light, showered thoroughly, scrubbing himself from head to toe, then ran a tub full and lay in the hot water, dozing blissfully, dreaming about a future with Hine and the girls, and a music studio that all the best musicians in the islands would come to.

Another going over with soap and a flannel, another rinse, and he was fairly sure he didn't stink any more. He was very tired, longing for bed, but he thought he'd better take care of the lunch kits first. It had to be at least midnight, if not later. Hatoe would be up in four or five hours, and the last thing he needed to start his day was a stinky kitchen.

Besides, Nat had to tell him that he was leaving weed collecting again, and he wanted to do it without a squabble this time, if he could. Wrapping a towel around his hips, he set out for the kitchen, taking care to make no noise so that he wouldn't wake his Dad.

The smell from the sink assailed him the moment he set foot in the kitchen. Scolding himself for being a thoughtless idiot, he took the food out of the kits and threw them both out onto the back lawn. They were light, so they didn't go very far, even though he threw as hard as he could. He was too tired to do anything about it, though, and stumbled back to put the food in a container that he hoped would block the smell and put the container in the chilly bin. After he'd had some sleep, he'd be in better condition to decide whether or not the food was still edible.

Something still stank, though. Cursing himself for bringing the kits inside, he sniffed, trying to identify where the smell came from. He expected it would be the sink or chilly bin, but it seemed to be coming from the door. Standing back and looking along the floor in the moonlight, he noticed marks on the tiles. Closer inspection revealed that, despite his effort to hose himself off, his footprints had left traces of mud on the tiles. If he didn't clean them up the whole house would stink by morning. He could hear in his head how upset his father would be to get up to a smell like that, and in the kitchen of all places! He wouldn't have a lot of sympathy for Nat being dumped out of the canoe by Ray, either. He ought to have taken more care. Plus, he still had to explain why Bessie was sitting on the slip overnight and work out a way to get her home.

Would this night never end? He was so tired he couldn't think straight. Wearily, he got a bucket, put water and bleach in it and picked up the dish rag. He stood, staring at the cloth in his hand, a pounding headache starting behind his eyes. He knew his mother would be upset if he used the dish cloth on the floor, but she wasn't there, and he had no idea where his Dad had left the mop. Wiping the sink out with the bleach-soaked cloth in hopes of getting rid of any lingering smell there, all he wanted was to be finished as quickly as possible so that he could go to bed without having to face the smell in the morning.

The headache was only from lack of sleep, he knew. As soon as he could get to bed it would fade. The sooner he finished wiping up the mud, the sooner he could go to bed.

Not wanting to wake Hatoe, Nat didn't turn on the lights. He could see the marks on the floor quite easily in the moonlight. Bending over made his headache throb. He could no longer see the humour in being dumped into the harbour. He got right down onto his hands and knees, calling Ray all kinds of names. "So much for trying to help the stupid clot."

He knew Ray wouldn't tell anyone what happened. For one thing Ray was not a talker, so no one ever heard things like that from him. For another thing, talking about it might bring out what it was that had made Ray so angry, and Nat was sure that Ray didn't want anyone to know that he kept a hidden flask of hard liquor with him, even on outings that were supposed to be alcohol free.

Just the same, Nat no longer felt bad about having to tell that to the Harbour Master. If Ray hadn't dumped him in the drink, he would be in bed now. Not only did Nat feel angry about that, but he also felt angry with his Dad. If Hatoe would put the mop back where Mum used to keep it, Nat would know where it was and wouldn't be down on the floor.

He could hear his mother's voice in his head, being upset that he was using the dish rag on the floor. "It'll never go in the sink again," he told the voice in his head. "It's been demoted to floor rag. After this it'll get recycled."

He sat back on his heels to rinse the rag out in the bucket, telling the voice in his head, "If certain people would rinse cups out and put mops where they should be I wouldn't have touched the stupid dish rag."

He froze then, staring at the kitchen door. There was a shadow there. A person holding shoes in one hand.

What on earth? Silently Nat crept over to the wall, so that as the door was slid open, he could stand up and turn the lights full on, saying with all of his pent-up anger, "What do you think you're doing?"

It was Hatoe, reeling back, sandals in hand, still dressed in his work clothes. Clearly, he hadn't been home.

"Where have you been?" Nat was incensed. Hatoe's stagger made it obvious he'd been drinking.

"I . . . er . . . you see . . . um . . . well . . ."

Hatoe's red face and stammering made Nat so angry that he shouted, "You're only going to get about three hour's sleep! Talk about irresponsible! It's not even enough time to sober up."

Hatoe's eyes widened. "I haven't . . . I'm not . . ."

After being with Ray all evening, Nat had no patience left for the denials of closet drinkers. The anger and disappointment that he'd felt towards his Dad was overlain with disgust that he would use the same pathetic pretences as a loser like Ray. He stepped closer to smell the booze and call Hatoe on it, saying, "How could you when so many people rely on you? You're letting the community down. What will your parents think?"

He saw the shock and shame in Hatoe's eyes at the same split second that he realized that he was not smelling alcohol. It was a scent. A familiar scent. Hine's scent. He couldn't think. He couldn't speak.

Hatoe was stuttering, stammering, but Nat couldn't understand him. Nor did he want to. "Get out of my sight!" he snarled.

Hatoe flinched, his hands up.

"You'd better go to bed," Nat turned away, unable to stand the sight of his father right then. He heard Hatoe's footsteps go to the hallway door, stop, and then carry on, slowly.

To keep himself busy until he was sure Hatoe was in his room so that he wouldn't see him, Nat finished the kitchen floor.

As he wiped the cloth rhythmically back and forth, the first numbness wore off. All he could think was, 'He was with Hine. He was with Hine.' The image of his father with someone only six years older than he was shook Nat to his core. "She's young enough to be his daughter!" In a wave of rage, he went to the door and threw the whole bucket, contents and all, not caring that the bleach could kill the plants it landed on. As roughly as he had slapped the wall to activate the light paint, he now slapped it to turn it off. 'We were supposed to be together,' he thought, hurt welling up inside him. 'Good thing I didn't tell anyone. Not even Ray.' He stopped at the hallway door to admit, 'not even Hine.'

He continued silently along the hallway. He had to admit that he couldn't be angry with them because neither of them knew he had any interest in Hine. As he walked past his father's door, he heard Hatoe pacing. 'Let him pace,' he glowered. 'What does he mean by spending most of the night with a young girl like that? Even if he didn't know that I was interested in her, what was he thinking?'

Everyone had been saying what a good bloke Hatoe was to take a fatherly interest in the poor young widow. What would they think when they found out about this? Some fatherly interest!

He closed the door to his room so softly that he was sure Hatoe couldn't have heard it. He threw himself down on his back on top of his bed, picturing how outraged the community would be about an older man taking advantage of a young girl like that.

And they wouldn't be able to keep it from the community, either, with those two little girls chattering away to all and sundry.

The image of Hatoe's face when Nat was scolding him flashed across Nat's inner eye. That hadn't been an alcoholic flush; that was embarrassment, pure and simple. As soon as he saw that, then he realised that the stagger hadn't been from drinking, either, it had been from surprise. Nat started to snicker to himself. Poor Dad. Imagine if this had been the first time he'd done anything like this. Then he'd tried to sneak into his own house so that Nat wouldn't hear him and guess what he'd been doing, only to walk into sudden bright light and a real earbashing. The idea of himself, the son, growling at Hatoe, the father, struck Nat as funny enough to prompt him to get under the covers.

He lay on his back, staring up at the ceiling in the moonlight. He had never thought about his father being interested in Hine, nor had he ever imagined that she would look at an old man instead of someone closer to her own age. He didn't know why he'd thought he might be able to get Hine to look at him. She'd rather go with someone twice her age than give him a chance. No, he reminded himself, she'd never been given the option. He wasn't heartbroken, he realised. He was angry, surprised, disgusted, but not grieving. Why? Well, obviously, because he wasn't in love with Hine. He rolled that one around his brain pan. No, he had never fallen for Hine, he'd fallen for Tia. He wanted to raise Tia. She felt so much like his own baby that he had planned to partner her mother and put up with her sister in order to take care of her.

This was a better solution, he realised. Remembering how Hatoe had handled Mere on the pier he knew that Hatoe would be a much better stepfather for Mere than he could ever be. And, if Hine had fallen for Hatoe, that was a much better basis for a partnership than his hairbrained plan had been. Plus, if the relationship between Hatoe and Hine did turn out to be permanent, he would be Tia's stepbrother and would have her right here in Hatoe's house all the rest of her childhood. All the benefits of having her around with none of the responsibility.

He pondered this new situation, trying to get used to the idea. That clarified everything for him: Hatoe had been happier in the last month or so than he had been since Annie fell ill.

He sat up on his bed. It was as if his Dad was coming back to life. If that was Hine's doing, Nat no longer cared about her age or what people might say. If Hine could bring his Dad back to him, Nat would do everything in his power to support and protect her and to help them.

Now that he thought about it, Hine had been happier lately, too. That was better for the girls. The best thing he could do for Tia was to give her the best stepfather she could have and a happy Mum. If it didn't turn into anything permanent, that was still good if it brought the old cheerful, easy-going Hatoe back.

Not only that, but he also figured out with a thrill of relief and a jolt of excitement, that would leave him free to pursue his dream of starting a band.

Now all he had to do was make up with Hatoe and tell him that he understood. He knew he could get Hatoe to laugh if he told him about Ray dumping him into the mud.

He lay down snickering at the image of himself in the mud and fell asleep trying to think of things to say to Hatoe that would make up for the way he'd spoken to him. When he'd been an errant teenager his Dad had never been as tough on him as he was on his Dad tonight. Perhaps he wasn't ready to be a parent yet.

His back-brain was on alert, listening for Hatoe while he slept, so as soon as the water ran in the bathroom in the morning, he woke up.

He got up and dressed, then waited quietly until he heard Hatoe go from the bathroom to the kitchen. He silently went to the bathroom, then slid into the kitchen. Hatoe's face was hidden behind his shipping charts. Nat hoped he could pour a cup of tea before he had to find the words to apologise to his Dad. To his knowledge he'd made no sound, but when he glanced at Hatoe, Nat nearly jumped out of his skin. The fierce look in Hatoe's eye was the stuff of nightmares. "Dad, I'm . . ."

"Where do you get off telling me to go to bed like a five-year-old?"

Embarrassed, Nat could only raise his hands in submission and agree. "Yes, I'm . . ."

"Who do you think you are to order me out of your sight in my own house?"

"You're right, I . . ."

"And what business is it of yours where I've been?"

"Yes, you're . . ."

"What gives you the right to wait up for me and give me an earbashing?"

"I didn't actually ..."

"It's none of your bee's wax where I spend my evenings or who with."

"You're right, it's not."

Hatoe's voice lost its harsh edge and took on a slightly pleading tone. "I've got the right to see anyone I want to."

"Yes, you do."

"It's my look out if I don't get enough sleep."

"As long as you let someone else skipper." Nat had the feeling Hatoe wasn't listening to a word he said. When that comment got no response, he knew he was right.

"If I'm invited for tea, I have every right to accept."

"Yes, you do."

"She's a grown woman."

Nat didn't answer. He sipped his tea, waiting to see whether or not Hatoe was really going to tell him everything. He could sense a struggle going on inside Hatoe.

"There's no reason we can't be together: we're both adults."

Unable to bear his father's embarrassment, Nat tried to give him an easy way out. "No reason at all. It's not as if it's anything serious."

Hatoe dropped his eyes. He folded his shipping charts with elaborate care.

Nat stood wordlessly, barely breathing. All his instincts told him that their lives were about to go in a whole new direction.

Creasing the folds of the charts, Hatoe asked very softly, "What if it is serious?"

Grinning, Nat exclaimed, "Then you'd better get over being defensive with me, mate! You're going to need someone rowing with you in that boat."

Hatoe's head came up with wide eyes and a slack jaw. "You don't mind?"

"I'm pleased."

"What was all that last night, then?"

"I was wrong. I'm sorry. I was taken by surprise, and I'd had a rough day."

"The girls are too much for you?"

"No, I loved every minute of it. After that I spent the rest of the day with Ray. Dad, I must tell you . . . you can't take Ray out."

Hatoe stared at him in blank amazement.

"He had a hidden flask of hard liquor on him. I took him out to the mud flats. We agreed to have no alcohol in the canoe. Do you remember that I told you this morning, that he was drunk all day when he wasn't hired this morning? Well, the Harbour Master was wondering if he was enough of a safety risk to ground him. Now I have to tell him it's worse than we thought."

"You'd better ring Kahu right now. He must know before the crews are hired, even if it means waking him up."

While Nat rang his grandfather, Hatoe made breakfast for both of them. He listened to Nat's side of the conversation, shaking his head, sadly. "I had no idea he was that bad," he said when Nat broke the link.

Nat felt sick. "I can't tell you how much of a rotter I feel for dobbing him in."

"Yeah, I know. It's never easy. Ray will thank you for it in the long run."

Nat appreciated the intention but wasn't convinced. "Ray will think I pretended to be his friend to trick him."

"Only until he's sober. Then he'll realise you saved his life."

Nat helped Hatoe put their breakfast on the table and made a fresh pot of tea, saying, "He dumped me into the mud flats. I'm surprised you didn't smell it."

Hatoe looked at him for a moment. "You know, I think I might have. I just didn't realise it was here and not blowing in from the harbour, eh?"

"You were otherwise occupied," Nat grinned, teasing him. "I hosed everything off as well as I could. I was wiping up drips off the floor when you came home."

Hatoe grinned. "Did I scare you as much as you scared me?"

"Oh, at least!" Nat chuckled at the memory, then he changed the subject. "Bess is still on the slip. I couldn't portage her by myself, and I didn't want to risk her by dragging her. I brought the tridents and lamps home. They're in the shed."

"We'll have to get her before we do anything else. Get any fish?"

"Not a one. Ray nicked the corner of a fin, that's all."

"Shame. I could have done with a feed of flatties."

"Are you sure Hine will let you eat something with a face?"

Hatoe got up to take his dishes to the sink.

Afraid he'd offended his Dad, Nat hastily finished his breakfast and joined him at the sink to help with the dishes.

Watching Nat thoughtfully, Hatoe asked, "Are you sure you don't mind if Hine and I become a couple?"

"Yes, I'm sure. I think it's good for everyone."

"Well, what was that all about last night, then?"

"I was caught by surprise, and I was wrong. I'm sorry."

"Nat, I saw the disgust in your eyes."

"I thought you'd been drinking."

"Me? Oh, right. I remember now, you said something like that."

"Sneaking in after midnight with your sandals in your hands, staggering, red-faced . . ."

"I did not stagger."

"Yeah, you did."

"Well, you nearly gave me a heart-attack."

Nat laughed. "I'll bet!"

They both laughed, then, turning to lean on their elbows on the counter, Hatoe saying, "I was trying not to wake you up."

Nat added, "I wasn't ready to hear you laughing at me for sitting in the mud. I was still trying to get used to the idea that I can't help Ray."

Hatoe took a deep breath and confessed, "I didn't want to see or speak to anyone. I'm still trying to get used to the idea of what I've done."

Nat's heart went out to his Dad. "You did nothing wrong."

"She trusted me."

"Still does, I imagine."

"You know what I mean."

"Yes, I do. Get over it. Hine is not some helpless child you took advantage of. You said it yourself: she's an adult."

"What will people think?"

"That she's young enough to be your daughter and they thought you were taking a fatherly interest in her."

"Tangaroa in the sea!"

"You knew that. There's no point in hiding from it. Hold your head up and live it down."

"I appreciate your support, but I can't do it. Hine is a beautiful young woman. She deserves someone closer to her own age, not an old fossil like me."

Nat straightened up and stood square in front of his father. "Listen to me, Dad. You can <u>not</u> hurt her like that. It's the women who choose. She chose you. Yes, she's younger than you, but she's six years older than me, and if I can make up my own mind who I want to be with, for my own reasons, even if it's someone unexpected, so can she. I might not understand it, but it is the right thing for all concerned. Hine was partnered, so she knows what she wants. She's been happier these last few weeks, and so have you."

"Really?"

"It's as if you've been away for a long time and you've finally found your way back. I don't care what anyone else says, I'm so glad that you're beginning to be your old self again that I'll do whatever it takes to keep this happening."

"I ... I'm . . . I don't know what to say. It does feel as if I'm coming back to life. It's like I'd forgotten how green the trees are, and the sun hasn't been warm. But I'm worried about Hine."

"Of course you are, you're in love with her. But, man, how can you love a woman and not see the change in her? She's smiling and laughing, teasing, and walking with a spring in her step. How could you miss that?"

"I thought I she had more energy, then I though it was wishful thinking on my part."

"Cor, what a doze!" Grinning, Nat ducked to one side.

Rolling his eyes, Hatoe straightened up, saying, "Let's go and get that canoe before we go out."

All humour instantly left Nat. As he went through the doorway, he said, "Dad, let Ben skipper today. You haven't had enough sleep."

Following Nat, Hatoe closed the door behind them, observing, "We seem to have exchanged generations."

Nat was embarrassed. "I'm sorry for blowing up last night. Before I have my kids, you'll have to teach me your secret."

"The two main points are not to jump to conclusions and not to get so angry."

Recognising that he'd done both, Nat snickered at himself. "Yeah, well, it's just as well I won't be a parent for a good, long time, eh?" He grinned at his Dad, "I still think it's a cheating way to get girls into our family when we've only had boys for generations."

"Oh, as if!" For the first time Hatoe actually chuckled.

They fell into step beside each other. Neither bothered to touch the light paint on the trees lining both sides of the path, being comfortable enough in the dark on the familiar path. Some windows were lit.

Softly, so that no one in the houses they were passing would hear him, Hatoe noted, "I won't be the first one out today, but you know something? It doesn't bother me like it did. Since your Mum died, I've dreaded running into anyone, but now I feel like I miss everyone and want to keep up with what's going on."

"That's what I meant by your old self coming back." Nat tried another tack. "You're not going to go straight out, anyway. I'm not available today, you can't hire Ray, and with no one to watch the girls I don't see how Hine can go out, either."

Hatoe stopped at the light pad at the top of the ramp. Once they were out from under the trees, the predawn light was enough to see each other's expressions. "You won't work, but you won't watch the girls so that Hine can work?"

"Bessie's over here," Nat hastily headed towards the slip, thinking he should have found a better way to introduce Hatoe to the idea that he was going to have a career in music, after all. He hurried down to the slip and piled the clothes in a heap. As Hatoe caught up with him, he protested, "It sounds so harsh when you put it like that. If we turn Bess over, we can carry these home in her. I'm sorry I didn't tell you earlier, but I had a visitor yesterday."

When they had the canoe on their shoulders, Hatoe admitted, "You did say something about it. I reckon you didn't get much chance to tell me the news, eh?"

"We were a bit distracted," Nat agreed. "It was Iggy, a well-respected musician. I made an appointment to meet some people in Tāmaki-makaurau today before I knew Ray was unemployable."

"It doesn't look as if you're willing to change your appointment for the sake of your family."

"Not at this point, sorry. There's no time to get a hold of everyone." Nat thought that lack of sleep had made Hatoe as cranky as he'd been before Hine. Plus, it was affecting his judgement if he was as oblivious to the need to have someone else skipper as he appeared to be. "It wouldn't be a bad idea to miss today if you can't find crew."

"Miss a day? Why should I stay in?"

"To find a permanent third, at least until Ray comes back."

He felt the canoe jerk as Hatoe reacted. "You can't be serious about doing that again! Remember how glad you were to be back home . . . why would you do that to yourself again?" He took a deep breath and asked gently, "This isn't about Hine, is it, son?"

Nat was startled. It had never occurred to him that his Dad might take it that way. "No, no, Dad, hold up."

"Because I just want you to know you don't have to get out of our way."

"Listen to me, Dad. I'm going back to Tāmaki-makaurau because I've been hired to work with Iggy on a piece of music. Apparently, I'm good with arrangements and interpretation. Good enough that the top musicians in the islands are willing to pay me to do the one thing in this life that makes me feel fully alive. Can you imagine what that's like?"

"Yes." There was a completely different tone in Hatoe's voice. "Yes, I can. That's the way I feel out on the deep blue."

Nat tried to reassure his Dad. "I'm not going to be gone for long, eh? A day or two." Then he pressed his advantage. "But you do need to come up with a permanent third person. I can help out sometimes, especially at first, but as things get going, I'll have my mind on other things."

"Yes, I can see that. Its likely time Hine and I talked about a routine for the girls so that she can earn a steady income."

"What about her widow's pension?"

"For her own sense of autonomy, she needs to be self-sufficient."

"Well, I'll tell you what, I can help a bit while we're all trying to sort ourselves out. Taking care of Mere is just a matter of before and after school and lunch. It's Tia who has to be watched every moment, but she's such a sweetheart there's no trouble finding someone."

"Now you're confusing me. You're staying here after all?"

"I'm going to be based here in Matapihi. One of the things I learnt was that I don't do very well in big towns. So, I need to come up with a way to make a living from music here. Iggy's visit gave me an idea. If I can do what he says I can do with this piece he's having trouble with, I can turn that into a business based in Matapihi."

"Sounds like a big fish on a light line."

Nat was thankful they couldn't see each other's faces while they were carrying the canoe. "Yes. But I think I can do this. I'm not a great singer, I don't compose original scores or lyrics, and I didn't do well as a solo act, so I thought my dream was fantasy. I gave weed heaps, but my heart wasn't in it. I have to know whether or not I can do this."

"I didn't know you felt that way about it. I thought you got your wandering itch out of your system, then came home and settled down."

"Sorry, I wasn't trying to fool you; I was trying to find my personal answers."

"What did you find?"

"That I'd rather be a third-rate musician than a first rate weed collector."

"Ouch!"

"Sorry."

"Don't be." They had reached their garden. They lowered the canoe, then Hatoe turned to face Nat. Rotating his shoulders, he asked, "Do you have a plan?"

"First: see if I do have a knack for arrangement and interpretation. Second: start a band with people who can write original stuff. Third: build a house with a recording studio."

Hatoe put his hand on Nat's shoulder. "You have the same need to go and find your happiness as I do, whether anyone else understands or not."

CHAPTER EIGHTEEN

Caleb

"Son of a bitch! *¡Que chafa!*" The unexpected headline drove Caleb Faithful into a thundering rage. Leaping from his chair, he was across the room with his finger jabbing the chest of the nearest pigeon. "You! Find out which double-crossing sum-bitches voted for that dickhead, Matthew Tigris!" The guilty secrets of the most likely Exodus Party members flickered through his mind's eye, along with the various ways he could ruin their political careers and personal lives.

His brother, Hanoch, asked him, "Didn't you say it don't matter who they nominate cuz we got Lucas Ebal in our pocket?

In disgust, Caleb snarled at him, "Don't you pay no attention to nothing? Matt Tigris will just eat up Lucas Ebal. The Genesis Party ain't got shit, and if the Destiny Party can't win over Tigris either, he's got it in the bag. The herd just loves the crap he's dishing out."

"You really believe the Exodus Party will win this time?"

"What did I just say?"

"What are we going to do? Do you want us to see what we've got on Tigris?"

"Yep."

One of the eager pigeons piped up with, "We'll bring him down, for you, Sir."

Caleb rolled his eyes. "No, you ass. Get enough on him that we can control him."

Hanoch looked confused. "Control him? What about Lucas Ebal?"

"The hell with him." Caleb dismissed his brother's confusion, turning to the pigeons. "We need plenty on Matt Tigris. He's going to be a hell of a lot harder to control than Ebal ever was. Lucas Ebal was a real politician, in it for the money and the fame. This asshole is the most dangerous kind of idiot. He believes his own bullshit."

Much as Caleb hated ass-kissers, he kept them around because they were useful. An informant among them said, "They say he's got ideals."

Caleb shrugged. "That's what I said."

There was a knock at the door. "Mr Faithful, Sir."

"What now?"

"It's about your nephew, Gomer."

"I'm sick to death of that useless shit! *Me Vale Madres.* Let him hang this time."

"Yes, Sir. It's just that he got pulled over again, Sir."

"Drunk again? Let him take the rap for this one. Teach him a goddam lesson."

"Not drunk, exactly, Sir."

"What? What?"

"Higher than a kite, Mr Faithful, with a whore in the car, and classified documents in the back seat."

"Shit! *¡A la verga!*"

"A male whore dressed as a chick, Sir."

"Keep that loser out of my sight! *Pinche* Gomer! I can't stand to hear him sucking up and making lame excuses."

"Yes, Sir."

Hanoch looked as fed up as Caleb felt. Gomer was nephew to both of them, their sister's son. "*De la fregada.* What's this one going to cost us?" he demanded.

The pigeon gulped. "The arresting officer wants to be persuaded to keep it quiet, Sir."

Caleb could feel his temperature rising. Sooner or later people would learn not to screw with the Faithful brothers. "*¡Desmadre!* Persuade him. Make sure we've got it all, and then take him out. Goddamit! With this new shithead running for the Exes I've got enough on without that stupid lunk-head running around with classifieds. Who let him have anything?"

"I don't know, Sir."

"Find out."

"Yes, Sir."

"Damn. You know, Hanoch, what we need is a distraction."

"What kind of distraction?"

"I don't know. Something brand new that will keep the herd busy."

"Something brand new? We can have a big victory against the Westers."

"Not new, and it's too close to the line Matt Tigris is feeding the herd about the Westers are lost children of God who should be treated with compassion and respect." He spat into the spittoon. "Can you imagine what it would cost if we had to pay wages to get those pagans to work? How stupid can you get? They're prisoners of war, for God's sake. We let them live. That's more than they do for our guys." He could see the glances and knew they'd heard the stories that GR soldiers captured by the West could earn their way to citizenship in the West and stayed there because they wanted to. He knew it was all crap, so he wouldn't even talk about it

Hanoch pointed out, "Matt Tigris ain't said nothing about paying the pagans, only that we'll convert more with kindness than with the lash."

"Bullshit! *¡Chingadazos!*"

"The voters are eating it up."

"Who gives a shit? It's more liberal left-wing lies. These whining liberals never think things through. They yap and yap about poor this and poor that, but they never think about who's going to pay for their stupid ideas. The first thing that'll happen if we give the enemy citizens' rights is they'll want to be paid. Are the liberals going to pay for that?"

"It's Tigris's platform that Jesus is the God of Love and the New Testament is good news."

"Once we get the right leverage on Tigris it won't matter a damn what he said before he was elected."

"If we're hanging Ebal out to dry, how do we stop Tigris getting at our guys?"

"Get the right things on him and he'll watch what he says."

"It ain't that easy to get anything much on this guy."

"Don't I know it! Why do you think I didn't want him to be the Exodus Party nomination?"

"What are you going to do?"

"Don't you listen to nothing? I'm gonna find a distraction that'll take everyone's eyes off the ball and find an angle on Tigris that'll bring him to heel."

Hanoch pulled a face. "Got any ideas?"

Irritated, Caleb glared at him. "That's your job."

"Execute that ex-son-in-law of yours publicly."

That amused Caleb. He let himself relax enough to throw his head back and roar with laughter. "I wish! Nah, he don't get off so easy. After what he did to my little girl, I'm gonna destroy him: his reputation, his name, everything."

Hanoch screwed his face up as if he didn't think that would work. "Lycus is doing okay so far: he pushed the Panhandle through to the coast and now it looks like he's pushing the Junta back."

The flash of rage hit Caleb so hard that he stumbled. He could barely see through the red mist that filled his eyes. "Out!" He yelled at his aids. They scattered as he rounded on his brother. "Don't you <u>never</u> praise that asshole again!"

Hanoch flinched. "I wasn't praising him. You know it's the truth."

Caleb felt betrayed by his own family. "Whose side are you on? The truth is what I say it is! You're either for me or agin me!"

"I'm for you Caleb, you know I'm with you to the end! We're brothers. Ain't I always got your back?"

It was true that Caleb wouldn't be where was without his brothers and his father, but he still resented it when any of his family showed anything less than total agreement with him. They were living off him; the least they could do was be completely loyal. "Watch your fucking mouth."

The pleading tone in Hanoch's voice irritated Caleb as much as anything else. "I got to keep you sharp. You said and Daddy said you'd lose your edge if no one never kept you in touch."

What infuriated Caleb the most was remembering their father talking about how easy it was to lose touch with the real world and how that undermined everything and remembering himself agreeing to guard against it. He sucked in the red-hot temper, knowing that being emotional would make him appear weak. Any sign of weakness left him open for exploitation, even by his brother. He corrected himself: especially by his brothers. Cold blooded again, he glared at Hanoch. "I don't want to hear nothing about that asshole unless it's to tell me his reputation is ruined. Got it? It ain't enough to tell me he's dead. Give me proof he's a coward or a traitor or a pervert."

"I hate to be the one to break it to you, but our best guys can't get nothing on Jaakobah Lycus that will ruin him."

"Give me something I can use or shut up about him."

"Look, it ain't working out no more, Caleb. It's time for other options."

Caleb was disappointed. He'd never taken Hanoch to be a quitter. "Like what?"

"You could run for President."

"Are you out of your fucking mind? I control the President! Why the hell would I give that up? You want me to jump through hoops to get the ignorant herd to vote for me, only to have all the leeches in the House stopping me at every turn? Then, even if I do get things done, I lose everything I worked for and built up because of something as stupid as a fucking election! Give your head a fucking shake!"

"You've got to know when to fold."

"I do, and this ain't it."

"Caleb, it ain't working no more. Your best shot couldn't stop the Exes from nominating the wrong guy."

"They're gonna pay for double crossing me."

"That don't change nothing. Tigris is still their nominee."

Caleb'd had the impression now and then that no one understood what he did, how he did it, or why. Partly that was because he never let anybody know what was really going on, he knew that, but it still disappointed him that none of them had the imagination to figure it out. "Yeah, it changes something. It makes damned sure the next time one of the shitheads tells me he's gonna do something, he won't even think about breaking his promise to me."

"That only makes a difference if you're still there."

"Right."

"You can't hang around after this."

"Watch me."

"You've lost your power base. Face it and shift your angle while you can."

Just in case Hanoch had heard something he'd missed, Caleb played along instead of shutting Hanoch down. "How do you figure?"

"You can't make the conventions vote the way you want them to anymore."

"Destiny and Genesis did, and most of the Exodus Senators and Members did. The ones that didn't will have time to be real sorry. Its two years to the midterm elections. That's more than enough time for them to tell all their friends how sorry they are for breaking their promises before they're out. When that word gets around the rest of the quail will be real careful not to cross me."

Hanoch hesitated. Caleb hoped that meant he was either going to give some information, or Hanoch had figured it out, but he challenged Caleb, "There's nothing to say they'll be sorry, much less say they are to anyone else."

Disappointed, Caleb growled, "I said it."

That should have been enough for his idiot brother to know that everything was under control, but, no, he went on, "No one can control all three major parties."

"No one needs to." Caleb was not about to tell Hanoch the secret of the light touch: of influencing as few people as possible as little as possible as rarely as possible to get the votes to go the way they needed to go without anyone catching on. If Hanoch was too stupid to figure it out for himself, then he didn't deserve to know.

"Face it, you ain't got the guy we worked on, you got this Tigris guy that's going to be a pain in the butt, and you ain't even trying to beat him. This never happened when you were at the top of your game."

Disgusted, Caleb shook his head. He got right into his brother's face, speaking very softly and with maximum malice. "Yeah, it did. It happens all the time. The reason you got that fancy house to live in and that rich, beautiful wife, and all those servants, and that willing mistress that keeps her mouth shut, and those useless sons of yours got commissions, is that I don't quit every time the quarry moves."

He felt better when he saw how much that hurt and upset Hanoch and they both knew there was not a thing he could say or do about it without losing his status and way of life.

To rub salt in the stinging wound, he aped the exact tone of voice Hanoch had used, to say, "I wasn't dissing the boys. You know it's the truth."

As much as he enjoyed causing the impotent rage he could see in his older brother's eyes, he despised Hanoch for not being man enough to stand up to him and take the consequences. That's why no one except their Daddy had ever understood what he did. He was the only one with the imagination to see the possibilities, the smarts to figure out how to pull off the manoeuvres, the patience to work out how to do it without anyone catching on to what he was up to or being able to trace things back to him later, and the balls to take the risks and actually make the moves. "Is that all you got?" He challenged Hanoch, taking a step back.

In a hissing fury Hanoch squealed, "You've shot your wad. The House and the Senate don't listen to you, if they ever did."

Caleb checked that in his mind. 'The vote was close, so most of the Exodus Party did what I wanted. The ones that didn't will be ruined. The Destiny Party are tearing themselves apart with infighting and scandals right on schedule and they've nominated a putz that even Ebal could beat.' Caleb hadn't planned that; it was one of the crops he got from tilling the ground right. And the Genesis Party still did anything he said. That would be useful after they lost. He made a mental note to prepare the ground so that when they lost, they wouldn't feel he'd let them down. He had more influence than anyone could guess. He turned his attention back to his brother's angry rant.

"So now Matt Tigris will be President, and good fucking luck getting him to listen to you or keep your office next to his. Or even in the Wright House. He's so popular because he always thinks for himself and not even the lobbyists can make him go against his conscience, so what are you going to do about that?"

"Everyone's got their angle. If we can't find a scandal, we'll use another pressure point. There's always something. His beliefs, his family, whatever." Caleb tossed the answer off casually because his mind was busy taking note of Hanoch's points. The biggest problem with Tigris was that he always thought for himself. Looking at him from that angle gave Caleb the best idea he'd come up with so far to handle him. Knowing that he never went against his conscience just meant that Caleb had to angle things so that what he wanted looked like it was in line with Tigris's precious conscience, and what he didn't want looked like it wasn't. Same beef, different gravy. This was going to work to his advantage.

"He's an honest man."

Caleb laughed. "He's a politician."

"You never figured on an honest politician, did you? Fucks you up, huh?"

"You better pray it don't." Hanoch faltered when he heard that, which made Caleb grin. "Your gravy train ain't dead yet. Honest men are the easiest of all."

Resentment flared in Hanoch's eyes. "I'm praying you have an easier time handling Tigris than you did with Jaakobah Lycus."

Caleb recognised the attempt to get back at him, and it cheered him up because it showed him yet again that no one could touch him. "Let Lycus think he's got away. El Presidente is the most dangerous enemy our officers face. I'll get Lycus promoted and see how he likes facing the Junta with brass on his shoulders. We got him then. If he wears it, he'll get killed, and if he don't we got him for disrespecting the uniform."

"Dying in battle won't ruin his reputation."

"No, you moron, that's not what the story will be." Hanoch's bone-headed attitude riled Caleb so much that he searched for something to snarl that would make Hanoch jump. Knowing Hanoch couldn't have two different thoughts at the same time like he could, he decided on a change of topic to rattle him. He knew Hanoch was expecting him to be furious that he was mentioning Lycus after he'd been told not to, so he said, "So what have you got for a distraction?"

Hanoch's jaw dropped. "What?"

"A distraction. I told you we gotta get something new to keep the herd busy."

"Give me a break! You ain't . . ."

Triumphantly, Caleb swooped in for the kill. "Sheeitt! I gave you one job. One! And you can't even do that much. Tell me again . . . what the fuck am I paying you for?" Before Hanoch could close his mouth, Caleb was out of the room and calling for a meeting of his top idea men.

In the couple of hours, it would take to get them all together he went home, so pleased with himself that he was humming as his brother trotted beside him trying to explain.

"Don't you got a home to go to?" Was all he said to Hanoch as he slid into the back seat of his armour-plated vehicle. That shot was satisfying, too. Now he had Hanoch coming and going. If he showed up at the meeting, Caleb could ask him what he was doing there, but if he didn't show up Caleb could slam him for being a dead-beat. The part he loved the most about it was that Hanoch knew he was caught but was never fast enough to stop it from happening.

Like a whipped dog, Hanoch was at the meeting, anxiously making sure everything was just right. Caleb accepted the coffee, cigars, bourbon, and food, but he despised Hanoch for being so weak.

"Of course we'll do everything we can to support the incumbent, Lucas Ebal, in this election," Caleb started, to make sure they all knew the public position, and to lay the groundwork for the 'insider leak' from the closed private meeting. "We all know he's the best guy, but the

Exodus candidate, Matthew Tigris, looks like he could sweep it. Any ideas?"

He took care to appear thoughtful while they ran through the usual round of ways to prop Ebal up and cut Tigris down. He let it go on for a bit, then said, "We done all them things. The voters're used to them. We got to come up with something new that nobody saw before so they ain't got no clue how to take it and they don't stop talking about it and trying to figure out what's going on."

There was a moment of silence as they tried to digest that, then a burst of conversation. Most of what they came up with as new and original were retreads of the same old political tricks that had been played since the Garden of Eden.

Caleb kept saying, "That's not new," until the group was frustrated.

"I don't know what you're looking for," Hanoch complained in exasperation.

"Something new."

"Like what?"

Even for Hanoch that was dumb. With withering sarcasm, Caleb answered, "Oh, I get it; you don't know what 'new' means. Why didn't you say so? 'New' means no one ever saw it or thought of it before. Not an old plan changed to look new, or a new way of looking at an old set-up, but the kind of thing that gets every man-Jack of them and their old ladies, too, saying, "I ain't never heard of nothing like that in my whole life." We do that and they'll talk about nothing else."

They stared at him.

He knew they couldn't come up with anything . . . he couldn't, either . . . but he had to keep the pressure on them to shake something loose, like sending the dogs into the brush to flush out the quarry. "Well, come on; don't just sit there like birds on a branch! Give me something or go home."

That jolted all of them. They all started talking at once, to each other and to him. They were more original, but it was still all about new ways of pulling old stuff. One man wasn't trying. It pissed Caleb off to see him just sitting there. "Resigning?" he demanded, suddenly.

Everyone jumped and looked around to see who'd got the boot. Seeing the eye was not on them, the others relaxed. Some carried on discussing their useless ideas, but most fell silent; watching to see what was going to happen to Caleb's victim.

His head jerked up; wide eyes focused on Caleb. He blurted out, "The only new things I saw in my whole life were the Panhandle and the comics about them savage islands. I been . . ."

Caleb felt a stir in his back-brain. "What did you say?"

"I was trying to think of . . ."

"That's what I'm talking about!" Caleb had the germ of an idea. "What do we know about the savages?"

They were all caught off guard.

"Um . . . they survived Judgement Day."

"They're ungodly."

Caleb realised that would get him nowhere. "Yeah, yeah." He stood up, signalling the end of the meeting. "You got one week to find out everything there is to know about those guys."

He didn't know what he was going to do with the information, but he did know it would be something no one, whether general public or politician, would be ready for.

Pleased enough to whistle through his teeth as he headed to his car, he ordered Hanoch, "Sort them out so they don't double up. Set up a meeting in a week. Check my schedule for when I got a two-hour block. If I don't got one, let me know. I'll have to make time for this."

Resentfully, Hanoch asked, "Are you going to tell me what this is about?"

At his vehicle, Caleb turned and patted Hanoch's cheek. "I already did. Like Daddy always said, listening is the greatest skill of them all." He knew full well he'd done no such thing, but he never said outright that he wasn't going to tell anyone what he was up to.

Once he was out of sight the smile faded from his face as he got down to trying to figure out what he was going to do while his driver took him home. He couldn't make any definite plans until he knew what he was dealing with, but he needed to be clear in his own mind of the general direction he wanted to take. To form an over-all picture in his mind, he recalled what had led to this situation. Reflection was not something he did. He only looked back to keep whatever he was doing at the time in focus and to maintain consistent strategies.

The unexpected survival of non-Christian people in some strange place had been very useful. It had been one of his major tools in reducing the once powerful Destiny Party to the in-fighting, disorganised mess they had become.

It was the military that had wanted to test the seaworthiness of the ships built by captured Westers. Caleb hadn't taken any notice at the time, seeing no profit in it for himself. It had amused him to suggest that the explorers should pay for the whole thing, when the military applied for research funds to equip the ship. It seemed only right that the curious idiots paid for their own deaths. The price of curiosity needed to be death, preferably at their own hands.

The whole thing had looked like a great idea to him. He was surprised the military came up with it. It got rid of the curious so that their nuisance ideas never could cause trouble, at the same time as testing the ship outside of the protected waters of the port. It would call the bluff of the Westers who had sabotaged the ship building by putting the leaders among them on it. A ship that was so unstable that it couldn't be used was deliberately chosen as an object lesson to the captive Westers.

Not only was it loaded with the worst Westers, and all the explorers, but also every slacker in the military. There was no question that was the end of them.

The shock when the ship was seen months later approaching the port on its way back home was the greatest Caleb had ever seen. It was as if the ship and everyone on board had returned from the dead.

Not being a believer himself, Caleb wasn't affected by the news from the ship that someone aside from them had survived Judgement Day. He didn't know what had brought everything down, but he was fairly sure it had nothing to do with the Judgement of God that His creation was so wicked that he had to destroy everything. That sounded like a baby's tantrum to Caleb, not the act of a rational adult, much less the most intelligent, powerful being in the universe. He didn't believe there was any such being, but if there was, it wouldn't smash everything every time things went wrong, it would know how to fix them.

He paid no attention when the President ordered the military to erase every sign that the men on the ship had seen anything. He was impressed by how quickly they moved and how thorough they were, but he had expected that kind of reaction from them. The Destiny Party was the most hard-line, right-wing, fundamentalist of the parties, so it was only to be expected that they wouldn't be able to handle any challenge to their beliefs without a violent over-reaction.

What happened that was so annoying to Caleb was that after that the government tightened up on everything, to the point where new laws, and enforcement of old laws no one took any notice of, threatened to undermine his businesses. When he couldn't get any of them to see reason, he could see no other course of action but putting the hysterical theocrats out of office. Their reasoning was that God had destroyed Western Civilization because of wickedness, and they were going to make sure that didn't happen to the GR by purifying it.

More strongly than any of the others, the Destiny Party believed that the GR had been spared to lead the world back to the Wright Way. The news that there were people living happily and well outside of the rules they believed were necessary for survival panicked them beyond anything Caleb had ever seen, and he knew that there was nothing he could do about it. Economic sustainability had no say against the furore of religious panic.

In keeping with his philosophy of knowing when to fold, he had walked away. Another part of Caleb's philosophy was always knowing where the skeletons were hidden. If he couldn't get what he wanted by talking sense, he would make it happen by getting rid of the people he couldn't influence and replacing them with people who did what he said. Making sure nothing could be traced back to him; Caleb assisted people to find out that the holier-than-God party had some dirty little secrets. Once the uproar started, it wasn't difficult for a man with Caleb's connections, abilities, ruthlessness, and timing to steer it in the direction he wanted it to go.

It was true he had fed members of the other parties certain details about where they might look to find scandals in the Destiny Party, and had pointed out how angry the voters would be if they knew that contact had been made under the Destiny regime and covered up, but it wasn't true that he'd controlled what they did about it. Some of the things they did with that information was unexpected. Scandals were exposed that he hadn't known about, and comics appeared about the savage islands after Destiny had been swept out of office and Genesis took over.

Remembering the sequence of events gave Caleb in idea. He arrived home in such a good mood that his whole family had a happy week with cookouts, touch football, and dog fights. He was even nice to Hanoch. It amused him to see that made Hanoch more nervous than threatening him did.

Wanting to see if that would work on Gomer, too, he let word get out that so long as Gomer never said one word about his latest arrest, he wouldn't be thrown out of Caleb's house. Until Gomer ruined it by downing enough bourbon to get boastful, it nearly worked. After that all Caleb really wanted from Gomer was to never see him or hear from him again. What he told Gomer as he threw him out was that he'd better smarten up if he wanted to stay alive.

At the end of the week, the pigeons sat around the meeting table with their sheaves of notes, all eager to impress him. That annoyed him. He never wanted anything on paper. When Caleb chose his pigeons, he made sure they were useful, had good memories, would keep their mouths shut, and were ambitious. Then he treated them as interchangeable, nameless non-entities. If he had to, he could remember their names, but he liked their reactions to knowing they didn't even make enough of an impression on him for him to know their names when they worked with him. In his opinion it made them work their asses off to break out of the pack and impress him so much that he would never forget their name.

The one who got his attention was the sharp eyed one who started with, "I'll burn my notes before I leave, Sir."

Caleb grunted.

All of the pigeons talked over each other to say the same thing.

Caleb ignored them, asking the first one, "What have you got?"

"This guy that writes these comics . . ."

"Just one guy?"

"Yes, sir. It looks like it's all drawn by the same hand."

"Who does he work for?"

"Looks like he's on his own, near as I can tell at this point."

"Huh. Private enterprise. I like it." Caleb was pleased. He could always manipulate someone who was trying to earn a living.

One of the other pigeons chimed in. "He was on some ship the purists didn't approve. He was in correction about a year, then, when he got out, he drew pamphlets showing all there is in the rest of the world is water and islands with fire coming out of the ground, with nobody alive and no animals. No, dogs, no cattle, no hunting."

Caleb was confused. That wasn't what he'd heard.

The pigeon rushed on, "When Genesis won the election, he started to write about islands with people on them."

Caleb leaned back in his chair, beaming with delight. "So, it's all bullshit." It couldn't have worked out better for him. Anyone who would change his story that much once could be made to change it again without too much effort. "What's his name?"

One said, "He signs his comics, 'Witness'."

Another cut in with, "His real name is Vince Thomas."

A third filled in, "Invincible-faith Pispah Thomason."

"CP," Caleb purred, unable to believe his luck.

"Sir?" They all looked confused.

Let them. If they couldn't figure it out for themselves, they didn't deserve to know. To him it was obvious that the only people who gave their kids names like that were hard right fundamentalists or those who were trying to look like hard right fundamentalists. Since was obvious from the fact that the guy had been on the ship that he was not a fundamentalist, he had to be trying to look like one, which was what the conquered people did. "Any of you ever read the comics?"

Most of them raised their hands.

The bright boy said, "I've got some here for you to see, Sir."

Caleb reached out for them without comment, making a mental note to have Hanoch remind him who that one was. The newer ones, with their stories of badly dressed, poor islanders with no shoes who lived in terror of offending the trees, were what he'd expected. He could see where the stories could be punched up to rivet the readers' attention and get everyone talking.

"These are older ones."

Caleb could see the development of the stories after the abrupt change from an uninhabited island to one with people on it. "Where did you get these?" He was surprised that there were any older copies around.

"I know someone who collects them."

"Who what?"

"People keep them. They trade them and sell them to get a copy of every last one."

Caleb couldn't have been happier. It was better than he could ever have imagined. If people were already collecting the comics, he was halfway to getting his distraction to work. As if it made no difference, he ordered, "Find this Vince guy after we're done, and get him in here. We're going to make his wildest dreams come true. Have you read any of these?" He looked around the table, expecting perhaps one or two to admit to it, but to his surprise, most of them had. He leaned back in his chair, chomping his cigar in satisfaction. "So, tell me . . . is any of this real, or is it all bullshit?"

For nearly an hour they went through the comics trying to sort out whether or not anything in them was true or based on fact. Caleb wanted an idea of what he was dealing with before any of them talked to Vince. He wasn't planning on seeing Vince himself, but on having one of the brighter pigeons, the ones he thought of as hawks, make Vince an offer. It would be a nice, friendly offer, and if all went well, that's all it would ever be . . . a friendly business arrangement where Vince made more money from his comics than he could any other way, and Caleb had a pet talent who produced what Caleb wanted the herds to read. It was in Vince's best interests to accept the deal and do what he was told from then on.

Caleb liked people who did what they were told. Which made him think of someone who didn't do what he was told and was running the risk of drawing attention to the family. Putting Gomer somewhere out of sight had been at the back of his mind during the whole week. Now he had a flash of inspiration about how he could put it all together.

"Looks like they found something, or the Destinies wouldn't have tried to cover it up. I figure we're never going to know for sure unless we look for our own selves." The nervous reactions pleased him. They should worry about what he was going to expect them to do.

For the first time he acknowledged that Hanoch was at the table with them. He fixed Hanoch with his 'no argument' eye. "Get that Vince guy on the payroll. Find the other guys who were on that ship, military and civilian. Find out what they saw and get it back to me. Find out what Westers they took. They might have saw something. We cain't question them without attracting attention, but if we know what ones we're looking for, we can work on that. Same with the others. Don't get people curious. If you get the idea there's anything out there that we can make a profit on, come straight to me with that. Anyone know who was the duty officer?"

"Yes, sir. Major Temperance."

"Where is he now?"

"I heard he was transferred to the swamps."

Caleb turned to his military expert. "Dig up his records." He nodded to the others. "Add him to your questions. There's got to be a reason he was sent to the swamps after bringing everyone back alive."

"The military or the civilians, Sir?"

He thought for a split second, and then decided, "Both."

He dismissed the pigeons, keeping Hanoch back. This was one time when his plans would work out better if Hanoch knew what he had in mind. He chose to 'confide' in his brother by a lowered voice in the meeting room to increase the chances that someone would overhear and start useful rumours. "First, a bit off-topic . . . we want the incursions into the swamps to come off. Records show that there is something worth having there. Now, for the rest of it . . . you got to keep your eye on the ball and your ear to the ground for a ship in better shape than the last one. They didn't want that one to come back. We do want this one back . . . if there's profit to be made, we want to know about it." He smiled at Hanoch. "I thought Gomer could lead the mission."

One of Hanoch's rare genuine smiles lit up his eyes. "His Mama will be so happy that you're giving him a second chance. I'll get right on it."

"I'll bet she will," Caleb said under his breath. If Gomer found anything worth having, Caleb would consider that he'd earned himself another chance. If he screwed this one up, he was done as far as Caleb was concerned. This was Gomer's last chance. The greatest threat to Caleb's way of life was members of his family who didn't know how to stay invisible. It was much more efficient to be the puppet master than the puppet. He not only had more power, but he also held on to it if no one was really sure exactly how much he had. He had a cattle ranch, like a lot of people did. He made sure it looked as if he worked on his land like everyone else, and that it appeared to everyone except a select few that his contact with the government was as a volunteer, out of a feeling of civic responsibility. The members of his family who needed shows of status or power threatened to destroy everything. They had to be stopped, no matter what it took.

Caleb was grateful that he'd managed to hang on to the office in the Wright House, next to the President, where he could quietly wield his influence. While he was waiting for the pieces to be put into place for a trip to the islands, he talked to the new President, Matthew Tigris, about God's Providence in having the oil, gas, iron, and other metals come under the control of those who knew what to do with them.

Tigris was worried. "There are riots and protests all over the Panhandle. I'm glad you believe we're in God's hands, but the newly conquered peoples had different religions, and they ain't taking to the Wright Way. They'll die before they'll accept salvation."

Caleb was unconcerned. "Happens every time God brings lost souls to us."

"They want everyone to know that the GR lied to them. If the citizens think I lied to these people, they'll lose faith in me."

"It wasn't you that lied to them; it was the previous regime. Besides, people forget. If a spaceship landed, they'd forget it inside of five years if you didn't remind them." Obviously, God put them in that position to do His work. In the two hundred and fifty years since God's Judgment no one had reunited the continent, but since Caleb had been given the gift of sight, more had been done than in the previous fifty generations. If they kept the faith, more would be done yet.

"God put me here to do His work."

Caleb spent the next several weeks adjusting the President's thinking until he understood he was where he was because of Caleb, and if he didn't do what he was told, he'd be replaced just as easily as he was put in. He needn't be so foolish as to think the people voted him in. Democracy was not God's Way. It was sinful to allow the masses to push and pull the direction of the nation back and forth according to the latest whims or fashions. The nation needed to be run by the righteous according to the writings of the prophets.

Tigris thought that Western Civilisation held things together for over three hundred years with the people governing themselves.

Caleb acted astonished that the President was so naïve. "The illusion of having a say was and still is an opiate to avoid the expense of subduing the masses. The idea of dozens of states all with their own State Governors all vying for their own moment of glory is ludicrous. All those states with their own police forces and their own laws so that all people needed to do was cross state lines to get away from the law. It created the instability which brought things down in the first place."

"It was God's Judgment which brought things down."

"If the nation had been efficiently run it would not have collapsed. No amount of disruption can put an end to a Government that's run properly. If we follow the Right Way the continent will be united under Righteous Rule, the Rule of Law, the Wright Way."

"But what about the riots? No matter how hard we try to stop it, word will get out."

"The best way to deal with the dissention is to distract the masses. Use the Panhandle in a way that benefits the people living there, then they won't want to do away with it anymore. Move loyal people in and set them up to dilute the natives, move the natives to better lands so that they loose their ties with the Panhandle, re-educate the children so that they turn their parents in and follow the Wright Way, and provide work for the people in the Panhandle so that they don't have time to cause trouble and are too well off to bother."

"What kind of work, what kind of distraction?"

"Something that hasn't been done before."

"Like what?"

Caleb let The President suggest things, waiting while he made all the same suggestions as everyone else always did. "You mean they've been done before?"

"Yes, Sir, and if we keep using the same old methods, they'll lose their effectiveness."

"I'll get a task force on it."

"No need for that, Sir. What we want is something that's happened recently that's new or at least a bit different."

After a few empty guesses, he finally asked Tigris if he would consider the exploration of the islands to be something brand new.

"I never thought of that!"

"Most of the citizens know nothing about it, except for the comics. The Church decided not to broadcast it because it flew in the face of the belief that God wouldn't have let the godless survive His judgment on a sinful population. Nothing will capture the hearts of the masses as much as an official exploration to find out what's really there, especially if they're going to profit from it."

"Do you really think the voters will accept it if someone else survived? What about their faith?"

"Yes, I really do. Even if they've survived, no one but us has got iron and oil, so it'll be the same in the long run." Caleb was thinking that if it was true that the GR were the only ones with oil and iron, then it was going to be a cakewalk to take anything the islanders had that was worth taking. Out loud what he said was, "If the ships come home loaded with riches, or with deals, the Panhandle will benefit in ways they never have before. Once they're better off in the Wright Republic than they could ever have dreamed of, they'll want to stay. Then we've got them"

"And if not?"

"If not, we'll have an off-shore base for taking over the West."

"You're going to give your money to the Panhandlers to hush them up?"

"Not for long. It's easy to get it back. They'll fuck up one way or another."

The President took a step back. "You're sure you'll get your money back from them?"

"Plus."

"What if it goes wrong? What'll you do if you lose your money?"

"The fastest, easiest, cheapest way to put an end to dissention is to make the masses think they want to do what you want them to do.

If you use only force all the time, the dissention spreads underground. You keep the force around so that they know what'll happen if things go wrong. A gun in one hand and cash in the other. They'll go for the cash every time. It's easier, no-one can resist a gamble, and they get to stay alive. No one can turn down the choice of getting what you want by going this way or going to hell if you go that way. Not even you or me. So long as they don't see that it's the same hand holding the cash that's holding the gun."

President Tigris asked, "And if I don't think this is right?"

"You think it's righter to keep fighting a losing fight? You like the idea of going down in history as the President that lost the Panhandle? The one that cost us the port we need to protect our nation from Western aggression?"

"Of course not! But there's got to be another way!"

"You can do the same old things with the same old results, or you can do something new and be a hero."

"And you get all the credit, I suppose."

"You never mention me. Not ever. Not if it succeeds, not if it fails."

"What's in it for you, then?"

"If the Panhandle fails, we all go down. I'm a rancher. I need the rails safe to get my beef to market. I've made a few investments on the side. To get my money back I need the Panhandle peaceful. Why don't you talk to the other presidents and find out who put the Panhandle through?"

Tigris stared. "You can't mean me to believe it was you."

Caleb narrowed his eyes, considering. "Ever ask yourself why the Panhandle reached the sea now and not sooner? We were trying to do it for a hundred years."

"We figured out how to do it."

"Next time you talk to other Presidents, ask if anyone said it was a good idea to have another go at it right then. When you get some spare time, go over what was different this time and ask yourself if there's some guy that would dare the President to try something new."

Tigris stared at him.

Caleb could see that he was putting it together in his head, so decided to press his advantage. "You saw that the port ain't named for me, huh? The President gave me the office by his instead, so that he had someone in reach for a touchstone."

"A what?"

"Someone who always tells him the truth. Some one not standing for election."

"With respect, Mr Faithful, both parties in power in the last two elections lost."

Caleb smiled. He had him. "Call me Caleb. Do you know who the commander was that pushed the Panhandle through?"

"A relative of yours?"

"The father of my grandson, Faithful Lycus." He waited a beat, then added, "The way of it is, I can tell them what's going on that their advisors don't know, can't see, or are too chicken to tell them, but I can't make them believe me over their advisors, or listen, or do nothing."

Tigris had a half smile. "So, if things go wrong it's because the President didn't listen to you, and when things go right he did?"

"Have you noticed there's been more progress in the last ten years than in the hundred before? Have you noticed some new ways of looking at things? Like how to beat the West in the Panhandle?" Caleb decided the best thing to do at that point was leave the President to think it over.

"We'll get a good ship," he assured Hanoch, when they were alone. "What we've got to do now is make sure they don't dump slackers on us." He gestured to the comics, indicating their on-going fact gathering. "The one thing all of them said is no one gets island talk, and they can't understand us. Looks like this one civilian, Willie Jay Rimmon got good at figuring out what they said. Get him and one of the other explorers on our ship to translate. And we got to get someone to go that can find the place. That's a neat trick, when we don't want none of the slackers. We got to learn to do this without no Westers. We got to take some this time. How's it going buying the ones that went last time?"

"We got the ones we could. Most of the ones that went escaped in that big break out."

"Shit! *¡Chale!* Question the ones we got. See if there's some that got missed. If we can pull this off we've got our distraction, and we make a profit, too."

CHAPTER NINETEEN

Ahnya

ive years after the visit from the GR, Ahnya sat on the bench in the shade with her mother-in-law, Donnurite Grahmore, Rita, watching the children play in the common area. Ahnya adored Donstan's mother, finding in her the support, guidance, and companionship that she didn't get from her own mother. Rita half rose to her feet, one hand partially raised, then sat back down shaking her head. "That child is determined to break her neck," she said, with a fond smile. Six-year-old Donya was fearless, clambering up the climbing frame, higher even than children older than she was, and climbing across the top. She seldom fell, and if she did, she shook herself off, inspected any scrapes or bruises, and climbed straight back up again. Eight-year-old Wynson was more cautious, got fewer bumps, and made a bigger fuss out of smaller incidents than any of the others, leaving himself open to jeers from the other children that broke his heart.

Ahnya's heart ached for her beautiful younger son. He was such a sweet personality, so gentle and kind, but his life was going to be difficult for him even if he hadn't been born so self-conscious and sensitive. Why couldn't he have been born with the outlook of gleeful deviltry that Ahnstan and Donya had? They were from the same genetic stock, after all, since his biological mother was Ahnya's sister, Wynlynya, Winnie.

Spoiled by their mother, Flynya, Winnie had been rebellious and sullen. She'd been their mother's pet, the precious third child. Ahnya and Winnie's parents had applied for a third child certificate after Ahnya and her brother, Flynirwyn, Flyn, had been born. Not everyone in their Hundred had two children, so a Third Child Certificate was granted to them in short order, so that there was exactly two years and two months between Ahnya and her brother, and between Flyn and Winnie.

But even though the children were so evenly spaced, they were not equal. Winnie, with blonde hair and big brown eyes, was delicate and pretty as a child, and had been the undisputed favourite. Resentful of the extra attention paid to their younger sister, Flyn had moved away at a very early age and had little contact with his family. Ahnya wasn't close to her family either, though she missed her brother. They had been very close as children, and it hurt that he included her in the ones he wanted to distance himself from.

Ahnya had been named Ahnirlynya, but she had never liked the long, cumbersome name that her mother insisted on everyone using in full, so she'd shortened her legal name to Ahnya as soon as she was old enough to do so, which was a constant source of tension between herself and her mother. Her father, Ahnirwyn, had preferred the shorter name, which didn't help smooth things with her mother.

Ahnya hadn't actually been all that surprised when the scandal broke that sixteen-year-old Winnie had found an unscrupulous doctor to remove her plugs without a certificate. Because she had broken the law, and had no parenting courses, no income to support a child, and no partner, the baby had been taken from Winnie at birth.

The usual punishment for having a child without passing parenting courses, or having a stable partnership, or a dependable income, never mind breaking the law by having the plugs removed without a certificate, was to have no chance of raising the child thus conceived, and of having little chance of ever passing a parenting certificate later. That discouraged all but a very few from attempting to have their plugs removed until they had all the provisions in place for raising a child.

Because Winnie refused to divulge who had fathered the child, Wynson couldn't be named properly. They didn't know his father's name to give it to him.

Donstan and Ahnya had partnered for a year and a day while they were in University; both studying technology. They'd partnered very young, but at the end of their year and a day, they had both decided to commit to a long-term partnership and had applied for parenting courses. Despite their youth, they had passed everything, even the maturity tests, so they'd gone together, certificates in hand, to the clinic to have their plugs removed. Once they had qualified to be parents, they were automatically entitled to two children, one to replace each of them. If they wanted a third child, they would have to apply for a Third Child Certificate, in the hopes that someone in their Hundred wanted only one child or couldn't have children. Ahnstan arrived immediately, when Ahnya was only nineteen years old, and they were both still apprentices.

Together they could have raised Ahnstan on their apprentice income, and completed their studies at the same time, but when the scandal with Winnie broke, they decided to offer to raise the baby. Two babies, less than a year apart, was a different proposition. To make it possible they had to have financial help, which meant Winnie was outraged to have part of her income diverted to Donstan and Ahnya, along with the assistance the authorities decided was needed. That caused a great well of resentment in Winnie.

Unwanted babies were unheard of in the islands, since both boys and girls had inert plugs inserted in their vas deferens or fallopian tubes before they reached fertility, so the only way a baby could be conceived was for both parents to have their plugs removed. Still, occasionally, there were children who could not be raised by either parent, and in those cases everything possible was done to place the children inside their genetic family, up to and including providing support to the people who took in the stranded child.

Ahnya's mother, Flynya, had assumed that she could persuade the authorities to allow Winnie to raise her baby if Winnie lived with her, but not only did Winnie have to do her time in behaviour modification, but Flynya didn't seem to grasp the reality that Winnie had broken the law, and was with-holding information from the authorities, such as who had done the operation, and who had fathered the child.

It was clear that Wynson's biological father had to be either a man who had had his plugs illegally removed or a partnered man whose plugs had been removed so that he could father a child with his partner. Sometimes, if people didn't conceive, they didn't have their plugs replaced. If people found out they were infertile, what would they need plugs for? If the father was ever caught, his punishment would be an irreversible vasectomy.

Flynya had next taken it for granted that she would raise her grandchild when Winnie was denied the right, but when she refused to retake the parenting courses to do so, she rendered herself out of the running. The resentment that Flynya felt that Ahnya, 'a mere child,' had been granted custody in preference to herself, had strained Ahnya's already fragile relationship with her mother. Her parent's partnership had dissolved while Ahnya was still in school. It was never considered that Wynson might have been raised by Ahnya's father, Ahnirwyn, who had shown no interest in doing so.

Ahnya was even less close to her father than her mother, a situation Donstan had never understood, coming as he did from two parents who loved each other and all of their children equally, even though individually.

Even if he didn't understand it, Donstan didn't like living with the tension in Ahnya's family, so he searched for an opportunity to complete his apprenticeship on a different island from Ahnya's mother. As soon as he had the chance, he and Ahnya moved away with great feelings of relief. Despite behaviour modification, Winnie remained bitter that she had used up her chance to replace herself. Even if she did qualify to be a parent later, she would only be granted one child, to replace her partner.

To take proper care of two babies so close together, Ahnya left her apprenticeship and stayed home, taking full responsibility for the house and the babies, so that Donstan could both finish his studies at night school and work during the day. They decided they might as well have their second pregnancy while Ahnya was already home, had their plugs removed again, had Donya, and retired from baby-making. Donstan hadn't wanted to apply for a Third Child Certificate, because he didn't want to try to raise four children. Ahnya wouldn't have minded, but it took two, so it didn't happen.

As soon as Donstan had completed his courses and could work full time as an engineer, Ahnya went back to school to complete her courses to be a communications technician. Once they were both working, they were able to relax into a more normal family life where each of them worked three days a week, so there was always one of them at work and one of them home with the children, and one day of the week when they were both home, just like everybody else with small children.

Now that Wynson was eight, he'd been asking questions about his origins. Ahnya didn't know what to tell him. She looked at his beautiful shining cap of blond hair gleaming in the sunshine and heard his laughter as he played with the other children. She asked Rita if she thought it would be a good idea to seek the help of a behaviourist. She wanted some way to avoid lying to her son without hurting him with the bald truth.

"He must know the truth, dear," Rita said, in a low voice so that the children couldn't hear. She looked over her shoulder to make sure Ahnstan wasn't behind them and added. "The worst thing would be if you said nothing to him, and he heard it from a third party. I don't know how I'd handle it in your place. Very difficult, dear, you must be careful. He's not a stupid child, but he's less than a year younger than Stan, who's advanced, so he feels stupid. Put that on top of being the odd man, and being sensitive, too, and you've got a recipe for disaster. I worry about that one. Lots of extra hugs and encouragement, I think."

Ahnstan was not playing with the other children in the commons; he was in the house doing one of his endless experiments. Somehow or another, as he'd grown, he'd become a thoughtful boy. He was still wild and loud when he played sports, but at home he had become academic and bookish. He even wore glasses. "Mum! Grandma!" he came pounding out of the house. "You must come and see this! The visitors have come back!"

They both jumped to their feet. Ahnya said to Ahnstan, "I can't come, love, I'm watching the children," then said to Rita, "You go, I'll be there in a minute."

"But Mum, the last time they were here I was only <u>four</u>."

Ahnya half got up. She hadn't thought about the visitors for years. "I can't son, not until I've sent all the children home. I'll be there as soon as I can."

Rita broke into a lope, catching her grandson's hand. "Come on, show me."

House lots were arranged in hexagons, three lots to a side. Each lot was almost a triangle shape from the walkways under the train tracks between each hexagon to a common area in the middle of each hexagon where the children played. Most of the commons had trees, climbing equipment, slides, pools, or swings for the children in the hex. Parents took turns watching over the children as they played. It was Ahnya's turn that day. She went into the commons, told the children that the visitors had come back, sent the neighbour children home, and took hers in with her despite their protests.

Ahnya couldn't help but feel relieved that she no longer replaced the Speaker of her Hundred. This time she would be able to speak up at the meetings. The reporter was repeating a broadcast that had been on a few minutes earlier, saying that a ship from the Gethsemane Republic had been seen by fishermen off the coast to the north, heading towards the Islands.

Ahnya began to chop up vegetables for their dinner with the wall unit on, so that they wouldn't miss anything.

"You don't usually have that thing on at mealtimes, eh?" Rita asked.

"Yeah, nah, but I don't want to miss anything today."

With only partial attention on what she was doing, Rita helped Ahnya prepare dinner, watching to see if there were any pictures of the new ship. So far it was just the reporter repeating what had already been said about the new ship, talking about the first contact, and showing the old images of that ship, taken five years before.

They had to turn the wall unit off to get the children to wash their hands and faces for dinner, but they willingly set the table while watching, even though they had to be reminded to put the knives and forks and plates down, since they tended to stand, transfixed, holding them in their hands.

"I think we saw that one before," Ahnya told Rita.

"Are you sure?"

"No, it's hard to be sure when they all dress alike and have those strange hats that shade their faces."

Rita nodded. "I wondered last time if they have no pride in their clothes, or if it's that their culture has a peculiar sense of style. They all wear long pants, no matter what the weather, all coloured blue, with boots that have built up heels no matter how tall or short they are, no matter how warm it is, or whether they're inside or outside, shirts with long sleeves that they roll up, kerchiefs knotted around their necks, and hats with high crowns and wide brims. I can't help but think that, aside from making them look like children at a fancy-dress party, encasing their feet in those boots all day every day cannot be good for their health, nor can balancing on those built-up heels all the time do their joints any good."

Ahnya agreed. "Perhaps they can't walk very far with such things on their feet, and wrapped in so many clothes, which was why so many of the ones we saw were overweight."

"That's a good point. Remember when the reporters were telling us how surprised the GR were to see octogenarians giggling and laughing while chasing grandchildren and great-grandchildren around? That makes me think that people don't live as long in the Gethsemane Republic as they do here."

"You could be right," Ahnya said, lifting her head at the sound of the door at the top of the stairs up from the kitchen.

"Daddy, Daddy!" Donya crowed, rushing to the stairway.

The first thing Donstan said as he rushed down the stairs from the second floor was, "Have you heard the news?" As he came into the kitchen, he altered that to, "Oh, I see you have," as he scooped Donya up, and reached out to ruffle the hair of each of the boys.

Ahnya and Rita had stir-fried fresh vegetables from the garden with little strips of smoked bean curd and a steamed fragrant mound of herbed wild seeds. They left the wall unit on to keep up with the news as they ate.

"What's going to happen, Daddy?" Ahnstan wanted to know.

"That depends on what they want," Donstan answered.

At five Donya was too young to understand what was going on, although she could tell it was something that was important, so she ate quietly, watching the others with her big brown eyes. She had Donstan's fair hair, along with brown eyes that she seemed to have come by all by herself, since her father's eyes were blue, and her mother's eyes were green. Ahnstan had his father's blue-grey eyes and his mother's dark hair. Ahnya assumed that Wynson must have got his blue eyes and blond hair from his biological father, since her sister had dark hair and dark eyes, in the same way that Donstan was blond like his father, when his mother was a brunette.

"They're further north this time," Donstan observed.

"Where did they go last time, Daddy?" Wynson asked.

"Don't you even know that? Tauranga-Moana." was scornful.

"Stan! Be nice!" Ahnya scolded. She said in a quieter tone, "I wonder why they're doing that?"

Rita explained, "When Olarine was the First Servant, she lived there, so the Servants met there. The visitors don't have any way of knowing that's changed, because the election was held after they left."

"I wonder how they'll take to finding out that Pitamete's the First Servant now, so now the Servants meet over on the west coast?" Ahnya couldn't help snickering. The mental picture of the visitors being bewildered and frustrated was just too delicious.

Donstan mused, "I wonder if they'll be as pushy as they were last time? They were so angry when they found out we had a King and hadn't told them. They were dead set that the King had to be some kind of mighty ruler. I don't think they ever did understand that the King has nothing to do with the government."

"Yeah, nah, I don't think they did." Rita agreed, adding in a disapproving tone, "They upset poor old King Uetaoroa so much that he retired."

"He was ready to retire, anyway. Probably past time, if the truth be known."

"Yes, but still."

Donya piped up suddenly, "Grandfather King gave me a lolly."

"Yes, he did, that's right, at his birthday celebrations. That is who we're talking about. You're a clever girl," Ahnya congratulated her, telling Rita, "We took the children to the King's party on the beach."

"Good memory, too. That was three years ago," Donstan added.

Ahnya was taken aback. "Was it really?"

Rita nodded. "Has to be, you were visiting me last King's birthday, and the one before that was filthy weather, remember? The storms and weeks of rain."

"Oh, right. You're right." Ahnya beamed at her daughter, delighted with her.

Wynson was determined to get some of the approval that was floating around the table. "He had two sticks to walk."

"Yes, he does."

"Why?"

"Sometimes when you get old, your legs aren't as strong as they were when you were young, and they need a bit of help."

"That's never going to happen to me." Wynson stuck his chin out.

His brother challenged him instantly. "How do you reckon?"

"I'll never get old."

Donstan and Ahnya exchanged amused glances with Rita. "Grandfather King has gone downhill quite a bit since he retired, hasn't he?" Ahnya said to deflect the conversation slightly.

"No doubt about it. The visitors won't find King Ngaronoa nearly as easy to intimidate as his father was," Donstan declared with a self-satisfied grin. "Olarine was a good First Servant, but it seemed like they didn't believe a woman would have won the election."

Rita snorted. "It makes me so mad that they think women should do nothing but stay home with the house and children. That's half the productivity of the entire population not being used. Ridiculous. I don't see how their country can run like that."

Donstan shrugged. "There were so many misunderstandings on both sides, Mum. We likely didn't understand what they meant. Anyway, this time they'll be dealing with Mr. First Servant Pitamete Meithei."

"For a little while, anyway. It's been nearly five years. We're just about due for an election," Ahnya shrugged, getting to her feet to clear the table. "Come on, children, clear your places." Ahnstan and Donya willingly clambered down and carried their plates to the sink.

Wynson remained where he was. "I'm not finished," he insisted, stubbornly.

"That's okay, you can say there and finish," his father told him, getting to his own feet to carry his plate to the sink.

"You don't think Mr. Meithei will win again?" Rita asked as she stacked the dishes neatly in the sink as Donstan handed each one to her after scraping the food scraps into the compost bin, and Ahnya got out the pudding.

"I'd say he has a good chance, actually," Donstan said.

"He might. I'll vote for him," Ahnya put down a tray of oranges, hollowed out and filled with orange gelatine.

"Oh, look what Mummy made!" Donya crowed at the sight.

"Grandma, actually," Ahnya smiled at her mother-in-law.

Wynson decided he was finished after all and ran to the counter to look.

"Where's your plate?" his father asked, sending him back for it.

The leftovers from dinner were wrapped and put in the fridge, the crumbs were wiped from the table, the bowls were given to the children to be set out, then the giggling started as the children scooped jelly from the oranges with spoons.

Still the reports came over the wall unit. The ship had put down anchor off Hauraki; flotillas of small boats and canoes had gone out to meet it and escort it in; a small motor boat had been lowered to the water from the ship; a number of men had climbed down rope ladders from the deck of the ship into the small boat and set off for shore, accompanied by the flotilla of welcoming boats and canoes. Even with the mixed feelings the first contact had engendered, the new visitors were still being given a warm welcome.

As the adults looked at one another, Anya felt an ominous shiver of apprehension.

Willie Jay

illie Jay could see that the white-haired lady was doing her level best to explain that she was no longer First Servant, but Gomer Jordan was too impatient with Willie Jay's struggles to translate to be able to understand. "We had an election after you left. We have a new First Servant now. You met him. He used to be Second Servant. Pitamete Meithei."

Willie Jay recognised Olarine Eidola. He was glad to see her, though he'd been hurt last time when he realised the islanders had a King and hadn't told him. At the time he'd felt that they'd made a fool of him. Now he was so pleased to see a familiar face that he was willing to forgive and forget. He was translating to her that Mr P. Gomer Jordan did not want to talk to any of the King's servants; he wanted to talk to the King himself.

"We've also had a royal election since you were here," she told Willie Jay. "Grandfather King, Uetaoroa, retired."

Willie Jay translated that for Mr Jordan, editing out his scornful, "Are they all quitters here? It's no wonder, when their King abdicates. Some leader!" by asking, "Your King abdicated?"

Olarine looked flustered. "Saying the old King abdicated makes it sound as if he shirked his duties, which he never did. He was nearly ninety, frail, and could no longer do the job as he would wish to do it. No, he fulfilled all of his duties. But you saw him at the Hui we had for you. Do you remember how elderly he was, then? We accepted his request for retirement. He is much loved. The Grandfather of the Islands. He'll live longer with less stress."

The only question Gomer had from all of that was, "He has to ask you if he can quit?"

"It's his duty to serve the Will of the People."

"Doesn't sound much like a King."

Olarine's eyes widened. "Do you know what he means?" she asked Willie Jay.

Willie Jay tried to think of a way to explain to Gomer what she was asking. He asked Gomer, "What's a King sound like?"

"Tyrants. We'll give them freedom from the rule of Kings."

He translated that to Olarine, who said, "No one rules us. We are free people."

When he translated that, Gomer scoffed, "How can you say you're free when you got a King?"

Olarine raised her eyebrows at that, and told Willie Jay, "Our King is not a tyrant."

Gomer scoffed again at the translation. "Not this one, maybe, but what about the next one? Why don't you do away with royalty if you want to be free?"

"Perhaps I should restate that," Olarine tried after Willie Jay translated. "Our monarchy cannot be tyrannical; they do not rule us. They are not government; they are the soul of the people. The government deals with the business, the King or Queen deals with pomp and circumstance, glory and history."

When he heard Willie Jay's translation, Gomer snorted, "You're sure his son didn't 'persuade' him to retire so that he could have the power?"

Olarine floundered, getting Willie Jay to repeat the question a number of different ways before she assured him, "Royalty has no power. If Ngaronoa was not to be trusted, we would not have elected him."

Gomer snorted impatiently when Willie Jay translated that. "Stupid old cow don't know the difference between a President and a King. Tell her she better take us to her boss or else."

Willie Jay hesitated, remembering what had happened to Vince when the islanders got upset. It had been a real chore to convince Gomer that no one could set foot on the islands with weapons. Willie Jay and Chuck had started working on that right at the beginning, before they were on board. Not wanting to find out what they would do to him or Gomer, he said instead, "I think we're on two different pages here, Ma'am. I was talking about the King's son, not your new President."

Gomer interrupted. "No matter what he's called, how do we get to see him?"

Willie Jay translated the question to Olarine, then translated her answer, "As soon as the word spread that the ship had been seen heading for Hauraki, I'm sure the First Servant set out for here."

P. Gomer Jordan did not like waiting. He acted as if waiting for the First Servant constituted a personal affront to him alone. "How long will it take him to get here?"

"I should think he would arrive shortly," Olarine said.

Willie Jay asked, "He wasn't at home?"

"Yes, he was. The First Servant does not live here."

Willie Jay stared at her. "This is where we met with you last time, isn't it?"

"Yes. I was First Servant five years ago. This is my home." Olarine sounded as if she was struggling to be patient as she repeated herself. "We've had an election since then."

Gomer lost interest and wandered over to the door to stare out. He looked lost without his posse. Willie Jay and Chuck had persuaded him that a large group of bodyguards would be a hassle.

Willie Jay continued to try to understand. "So you said. The King's son won."

"No, no, no. King Uetaoroa's son is Ngaronoa. Ngaronoa was elected King when Grandfather King retired. Pitamete Meithei was elected First Servant. We meet at his house, now."

"Wait a minute, you had <u>two</u> elections?"

"Yes. The government election and the royal election."

"You <u>elect</u> your king?"

"Of course. How else do we know the people's choice?"

"Is it a real election? I mean, his son got the throne anyway."

"It was a close race with his cousin, Wineera. She is very popular."

"His cousin? So, the crown might have gone to the King's niece and not his son?"

"Yes, it looked like she was going to win for a while there, but in the end, King Ngaronoa earned more votes. He's not only popular, he has distinguished himself by outstanding service to the community, and also achievement. He's a three voter, but Wineera's only a two voter. She's earned a second vote for her service to the community, but she doesn't have the achievements Ngaronoa has. If it had been anyone else but Ngaronoa, she would have walked away with it."

Willie Jay was startled. "Whoa, whoa, whoa. What's a 'three voter' and a 'two voter?' You can't mean they vote more than once."

It was Olarine's turn to stare. "Can't you earn a second vote in the Gethsemane Republic?"

He felt offended. Didn't these people know the basics of democracy? "Of course not! One man, one vote. Do you mean in this country some people do vote more than once?"

"Of course. How do you acknowledge people who have distinguished themselves by outstanding service to the community if their Hundred can't award them a second vote? King Ngaronoa dedicated his whole life to service when he was only a schoolboy. He has given of himself selflessly to the community, while managing to never neglect his family. That's such a difficult balance to achieve that he earned a second vote when he was still in University, which doesn't happen very often. I didn't get mine until I was middle aged. Wineera got hers when we had a volcanic eruption, and she worked tirelessly in the Disaster Relief. King Ngaronoa already had his second vote when Tarawera blew. All we could do to acknowledge his incredible bravery was give him a third vote, his achievement vote. We haven't had such a man for King in a long time."

Willie Jay translated for P. Gomer Jordan. Then there was a strained silence as they tried to digest what they'd heard.

In the silence, Willie Jay heard the pleasant sounds of children playing. He listened to them, remembering that there were safe play areas in every block. He was trying to recall the name of them when he heard the faint whine of an electric motor. He remembered the sound from the first visit. He heard the motor slowing down, then it stopped and was followed by the vague creak of floorboards in the second-floor entrance. Then he heard muffled thumps and figured that someone had arrived and was taking the outside stairs down to ground level. He remembered enough about the island houses to guess that the person was going come in through Olarine's garden and make an entrance into her courtyard. He could tell from her expression that Olarine had heard the same thing and was pleased about it.

She smiled at them both. "I am sure the First Servant will be here momentarily."

The children's play hushed to whispers in the distance. "Look! It's the King!"

Willie Jay glanced around to see if the others had heard. Olarine was looking at the door in anticipation. Gomer and his bodyguard were muttering to each other that they were fed up with the stupid old servant jerking them around. He felt very nervous, wondering if he should say something about what he was hearing. He knew the thud, thud, thud was heels hitting the earth in unison, but he had no idea what the faint clack, clack, clack was.

Nothing prepared him for the first sight of them at the door. Suddenly there were two huge men right at the glass doors, who flung them wide, ducked together to get their head-dresses through the doorway, and stood side by side, astride, bringing their spear handles down on the stone tiles with one mighty synchronized crash.

It was King Ngaronoa and Pitamete together, both in full ceremonial garb, the reeds of their 'grass' skirts swinging with each step back and forth, clacking in rhythm over their red linen underskirts, ceremonial feather capes billowing from their shoulders, ceremonial spears in their right hands, feathers standing high from top-knots of hair on the backs of their heads, making the two tall men seem like giants.

P. Gomer Jordan was suddenly behind Olarine and Willie Jay, both of whom were on their feet, staring. Pitamete was a big man, but King Ngaronoa was massive. The King spoke in a booming voice. "Tana koutou! Tana koutou! Haere mai!" Then they both said, "He!" and slammed the butts of their spears on the stone again, as one.

Both were bare-chested, except for a ceremonial sash woven of reeds, bearing the patterns of their stations. The ancient, stylized tattoos showing their lineage were carved on their faces, woven headbands with stylized patterns sat tight on their heads, holding the head-dresses in place. Their bare feet were planted far apart, giving them the appearance of cats ready to spring.

Willie Jay could see that Olarine was delighted by the effect. His heart sank. If the islanders thought the GR would show some respect after that, they were so wrong. All the islanders had done was prove that they were savages.

Olarine greeted the men, "Mr. First, King Ngaronoa, we were waiting for you. Come in and meet our guests. You remember Mr. Willie Jay Rimmon don't you? And this is Mr. P. Gomer Jordan. Mr. Jordan, I'd like you to meet the Island King, Ngaronoa Turikora, and First Servant of the Islands, Pitamete Meithei."

"Pleased to meet you. I'm sure." The men shook hands, the islanders briskly and with smiling confidence, the GRs awkwardly, all murmuring the insincere pleasantries demanded by politeness. Willie Jay translated with all the sincerity he could to make up for Gomer's lack of it. He was embarrassed, as if an idiot cousin had spat in the lap of the mayor.

Olarine was smiling, looking more at ease and sure of herself. "Welcome, gentlemen, do sit down. Would you like something to drink?" Her grey eyes sparkled.

Keeping their faces as expressionless as stone, Ngaronoa and Pitamete strode with dignity into the room, and seated themselves on large, strong chairs.

"Tea, please," said Pitamete.

The King wanted juice.

"I don't suppose you have any bourbon, do you?" P. Gomer Jordan asked plaintively, sighing at the look of puzzlement his request earned, and opting for coffee.

"At last, you have returned to our islands," the King said in his deep voice as Olarine left the room.

Willie Jay fidgeted. "Well, yes, you see, when Mr. Jordan, here . . ."

"Just call me Gomer."

"When Mr . . . . er . . . Gomer, here, wanted to come to see you, he asked me to come with him to translate, so that you and he could understand each other."

"You wanted to see our beautiful homeland, Mr. Gomah?"

"Just Gomer, Mr. . . . er . . . ah . . . I . . . ah . . . don't rightly know how to address a King. I never met one before, you understand."

"Ngaronoa."

"Non . . . er . . . Na – Naron . . ."

"Ron."

"Thankee kindly, Mr. King Ron, that's much better. Well, now, I never thought a King would sit so nice and cosy and friendly like. Thought you'd be in a palace."

Ngaronoa and Pitamete both turned to Willie Jay to translate for them.

He stammered. "Er . . . ah . . . a mansion. The place where the King and Queen live."

"My house is on the west coast, across the island. You came to the east coast, so we thought it would be easier for you if we came to you."

Olarine returned bearing a tray loaded with a pitcher of juice, drinking glasses, and a bowl piled high with fruit. She was followed by her partner who carried a tea tray with a tea pot and cups, and a coffee pot and mugs. Proudly she introduced him as they set their burdens down on the tea table. "I think you didn't have a chance to meet my partner when you were here last, did you, Willie Jay? Abernaud Eidola, my partner these last thirty-six years. Bernie, this is Willie Jay Rimmon from the Gethsemane Republic."

Willie Jay rose back to his feet to shake Abernaud's hand, saying, "Pleased to meet you, Sir."

Abernaud turned when he'd set the tea tray down, took Willie Jay's hand and shook it firmly, saying, "Welcome to our home."

When Olarine introduced Abernaud to Gomer, he commented as they shook hands, "Just call me Gomer, Abe. May I call you Abe? Thirty-six years, huh? Now ain't that something. Never got more than eight years, myself. Don't know how you do it. My hat's off to you."

This puzzled the islanders because they could see that both men had their hats on.

Gomer remained on his feet, standing back where he could command the attention of everyone in the room. "Well, now, gentlemen, Mr. King Ron, and lovely lady, shall we get down to business?" Without waiting for anyone to respond, or even for Willie Jay to finish translating, he launched into an animated sales pitch. "I am so glad to have you all assembled here, the King and all, because I have a proposition for you that will make all your dreams come true. I heard so much about your beautiful land when Sam Jonson's expedition returned, that I thought to myself, P. Gomer, I thought, there's a people who need you. You see, folks, I can make you rich beyond your wildest dreams. Just think what it can be like here with some real development. Tourism. Hotels. Happy people paying to vacation on these beautiful beaches. And guess where all the profits will be going? Into your pockets." He pointed playfully at the King, then wavered, because it was obvious that the King had no pockets. Nor did anyone else in the room except himself, the bodyguard, and Willie Jay, who was signalling frantically to him to slow down so that he could translate. He took a slurp of his coffee, and stalled, a stricken look on his face. "What in Sam Hill is this?"

Willie Jay hastened to explain, "Their coffee tastes different from ours."

"You ain't kidding!"

He smiled at Olarine, who was asking, "Is something wrong?"

"Don't you worry your pretty little head about it, dear lady." He turned back to the men. "The profits will go to you, as I said, and I will have a modest commission, of course, as developer, but that harbour we sailed into is perfect for a vacation spot. Picture it bustling with life. Why, we'll build wharves for the passenger ships, and then you can use them to bring in cargo, to start to buy all of those things you've had to go without for so long, things like . . . " he faltered again, realising that none of the island men were wearing what he thought of as men's clothes. The King and his servant had on what looked like grass skirts, and the hostess's partner had on what looked like the kind of wrap someone would put over swim trunks. And they were all barefoot. "Like shoes, and jeans," he finished, triumphantly. "We'll build roads for you, of course. It won't take your country long to pay that off. It'll be your leg up back to civilization! Can't you just picture this land prospering again, bustling with industry? You'll be known in all history as the King who rebuilt the nation. King Ron the Great. How do you like the sound of that?"

"No."

"Now, don't be too hasty, there, Mr. King Ron, think about it. You owe it to your people."

"I cannot say. It's for the People to say."

"It's for their own good, though, you see, and as their leader . . ."

"Please excuse the interruption, but I do not know that word, 'leye-der.' I am the King. I do not decide. That is for the people."

"Well, you've got to show your people the way."

"I do not. The Servants will talk to the People, then decide if there needs to be a counted vote or if the Will of the People is clear without it."

"The servants decide? But you tell your servants what to do."

"A King cannot meddle in government. It is forbidden by the Charter. They are not servants of the King; they are the Servants of the People."

Willie Jay had a flash of stunned comprehension. 'Servants of the People?' He turned to Pitamete. "Then you are the head of the government."

Pita nodded.

"Of course," said Olarine.

"But Ma'am, you don't understand, when you told us you were the First Servant, we thought you were like, you know, the head maid or something. We never realised <u>you</u> were the leader." he felt sick with embarrassment. He pulled his hat from his head and held it in his hands. "Oh, Ma'am, I am so sorry, Ma'am. Begging your pardon, Ma'am, we don't see ladies running countries where we come from. It was an honest mistake. On behalf of myself and everyone else in Sam Jonson's expedition, I do apologise. I am sorry for any offence, Ma'am."

"Please convey my acceptance to everyone else. We all misunderstood many things that first time. We are so different that both of us were confused."

"Thank you, Ma'am. That's very gracious of you, Ma'am."

"Well, if that don't beat all," Gomer mumbled to himself, trying to find a way to get his sales pitch back on track after Willie Jay had translated. "You got me pitching to the wrong person. So, who all makes the decisions here?"

"That'd be the First Servant. These folks say 'First' the way other folks say 'President.'"

Gomer turned to Olarine, "So you get my point, Ma'am, about the benefits we can bring to your beautiful country and your people."

She smiled at him. "It's not for me to say."

Gomer turned back to Willie Jay in defeat.

Olarine relented, slightly. "I was First Servant when Willie Jay was here five years ago. We have had an election since then. I am now Second Servant, and Pitamete Meithei is now First Servant."

"Um . . . er . . . Peter- mettee My-tie, may I call you Pete? As I was saying . . ."

Pita held up one hand. "I don't mean to interrupt, Mr. Gomer . . ."

"Just call me Gomer."

"Yes, Gomer, I must confess I don't understand some of the words you used. What is 'taw-er' . . . um, I'm sorry, I don't remember the rest of the word."

"Pardon me? I didn't catch that."

Pitamete turned to Willie Jay. "When Gomer was telling us what it could be like. Beyond our wildest dreams."

"Tourism?"

"Yes, that's the one."

Gomer spoke as if Pita were only six years old. "That's when people come from other places to see your beautiful beaches and forests. They spend their vacations relaxing, living the good life, and they spend big. Lots of lovely bucks, and it'll all be yours."

They looked just as lost as they had before he'd explained. "What are bucks?" Pitamete asked.

"Deer," Abernaud supplied.

"Oh." Pita nodded, then said to Gomer before Willie Jay could explain, "I don't think the People will agree to having wild animals back. The deer were all hunted out in the Dark Days, before the Freeze. We preserved what native life we could during the Freeze, but not the imports. We couldn't save everything, and deer weren't native to the islands. They were not a benefit to our wildlife."

"You got no deer? What do y'all hunt?" Gomer was too taken aback to keep to his pitch.

"We do not hunt," Ngaronoa told him flatly. "We are proud that our ancestors developed a non-violent society."

There was a stunned silence, which Willie Jay broke by explaining that Gomer had not meant deer when he'd said 'bucks' but had meant money.

"Ah." They looked at each other. "Beads," said Pita.

"We will have to ask the people of Tāmaki-makau-rau if they want ships that belch smoke coming into their harbour," Pita told Gomer. "Our ancestors did have big wharves there, but they took them all out to use the metal."

Gomer's carefully rehearsed argument against environmentalists preventing development evaporated in his surprise. What he said instead was, "They did WHAT?!"

"They took them all out. It took a long time for the forests to recover from the Freeze. Until then our ancestors had to use what wood they could find, and to scavenge metal. The islands don't have mineral riches. Before the Dark Days such things were imported. Since then we have conserved what we have, and learned to live without it."

"But to take all your wharves out. How could you defend yourselves?"

"Defend ourselves? Against whom? We have seen only your people in two hundred and sixty years."

"Well, now, you see? That's what I mean. You can open this country back up again, and let the world know you're here. Ready for business."

They looked at one another again. Pita got to his feet. "I will convene a meeting of the Servants to discuss this. We will put it to the Ministers to spread the word among the People. Then we will wait to hear the Will of the People."

Before Gomer had a chance to protest, Olarine and Abernaud also stood up, so Ngaronoa rose to his feet as well. Without the head-dress the King towered over everyone. With the head-dress he nearly touched the ceiling. He and Abernaud started to talk and argue about boat racing. Olarine asked Willie Jay about the other members of the first expedition, and Gomer found himself being questioned by Pitamete in a way he didn't expect and wasn't sure how to handle. Even without Willie Jay translating for them, they understood each other well enough, with hand gestures to assist in making their meanings.

"How are you going to build wharves when we do not have the metal that our ancestors had?"

"Well, now, we'll have to talk about that."

"How are you going to build in Tāmaki-makau-rau without spoiling it?"

"Oh, we're not going to spoil it, we're going to develop it. That'll be our slogan, "The unspoiled paradise." Can't you just picture it?"

"The records show that before the Dark Days, when there were cities there, the fish and the land were dying. The people do not want the old ways back. The old ways led to death and illness. This is a better life."

"Well, now, you can't rightly say this is a better life when you ain't seen nothing else. Why, you don't even have bourbon here. You should come with us for a visit and see what y'all are missing."

"How will we know that the taw-rists will not have violent ways? We have made a peaceful society."

"Now all this talk about a pacifist society. Old ladies have dreamed about that since before time, but you all can't change human nature."

"We did not change human nature; we worked to understand human nature so that we could learn other ways to cope with daily life. Our ancestors had to change everything about their lives and their society to survive. It wasn't easy, our People had a proud warrior tradition. The training starts in the cradle. In a violent society children learn from the cradle that violence is successful. In our society children learn from the cradle that violence is not successful. By that means we've had two hundred and sixty years without the horrors of the past."

"That's all very well in theory, but it don't work in the real world."

"Our world is real to us. I do not think the People will want to risk going back to the way it was. If your world can't exist without aggression, we are better left alone."

*   *   *

Willie Jay and Chuck could see that P. Gomer Jordan was not a happy man. He was not finding it at all easy to recover from his upset stomach with the motion of the ship on the open ocean. He insisted that he had to cut the visit short because of a touch of food poisoning from the pigswill the islanders had served him, even though nearly everyone on board had also fallen ill.

Belatedly, Willie Jay remembered that people had been sick on Sam's trip, too, but Chuck thought it wasn't in their best interests to mention that at this late date. They were nowhere near as queasy themselves as they had been the first time. Perhaps they were more used to the food, or the water, or whatever it was. Willie Jay had vague memories of Doc Hosannah saying something about bugs, but Chuck decided it was better for their well being to say nothing.

There was no other word for it, Gomer was ranting. "I knowed I shoulda taken Chuck with me every time I went on land, Rimmon, instead of leaving him here to find out what he could when I went to see that Servant woman. You screwed up the introduction for me, and its first impressions that matter the most! Once a sales relationship is tarnished, it's tarnished. The least you could have done is warned me how bone headed stupid and ignorant them islanders is."

Chuck stayed very quiet and still, so as not to attract Gomer's attention. Willie Jay couldn't get a word in edgeways, "But . . ."

Gomer carried right on as if Willie Jay hadn't said anything. "Chuck here couldn't do nothing to sort things out after the balls up you made of it, Rimmon. What have you got to say for yourself?"

Willie Jay had no idea how to defend himself. "W – w - well, now, G - gomer . . ."

"You've been here before, you knew they live like savages, it was your job to tell me!"

"Well, I wouldn't rightly call them . . ."

"What do you think I brought you for? Because if you think it was just to lay in the sun you need setting straight about that! You was supposed to help me with them! Tell me what makes them tick, for God's sake, so that I could get them to understand."

"Well, you see . . ."

"No, I don't see, and that's the truth. What I can see is you got a free trip back there on my dime and did nothing to earn it. You didn't even tell me which one of them savages was the one in charge. Coming in like that, all dressed in feathers and grass skirts with spears, for God's sake! Spears! And tattoos. On their faces, for God's sake! Both of them, their King and their leader. No wonder this country's gone to the dogs. I never saw anything so pagan in all my life! Abraham Mahlon Wright couldn't have done nothing with godless heathens like that! You should oughta told me how bad it is!"

"We didn't know . . ."

"What do you take me for? I know you do know! Pulling your hat off and acting all humble in front of godless pagans! Don't you got no pride? When that Balaam guy wouldn't come, I was told you were the one who took over for Balaam."

Stung, Willie Jay felt his cheeks getting hot. "Johnny Balaam didn't find out how their system worked. We found out <u>this </u>time that they call their rulers 'Public Servants.' Johnny thought the Servants were the King's servants, just like the rest of us did."

Gomer sneered. "The 'King's servants.' What sort of a King is that? Prancing around wearing skirts and feathers like a show girl, got no say in nothing, can't decide for his own self. Can you imagine what his palace must be like? Probably got to ask the 'People's' permission to take a leak!"

"When we left last time, we sailed right down to the second main island and some of the smaller ones before we left. We didn't see no sign of nothing like a palace or a capitol building, or even any cities. Most of the coastline had hardly any sign of people at all. Just trees and grass and sand."

"All that undeveloped land, and these idiots vote to leave it that way. It's a crime. They don't know what's good for them. They got no decent leadership, no decent clothes, no decent food, not even bourbon. They go around barefoot. None of them even know what a cigar is. There's a fortune to be made here, and they're too stupid to see it when it's right under their noses. I surely do wish Wright was still alive to bring them back to right thinking so's they could understand what's good for them."

"I think they understood, they just decided they didn't want it."

Gomer exploded again. "Boy, when they said you weren't too bright, they didn't know the half of it!"

"No one said that!"

"Oh, yes, he did, and he was so right! Stupid I said they are, and stupid I meant. Do you know what that First Servant of theirs, the other one prancing around in skirts and feathers, said when I told him we'd build roads for them? Tell him, Chuck."

Chuck quoted, "It took us a hundred years to dig up all of the roads. The People might not agree to spoiling the land like that again."

Gomer spread his hands. "They spend a hundred years digging up their roads! How stupid is that!"

"They get everywhere on that train thing of theirs, the Flying Fish."

"The first good wind will blow that thing over. They just don't know nothing about engineering. And it's all shiny and pretty like everything else in this sissy place. That's what comes of letting women be in charge! 'Fish' for God's sake! When they said, "We'll catch the Fish there," I thought they were going fishing or some other damned thing. And it looks like a fish, too, a fish lying on its side, flat on the front and the back and rounded over in the middle, with all them little pretty shiny bits on it like fish scales. That's not a train!"

"It gets them around, and when they hook more than one carriage together, that's like a train . . ."

"Oh, give me a break! It don't even shake the ground. A girly little shiny glass toy humming along, "I just love being up with the birds in the tree-tops," "Look at the view from up here." It's pathetic. They're pathetic. I'm going to tell my uncle, Caleb Junior, that we got to help these here people. As soon as he's done putting down that rebellion in the west, them islanders got to have some government advisors to make a proper democratic government and get rid of that King, some proper schools, Wright missionaries to bring them back to God and put an end to people walking around half naked. They don't even get married proper. Did you hear that old crow? She's been living in sin with that partner of hers for thirty-six years! And that's who they elected to head up their government?"

"Well, now, Gomer, it seems like they do get married, they just call it partnered. It's like they got a different word for everything."

Gomer stuck out his chin belligerently. "I'm telling you they need religion! That's what comes of going pagan, they lay around like bums on the beach all day waiting for hand-outs."

"And I'm telling you they got no beggars on the streets like there is back home! They are all working, they just do things different from us."

"You don't tell me nothing! If you'd told me what you was paid to tell me, I'd have a big fat contract in my hand now! I got a good mind not to pay you no more."

"I have a contract! I'll sue!"

"You forget who my uncle is, boy. I ain't paying for what I didn't get."

Kiri

Kiritoe took a breath and looked around the lab for a moment to break the tension building up inside. The adjustments he and Fedrack were making were so precise they were like surgery, and Kiritoe's hands were cramping from making attempts to have fine control over his fingers. His great big, sausage-like fingers were not intended for delicate work like this, but he couldn't complain, it was all his idea.

The lab they were working in was semi-underground, the windows up near the ceiling, letting in a muted greenish light because of the ferns growing over them. Even the lighting inside the lab didn't completely overcome the faintly greenish tinge this gave to the room because the sterile white walls reflected the green. All of the surfaces of the lab were slick for easy cleaning, all silicates of one kind or another: glass, fibreglass, and various silicate plastics.

Fedrack finished recording the data from the last experiment, made a minute adjustment, and said to Kiritoe, "Ready?"

Kiritoe nodded, rolled his shoulders in an effort to relax them, and poised himself for Fedrack's signal, his fingers on the dial as delicately as he could manage.

"Kiri! Brain! You'll never guess what's happened!" Tui ran full tilt into the lab.

"Oh, for goodness sake, Tui, you know these experiments are sensitive!" Brain was quite irate.

"Sorry, but . . ."

"You're not making it any better by keeping on talking! We're testing sound waves, you know."

"Just listen! They're back!"

"What?"

"The visitors, the strangers, the men from the Gethsemane Republic."

"What!" In his surprise, Kiritoe didn't notice his fingers twitch on the controls. None of them heard the new sound waves thus generated, but they felt the effects as, in a single stunning moment, all their sphincter muscles released at the same time. In the shock, horror, and humiliation of messing himself, wetting himself, and throwing up all at the same time, Kiri didn't realise what was causing it until a similarly afflicted Brain hit the kill switch.

They stood, stunned for a moment, their minds refusing to accept that they'd just all filled their pants, and lost their lunches, without any warning or any control over themselves.

"Oh, man, what happened?" Tui was weeping, standing still, her arms limp at her sides, too mortified to move.

"Sound," gasped Fedrack. "It's got to be the sound waves. What an interesting result."

"What were you fellows <u>doing</u>?!" Tui's voice rose to a piercing shriek.

Kiritoe spoke in his deep, calm voice, wiping vomit off his chin. "Experimenting with sound waves. We want to be able to communicate with whales."

"Like <u>this</u>?"

"No, no, we didn't know anything like this was possible, eh? We wanted to find a way to make those low sounds they make that travel through the water for miles."

Tui was starting to shiver. She was going into shock. Kiritoe came out of his daze at the sight of that.

"Brain, we have to clean up in here. We have to get out of these things and get some tea into Tui."

Born devoid of a sense of shame or disgust, Fedrack was recording the data.

"Leave that," Kiritoe shouted at him.

"What? We must record this data, we can't . . ."

"Py korry, Fedrack, if you don't get some help . . ."

Tui screamed. "Don't you go out there!!"

Fedrack turned to look at them both, bewildered.

"Don't you bring anyone in here! Don't you dare let anyone see me like this!"

Despite the mess and smell, Kiritoe took her in his arms. "It's okay, Tui. All we need is to get cleaned up and calmed down, and everything will be all right."

"As long as no one ever knows what happened."

Brain took a step back towards them. "It was an accident with an interesting result. As scientists, we have to . . ."

"Just go and get something to clean us up. And get something for us to wear." Kiritoe was stern. He couldn't do it himself because that would mean leaving Tui alone with the oblivious Fedrack.

Tui was nearly hysterical. "Fedrack Rianploot, if anyone ever finds out about this, I'll never forgive you, never!!"

"It's all right, Tui. We aren't going to tell anyone. Brain, there are some lab coats just on the other side of the door. Bring them to us, would you?"

"Not tell _anyone_? But this is . . ."

"BRING THE LAB COATS!"

"All right, all right, you don't have to yell." Fedrack slipped around the door and reappeared with three lab coats. They stripped, dropping their noisome clothes where they were, then padded off to the facilities to clean up as best they could. Although they were all used to using one facility, Tui couldn't bear to have the men see her like that, so they let her use the showers, while they cleaned themselves as best they could, using the sinks in the toilets.

Fedrack complained to Kiritoe, "We should have protected the data before we left the lab. What if the cleaners go in there and touch something? You're not really going to keep this a secret, are you? You can't do that!"

"We'll talk about it later, Brain. Right now, Tui is too close to going into shock. We have to take care of her."

"But, but, but. . . ."

"Brain, for once, just pretend you're part of the human race and actually care about other people."

"What do you mean by that? I don't know what's got into you lately. Ever since you took that year off school to go fishing with your Dad there's been no talking to you. You just don't care about the science anymore."

"I'm a history major, remember?" Clad only in a lab coat, ignoring Fedrack's protests, Kiritoe walked out of the toilets and tapped on the shower room door. "Tui, are you alright?"

A sniffling voice answered him. "No."

"Do you need for me to come in?"

"No!"

"I'll wait here."

"Thank you."

Fedrack came out of the toilets. "We have to protect that data, Kiri..."

Kiritoe turned on him fiercely, took him by the arm and hissed in his ear, "Shut up about it. Just shut up about the rotten data." Dragging Fedrack by one arm back to the lab door, he continued to whisper fiercely, "You just get started cleaning up in there. We'll be there to help you as soon as I make sure Tui's okay. You got that? Not one more word. Get the clothes picked up and wrapped in something, then mop the floor and don't forget the footprints."

In the five years since they had started University together, Kiritoe's group had gone in several different ways. Kiritoe had worked hard and passed his bachelor's degree at the end of his second year. He had not gone directly into teaching but had taken a year off to spend time with his father on the fishing boat, to work that burr out of his system. He and his father became close, but it was very clear to them both before the year was out that Kiritoe was no fisherman. His scrawny musician brother had more aptitude for the life than Kiri had.

He found it easier to cry for his mother on the fishing boat when everyone's faces were wet with spray. At first resentful of the young woman his father was spending time with, Kiritoe came to see Hatoe's loneliness, and in the end was able to give his blessing on his father's new relationship.

The brothers couldn't have been more different. The older one, Anatoe, could play any musical instrument invented by man, and sang in a bell-like tenor. He was a slender man, with pale skin, stringy brown hair, and hawk nose, delicate lips, and hunched shoulders, who scuffed his feet when he walked. The younger brother, Kiritoe was tall and broad and brown with a wild mop of curly black hair, a broad flat nose, full lips, a rumbling bass voice, and a strong stride. He'd never been much good at playing instruments, being too uncoordinated for strings and most wind instruments, and too impatient to conquer the complexities of keyboards. The only thing he played well was drums, which he pounded with more gusto than finesse. But on the boat, he found himself composing, to his own surprise as much as anyone else's. Haunting, elusive songs of loss and loneliness that Anatoe played in the evenings at home on his guitar with such depth of feeling that Kiritoe couldn't believe he'd written them himself.

On his return to the University, Kiritoe majored in music composition, earning his bachelor's degree in two years while Anatoe became famous for singing and playing Kiritoe's compositions, and Hatoe inducted their cousin, his nephew, Benatoe, into the intricacies of owning the fishing boat.

Kiritoe thought he would be more at ease with himself now that he knew there was no chance he would ever make a fisherman, and now that he knew his father was not disappointed in him for taking another path, but, in fact, he still felt restless. The sea still pulled at him. He answered that call by combining his love of music with his love of the sea and started experimenting with whale communications.

After he had his degree in music, he didn't know what to do with it. He didn't want to teach music, or study it any further, so he started to work on his master's in history, spending every spare moment studying underwater sound waves.

To help him he sought out his friend Fedrack Rianploot, recently returned to the University after spending some time in behaviour modification.

Fedrack had started out well, there was no denying he was brilliant, but he'd been distracted by drink and other mood-altering substances to the point where his marks slipped, and he failed his second semester. A course in behaviour modification in the evenings after school had him clean and sober, though a semester behind his friends. When his behaviour became erratic and his marks slipped again, he was sent off to live in a behaviour modification village, a mod vil, where it took him half a year to come to terms with his inability to connect with others, to get to the root of his need to drown his feelings in beer, and to return to the school able to stay clean and sober. By that time, he was a year behind his classmates, and the difficulty he had settling in with a younger group sent him back into the bottle and back to the mod vil, this time for a year.

At the end of five years Fedrack had his Bachelor of Mathematics. The mathematical components of Kiritoe's experiments fascinated him. His difficulty lay in his tendency to obsess over the project, and to leave no time in his life for other things, like socialising. Even though he'd learned that if he didn't cultivate companionship the loneliness would drive him back into the bottle, he still had trouble tearing himself away from his numbers to take notice of people.

Tui had stayed at the University the entire five years. She didn't get her bachelor's degree quite as quickly as Kiritoe, but by the end of five years she had both her bachelor's and her master's and was working on a thesis for her doctorate while working as an associate teaching language courses. She had brown eyes, bright red hair, and an infectious laugh. She didn't have much time for Fedrack, but she adored Kiritoe and put up with the one to be able to spend time with the other. She loved to dance, and to sing, and Kiritoe's bass voice melted her at the knees. She had thought that if she was the one to give Kiritoe the news that the strangers were back, that he would have come rushing upstairs to find out what was going on. They might even have sat next to each other, or perhaps he would forever after have remembered that she was the one who told him the news.

What he did was see her back to her residence, both clad only in lab coats, saw her in, told her roommates she'd had a bad fright, promised to have her clothes cleaned for her, and then left, saying he had to get himself dressed now that he knew she was all right.

As soon as they'd taken care of everything else, including keeping the data, and getting dressed, Kiritoe and Fedrack set out on the Flying Fish in search of Calline Digan, now in residence at the University Hospital. They sat in the doctor's lounge, talking about the return of the strangers to the doctors who came and went, waiting for Calline to get off duty so that they could talk to her about the unexpected result of the sound waves.

"Have you heard the news?" Kiritoe blurted out when Calline finally came through the door. It was a stupid thing to say, he knew, but he was always tongue tied around her.

"Nah, yeah, of course, it's all anyone's talking about. Look, you two, I'm really tired, eh?" She was rubbing her neck absentmindedly with one hand, trying to toe her shoes off as she stood.

"Shall I rub your neck?" Kiritoe asked, red faced.

Fedrack leaped into action. Adam's apple bobbing alarmingly, hands jerking, eyes on the floor, he offered, "I could rub your feet. I can give a good foot massage. I learned in the mod vil. Your feet are sore. Aren't they? Don't you have sore feet? You could sit down. Here. Or here. This one, sit in this chair. You can take your shoes off. Or I can. I can take your shoes off. And your stockings. No, no. You can. Are they socks? I can do it with your socks on if you like. Or you can take them off. If you like."

With Fedrack massaging her feet through her socks, and Kiritoe's big hands soothing the tightness out of her neck and shoulders through her lab coat, Calline relaxed with her eyes closed and a huge sigh of relief.

"Hey! How do you rate this?" one of the other doctors asked, walking into the room.

Fedrack jumped back as if Calline's feet had become red hot, but Kiritoe brought his hands to rest on her shoulders, just the pads of his thumbs gently stroking the back of her neck under her fair hair out of everyone's sight. "Brain and I were doing experiments with sound waves, and we had an interesting physiological result that we wanted to discuss with Dr. Digan."

The student doctor eyed the three of them sceptically. "Right," she said. "And I can breathe underwater, and all."

Fedrack went beet red and stammered.

Kiritoe leered at the student doctor and said, "That could be a good thing. We could use you in our experiments if you can breathe underwater."

Calline grinned. "They're just friends of mine. We started first year together. They were in my Language class." She got to her feet.

Giggling, the three of them left the doctor's lounge and walked to the train, Fedrack carrying Calline's shoes. She took them from him and balanced herself with one hand on the wall to slip them on before they went outside. "What's this experiment?"

Before Fedrack could expound, Kiritoe cut him off with a wave of his hand, saying, "As soon as we're somewhere where we won't be overheard. We promised someone not to let word get around."

"Now I'm intrigued," Calline smiled. "And I'm nowhere near as tired as I was, but I am starving."

"My place, then," said Kiritoe with great satisfaction. "I can fix us all a feed." He knew there was no chance Calline could have considered going with him to his flat if he'd been by himself, so he was grateful that Fedrack was there, even while he resented his presence.

The medical school and University Hospital were in the beautiful park-like Turitea campus, with its huge trees and attractive gardens, but Kiri's rented flat was near the lagoon on the city side of the Manawatu River, because most of his studies and teaching was done in the Hokowhitu campus.

On the Flying Fish from one campus to the other, Fedrack tried to talk about the experiment, but Kiri reminded him that they'd promised not to mention it in public and changed the subject. "It looks like the strangers are going to be a part of our lives from now on."

Calline lost her usual cool manner. Her eyes gleamed with intensity. "The virus that causes the contact reaction is very interesting. I think it comes from the common cold mutating in isolation."

Fedrack said, "Good for you!" in tones of extravagant admiration.

Kiri looked into Calline's eyes to see how she took Fedrack's undying adoration. He'd always liked Calline because of her intellect and integrity, but he'd never been attracted to her because he'd thought she was cold. A highly emotional person himself, he couldn't relate to people who had no passion. What caught his attention was the spark in her eyes. He noticed for the first time that they were a beautiful grey blue, with clear whites and startlingly black pupils, and a fire behind them that he hadn't realised was there. It dawned on him that she was passionate in her own way. She was as zealous about this as anyone was about anything. "What does that mean for us?" he asked.

Calline leaned forward, eagerly. Kiri was struck by how attractive she was. He wondered how he could have missed that classic bone structure. He listened to the intensity of the way she said, "Both times the GR have come here people have come down with virus-like symptoms. Whatever it was, we've contained it by isolation techniques, but we still don't know what it was. It wasn't any virus that we'd seen before, and I've heard the GR got sick, too, so I think common cold and flu viruses have mutated on both sides of the ocean. That would mean they have no resistance to ours and we have no resistance to theirs."

Feeling overwhelmed by her beauty and intelligence, Kiri asked, more to keep her talking than from any real grasp of the implications, "What should we do?"

"I want to get a research grant to find out if there's a way we can inoculate ourselves so that we don't end up with an epidemic."

"An epidemic?" Kiri suddenly realized what Calline had been saying. "How bad could it get?"

"Flu epidemics can kill. The worst thing about them is they don't only kill frail people, like the very old, or the very young, or those who are already sick, but they kill people in the prime of their life."

Kiri felt a creeping horror. "You don't mean this GR bug could kill me, do you?"

"Not if I have anything to say about it," Calline declared in her soft voice.

Kiri could see now what he'd missed before: despite her demure manner and tiny voice, this woman was implacable. He remembered that when the GR had arrived the first time, that Calline had started studying for her citizenship while the rest of their group was still thinking about it, even though she was so shy that she dreaded going to meetings without her parents. She fascinated him. The mixture of hardness and softness intrigued him. "You're going to work on this all on your own? Why aren't the authorities taking care of it?"

"Most people haven't faced what it means that they've come back."

They shook Fedrack's shoulder to wake him up. "Next station, Sunshine," Kiri sang out, getting to his feet. "Just the same," he said to Calline, "You'd think the School of Medicine would bust a gut to find some kind of preventative medication." As the Flying Fish slowed down, he pushed Fedrack's leg with his toe. "Rattle your dags, old son. We're here."

Moving towards the carriage door, she explained, "Not everyone puts things together. People in the School of Medicine know medicine. They don't know a lot about things outside of that, like whether or not the GR will be a permanent part of our lives."

Glancing over his shoulder to make sure Fedrack was following, Kiri argued, "It's obvious. One bunch found us and another lot came to sell us something five years later. From now on whenever one of them has a bright idea about something they can get from us or sell to us they'll chug on over in those smelly ships of theirs. Even if they only come once or twice more, we still have to have some kind of protection from a potentially deadly epidemic."

Running lightly ahead of him down the stairs from the platform, Calline pointed out, "But not everyone thinks they'll be back again after this. They didn't get anything they wanted from us."

Kiri snorted. "Only a doze would think that. You can't put the egg back together once it's cracked. This egg is broken wide open. Our isolation is gone. They've found us and they've come back."

Fedrack disagreed. "The numbers don't add up. It's a long way to go. Expensive. If they don't make enough money to pay for it, they won't do it again."

Kiri waited for him at the bottom of the stairs, disputing that. "Not every part of life revolves around numbers. They could come back to learn something, or for a holiday, or any one of a thousand other reasons that don't have to do with numbers adding up."

Fedrack waved him off and changed the subject, turning to Calline and telling her the story of the strange side-effect they'd had from their attempts to create the very low sounds the sperm whales made.

Kiri chipped in to clarify points when Calline looked too confused. Mostly, he let Fedrack tell the story while he let them into his flat and whipped up something for them to eat.

Calline was fascinated by their story and agreed to take notes on her day off when they re-created the waves that had caused the phenomenon. They planned with some hilarity how to prepare to cope with the consequences if repeating the exact sound waves had the same effect on them as it had by accident, but ultimately they agreed that even if it did, it was just an interesting anomaly that had no bearing on Kiritoe's experiment, and records of it wouldn't be included in the findings on communication with whales.

All Kiritoe really got out of the evening was successfully finding an excuse to spend time with Calline. All he had to do now was find a way to do that without Fedrack. It surprised him to realise that he'd been so caught up in the events of the evening that he'd hardly given another thought to the return of the strangers and the threat that came with them.

CHAPTER TWENTY-TWO

Sam

Sam and Johnny tried to calm Willie Jay down, while Chuck grinned a bit at how worked up Willie Jay was.

Relieved beyond words that Willie Jay and Chuck had come home safely from their second trip to the islands, Sam spoke to Willie Jay like a grandfather, "Now, just you settle yourself down there, a bit, Willie Jay. You're running hotter'n a cracked radiator."

Willie Jay jumped up from his chair in Sam's front room. "*Agarrar la onda,* Sam, he's just plain lying!"

Sam shook his white head, "Well, now, it don't pay to say things like that too loud. *Aguas.* You could get yourself sued that way."

"You know I'm right!"

"All I know for sure is them Islanders was some real strange folks. I never saw the things Vince is talking about, but that don't prove they ain't there."

Johnny Balaam was sipping his mint julep quietly. Willie Jay turned to him, "Johnny, you know he's lying."

Johnny shook his head.

Chuck commented, "I know he makes a lot more money from it than any of us."

Willie Jay started to pace up and down the room, out on to the porch of the farmhouse and back again. "It ain't right. It just ain't right.

We went over there to find out if anyone was alive, and to tell the folks here what'd happened to them. Vince is making them look like savages running naked in the jungle and sleeping with their sisters, and you know that ain't how it is there."

Chuck winked at Sam when Willie Jay was out of the room in his pacing, and said to Willie Jay when he came back, "Why make such a big deal out of it? You know no one's ever going to know if Vince is telling the truth or not. He's making a million with his comic books. Everybody loves it. Sounds like you're just jealous that he's the only one of us who really got rich out of this deal."

Willie Jay's voice went up almost to a squeak. "That's not true! Johnny, you know it! Vince is selling a pack of lies, and we have to tell everyone the truth! Otherwise, someone like that Jordan's going to go over there and screw the islanders, and they don't deserve that."

Chuck blew a raspberry. "Oh, give me a break, Willie Jay! No one believes P. Gomer Jordan! You were there with him, you know he's as useless as tits on a boar hog."

Sam shook his head again and shifted his feet on the footrest of his comfortable chair. "Boars got tusks, Chuck. Don't count Gomer Jordan out too fast. He might not have the common-sense God gave a skeeter, and the God's honest truth he tells today might be the opposite of the God's honest truth he told yesterday and different again from what he'll say tomorrow, but he's oil money, and oil money talks." He frowned at Willie Jay. "Sit down, boy, you're making me tired. Gomer ever pay you?"

"Not one thin dime, Sam, and he paid Chuck in full."

"How'd you do in suing him for it?"

"I can't afford a lawyer. Every time I found one who would do it for a cut, soon as they seen who it was I wanted to sue they backed out and billed me for the time they spent to find out. One guy told me I could do it myself, but when I talked about that to the others when they turned me down, so many of them told me what could happen to me if I did, what with counter suits and all, I just plum gave up. Paying lawyers to tell me they couldn't help me pretty near bankrupted me. My Daddy wouldn't help me no more, he told me to get out while the getting was good, afore Gomer got wind of what I was fixing to do and sued me or got me arrested."

Chuck grinned, a look of comprehension in his eyes. "That's what this is all about! Gomer ripped you off, and you're madder than a hornet with his nest knocked down! Well, you should've known better than to go along with him."

"You went," Willie Jay retorted. "And you got paid."

Johnny put in, "I wouldn't go. No, Sir, no how."

"That's got nothing to do with it! Vince is lying, and Gomer's lower than a road-kill snake!"

"Well, Willie Jay, take my advice and leave it alone."

Sam nodded in agreement. "I knows you don't like it, son, and you ain't no quitter, but if you try to go around and say that, you're just pissing into the wind. It'll get all over you and make no never mind to them. Like as not it'll give Vince free publicity and help him make more money out of the deal, and for sure it'll give Gomer a way to finish you off. You don't want the sheriff to find some violation in your Daddy's gun shop, do you, son? Now you know the sheriff where your Daddy has his gun shop is a cousin of Gomer's or knows him real well. That's the way these things work."

Willie Jay jumped up from his chair again and stormed out of the room. Sam shook his head, and Chuck grinned. They heard the screen door slam behind him. Johnny sipped his mint julep and murmured to Sam, "He never was cooking on all burners, that boy."

Sam shrugged. He sympathised with Willie Jay. "He's an idealist. That's a hard way to live. After a bit no one will listen to you. Even his Daddy don't listen to him no more."

Chuck snorted, "His Daddy ain't listened to him none since he shot him hunting. Nothing ruins your credibility like a bullet in the ass."

Sam nodded, remembering the story and trying not to laugh. "There is that. And the little matter of the time the con man got all the money in the till from him, and he had more in the till at the time than he should have."

Johnny nodded. "His Daddy never did want him in the gun shop, he said Willie Jay's a walking accident looking for a place to happen, and you don't want someone like that running loose in a gun shop, but he had to give the boy a job when he couldn't keep a job no place else for more than a few weeks and the army wouldn't have him."

Sam nodded. "I'd guess his Momma didn't want him in the army anyway after they lost their oldest boy in the Sierra Massacree. Reckon the only reason that boy's alive is that his big feet were too flat for the army. No wonder he trips over his own feet all the time if they're too big and too flat for the army, when all the army wants is that you look like you're breathing."

Chuck snickered, walking across the room of the house Sam had acquired from the old man who'd hired him after he got out of prison, Hosea. Pouring himself a drink, Chuck commented, "There's one in every family. I ever tell you about my cousin Lemuel?"

Sam shrugged, not really wanting to hear about Chuck's cousin. "Willie Jay's a nice boy but the sky ain't blue in his world, its rose coloured. I knows Vince is inventing these stories, but so does everyone who thinks about what a little time he was there and what big stories he's got to tell. It's just comics. Once something like that gets going, you're putting yourself under falling rocks if you try to stand in the way of it. It's the flavour of the month. It'll wear out when the next thing comes along. Then people will start to question it, then you can stand up and say, "I was there, and this is a load of horse hockey." As for Gomer — my take on that is he's found a way to make money over there and he's trying to drum up political support for it so he gets to spend public funds to go over there. That ain't right, but you can't do nothing about that, neither."

Chuck shrugged, "Can't see what he's going to make money off of in that place. There ain't nothing there worth having. I got more time to do the kind of exploring we wanted to do. You know what the islanders do with their city blocks? They build them in circles instead of squares."

"That don't make no sense," Sam objected. "They wouldn't fit together like that. What about their roads? How would that work?"

"Even when we was there before, we saw they don't got no roads. They got paths for walking and riding bikes, and they ride in that Flying Fish."

Johnny nodded, sadly. "They can't do no better on account they got no morals."

Chuck frowned. "I wouldn't say that. I saw more morals from the islanders than I did from the GR. What I don't get is how the Faithfuls figure to make any money off those guys. I never saw no sign of riches of any kind."

"If we saw things the way guys like the Faithfuls do, we'd be millionaires too. Something got Gomer's attention enough that he got there only five years after we did. It took me my whole life to get there, and that was building on a lifetime of work from the guy ahead of me, and I've been in debt ever since. My savings are gone, my wife's left me, and I lost my kids and my home. If I get sick in my old age I don't got no way to pay a doctor. But Gomer saw something in what we found and high tailed it over there. Got a ship together and money to run it in only five years. Either him or someone in his family sent him, and they've kept quiet about it so if it don't pan out he takes the fall. The Faithfuls control one fifth of all the oil on the continent, and they're related to most of the other oilionaires. They can do anything they want, and you and me can't do squat about it."

Willie Jay came racing back in. "Sam, I know what Gomer's up to. He wants to build resorts there."

"That'll never get off the ground. It's a long way to go for a vacation. There ain't enough money in it to make back the investment."

"You're not looking at the whole picture, Sam," Johnny said slowly, twirling the sprig of mint around in the top of his glass, with his bottom lip folded over his top lip.

"What're you talking about, boy? You just thought of something?"

"Gomer's slipperier than a greased pig. He'll make money on that coming and going."

"I don't see how. He's got to get builders and materials there to build the hotels and the wharves, ships to take that stuff there, and to take passengers there, get passengers on his ships, and get them there and back. It's not like a cruise down the coast. Look how long it took us to get there and back. That'll cost more than people will pay for a vacation and take too long."

Chuck leaned his elbows on the table. "Ah, but that's the point, you see. It's getting more and more dangerous to take vacations along the coast here, what with every tin-pot nut group taking pot shots at the rich. Ain't nobody going to do no shooting over there, and I'm betting his plans include getting us to pay for it in taxes at this end, and the islanders to pay for it at that end, right, Willie Jay?"

Sam snorted. "More fool him. How're they going to pay for it? They got no money."

Willie Jay looked stricken. "He told them he would build roads for them, and it wouldn't take their country long to pay it off."

It was Johnny's turn to snort. "No, not long. Only a lifetime or two. That's what he's fixing to do right enough. He'll end up owning all those islands, and all those naïve people will be working for the Faithfuls all the rest of their days."

Chuck added, "Don't you see, Sam? It's a new place to go, somewhere none of them oil-rich bastards that can afford cruises have ever been before, and ain't nobody going to shoot at them, neither. They'll pay top dollar for that, and it don't hurt none that they've heard Vince's stories about natives running through the jungles naked, neither. Now how much do you bet his evangelist cousin gets in on this and gets the faithful to pony up millions of bucks for God to send missionaries over there? All in the name of A. Mahlon Wright. He's going to rake it in, no doubt about it."

"That's the riches he sees," Sam was disgusted by what he saw in his mind's eye. "He sees a South Pacific paradise as the private playground of P. Gomer Jordan. There's not a cotton-picking thing anyone can do about it."

"Sam!" Willie Jay was aghast. "We led him there! We have to do something to stop him!"

"Like what? We can't stand up against the money and connections of the Faithfuls. If I try to say anything, I'll end up back in the joint. All I've got to make my way is my reputation for the straight scoop. As it is the truth is getting harder to tell thanks to Vince's fictions."

Willie Jay continued spluttering loudly that they had to do something.

Leaning in close to make sure he was heard under the noise Willie Jay was making, Johnny said to Sam, "It's a shame we can't let people know what the Faithfuls are up to this time. They've about had their fill of P. Gomer and his hog-in-the-trough ways."

Sam looked at Johnny, thoughtfully. "Willie Jay, hush up, boy, and let me think. Go out to the kitchen and get Maria to rustle us up some grub. You know, Johnny boy, I'd be mighty happy if I had a hand in bringing the Faithfuls down, and you didn't hear that here."

Chuck grinned. "Hear what?"

"Just you remember that; you didn't hear nothing here. Now, we can't just go and say this, we need to put it in the underground press, and we need to find out how to get hold of the underground press to get it in."

"You know, I heard tell they used to have a radio with pictures before the Liberty Wars. How come we ain't got that back? It would help us out here."

Sam shook his head. "We only get back what the oilionaires want to pay for. They can't see any profit in funding it, it don't happen. Personally, I think what they've got against moving pictures in everyone's homes is that we'll be able to see what's really going on. We know what's going on ain't what they're telling us, but we cain't see what it is, so we don't know what we're up against. But if we c'n get someone on the ship with Jordan when he goes back, we can get pictures of what's really going on there and let the folks at home know they're being had; again. It'll do two things. It'll make up to the islanders for putting the vultures on them, and it'll prove one of the things we've all suspected about the Faithfuls and their greedy friends and family."

Johnny protested, "Now hold on there, Sam. I ain't going back there. You guys got a bit sick, but I was real poorly. That ship doctor we had said I had a strong allergic reaction. It could kill me to go back there."

Chuck suddenly laughed. "That would help, wouldn't it, if they all got real sick from going there?"

Sam couldn't help snickering even though he thought it was a serious subject. "You know, the biggest thing we got against getting folks to think about what the Faithfuls are doing, is that they're working on the foundation laid down by good ole A. Mahlon Wright."

Johnny stood up. "They ain't doing what he did, though, Sammy. They're twisting his work to their money-making schemes."

"That's what they're doing right enough, but they don't want no-one to see it." He had a sudden desire to make sure people saw what it was the Faithfulls were trying to hide. Willie Jay was the best one to get it right under their noses. "Where is that boy? Willie Jay!" He swung his legs off the footrest and stood up, shakily. He put his hand on the small of his back and groaned. Lately he hurt every time he moved. Maria had brought him some herbs that were supposed to help, but they might as well be magic beans for all the good they did.

Willie Jay ran back into the room. "I was just coming, Sam. I told Maria you're hungry."

"Now listen to me, boy. I can't go back to the islands, I'm too old. But you can. Question is, can you keep you mouth shut?"

They all stared at him. Chuck asked, "What's this all about, Sam?"

"Come out to the truck. We don't want no one over-hearing us, and remember, you never heard nothing here."

Willie Jay looked from Johnny's face to Sam's, then Chuck's, and back again, a slow smile spreading over his honest, round, tanned face. He fell into step with the others. "I can do that, Sam, trust me."

Sam lowered his voice. "We'll see, boy." They crammed into the old truck. Sam drove it slowly around the side of the hay-barn, out of sight of the house. When old Hosea had taken him in, still suffering from a bad case of the joint-jitters, Sam was supposed to work for the old guy as a hired hand because his sons had been taken in a purification raid and no one else dared to work for him in case that made them look like sympathisers. In a short time, the two old men had become close friends. They worked together rather than one working for the other. Hosea gave Sam all the information and contacts he had to do with subversive activities. As Sam gathered the explorers around him, Hosea stayed out of the way. Anything that went against the GR was a good thing in his eyes, but he wouldn't join in so that he didn't know.

Sam didn't know whether Maria was a relative or friend of Hosea's or hired. She cooked and cleaned, taking care of them, their clothes, the house, chickens, and gardens. They couldn't have made it without her.

When he was sure no one could over-hear them, he said to Willie Jay, "Now, you took some mighty fine pictures of our trip, huh? And you took photos when you went hunting, huh?"

"Yeah, Daddy won't let me take my camera with me no more. He says it distracts me."

"You shot him in the ass, Willie Jay. It makes a man a might tense to have his son shoot him that close to where it counts most. But I don't want you to take cameras deer hunting, I want you to take cameras truth hunting. Is Jordan fixing to go back?"

"Reckon so."

"Then you're fixing to go with him."

"Sam! Jordan never paid me last time!"

"I know, and like as not he's going to get out of paying you this time, too. But if this works, it'll be one more step towards the good folk of the Gethsemane Republic getting those boys out of power. Now don't try to be clever, Willie Jay, just take pictures. If they think you're smart they'll get suspicious of you, and you know what'll happen to anyone who gets in the way of their plans, but they ain't going to look at a good ole boy who just takes pictures and can help them talk to the islanders. Don't talk to no-one about us, you got it? Just tell me one thing, Willie boy, was any of them sick this time?"

"Well, yeah. Me and Chuck wasn't sick this time."

Chuck added, "The others that were with us on the first ship didn't get it again, either, but all the first timers got it just like last time, and Gomer was pitiful sick."

Sam turned the truck back to the house. "Explorers, I got us a plan. Let's go in and have some grub, but don't talk about this in the house. Maria's a good girl, but if someone pays her, she just might tell them what we said."

Ron

One of the things First Servant Pitamete Meithei and King Ngaronoa Turikora enjoyed the most in all the world was going fishing together. They took turns with whose canoe they used, each one feeling that he was in charge of the fishing expedition when his canoe was used. The two men said little to each other, aside from the friendly sniping born of years in each other's company, until they were well out of earshot from the reporters on the shore. Even then they pitched their voices low so that their conversation wouldn't carry over the water.

"Do you think we can keep on doing this now that you're King and I'm First Public Servant?"

"What do you mean?"

"The King can't take part in government, and I'm the head of the government. Doesn't it look wrong if we go off by ourselves like this?"

"We've been going fishing since we were little kids, Pita. We can take someone else with us, but when everyone's busy, or we just want to talk to each other, I don't see any reason we have to stop the habit of a lifetime."

"Propriety."

"Propriety? You? You're the least proper person I've ever met! That's why my parents didn't like me to play with you when we were kids. What's happened to you?"

"I've been elected First Public Servant. It's a big responsibility. Perception is reality, remember. I can't be seen to be doing anything questionable."

"Who are you and what have you done with my friend, Pita?"

"No, Ron, I'm serious."

"I suppose you had to grow up some time. Better late than never, so they say, but I think you're taking it a bit far. Look, going off fishing isn't a crime, just so long as I don't tell you your job or try to influence you, alright?"

"But you did influence me to wear my ceremonial piupiu," Pitamete said in a mischievous tone.

They both burst out laughing. "Did you see the look on the face of that blowhard?"

Ngaronoa chortled. "Pete, may I call you Pete?" he mocked.

"P. Gomer, just call me Gomer," Pitamete, countered. "Mr. King Ron."

"No, no, no, King Ron the Great, don't forget that part." Ngaronoa pretended to preen.

"He didn't seriously think we'd be impressed by that load of bird droppings, did he?"

"You know, nothing has helped me sort out my life as much as the training I took to be a Calmer, and my training to be a Calmer tells me he honestly did think he was impressing us."

"Not that you were a Calmer for long."

"I only went into it because you were going into it, and I had no idea what I wanted to do after school, and I might as well make use of growing so big."

Pitamete snorted. "You can't have that! I only went into it because you were going into it and I had no idea what I wanted to do after school, and I might as well make use of growing so big." They both laughed again, but more quietly this time, remembering the reporters on shore.

Ngaronoa said, "I don't know if I buy that. I had no idea what I was getting myself into. You must have been better prepared; you stayed in it."

"I had no idea what I was getting into, but once I was in it, I found it was a combination of fascination and feeling like I was doing some good. By the time those poor souls need a Calmer, they're in a real fix. Some of them are never free again, you know."

"That's what I couldn't handle. I overdosed on human misery."

"But you said it was the most helpful thing in your life."

"The most helpful thing to help me sort out my life. All those courses in human behaviour, why we do the things we do, how to get people to do the things you want them to do, how to tell the difference between what people say and what they mean, how to read people. That's what's been helpful to me. Trying to get some poor sod to calm down or you'll take him away was too stressful to me, I couldn't deal with it. Every time I took someone to a mod vil against his will I thought I'd failed. I couldn't sleep at night, remembering the begging and pleading, or crying. I'd always think how I'd feel if that was done to me."

"It's not just 'done to' people. Everything possible is done to help them. It's only the ones who are a danger to themselves or others that are put in secure mod vils. Most people can be treated at home, or by short stays in neighbourhood open mod vils."

Ron rolled his eyes. "I know. I was there. I did the job. I still couldn't stand it when I had to take someone in, and I knew they weren't going to be free again any time soon."

"That's why you quit?"

"Tarawera erupted."

"So, you ran off to pull people out of burning buildings and run around under falling red hot rocks and get yourself a third vote. You left your station to do that, you know."

"You don't know what it was like. You can't walk away from someone who's going to burn to death to calm down someone who's frightened. Life is more important than shattered nerves."

"I suppose that's true. There's nothing to calm down if the person doesn't survive."

Ngaronoa snorted. "You're so crass sometimes it isn't even funny."

"You're too sensitive sometimes. You didn't think about becoming a behaviourist?"

"Yeah, nah, I lost patience with them after Tarawera threw hot rocks and boiling mud at people. I saw things I've never been able to forget, eh? A man who had lost a leg pulling himself out of the wreckage. I saw people who burned to death or drowned because we couldn't get to them in time. After that I could never have any sympathy for people who were throwing tantrums because they couldn't get their own way. I'm surprised you didn't become a behaviourist, though."

"I failed the tests. I never told you that, did I? Not sensitive enough, they said. Too crass, you'd say, I suppose."

"Yeah, nah, I didn't know you'd failed. I didn't even know you'd sat the tests, eh? How was it you never told me?"

"Embarrassed."

"Why are you telling me now?"

"Doesn't matter any more. It was so long ago, thirty years or more. It was a good experience for me to fail like that, eh? Made me think."

"I was too sensitive, you were not sensitive enough? But you were a Calmer for a long time."

"You need to be a bit insensitive to be able to calm someone down, at the same time as being sensitive enough to be able to at least make it appear as if you're sympathising with them. They have to be able to sense that you'll have no trouble putting them out and carrying them off, or they won't listen, just as much as you have to be big enough that they know they can't get free of you if you do have to take hold of them."

"Think you could have held Gomer?"

"No doubt about it, even though it's been years and I'm really out of practice in how to subdue someone without hurting them."

Ron looked at Pete thoughtfully. "Have you noticed that when the GR uses the word, 'subdue,' they don't mean calm someone down by talking to them, or physically restraining them so that they can be given a shot, they mean killing and injuring people until the survivors are too afraid to resist?"

"I've tried to avoid thinking about it. I can't imagine how people can do that to other people."

"Now that they've been here twice, it's my guess that whether we want them back or not, they're going to keep on coming. I just hope some of those people who are capable of hurting and killing other people aren't among them."

Pitamete was silent for a while. The only sound was the water slopping against the sides of the canoe, and the fishing reels. Pitamete reeled his in and opened the thermos, pouring himself a hot tea and offering the thermos to Ngaronoa. "Do you think our behaviourists and mod vils would be able to help people who have been raised to think aggression is normal behaviour?"

Ngaronoa continued the silence for a moment. He accepted the thermos, and put it between his feet while he reeled his line in. Then he picked it up and poured himself a cup of tea, saying softly, "They don't only think it's a normal way to behave, they're proud of it. We might be able to re-train children, but by the time they're adults, living a whole life thinking like that, I don't think gentle methods would work with most of them."

"What can we do if they do come back, then?"

"Pray."

"That's the best you can do? You said the behaviourist training to be a Calmer had helped you sort things out."

"It didn't cover anything like this. Besides, you got more out of it than I did. You worked as a Calmer for years, and you met Leora there. I didn't meet Emere there; I met her after I left."

"At the boat yards? Why'd you go from being a Calmer to building boats, anyway? It's quite the switch."

"I couldn't face working with people any more after being a Calmer, and after the things I saw in the eruption. I wanted to do something completely different, and working with my hands appealed to me. I heard someone in Otaki was looking for an apprentice, and thought it looked like a good idea. Good thing I did. Emmy was a sailmaker. Why are you surprised I did something different when you went and grew fruit? And that's with the both of you in the business."

"One of us had to get out of it if we wanted to have a family. We couldn't both be on call. You've no idea what it does to your family life if you can both be called out in the middle of the night at any time. People always seem to have their emotional disasters in the wee hours of the morning. With Leora being a behaviourist, it seemed like a good idea for me to get out of it. I'd had enough. Trees don't make scenes or argue. I've found them peaceful to deal with after being a Calmer, bruised fruit and all."

"So, then, you've had more behaviourist training than I've had, plus you live with it all the time with Leora's work. You tell me what's going to happen with the GR."

"One of two things. They'll either come back or they won't."

"That's mighty helpful."

"One thing that's been bothering me: when Gomer asked us how we defended ourselves without big wharves, do you remember?"

"Yes. You said we hadn't had anyone to defend ourselves against."

"I asked whom we would need to defend ourselves against since we hadn't seen anyone in two hundred years until they arrived. He said, "That's what I mean," and it gave me the shivers."

"I think he just meant that now that we have been contacted, we can't carry on in the old way."

"Nah, yeah, I think that's what he meant. But what does that mean? If we can't keep on as we are, what do we do? We can't become like them, that's not who we are, eh?"

Ron took a long drink of his tea. "They can't expect us to be like them. That doesn't make any sense."

"Even so, it was like a ghost walked over my grave. Either Gomer was disappointed that we weren't thrilled with his idea of bringing roads and cities and animals back, and will give us up as a lost cause, or he'll be back to try again to persuade us."

"It's a very long way to travel. It isn't likely they'll keep on coming if they don't get what they want."

"Did he look to you like the kind of man who accepts 'no' graciously?"

Ron shook his head. "He seemed to take it as a challenge to go at us harder. I think the only reason he left is that he came down with contact reaction."

Pete nodded. "That's what I thought, too. That's why I think we'd better brace ourselves for that silly bugger, or another one just like him, to come back."

"And if he does come back to try to persuade us?"

"He'll either try to talk us into it, or he'll try to bully us into it."

"Great Tane, that's a horrifying thought! You were right in the first place; we shouldn't have come out fishing by ourselves."

CHAPTER TWENTY-FOUR

Dinah Rose

$\mathcal{D}$emas Luke Flynt 4th, known as Tuffy, and his wife, Dinah Rose, were having breakfast with their three children when the courier arrived with the diplomatic pouch.

"I better see what this is," Tuffy said, giving Dinah Rose a brief peck on the forehead, ruffling Effie's hair and telling the boys to be good soldiers.

Dinah Rose carried on supervising breakfast. It made no difference to her whether Tuffy was there or not. He was away so much that she was used to taking care of the children on her own. Her eldest son Faithful Lycus was from her first marriage to the soldier, Jaakobah Lycus. It had been a mistake that Daddy had rescued her from. No one was supposed to divorce, but Daddy had managed to get a special dispensation for her. She didn't feel grateful exactly. It was, after all, her due as the beloved only daughter of Caleb Faithful that she never had to put up with anything she didn't like, and rules, or even laws, were adjusted to suit her. Her second son, Demas Luke Flynt 5th was Tuffy's son, and nicknamed Quinn. She'd had a few anxious weeks when Quinn was born looking so much like her that she couldn't tell if he was going to look like Tuffy or not. She'd tried to cover her tracks by saying how much the baby looked like Caleb. Despite her relief at finally seeing

Tuffy's distinctive features emerging in her baby son's face, Dinah Rose never lost the resentful feeling towards Quinn that he'd come close to betraying her.

Because both boys made her feel uncomfortable by reminding her of her despised first husband, and Quinn by bringing back the heart-stopping terror of being caught out in something not even Daddy would forgive, the one of her children who brought her unlimited joy was the daughter, the youngest of the three, Ephrath Ahlai Flynt, Effie. Not only could Effie do no wrong in Dinah Rose's eyes, but she was also Tuffy's little princess and the apple of Caleb's eye. In vain Dinah Rose's mother, Minnie, warned her that Effie was badly spoiled, none of them were listening.

Not trusting the nanny to take proper care of her precious, Dinah Rose was kneeling beside Effie's chair trying to persuade her to eat yet another delicacy after all the others had been poutingly rejected when Tuffy put his head back around the door to call her. "Can't it wait?" she snapped at him, not wanting to leave Effie's side until she was satisfied the little darling wouldn't go hungry.

"No!" Tuffy said in a tone that made her instantly angry.

She leaped to her feet, rushing to shut the door behind them so that she could give him what for. Effie immediately started to cry. "Now look what you done!" she scolded.

"What I done? *¿Qué chingados esta pasando aqui?* I want to know what you done!"

She was startled to realise that he was at least as angry as she was. "Don't you . . ."

"Your Daddy wants us to have supper with him next Friday. You been careless!"

"Me? I've been way more careful than you, you *culero!*" Dinah Rose was outraged. Even so, she lowered her voice from her usual indignant shriek so that she wouldn't be overheard by Caleb's spies, hissing in a whisper that only Tuffy could hear, "If Daddy's found out you been selling arms to the enemy we're done for, you *pedero*. He'll never believe I didn't know about it." She was pleased by the shock on Tuffy's face. Did he really think he could hide something like that from her?

Her pleasure instantly turned to fear when Tuffy pointed out, "You did know about it."

She tried to hide her fear behind bluster, "You cain't keep nothing from me. I know everything you do."

"Yeah, right." He acted nonchalant, but she didn't buy his effort to bluff her. Not only did she know him too well, but she'd seen the look in his eye: he'd had no idea she'd known about his arms dealing. But her feeling of superiority evaporated when he added, "Just like I know all about your little scheme to move the jewels without paying Daddy his cut."

"You still had to do something for him to call us back home in the middle of negotiations," she reminded him.

"I never. You did. You think none of those guys you had digging in the Ashlands could be bought off by Caleb?"

She retorted, "You think none of the guys you got doing the deals for you could be bought off by Daddy?"

They stared at each other for a moment, and then Tuffy suggested, "Your Dad might not be mad at us. Maybe he finally noticed my hard work. Look what I done for him. I found out where the smugglers were getting across the border, and it was me that got the Ashies to understand that they better not fuck with the Gethsemane Republic if they knew what's good for them. That was me. Caleb's got to know there ain't no one else taking care of business for him like I done."

Dinah Rose had a sudden image of beating her brothers out for her father's approval. She beamed at him. "You got to be right. Daddy wants to see us to promote you. After I'm done telling him all what you done for him, you'll be his favourite, I just know it! How much time we got?" She realised that she had a lot of work to do before she could leave this place. She would have to arrange something with her teams of treasure hunters digging down through the deep layers of volcanic ash to the houses down below to find the buried valuables. It would be disastrous for her if her father ever found out that she'd uncovered twice as much as she'd told him.

Tuffy looked pre-occupied. Dinah Rose had no doubt he had as much tidying up as she did, just in case they were sent somewhere else and never got to come back.

"Tell Daddy I miss him whole bunches, and so do the kids, so we're all coming home to see him. Send that in the diplomatic pouch today, and say I'll write to him tonight." Tuffy might have believed he was acting the strong and silent male, but she could see the relief in his eyes as he nodded and let her out of his office.

It was up to Dinah Rose to organise the staff to run the household in her absence. In fact, since it was a diplomatic residence, it was set up to keep running whether there was any current diplomat in it or not. The exercise not only served to make her feel important, it was also the ideal disguise for her activities in covering her tracks from excavating several times as much treasure as she reported to her father, plus it genuinely did get all of them packed for the trip.

She had to set it all up as if they would be right back, because there was no indication that they wouldn't. At the same time, she had to set it all up as if they wouldn't be back because there was no way to know what Caleb was up to. If he was getting them out of the way to check up on them, it would be suicidal to leave the evidence behind.

Even if she could convince Daddy that she was innocent, Dinah Rose knew it would be at the expense of Tuffy. When it was staring her in the face like that, she had to admit she didn't want to see Tuffy treated the way her first husband, Jaakobah, was being jerked around by her father. And if Daddy couldn't be convinced who knew what might happen to her.

Being Caleb's beloved only daughter wouldn't save her. Her cousin, Gomer, had made the mistake of failing on the last job her father gave him. Now he was in clear and present danger in the Panhandle. Jake had been sent there on their divorce, too. Somehow, he had survived, but that didn't mean he was forgiven. Once Daddy decided you'd betrayed him, he never forgave you. When Jake had not only survived but had been the one to put the Panhandle through to the coast, Daddy had been furious instead of pleased. He'd had Jake demoted on a technicality and moved into more danger, instead of promoted and acknowledged.

Fear drove Dinah Rose to do an obsessively thorough job of leaving no trail for Caleb's investigators to follow back to her. The moment she was sure her Daddy couldn't discover what she'd been doing, she forgot her fear and went back to feeling superior to everyone else. Priding herself on how quickly the kids and the household were organised, she was on top of the world when Tuffy got home.

Running his hand through his sandy hair, making it stand on end in the way that made her crazy, he said, "I'm pretty sure your Dad ain't kicking us out of here, or he'd've had our replacement on us before we knew it was coming."

His nervousness enraged her. "You pantywaist! Always snivelling like a two-year-old! Comb your hair!"

"Sheeitt! Can't a man even come home for his supper after a hard day without getting his head bit off?"

"Like you had a hard day," she sneered. "What did you do that was so almighty hard?"

His voice and eyes went cold. Flicking glances left and right to remind her that there were always spies, he said, "I did the same thing as you."

"The hell you did! I had to get the whole house set up for us to be gone, who knows how long, or even if we'll be back, and that ain't easy, let me tell you, Mr Big Shot!"

"Yeah, that's a real hard day's work. I bet it took a whole two seconds to tell the housekeeper we're going away. You poor dear. Boy, I bet you had to lay down and rest after that."

"You asshole! You know I got more than that going on! I got all our stuff and the kids ready to go, too."

"Oh, well, excuse me. Not two seconds. That must of took at least five seconds to tell the maids to pack our stuff and the nannies to pack the kids, too. You talked to what, three people? Or did you just tell the housekeeper and get her to tell the others?"

Dinah Rose had gone past being angry with him to being scared that Daddy would demand an accounting of her time. Almost in tears, she pleaded with Tuffy to understand, "You can't just tell these foreign types what you want. You got to watch them every minute or they don't do nothing, and if they get any chance to get behind your back, they do stuff to screw you up. I had to have eyes in the back of my head the whole blamed day long and be everywhere at the same time."

"They would've got it done faster if you'd quit nagging them."

That made Dinah Rose mad all over again. "Oh, as if you know damned thing about it!"

"Yeah, I do. You nag me day and night."

"Somebody's got to get after you, or you don't do nothing. And they would not either get it done faster without me. If I never kept them moving, we'd still be waiting for them. I made them get it done so we can leave first thing in the morning."

"Like as not they went as fast as they could to get you out of their hair."

Furious, she shouted, "I made them move it! Me! They did not do it their own selves to get away from me!" She always promised herself that she wouldn't let him get under her skin, but he always found a raw nerve so that she reacted before she knew it. Usually, it was because he said out loud what she feared the most.

"I seen them roll their eyes when you weren't looking."

Beside herself, she shrieked, "Tuffy Flynt, they do not roll their eyes at me behind my back!"

The fight went on all evening and into the night, picking up again the next morning the moment they were out of sight of the official farewell party, and could turn their diplomatic faces off. They sniped at each other during the first day of the journey, but after that they were both more concerned with making a good impression on Caleb than they were in getting even with each other. Knowing that the best way to please Caleb was to prove to him that they had been busy doing things he needed done, they concentrated on feeling each other out for things they could creditably lay claim to or had actually done.

To set up relations with neighbouring nations, the Presidents sent envoys. Once trade was established, diplomats were exchanged. Whenever he could, Caleb had someone he controlled chosen for the diplomatic posts. They were responsible for making the host nation believe that the GR was there only for peaceful trade. At the same time, they were to find anything that Caleb could make a profit from and anything the nation was doing that could be used to make them appear untrustworthy in case at some time in the future something went wrong with the planned peaceful trade.

Dinah Rose had grown up overhearing such things. Although good little girls didn't take an interest in the man's world of politics, Dinah Rose had avidly absorbed every scrap of information she could from the odd word she overheard now and then. So great was her love for her Daddy that his every word was magical to her. She so wanted to be like him that she memorised everything he said, spending hours trying to figure out what it all meant. At times she sassed her mother just so she would be locked in her room with nothing to do. That was the only way she could get hours to herself without interruption to puzzle out something she'd overheard her father say to one of his men. She never accepted that there were things boys could understand but girls couldn't, especially when the boys involved were her brothers and cousins, and she knew that she was way smarter than most of them.

Bit by bit she pieced together a grasp of what was going on. She was sure her Daddy would be pleased when one of kids gave him the right answer, even if he was surprised by which one it was. She concealed herself outside of Caleb's office where no women were allowed. She timed it perfectly, stepping into the room as Caleb was screaming, "Good God Almighty! Ain't none of you got the smarts God gave a wet sock?"

Confidently, she gave the answer she knew her father was looking for. She wilted almost at once. Instead of being pleased, Caleb laughed. Worse, her brothers and cousins weren't impressed. "What's she doing here?"

"Go back to the kitchen."

"No girls allowed."

"But I was right, wasn't I, Daddy?" she pleaded.

He patted her butt kindly. "Don't you worry your pretty little head about it, Precious. What did Mama send you here for?"

Defeated, Dinah Rose pretended that her mother had sent her to find out if the men needed a snack. To add insult to injury, her mother slapped her when she heard the message, saying there was no way Dinah Rose could have got it unless she was hanging around where she had no business being.

Alone in her room as punishment, Dinah Rose figured out that her mistake was saying something in front of the boys. Caleb was trying to make them come up with the right answer, and she'd gone and given it to them. But her Daddy knew she could do it. That was more important to her than showing the boys up, much as she'd wanted to do that as well. As soon as she had a chance, she planned to quietly let him know she realised what she'd done and was sorry.

Once again, he caught her off guard. He didn't remember that she'd said anything. He only remembered that she'd had a message from her mother. No matter how hard she tried to explain that she understood what he was doing and wanted to be part of it, all he would do was pinch her cheeks or ruffle her hair and chuckle. When she started to get frustrated, he kissed her and told her to run along like a good girl, saying, "That's why it's not good for pretty little girls to worry about men's work. Girls are too emotional to do men's work. You don't want a nasty old wrinkle on your cute little nose, do you?" He tapped the tip of her nose with his forefinger.

The bottom dropped out of her stomach. She was too stunned to be able to make any more tries to get through to her father. Her life changed at that moment. From then on, she knew that if a female said something no one heard it. It wasn't right or wrong if a girl said it, it just didn't exist.

From that day, Dinah Rose had been trying to get Caleb to see that she had something more than cuteness to contribute. It got her nowhere, of course: Caleb didn't notice, and Minnie punished her for being unladylike.

Every year high society attended the graduation ball for the young officers. Most of the officers were from that social class, so the yearly ball was a good place for society girls to meet suitable young men. Once in a while a boy from lower down the social scale would be such a talented soldier that he'd be sent through officer training. They were honoured as the ones who were the most likely to save lives in battle, and to protect their way of life, but they were not husband material for the likes of the only daughter of Caleb Faithful.

It was sheer rebellion that drove Dinah Rose slip away from her chaperone to follow a handsome, tall graduate outside. It seemed to her that he liked her as much as she liked him, so she figured out ways for them to get together again after the ball.

Because she had been raised as a nice, innocent little girl, she had no idea that what they were doing would make her pregnant. She knew she shouldn't do it, of course, but she thought it was only something that made her feel real good and would make her mother mad if she knew about it. Taught that God blessed some women with babies and not others, it never occurred to her that she had anything to do with it.

Minnie figured out that Dinah Rose was pregnant at fifteen and gave her such a beating that she couldn't sit down for days.

Caleb didn't blame his little peach for one second. She was a pure child. It was all the fault of that young officer. "He's CP!" he thundered in outrage.

"Is the blood of our families to be muddied by the likes of that trash?" Minnie sobbed, dabbing her streaming eyes. "Slut!" she screamed. "How could you after everything we did for you?"

"Hush, Mama. We got to figure out what to do."

"No matter what we do, someone's gonna figure out this baby came too quick."

"I can talk to Bela. He wants to get married again, and he likes them young."

"What about the baby?"

"I'll pay him to say it's his. It's the only way he's going to have a kid by the look of things. We're doing him a favour."

"People will still figure out the baby was too quick."

"Not if he's sent into the Ashlands before she starts to show, and no one says nothing about no baby."

For the first time in her sheltered, well ordered life, Dinah Rose had no idea what was going to happen to her, and she was terrified. She'd always dreamed of marrying some handsome young man, not being sold off to ugly old drunk who was at least as old as her father, and who'd had two wives die. She trembled as she asked, "What happened to Bethiah?"

Minnie scolded her, "Serves you right! The wages of sin are death." But she told Caleb, "Silly old fool will get drunk one day and say too much."

"Yeah. Forget Bela. Boaz talked to me about joining our families."

Minnie looked at him. "Do you want his blood in the veins of your grandkids?"

"No! I God-damned don't! But that CP ass-h . . . well, begging your pardon, ladies. I know how to fix the likes of him so he can't never mess with nobody's little girl again. But we still got to get someone to take her and her bastard."

Minnie frightened Dinah Rose even more when she smiled at Caleb and forgave his cussing and taking the Lord's name in vain by saying, "That's alright, Big Guy, I'm sure the Good Lord knows you been pushed too far. We got to make sure it's somebody who'll keep his mouth shut and not get too fussed about where the baby came from."

Caleb smacked one fist into the palm of the other hand. "Ain't no way Boaz'll take in a half CP bastard. Blood will tell. We gotta come up with someone he'll believe, whose kid he won't mind raising like it's his grandkid."

Minnie nodded, "Someone married, so they don't ask why he never married her; someone you'd trust with your daughter, so they don't ask what we were doing, and someone whose kid they'll be happy to hide in their bloodline."

"Yeah? And what do we do when the guy we finger says he never did it?"

"We never say it outright. We can't help rumours, huh?" They laughed, and then both turned on Dinah Rose, impressing on her how important it was for her to never let out to her husband who the father of her baby was.

Dinah Rose was overwhelmed by the vision of being married off like a dog being bred, while who knew what was happening to Jake. Even as they were pounding on her mentally and emotionally, trying to force her to promise to keep the baby's father secret to protect the reputation of the family, all she could think about was that Jake was the only man who had ever said she was smart. All at once she knew she couldn't bear to live without that. No matter what happened, she couldn't give in to their demands.

It took her a while to figure out who her father's friend Boaz was, but once she'd placed him, she recalled what complete jerks his sons were. The idea of letting any one of them do what she and Jake had been doing revolted her so strongly that she nearly gagged right then and there. She fought in every way she knew of against their plans for her. She tried tears and begging, then, when that didn't work, she switched to letting them know that she would not keep the father of her baby secret.

Pitting herself against her mother wasn't hard. She had no trouble sticking to her guns while her mother wept about the dreams she'd had of a beautiful wedding for her only daughter. She was unmoved by her father's accusations that she was making her mother cry. It never seemed to mean anything to Minnie when she cried, so she didn't feel any particular distress when her mother cried. If anything, she felt a sense of satisfaction: 'serves you right.'

Caleb muttered, "If we could get rid of it . . ."

Minnie sniffled, "I could find out where the servant girls go."

Dinah Rose was horrified. She didn't know happened to girls that people snickered and whispered about: "She did something about it." What she knew was that they were, "Never the same again," and some of them died. In desperation, she said the only thing she could think of that would affect them both immediately: "The gossips will love that if it ever leaks out."

"You would love that, wouldn't you? Do you want to see your mother dead of shame? Because that's what you're doing; you're killing me!"

After all the fussing was done, Dinah Rose married her CP lover and had his son. The trouble between them started before Faithful Lycus was born. Pleased and proud that Jaakobah thought she was smart, she showed off to him the cleverness she was the proudest of: her deviousness. She couldn't believe it when he didn't approve, telling her she had the wrong attitude. Life together quickly became impossible for them. By the time the baby was born she no longer cared what her father did to Jaakobah Lycus, just as long as she never had to see him again and listen to his lectures on ethics.

She had less respect for Tuffy, but at least he knew what was what. She couldn't help worrying, though, that this summons to see her father was bad news. It was too likely that Tuffy had thought he was smarter than he was, and Caleb had caught him out. She had to decide whether she would be better off supporting Tuffy or making it look as if she had no idea what he was up to.

She decided that they had the best chance if they appeared to be a tight unit. Tuffy didn't need any convincing. She swallowed her harsh words about his backbone of jello and concentrated on figuring out all the things they'd done that Caleb would be pleased with. She could always punish Tuffy later.

Minnie welcomed them at the door, gushing over her grand kids, and saying to Dinah Rose, "Oh, that a shame you had to be so long in that backward place where it didn't matter what you looked like, Dear. We'll just have to go out today and get you some style before anyone sees you like that. Don't you got nothing that's in?"

Visions of being pampered in beauty salons danced in Dinah Rose's head. "I'll be ready to go as soon as I get the kids settled," she said.

Minnie beckoned impatiently to a servant to come over and help the ones taking the children, saying, "Your Daddy's been tending the brisket for hours."

Dinah Rose swallowed. "My mouth's watering just thinking about it." She frowned at the servant, asking her mother, "Who is that? I never saw her before."

"Abigail Capernaum. Didn't I tell you? Old Gabby died."

"Yes, you wrote to me about it."

"Well, I had to get someone, didn't I?"

"But I've never seen her before. She don't look like none of the others." Dinah Rose turned to watch the servants go, trying to place the stranger's face. "Who is she related to?"

Minnie's voice got hard and shrill. "Are you saying I don't know how to hire my own staff?"

"No, Mama, I didn't mean that. I just never saw her before, that's all."

"So, you right away question me like I don't know what I'm doing."

"No, for real I never meant it that way. I feel . . ."

"Well, I feel hurt! After all I've done for you . . ."

"Well, I'll get you a special treat."

"I don't feel like going, now."

"I don't feel like going without you, but I can't let anyone see me like this. What would people say?"

"Serves you right," Minnie sneered, but she started to get ready to go. "You don't got time. You got to be back before Daddy's brisket is done."

"We will," Dinah Rose assured her, knowing that what had got her mother moving was the fear that if the daughter looked bad gossips would point at the mother.

Relaxed, massaged, coiffed, manicured, pedicured, and wearing the latest fashions, the women returned ready to face anything. At least, Dinah Rose thought she was ready for anything until Tuffy hissed in her ear, "You'll never believe what your Dad wants us to do."

"Keep your cool," she murmured, turning his whisper into a kiss on her cheek by tilting her head into his lips and pulling back to smile at him like a young girl in love. Everyone who was anyone was there, and she didn't want any of them thinking Tuffy was scared.

She was surprised to see her cousin, Gomer there. She hadn't expected to see him again until he redeemed himself from failing at his last assignment. Without appearing to do so, she watched him to see if she could figure out why he was there. Tables were set up under awnings so that they could sit out of the sun to eat. Instead of keeping Gomer at a distance, as she would have expected after a screw-up, Caleb and Minnie sat at the same table with him, beckoning Dinah Rose and Tuffy to join them.

"Tell Tuffy what them ignorant savages said about roads," he ordered around his mouthful of brisket.

Preening in what he saw as Caleb's approval, Gomer said, "I said we'd build roads, and they said it took them a hundred years to tear up all their roads the first time and they didn't want to go through all that again."

Dinah Rose could see the problem with that right off. There had to be some kind of trail or road for people to get around or they wouldn't have survived. She glanced at her husband and father to see what their takes on it were. Caleb was watching them in such a calculating way that she knew that's what they were there for.

She was very glad that Tuffy didn't fall into Gomer's way of looking at things. She could have hugged him for asking, "Why would we build roads for them?"

Gomer rolled his eyes. "Because they don't got none."

Dinah Rose saw her chance. "But how do they get around, then?"

Gomer tried to ignore her, but Caleb pressed the point. "Yeah, tell us how they get to market with no roads."

"I never saw them go to market."

"So, they just go hungry?" Dinah Rose thought Gomer was making it up.

"No, they put a lot of food out for us. If it wasn't such crap it would have been a feast."

Caleb licked his lips like someone who knows no one on earth can BBQ like he can. "Stands to reason pagans can't handle a good piece of meat right."

"Yours is the best, Hon," Minnie smiled.

Gomer muttered, "Never saw no meat."

"What?" They all stared at him, dumbfounded.

"Vegetables, fruit, fish, eggs, and some stuff I ain't got no idea what it was, but no meat."

Assuming that Gomer was exaggerating for effect, if not making it all up, Dinah Rose ignored his attempt to distract them with such BS and drilled in on what she considered the main point. "So, if they got no roads how do you figure they got to the feast? Or got it together?"

He tried to avoid her by starting to say something to Tuffy, "You . . ." but Caleb cut him short. "Answer the lady!"

That was too much for Minnie. She got to her feet, urging Dinah Rose to go with her. "It's time for us to make the sweet. We'll leave you men to your . . ."

"Leave her be!" As Minnie left by herself, Caleb frowned at Gomer. "Well?"

"They got this stupid little thing. It's kind of like a train, only it ain't."

Caleb glared. "What the hell does that mean? Is it a train or not?"

Gomer went red. "It don't run on no proper rails on the ground. It's up in the air, like higher than the house." He looked around at everything tall, nodding to himself. "Higher than your barn, Uncle Caleb."

Caleb looked from Tuffy to Dinah Rose. He didn't need to say anything, she knew that look meant, "Can we make money off that?"

"Like a bridge?" she asked, trying to picture it, feeling faint that her father was finally recognising her abilities.

"But everywhere. And not like a real bridge. Bridges are strong, you know, cement and stuff. This is like a mess of sticks."

Tuffy squinted. "They run their train over sticks? Do you mean they got no rails or they put sticks on the rails?"

"No. It's like a bridge made out of big logs, only it ain't made right so it don't look like no regular bridge, it looks like a mess of sticks – um - logs."

Dinah Rose could feel how hard Gomer was struggling to explain it to them, which convinced her that he was telling the truth. If he'd been making it up, he would've taken the easy way out. She couldn't see how they might make money from a badly built train, but she was willing to follow the line of questions to see where it went. "So, they don't know how to build bridges."

Gomer put up his hands. "You ain't kidding! It don't go nowheres . . . not across a river or nothing like that, just around and around the houses."

Tuffy raised an eyebrow. "Their train goes around their houses."

Gomer leaned forwards. "Yeah. They're so hopeless at building that they don't even make proper stations or front doors. They got stupid wooden platforms up in the air and you got to walk down to the ground. You ain't never seen nothing so stupid. Their front doors are up on the second floor because of it. You got to walk on a bridge from the platform to the house."

Tuffy sat back. "So, they do know how to build bridges."

"Only from the train to the houses, not for cars or the train."

Caleb tapped his fingernails on the side of his plate. "I wouldn't like to have a train going past my house all the blamed time. How the Sam Hill can they sleep with their houses shaking all the time and the whistle blowing right beside them?"

"Oh, it don't shake the houses."

Tuffy snorted. "The train goes right up to their houses without shaking them."

"Yeah, for real. Now that I think about it, I stood on the platform with the train coming in, and it never shook like ours do."

They exchanged sceptical glances. Tuffy said, "There's still the whistle."

Gomer shook his head. "I never heard a train whistle the whole time I was there. When you're inside the houses you can't feel the trains go past, and you can't hardly hear them, neither."

The men winked each other, but Dinah Rose had the feeling they were getting close to something. "You didn't even hear the steam?" she asked, quietly.

He stopped, frowning and chewing his lips. "I never saw or heard steam around their train, or anywhere else over there."

Dinah Rose wanted to be sure she'd heard what she thought she'd heard. "But … then they've got a quiet motor that's strong enough to pull trains and runs without letting off steam."

They all went still.

"Yeah, I guess so," Gomer shrugged. "They don't got no industry or nothing. They sure are backward."

"You can not be from my blood line!" Caleb screamed at him. "I sent you over there to find anything we can use and you miss something like that?"

When all the yelling was over with Tuffy and Dinah Rose were invited to join Caleb as he rode around his property. They both knew that it was more of an order than an invitation, but they were fairly sure they weren't in any trouble with him, so they didn't have to pretend to be pleased to go. Dinah Rose tried not to have her excitement show. After a lifetime of being shunted aside, she was finally being recognised for her abilities. It took every ounce of her self-control to calmly say, "Thank you, Daddy," when Caleb told her, "You're my secret weapon."

She knew they were riding with him so that no one could overhear them. She did her best to stop herself from glancing nervously at Tuffy all the time, so that her father wouldn't get the idea she had no guts. When they were well away from everyone and all buildings, Caleb started: "If it's true them islanders got a quiet train, think what we can do with it! If the enemy can't hear a train coming, and if it don't shake the ground to warn them, we'd have an advantage none of them could touch. We'd go straight through the swamps like a hot knife through butter. We'd drive the Westers and the Junta right the hell out of the Panhandle and away from the port once and for all. Then we can get on with what we put the port there for in the first place. We could get to the Gulf and have a port there, too. That would open the whole Eastern Alliance to us. No more of those bastards hiding from us behind the swamps. We'd just go right through the swamps and, "Hello, boys!" It'll change everything."

Something was niggling at the back of Dinah Rose's mind. "Why would we still want to go through the swamps if we could go around them?"

Caleb winked at Tuffy. "You watch your back around this one, Boy. She's dangerous." Under the pretext of pointing out the herds of cattle and horses roaming free as far as the eye could see, he checked that there was no one anywhere near them. Even then, he lowered his voice. "Because there are some old documents that show the ancients had huge gas stores in underground bunkers here."

"But it wouldn't be any good anymore," Tuffy objected. "It's been too long."

"Yeah, for our way of doing things, but the ancients knew more than we do about stuff like that, no matter what the Wright Way says."

Dinah Rose nodded. She'd always suspected as much. "Knowing you," she grinned at her Dad, "There's no doubt these are real."

He cocked his head sideways. "What do you think?"

"I'm thinking you don't waste your time on things you ain't sure of."

"Told you she was dangerous," he grinned at Tuffy, who nodded back.

Dinah Rose didn't know whether to be relieved that her father was so relaxed or not. He might be pleased with them, or he might be setting them up. She badly wanted his comments about her to mean he had realised she had a brain, but she knew all too well that it could just as easily be a veiled threat.

"Even when the Purificators went after military records, they couldn't get everything. Some classified files were kept from them. They destroyed more than we'll ever know, but they never got everything. The military's got a way of protecting itself."

They rode on in silence for a bit, and then Caleb told them, "I got to know what's on them islands. If that quiet motor is half-way true, I got to be the one that gets it. The military will pay handsome for something like that."

Tuffy sounded surprised. "Do you believe Gomer?"

Caleb snorted. "Gomer's a useless tit. But there is for sure something weird in that place."

Dinah Rose dared to give him her observations. "He for sure saw something that he's never seen before."

Caleb turned his piercing gaze full on her. Braced for the usual dismissive comment, she could only gape when he demanded, "Do you read the comics about the islands?"

She was relieved when Tuffy jumped in with, "I thought they were bull."

"Yeah, more now that the guy that writes them works for me. I looked at everyone that went there. Some seriously strange stuff, but none of them said nothing about no quiet engine. I heard about weird food, no dogs, freaking out because one guy shot a tree, and a whole bunch of other stuff, so I sent Gomer over to find out if there was something there we could use. Now he's come back bleating about guys wearing skirts and they don't want no roads, and he never brought home one thing we can sell. So now I still got to find out what's there. You two talk to Vince, the comic writer. I'll show you the file on him so you're up to speed. Get an idea of other stuff like that train thing that Gomer missed."

They took a day to familiarise themselves with Vince's stories, conferred with Caleb about it, then set off the next day, excited that Caleb was trusting them to do work for him that they'd never been given before.

"I'll do the talking, you just listen," Tuffy decided.

"Daddy said both of us," Dinah Rose protested.

"He still expects you to be lady-like."

Resentfully, Dinah Rose sat and watched as Tuffy questioned Vince. Something about him caught her attention, and she started to listen more intently, forgetting to be annoyed. She hid behind her fan, becoming invisible to the men. The more she tuned in to Vince's body language, the surer she became that he was not telling the whole truth. When Tuffy paused, she asked, "How much time did you spend on the islands your own self?"

She knew she'd made the right call when he jumped and spluttered. Even if she made allowances for the unexpected change of subject and that he'd forgotten she was there, it was still obvious to her that he either had never been off the ship or hadn't been off for long. Very little of what he was saying was personal experience. It didn't matter what he said after that, she didn't believe him. She went back behind her fan, watching how he answered Tuffy to see if she could pick out what was from things he'd heard and what was made up out of his head.

Tuffy was furious with her, shouting on the way back to Caleb's ranch, "I told you to let me do all the talking! You threw us both off! You and your big mouth nearly ruined everything!"

She smiled at him. "I'm mighty glad you saw it for your own self."

He sighed. "Saw what?"

"He's full of it."

"You can't know that."

"Yeah, I can. I was watching him the whole time. We can't find out what Daddy wants to know from him because he don't know."

"Do you think your Dad knows that?"

"He might be testing us."

"Then he'll be pleased if we tell him."

"Or he might think we can get it from Vince."

"Then he'll be pissed if we tell him."

"Less than if we feed him what Vince was feeding us, and he sends someone over there on the strength of it."

"Ain't that the truth!"

They expected Caleb to be pleased with them if he had known Vince didn't know anything, or annoyed if he hadn't realised. What they didn't expect was to be given the files on everyone who had been on the first ship and told to find as many of them as they could.

Dinah Rose was grateful they'd taken precautions before they'd left their last assignment, because it was looking as if they weren't going back there any time soon. "We'd better start with these two translators that went with Gomer," she told Tuffy. "They've been there twice."

When they told Caleb how they planned to start, he slapped Tuffy on the shoulder and squeezed Dinah Rose in a one-armed hug. "You two got it! I'm gonna give you a promotion. You take the next trip out there. See what you can find. Get them ignorant savages ready for the exchange of diplomats so when the President reaches that point, we're all set. I'm gonna get the same guys that went with Gomer, so you don't have to talk to them now, you can do it on the way. You can start hunting down the others tomorrow, but you better talk to Gomer today. He ships out tomorrow."

"Gomer?" Dinah Rose had her doubts that would do any good.

"The useless tit might have seen things he don't know he saw. You might get more out of him if he's showing off. He's playing on the four-wheeler hills with the boys."

Tuffy and Dinah Rose set off for the dirt tracks in shock. "He knows you stole the loot from the buried houses, you stupid bitch. Now look what you did. You got us sent on a suicide mission."

Dinah Rose was badly scared, but she wasn't going to let Tuffy see that. "Who was it that sold arms to the Ashies?" she sneered.

"You stole from him!"

"You betrayed the whole nation!"

"He wouldn't care about that, as long as I ain't caught."

"He would so!"

"Nah. If you don't get caught, he admires your balls. It's what he does. He only gets mad if you cheat him, like you did."

"Oh yeah . . . like you can keep something like that from him!"

"If he figured it out, he ain't mad about it. You heard him say I got it."

"We got it. Both of us together. I'm his secret weapon."

"What are you worried about, then?"

"You're the one that said it!"

"You're the one that did something to worry about!"

Dinah Rose tried to defend herself. "Either he don't know, or he knows and don't care, 'cause he's real happy with me."

Tuffy stopped. "He knows," he said in a different tone of voice.

"Why do you say that?" Dinah Rose felt cold inside. She knew Tuffy was genuine this time.

"He said you're dangerous. He said I got to watch my back around you."

"He was just saying that." She swallowed. "It don't mean he knows."

"Yeah, it sure enough does. He knows what you did and what I done. We screw this up and we're done for. He knows if there's anyone who can find out things people don't want no one to know, that's you. You saw right through that Vince character. You were right. It was a test. He knows if there's any way to make money, we'll find it."

Holding on to her one hope, Dinah Rose whispered, "Even if I messed up, he'd never send me away from my babies. He knows they need their Mama."

Tuffy stopped and put his arms around her. "Gomer's wife and kids need him, too, but he's shipping out, and you can bet it's to no soft desk job. He's going back into danger, just like Lycus."

"But he can't have me shipped out."

"Let's see if he lets us take the kids with us."

Realising that Caleb already had all her children under his control, Dinah Rose's heart sank. Feeling that there was nothing she could do except try to please her father, she turned and started off for the four-wheel track again. They walked hand in hand towards the sound of the revving engines.

Her brothers and male cousins were showing off to one another, doing dangerous stunts with their souped-up machines. Gomer was being even more reckless than the others. Spotting Tuffy and Dinah Rose, he roared off the track, bouncing over the uneven surface until she was afraid he would flip his buggy. Somehow, he made it, shut the motor off, slid down to the ground and came weaving his way over to them. She could see that he was more than halfway drunk, but wasn't too concerned, since he wasn't driving any more.

She thought he might be able to get him talking unguardedly while the alcohol had him loosened up, but she couldn't get anything sensible out of him. His attention was on the other men competing in jumping their buggies off the crests of hills they'd built in the dirt. "I can do better than that," he said, throwing back another beer and belching.

"Maybe you should take a bit of a rest before you go back out there," she murmured, trying to keep him on the ground without mentioning the alcohol.

He wasn't fooled. "Nah, I can drink twice this much and still drive better than any of them."

"But we wanted to talk to you," Dinah Rose wailed in a desperate last attempt to stop him.

"I'm just gonna show those guys how it's done. I'll be back faster than a coyote grabs a chicken. Here, hold my beer and watch this."

Those were his last words.

CHAPTER TWENTY-FIVE

First Shake

Kiritoe Amaru

"The next stop on our historic tour," Kiri told his class as the Flying Fish sped along up the hillsides away from the steam clouds of Wairakei, "Is Heretaunga Bay, to take a look at Te Mahia, so you can see how our ancestors in that part of the country dealt with the Freeze. It's not going to be a long trip, but you will have a couple of hours to get your notes on Wairakei in order, and to bone up on Te Mahia so that you know what we're looking at when we get there. We'll be there in time for lunch."

He was standing at the front of the carriage, where the ceiling was still high enough for him to stand upright. The carriages had no real 'front' or 'back' since they were the same at both ends. The carriages of the Flying Fish didn't turn around, they simply reversed direction at designated points, switching from one track to another so that they didn't run into oncoming trains. Trains heading east were always on the south side; trains heading north were always on the east side, the oncoming train was always on the right of people facing forwards. Half of the seats faced forwards; half faced backwards. This meant that the 'front' of a carriage referred only to the direction they were going. The foremost and hindmost seats, one seat in the middle, were usually used only by children because the ceiling sloped down so much at those points that it nearly touched the seat backs. The inside of the carriages was smooth and glassy, of a coloured fibreglass, with the 'ribs' of the triangular framework making a waffled effect. For standing passengers there were floor to ceiling poles at each seatback to hold on to, polished smooth as glass by many hands. There were also long poles running the length of the carriages, above the heads of most people, for people standing beside the seats to reach up overhead and hold on, until they curved down at each end.

The reassuring rustle of papers told him that his students were taking his instructions seriously. He really liked these field trips much more than lecturing in the university lecture rooms and found teaching mature students more to his taste than dealing with multitudes of children. All he needed to do by way of instructions with this group was give hints and advice, he didn't need to supervise.

Lucy, a slender young red head who had her bachelor's degree in sociology, asked, "Will you be answering questions while we're riding the Fish, Professor Amaru?"

"Nah, yeah, of course." He reached his hands up over the poles that ran along the carriage, and hung both his forearms over them, letting his hands flop down near his face. He noticed that Lucy looked at that with a wry grimace. She would have had to stretch uncomfortably to even reach the overhead poles, and here he was draping his arms over them.

"Professor, I was wondering, is the conventional history; that the movement underground during the Freeze started in Wairakei; the actual truth?"

"Seems to be."

"Why there?"

"Maybe it was more obvious there that the warmth was underground, since they're surrounded on all sides by heat coming up from underground."

"But there wasn't much in the way of cave systems there, was there? Not like some other places. Wouldn't the movement underground have started from places where people took shelter in caves?"

"Not necessarily. Caves are pretty difficult to keep warm and dry. More likely to have started from buildings that went deep enough underground to be warm: tunnels and mines and that sort of thing. Remember, they lost all power, so they had no way of heating their buildings, except for the ones that had fireplaces."

"One thing that's been on my mind, Prof." Rahari, a history student spoke up.

Kiritoe looked at him.

"Wairakei has so much power, why don't we pipe it all over the islands?"

"That's how things were done before the Freeze. Mostly they were underground to the buildings and roads. Aside from the underground power it was also sent through lines overhead, wires, to every building. We've all seen the pictures. What an ugly sight, aside from the fact that every time there was a strong wind, or an earthquake, or an eruption, or a landslide, or something happened to one of the power poles, a great many people had no power. Sometimes whole districts, which left hundreds, or even thousands, of people without power. Before the Freeze the population was three times the size it is now, so people were more crowded, and more people went without power every time the power grid was disrupted. In the Freeze, which was really a short Ice Age, power went out all over the islands, both the underground and the overhead types, leaving people with no way to get warm, no way to cook, no hot water, no way to get information. That caused enormous loss of life, except the people who were off the power grid. Our ancestors decided that the best protection against another catastrophe like that was to make every building self sufficient. Nowadays if we have a disaster, even damaged buildings still have power and water, unless they're badly damaged. They used to move water around by pipes, too, which was another part of the loss of life. When the power system broke down, so did the water system, yet we're an island nation which has wet winds from the sea all year round. All that rain running off the buildings, being wasted, while water was piped in at great expense from reservoirs. Made no sense to rebuild that system when layered roofs could catch the clean water and store it in the walls and roofs and in cisterns under the houses to keep each house self-sufficient."

Lucy spoke up again. "Most of the rest of you are history students, but I'm a sociology student, so forgive me if my questions aren't on topics that interest most of you. We used to have a really different kind of society. Do you know why we changed so much, Prof?"

"Well, you know, history isn't only about what happened and when. A big part of it is understanding why things happened. A big part of what happened here was the realisation that we were totally on our own. Once our ancestors had lost touch with Australia, they knew all they had was themselves, and all they were going to have for an untold length of time, was just themselves and good old Kiwi ingenuity. So, when the Freeze hit us, not too long after that, we were already thinking that we had to find our own solutions. Well, not us, but our ancestors who weren't any different from us, you know.

The first thing that happened, of course, was that huge numbers of people went bush. Not only did that hunt out all of the deer, pigs, goats, rabbits, and anything else that moved, but the farm stock was gone within the first weeks. Without power the farmers couldn't take care of them, and the population of penned animals collapsed. Meantime, people were crowded together for survival. Wood fires could only do so much before the forests were being destroyed, and they were not re-growing because of the weather change. No-one knew the Freeze would only last sixty years. There was no way of knowing if it was like the Mini Ice Age of the fifteenth century, or if it was the return of the big ice sheets from twelve thousand years ago. So, they started planning for a big Ice Age as the best way to survive.

They dug out whole cities underground where it was warm, but it was crowded. The only way to survive such close quarters was by developing ways of dealing with disputes non-violently, so the system of behaviour modification grew, and children had to be trained right from the beginning how to interact peaceably. The only way to keep what population had survived from outgrowing their limited resources was to keep the numbers steady by allowing only replacement of the existing population, no increase. The only way to feed everyone was to grow vegetables and algae, so the extensive glass-house complexes were built to create the right climate for vegetables, and that was extended to preserve what wild-life and plants they could save. They chose the indigenous species first, which meant virtually everything that wasn't native to these islands, except people, died out.

As a land mass we don't have many natural mineral resources except sand, so our ancestors developed our silicate technology, which gives us the modern conveniences we enjoy today. That's another reason against your idea of shipping power all over the islands, Rahari: not only is it impractical to have a system that's that fragile, the sheer amount of metal it takes to string wires to every building is prohibitive. Our ancestors pulled down all of the wires in their search for metal, the same way they pulled down the high buildings and tore apart the big ships that they couldn't run without fuel."

Rahari nodded his head, then asked, "So it is true our ancestors lived underground, then? I'd always kind of thought those were fairy stories."

"Yes, it certainly is true, especially in places where the geothermal heat, that protected them from freezing, is right close to the surface."

"Then why don't we ever see the tunnels?"

"Because children exploring had a habit of getting lost in them and dying before they could be found. All of the tunnels were sealed over and hidden. We don't need them anymore."

"Does anyone know where they are? They could be of historical interest."

Kiri shrugged. "Someone must know. Even after over two centuries there must be records somewhere."

The students settled into discussions and arguments among themselves, considering what they'd seen and heard, and preparing their notes. Kiri wandered to the back of the carriage, where there was only one couple sitting. They nodded to him. "You're a professor?" the woman asked as Kiritoe chose a seat and settled himself.

"Of history, yes, at the University of Manawatu," he answered. He knew they expected someone who looked like him to be a Calmer or a logger. He took the first seat behind the door, because it had more leg room. The seats right behind the doors were designed to be folded up to make a space for a wheelchair, but there were no wheelchair passengers in the carriage, so the seat was free.

"They're not school kids, are they?" The man was looking at Kiritoe's students, all busy with their papers, and talking quietly. They formed a group in the front of the train, being carefully ignored by the other passengers.

Kiri set his briefcase down on the seat beside him and opened it. "Yeah, nah," he chuckled in what he hoped was a friendly way. He really didn't want to talk. He hoped to get in a short nap before they arrived on the coast. "We're all from the university. Most of them are looking for subjects for their theses for their masters' degrees or doctorates." Perhaps if he looked like he was working, they wouldn't talk to him too much. He didn't want to be unfriendly, but he wanted time with his own thoughts.

He peered out of the window of the Flying Fish to see if he could catch a glimpse of the sea. They were down in a ravine, steep on both sides, and instead of running along high up to get as much light as possible to the solar panels, in this kind of area the trestle was only about two metres from the ground, just enough to give it the flexibility needed in an earthquake, so that if the Flying Fish did fall the passengers had a better chance of not being killed by the fall itself. Down in the ravine, Kiri had no chance of seeing anything but the forest flashing by, some fern fronds brushing the tracks.

His fellow passengers didn't speak to him again, so Kiri began to relax. He had nothing to do and couldn't see anything; this was as good a time as any to take a nap. He closed his briefcase, then pulled off his jersey, rolled it up into a pillow, and leaned his head against the wall of the carriage in between two windows, moving it back and forth a bit until he'd found a comfortable spot between the ribs of the carriage. The bar for the use of wheelchair passengers was bolted to the wall beside the seat, right where he wanted to put his elbow. It annoyed him until he found a way of curling up where he didn't come in contact with it.

As he dozed, he thought of his father. Perhaps he wouldn't go back with the students after this stop. Perhaps he could carry on up the coast to the north and visit his Dad, Hatoe. He hesitated a moment, wondering if he shouldn't check first, to make sure his father wasn't out on the sea, then he relaxed again. If Hatoe had the Laughing Dolphin out at sea, Hinerehia wouldn't object to a visit. She seemed to want to be friends with Hatoe's sons. He should give her a chance. He had to admit he'd never really given her a chance. He'd given his father his verbal blessing on his wish to partner her for a year and a day, but mostly he'd just stayed away. Stayed 'out of it.'

Hine was younger than Hatoe, only six years older than Kiri's brother, Anatoe. Nat had seemed to be all for it, urging Kiri to give his blessing, which was why Kiri had said that he did, when the truth was that he disapproved very deeply. He hadn't expected the year and a day to turn into a life-time commitment. Her husband had been lost at sea in an ill-advised attempt to cross the roughest piece of ocean in the world to try to reach Australia, leaving her with a newborn baby and a two-year-old. Hatoe had been part of the community of fishermen taking care of the young widow and had fallen for her and her two little girls.

Kiri had attended their bonding feast all smiles in place, but if he was honest with himself, he hadn't felt supportive. Because he'd been away at university when the Kaumoana went down, he'd never had the chance to come to terms with the gaps in the township as the ones living there had. He couldn't shake the feeling that Hine should have gone to her family instead of the fishermen. He repeated her nickname to himself, "Hinny, Hinny," hearing his father say it in that special way he had, that made Kiri think of his mother and the way his father used to talk to her. It brought a lump to his throat. In fact, if he thought about it, he had to admit it hurt deeply that his father had made a permanent commitment, combining his family name with Hine's, which meant he'd dropped the part of his name that he'd had from Anakiri; Anatoe and Kiritoe's mother. Her sons still carried her name, of course, and always would, but it still hurt. He'd even told Hatoe he thought he was right out of his mind to apply for a third child certificate so that he and Hine could have a baby together.

Now he told himself firmly it was time to grow up and cope with it. His father was happy and looked years younger, and that's all that mattered. Kiri had to live his own life. He fell asleep on that firm resolution.

Donstan Seamore

The three children raced home for lunch with their friends and neighbours down the wide grassy path under the train tracks. As usual eleven-year-old Ahnstan was in front, eight year old Donya close behind him, and Wynson pounding along right on her heels. She could usually outrun Wynson, even though he was two years older, but she could never catch Ahnstan. The other children in their hex peeled off to go down the side paths into the hex, but the Seamore children weren't going to delay by even the split-second it would take them to go down the path and in through the garden to the kitchen door. Calling, "See yah!" to their friends they pounded up the wooden steps to their front door, thundered across the planks of the veranda making it ring like a drum, and flung the front door open, heedless of the beautiful stained-glass window in it, bellowing, "Dad! Dad!" as they crashed inside, sending the caged birds shrieking in panic.

Donstan shouted, "Shoes!" at them, even as he leaped from the chair in his office to see why on earth they'd come in the front door.

Spinning in mid-stride, Ahnstan ran at full tilt back to the door to yank his shoes off. By that time Donstan could see that they'd left the door wide open and was scolding, "Shut the door! I'm not trying to heat the whole outdoors!" Then he saw the mud they'd tracked in and added, "What do you think your mother's going to think of the mess you've made of her hallway?"

"Dad! We've got our marks!" they shouted, tossing their shoes in a heap.

"Where do they go?" he demanded, pointing, so they caught their shoes back up and ran in their socks through to the kitchen where they lined their shoes up almost where they should be by the sliding glass door.

The pale beige stone tiles of the heated kitchen floor were warm under their sock-feet after the chill outside, so they slid across the tiles, pretending to skate to the table where their father had seated himself so that they could show him what had excited them so much. Noses blue with cold were pinking up in the warmth of the kitchen and beginning to drip. He handed a box of hemp tissues around, beaming at them, taking it for granted that they had done incredibly well in their Saturday morning disaster relief training, because, after all, they were his kids.

He remembered being exuberant like that when he was their age. It was like living those happy times all over again to watch his kids' excitement. Being their Dad was the deepest joy of his life. As the middle child, he had never gone first, so he took pains to make sure his middle child went first some of the time. "How did you do, Wynn?"

Wynson slipped his satchel off his back, fishing into it, saying proudly, "I got a gold, <u>two</u> silvers, and a bronze."

"Hang your satchel up, Chum, and show me," his Dad said, nodding his approval at the other two for being able to pull themselves back. Wynson dashed over to the sliding glass doors to hang his satchel on its hook, then slid back in his socks on the tiles.

Out of the corner of his eye, Donstan noticed that Ahnstan had suddenly lost all of his liveliness. Watching Wynson, he slipped his satchel quietly off his back, emptied it onto the chair seat out of sight on the other side of the table, walked to hang the satchel up, and returned slowly, hanging back on the other side of the table while the younger children boasted about their prowess.

Donya leaned against her Dad, watching as Wynson explained each of his badges. The bronze for knowing the correct sequence of what to do in an emergency, one silver for making a shelter in the woods out of branches, vines, and ferns, one for raising a tent without help. "But I got the gold for making fire without matches," he positively glowed with pride.

"Pyro," Donya taunted.

"Was that nice?" Donstan frowned at her, then smiled at Wynson. "Four badges is very good. I'm proud of you, son."

He wondered what was going on when he saw Donya react to Ahnstan by quietly standing up straight and walking over to hang her satchel on its peg. She hopped on one leg back to her father, hopping from one tile to another, zigzagging to keep to only one colour of stone tile, then without a word, but with a shy smile, handed him a little stack of cloth badges, suitable for sewing on disaster vests.

Puzzled that she seemed embarrassed, he flipped through them. She had three golds, two silvers, and an honourable mention. She'd rappelled down a cliff-side carrying emergency supplies, she'd known how to immobilize a victim in case of back or neck injuries using only what was found in the forest, she'd swum to shore towing someone bigger and heavier than herself in a simulated sea rescue, as well as knowing what to do and in what order in different emergencies, how to make tea from manuka leaves, and how to prevent hypothermia. She was only eight. Some of the disaster relief skills she'd mastered were intended for older children. In any other family Wynson's achievement would have been outstanding. Here he was being bested by a little sister who was casually achieving things most kids her age didn't even aim for.

Donstan realised then that the other two were trying not to overshadow their brother's achievement. He was proud of them, thinking that he probably couldn't have done that at their age. Not wanting to make Wynson's achievement seem less than it was by making too big a fuss over Donya, Donstan hugged and kissed them both, saying, "Two brilliant kids! In one family! Just wait 'til your mother gets home and sees this!"

Ahnstan was still standing back on the other side of the table, quietly watching. Donstan looked at him, his arms still around the other two. "Well, son?"

Without a word Ahnstan slowly pulled up a disaster vest off the chair. There was a moment of silence. Wynson and Donya turned to look.

"A yellow vest," Donya announced, as if Donstan couldn't see that for himself.

"How old were you when you got your yellow, Dad?" Wynson asked.

"Fifteen, I think," Donstan said, trying to get his head around it. "You earned your yellow vest at eleven?"

Ahnstan picked up the envelope he'd kept hidden and handed it across the table.

Donstan read the certificate and the accompanying letter inside. "Well, well. They feel that you have not only learned all of the necessary skills, but you also have enough size and maturity to take an active part in disaster response."

He'd expected Ahnstan to do well, and he'd known something was up, but he didn't know what to say to this. "I thought you all did well at the trials. Everything I saw you do was top notch, but I didn't expect this!"

He ruffled Wynson's hair, "I couldn't light a fire with sticks when I was ten. I'd have trouble doing it now."

He hugged Donya again. "I can't rescue a drowning victim now, never mind someone bigger than myself, and I certainly couldn't have done it when I was eight."

He looked across the table at Ahnstan. The boy looked partly proud, partly embarrassed. He didn't feel as if he was talking to a child anymore. "I couldn't have been a yellow when I was eleven, and I didn't want to, either. Leave me in the greens as long as possible; less scary. I was really glad that the first disaster I had to take part in didn't happen until I was seventeen." Then he grinned, his usual relaxed, casual feeling coming back. "Well, son, you'll never be a greeny again. Show that to your mother before you put it in the earthquake kit."

He got up from the table. "Off you go now and clean up that mess you made in the hallway before your mother sees it." He handed the children a broom, a mop, and a dustpan, musing out loud, "Let me see, what should we make for lunch? This calls for a celebration."

Trooping off with the others to the hallway, Wynson called out, "Barbeque!"

"It's the middle of winter, Chum. I'm not standing out there in the cold, freezing my bones to barbeque, even on a day as special as today."

"You always want barbeque," Donya commented, putting the dustpan down by the first pile of dirt for Ahnstan to sweep.

"It's my favourite," Wynson shrugged, standing back with the mop until the sweeping was finished.

"Can you make a cake?" Ahnstan shouted from the front door, sweeping dirt into the pan.

For the sheer joy of it, Donstan shouted back, "No time! Your mother will be home soon."

"I love your berry tarts," Donya yelled.

"Don't yell through the house!" their father yelled.

"Okay!" they all shouted back as loudly as they could, cupping their hands around their mouths to make it louder, giggling.

He snickered to himself, amused to hear Donya whispering, "He's going to make berry tarts."

"Yummo," the boys chorused.

Herding back to the kitchen when they'd finished cleaning, the children shouted at the tops of their lungs, "We won't yell any more!"

"I'm glad to hear it!" Donstan roared, frightening the birds just as much as the crashing door had.

By the time Ahnya got home the table was set, a casserole was bubbling in the oven with karengo biscuits browning on top of it, the table was set, and the entire family had shouted themselves hoarse and were giggling helplessly.

"What's the matter with your voice?" she asked Donya anxiously, setting off another round of laughter.

As she looked around, bewildered, all of the children collapsed with laughter, Wynson staging a fall from his chair to the floor.

"Its good thing no one yells in this family," Donstan remarked, sending the children into more fits of laughter, and getting a suspicious look from his partner.

"Your voice, too. What's been going on here?"

"Sheer high spirits," Donstan said, putting the casserole on the trivet in the centre of the table with a flourish. "Madam Mother, you have just the most brilliant children in the hex, in the row, in the town, in all three thousand islands, in the whole wide world!"

"Your marks came in today?" Ahnya asked, spooning the fragrant vegetable casserole into bowls, making sure to put a crisp-topped biscuit in each bowl, finishing by setting the lid back on the casserole to keep the heat in. "Oh, this smells so good. I wasn't hungry until I got a whiff of it, now I'm starving."

"Wynson," Donstan prompted, wanting Ahnya to see them in the same order he had.

Wynson got down from his chair to stand beside his mother. He spread his badges on the table to show her. Ahnya exclaimed, "Four! And a gold! Oh, that was for the . . ."

"For being able to make fire."

"Yes, I was impressed when you did that. You deserve a gold for that. Well done." She hugged and kissed him.

He went back to his seat and tucked in to his lunch. Donya picked up her badges from her lap and handed them across the table to her mother without getting up, and without taking a pause in her lunch. Ahnya's eyes widened as she saw the three golds.

Donstan gestured with his mouth full. "One of them is for pulling Stan from the water when he was pretending to be a drowning victim.

He's bigger and heavier than she is to start with, then he was fully clothed, and she towed him from the buoy to the shore."

"Oh, right, yes, of course. That was amazing, Donnie. And rappelling with that heavy load was outstanding. And knowing how to protect back and neck injuries is a life-saving skill. Congratulations, pet. I'm very proud of you."

Donya continued to eat as if lunch was the only thing of importance, swinging her long thin legs back and forth under her chair.

Donstan nodded to Ahnstan, but he continued to eat without looking up. It looked to Donstan as if he was going to have to tell Ahnya, so he said, "Stan's not a greeny anymore," as he got up to take the little tarts out of the oven.

She looked up with a puzzled frown.

He grinned at her, cocking his head. "It's true. He earned his yellow."

"He's eleven! They can't do that."

"Still. So, we voted to have these to celebrate." He showed her the tarts, then set them down on the tiled counter to cool and covered them with a clean cloth. As he walked back to his chair the glasses on the table clinked together.

Everyone froze in place and looked at each other.

"Tremor or pre-shock?" Donstan asked.

"I didn't feel anything," Wynson declared.

Ahnya looked over her shoulder at the bird cage. They were all huddled, feathers fluffed, murmuring softly, on the floor of their cage. "Uh, oh," was all she had a chance to say before they heard a deep rumble, deeper and lower than thunder.

"Outside!" both parents bellowed, making a dive from the table to the door.

Ahnstan grabbed his new vest, the others all dashed at full speed for the line of shoes, even as Donstan roared, "Shoes!"

Pitamete Meithei

Pitamete was sitting across from the Minister of Education, trying to understand why he needed more in his budget than had ever been allotted to education before, when the number of children needing education had not changed for two hundred years, when there was a tremble under his feet. He looked up. "Did you feel that?"

"Feel what?"

"I thought . . ." his wall unit chimed, the annoying, insistent sound of the emergency chime. More out of sheer self-preservation than alarm, Pitamete scrambled for his clicker and answered the ringer. "First Servant!" a man demanded urgently.

"Speaking."

"Massive earthquake. 7.5 at least, maybe bigger. Heretaunga Bay, don't know where exactly."

"Right. Full red alert. Thank you." Pitamete broke the connection, already on his feet. He gathered up the papers and handed them back to the Minister who was on his feet, eyes wide. "Sorry, Poul. You're needed at your station."

The stunned looked flickered out of the Minister's eyes as he grabbed the documents, crammed them in his briefcase and left at a run to return to his home hex, without saying goodbye.

Pitamete didn't notice; he was already slipping his gold vest and hard hat on, with their big silver '1' and pressing the button that set the sirens wailing. He stood carefully on the spot marked with a red X as the communications people had taught him, then, hands shaking, looked at the spot in front of him where he'd been told to look, cleared his throat, and pressed the button he'd been told would cut straight in to the communications network so that he could announce, "This is the First Public Servant, Pitamete Meithei. There has been a very big earthquake in the Heretaunga Bay area, the epicentre is not yet determined, the exact level on the Richter scale has not been determined, but it will probably turn out to be a minimum of 7.5. All islands on full disaster relief, stay tuned for reports from affected areas. Full red alert, People, level one emergency response."

He rang off, praying he had got all of the instructions of how to do an emergency bulletin right, and the People had actually been able to see and hear him. They had run a test of the emergency bulletin system right after he'd been elected, but he wished he'd practiced more.

Glendrona Tomptell

Glendrona was seven, plinking away conscientiously at her music lesson, over six hundred kilometres to the south of the epicentre, thinking that the lesson would be over soon, and she could go back to her own, familiar hex for lunch, and then she'd be free to play all the rest of the weekend.

Then the entire room swayed.

Glendrona froze for a moment, looking up at her teacher, Ms. Sergill. The moment she heard the word, "Earthquake," her disaster relief training kicked in, she dropped her violin and made a dive under the music room table with the other nine students. The shaking wasn't very hard, but it was distressing and seemed to go on forever. What she hated the most was seeing her teacher's cupboards opening and shutting themselves, things falling out of them, and the hanging plants swaying as if they'd come to life.

CHAPTER TWENTY-SIX

Meanwhile

Sam was on his way out to the fields at first light when the guard dog sounded the alarm. He stood still, the hair up on the back of his neck. A feeling of doom froze him in his tracks. The only thought in his head was that the PPL had found him, before his heart started pounding so hard that he couldn't breathe.

The farm dogs joined in with the guard dog, their menacing barks changing to yelps as shots rang out.

'¡*A la verga!* They've shot the dogs,' went through Sam's mind as his vision clouded over and he started to shake uncontrollably. Dark shapes ran towards him around both sides of the house.

He was done. No point in trying.

"What are you, stupid? Get the fuck outta the way!" The soldiers bursting in the back door knocked him down.

He fell and couldn't move. He could hear Maria screaming and Hosea yelling, "Angelo! Angelo!"

"You Angelo?" The soldier who'd stayed out the back with a gun on Sam demanded.

Not realising he was being spoken to, Sam didn't answer.

The soldier kicked him. "Answer me, Boy!"

Sam heard Hosea yelling, "My little brother, Angelo is out there! He ain't right in the head – he'll starve without me! *¡lo quiero!*"

"Oh, shit. You're a fucking retard." the soldier gave Sam another kick and went inside, calling, "Sarge, I got the idiot brother. He's drooling on the back step."

"Well, he's gonna have to starve without you, Hosea Miguel Perez. You're under arrest for crimes against the Nation, hostile activities, unpatriotic activities, and disobedience."

The chink and clatter of shackles and cuffs made Sam shake so hard that he curled into a ball, his arms wrapped tightly around his head.

Hosea was protesting, "*¿Es neta?* I never did none of them things."

Sam knew that wouldn't make any difference.

Sure enough, they were sneering at Hosea, "You dissidents are all the same; you never did nothing."

"No, really . . ."

"Tell it to the Judge."

"Yeah, how come your name came up when we bust up a smuggling ring, huh?"

They hauled Hosea off as Sam had known they would. He was still trembling so violently that he couldn't get up.

There were sudden shouts, squealing tires, and a crash from the road.

Maria tumbled down the steps, sobbing. She flung herself on top of him, putting her arms around him. "*De la fregada.* You're all I got now." She stroked his hair. "What did they do to you? Even your bones are shaking."

That was what he needed to try to get up.

Maria helped him, urging, "Come on, I'll make something nice for you."

"Don't be nice to me, Maria, I'm not worth it."

She picked up a chair and set it back on its feet while he turned the table over and balanced it against the wall, thinking he'd fix the leg later.

"Don't you talk like that. Hosea is a good man, and he hid you by saying you were Angelo."

He didn't like hearing her talk about Hosea as if he was still alive when it was obvious to him that the arresting officers'd had one of their 'transport accidents' and Hosea was dead. "Yeah, he did. That's the problem. They should have took me, not Hosea."

Maria frowned. She stopped straightening the house up to give Sam a long look. "Hosea maybe gave his life to save you."

Sam couldn't bear to think about that. He looked around wondering why he hadn't heard the GR trashing the house.

She coaxed, "Hosea had faith in you."

That cut Sam to the quick. "Well, he was wrong." He flopped down on a chair by the table and put his head in his hands.

Busying herself with stoking up the wood stove, she asked, "How can you say that?"

"I did nothing. You saw that. I couldn't even get up."

"You did the right thing. If they saw you ain't loco, they would have took you, too, and Hosea would've paid bad for lying."

"You don't get it. I didn't do the right thing; I lay there like a goldurned coward."

"No, not like a coward, like a man that got worked over in the joint."

"How do you know about that?" Sam raised his head to watch her puttering around the kitchen.

"I figured it out. You don't want to know the things I've seen."

"You're right, I don't." Sam was at his limit. Pressing his hands together to stop them from shaking, he forced himself to confess, "I did the same thing to my son, Rubin. The dogs barked, and, instead of helping him protect the family, I hid in the corner of my room. You see? I ain't worth the life of a good man like Hosea."

"Yeah, you are. Hosea knew about joint jitters. The GR know how to break men."

Neither of them put their fear for Hosea into words.

Maria didn't seem able to keep still. All day long she cleaned and tided, fussed and puttered.

Sam, on the other hand, couldn't move. It felt as if his body had turned to lead. No work was done on the farm that day. Neither of them could go outside. The only time Maria opened the door was to feed the chickens and surviving dogs.

Then she set Sam's shakes off again by crying out that an injured dog was crawling up to the door for help. She gathered it up and carried it to the fireplace. On its bloody fur she shed the first tears Sam had seen from her since the PPL had left.

As she tended the dog, weeping over it and crooning to it, Sam knew that the only humane things to do were to put this one out of its misery and search the farm for any others that had been shot but not killed, but he couldn't bring himself to do it. Every time he thought about getting up to take care of his animals, the image of those dark shapes running towards him would knock the stuffing out of him.

His heart practically stopped beating when he heard a tap on the back door just as dusk set in. He went rigid. "They're back." He couldn't form the thought that they'd come for him: it was too much. He could feel his brain shutting down as his body shook so much that he couldn't have made a run for it, even if there'd been any point to it. He hated himself for being frozen by joint jitters. He would sooner be cut down in a hail of bullets trying to escape than get carted off like a lamb. It was good that Hosea had never been able to afford glass so there was no window for the PPL to see him sitting like a lump.

*   *   *

A member of the underground came in a flat-out race to Rubin's, gasping, "The PPL got a pile of men and equipment heading for Hosea's place."

Rubin didn't hesitate. He raced to let Dixie Rae know he had to go, and he was galloping along the back ways towards the road. There was a promontory that they could hide and get a good view, providing the soldiers weren't guarding it.

As he drew closer, he slowed and quieted his horse. It was clear that there were no PPL around. Wondering what the soldiers were doing, he hid his horse and slowly climbed the hill, watching every moment for an ambush.

At the top he could see in both directions for quite a way. What caught his attention was groups of people milling around down there. It was clear that the military had gone by and caused unrest by doing so. Rubin tried to figure out what they were doing. He could tell that they'd gone to Hosea's place. He lay there trying to distract himself from fretting over whether they were at the house, and whether he could go and see his poor old Dad.

Chuck made his way towards the hill. Rubin only caught sight of him once, but that was enough to let him know. There was one group of troublemakers and Chuck, who didn't seem to be aware of each other. He looked more closely to see if the people were one group or not. He heard Chuck climbing the hill behind him.

Chuck crawled the last few feet so that his head wouldn't be seen from the road. "God, I'm sorry, Buddy," he apologised as soon as he was close enough to Rubin to speak quietly. "I didn't make it. Maybe Joe Mack had a faster horse, or he rode harder, or his route was shorter."

The look Rubin gave Chuck froze the words in his throat. He turned to watch the road below them.

That was when it hit Rubin how much danger they were in if Sam was in the prisoner's box on the back of that truck. Sam had never been the same again since his brainwashing. If they broke him this time, he might not be able to keep the information from them: the Underground, who was in it, and what it was doing. Perhaps the test of their escape route would be themselves – if they were lucky enough to hit the road before the Security Shield sent the PPL to hunt them down.

Chuck asked, "What's that?"

Rubin was looking the other way. "It's Joe Mack."

"Not over there. Down there."

Rubin didn't look. "He's by himself." He was choked by the thought that his Dad was not with either of the guys. He didn't move or talk for several minutes.

Joe Mack's voice came from behind him. "Sam ain't here?"

Chuck answered quickly, "I was too late."

"Me, too. You see if Hosea's okay?"

"I couldn't. The transport convoy was a troop truck with a jeep front and back. The truck had a prison box down near the tailgate instead of up behind the cab. The truck bed was covered from the box to the cab."

Joe Mack frowned. "That don't make no sense."

Chuck swallowed and explained, "They could have hid a whole platoon in there to set up an ambush."

He could see in Joe Mack's eyes that he knew what that could mean, though Joe Mack didn't say it out loud. "I never stopped, either. It don't help no one if we're all scooped. Hosea's kids tried to support one another and ended up with all of them took. Didn't the truck go past here?"

"No. they went the other way."

"Are you sure? The processing compound is this way."

Rubin suggested in a flat voice, "They're picking up someone else."

"What makes you say that? Is there someone else we don't know about?"

"There's a lot we don't know."

They sat quietly for a bit, hearts thumping painfully. Rubin watched the road.

Then Joe Mack crawled on his belly up beside Chuck. "What are you looking at?"

"Those guys down there."

"It looks like they're laying low to wait for the convoy to come back."

"What!" Chuck joined them. "How much do you want to bet they're the idiots that got us in this?"

"You're right," Joe Mack exclaimed. "Can we get down there before the convoy gets back?"

"No. They're coming," Rubin said.

Chuck and Joe Mack were cussing the hot heads so intently that they didn't hear Rubin add, "What the hell?"

"If we can't stop them, this whole Parish will be too hot to live in," Joe Mack growled.

Chuck shook his head. "We seriously don't have time to get to them."

"Why try and ambush? What's the gain? Just to mess with the PPL? That ain't going to save Sam, and it'll for sure set off a whole new round of re-education. What we don't want them to do is start a near war or insurgency type of out-break."

"Can you make it out?" Rubin persisted.

"What?" That was when Chuck realised Rubin had said something earlier. He turned to see what was up. The dust of the convoy was coming towards them at about forty miles an hour.

He peered into the distance, trying to figure out what had got Rubin's attention, ignoring Joe Mack's commentary: "It don't look like they're setting up an ambush here. They're spread too thin. I bet it's a message relay. If they're going to mount an attack, it'll be where the road takes that big ess around the gulch. Lots of cover there and, the vehicles have got to slow down to make the corners."

A puff of wind cleared the clouds of dust away from the convoy for a moment. For an instant Chuck got a clear view. "Pronghorn!"

CHAPTER TWENTY-SEVEN

Earthquake

Kiritoe Amaru

Kiri came awake in a bewildered feeling that he was upright. He'd gone to sleep curled against the wall of the carriage, which seemed somehow to now be the roof. The soothing movement of the Flying Fish didn't seem to be happening. They were sort of – still. What an odd dream. He must be really, deeply asleep. He shook his head to clear it, trying to pull out of the dream, only to realise that his head was between his two arms, which were over his head. What? Still groggy from sleep, he realised he was holding on to the bar that was bolted to the wall beside his seat, hanging from it. What?!

Kiri reached down with his toes and found they were in mid-air. He could feel that he was stretched across the centre aisle and along the seats on the other side. The carriage was definitely on its side. Everything was pitch-black. It shouldn't be dark. It should be nearly noon. He shook his head again. He could not come out of the dream.

Reaching around with his feet, cursing that it was winter, and he didn't have bare feet because he couldn't feel properly though shoes, he worked out the edges of what he took to be the people who had been sitting on the other side. Best not to land on them. He found the sides of the seats they'd been sitting on and put his weight on them. Letting go with one hand, he felt for a hand hold on the back of the seat he'd been sleeping in, to ease himself down gently. He couldn't shake the detached feeling, as if all of this were happening to someone else, or in a play.

He wormed his way in among the people crouched on what had been the windows on the other side of the carriage but were now the floor. "Are you all right?"

The woman's voice answered, "I am, but I think my partner was hurt."

"Something fell on me," the man's voice said thickly.

"Where are we? If we can figure out what part of the carriage we're in, we can find the emergency kit and get some light." Then he remembered that the emergency kit on his side of the carriage had been on the wall of the carriage right above the bar beside his seat. He could have opened it while he hung there. But that meant there had to be another one just about where he was, since the small first aid kids were paired on either side of the carriages beside the doors. He fished around beside him, then re-oriented himself, remembered that it was the ceiling that was beside him, and started to fish around on the floor, wishing he could snap out of the woolliness that seemed to fill his head. He told himself firmly that this was an emergency, something was seriously wrong, the sounds he could hear were frightened and hurt people, and he had to pull himself together.

Finally, he found the box virtually under the injured man, who moved awkwardly trying to get out of the way. At last Kiri had the box open and took out a light-stick, snapped it, waited for the green-tinged glow to start, then shook it and held it up over his head. An eerie, green-tinged light revealed the carriage lying on its side, the passengers in tumbled heaps. Most of the people who had been sitting on the downside had bruises or abrasions from being the landing cushions for people falling down from the high side.

Still feeling numb and unreal, Kiri called out, "What injuries do we have? Don't forget, the first aid kits by the doors are only small. The bigger ones are under the first and last seats."

Someone cracked another light-stick, which they used to check themselves and each other. The most serious injury in the carriage was Lucy's foot. She had curled her legs up under her in the front seat while she studied, and had become tangled in her long, heavy skirts when the carriage tipped over onto its side. Aside from Lucy's injury, all of the other hurts were bumps, bruises, and various contusions caused by falling from one side of the carriage to the other, or by being landed on. He was surprised there weren't broken arms or ribs.

Kiri held the light-stick up close to the windows on the high side. They could make out the fabric of what they supposed had to be the airbags outside the windows, but the big clue was earth on the windows where little bits had managed to get in under the airbags. "Look at that," he said, holding the light-stick up against the glass. Things felt more unreal to him than ever.

"We're buried," one student said.

"We couldn't be," someone argued.

"Nah, yeah, we are," someone else said. "I saw the hillside give way."

"No! We couldn't be!"

That was panic, Kiri realised, his mind flashing quickly through a sequence of: 'this is an emergency; panic kills in an emergency; got to keep everyone calm.' "Rahari," he called, hoping that was enough to prompt Rahari and the other students to comfort and support strangers as well as each other. "Listen," he said, and everyone quieted and listened. They could hear nothing. No birds, no sound from outside the carriage at all. "We're buried," he had to agree. Seemed like they were looking to him. He wished they wouldn't, he still felt as if he were dreaming. Just because he was big, with a deep voice, didn't mean he knew what he was doing. "Well, we have to take care of ourselves. Does anyone have any food?"

Some people had food with them, and some had bottled water. The whole carriage shook while they were working that out. Everyone froze. Kiri had a horrific image of them tumbling over and over down the ravine, unable to do a thing to save themselves. But that seemed to be all there was to it, just a small shudder. When he heard someone else let their breath go, he realised he'd forgotten to breathe.

"Earthquake," someone said.

"Aftershock," someone else corrected. "It was an earthquake that put us here."

"Must have been a doozy."

"I hope my mother's all right."

Kiri had to stop everyone's thoughts from going in that direction. They couldn't worry about their families; it would make them feel even more trapped. "The emergency supplies in the carriage will have some rations and water, but the more we have to add to that the better. We don't know how long we're going to be here, so the priorities are to take care of the injuries," he looked at a young mother with a nursing baby, and added, "And the baby. The baby's needs have priority. Now, we know they'll find us, so we just have to sit tight until they do. Since most people are in the front of the carriage, we'll make a toilet in the back."

There was a vague groan of protest.

Kiri pointed out, "We have no other way of relieving ourselves. We daren't make a hole in the carriage, we don't know what'll come in if we do, because we can't see what we're buried under."

There was an indistinct muttering of consent. Kiri made his way into the area of the seat under the low ceiling at the back of the carriage, forced open the emergency cabinet, and pulled out the earthquake kit.

In the front of the carriage, his students were working together to try to ease the injured Lucy out of the small space in the front of the carriage.

"What are you doing?" he called to them.

"Trying to get to the earthquake kit, Prof."

"Hold up a mo. There are splints and blankets and stuff in the one down this end, too. We can use the things in this one to take care of Lucy, and then get into that one."

"Right you are, Prof."

"What's your name?" Kiri asked the man he'd avoided landing on.

"Jerry."

"Hi, Jerry, I'm Kiri."

"Hi. This is my partner, Edie."

"Hi, Edie. Pleased to meet you. Jerry, can you give me a hand to get a couple of the blankets out of the earthquake kit, and curtain off this corner of the carriage? That'll give us a bit of privacy, at least."

"I suppose." Jerry got to his feet and made his way over to Kiri, followed by Edie, all of them bracing themselves against the ceiling so that they didn't stumble over the window frames in the dark.

Kiri handed the light-stick to Edie to hold for them as they pulled everything out of the earthquake kit, handing most things to Edie, who piled them behind her. Kiri and Jerry kept three blankets, the hammer, and some nails, and the roll of heavy tape.

"Maybe they'd be better taped up," Edie suggested.

"You have a point." Kiri looked down the front of the carriage. They had several light sticks glowing. He handed the light-sticks from the earthquake kit to Edie, saying, "I think we should conserve these. This one will stay here, so that we can always see our way into the toilet, and we'll just keep one glowing at a time down there."

Edie handed the light-stick back to Kiri, then loaded herself up with as many items as she could carry, making a carry-sack out of one of the blankets, then made her way cautiously and slowly down to the other end of the carriage with the bundle on her back. Kiri opened the multitool from the earthquake kit and cut a piece of tape that he used to hang the light-stick up.

He tried to look through the window at the back of the carriage to see if they were still attached to the carriage in front of them, but all he could make out was dirt.

"Could we crack that window, say, the one we'll be standing on in the toilet, to make a bit of a drain?" Jerry asked quietly.

Kiri nodded. "Good idea. We'll hang this wall first, so no one sees what we're doing. Don't want to scare them." They taped one blanket to the wall that had been the ceiling, and to the ceiling that had been the wall, taking care to arrange it behind seatbacks and tape it down. When it was a satisfactory curtain/wall between them and the others, Kiri got Jerry to pull the tape loose around the light-stick and hold it close to the window where they were standing, so that they could see what the window was resting on. They crouched down like two little boys at a mud puddle. All they could see was the inflated airbag that had covered the window, preventing it from breaking, and had softened their fall. "That shouldn't be a problem as long as we don't smash it hard," Kiri murmured. "I don't think it'll cause a collapse, or have the earth pouring in."

Jerry nodded, so Kiri wrapped the hammer in the other blanket, which both muffled it and made a softer striking head and gave the glass a few carefully placed blows. A network of cracks spider-webbed across it.

"Stop," Jerry hissed.

They peered at their creation. Jerry held the light-stick over it. "There's one complete chip here," he pointed. "If you can knock that one out, we'll have a drain hole."

"Without risking the structural integrity?"

"Yeah."

Kiri stood up and pushed down on the cracks with his heel while Jerry practically put his nose under Kiri's foot to watch the progress, signalling when he was satisfied, so absorbed in the task that he'd forgotten all about his bruised face. Kiri was glad of that; it had been his briefcase that had done the bruising.

They taped the other blankets up more loosely, so that the centre one could be used as a curtain/door while the one attached to the seats was stationary like a wall.

Then they taped the light-stick to the wall in the space inside the blankets and gathered up all the rest of the supplies. They made their way down the carriage to the others as self-satisfied and smug as two little boys who have raided a neighbour's orchard.

Ahnya Seamore

In the split second it took the Seamore family to race across the room from the table to the door, the earthquake hit, the floor jumping up to meet them and knocking them off their feet. Ahnya hit the floor hard, giving her knees and one wrist a painful jolt. Donstan was wrestling with the sliding glass doors that were refusing to slide, the frame already twisting as the floor bucked and heaved.

He was knocked away from the door, when he'd got it open only a crack, but it was enough for Ahnstan to get his hands into the space and force it bigger using his body as a wedge. The children squeezed through the narrow space, and rolled across the paving to the grass, unable to get to their feet. At the grass they swam across it against the bucking ground, by taking handsful of grass and pulling themselves along, their parents right behind them. Once they were far enough that if the house fell it couldn't fall on them, they turned and lay on their stomachs beside the earthquake kit watching the houses and trees dance and the train trestle writhe.

Donya lay with her head down, and shoulders hunched. An effort to sit up had brought her chin into harsh contact with her knee, causing her to bite her tongue painfully.

They couldn't hear each other over the noise of things breaking and the rumble of the ground beneath them. In a pause Wynson could be heard crying.

"What is it? Are you hurt?"

"I only got one shoe," he sobbed. "I have to get the other one."

"You'll do no such thing! There's broken stuff everywhere!"

As the houses flexed, the windowpanes did not, and the glass cracked, shattered, and popped out of its frames to crumble into fragments on the stone paving outside the houses. Judging by the sound of breakage inside the houses, even things they had thought were earthquake secure hadn't survived this one.

No more could be said, because it hit them again, and they had to lie and watch. Ahnya had noticed something was amiss with Donya but could do nothing but try to put a comforting hand on her daughter's shoulder.

It seemed to go on forever, but it did, finally, stop. "Big one," Ahnya said, unnecessarily when she finally dared to sit up in the eerie silence that followed.

"High sevens, or maybe even eight," Donstan agreed. "Everyone got your shoes on?" He put his on, then tentatively stood up. "Get into the earthquake kit and get the boy shoes while I secure the house."

Ahnstan opened the earthquake kit, a weather-proof box that was in everyone's garden a safe distance from the houses. He took out the vests, green for Donya and Wynson, bright orange for his parents. His father had a fluorescent lime-green 'E' on the back and front of his for

Engineer; his mother had a 'CM' for Communications. He put his own, new yellow vest on and handed the others out, then picked up the hard hats for everyone, which were in the same colours, except he only had a green one despite his new vest. There were sandals for everyone in the kit. He reached in to get Wynson's.

Ahnya was looking inside Donya's mouth at her poor tongue. "It's going to be very painful for a while, lovey, but it doesn't need stitches." She helped Donya on with her vest, put her own on, and reached for her hat. She noticed Wynson was sitting watching his father, not taking any notice of anything else. "Wynn? Put your vest and hat on, son."

Donstan was struggling to get the weather cover open from the controls that were on the outside of every house in case of emergency. The powerful earthquake had shifted the walls of the house out of alignment, which had pulled the hinges out of true. Finally, in frustration, he found enough strength to yank the cover open. He turned off the controls for the power in the house, even though there was no likelihood that the solar panels or windmills were trying to produce any electricity. Many of the little windmills were hanging at odd angles, not turning at all. Then he opened the valves that would allow all of the water from inside the walls, the roof, and the cistern under the house to drain into the storm drains. Then he went along the width of the house to a little trapdoor and opened it so that any of their caged birds that were uninjured enough to fly could get out and not be trapped inside to starve.

Wynson was fixedly watching every move his father made. Ahnya put his hard hat on his head for him, which got a reaction. "I didn't put my shoes away properly. I didn't know we were going to have an earthquake today. I couldn't find it. What if Daddy has to go back in the house to get it? What if the earthquake comes back? He could get killed, and it's all my fault." His teeth started to chatter convulsively. He was going into shock.

"Stop it!" Ahnya said sharply, to break through. "Put your vest on!" Mechanically Wynson obeyed.

"It's not your fault, sonny," she said softly, when she saw the shuddering lessen. "That's why we have spare shoes for everyone in the kit. Ahnstan already has yours for you. Besides, your Dad's an engineer. He knows what he's doing. What did your training tell you?"

"When there's water on the walls, keep out of the house, it's not safe," he said like an automaton. "If the walls are cracked, the water is contaminated, drain the cistern." Then he wailed suddenly, "Mummy! Our house is broken! What's going to happen to us?"

Ahnya looked at the house again. She could feel her own chin quiver as she noticed the tell-tale sign of water running down the weatherboards. She couldn't think about her home, or she'd be useless. "We have to get to our stations," she said briskly, getting to her feet. "What do you do?"

"We have to stay with the hex chief," Donya said thickly, around her swollen tongue.

Ahnya's knee was swelling up, too.

"But what about me, Mum? I've got a yellow vest, but I've still got a green hat."

"You're with me, so don't worry about it. It doesn't matter if a vest doesn't fit properly, but hats have to fit exactly to keep your head safe, so you have to be fitted for one. Bad luck the quake happened the day you got your vest. If we can, we'll paint yellow on your hat."

Donya and Wynson were getting to their feet, turning in a numbed way towards the commons. "We haven't got our badges," Wynson wailed. "Chief won't know what we can do."

"Everyone was there at the trials. Everyone will know what you can do. No one else has their badges either, the earthquake happened to everyone. You can come back to the earthquake kit for your tents and supplies when Chief says to." Ahnya shepherded her shocked children towards the commons. Behind them Donstan looked over, saw no-one was looking, assessed his likely risk, and slipped quickly inside his shattered house.

In the commons the neighbours were gathering. Some were crying, some were injured. The person wearing the white hat was the one in charge of the hex in times of emergency. "Got an injured one here," Ahnya called out, pushing Donya in front of her. Immediately someone wearing a blue vest and hat with a fluorescent white square front and back and a red cross in the middle of the white square, bent over Donya to assess her. "Get everyone out?" Ahnya asked.

"Even Grandmother Lilliprom."

"We were lucky." Ahnya looked around the damaged buildings of the hex, unable to believe that everyone had got out alive. "I brought just the children, not any of our kit; you can decide when you need things from our kit. I have to go."

"Right. You're Communications. We can't get through."

"Yes, I'm heading out right now. Wynson, dear, take care of your sister, she's hurt." Ahnya bent down and kissed each of them, then said briskly to Ahnstan, "Well, Stan, we have work to do."

Pitamete Meithei

It seemed as if only seconds passed after Pitamete Meithei made the announcement to the People before he heard from the Second Public Servant, Olarine Eidola, that she was on her way, and would arrive in two or three hours, and from the Tertiary Servant, Quanita Muliania that she would be there as soon as she could. He expected the King, Ngaronoa Turikora, to walk in the door any minute. Olarine had to take the Flying Fish south and west from her home on the north-east coast to Pitamete's home on the south-west coast of the island of Te Ika a Maui, and Quanita had to travel all the way up from the mid-west coast of the island of Te Wai Pounamu, so they couldn't expect her before tomorrow at the earliest, but Ngaronoa lived only a few kilometres away.

Before he had time to move, the chime went again. He stayed where he was and clicked respond. "Mr. First! She's lifted land up out of the sea. Massive. Sudden. Prime cause of tidal waves. It should head south. Warn the whole east coast and all islands south of Heretaunga Bay to evacuate to high ground. Some places have likely already been hit."

By the time Pitamete had finished giving the evacuation announcement, his home was deep in the business of dealing with the disaster. When he was elected First Servant, his office had been equipped with extra fibre-optic lines in case of emergency, and now they were lighting up like a fireworks display. His meeting room was Command Central, his office was the War Room, filled with people in black vests with black hard hats whose stations were central command. Every few seconds someone was demanding his attention with an urgent, "Mr. First!" He longed to hear someone, anyone, call him Pita in a normal tone of voice.

"Mr. First! There's been a landslide in the Panakiri Range. A six car Flying Fish was caught in it."

"Tanemahuta! How many people were in it?"

"We don't know that yet. They've only just realised what happened to the Fish. The sensors set off an alarm that they'd lost touch with it, which meant it was off the tracks, or that contact with that part of the track was disconnected, but it's not either side of the landslide, so it has to be in it. Search and Rescue is going in by centipede."

Pitamete looked around himself, aghast. It wasn't his place to make that kind of announcement. He was shocked to realise it was only an hour since the earthquake had first hit. He felt as if it had been days. Ngaronoa would have to announce this one. There was no sign of Ngaronoa. "Where's the bloody King?"

"Sir?"

"Has anyone heard anything from King Ngaronoa? I need him."

It wasn't the job of anyone there to look for anyone. People went to their stations and did the tasks they had been trained for. No one offered to help Pita, they just shrugged, said, "I don't know," and continued with their work.

Pita stepped on to his marker again, grumbling, "Everybody else is where they're supposed to be! Of all the people to muck it up! I thought I could count on him more than anyone." Then he made the announcement about the missing six carriages.

Glendrona Tomptell

As soon as the shaking stopped, the children wanted to go home but had to be reminded of the rule they'd been taught. If a disaster happens when you're not at home, stay where you are. "I don't like that rule," Glenda protested, her bottom lip sticking out.

Ms. Sergill decided that what they'd do while they were waiting to find out what had happened, was put all of their instruments away.

Glenda immediately felt guilty that she'd dropped her violin. Forgetting all about what was going on, she picked the violin up and looked it over, anxiously. She couldn't see anything wrong with it, so she put it in its case, and tucked the case into her satchel, hoping no one had noticed.

Ms. Sergill turned on her wall unit as she put some biscuits in her oven to heat through. She poured large glasses of sea moss drink for everyone, while watching the wall unit with half an eye, distributing hugs indiscriminately, and sending the children off to use the toilet. Some of the younger children were crying for their parents, some of the older ones were worrying about theirs. The teacher had the older children take care of the younger ones, even though the age range was only from five to nine.

As comforting as Ms Sergill was, Glenda found the announcement from the First Servant to be terrifying. Not even the wonderful smell of the biscuits helped.

Ms Sergill called everyone together. "Children!" she clapped her hands. "Now listen to me," she said firmly. "The earthquake was a long way from here, up on the east coast of Te Ika a Maui. It was very strong there, but we don't need to be afraid down here in the south. What we felt was like a ripple in a pond. You know when you throw a pebble in a pond, how the ripples spread out right across the pond, but they get smaller the further away they are? It's like that. We might even feel some more shakes, but they won't be as big as that one was. All we have to do now is stay cheerful and happy until it's time for you to go home. Now, before we have our biscuits and sea moss, let's go out to the earthquake kit. Everyone get your shoes on, then line up two by two, bigger children hold the hands of the smaller children. Now, who can tell me what's in the earthquake kit at your house?"

"A tent."

"Right, what else?"

"Light sticks."

"Right, what else?"

"Biscuits?"

"Probably not, but food that will keep, so I'll give you a half-right on that."

They fell silent, not wanting to admit that they couldn't think of anything else. One of the little girls started sucking her thumb.

Ms Sergill helped them out. "There's also medical supplies so you can help someone who gets hurt, rope, matches, wax, things to cook with, clothes, blankets, plastic sheets, disaster vests, hard hats, and a ringer link." She opened the lid of her earthquake kit. "Can you guess what's in the earthquake kit at my house?"

The oldest girl, Moana, said smugly, "The same as everyone else."

"Yes, dear, but I have something else, as well. Because I'm a teacher and I often have lots of children here, I have lots of vests. Does anyone know what colour?"

"I got a badge," Glenda said proudly, "Because I'm learning the colours of the vests."

"Good girl. What are they?"

Suddenly overcome, Glenda couldn't say. She could tell her disaster relief class, but not her music class.

"Who wears green?"

"We do!" The children were triumphant.

"You're right! Now, everyone put these on. Does anyone know what colour I will wear?"

"White," said Glenda confidently.

"No, not white, that is what the Hex Chief wears," one of the boys, Alan, said with scorn.

Ms. Sergill nodded. "Yes, that is what the Hex Chief wears, but it's also what I wear, if I have children in my care when there's a disaster. I wear a white vest with green bands."

They started to giggle as they tried to find approximate sizes for everyone so that their vests weren't so small that they wouldn't do up, nor so big that they wouldn't stay on. They were still trying to achieve this when the Hex Chief ran up, breathless. "Paki, get the children organised. The earthquake's started a tidal wave, we have to get them to high ground. We've got about an hour before it hits."

"But I was just watching," Ms. Sergill gestured towards her house. "It didn't say anything."

"Just came in right now. Evacuate. Hurry, girl, hurry. I'll be back in a tick."

"Right," Ms. Sergill said, clapping her hands again. "Come on, children, quickly now." As she did so, the sirens started wailing. The children went silent, white faced, and large-eyed. Ms. Sergill picked up a coiled rope from her earthquake kit, and all of the packages of food, giving them to the children to run into the house with and set them on the table and run back for more. She also took out the bundled waterproof sheeting and blankets, then followed the children inside.

"Now, children, bring your satchels here." She set the two eldest, Moana and Alan at the table to tie knots in the rope at evenly spaced intervals, and while that was being done, she pulled the musical instruments out of the satchels, stuffed food, bottled water, and the small bundles of tightly rolled, light thermal blankets into each satchel, cramming them until they would hardly close. She got the children to put on all of the warm clothes they had with them, being thankful that they had all worn coats, warm pants, and warm socks in the chilly weather, made them try to go to the bathroom again, even the ones who had only just gone, then settled each full satchel on its owner's back, bidding them line up at the back door two by two as she finished each child, giving each child another glass of sea moss to drink and a warm gooey biscuit to eat while they waited.

She raided her kitchen to find more food that would travel well, and raided her house for more items to keep the children warm while they waited for wherever it was they were going, and packed a full load in her own satchel, including the waterproof sheeting and the rest of the biscuits, took three copies of the list of the children in her class from her lessons records and checked the children she had with her, crossing off the ones that were not there that day, then stuffed two lists in her pocket, and set one on the table with a cup on it to make sure it stayed there. She did all this at a flat run, assuring the children they would be all right, but they had to do exactly as she told them, encouraging them to remember their evacuation drills, and telling them to set their empty glasses on the floor this once, they were not to leave the line to put the glasses on the counter or table.

The Hex Chief, Ngaire, arrived with the children in her care just as Paki Sergill was finishing. Ngaire started to hustle the children, but Paki called to her, "Wait a moment."

Paki took the rope from Moana and Alan, quickly counted how many pairs of children there were, tied a few knots swiftly into the rope, then re-arranged the children's pairs in their line so that she had an older child with a younger child, the youngest of the music students right at the front of the line, then put the rope between them so that every child was hanging on to a knot in the rope. Then she shouldered her own satchel, found a stout walking stick, put herself at the head of the rope and placed Ngaire at the end, with the children in Ngaire's care closest to her. Some of the children with Ngaire were younger than the music students.

"Got your lists?" Ngaire asked.

Paki patted her pocket, indicating that she had. "Now we go. Anyone know any marching songs?" Off they set at the fastest clip the youngest child could manage, straight to the train trestle and up the steps, round and round for the height of three floors, onto the platform, all of the children being held together by holding on to the rope, Ngaire scolding any child who didn't keep a tight hold of it.

CHAPTER TWENTY-EIGHT

Insurrection

As hard as Chuck Damascus had ridden, he was too late. He could see the truck leaving Hosea's farm with a jeep in front of it and another one behind. It was the standard formation that the Purity Protection League used for arrests. For the fear factor the PPL were always scarier than the regular military.

Sick at the thought that Sam had been arrested again, Chuck headed off to the underground's meeting place as fast as he could without lathering his horse. He couldn't imagine what the Underground would do without Sam. All he could think to do was pray that Joe Mack Capernaum had got there in time to warn Sam that the PPL were planning to arrest him.

Joe Mack had taken a different route to double their chances of one of them getting there in time. They had both stayed off the well patrolled routes; not only to duck patrols, but also because it was way quicker to take shortcuts that the PPL didn't know about and couldn't see from the main road.

Praying for something – anything – that would have made it possible for Joe Mack to have got Sam out of there before the detail arrived, Chuck stopped at a stream to let his horse drink and graze while he climbed up to the spot on foot. Rubin's horse was there already.

Lying quietly on his stomach watching nothing, Chuck felt his pounding heart calm down.

Joe Mack shifted so that he could see in that direction without showing himself. "Where?" he asked after the pronghorn.

"Racing the truck. It's passed the rear-guard jeep and it's gaining on the truck."

"That's what I saw," Rubin let his breath out. "Couldn't quite make it out. Your eyes are sharper than mine. They'd better stop before they get to them. They are young guys. They'll be all sorts of emotional after what's happened and pumped right the hell up, so they'll be boiling to just act without thinking."

Joe Mack was all business. "Do you know who's doing it?" he asked after the road stoppage.

Rubin shrugged. "It's got to be local boys. I think the surge in sabotage around here started when we brought Hosea's son, Emmanuel, back when he'd served his time."

"Do you think he's doing it?"

"Nah. When he did his tour of duty, he saw things he couldn't live with, just like we did, but he never found anything like the Explorers when he got home. He got in with young guys that did anything and everything that would mess with the GR. He got himself and everyone else except his Dad thrown in the hole. He blames himself. Ain't no way he'll do that again. He's stayed out of sight so he wouldn't lead the Purity Protection League to his Dad. It's not him doing it, it's guys who knew him before he was tortured. Re-education made him nuts. Not shocky like my Dad, but real loco. The Rebels are messing with the PPL to get back at them for what they did to Emmanuel."

"Stupid shits! One slip, just one slip here endangers all of us and them. It could tip our hand."

"Oh, hell yeah. They're going to get all the farms around here torched and the farmers captured or killed . . ." Chuck stared at the convoy, willing the drivers, "Stop, you dumb fucks. Stop right now."

"Hmmm." Joe Mack chewed his moustache. "I think maybe they won't."

Rubin caught his breath. "Even little kids know you can't out-run a pronghorn. You got to pull over and let them win."

"Yeah, everyone from pronghorn country knows that, but the PPL guys ain't never posted near their home territory."

"Oh, no! You don't really think . . ."

Joe Mack muttered, "Yeah, I'm afraid so. There's a good chance the commander don't know a pronghorn ain't no regular deer."

Chuck's heart started pounding. He couldn't get past the image of Sam in that prisoner box, shackled and cuffed. If the pronghorn cut in front of the truck to do its victory run the way they do, Sam would be thrown around like corn in a popper. "The guys will tell him. It's their hide too. Maybe one of them will shoot it."

Joe Mack looked back at the rebels. "The only good thing, if they don't stop or shoot it, is it'll pass them before they get to the ambush."

Chuck couldn't believe his ears. "How's that going to help? Sam's in that box!"

"Yeah, I know. Begging your pardon, Rubin, but you know we can't do nothing for your Dad. It'd be a mercy for him to be killed outright so they can't use him to teach the locals a lesson. Standing in front of a tribunal of inquisitors of the Purity Protection League is hell on earth in normal times, but when something like this has gone down then torture ain't to get a confession or save souls: it's a warning to others so that they won't want to join the resistance. That's why it's more and more public and grisly these days: it's not about truth; it's about power and control through fear."

"I know you're right." Rubin put his head in his hands. "If they crash and it kills him, it'll still be a rescue to him. He'd be better off that way than going through it all again. He ain't never got over the first time."

Chuck felt sick. "Oh, hell, man, that's harsh. They got to stop. One of them's got to know about pronghorns. They're everywhere."

Joe Mack shook his head. "It's better if they don't. If the rebels ambush these guys Sammy's in just as much shit as if they hit the pronghorn. Difference is, one's a pure old act of God and the commander might even get reamed for it and the local hot heads ain't close enough to get blamed. The other one's a straight-out attack on the GR by the enemy within. That'll get all the farms in a day's ride burnt to the ground. The PPL won't care who done it. The farmers and their families will go down dead or wounded and captured. The young guys ain't just risking their own sorry hides but everyone they know. They got a fire under them after what's happened to Emmanuel, but there ain't enough of them to do anything but get the whole thing busted and everyone pulled in."

"You're right, but how can we do anything about it?"

"No time. Pray there's no ambush, or else Sam's lifetime of effort won't mean nothing."

After that the three men sat silently watching the pronghorn race the convoy until Rubin slid backwards on his belly away from the prow of the hill, saying, "That loco buck's going to pass them way before they get to the ess bend."

"What are you doing?"

"I'm going down there in case I get a chance to go after my Dad."

He was gone before Chuck and Joe Mack could say anything. Joe Mack cussed and followed him, saying, "We got to stop him. It's too dangerous. What if someone gets shot?"

Hurrying to catch up, Chuck reminded Joe Mack, "It's his Dad."

"Yeah, I know. I'd want to save my Dad, too, but we can't allow it no matter how bad he wants to. There ain't enough of us to carry on Sam's work without him. It'll all be over for the

Underground if we lose any more."

Trying to think of a way to survive it if they couldn't stop it, Chuck suggested, "Any injured or dead can be hauled onto horseback and brought back to Hosea's."

"No, that's the first place they'll look. That's where they just got Sam from. The early stages are the most dangerous for accidentally revealing the whole thing."

When they reached their horses, Rubin was already out of sight. Chuck argued as he mounted, "Hosea's is still the safest until we find someplace else for anything more than first aid. We can hide them till they recover enough to move them someplace safe. Hosea's is the best place to base out of. He won't talk, but there ain't no guarantee of another farmer keeping quiet around the pickle barrel."

"You missed the whole point. The Ashies that have been keeping the northern border from being pushed further north have been messing with the GR for generations. When I got there to see if we could set up some place for people to go when we got them over the border, they were already rescuing people that made it that far, so they're not only all set up to move escapees, they've had lots of experience. They're real pleased to help us with something bigger and gave us some good tips on how to set it up without painting a target on our heads. What they pushed real hard is it's too easy to stay with places that you're used to. Too many groups get busted because all the Security Shield must do is keep an eye on them and they lead the way right to their base. We can't go to Hosea's until we're real sure it ain't staked out, just like we never checked on Hosea and Maria after Sam got snatched."

They reined in before they could be seen from the road. Chuck tried to spot Rubin without sticking his head up too far, telling Joe Mack, "That's the same as everything else. It's no different taking wounded guys there than anything else we do."

"You still don't get it. We ain't got enough guys to have an Underground if we lose any more. We got to get bigger before we take risks like this, or Sam's sacrifice is all for nothing." He pointed, "I'll go this way, you go that way, and if you see Rubin sit on him and make sure he don't run off half cocked and get himself killed or captured."

Chuck tethered his horse and set off on foot. There wasn't time to do anything before the PPL was on top of them. Chuck flattened himself so that the soldiers wouldn't see him. The heavy breathing and thundering hooves of the pronghorn were almost drowned out by the roar of the motors, but that was nothing when compared with the ear-splitting racket from the truck. It was obvious to Chuck that its engine was on the edge of seizing up. Whether they'd damaged the engine by pushing it too hard, or didn't dare stop in case it wouldn't start again, it was only too clear that they had no chance of avoiding the pronghorn unless they slowed right down, right then.

The animal was drawing ahead of the lead jeep. It was running beside the passenger side front wheel, and then it put on a burst of speed and started to pull ahead. "Stop now!" Chuck willed the driver.

But no one stopped or even slowed down. As if he was dreaming, Chuck watched the pronghorn pass the jeep and take a sudden dodge to the left without even bothering to clear it completely.

With a scream of tortured brakes, the jeep swerved violently. The truck stood on its nose, trying to avoid the skidding jeep but still smacked into it. The jeep clipped the pronghorn, flinging it up into the air. The pronghorn came down on the truck's radiator cap with a sickening crunch and slid along the hood and through the windshield into the soldier riding shotgun.

The rear jeep came to a stop beside the smoking truck, the two men leaping out to run to the aid of their buddies.

In the eerie silence that followed, a horse and rider appeared galloping full speed across the fields towards the ess bend. Chuck half expected a detail to take off after them, but it seemed that the rebel had guessed right: the soldiers were all too busy with the accident to do anything about him.

The lead jeep was out of Chuck's sight, but that didn't matter: all of the activity was around the truck. They had the cab doors open and were struggling frantically. Chuck couldn't make out what they were doing through the moving backs, but he could guess that the guy who had been riding shotgun was trapped by the body of the pronghorn.

Two guys were standing guard in the back of the truck, guns drawn, watching the prisoners as well as all around. 'They're expecting an ambush!' he thought, praying that Joe Mack had found Rubin and was keeping him from trying to rescue Sam. He was sure that he and Joe Mack were right that there were extra men hidden in the truck

"Typical PPL operation," he muttered. "The reason for the raid in the first place was to try to root the rebels out. They want to be attacked because that will draw out the bulk of the rebels. They let that guy go so that he'll bring the whole group back here."

Remembering some of the action he'd seen, Chuck figured the commander might be hoping for an ambush. The pronghorn was a tactical surprise, but they weren't startled strategically. They were hustling to get set up while they waited for the rebels to come riding on the attack. It would look like the rebels had the PPL, something that didn't happen much or for long, so angry young men wouldn't be able to resist.

To check his theory, he took a closer look at the number of men. There were too many. He counted again. There had been a driver and relief in each vehicle; that's six, plus two visible guards in the back of the truck. He should be able to see no more than eight . . . seven, if it was true that the guy in the truck was hurt. Yet he could see seven around the truck plus the two guards. That cover . . . he looked to see if there was any movement under it. It was suspicious all by itself because the PPL usually let prisoners be seen as a lesson. Why cover them this time unless it was to hide troops?

Convinced that the rebels were riding into an ambush, Chuck tried to figure out how to warn them. He slid carefully away from his hiding place making sure that the soldiers couldn't catch sight of him, then raced to his horse and galloped along the crick.

Knowing he couldn't be seen from the road; he gave it everything he had until his horse pricked its ears forward. Not wanting to be taken by surprise by whatever it was that caught the horse's interest; he pulled it up the bank out of sight. As soon as they were standing quietly, he heard the sound of many horses running towards them along the crick. He slid down off his horse and put his hand over its muzzle to keep it quiet. He wanted to be sure it wasn't some sort of PPL rear-guard action before he made his presence known.

It was clear that this was not a PPL detail. Not only were they not in uniform, they were young kids, right in that age when boys think they're invincible – between twelve and twenty. He needed to let them know he was there without scaring them so much that they shot him, so he let his horse greet the other horses, and waved his hat.

As they clattered and splashed to a stop, Chuck was looking down the barrels of a half a dozen assorted guns. It was just as bad as he'd feared. These kids had no chance against battle hardened troops. Not only were they seriously out-gunned – some had only sling-shots – but they hesitated and didn't act as one. He ignored their weapons – if they were going to shoot him, they would have – and called out to them, "You boys know the PPL hit a pronghorn back there?"

"What about it?"

"You got to know they got a heap of guys sneaked under the truck canopy."

"Yeah? How do you figure that?"

"I saw it."

"Oh, yeah . . . they just happened to let you see, huh? How come Mike was there and never said nothing, huh?"

"If Mike's the guy that took off on horseback galloping in a direct line across the fields, he was gone before the hidden guys moved. I only seen one, maybe two, extra guys."

"You don't know? Can't you count?"

Chuck could tell from the reaction to his description of the ride who Mike was. He looked Mike in the eye as he said, "Just a few points . . . the PPL might not have lit out after you, but you can be sure at least one of them paid real close attention to where you went and what you're wearing and the brand on your horse. So, if you're planning on going near them don't take any horses with that brand; swap your shirt, hat, and saddle blanket with different guys so no two pieces are together; if you had anything in that direction, move it now before they get themselves organized; and stop using your real names."

"We ain't got time for this bullshit." One of the older boys slammed his shotgun into its holster and turned to ride off.

Chuck remounted to ride with them. Because they all put away their weapons and turned to continue their ride when he did, Chuck assumed the boy was their leader. He studied the young man as the ride resumed its course along the shallow crick back towards the crash. He figured the leader was less than twenty years old and had probably spent no more than the minimum one year in the military, being excused from full service to the nation by either land deferment or some kind of physical problem. Chuck would have put money on something physical that left the would-be hero trying to prove that he was as good as everyone else, with enough time in the barracks to think that he knew all about the military, but not enough to get that there were things he didn't know.

If he was right about this guy, Chuck had his work cut out for him to convince the kids not to play right into the soldier's hands. Seeing that the boys riding behind the leader were switching clothes around gave Chuck the idea that they maybe didn't follow their leader blindly.

He tried talking directly to the followers. "There's a good reason for never using your real names."

"Like what?"

"The investigators can't get out of you what you never knew."

They jeered. "Making up names don't mean we don't know who we are . . . we grew up together."

"I did not know that. I'm not from around here. Neither are the PPL. So now you gave me info you don't want no one outside your families to know."

The leader turned on Chuck in a rage. "You planning to turn us in, is that it?"

"If I was, you would've never seen me. If I'm arrested now, I'm as dangerous to you as any of your family or friends."

"Ain't none of them will talk!"

"No? What about a six-year-old boy or a ten-year-old girl under a lash?"

There was an uneasy silence broken only by the splashing of the horses' hooves in the crick and the creaking of the saddle leather.

That was too much for the would-be hero. "Hey, old man, we never asked you to ride with us."

Chuck refused to be riled by a smart-mouth kid. "True. But you don't have to thank me. It's my way of supporting your cause – by keeping you all alive and seeing that your Parish ain't burned to the ground or re-educated."

"Don't listen to him! He's just trying to scare you. Look, old man, if your generation never had the guts to stand up for what's right, that's your failure. It don't mean we're gutless like you, and it don't give you the right to horn in on our action to make up for not doing what you should have done when you should have done it."

There were mixed sounds from the others. Chuck could see that some agreed with the know-it-all, and some didn't. Splitting them up would slow down their activities. That was a good place for him to start. "I've been standing up for what's right since before you were born. My friends were just as brave as you. The only difference is that some of us found out how guys stayed out of the gun sights of the Security Shield and some of us didn't. All my buddies that did things the way you're doing them are dead. All of them. So, you don't need to worry about me horning in on your action . . . I want to live longer than this. I'm here to make sure you know they got an ambush set up for you, and to give you some pointers on how to stay alive and not get your Mamas burned up in their houses, then I'm gone. I ain't fixing to go down with you."

All the boys were reacting in different ways. As he expected, the leader was so angry that he hardly made sense. The ones who agreed with him were muttering dangerously, but the others were having a variety of reactions, from fear or concern to curiosity.

They interrupted their leader's rant. "No, wait. He's got some good points."

"I told you not to listen to him! You're either with me or against me."

"It ain't about you. It's about us watching each other's backs and getting out of this together."

"If you want a safe job, why are you here?"

Chuck was pleased that the rebels were disagreeing with each other, but he didn't want them to get into a full-on fight during the ride. "You have to be sure what it is you're trying to do."

"Don't pee on my leg and tell me it's raining! It's obvious to anyone that really was doing this since before we were born, but not so much to someone from the Security Shield trying to find out what's going on, huh, Mr SS Spy?"

It was so stupid that Chuck would have laughed if he hadn't been so very aware that this aggressive ass and his hairy little buddies were armed and dangerous. "If the SS was on to you, they would send the PPL after you. The PPL don't do things like spy. They do things like set up an ambush to kill you all."

"You're full of shit. The SS's got to tell the PPL who they want."

"They don't care who you are. It's easier and faster to set a trap, kill a lot of you, and interrogate the captured survivors. So, you still have to figure out what you're putting your lives on the line for. Is it to make a long term difference, or is it to go out in a blaze of glory?"

There was a mixed reaction to that, too, ending with one of the boys pressuring their leader, "We got to hear what he's got to say. It might help our cause."

"Yeah, right, like making up names will stop the PPL from finding us."

"Well, no, it's . . ." the boy looked at Chuck in confusion. "If you don't use no name, what can we call you?"

Chuck grinned, "Oh, I can't think of a better name than the 'Old Man,' can you?"

There were grins and sniggers from some, glares and sneers from others.

He went serious. "Of course it won't stop the PPL, but it will help you keep from giving yourselves away by accident. Pick names that don't mean nothing, like you can be 'Blue' because you got blue eyes." He turned to the others, "And 'Shy' if you don't talk much or if you talk a lot, and 'Rider' for a real good or a real bad horseman. That way if someone overhears you, you don't give away the guys that are not there."

Blue protested, "I ain't using no stupid name like, 'Blue'!"

"For your own sakes never use a name like 'Ace,' or 'Boss,' because that will paint a target on your head. The interrogators will figure you're the leader and that you know way more than you do. If you can't give them the answers, they want the torture is worse and goes on for longer."

Blue boasted, "They got to catch us first."

Chuck tried sarcasm. "Yep. And it ain't such a bad idea to ride right into the trap. Once the unit can show enough heads to satisfy the brass that they got the rebel leaders and punished their followers and hurt them bad enough that there won't be any more trouble from this group, the government probably won't burn your Parish to the ground. It ain't for sure. They might want to make an example of you to make sure it's a long time before anyone else has the balls to stick their neck out."

"We ain't riding into the trap!"

No matter how angry or defiant Blue sounded, Chuck could see that the others were not so sure. Even the boys who had been loyal to Blue were starting to look uneasy. "That's the idea! What's your plan? You'd be smart to use the advantages you got over the PPL."

"Oh, now we're better than them?"

"You got some strong points, they got others. You're all from here and familiar with the area: they're not. They don't even know enough to pull over for a pronghorn. They got you beat in military training: only you guys over sixteen have had any, and you had just a taste or else you wouldn't be here. You can cut across country, but they got to stick to roads where they can run their vehicles, especially when they got two prisoners to keep from rescue."

"Two? What makes you think they got two?"

"After they took Sam, they went east for about long enough to get someone else before they headed west towards the prison."

All the boys spoke at once. "Took who?"

"Who's Sam?"

"The guy that's helping out Emmanuel's Dad."

"That just proves you don't know dick all, Old Man! You don't even know who they got."

"It ain't Sam?" Chuck was so thrown by the news that he distracted his horse, which stumbled. The other horses reacted to the floundering one, so the whole ride had to slow down while the horses were sorted out. "Are you real sure?" he asked, desperately, as he settled his horse. "Why the hell would they go for Hosea? He never had nothing to do with it. He don't even know what we're doing." He bit his lip, annoyed with himself for his careless words.

It was too late. The boys talked over each other again.

"Yeah, I'm sure. I watched them march Hosea out of the house in chains."

"Nothing to do with what?"

"How do you know Hosea? You ain't from here."

"What do you mean, 'what we're doing'? We who? Doing what?"

They had come to a stop, the rebels surrounding Chuck. "I can't tell you any more than you can tell me who you are or what you've been doing. What you've got to understand is you didn't invent resistance. There are a lot of men and women working in a lot of different ways and places. You can learn from their mistakes, or you can make the same mistakes all over again and learn the hard way. Your choice."

For once no one had anything to say, so he added, "Your best bet is to stay away."

In the yelling that followed, Chuck heard one voice of reason. "We can't stay away, Mister. Someone's got to watch for Emmanuel and stop him from doing something stupid."

"That's a good reason. Where is he?"

They started off again, one of the boys telling him, "We don't know, but if he heard that it's his Dad that was took. . ."

"Yeah." Chuck knew what he meant. "Emmanuel got the worst case of joint jitters I've ever seen. Not just the shakes like S – some people, but the cheese done come right off his cracker."

"How do you know Emmanuel?"

"Ever wonder how he got back here when he got out? There are more people doing more things than you think. Emmanuel stayed away from Hosea because he didn't want to lead the PPL to him. If he finds out his Dad got picked up anyway, there's no knowing what he could do."

"That's what we figured."

"What's your plan?"

"We'll see when we get there."

"No, no, no! You got to put it together like a military op. You got to do a real full recon. If you run out and try to save Hosea before you've done recon, they'll get the lot of you."

"Who said we're going to spring Hosea?"

"If all you're planning to do is find Emmanuel and sit on him, you still must plan and stick to it. And you must cover your horse brands, so they won't be able to trace you back to your farm and torch it."

Blue scoffed, "You don't know shit, Old Man. We want them to see the brands."

Chuck scratched his head to try to come up with a way to persuade the young rebels that was the last thing they wanted. "Uh . . ."

One of the riders took pity on him and explained, "We changed the brands, so they look like brands from original GR families."

Chuck stared for a moment, sorting out what he'd just heard. "You re-branded your horses?" He stared at the brands, seeing what they'd done before Blue finished snorting in derision. "Paint!"

They laughed, proudly. "Yeah, mine's the President's."

"Mine's a general."

"Mine's a senator."

Laughing, Chuck held up his hands to stop them from all listing where their fake brands came from. "I get it. Real smart. It'll work if they don't get close, but you know what'll happen if you get caught. That's worse than ghost horses, and you know the penalty for running unbranded critters."

"I guess you're going to tell us we didn't ought to it."

Chuck sighed, "None of us should be doing any of the things we're doing. It's a matter of not taking unnecessary risks. Use them if you got them, but don't forget what'll happen to anyone caught riding re-marked horses. If any of you get caught it won't matter to you a whole bunch if you're on ghost horses or not. Where it will make a difference is when the SS is deciding if this Parish should be punished."

"Oh, Holy Hannah! These guys are serious!"

"Yeah, they are."

"What if Emmanuel tries to spring Hosea tonight?"

"I thought you were out here to stop him."

"Yeah, what if we can't find him in time?"

Blue spoke proudly, "We have his back, of course! If Emmanuel goes for it, maybe we can get Hosea out."

That was exactly what Chuck had feared the most. Knowing that the young man was deliberately challenging him, Chuck did his best to stall them without taking the bait. "Don't even try without more guys."

"If we can't get him now it's going to be a hell of a lot harder to do it after they are taken off to the facility. Even the barracks is too well defended."

"Just the same, don't try it without more guys and a good battle plan."

"Standard military tactics: first disable the lead vehicle, and then while the convoy is stopping, you disable the rear vehicle so once they're stopped, they can't back out of the trap."

"It's nice to know you paid some mind in basic training but that's so basic that it's the first thing they'll be ready for."

"You don't get it, Old Man! The pronghorn already done it all for us."

"Yeah, I get it all right. The SS ordered a raid to take out what they believe are the heads of the rebels. The PPL sent a small but real good force that's smart, well armed, and well trained. From the military point of view, they're good soldiers that don't panic when they're outnumbered or hit by surprise. They're probably not even hand picked, just a good, highly rated group that's battle proven and has a good reputation for getting the job done. Perhaps the higher ups wanted two men, but the unit decided on their own hook to see what else they can flush out. Good soldiers take the imitative. After all, there's nothing like being sent for two men and coming back saying you have crushed the whole thing."

"Or maybe they were ordered to get all of us."

"True. The difference is that if it's the guys no one knows exactly where the rebels came from. They're hoping to get lucky. If it's the SS they're onto you."

"You don't know. You're making it up as you go."

"I know that if you make it through this damned fool try to spring Hosea, the PPL will take it out on everyone in a day's ride of here."

"They can't say who staged it."

"I told you before, they don't care. They're just as happy to torch the whole Parish and use you as an example to scare everyone out of rebelling."

"They can't burn the farmland! This is the breadbasket of the GR – ain't no President going to start a famine."

"If they think the farmers helped in any way, they're gonna kill everyone and torch the place in retribution. It used to be we were fighting to build the republic and to stamp out the perversions that destroyed the old one, but now things have got all twisted. The young ones take too much joy in their power over people. Some are truly cruel and sadistic. More and more is considered a crime every year, and less and less gets you before the inquisition. The efforts to stamp out resistance and rebellion and heresy have gotten stronger and more grisly and more methodical. Didn't you hear about the punishment handed out along the northern border?"

"Yeah, but they really deserved it."

"They were blowing up communications. Conquered farmers fighting to get their freedom back. What do you think the news will say about you? You got to have it all planned. Horses are harder to hide than people. Disguising your brands will only help if they know the brands you're showing and if they don't capture a painted horse. They don't know local faces or family groups all that well. They're not local so they can only recognise markers like clothes, boots, hats, saddles, blankets, horses, and brands. So, stay out of sight or at least far out of range. Switching stuff will only work once or twice."

"I ain't worried. Horses can go where deer go and vehicles can't."

"You're not just farmers; you're all hunters, too. Use your hunting skills. If the idea was to chop off the heads of the rebellion, and the guys planned a strike so that they will get promotions or commendations for killing or capturing the body of the rebellion, they would need something to get their target to come out where they can find it. Not a convoy so big that it scares you all off, and not so small that it gets destroyed, but something small with concealed firepower. They are not as thrown by the accident as you'd think because they were expecting an ambush so that they could report that they 'handled' the situation by getting the leaders and killing the rebels when they were ambushed. The pronghorn saved your sorry hides."

Blue was scornful. "Just how can you get all that from a fuck-up because they are too stupid to stop for a racing pronghorn?"

"The PPL always show their prisoners so that their family and friends and neighbours get taught a lesson. This prison box is covered and there is a squad under the cover. I served in the Panhandle under Magic Jack Lycus, the master of tricking the enemy. I seen this before. They can go back heroes with losses, but a huge enemy body count and they took out the heads as well. All legit if the commander reports the rebels tried to free the prisoners. So, to say they cut off the head and seriously pruned back the hands of the rebels, the squad's got to have something to give a harder punch than their ambushers expect."

Finally Blue was quiet.

"We got to find Emmanuel," one of the kids told the others, forcefully.

With great relief, Chuck told them, "I'll leave you here. Stay alive so that you're around for bigger and better things than this."

He rode back to the vantage point. It was a huge relief to see Joe Mack's and Rubin's horses were there. He hurried up the hill, creeping as quietly as possible. "Rube, it ain't your Dad."

Rubin just stared.

Joe Mack demanded, "What?"

"They arrested Hosea, not Sam. I found the rebels. They saw the PPL coming and rode to Hosea's farm to head Emmanuel off if he tried to save his Dad. They saw Hosea marched out of his house in shackles and cuffs."

"You found them? Where are they?" Joe Mack demanded.

"Trying to find Emmanuel so that they can make sure he doesn't get himself killed trying to rescue his Dad."

"Yeah, they better feel guilty," Rubin growled. "This whole raid is their fault."

"They're just kids. The oldest is trying to pass himself off as a grown man, but I'm putting him at seventeen or eighteen, and they go down from there to maybe fourteen, but the youngest might be as little as twelve." Chuck crawled up to the edge of the slope while they were talking. "Holy . . ." he'd expected to see the PPL further along than they were.

The lead jeep had been hauled out of the ditch, and the body of the pronghorn had been pulled from the truck, but nothing much else seemed to have been done. "What have they been doing?"

Rubin pointed out, "See that tarp over the back of the good jeep? It's covering their commanding officer. When they got the buck off him, he was dead."

Joe Mack intoned in a graveyard drone, "Beat by the buck's butt."

Chuck couldn't help snickering. He slid back from the edge so that he wouldn't make the grass tremble and catch the guard's attention. "What a shitty way to go," he said, all the tension boiling over into laughter. He pressed his mouth into his sleeve to keep the noise down, but he couldn't stop.

Joe Mack didn't help when he slid down beside him and added, "Would that make him pissed off or pissed on?"

Even Rubin joined in. "One thing's for sure . . . the pronghorn ain't got the guts to do that again."

Still laughing, Chuck managed to gasp out, "Spilled his guts, did he?"

"Filled the front seat with broken glass, and shit and piss and blood and guts," said Joe Mack, who couldn't keep up his mock-solemn tones and collapsed flat to the ground with muffled laughter.

Rubin was the first one of them to be able to pull himself together enough to bring Chuck up to speed on what had been happening. "They had to get the buck off their CO and try to clean him up."

Chuck couldn't help it, he had to ask, "Did they give him mouth to mouth? That'd be a crappy job."

"You said a mouthful," Rubin snorted, losing his fight to stop laughing.

They laughed until they were weak.

Rubin rolled onto his back, wiping his eyes. "I thought for sure they took my Dad."

Chuck and Joe Mack instantly sobered up, caught each other's eye and sneaked back up to the prow of the hill to peer through the brush.

Joe Mack filled Chuck in. "Looks like the pronghorn hit the radiator cap and knocked the rad into the fan. When they got the buck off the truck, the hood was caved in, so they had to pry it open to get the radiator off the fan. They pulled the jeep that clipped the buck out of the arroyo with the other jeep. They been working on it ever since."

Chuck tried to figure out what had happened to the jeep. "It hit the buck hard enough to throw in it up onto the hood of the truck. That could have wrapped the fender around the wheel, and it would have to be pried off or the jeep ain't going nowhere."

Rubin disagreed, "Nah, if that's all it was they'd be done by now."

"Maybe the fender cut the tire," Joe Mack suggested. "Remember that time on the Northern Front when that jeep hit a boulder? The fender got bent into the tire. It blew the tire out, and the bits of tire tore the wires and hoses under the hood to rat-shit. The spare tire never did a thing to get them going after the damaged tire ripped the guts out. It took them forever to walk to where they could send for parts to splice and patch the gas and fluid lines."

Chuck grunted acknowledgement, remembering not to nod his head because the movement would give the guards something to focus on. "I remember those guys caught hell because they'd took the pieces off." He could see the guards constantly scanning in all directions, paying careful attention to any place that could hide a sniper, like the high spot where he was hiding. He watched the soldiers struggling to pry the fender off the wheel, and realised, "They got more problems than the wheel. That's a steep ditch full of rocks. They had the fender off. It's holed the oil pan.

You can have extra oil, but you can't put your finger in the hole to get you home."

Rubin questioned that. "Are you sure? I don't see no oil on the road. Maybe they broke or bent an axle and they're trying to free up the wheel enough that it rolls and tow it."

"Military vehicles got tough axles, so it would be a bang to snap it. I can see a dark patch that I think is oil, not shadows."

Joe Mack added, "They got themselves in shit if you're right. The truck's got a broken rad. It's undriveable even if it ain't full of blood and guts and crap. Ain't like tearing off the quarter panel will get it rolling. It needs parts that they don't got with them. If they don't get the jeep rolling, they're screwed. It ain't as bad if that dark patch you can see is gas. They got extra gas. Oil pan is harder to deal with. Running out of gas is annoying. Running out of oil breaks engines. If all they got wrong with the jeep is a bent but usable axle or tie rod or busted steering, they can make it to the nearest farm and bunker down, but with busted transmission lines or holed oil pan they're sitting ducks."

Chuck was surprised by Joe Mack's tone. "You say that like it's a bad thing."

"I wouldn't want to see a shooting war all up and down the road. You know what the end of that would be."

"Yeah, you're right, but the rebels ain't going to attack. They get that it won't help their cause, and it'll set the SS off on this Parish, wiping out everything they're fighting to save."

Joe Mack snorted. "I'll believe that when I see it. Ain't no sabotager in the whole GR going to pass up a crippled platoon that's got two of their relatives, or neighbours, or even friends. It ain't natural."

Rubin commented, "If they can pull that off, we should get together with them. If they've got smarts like that, it will be the beginning of the Underground as an organized and active thing."

Chuck told them, "You both missed the biggest problem. Why is the prison box covered?"

Joe Mack grunted, "Yeah, we talked about that. We would have seen them when they crashed if there were extra guys there."

"Oh, yeah? How many guys can you see?"

"Eight."

"That's one too many."

"It's only one."

"I saw two extra before. They got room to hide a squad. I been thinking. A twelve-man platoon of three four-man squads."

Joe Mack insisted, "We would have seen more of them when they hit the buck."

"No, not if it was an ambush. It looks to me that one platoon was sent on a raid mission and this lieutenant assigned duties in four-man squads. Squad one is four guys who are great drivers, one in each truck with a spare driver to ride shot gun in one of the other vehicles. Squad two is the quick response troops of hardened infantry geared for everything from long range shootouts to hand-to-hand combat. Squad three is the heavies that they're hiding. They're specially chosen weapons experts or mission specialists or something like that. Some kind of weapons or strategy to make it worth it to sucker the rebels into ambushing them."

Joe Mack was starting to say that he thought Chuck was wrong when a change in the activity distracted all three of them.

The soldiers stopped working on the damaged jeep. They were going to the truck and moving the good jeep.

Rubin muttered, "They can't fix the jeep. They got to tow it."

As soon as Rubin said it, Chuck could see that was what the soldiers were doing. "Ain't no way they can get everyone in the jeeps."

Joe Mack added, "They ain't going back to the prison. They're turning around."

"Yeah, I bet they're going to limp to a farm for repairs." Chuck had no sooner said that when a horse and rider erupted out of cover and high tailed it towards the farm.

"Damn, those kids are good!" Joe Mack exclaimed. "I was watching for them, and I never saw them. They must be going to warn the family."

"The PPL won't be able to see him from that angle," Chuck observed. "They won't know that the farm was warned."

Rubin explained, "The closest farm that the PPL could see from the road is old man Comfort's place."

"Now I can see them," Joe Mack said in satisfaction. "They're in the trees and scrub around the convoy."

Chuck watched in tense silence as one jeep towed the other back past the truck. He was praying as hard as he could that the rebels wouldn't attack anyway, despite everything he'd told them.

It gave him a certain amount of satisfaction to hear Joe Mack say, "Holy Smoke! You were right!" as a whole squad emerged from under the cover on the back of the truck, marching the prisoners ahead of them.

"Oh, God, it is Hosea," Rubin breathed. Relief flowed from in waves so strong they were almost solid.

"It wasn't Sam," Chuck agreed.

"We got to get to Hosea's and make sure Sam's okay," Joe Mack decided. "Hosea's is safe for the moment while the whole platoon is busy here. You can bet if they left someone watching, they would have gone and got them to help with this mess."

Hosea was being prodded to the front, the other prisoner stumbling behind him, hampered by the shackles. Chuck could see the formation that the PPL was going for. The jeeps at the rear, the body in the good jeep; two men in the towed jeep, weapons raised, facing back to the abandoned truck; the soldiers marching beside the jeeps, behind the prisoners. "Using them as shields," he thought. It was overkill to have so many heavily armed men against two old guys who could barely walk in their shackles and chains. Chuck would have made a sneering comment about it, but he was distracted by Rubin grunting his agreement with Joe Mack and starting to move.

An explosion of noise from the road made him jerk his head back around, terrified that the rebels had attacked after all.

There was such confusion that it took Chuck a moment to sort out what had happened. The soldiers were firing on a strange man who was charging the prisoners on a big horse that Chuck had never seen before.

Joe Mack started, "See, I told you . . ."

Chuck cut him off. "It ain't them."

Rubin announced, "It's Emmanuel."

"How the . . ."

"He came from nowhere!"

They watched in heart-pounding horror as their worst nightmare unfolded on the road.

Before the clouds of black-powder smoke got too thick for them to see through, they saw Emmanuel gallop straight at Hosea who sort of jumped, chains and all, was caught by his son, thrown across the horse's shoulders, and whisked away, amid gunfire and blasts from flamethrowers.

The men covering the rear turned, and as they did both sprouted arrows out of their backs from invisible rebels. As they went down, one of their weapons fired.

The other prisoner and the man behind him went down.

Gunfire erupted in all directions.

The blue smoke hung in the air, so heavily that they couldn't see what the soldiers were doing.

All they could see clearly was the horse bolting headlong across the fields. It's screaming told them that it had been hit. Hosea bounced on its shoulders like a sack of potatoes. Emmanuel was curled over his Dad until his head was almost on Hosea's back. Emmanuel wasn't dead or unconscious because he was staying in the saddle and holding Hosea on, but he wasn't controlling the animal, which was in a panic-stricken stampede.

"If he pulls this off, Hosea can be the test of the over-the-mountains network we've been trying to set up," Joe Mack suggested.

"If they didn't get him, being beat up like that would do it," Chuck pointed out, adding in anguish, "They're hitting kids with flamethrowers, the pig fuckers!"

A rebel was spotted by a man armed with a flamethrower. The flamethrowers opened up blasting the rebel and cooking him, his screams turning Chuck's stomach.

When the flame throwers kicked up, a half a dozen rebels bolted at once. Harrying fire dropped some. The rest disappeared so fast in the rugged terrain that Chuck figured they might survive.

Others stayed hidden until the burning sagebrush forced them to move.

Joe Mack approved, saying, "I'd rather get a bullet in the back than get cooked, too."

Chuck couldn't speak, it was so devastating to him to watch the very thing he'd tried so hard to prevent playing out right in front of him. He knew that a direct hit by a flamethrower was not survivable. Even a near miss at short or medium range would scar the boy terribly, branding him for life as one of the rebels – if he didn't die of infection. One poor kid jumped up with his clothes on fire and was pumped full of shot as he rolled around on the ground to put them out.

A mass bolt brought a hail of fire, but Chuck had hope that some might have made it. He knew from experience that except for luck you couldn't hit targets in the back that ducked from side to side and up and down like those fleeing kids did.

When there was no more movement, the soldiers grabbed up their own fallen, both injured and dead. They put their injured in the front seats of the damaged jeep, putting the bodies in the back with the dead commander, the dead men's weapons, and the cans of extra gas. They limped for the farm without looking at the rest, not even checking their remaining prisoner to see if he was alive or dead.

"You rally up to Sam's farm," Joe Mack ordered Rubin. "We'll see if there are any kids alive that we can help."

Rubin hesitated. "I don't want to lead them to my Dad."

Joe Mack shook his head. "This is the one time you're safe. They just hit Sam's, and they got hit back, so they will think they got the right guys for the rebels to risk so much to try and rescue them. Ain't no reason for them to go back there even if they could, and right now there ain't no way they can. They're wounded and limping to a safe house. They'll send for re-enforcements and hunker down in the house until help arrives. So long as no more rebels stick their noses out, they will think that was the last of them."

"How can you be so sure?"

"You're a farm boy. You had one year when you were a kid, and maybe a few weeks' refresher once or twice. I did ten year's straight service. I seen it all. I know how these guys think. Chuck was right. They were using the raid to lure out more rebels so they could wipe out the rebellion. They were supposed hide the firepower advantage until they were ambushed. The pronghorn messed that up. I know that kind of battle-plan. You're the decoy, the hunter, and the trap, all at the same time."

Chuck assured Rubin that Joe Mack was right. "That's what I told the kids."

"They already knew that they were playing with fire. I know them, and their families have been scared for months that the re-educators would come."

Joe Mack nodded. "They were right, but they never would've expected this. It used to be just to keep all GR citizens on the Wright Way. It's changed. They used to try to target the punishment where it was really warranted. We were ordered not to create more rebels by acting out of hand, but these days that don't seem to matter. They were here to mop up as many as they could but survive if possible . . . to fight and win the day enough for some to limp away. This ain't a surprise or defeat for them. That stupid buck saved a bad deal from being a hell of a lot worse. You'd better believe they are taking all their dead back to build a story that will cover their own asses."

Blind-sided by that, Chuck objected, "They got to report and bury the dead and get re-enforcements."

"Yeah, and they took all their own dead, so they can show their Commanding Officer got wiped out by an animal and two men were killed by arrows. They can claim to have killed the whole gang or whatever's reasonable enough that the officers don't go to the trouble and expense of sending out a re-education posse, so they won't have to come back here. The rate these folk are moving their wounded and dead, by the time anyone gets here to check the story there'll be no way to confirm or deny it, so the soldiers can cover their own asses by inflating the body count. It always was the plan to retaliate with devastating force, even if the resistance was six-year-olds with toy guns. That's what the General meant when he said for the security of the GR all malcontents must be punished in a way they understand."

The three of them stayed where they were for a moment more, each lost in his own thoughts.

Staring into space, Chuck was trying to get his head around what it meant for his homeland to be going further and further down this path away from the decency he'd been raised with and that the GR claimed to be defending. "We got to do everything we can, so our kids don't grow up in a nation of lies and torture."

"Look at those kids go!"

Startled by Joe Mack's exclamation, Chuck took a better look at the road. The local kids had started stripping the truck the second the soldiers had marched away. Using the truck for cover while the platoon was still in view, they had started working on it. There were men and women on horseback collecting the injured and dead, and putting the fires out, but swarming over and around the truck were nimble-fingered little boys. "Where's the pronghorn?" He hadn't noticed anyone moving it, but it was clearly gone.

"On someone's table."

Suddenly everybody vanished, dropping whatever they were doing and racing or galloping to cover. Before Chuck could complete his thought that there must have been some kind of signal that he didn't see or hear, the hammering of a jeep motor being pushed to its limit reached him faintly. He had a deep feeling of foreboding at the sight of the military truck missing its hood and all the doors, seats, gas, oil, and every part of the motor that wasn't too big to carry. "The PPL will burn this whole parish to the ground for this!"

At least Rubin agreed with him. "Everything is going to change around here after this."

The good jeep came roaring back with all the dead PPL lain on top of each other in the back. It slowed down when the driver saw the stripped truck. For a moment Chuck thought the guy riding shotgun was going to stand up, but the jeep picked up speed again and they carried on without stopping.

They could hear the jeep long after it was out of sight. The locals didn't wait until the sound faded. They went back to shovelling dirt on the flames to smother them and beating them out with the shovels as soon as there was a chance they were out of gunfire range. Chuck was afraid that the jeep would come back, but it didn't even slow down again.

"It's okay now for all of us to go down," Joe Mack said, getting to his feet. "That'll give you more information for Sam," he nodded to Rubin.

Chuck felt nervous for a moment, then got up and followed the other two. It had been so important that no one saw them that it was hard to turn that fear off. Hardly a glance at the folks below assured him that everyone was too busy putting out the last of the fires, stripping the truck, or loading the pieces onto horses or carts to pay them any mind.

They collected their horses and rode slowly along the middle of the road until they were sure everyone had seen them. People waved to Rubin but stared suspiciously at the other two until one youngster yelled, "Hey, Old Man!"

Overcome at seeing one of the rebels unhurt, Chuck slid to the dirt and ran to clap the boy on the shoulder, knock his hat off, and shout at him, "You stupid little shit!"

Grinning sheepishly, the boy caught the dog that had rushed to his defence, holding it back from attacking Chuck, and explaining to the man who came striding up, "Dad, this is the guy that told us about the PPL trap."

Chuck straightened up to look the man in the eye and shake his hand. "I tried to stop all this." He gestured around at the fires and the blood soaking into the dirt. "I'm real sorry."

The Dad shook his hand and went to introduce himself, but Chuck stopped him. "No names. They can't get out of us what we never knew."

"We know each other," the Dad pointed out, nodding to Rubin.

Joe Mack gave him a half-smile. "Yeah, we never thought of it until it was too late for some of us, but we must start somewhere. Maybe the next lot can learn from our mistakes."

Chuck cut in so that there wouldn't be an awkward moment. "Do you know who the other prisoner was?" He looked at the patches of blood on the road. "It's too bad they got him, but if you know who he was at least his family will know what happened to him . . . and, seriously, he's better off gunned down than being questioned by the interrogators. I guess it was too much to hope that him and Hosea both got away."

The locals looked at each other. Chuck had a very bad feeling.

It was the Dad who broke the news. "Hosea never made it."

Joe Mack yelped, "What do you mean?! We saw Emmanuel take off with him!"

"He was shot. Back of the head. Like as not, he was dead before he hit the horse. Emmanuel's burnt bad. He might lose his eye."

Chuck had to admit, "We heard the horse scream."

"Yeah, the flamethrower nicked it. Not as bad as Emmanuel. Don't want to shoot it, but don't want the investigators to see it, neither."

Chuck had a sudden flash of insight. "Swap you. No one can afford to lose a good horse, and we can't let them find a horse matching the description of the one that took off with their prisoner and has got flamethrower burns. They can't find any of your sons with burns, either. Your only hope to stop them from torching or re-educating your whole Parish is to make them think the rebels ain't from round here."

Joe Mack got excited enough to slide down from his horse to talk eye to eye with the farmers. "Yeah, we can switch the wounded horse for a good one, so no one is short one. If it dies, we'll have to get ours back, but if it does okay you never have to explain its scars. All the burn survivors must come with us, too."

"Where are you going to take them? There ain't time . . ."

Joe Mack interrupted. "I'm betting that the PPL won't come back until day light. They've lost too many guys at night on empty roads in areas with high sabotage. The barracks ain't going to send a full escort just to pick up a few guys. More likely they will send another transport truck and a jeep or two."

Chuck could see the sense in that. "Yeah. They probably won't be back before sunup, so we got time to get the burnt wounded and the horse someplace that the PPL ain't never going to look for them." He turned to Rubin. "When you give the news and find out how they're doing, see if they've got any ideas what we can do to help, and how to make it look like the rebels are raiders from someplace else."

Rubin turned his horse to head back towards Sam's. "Meet you here or there?"

Joe Mack and Chuck glanced at each other. "There," Joe Mack suggested, tentatively.

"There," Chuck agreed, realising that they had no plan for getting a bunch of injured people and a horse through the Underground unnoticed. Thinking that Sam's place was as good a place as any to get everyone together, he gave up on the idea of not admitting openly that Sam was part of it. Watching Rubin riding away, Chuck suggested, "We could have a funeral for Hosea to cover up the cart tracks coming from all over to Sam's place."

Joe Mack caught on like he'd read Chuck's mind. "We should make two graves, one for Hosea and one for Emmanuel. They ain't going to look for him if he's dead and buried."

"We'd better have a funeral for the other prisoner, too."

"Yeah, that gives us two places to hide guys with suspicious wounds until we can move them all out into the pipeline. We just got to move them before the investigation starts." Joe Mack asked the farmer, "His folks won't be too scared to help guys that got burnt trying to save him, will they?"

The farmer shrugged. "I dunno, I'll ask him."

In shock, Chuck and Joe Mack yelled together, "ASK him?! Ain't he dead?"

"No. L . . ."

"Don't say his name!" Chuck interrupted. "Just call him 'Lucky'. We saw him go down."

"Yeah, he sure did. He hit the dirt and stayed there. Played possum and them PPL never did check him."

"Well butter my butt and call me a biscuit! That's the best news I heard all day!" Joe Mack was so pleased that he slapped the farmer's back as well as Chuck's.

"Well, he was covered in blood, and he did manage to fall off the side of the road when he went down."

They grinned at each other like idiots.

"Just 'managed' to . . ."

"Yeah, like it was an accident. But it wasn't his blood."

"No, sir, it wasn't his blood."

Chuck sobered up first. "We still got to make a grave and a cross with his name on it. They won't hunt for him if he's dead, plus if they can report that they killed the rebel leaders and wiped out their followers, I figure the Security Shield will only check out their story, it won't go to the trouble and cost of re-education."

Joe Mack assured the farmer and his son, "He's right. The SS can't get the PPL to torch the whole Parish when the GR needs all the farms we can get to supply the troops, unless they can prove imbedded traitors. And they got to account for the costs and manpower of re-educating a whole parish. Give them a way to duck it and they will. So, if you bury your boys where we're saying Emmanuel and Lucky are, then you got no fresh graves to explain."

"We lost more than two of our boys."

Thinking of his own little son, Chuck choked up. "Yeah, man, I'm sorry. But you can't have fresh graves in your churchyard or farms if the rebels were outside raiders."

Joe Mack asked, "What about the folk where the PPL holed up? Will they give it away?"

The boy shook his head strongly. "No, sir! Their son is one of us."

Chuck nodded. "Yes, we saw him high tail it to warn them, but they don't know to say that the rebels were raiders from somewhere else."

The farmer assured them, "I know those guys. They'll be desperate to get the PPL to think that they're loyalists so their place ain't torched and none of the family gets shot or arrested. We already know that they met the PPL at the gate and welcomed them with open arms. They're helping with the jeep repairs."

"That makes sense. The soldiers will really think the farmers are on their side if they're helping them."

Joe Mack put in, "You got to help the guys with guns in your house. That ain't got nothing to do with their side."

The boy objected, "The Comforts ain't working at gunpoint. The jeep's at the back door in between the house and the barnyard. There's a couple or three of them working on it with the PPL. Mrs Comfort and one of the girls took a basket of food and drink to them and they all chowed down."

"So, you're watching them."

"Yeah. It ain't no trouble to get a message to them that the sabotage was from raiders."

Joe Mack grabbed the boy's arm. "Hold your horses, little buddy. I get it that you could watch the PPL limping to the Comfort place and getting set up, but during the time the five that are left at the farm are waiting for the re-enforcements to arrive, they'll secure the area. One or two will be working on repairs through the night or until it's done, and the rest take up positions around windows and doors to cover them. They can't cover the road and gate from there, so there will be a sniper in the house watching the gate."

Nodding, Chuck added, "And another sniper posted in the hayloft looking out over the grazing land for anyone trying to sneak up. If the Comforts can get the men to feel that they're among friends enough to split up, then anyone free could float for relief or naps so they can drive when help comes or fight harder if there's an attack."

The farmer stared. "An attack? What do they think we'll do?"

"They think there are rebels here that were fixing to ambush them when they were at full strength, so now that they're below half strength, they got to stay alert."

"As if we'd attack a house with women and children in it!"

Joe Mack explained, "I know, but the soldiers don't. They got to watch their backs all the time anyway, and now that the kids have stripped the truck . . ."

Chuck nodded. "It would be a real good idea if no piece of that truck ever showed up in these parts. It's going to be tough to get them to believe that raiders from somewhere else stripped it. If they see anything that might have come from it, the game will be over, and the Parish will burn."

The farmer went pale, staring at the remains of the truck being towed away like a cart behind a team of horses.

Swallowing hard, the youngster asked, "How long do we got to hide it?"

Joe Mack glanced at Chuck. "It ain't that easy to keep a military truck out of sight."

"Pieces of truck," Chuck reminded him. "It's easier to make the odd wheel look like something else."

The farmer said, "We can stick it in a barn."

Joe Mack jumped on that. "First place they'll look."

The farmer blinked. "An abandoned barn."

Remembering now just why he and his classmates had always been down on the farm boys, Chuck did his best to sound respectful. "They'll look inside everything big enough to hide anything; no matter how abandoned it looks. If an abandoned barns got tracks up to it like something was towed there in the last day or so, what do you think they are going to do? You're a hunter, what would you do with a fresh trail?"

The farmer gaped at them. It was the boy who had the presence of mind to ask, "Are we done?"

Joe Mack assured them, "Not if you think like hunters. Lay trails to dead ends, like the whole Parish making tracks to Hosea's and Lucky's funerals. Put the parts of the truck where they can't be traced back here if anyone finds them. You want it to look like you're all loyalists and the rebels came from someplace else and took their loot with them. The PPL might not buy it, but it's the only shot you got to take the heat off here."

Chuck remounted, turning his horse back towards Sam's, saying, "We'll go and get things ready for the funerals."

As he mounted to ride with Chuck, Joe Mack warned them, "Stay away from the guys that are holed up waiting for reinforcements. They'll have snipers in the attic and the barn so the guys working on repairs to the jeep are covered from both sides between two the buildings. They could rig a grenade to the main gate to make a nice doorbell. The snipers see will see anyone crossing the fields, as well as seeing the reinforcements coming down the road so they can get to the gate first to let them in. if they see anybody sneaking across the fields, they won't only shoot, they'll blame the Comforts. No matter that the Comforts welcomed the troops with open arms, fed them, tended their wounds, and helped them repair the jeep, if the PPL thinks there's anything at all the least bit suspicious, then they'll punish the Comfort family so you all can't miss the message: "Don't fuck with us!" they ain't going to wait and find out first if they're right or not."

As they rode off towards the ranch that was now Sam's, Chuck asked, "Did we do any good at all?"

Joe Mack grunted. "They know what they're dealing with. They might be more careful. The kids will still try to find a way to warn the family."

That's what Chuck was afraid of. "I put everything I had into stopping those boys, and they did it anyway."

"On the road past the squad or across the fields out of range?"

Chuck swallowed his regrets. "Out of range – and out of sight if we can."

CHAPTER TWENTY-NINE

After Shock

Kiritoe Amaru

To pass the time while they waited for rescue, the group buried in the carriage rationed the food and water, kept the baby entertained, tended Lucy and her injured foot, sang songs, told stories, got to know each other and their life histories, and worked at loosening the seats and back rests from their frames to put down over the windows and ribbing of the carriage wall so that they could get comfortable. They tried not to be too active, so that they wouldn't use up the oxygen any faster than they could help. They gathered up the student's papers and helped them sort them out and put all of the papers in bags, satchels or briefcases, depending. They listened to each student talk about what they were planning for careers and gave useless advice. They took pieces of paper and pens to write a list of their names, ages, places of origin, next of kin, and contact information. As a sailor, Kiri knew Morse code and wrote out the sequence to say how many of them there were, and that there were no deaths. Practicing it helped them all keep hold of the hope that they would be found before the air ran out. They made it into a kind of chant, clapping their hands in a rhythm of long, short, and pause, with Kiritoe calling it to them like the stroke caller in a canoe.

The worst times were the aftershocks, which not only shook the carriage, but also brought frightening noises. The little tremors weren't so bad. They were like a wave passing through them. Even then, no matter how determined Kiri was to keep the conversation going, he would freeze at the slightest shift, every time, and forget to breathe with everyone else.

Bigger aftershocks were harder to bear. They didn't only shake the carriage, sometimes they settled it or changed its angle, or made the earth groan. Worst of all was the eerie clinking, almost like a cloth bag of china.

"What *is* that?" Edie demanded, clearly reaching the end of her endurance.

"Rocks settling."

Kiri was glad somebody knew, because he had no idea.

But it wasn't good enough for Edie, who retorted, "Rocks do not sound like that!"

Everyone who knew anything about it worked to explain to everyone else how it could be that solid rock could sound like delicate china. It seemed to Kiri that the main reason the whole group was holding together so well was that whenever one started to panic, the others drew on their disaster relief training to keep everyone calm.

Following every after shock, no matter how small, they chanted to Mother Papatuanuku to preserve her People inside her and asked her to calm Ruamoko down. No one had much faith that it would do any good to ask the volcano god directly to stop throwing a tantrum, but it made them feel better to chant to Ruamoko, so they did.

Once in a while there was the sound of a whoosh of air. The first time it happened some people thought it meant the rescuers were reaching them. No one thought about the air bags until they heard earth and stones settling onto one of the windows. After that the sound of escaping air had them all holding their breath, watching and waiting to see if the windows held. One of the passengers would take a light stick and hold it by the window so that they could see if there were any cracks. Kiri wasn't sure that was a really good idea, since he couldn't imagine what they could do about it if one of the windows did give way, but he didn't say anything because it seemed to be something everyone needed. There was no denying that there was a lot of reassurance in seeing a deflated air bag covering the window like a blanket. Even if some dirt piled on the window, they still felt protected by the sight of the tough pale grey fabric shielding them. Knowing that the windows were impact-proof didn't give the same feeling of protection as the sight of an impenetrable layer between the earth, its rocks, and the glass.

"Shouldn't there have been emergency lighting?" someone asked at one point, and they all agreed there should have been, but for some reason it hadn't worked.

Eventually they heard a thumping. They spread themselves out along the carriage and beat out their rehearsed reply in time with Kiri's chant. The answer came. Kiri sagged, listening for it to be repeated, so he could be sure of what he'd heard. Then he beat back, "Understood."

"What did it say, Kiri?"

"We're not a priority."

"But tell them we don't have enough air."

"We can wait a little while longer."

"Tell them Lucy's hurt."

"Come on, everyone. We know what that means. It means there's someone worse off than we are. We're in a six-car train. Who knows what happened in the other cars? Let's eat now, we don't have to ration any more, we know they're right there."

Knowing they were right there, and were not coming for them right away was harder than being trapped in the first place. They could hear occasional thumps. Efforts were made to pass the time again but were always quickly shushed as someone thought they could hear something. Eventually all they were doing was sitting tensely, listening, trying to keep the baby quiet.

Then the thumps were closer. Something pranged against the carriage, and again, and again. "They're poling for us, trying to find out where the carriage is. We're really buried."

Then there was a sort of a silence, in which muffled thumps came steadily closer. "Digging," they guessed.

A shaft of strong light came in one window as the airbag was removed, and they all winced and covered their eyes. The earth was swept off the window with a straw broom, until people could be seen through it shovelling earth back up a slope away from the window. When the space over the window was cleared enough, the emergency door function of the window was popped off and fresh, earth-smelling air poured in. A huge head and shoulders filled the window. "How many of you are there?" a deep voice called over their cheers, and the baby's startled wails.

Kiri handed up the list, and called up, "One broken foot, one baby, the rest of us either unhurt or cracked ribs, pulled muscles, bumps and bruises."

"You're the best yet," the man said cheerfully. "Hand up your injured." He lowered a ladder down into the carriage.

"Mother Papatuanuku," Edie breathed, "I think that's the King."

"I shouldn't go first," Lucy was protesting.

They handed the baby up to Ngaronoa, then helped its mother up the ladder, then simply picked Lucy up and carried her gently to the ladder, ignoring her protests. They reached as high as they could to put her on the ladder as far up as they could manage, where she clung, gasping, pale and sweating, her broken foot hanging. Kiri climbed up the ladder behind her, and half over her, so that he could lift her up to another rung. Carefully he helped her up, gritting his teeth against the sound of her yelp each time she was moved, until Ngaronoa could lift her out and carry her away. Kiri jumped back down and helped all of the others out. He was the last one to leave their prison.

Ahnstan Seamore

Ahnstan looked back as he walked away, to see his brother, Wynson, standing with an arm protectively around Donya's shoulders. He could tell from his mother's tight jaw that it bothered her to leave her children. He wished he could stay with them. He knew what to expect, then. He felt terrible leaving Donya when she was hurt. He was the oldest. If his parents couldn't be there, he should be. He had his head turned, watching his brother and sister, so he didn't see his father coming. He heard his mother say, "Don, what were you thinking?" and turned.

Donstan was walking across the pavement carrying the pan of berry pies which had been set on the counter to cool under a cloth, and the casserole dish which had been covered to keep it warm. "It was safe enough, and the food is needed," he started, but a tremor hit, and he said, "After shock! Sit!" instead of continuing his explanation.

They sat on the ground, but it was clear Ahnya didn't sit down easily.

"What is it?" Donstan asked.

"I banged my knee."

"Get it seen to?"

"Don't have time for that now, I have to restore communications as fast as possible."

Donstan gave her a measuring look. It was clear there was going to be no discussing it, so he shrugged, waited until the shaking stopped, said, "That wasn't too bad. After a really big one like that sometimes the aftershocks would be full sized earthquakes if they were on their own."

He helped Ahnya back to her feet, and held out the tarts to Ahnya and Ahnstan, who shook his head. Much as he loved his Dad's tarts, he had no appetite.

"Take one, son, we'll be glad of them later," Ahnya told Ahnstan, taking one herself, which she cradled like a baby. She turned to Donstan. "Don, talk to that boy. He's blaming himself for not having his shoes."

"He can't. It's my responsibility to make sure they put their things where they should be."

"Will you tell him that? Please, dear."

Donstan said, "I'll be back in a tick," and went off to the commons.

Ahnstan couldn't bear the naked pain on his mother's face as she looked at the wreckage of her kitchen through the broken glass doors, cradling the tart in both hands, so he watched his father instead. He knew they were rushing, everything was actually going quickly, but he felt as if everything was slowed way down, and they were taking hours to do anything. Most of the people in the commons were still wandering about slowly, dazed, or comforting one another. Wynson was standing stoutly, his arm around Donya's shoulder as they talked to their Dad. She had a fixed look on her face. Ahnstan knew that look. She was determined not to cry, and wouldn't, either. Were they ever again going to be able to play their game of hopping from tile to tile, keeping to only one colour across the kitchen? What did it matter that they'd all done so well when now everything was broken, and they didn't even have their badges so prove what they could do? Now Mum would never have known that they'd tracked mud into the house, even if they had been made to clean it up.

"Wynson will be all right, won't he, Mum? He'll take good care of Donnie. He's good in a crisis, isn't he?"

"Yes, he always comes through in a crisis, that one." Ahnya put her arm around Ahnstan. "We'll be all right."

"They're waving to you, Mum." Ahnstan waved back. He looked up at his mother, saw her swallow hard, then put on a smile and turn to wave gaily at the younger children as if they were just off to a picnic, then turn and walk quickly to the bicycle shed as if her knee was giving no trouble, and disappear inside. He waved again, then followed his mother, standing back to let his father pass him as Donstan came loping back up.

"We've got to get going. Time's awasting, I bet I have to assess every single building in the whole town," Donstan said, lifting the bikes out of the shed. "Hold mine," he told Ahnstan, then went to the earthquake kit and got out packs of food and clothes for each of them, which they strapped on the bike carriers.

"Can't you assess our house first, Dad?"

"You know I can't. I have to be where I'm expected to be, at my station like everyone else. I can't assess by myself, it takes the team, and the equipment. We have to follow the plan that was decided on." He hugged Ahnya, held her close, and kissed her. "See you."

"I'll get the lines back up so I can call you," she grinned, but Ahnstan knew it was a forced grin.

Donstan hugged Ahnstan. "Hang in there, Son. We'll get through this." Then he was off, speeding away on his bike with a wave over his shoulder for everyone.

Ahnya and Ahnstan mounted, waved again to Wynson and Donya, and pedalled down the path. "Should we be riding under that, Mum? It was moving a lot. What if it comes down?" he looked up at the train trestle.

"It's designed to flex in an earthquake. It's made that way. Get Dad to explain the engineering to you. If it hasn't come down, it isn't going to. I'm glad I wasn't on it when that one hit, though."

"Yeah, wow. It would have been horrible to get shaken like that up there!"

"That's what I was thinking."

"What if it fell down, though, Mum? Wouldn't the Fish be smashed to bits?"

"It only looks brittle, because the surface is covered with solar panels. The skin of the carriages under the solar panels is a very flexible, very tough, very light material. The solar panels will break off if it falls, and the people inside would be bruised, but the Fish itself would deform without breaking open. It can take more impact than falling fully loaded three floors. It's very tough. The weakest part is the windows, but there are bags full of air that will puff out over the windows if anything drastic happens. The idea is that the windows will be cushioned and covered. The airbags should also help cushion the impact if the trestle fell down or the Fish came off the rails."

*   *   *

Ahnstan was fully occupied weaving around bits of debris on the path. He was surprised by how few people there were on the paths, even though he knew everyone who didn't have an essential job would be inside the commons of their hexes taking care of the injured, preparing tents and food and assessing water for drinkability. He'd been trained on what to do inside his hex as a greeny, and why the adults were doing what they were doing. What he didn't know was what to expect outside of the hex. Everyone he saw was in a hurry. There were people testing the trestle to make sure the train was safe for riders. At the slightest sign there might be an aftershock, everyone dropped to the ground. "This is different from rehearsals," he grumbled.

"Well, yes," his mother agreed. "In rehearsals the ground isn't shaking, and your house isn't wrecked, and no one is hurt."

"Can we fix our house, Mum?"

"It's better if you think that it's gone. Then you'll get a nice surprise if it's not, and it won't break your heart if it is."

"But really?"

"Really, I think it's gone, son. The cistern is probably cracked, the piping is obviously ruptured: the walls are askew. I think that one's a memory, and it might not even be safe for us to go in and get our stuff."

"But Mum!"

"It's just things, Stan. Things can be replaced, but people can't. We still have each other, and we're lucky we have all of us. You wait, you'll meet people who don't have everyone."

"How do you know?"

"You can't have that big a quake and not have some losses."

To keep his mind off the idea of his home being gone, or that some people died that morning, Ahnstan went back to the subject of the Flying Fish. "Mum?"

"Yes."

"What's the Fish made of?"

"Mostly hemp fabric impregnated with fibreglass with carbon fibres in it, put over a silicate frame. The frame is a network of ribs in an interlocking pattern. It's based on something called a geodesic dome, though it's not a dome, because it's got to be aerodynamic."

"What does that mean?"

"A geodesic dome is a dome made of triangles, because the triangle is the strongest shape in engineering. Aerodynamic means that it slips through the air with the least amount of drag possible, like making a boat slide through water. You know the shape of boats, or dolphins?"

"They're not the same shape."

"Pointed at the front and back, smoothly rounded in the middle."

"Like fish."

"Yes, exactly."

"The Flying Fish is sort of like a flatfish, not like an ordinary fish."

"That's true."

They were arriving at his mother's work. Ahnstan was astonished by how busy it was.

Command Central

As soon as he'd finished the emergency announcement, the First Servant, Pitamete Meithei went looking for someone who he could commandeer to pay attention to his concerns. He simply couldn't understand why Ngaronoa hadn't been there in minutes giving his support. "Nothing can happen to him! We can't afford that right now!" he told himself, to calm the voice inside him that was warning, 'Anything could have happened to him.'

Pita pulled his hand down over his face. His partner, Leora, had been at work when the earthquake hit, so she would be at her station there, which meant he couldn't talk it over with her. In the kitchen people were making refreshments for the emergency command team. They were wearing black vests, so obviously they were part of the command team. Pita's station had never been near Command Central. Being taught about it, even seeing pictures and having black vests visit his school when he was a child, had not prepared him to be right in the middle of it, surrounded by busy professionals who knew more about what to do than he did.

"Mr. First, have you had anything to eat or drink?"

"No, I . . ."

"You must, Sir. You're under a lot of stress. Everyone's looking to you right now."

"This is your station, then?"

"Command Support, yes. We keep the nerve centre at peak function. Would you like tea or juice, Mr. First? I recommend something hot. Hot tea or soup, or hot apple cider, and some of these. They're very small, each one is less than a bite, but they're chewy and tasty, and they all have the right balance of carbohydrate, protein, and oils for high stress. Did you have lunch?"

He couldn't possibly remember that far back. That was before the earthquake, in another life. No, maybe he'd been planning to have lunch after he'd dealt with the Minister, then the earthquake had happened. To escape the support staff, he took a tea with him in a covered mug so that it would stay hot and wouldn't spill, and a handful of the hot little bites. He was surprised to find his head clearing moments afterwards and made his way with more purpose and less feeling of confusion through the babble of voices speaking earnestly into headsets.

Disaster Response was so much a part of all of their lives that the various parts reacted automatically. It was inconceivable to him that Ngaronoa wouldn't have headed straight for Command Centre. The Public Servants had to concentrate on the details of the disaster and its relief; it was the King's responsibility to lead the people emotionally. His problem was not only that he was coping alone, receiving reports of the disaster, giving encouragement and assurances, but that as time went on without a word from Ngaronoa he became more and more filled with dread that something had happened to him. He couldn't imagine life without his closest friend.

Quietly he asked the Commander, "If we've lost the King, what's the procedure?"

He got a look that meant, "You should know that." The Commander answered equally quietly, "Do you have reason to believe we might have, Mr. First?"

"Don't know where he is. It's been hours."

"The Public Servants appoint someone until the emergency is over and an election can be called."

"Wineera. She came in second."

The Commander turned back to his screen. "Not my department."

Pitamete touched his shoulder. "Whose department is it to find her so that I can call her in, just in case?"

"I'll deal with it."

"Thank you, Commander."

Another voice, before he had a chance to think. "Mr. First! The seismologist."

Automatically he answered the ringer, "Pitamete Meithei here."

"Mr. First, although it's a mathematical fiction to talk about an epicentre when a long blind thrust fault line slips, for the sake of focus, we could say the epicentre was mid-town Wairoa. The People can focus on that, they can see the damage. The Earthquake was 7.9, with the seafloor uplifted in the same manner as the earthquake 357 years ago that raised what had been the Ahriri Lagoon and turned it into land. The 1931 earthquake was 7.8. The earthquake today is bigger than that one was, and caused a tsunami, which travelled down the west coast reaching heights of five and six metres on long shorelines, higher where harbours and fjords funnelled it. The uplift today is likely to be correspondingly bigger. I've sent you copies of the seismic reports, which we can go through together, if you like."

"Yes, please, I need it explained to me so that I can tell the People what happened."

Pitamete was concentrating hard on the seismic reports, and the seismologist's explanations of them, when someone called him. "Mr. First! Mr. First!"

"What now?" he looked up from the seismic reports with some irritation.

"You wanted to know the whereabouts of Wineera Rangituri."

"Yes, yes, I do, thank you. I'll be right there." He told the seismologist, "Mr. Wattigan, can you tell the People this now, please? I think I've grasped enough to put it in lay terms after you've made your broadcast. There's something I have to take care of right now."

He followed the person who had come to fetch him into what had been his living room. The wall unit there was playing the news reports. The young man assigned to keep track of the public information said to him, "Mr. First, Princess Wineera is at the derailment site. There are no pictures from there yet, the fibres are out, but the reports that are getting through are saying she's there. The Fish was buried by the landslide. Some of it was crushed."

"Oh, no. I was hoping they would find it had just been stranded." Pitamete swallowed. He would have to announce that, too. He really wished Ron was there, he'd have handled it much better. At least they'd found Wineera. "I should have known she'd be right there, where so many people are in danger. Now all I need is to find a way to talk to her to tell her she might be appointed Queen, at least until we find out what happened to the King."

"Oh, but Mr. First, the King is there, too."

"What?!" Pita was so jolted that he could help shouting.

"I'm sorry, Sir, they didn't tell me you were looking for the King, they only told me you wanted Wineera. King Ngaronoa is digging people out of the buried carriages."

"The King! He's digging people out of the freaking Fish!! He could get killed going that! How are we going to get a hold of him?"

"So, you need to speak to the King as well as the Princess, Sir?"

"No. I need to speak to the King instead of the Princess! Once I have him, I don't need to bother Wineera." The combination of relief that his friend, Ron, was alive and unhurt, and anger that the King wasn't where he was supposed to be, hit Pitamete so hard he couldn't think straight.

"Yes, Mr. First. Will you be making your broadcast now, Sir?"

"Pardon?" Pitamete blinked, momentarily unable to figure out what he was talking about.

"The broadcast to tell the People about the earthquake, Sir."

"Oh, yes, right. And, since the King is there instead of here, I have to talk about that buried Flying Fish, too. Do we know if all of the carriages were buried, or just some of them?"

"No, Sir, we don't have many details yet."

The news broadcast switched from the buried train to the scientific explanation of what had happened. Pita watched the seismologist's explanation on the wall unit for a moment, then grinned. "I'd better do that right away. No-one can make head nor tail of that gobbledygook."

The young man monitoring the public broadcasts grinned back in relief. "That's what I was thinking," he confessed. "I'm glad you can understand it, Sir."

"Barely." Pita walked dutifully to his marker in what had been his office and talked in what he hoped was a readily understandable way about what had happened to their fair land.

Glendrona Tomptell

"Evacuation!" Ngaire called out to the people on the platform as the children reached the top. "Hex nine, Akaloa row," she said to the harried looking young man wearing the bright crimson vest of an organiser.

"All children are evacuating to the summit above Ōtautahi Harbour," he told her, indicating which side of the platform they should take.

Ngaire and Paki Sergill handed him one copy each of their lists of who they had with them. They got the children to line up where the door of the Flying Fish would open by the simple expedient of making them keep hold of the rope and keep the rope straight between Paki and Ngaire.

"Children first!" the young man called out as the Flying Fish pulled smoothly into the station. Adults quietly got off to give their spaces to the children, since each carriage couldn't seat more than twenty, and they had a party of eighteen. They got on and settled as quickly as they could, the youngest children in the laps of Paki and Ngaire, to comfort the little children, and to take up as few seats as possible, the rest crammed in as tightly as they could be. The adults filed back on, as many as could fit all standing squashed together. Even though it was winter, they opened windows a crack for fresh air.

As the Flying Fish's sensors indicated it was full to capacity, it didn't stop at any more stations. Glenda was crammed with three other children in a seat meant for two, and could see how many were standing, but she still felt sorry for all of the people waiting at the stations they passed.

Evacuate. It was a big word. Their disaster training instructor had made them practice it and repeat what it meant. If something dangerous happened, everyone had to go away. They would be taken care of, kept safe, and then they would go home afterwards. But she thought that had meant she would go away with her Mum and Dad. She didn't know it could mean going away with her music class. She didn't want to cry like a baby, so she tried to think of something more fun than being squashed in this over-crowded carriage.

She wanted to go to Nana's. Granny lived with them, upstairs, but Nana lived a long way away and it was fun to go and stay with her. Glenda didn't want to ask if they were going to Nana's in case the bigger kids said she was a baby, but she couldn't tell which way they were going once they got on the Flying Fish. The Flying Fish always looked exactly the same, no matter where you were.

Anyway, it wasn't flying any more. It was stopped in the middle of the track. She couldn't see why. All she could see out of the window beside her was the treetops. "Why are we sitting here?" she whispered to the girl beside her.

Kim shrugged. "Dunno."

A man leaned down and said to them, kindly, "There are trains ahead of us, blocking our way."

Kim got scared at that. "What if the water comes while we're stuck here?"

They moved at that moment, speeding along again. One of the adults pressed the button so he could get off at the next stop and started wriggling his way through the crowd in the carriage as the Flying Fish sped along. When they stopped and one person got off, five tried to get on. "Move back, can't you?"

"Yeah, nah, we can't, eh? There's nowhere to move back to."

"Come on, you fellows, I've waited through eight trains!"

"Sorry, man! Good luck!" the people called out as the doors swished shut and the Flying Fish started flying again. They were away from the town, so the track didn't make its familiar jog left, stop, jog right, jog left, stop as it made its way along between hexes, but went straight with a long way between stops, getting to a much higher speed than it did in the town. It felt to Glenda as if she'd never gone so fast in her life before. She hoped they really were going to Nana's; they'd come far enough.

They went as high up the hillsides as the Flying Fish tracks went, then got out, Ms. Sergill anxiously counting them over and over. It seemed to Glenda like they were nearly at the top of the hills when she looked out through the glass walls of the station. Then they had to keep a tight hold on the rope and march on, at first down from the platform to the ground, not round and round for three floors here, but only about the height of a tall man, then along up the last part of the hill over the tussocky grass, keeping the rope straight between them. Three-year-old Morehu started to cry.

"Ms. Sergill, I don't know what's wrong with him!" Alan called out in panic.

They stopped their march, and Ngaire bent over Morehu, who wailed, "I have to go wee wee!"

Glenda had to, too, but she was big enough not to say anything until they got there. She didn't think this was where Nana was. They'd come a long way, but this place wasn't like the place where Nana lived. While they stopped to tend to Morehu, Glenda looked around. She knew this place! This was the hills where she'd picnicked with Mummy and Daddy. That's what they were doing, they were going to have a picnic. She didn't feel nearly as scared any more.

While Ngaire took Morehu behind some tussock, Ms. Sergill raised her walking stick in the air. "Off we go, children! We must keep going. Ngaire and Morehu will catch up." She planted the walking stick down and off they set again, keeping a tight grip on the rope, up and up. Part of the nagging fear came back to Glenda. This wasn't just a fun picnic. The feeling of something terrible kept hovering. She looked back but couldn't see Ngaire or Morehu. What if they couldn't catch up? What if they got lost?

On and on they went, Ngaire taking someone off to the side to go to the bathroom every now and then, then catching back up, until they reached the summit of the hills 600 metres above Ōtautahi Harbour. Glenda was glad the Fish had taken them so far up; they could never have walked all that way. They went over the top, to where they could see down into the harbour. By that time Ms. Sergill, Ngaire, Moana, and Alan all had little children riding on their backs, sitting on their satchels, and some of the other children were carrying two satchels for the ones who had been unable to keep going under the weight of theirs. Glenda's satchel straps were cutting into her shoulders, but she refused to say anything about it. She wanted to be like the bigger children; to keep on and keep on without a word, helping others, taking the smaller children's satchels as well as their own. They hadn't let her carry two satchels, telling her it was too much for her when she'd offered, but she could at least carry her own the whole way and prove that she was a big girl.

Yet, when Ms. Sergill told them they could stop, her legs simply buckled beneath her. She didn't have the strength left in them to get back up and hide behind a bush to pee, nor even to take her satchel off. She just sat there, on the grass, looking down the hill at the harbour, leaning back on her satchel as if it had been a chair-back.

Ms. Sergill spread the waterproof sheets out on the hillside, getting the boys to find rocks to weigh the corners down, then covering the waterproof sheets with blankets, and getting the children to sit on the blankets, close together for warmth. She wrapped each pair of children in a blanket and soon they were all in cosy little heaps. Some of the littlest ones tipped over sound asleep, their heads on the laps of their companions. Glenda watched them with the detached disinterest of weariness.

"What a little trooper you are," Ngaire said to her, softly. She sat in the grass beside Glenda. "You're Judge Tomptell's daughter, aren't you, pet?"

"Mummy's not a judge, she's a Mummy, and Daddy's name is Glendritz. Mummy calls him Glen."

"Yes, he was Tertiary Servant. He resigned when you came along, did you know that?"

Glenda shrugged. She hadn't known, really. She didn't like talking about her parents. She'd always felt embarrassed that they were old and grey like everyone else's grandparents. She dreaded when they came to the school or music recitals, or disaster relief trials, because she hated the tone in the voices of the children who asked, "Is that your <u>Dad</u>?" or "Is that your <u>Mum</u>?" and she hated having to explain if someone said, "Your Granddad is here to get you." Her grandmothers were as old as other people's great-grandparents, and she didn't have any grandfathers or great-grandparents of her own. She loved her parents when she was by herself with them, she just didn't want anyone else to see them or talk about them.

Ngaire slid Glenda's satchel straps off her shoulders for her, asking gently, "Do you need to go to the toilet?"

"I'm big enough to go by myself," Glenda said primly.

"I can see that, dear, but you're just about done in." She took Glenda's hand, pulling her to her feet against her will. "Come with me, we'll just slip behind those bushes, then you can have some biscuits with everyone else."

When they were out of earshot of everyone else, Glenda took the chance to ask, "What water is coming?"

"Have you learned about tidal waves yet?"

"What's that?"

"Sometimes when an earthquake shakes the land, it makes the sea slosh, like water in your bathtub if you slide back and forth. Have you ever done that, and made a big enough slosh that the water came out and went on the floor?"

"No, Mummy said not to."

"But you know it can, right?"

"Yes."

"Well, the sea is bigger than your bathtub, so its sloshes are bigger. Very big. Big enough to go right over your head. So, we came up here where it can't reach us."

Glenda felt a lot better. Things made more sense, now, and she was vastly relieved once she had relaxed enough to go to the toilet behind the bush. "Why does the ground shake?"

"Once upon a time Maui went fishing in a huge canoe, his waka. Because Maui was a god, his waka was not like our canoes, it was so big that it's now this land, Te Wai Pounamu."

Glenda was having none of that. "This is not a waka; this is an island." She pulled her pants up and came out from behind the bush to tell Ngaire firmly, "It's dirt and grass and trees. You can't have hills in a canoe."

"But it's Maui's waka, so it's magic. See the shape of the peninsula? Sticking out from the mainland, then it's round? We're on the canoe paddle."

They walked back to the group, arguing. "This is not a paddle, this is hills."

"In the story, it's the paddle of Maui's waka."

"I didn't want a pretend story; I want to know really and truly."

Ms. Sergill looked up as they approached. "What story is that?"

Ngaire answered, "The story of Maui's fish, and why we have earthquakes."

"Oh, yes, tell that story!" several children called out.

Ngaire started again, while Glenda settled herself comfortably under the blanket with Kim, sitting on another blanket that was over the waterproof sheet. She was soon feeling warmed through and quite comfortable, even if she did think the story was dumb.

"One day Maui went fishing in his waka. Who knows what Maui's waka is?"

"It's this land, Te Wai Pounamu," Alan said. "It's also called 'Te Waka a Maui'."

"That's right. And does anyone know what part of the waka we're sitting on right now? Let someone else answer, Alan."

No one did, so she let Alan tell them they were sitting on the paddle.

"Maui dropped his anchor, then cast out a magic fishhook made from his grandmother's jawbone."

"Eewww."

"Gods do things differently from the way we do things. His grandmother's jawbone was magic, and caught a huge fish, which is Te Ika a Maui, the fish of Maui, a land nearly as big as Te Wai Pounamu. Now, do you know what happens when a fish is out of the water?"

"It dies if you don't put it back."

"Well, yes, but it flaps and flops around, doesn't it?"

"Yes." Alan had to get up and throw himself on the ground, doing an imitation of a stranded fish, complete with sound effects.

"Yes, sort of like that Alan. Thank you. Well, Te Ika a Maui is a magic fish. He isn't dead, even after all these years, and sometimes he still twitches. So don't worry about earthquakes, they're just the fish of Maui letting us know he's still alive, and the tidal wave is just the water flicked up by his tail. We just have to get you out of the way because it would be over your heads."

"Because the fish is so big!" Glenda finished triumphantly, feeling so much better that she accepted the biscuit handed to her, and sat nibbling it, looking down at the slopes of the hills around the harbour, idly wondering how far up the water would splash. She had a picture in her head of the tidal wave being like the time she tripped, and her water splashed out of her cup, getting all over Granny, who had said, "I wish you'd be more careful!" It would be like that, she thought, only bigger. She hoped someone had told Granny about this. She would be really mad if she got soaked with a big splash.

Underground

Since Hosea's arrest times had been hard for Sam and Maria. They couldn't do everything by themselves. They were helped by some of Maria's family until they realised that they couldn't convince her to leave Sam. Then they called her loco and stopped coming around.

Sam knew that they were staying away from the place where someone had been arrested so that they wouldn't run the risk of coming under suspicion. He kept his own family away for the same reason, as well as not wanting them to lead the PPL to him. That left him relying on casual labour when he could get it. Aside from the problem of paying workers, there was always the fear that any stranger who showed up looking for work could be there to spy. What's more, if any of the hired hands ripped him off, there was nothing he could do about it, because filing a complaint would expose him to the very people he was hiding from.

He hadn't been able to pay Maria since Hosea was hauled away. He didn't know why she stayed with him instead of going back to her family, but he knew he couldn't make it without her.

Hosea had kept game on the table, so they didn't need to eat their beeves. Sam couldn't even hunt because of his arthritic legs. He used to be as stealthy as a cat. Now he lumbered around like a blind bear. He couldn't stalk the prey anymore; he had to lay in wait and hope they would come to where he could ambush them. He depended on Maria's gardens and chickens to keep them from starving. The amount of work he could do got less and less every day. No matter how hard he fought the pain to keep going, he always needed to sit down too often to get all the work done. They got sick of eating chicken and jackrabbit, and the farm quickly started to run down.

A few weeks after Hosea died, Maria told Sam, "Your friend's here."

Sam straightened up slowly and painfully.

Joe Mack came into the room asking, "You ever see a doctor about that?"

"Yep. Waste of money. He said I got arthritis, which I knew, and he said there ain't nothing can be done. Then how come Maria's herbs help?"

"I don't know nothing about that. Now that the PPL have given up poking around this

Parish, we got to have a meeting."

Sam immediately had an image of the PPL watching them and struggled to speak through the panic attack that brought on. "Just because they're gone don't mean they ain't keeping an eye on us to see what we do when we think the heat is off."

"We know, Sam. We're watching for them, but it looks like they figure they killed the sabotage with Lucky and Hosea."

Sam couldn't help reliving that horrible morning. It replayed in his mind's eye no matter what he did to stop it. He tried to explain, "Hosea saved me. Once they thought I wasn't all there, they never looked at me again. If it wasn't for Hosea, the PPL would have took me. He knew what he was doing: he lost his family because they were rebels, remember?"

"Right. We don't want to give them a way to figure out it's you here."

"What?"

"They don't know it's you here. We been telling everyone you died."

It made sense to Sam now. "That's why they believed Hosea when he called me 'Angelo' and said I was his retarded little brother."

"Okay, from now on you're Angelo. It gives us a good reason for helping and sending guys here if Angelo's a few cents short of a full dollar. If we work it right we can cover up a lot of coming and going."

Not wanting Maria to overhear, Sam indicated with his eyes and a tip of his head that Joe Mack shouldn't say anything else.

Joe Mack nodded, "We got to go hunting."

"I ain't no good . . ."

"That's why I come to fetch you." Joe Mack herded Sam outside and into his old banged up farm truck with the gun rack across the back window and eager hunting dogs in the truck bed barking challenges to the farm dogs. While Sam struggled up into the seat, Joe Mack settled his dogs and swung himself up into the cab with an ease that Sam envied. Bad enough that he'd been tortured without arthritis setting in at the points of injury. Joe Mack gunned the protesting motor and lurched the rattling truck over the farmyard ruts to the equally rutted road. It's worn-out shocks beat up on Sam's sore joints like he was being tortured again.

"Ain't no one can hear us here," Joe Mack said. "Did you know they're asking questions again?"

"Who is asking questions and why?"

"I was kind of hoping you could tell me."

"All I know for sure is the PPL talked to Willie Jay, and Johnny's vanished."

"Did they take him?"

"No, he's hiding so they can't take him back to the islands."

"He ain't too far off. They've questioned me and they're hunting for you in case you ain't dead."

At least some of it became clear to Sam. "Well, what did they ask you? That'll give us an idea of what's going on."

"Same as before: what are the islands really like?"

"That tells us two things: they ain't depending on what Vince says, and they're thinking about going back."

"Oh, for sure they're going back. They already told Willie Jay he's going."

"So he'll go for sure?"

"He ain't got no choice. I'll go with him this time to give Chuck a break."

"That opens up another bunch of things." Sam clenched his teeth against the pain in his joints. "First, have you heard any rumours about Vince?"

"Not a word."

"That means something, too. They're letting him write these things, but they don't believe them. Why are they spreading information that they know ain't true? We can work on that later. Right now we got so much to figure out at once that we got to figure out what comes first."

"Oh, I got more to tell you yet, Sammy boy. Your daughter, Beulah, is working in the charity kitchen outside the prison."

"What!" He was horrified that Beulah had left the comparative safety of his brother's farm to be practically in the SS's faces.

"She's the best recruiter we're ever going to find, ever. She can smell a double player a mile off. You got a message from Beulah – Orpah and Paari both got out."

It was bitter-sweet for Sam to hear that. He was glad another daughter and son of his were free from their stepfather, but he couldn't see them, and he was worried about what would happen to them. "Not that that they're any better off."

Joe Mack peered at Sam out of the corner of his eye. "What do you mean?"

"They can't come to me, and who knows if my brother or Rubin can take them in? What have I got to offer them?"

"Hope for the future and a cause to work for."

"No, I don't want them mixed up in this."

"They're in it up to their necks whether you like it or not from leaving without permission."

Sam sighed. He knew that was true. "Can we get them out in the pipeline?"

"They ain't going to go. They want to help free the younger ones."

Sam just stared at him, unable to speak. He couldn't bear to think of his daughters, Beulah and Orpah, mixed up in the underground. He had vivid memories of what happened to women in custody. It flickered through his mind to ask whether Beulah was dressing as a man or a woman. He choked over the image of how she was likely to be treated if she was arrested as a man, then they found out she wasn't.

"I guess we can't just send all our women folk to foreign parts. We ain't really got that far along planning underground ops yet. Up until now it's just kicking around ideas and talking."

"We did more than that. We got messages all the way to the Free West and back. Rocky, Sage, Cliff, and Skipper all escaped. They helped convince folks there that we're for real. Because of them Radio Free West is up and running. We got allies in the Ashlands that I talked to."

Sam stalled. The delight of finding out that the Weskies he'd befriended had survived momentarily distracted him. "God must be on our side," he mumbled.

"Huh?" Joe Mack stopped the truck deep into the woods.

Sam had to sit for a moment. His joints had locked up so that he couldn't move right away. "Kind of big odds against any of those guys still being alive, and here you are saying they made it and got back home, and you got in touch with them."

"Yup. I guess our guys were behind the big slave revolt the government kept announcing never happened."

Inside Sam something percolated. Could it be that the explorers had made that much difference to the Weskies they'd befriended? His jitters faded as he got the feeling that it might be worth it after all. If such a small act as listening to the Weskies on the island could lead to such big events as a slave revolt and mass escape, then they really were going to have an effect. He hauled himself out of the truck saying, "It might just be possible to turn the GR back into the good place it used to be. You got Emmanuel out in the pipeline, huh?"

"Sure did. Him and the other prisoner, plus some of the kids that got burned."

Walking awkwardly and painfully on the uneven forest floor, Sam tried to distract himself by talking. "Didn't some kids get shot too?"

"Yeah. One guy. We took him to another farm and said it was a hunting accident."

Caught by surprise, Sam grinned, "And the farmer went for that?"

"He looked like he didn't buy it, but he never said nothing."

"He had to hear the exchange of fire. That stuff can be heard a long way off so long as there's no motors running near you when it goes down."

"He raised his eyebrows, but he never asked any questions. He patched the kid up so that we could move him before the search got there."

"Yeah, that's what makes a good GR citizen these days – ask no questions. We got to develop something more reliable than going to a guy's house and saying we had a hunting accident. This just shows why we can't move too fast. If we get this running, we'll do more than rescue a few people: we'll shake all the GR back to its foundations." He was startled to silence by the sight of the explorers, with Rubin, some of the members who had not gone with them to the islands, some of the locals, and a few people Sam had never met before.

Joe Mack gave a whoop at the sight of Johnny Balaam. "Johnny! As I live and breathe, I'm surprised you showed yourself, son. If they followed any of us, they might see you."

Johnny smiled, "Now that they got their translators, it's no different if they see any of us."

Sam told him, "Ain't no reason you'd die if you went back to the islands."

Chuck stood up as they reached him, adding, "Sam's right, Johnny. Me and Willie Jay weren't even a bit poorly when we went back." He guided Sam to a fallen log they'd picked as a seat for him, while the rest of them stood or sat on the ground.

Johnny argued, "I was the worst. My life was preserved by prayer that time, but I won't get through it again."

"Bless your heart," Willie Jay said. "You don't gotta live in fear. The Good Lord will keep you safe. Nobody who was with us the first time got sick again."

Johnny put his hands up. "I don't care if you all think I'm plumb loco, I know I'll die if they make me go back there, so I ain't going."

Sam waved the others to silence when they started to argue with Johnny. "Is that true, Chuck? You only get sick once?"

"I can't say I paid a whole lot of mind. Gomer was real bad off, so we left earlier than we were supposed to. Me and Willie Jay never got sick this time, but . . . oh . . . now that I think about it, the Weskies that were there before were okay, too. Is this a big deal?"

Sam had a feeling it was going to mean something, but he couldn't put his finger on it right then. He made a stab at it. "If you only get it the one time, like chicken pox, Johnny don't need to be scared no more."

Johnny shook his head. "You don't get it. I'll die if I go there again. The Lord warned me in a dream."

Feeling like his old self, Sam took control of the meeting. "If we're all here we'd better get on with it before someone wonders where we are.

First, it looks like they're going back for a third time to our islands. Joe Mack and Willie Jay are going with them this time."

Willie Jay's voice rose. "They never gave me no chance, Sam. They came right to the house and said I was wanted and now Daddy thinks I done something."

"You did," Joe Mack grinned. "You went with us."

"No, not that. Like a sin or something."

"Does your Dad know what you been doing?"

Not wanting them to get too far off the topic, Sam frowned at Joe Mack. "Let it go. This is more serious than it looks. We were going to watch out for the folks of the explorers who're away, but if the PPL are going to his folks' house to get Willie Jay, then maybe we ought to back off some."

Joe Mack sobered up instantly. "None of our guys better go near my house while I'm gone. If they're watching the explorers . . ." he stalled.

Sam nodded. "I know what you mean. It could go both ways: if they're watching our homes that'll lead them back to us, and if they're watching us, it'll drag our families into it."

"We might not be able to keep them out of it," Chuck pointed out. "It's no secret who went on the exploration. We never guessed it would be like this, or we would have been more careful."

"Damn! You're right." Joe Mack exclaimed. "What can we do?"

"Not a whole lot except maybe stay away from them."

"Oh, hell."

Sam felt sorry for all of them, and a bit irritated that Johnny had to jump Joe Mack immediately for saying, 'hell.' He interrupted Johnny to prevent an argument. "I wish it wasn't like this. If I knew it would get like this, I would've done something different or set things up different, or something."

"But it's too late now," Chuck finished for him.

Joe Mack. "Yeah. They know all our names and where we come from because we never thought to cover our tracks."

"It would've been worse if we did."

Sam was surprised by how certain Chuck sounded. "Why?"

"They would have got it out of us when they had us in the joint."

Sam could feel the familiar shaking starting just from the mention of it. Interlacing his fingers and pressing his hands between his knees so that no one would see them shake, he hurriedly changed the subject. "The main things for Joe Mack and Willie Jay to find out are: who's behind this trip, what's it for, and does anyone get sick more than one time."

Willie Jay had been looking miserable since they'd started talking about staying away from their families. At that he let out a wail. "My Daddy ain't never gonna let me do that!"

For the hundredth time Sam wished he hadn't taken along someone as immature and naïve as Willie Jay. "He's got to know you ain't got no choice, son. Wasn't he there when the PPL came for you?"

"Well, yeah, but I been arrested when we got home and now the government men want me, he says I broke some law of God or man somewhere. If I stay away from him ain't nothing in the world will get him to think I ain't guilty as sin."

Johnny reassured him, "They want you because you're the best translator. Your Daddy will be proud of you when he knows they want you for a good reason."

Willie Jay gave Johnny a pitying look. "My Daddy ain't gonna think this is good."

Johnny wasn't about to give up so easily. "You're always saying that your Dad thinks you're dumb . . . well, he's going to think you're way smarter than he figured. . ."

"No!" Sam had to put a stop to that. "Let them think you're dumb."

"I don't let them, they say it all the time, even if I do something that ain't so dumb."

"That's okay. It might save your life. When the PPL got Hosea, he said I was his retarded brother, Angelo. They never even got a proper look at me after they figured I was stupid." Willie Jay stared at Sam with his mouth half open. Sam couldn't help thinking that he understood why Enos Rimmon thought his youngest son wasn't all there.

Johnny tried to reassure Willie Jay that the explorers didn't think he was stupid, but Sam cut him off. "Don't try to act smart, Willie Jay. That'll get you in big trouble. Being dumb might save you, son. Hosea was on to something when he told the PPL I'm not right in the head. They never even tried to talk to me after that. Don't try to be smart. If they catch on that you ain't as dumb as they think, it'll be all over for you."

Joe Mack grinned. "Don't worry, Sammy, I'm gonna make sure none of the PPL gets any idea our boy's got any brains."

Sam was afraid of that. "Don't go too far with it, Joe Mack. The tiniest hint that it ain't real and you'll be sorry you were ever born."

Joe Mack settled down some and promised, "Okay, Sammy boy, you can count on me."

Sam warned Willie Jay, "Don't try to play dumb, either. Just be your own self, and if they think you're a few rounds short of a full chamber, let them, it's good for your health."

Willie Jay looked at Sam with such hero worship that he made Sam feel like a bad-tempered old man even before Johnny said, "I had sinful thoughts when I heard what happened. I was glad it was Hosea and not you."

Willie Jay's head hung down as he muttered, "Me, too."

Joe Mack snorted, impatiently. "We were all mighty relieved it wasn't Sam. Ain't nothing sinful about that. It don't mean we wish any ill on Hosea or his family. Dang, we saved his son, didn't we?"

"Yeah, we did," Sam agreed to stay in control of the meeting. "We ain't just the explorers no more, now we're a real honest to goodness underground. We got to plan for a more secure longer-term place to base out of and to take the wounded. We got to make better plans. Like, when we meet like this, we got to have lookouts."

Chuck assured him, "We got lookouts."

"Are you sure we can depend on them?"

"It's my brother and a couple of the local guys. I'd trust them with my life."

"We are trusting them with our lives," Sam pointed out.

A woman's voice asked, "What about people trying to make it to the border on their own?"

The men glanced at one another. They hadn't thought that far, yet. "They'll just have to do what they've been doing," Sam told her.

"We got to come up with some kind of signal," she insisted. "So, they know if they've come to a safe house."

"We ain't got a whole lot of safe houses set up," Chuck explained.

Sam had a flash of the obvious. "Listen, you guys. When we're moving folk, we got to know if the place we're taking them to is still safe when we get them there."

"Yes," the woman agreed. "And it's got to be something that won't make the PPL suspicious if they took over the house."

Sam had a sudden insight that the female subversive was Mrs Comfort. "Men know nothing about women's work," he said slowly, searching for inspiration as he spoke. "If you could do something that you could pass off as normal work . . ."

There were few women there, but in a moment they all had their heads together in an intense whispered conversation.

Turning back to the men Sam said, "If we had a better idea of who is behind the President pulling strings, we'd have more of a chance of figuring out what's really going on."

Joe Mack told him, "That's one report I never got a chance to tell you yet today. When you said we needed people in the house of everyone with likely influence on congressmen or senators we never got to everyone, but my sister is working inside the Faithful house as a maid."

Sam could feel his jaw drop. "Caleb Faithful? He's the last one I would have picked. He's never around when anything goes down and most people have never even heard of him."

"We used your points." Joe Mack counted off on his fingers, "Who's doing better than he should; who knows everybody who's anybody; who's got access that makes no sense; who's power or fame hungry; and who is always around when anything goes down. No one fit them all, so we went for four out of five. Faithful had them all except the last two. His wife was hiring maids, so we got someone in. Now we're thinking he's a whole lot more power hungry than he looks."

Sam felt himself going cold. The most chilling realisation dawned on him. "Holy Hannah! The power-mad are real set on making sure everyone in the whole blamed world knows who they are and what they did and that they're better and smarter than everyone else. If this guy can get the government to do what he wants, <u>and</u> keep quiet, then we are up against something smarter and way more dangerous than any of us ever dreamed up. That's scarier than a sidewinder with no rattle. It means we don't know where he is, how poisonous he is, when or what he's going to hit, or why. Usually, it's easy to see what they're after – fame, power, greed, money, or whatever. If the f . . ." Remembering that there were ladies present, he stopped himself from cussing. ". . . guy stays low how in hell can we figure out what's going on?"

"My sister heard them say that they had to get 'them' to pick up the 'old guy.' That's why me and Chuck took off to warn you they were coming. We figured 'them' was the SS or the PPL and 'the old guy' was you."

Chuck stepped closer, adding, "We tried to tell you after the ambush, but you were too shook up to get what we were saying. They knew someone went over the northern border and came back. They figured someone based here was working with the Ashlanders, so we thought they meant you. We never thought they'd go after poor old Hosea. He took the rap for what we've been doing."

Sam worried about Joe Mack's sister almost as much as his daughters. He had to force himself to accept that he couldn't do anything for any of them. He fought hard to drag his thoughts back to the conversation. "What does your sister say about what's going on inside the Faithful household? If we're right that Caleb's the one that's influencing things, what she sees will tell us what's going to happen."

"Ambassador Flint and his wife and kids are there."

"That ain't news. They'll be there for the funeral of Caleb's nephew. That Gomer what's his name that took you guys back to the islands. Flint's wife is Caleb's daughter."

Joe Mack tipped his hat back and scratched his head. "We figured it was Flint that got the info from the north."

A light went on in Sam's head. "We'll have to see if we can find out if that's right. When you think about it, why would the whole family come home for the funeral? The Ambassador would stay at his post, huh? Only the wife would come home, if anyone did. It's her cousin. We'll see if your sister can find out when they got there. What we want to know is if they started asking the explorers questions before or after the Flints got there."

Chuck nodded. "I'm thinking they started to look for us about the time the Flints got there, right before the news hit the streets about the nephew's accident."

"I'm guessing we got the right guy, then. I'm guessing the best thing we could do is get more people inside the family homes of all of Caleb's kids and nephews."

Joe Mack settled his hat back on his head. "Something's incoming."

Even Willie Jay snorted at that.

"We got that," Chuck told him in crushing tones. "What we got to do is be sure."

After a short silence Johnny offered, "So we know one of them is going back to the islands again, but we can't figure out why."

Sam nodded. "That's only part of it. The next thing is to find out where Caleb was before and after everything; he might have a hand in it."

Joe Mack blinked. "I wonder if Tuffy Flint will go back after the funeral."

Chuck and Sam caught each other's eyes. "Good one."

Chuck asked, "Do you think he's got enough pull to get his family out of the line of fire before it happens?"

Sam could tell him was, "If it's true that Caleb Faithful is the secret power we always figured was there, then we're up against real evil. If his family gets moved out of the way before things get hot then we'll know."

"We got to do what we can against the likes of Faithful," Johnny growled. "He's doing the opposite of what the Good Book says."

"If it's really him that's our spoiler," Sam reminded Johnny, amused to see how aggressive the normally laid-back guy was suddenly.

"How can we figure out what Caleb Faithful's up to or if it's him?" Johnny demanded.

"We got to get people in places where they'll hear if any of the family moves; we got to set up a way of getting the info from them to us . . ." Sam turned to Joe Mack, ". . . and part of that is figuring out how to get information from your sister while you're away in the islands."

Joe Mack nodded. "I never got a chance to tell you what the Ashies taught us. One of the things was not to have family passing messages, so we're already working on that. We figure it's less suspicious if she eats lunch with a girlfriend on her day off, and there's no tie to me."

"Except for the name."

"Yeah, that's another thing. We got to get code names for everybody, so the new recruits never know our real names."

Sam could see that. "That makes senses. It's too late for us, but it will make new recruits safer."

Chuck said, "That's what I told the rebels. I been thinking about this info, and I figure we can use the radio."

Joe Mack snorted. "How do you figure? Ain't only us got radios, and the moment we start to use them for sh . . . stuff like that the PPL will be down around our ears like a hive of wasps."

Chuck looked unconcerned. "Yup. Got that. What I figure is that the more people who know what it takes to make a radio, the more news can get around that the PPL don't want getting around."

Sam suddenly felt dizzy with excitement. "They can find and destroy radios here, but there ain't a blind thing they can do about Radio Free West!"

"All they can do is try to find out who's receiving it."

"When citizens find out the truth about what's been going on, it's going to move the foundations of this nation."

"Hopefully back to what it used to be," Johnny growled.

Joe Mack was insistent. "That's what we're all aiming for, but I still want to know how we're going to get messages back and forth. We can't carry radios around, and there ain't enough of them around to spread the word."

Sam could hardly contain his excitement. "I just know we're going to make this work. First thing we got to do is teach folks how to build radios and find out how to get the parts. We find out how to keep an eye on Caleb Faithful and his family. We find a way to get info to everyone in the underground without getting all of us together. It's too dangerous."

Mrs Coyote said hesitantly, "We think we got an idea."

"Okay, shoot." Sam didn't think it would do any harm to hear what the women had come up with.

"We never wash feather quilts, so if there's a quilt hanging on the line to dry then it's a signal. Bandanas hanging by them give the signal. Red means don't stop. Blue means welcome."

"Thanks," Sam couldn't believe how simple it was.

Even Joe Mack grinned. "That'd work."

"We could use it, too," Chuck's eyes lit up. "We could leave bandanas on fences."

"Yeah." they beamed at each other.

"Don't tie them, though," Sam warned. "They'll look like a signal then. Catch them on the wire or something so it looks like it was lost."

"This is going to work," Johnny beamed.

Joe Mack thumped him on the shoulder. "If it works, you'll hear from Radio Free West."

"Let's get out of here before they catch us all and wipe out the whole underground."

When they got back to Joe Mack's truck there was a butchered deer in the truck bed. "What's this?"

"We went hunting, remember? If they were watching, there ain't nothing strange about two guys going out and coming back with meat."

"Well put it in the cab with us so the dogs don't get into it." Sam didn't like the idea of taking charity, but it was going to be easier to explain to Maria where he'd been if he went 'hunting' and came home with something hunted. "Watch out for Willie Jay on this trip, son. He ain't like rest of us."

Joe Mack laughed. "You can say that again!"

"I'm serious. Those guys can tie him in knots."

"I'll do my best."

CHAPTER THIRTY-ONE

Aftermath

Kiritoe Amaru

The smell of the earth and the fresh air made Kiri temporarily dizzy. They'd been more short of oxygen than he'd thought. He climbed up the slope of the hole that had been dug down to the carriage, noting how carefully it had been done so that earth didn't fall in on them when the emergency exit was popped. He was surprised to realise that the bright light that was making his eyes water was actually muted because it was evening, the sun was going down, and they were in the ravine. They couldn't have been down there that long. The last thing he remembered, it had been lunch time, now it was dusk.

He stared around, trying to orient himself. It looked like the whole side of the ravine had fallen down, taking the Flying Fish with it. "Come on, man. Don't stop or you'll pass out," a rescue worker urged him.

He turned towards the sound of the voice and caught his breath in shock. The remains of a large tree were sticking out of the carriage that had been directly in front of the one he'd been in. What miniscule difference in speed would it have taken for that tree to have penetrated his carriage instead of that one? He felt light-headed and unreal. How ridiculous to tell him he would pass out, there was nothing wrong with him. He hadn't even been bruised. Or scared. He'd functioned on automatic, all those years of disaster response training making everything come to him without even having to wake up to do it. He still felt as if he was in a dream as he climbed out of the hole and down the slope on the other side.

What if he'd got on that carriage instead of the one behind? He couldn't imagine, simply couldn't imagine being in that carriage instead of in the one where the worst problems were a broken foot and a crying baby. The thought of it made his knees go weak. How close was that? The back of that carriage was no more than a metre from the front of his carriage, the trunk of the tree no more than two metres from where Lucy had curled up so comfortably in her seat.

There was another smell there. A particular smell that made him want to cry, to throw up, to run away, or to get busy and help out. A smell of blood, of medicines, of upturned earth, uprooted trees, torn plants. And something else, something indefinable that put the hair up on the back of his neck. He stumbled down the slope where he was told to go. He noticed a row of people covered in sheets to one side on a patch of grass, lying side by side, not moving. The sheets were tucked neatly under their feet and right up over their faces. It didn't register what that meant, but he did notice that the grass they were lying on seemed surprisingly undisturbed. He stumbled, someone caught him and helped him, but he shook them off without looking at them and staggered on towards a tent he was told to go to.

Suddenly he was assailed by someone weeping and calling his name. He almost lost his balance as the person ploughed into him. He blinked, bewildered. She hugged him tightly, sobbing, "What are you doing here? Great Tane, Kiri, you were in that Fish? I can't believe it! You're alright? Tell me you're alright!"

Someone pulled her off. "Leave him alone, he's in shock."

"Oh, Tui, hi," Kiri said, realising who it was. He stumbled on towards the tent, thinking how absurd it was to say he was in shock when he was just tired. It was just that he still couldn't wake up properly, that was all. One part of him insisted he wasn't dreaming, but the rest of him was just as sure he was.

At the tent he was checked over carefully, given a clean bill of health, and sent to sit down. He made a comfortable seat on a mound of earth and sat obediently. He was given a paper cup of juice and told to drink it all. He idly watched the people going into and out of the tents. Some were able to walk, some were helped, and some were carried on stretchers.

As he watched he saw someone familiar. He thought of Calline, and his heart leaped within him. She couldn't be here! He took a closer look. A slight, blond woman, efficiently dealing with a bleeding child. Calline! What's she doing here? Oh, of course, she's a doctor. She'd have come in because of the disaster. His head cleared suddenly, and he got up and walked briskly over to her. She looked so worn; he had to make her take a break.

"Lina, are you alright?"

She gave him a quick glance. "Hi, Kiri, are you here to help? We need some blankets brought in and find a way to warm them."

Automatically he turned to do her bidding. She'd already turned away from him, busy with the injured child.

A large woman intervened. "Yeah, nah, he's not helping, he's a victim. He's shocky, eh? Come with me, Sir."

He blinked at her. He'd seen that face on the news. Wineera. The hero princess. Of course she'd be here. They could depend on her in a disaster. He suddenly felt that everything was going to be all right. He obediently followed her, saying conversationally, "Looks like the whole side of the ravine just came down on the rail."

She glanced up at him. "I know you don't believe you're in shock, Sir, but believe me when I tell you, you are." She took him back to his seat on the mound of earth, telling him, "We've had a massive earthquake."

An earthquake? That's nonsense. He'd have remembered an earthquake. "Dr. Digan needs blankets, and she wants them warmed. It helps people in shock, you know. I have to get them for her." But even as he said it, she was pushing him back down on to his seat.

"Did you drink all of your juice?"

He couldn't remember.

"You need to drink it all. You need it. What's your name, Sir?"

"Kiritoe Amaru."

She blinked, dropped her stern look and asked, "The composer?"

It was his turn to blink. "I suppose so. I wrote something once."

She shook his hand, grinning down at him in shy delight. "I'm so glad to meet you. I love your music. Are you going to write something about this?"

"What?"

In a tender voice, nothing like the powerful manner she'd had before, she urged him, "Now you sit right there, Mr. Amaru, and don't move until I get back. I'll get you another glass of juice. You have to have it. And don't you worry about Dr. Digan's blankets, I'll see to it. Will you sit there until I come back?"

It seemed to be important to her, so he agreed, feeling that his knees were weak, and he needed to sort something out, though he wasn't sure what that was. She was gone, leaving Kiri feeling more lost and confused than ever. It was getting dark all around him now, the sun was low behind the trees. The insides of the tents were lit with lamps, the sides of the tents glowed, light poured out through the openings, and shadows moved about inside. He could see Wineera directing people, taking care of Calline's need for warm blankets; suddenly feeling chilled himself as the sun went down.

The ground shuddered. That's all we need, he thought. An earthquake on top of this. Wineera arrived beside him with his juice and stood over him to make sure he drank it. "That aftershock was only a little one."

"Aftershock?" he looked at the gash in the hillside. Clods of earth and rocks were tumbling down the raw face.

"From the earthquake that buried the carriage you were in." She watched his face closely as she spoke. "What do you do for a living?"

"Professor of history at the University of Manawatu. My students. Where are my students? They're my responsibility."

"That's better; you're coming back to yourself a bit now, Professor Amaru. Don't worry about them; they've all been taken care of. You did more than your responsibility in that carriage, you held everyone together. Don't feel badly, it's quite common that when people have shouldered the burden of everyone else's safety, when that burden is suddenly lifted their minds blank out about what they've gone through. You did a great job. You'll be recommended for that, you know. Your carriage came through better than any of the others."

Kiri was appalled. He couldn't be recommended for that! He hadn't done anything. He'd been asleep. He'd never woken up properly. Tears filled his eyes. He pleaded with Wineera to understand, he shouldn't get anything, he hadn't done anything, it wasn't right, he wasn't even bruised, and other people . . . his voice trailed off, and he gestured in a circle encompassing the hospital tent, the steady trail of people making their way away from the site.

"You're going to be all right, now," the princess said, patting his hand. "When you're ready, walk over that way, around the other side of the admin tent. You can sign up there to help here or find a way to leave from there. Report in so we can record what you decide in case anyone's looking for you."

She left him again, and he put his head down in his hands. It wasn't right, it just wasn't right. The world had gone mad. Young girls like Lucy got hurt, and a big clumsy albatross like him got recommended. Then there was Lina, doing such terrible work in appalling conditions. She was so slender, such a shy personality, this had to be harder on her than it would be on a tougher person. She was so incredibly stoic. She probably had more guts than he did. He had to go to her. He got up and walked back to the hospital tent, annoyed to realise he was still stumbling. There might have been something to this palaver that he'd been in shock. "Where's Dr. Digan?" he asked a nurse.

"I can help you."

"Yeah, nah, I don't need help, I'm a friend, eh?"

"Just what she needs. She's taking a break out the back."

He walked to the back of the tent. Calline was squatting on her heels, staring off into space. "Lina?" he said softly.

"Kiri!" she got to her feet. "Are you okay? They made me come out here, but I can . . ."

"Shh, no, I'm good as gold. I'm going to see my Dad, make sure he's okay. They were right to make you come out here for a minute; you have to take a break now and then. You're only human, you know. You won't be any good to the ones who need you if you wear yourself out." She came into his arms, head down, and he held her. Tiny little thing, she didn't reach his shoulders. He bent down to enfold her like a child and just held her gently with his cheek against the top of her head until she was ready to stand up straight. "When this is over, we'll go someplace together, and you can tell me all about it." He brushed a stray hair off her forehead.

She nodded and went back into the tent without a word.

Kiritoe turned and strode around the tent with a long stride and firm step. He caught sight of Tui out of the corner of his eye, nodded to her with a vague memory of having seen her here earlier, and continued without breaking stride to the admin tent. It was still in the process of being erected. He casually lent a hand to a young man struggling to put an awning on a pole, while asking, "Do you know who I'm supposed to report to?"

"Thanks, mate. Nah, yeah, you go over there where those fellas are, eh?"

There was a straggly line in front of a table lit by lamps hanging from pieces of branches rammed into the dirt. He joined the back of the line behind a stranger, but he spotted several of his students. They called to each other, things like, "Are you okay?" and "Where are you going to go?" The unreality of it all settled on him again, like a shroud. This couldn't be happening. The continued tremors in the ground just added to the unreality. They were learning to walk on shaking ground as if they were at sea on a boat. No one paid it any mind anymore, and that just couldn't be right. The man in front of him said, "I've heard they've set up a kip tent over there. Are you going to kip here for the night?"

"Yeah, nah, mate, I've got to get out of here. I've got to go up coast and see my old man, eh?"

"You better wait 'til morning. What if another biggie hits us in the night?"

"It'll hit here, and I'll be there."

"Yeah, nah, mate. The epicentre was up coast. She could hit again while you're on the way. In that Flying Fish and Pwoing! Down on the ground again."

Kiritoe hesitated, but he had to get out of there, even if he had to walk the whole way. "I've got to get out of here, mate. No matter what she takes, I've got to do it."

He gave the people at the table his name, where he'd come from, and where he intended to go. He nodded politely at their urging that he stay until daylight, then walked over towards the tent that was being set up, along with the others who had been in the line.

He saw the couple who'd been in the carriage with him. They greeted him like a long-lost relative. He shook Jerry's hand. "Fine job there, Prof, we owe you."

"Yeah, nah, you don't, eh? We were all in it together." He hugged Edie, then excused himself and turned to Rahari and clapped him on the back. "We made it, eh?"

"Too right, Prof. Good thing you were there with us."

"Where's Lucy?"

"They took her out. Search and Rescue have a centipede. Weirdest thing I've ever seen." Rahari looked over his shoulder between the tents.

Looking in the same direction, Kiritoe spotted some movement, lamps swinging, over to one side between the tents. He excused himself and jogged on over there, ignoring the calls behind him. It was the Search and Rescue in their fluorescent orange uniforms bringing in supplies and medical staff and taking out the injured that could be moved to hospitals to relieve the pressure on the field hospital. He saw his chance, added his size and strength to their manpower, and quickly was balanced on the back of the centipede as it picked its way over the broken terrain with its six enormous balloon tyres moving independently up and down over rocks and logs.

"What powers this thing?" he asked in fascination.

"Fuel cell battery."

"I've never seen anything like it."

"Hope you never have to see anything like it again, too."

He couldn't argue with that.

As soon as they reached the closest part of the Flying Fish tracks that were safe to use, the centipede stopped at the lift. Kiritoe helped the doctors and Search and Rescue people take the stretchers to the lift and take them up to the platform, then, without remembering what had happened in between, he was flying along in the familiar kind of smooth quiet ride he'd known all his life, northwards.

Ahnstan Seamore

"Ahnya Seamore," his mother announced herself, and was welcomed with cries of delight.

Then Ahnstan saw an aspect of his mother he had never seen before. Once she'd assessed what the people already there had done, she was in charge.

Ahnstan was taken aback to see the way everyone there obeyed his mother. Not like at home where she and Dad talked about things, and not like she was Mum, but like she was the team leader. People snapped to when she spoke. He discovered that it felt wrong to call her 'Mum' so he called her by name, and she treated him the way she treated every other helper – briskly.

He'd visited her at work, but he'd never seen anything like this. He was astonished by how different everyone was, how focussed. No one was casual and friendly and slow moving the way they usually were. He lost all track of time and was surprised to be ordered to take a break. There were cots made up, in fact he almost remembered being part of that, but he'd done so much, so much had happened, that it had all become a blur.

He was fed a hot meal and ordered to lie down. He found the tart his Dad had baked, still in his satchel, and sat cross-legged on the cot, holding it in his hands, and looking around as if he was seeing everything for the first time. He was confused to realise it was dark. He didn't know where the day had gone. He realised it was better to be busy, to be part of the repairs, than it was to be a small child in the commons wondering what was going to happen. He thought he wasn't tired, but he hardly had a chance to finish the berry tart, wondering about his father and brother and sister, before he was sound asleep.

The Leaders

Pita had never felt quite as relieved as he did when Olarine arrived at Command Central, wearing her gold vest and hard hat with a big silver '2' front and back. He was so thankful to see her, and to have her take some of the burden, that he hugged her.

"Mr. First, you look like you've been coping on your own," she teased him.

"Ollie, Ron's not here."

She gripped her open mouth with one hand, her eyes bugging out over it. "Great Tane in the forest! What happened?"

"The sod went to the quake-site instead of here."

"He's in Wairoa?"

"Worse, he's digging people out of the landslide, going inside the buried Fish to get the victims out, and there's aftershocks bringing more of the hillside down. I haven't been able to get hold of him yet."

"People were asking questions on the way here about why he hadn't been seen on the wallie. They need to see him. It scares them when they don't. They're afraid he's been caught in it."

"I'll be sure to tell him that when I get hold of him. Command Support's been trying to get an open line to him for over a half an hour now. How'm I going to explain this? A big chunk of how people get through things like this is how they feel, and a big part of that is having confidence in the system. How can they have faith in the system if one of the gold vests isn't at his station?" Only four people in all of the islands wore gold disaster vests and hard hats, the three Public Servants and the elected Royal.

Olarine said, "You would have sent him to Wairoa, anyway, to lift the spirits of the people who're at the epicentre. All you need to do is make known that he was on the way to being at his station and stopped to rescue people. Make it sound like it's a great thing. The derailment is more or less between here and Wairoa, isn't it?"

"Yes, it is. Olarine, thank you. I was so caught up in it I couldn't think what to do. You wouldn't expect someone like Ron to go on by and ignore people who needed help."

"I thought it was tough to be First Servant when we had first contact with the GR, but at least I didn't have to deal with a major earthquake, a tsunami, and a missing King."

"Swap you."

"Not on your life!"

They set back to work, Pitamete feeling vastly relieved. His partner was now home giving him comfort and support, and his right-hand woman was taking half of the burden from him. Just the same when command support told him that the King was on the line, he made sure he had a private place to take the call so that no one could overhear him, then he exploded. "What do you think you're doing?" he shouted.

"What do you mean?" Ngaronoa sounded genuinely surprised.

"You're the King, your station is Command Central."

"But I've always . . ."

"Look, when Tarawera went off your _Dad_ was the King. You could do things like this then. What did he do? He went straight to the First Servant and bloody well stayed there until he was told otherwise! The people need you."

"Well, then, that's what I'm doing, Pita. I'm helping the people who need it."

"We've got thousands of trained rescue workers; we've only got one bloody King!"

"People died here, Pita."

"People died in Wairoa, too. Get your royal rear end over there."

"I don't appreciate being reamed like a relief player that bounced the ball out of play."

"You <u>did</u> bounce the bloody ball out of play! In the biggest match this century no less! The ball's in play on the west side and you went to the bloody middle! Leave the hero stuff to Wineera from now on. You do the King stuff. I'll tell the people you were on your way to Wairoa and had to stop to give a hand because you couldn't go past people who needed help, so they don't get the idea you forgot what they elected you to do. You get your King face on and go where you're needed most."

"Ouch. Right. On my way."

Pitamete found Olarine and muttered to her, "That boy's got more sand than sense."

A command support medical officer walked in on them and told them, "Mr. First, Ms. Second, you can't work too long. You need rest."

Olarine said quickly, "I'll take over. Pete's been on his own for hours, but I've just arrived."

Pitamete protested, "I'm needed here. It's my responsibility."

The doctor told him firmly, "You can't go on without a break. You'll be called the moment anything drastic happens. You took it all on your own for hours. You're worn down. Get a few hours sleep, then relieve Ms. Second."

"Sleep? It's not even teatime yet!"

Olarine nodded to Pitamete. "You still need a break. Once Quanita gets here, we can run eight-hour shifts around the clock, with two of us on at all times, but while it's just the two of us we have to spell each other or there'll be no one capable if something else happens."

"It's not that late yet."

"Mr. First, it's important that you rest before you're tired so that you're always at your peak . . ."

Olarine saw Pitamete's partner and beckoned to her, interrupting the doctor. "Just go, Pete. Leora, can you take him?"

With the combined forces of the doctor, Olarine, and his partner against him, Pitamete gave in. "I'm not going to be able to sleep, you know," he confided to his partner, Leora.

The doctor spoke up before Leora could. "You'll need to do relaxing exercises, Mr. First. Do you need for me to coach you?"

"Yeah, nah, thanks all the same, I'll be all right."

"I feel like a child being sent to bed," he grumbled to Leora.

She giggled.

"I'm glad you're home," he said and hugged her.

"We didn't need to stay at our posts all night. Life can continue as normal for everyone but you this far from the quake, except for taking in evacuees if any come this far, and sending relief boxes there and where the tidal wave wiped things out."

He lay on his face on the bed watching the wall unit in their room while Leora gave him a massage. Ngaronoa was being touted as the hero of the hour, with pictures of him carrying a red-haired girl with a broken foot out of the buried Flying Fish. Because she only had a broken foot, she was able to give an interview about what it was like to be buried for hours. She told the reporter how her history professor had kept them all going, even building a toilet in the carriage, and teaching everyone in the carriage how to pound out in Morse code a message to their rescuers of how many of them there were. She credited him with the good condition of the passengers in that carriage, and the lack of panic. In another carriage panicked passengers had tried to dig their own way out, causing the carriage to fill with earth and smother some of the occupants. She also described how the sight of the King's huge frame filling the emergency exit had been an indescribable feeling of relief. "As soon as you see the King, you just know you're going to be all right, no matter how bad it really is," she said.

"He did it again, didn't he?" Pita muttered.

"You shouldn't be watching this, Love, it isn't helping you relax. You're only going to get a few winks before they wake you up to take over for Olarine."

"Remind me in the morning that we have to find out who it was in that carriage." Pitamete said, not making a move to turn the wall unit off.

There were pictures of Ngaronoa striding about the shattered towns of Wairoa, Tuhara, and Mohaka. He'd shifted rubble with his bare hands, he'd taken part in digging trapped people out, he'd held rubble up so that others who were smaller could get into tight places to pull victims out, and when a reporter had caught up with him, standing up on the rubble of someone's house, he'd given a ringing impromptu speech that people all over the islands were quoting lines from.

"Look at that bloke," Pita said, part in admiration, part in chagrin. "A one-man rescue team, and an orator to boot." He sighed and rolled over. "Now I can sleep."

Glendrona Tomptell

"Tangaroa in the Sea!" Ms Sergill exclaimed.

Glenda knew that exclamation meant the tsunami was starting. Frightened, she rushed to Kim's side and sat very close to her, leaning on her and holding her hand. "It can't reach us, can it?" she whispered.

"No," Kim whispered back, holding Glenda's hand just as tightly as Glenda was holding hers.

The first thing that happened was that the water flowed out of the harbour. Glenda watched with mounting puzzlement as more and more of the harbour bottom was revealed as being brown and muddy looking. She was fascinated to see the dips and mounds on the bottom of the harbour. It wasn't flat underwater; it was just like the land, only wet. Further and further the water drained away, until large areas that had always been water were just mud. If any boats had been there, they would have been lying on their sides, but they'd all been taken out to sea.

Glenda remembered hearing people on the Flying Fish talking about that, that the safest place to be was out on the water because in the deep water you wouldn't even be able to tell that the wave had passed by. It made no sense to her, any more than the sight of the harbour emptying did.

Then the water started to come back. Waves came in, further and further across the harbour. For a split second it looked normal again, but the waves didn't stop where they should have. They kept on coming, up the beach, then over the beach, all the way up to the verges, then over the verges, over the paths, over the jetties, up around the buildings down on the waterfront, past them through lawns and gardens, up the sides of the buildings, over the windows. This was wrong. This was frightening. What if this was happening at home? What about her dollies, and her stuffed kiwi bird?

Morehu wailed, "I can't see." He grizzled to Ngaire, "Nyreeee, Niiiirreeeee!! I can't seeeeeee!"

Glenda felt annoyed with him. He was distracting. She was just starting to wonder where she was going to live if her home was underwater, and what would have happened to Granny upstairs, when the water started to leave again. It was no longer getting higher and higher; it was getting lower and lower. Her small trill of relief quickly flickered out as she realised the water was taking things with it. Pieces of houses, gardens, bushes, and sheds were being pulled along by the water, past and over everything between where they'd come from and the harbour, being smashed into pieces and smashing everything they were pulled across or into. Soon the harbour was a brown confused mass of floating debris.

"That wasn't so bad," Ms. Sergill was saying to Ngaire as each time the water came back it was smaller. "It must have gone past the harbour, and didn't come in. The impact must have been on the north coast of the peninsula, so it just sort of sucked the harbour dry as it went past."

"You're right. They got off lightly on this side. I think we should go down this face and try to have the children down before dark. We have a better chance of being able to get them to an emergency shelter on this side than we will at home."

Glenda couldn't believe her ears. It was the worst thing she'd ever seen in her life, far different from anything she'd imagined, and they were saying it wasn't so bad?

After they'd had a picnic dinner from the food they'd carried up with them, they packed everything up, loaded up their satchels onto their backs again, took up the rope, "With your same partners, children, please," stood to be counted one more time, then made their way carefully down the much steeper side of the hills towards the harbour, Morehu complaining about having to walk. "Come on, Morry, you're a big enough boy to walk at least part of it. I can't carry you the whole way. Everyone else is walking." Morehu sniffled and managed to trip every few steps, slowing them all down, until Alan got a chance to whisper to him without being overheard by the adults, that he was a sookie baby, then he shrieked, "Am not!" but after that he stomped along in sullen silence without falling over anymore, and they made better time.

As they got closer, strange smells and noises met them. The town smelled of mudflats instead of trees and grass, the noises were of disruption, not of peaceful routine. There were no birds singing, only gulls screaming. They were not the only ones coming down from the hills. Although no one had been near them on their perch, they could see other people trekking down the hillside towards the town, meeting up and walking with them, bigger people going faster by them, helping with the smaller children at the steep parts. Ms. Sergill and Ngaire wouldn't let any helpful strangers carry any of the children and split the group up. "We have to stay together."

It was scary to climb down the steep side of the hills. Glenda wished they could have gone back the way they'd come; it was an easier walk. No one mentioned what might be on the other side of the hills, so Glenda said nothing about it, but she was afraid just the same. It seemed all of the peninsula, both the north side and the south side, were walking down the south side, not even thinking about what had happened on the other side of the hills.

Organisers in their crimson red vests met them at the foot of the steps up to the Flying Fish rails. "These tracks weren't touched, they're way above where the water reached. This high part of the rail is safe. If you're going down to the harbour, you'll be told where to get off for safety."

"We have evacuated children from Le Bons Bay," Ngaire told them.

The young lady consulted her pad. "Take them to Hilltop, where emergency shelters are being set up. Children first. Do you have a list of them?"

Ngaire and Ms. Sergill handed over copies of their lists, saying, "These are the last copies we have."

The organiser nodded, tearing a sheet of paper from her pad. "Can you copy your list out, please?" She turned away from their group and raised her voice. "Everyone else, report in so that your relatives can find out where you were, then we need able bodied adults without other responsibilities to go over to the west coast. Bad hit at Otanerito. Just a glancing blow, it went past, it didn't hit head on, thank Tangaroa."

The next thing Glenda knew she was on the Flying Fish again, nowhere near as crowded this time, heading out to who knows where. She felt angry and let down. She badly wanted to go home, but was too terrified to ask about it in case someone told her that something bad had happened to her home. She could hear adults talking to each other about damage estimates, and repairs, and how long it would take to get back to normal, and she didn't understand half of the words and it filled her with dread.

CHAPTER THIRTY-TWO

Transfer

"Mail, Sir."

Jaakobah Lycus looked up at his adjutant in surprise. "We got mail yesterday." His first thought was, "What are they up to?" He nodded to his adjutant, who put a sealed folder on his desk and left, closing the door.

Lycus checked the seals on the folder to make sure they hadn't been tampered with before he broke them. He poured himself a shot of moonshine and took a sip of it to steel himself for the coming headaches. New orders, no doubt. Some stuffed shirt who had never seen the reality of the front line in the south telling him he was doing it wrong: ordering him to do things that looked good on paper, but that wouldn't work.

He took out the envelope and looked it over, front and back. Well, he couldn't make it go away, or pretend he'd never got it, so he might as well get it over with.

His heart sank when he saw that he'd been transferred to the south-eastern front. Once again, he was being punished for his success.

The long nightmare had started when he'd married pretty little Dinah Rose Faithful. He could hardly remember back that far, back when he'd been young and idealistic and full of hope.

Of course he had loved her, sweet little thing, only fifteen. He hadn't been much more himself, only seventeen. Of course, the old man had hated his guts. No marriage could have lasted under those circumstances. But Jaakobah had never expected to pay so high a price. The talk was that he'd seduced Dinah Rose to get a share of her Daddy's money. He wished it had been like that. Instead, he'd been plumb young and stupid, and so had she. Then she'd married someone more to her Daddy's liking, someone old Caleb could intimidate, Tuffy Flint, and Jaakobah, had paid the price of deflowering the Faithful princess by spending the years since then in harm's way.

He knew Caleb was disappointed that he hadn't been killed.

Every time he managed to get himself settled, and make a bit of progress, he'd be moved again. Usually to somewhere more dangerous. It had reached the point where Jaakobah's superiors felt sorry for him, and said things like, "You sure got on the wrong side of somebody with pull, boy." Some of them did what they could to ease up on Jaakobah some, without getting their own necks in a noose. Jaakobah was careful never to say that all he'd done was get Caleb Faithful's daughter pregnant and marry her when they were both kids. He kept his mouth shut and took whatever was dished out, year after year. He was numb to it all, now. He didn't even sigh at night over never being able to see his son, anymore. Of course, he drank a bit too much, but who didn't?

His reward for creating the Panhandle by wrestling a narrow strip of land from the Free West to the north and the Yucatan Junta to the south and getting it under control to the point where it was safe to build the railway and the shipyards, had been demotion over some invented charges that he had mistreated the locals. The locals had been shooting at his men and they'd shot back. That's what you did in a shooting war. But when a new President was elected who wanted to change the GR image from conquerors to lawful democratic government, people who shot at you were not fired on in the street, they were arrested and tried.

The rules had been changed, but his orders had not. Just the same he'd been demoted to a more dangerous place, the front lines of the battle to hold the new southern border. In the time he'd been there he'd pushed the border further south into Junta territory and had been pushed back again, several times. Where he'd ended up was some miles south of where he had started.

His promotion back to Colonel came when his commanding officer had been killed in a raid. The life expectancy of commanding officers on the southern front lines was so short that being transferred there was thought of as a death sentence.

He wondered what his replacement had done to be sent to a certain death. He wondered what he'd done to survive.

He looked at the letter again. They were sending him to the steamy, hot, smelly arm pit of the world. He wasn't being demoted again, but he couldn't take any of his men. 'What the hell,' he thought. 'It's true they're trying to get my ass shot.'

After all the hard work he'd put into the Panhandle, he was sorry to leave it with the job half done. He hated the idea of any ground being lost. They'd fought hard for it, at great loss of life. He had no doubt that at least some, if not all, of the gains he'd made along the southern border would be lost, no matter who relieved him, because he didn't do things the traditional way and nearly everyone else did.

When Dinah Rose left him, he was transferred to what was then the Western Front. He had known then that it was a way to get rid of him. He figured Caleb had pulled strings to make sure he would be as far away from his wife and son as possible. It did cross his mind that Caleb wouldn't be sorry if he didn't make it, but he didn't think Caleb was trying to destroy him. That came later.

For a hundred years the GR had depended on their superior weaponry and equipment to expand, getting bigger and stronger as they conquered their neighbours. Every few years they had another attempt at reaching the sea to the west or the gulf to the south. Not only did the nearby nations fight to drive them back each time, but they sent troops to help each other every time news arrived that there was another incursion by the GR.

The Free West didn't work with the Junta or the Gulf Entente, nor did either of them work with each other. Coming to each other's aid was a matter of individual survival. Scouts for each group would report home that there was activity, and various armies would show up. Whenever the GR was present, all the groups of small nations would assemble and go to drive the GR back. For generations the GR had been unable to withstand surprise assaults on the flank or rear while they were in a shooting war with whoever was in front of them.

None of the small nations trusted the others enough to give up their independence and join together to form larger nations to stand against the GR. They were successful as small, mobile, independent armies that could combine at a moment's notice against a mutual threat. Attempts to divide and conquer never worked long enough for the GR to be able to reach the coast.

Jaakobah was promoted to Major when his commanding officer was killed. By then he'd figured out ways of getting around the enemies' strategies. It was the opposite from the way they'd all been trained. Instead of pushing forward aggressively, he stayed still whenever his men had good water, watching to see what the enemy was doing. He'd strike hard and fast, in unexpected ways, times, and places. He broke all the rules by having a retreat planned into every foray.

'Old Jack,' as his men called him, was only trapped between the armies of the Free West and the Yucatan Junta once. He didn't retreat all the way back to the GR, even then, but managed to angle his withdrawal so that he made his stand where he knew there was fresh water. Not many GR leaders had pulled that off, and those who had done it had not been able to last long. The desert dwellers were practiced in diverting and poisoning streams.

Jaakobah was ready for that, too. He mounted a fierce attack before the enemy had a chance to touch the stream, catching them by surprise by striking from the other side of the stream from his camp. That was the turning point. From then on, the enemy was less confident, and his men were more confident. By tactics of outsmarting the enemy instead of relying on strength, he forced a corridor through to the sea.

He had made it to Colonel by the time he'd reached the coast. His thanks for that achievement was to be busted back to Major and sent to this hell hole. It wouldn't look too bad for him if things went downhill when he left here, the same way it did when he left the coast. Maybe someone would notice that he pulled off things no one else could, and things went down hill every time he was kicked out.

He knew for sure that this transfer to the swamps was mean to kill him. He'd been transferred to the Western Front when it had the highest rate of attrition. He'd survived that, turned it around so that more men went home alive, and pushed on through hundreds of miles of hostile territory. As soon as it was safer for officers, he'd been transferred to the next most dangerous posting, the Southern Front. Now that he'd turned that around too, he was being transferred to the latest most lethal place in the GR occupied lands, the swamps.

He had his orders in his hands. He read them yet again. This was not a dream. The moment he walked through that door and admitted he'd read the orders, he was on his way, yet again, to the place most likely to kill him. He'd had promotions given, then taken away. He'd learned not to hope, not to plan, not to count on things. But this! This was different. This was the third time. Now there was no doubt that there was a deliberate intention to put him in harm's way. "Once is a glitch, twice is a co-incidence, three times is a pattern, and four times is a habit," he chanted.

He shook his head. It didn't have to happen four times to him, personally, for him to see it as a pattern. That nephew of Caleb's had been assigned to Jaakobah's old post in the Panhandle, once it was dangerous again. The rumours were that there was a row with the old man. For some reason, going to those pagan islands was a bad idea: Captain Jordan was dead, and so was the Major who had discovered the islands. It gave Jaakobah no comfort that the story was that Gomer Jordan didn't die in combat, but home on a weekend pass. He didn't believe official stories at the best of times, never mind when any of the Faithful family was involved. Why would a commanding officer get or take a weekend pass while his men were under fire? At least some parts of the story didn't add up. Since he didn't know what was truth and what was deceit, he stayed with what he knew to be true: two of Caleb's family members had been put in danger.

In Jaakobah's view that made four times that someone who'd got on the wrong side of Caleb Faithful had been posted to the most hazardous arenas.

What worried him were the stories about Major Temperance. Jaakobah didn't know the man, and he had no idea what Caleb had to do with the journey to the islands, but when the ship returned, the commanding officer had been posted to the swamps. What he had done or had not done that had got him sent to the armpit of the world, Jaakobah didn't know. He'd heard that Temperance drank too much, but who didn't? What he'd heard that really ate away at him was that Temperance had been fragged by his own men. Of course, the official story was that the enemy got him. But there was something about the whole story of Major Temperance that put Jaakobah's hair on end.

It only made sense to be wary of official news after Dinah Rose had told him how it was manufactured, but the problem was that rumours and gossip weren't any more likely to be true. But if there was any truth to it at all, he had been posted to a unit that had gotten away with murdering their Commanding Officer. He'd heard nothing about a court martial from either source. As careful as he was, this raised watching his back to a whole new level.

He noticed that his replacement hadn't arrived with the orders. That was unusual enough to get him wondering why. Somehow or another it had to be part of the constant effort to break him or discredit him. The only way Jaakobah knew of not letting Caleb win was to maintain his dignity and personal ethics . . . and to stay alive.

He was not going to give Caleb the satisfaction of getting to him. Assuming that someone somewhere under his command was being paid by Caleb, Jaakobah made sure he showed no signs of stress or disappointment. If any reports were going to Caleb, they were going to be reports of how he wasn't bothered by anything.

Jaakobah didn't survive for his own sake alone . . . he survived to spite his ex-father-in-law. Nothing pissed Caleb off like not getting his own way did.

He knew he was being spied on because one of the reports had fallen into his hands. It had been among the personal effects of someone he'd trusted. From then on, he trusted no one, confided in no one, and let no one get close to him. He wasn't going to make it easy for anyone to kill him.

New Beginnings

Kiritoe Amaru

Kiri's father had moved out of Kiri's childhood home into a bigger house when he'd partnered Bram's young widow. Kiri had stayed there when he went home for Hatoe and Hine's bonding ceremony. For some reason, however, making his way to the new home after the earthquake upset him to the core.

He went to the house that held memories of his mother and stood in front of it feeling deeply angry at the people who were living there for having changed the colour of his mother's house, and replaced all of the fish windmills that had advertised that it was the home of a fisherman, and the dolphin windmills she'd loved, with flowers and birds. It no longer said 'Amaru' over the veranda. He refused to look at the new name and stormed off in a temper.

He knew that Hatoe and Hinerehia had found the house together so that it was 'their' home instead of his or hers. He also knew she'd given up the home she'd shared with Bram, to be fair. Mentally he could see that it was fair, but emotionally it tore his heart apart. Not even the knowledge that they'd chosen a house that could accommodate her two daughters and have room for his two sons to stay when they visited was sufficient to ease the ache he felt at being unable to go into his mother's house and feel her presence or touch her things.

All of a sudden, he couldn't remember the directions to his father's new house, and he had no idea what had happened to his briefcase. He couldn't remember if he'd had it with him when he'd left the carriage. He knew it had been beside him on the seat, and it had slid down and hit Jerry in the face, but after that he had no memory of it.

He saw chairs and tables on a large veranda, and windmills in the shape of knives, forks, and cups, and decided to have a cup of tea and think. He ordered a tea, then remembered that he had no idea what had happened to his jersey or his wallet. He blinked at the girl behind the counter, confused and lost. "I'm – I'm sorry," he stammered, not knowing where to start to explain himself. It was his hometown; how could he forget his way around?

"You all right, mate?" A rangy looking man got up from one of the booths and sauntered over with a loose-limbed walk that made it look as if he had extra joints in his legs.

"I'm – I'm . . ."

"Here, mate, sit down, you're all in. I'll get his, Sandy. Put some honey in it."

"I don't like it sweet."

"You have to have the sugar lift, mate. You'd better have something to eat, too. When did you eat last?"

"Dunno. Can't remember."

"I'll get that," the girl behind the counter said quickly before the man could say anything. She asked as she pulled a hot pie from the warmer and slapped it on a plate, "What happened to you, mister? Were you in the quake?"

Kiri didn't want to tell them he couldn't remember any earthquake, since he knew he should. He told them, "I was in the Flying Fish, coming from Wairakei, and we got buried."

"Great Tane in the forest!! You were in that? How'd you get out? They're still digging people out of that thing. Reckon it'll take till morning. They don't think there's any more alive."

Both the man and Sandy were sitting across from him in his booth, leaning across the table at him, pushing food and tea at him. He blinked at them, feeling dizzy. What they said made no sense. No one had died. Just Lucy broke her foot and they'd taken her to a hospital. The King himself had carried her. He could tell them that. "The King was there, digging people out, and Wineera. You should have seen Wineera. I got to meet her. She shook my hand." The tea was sliding down nicely. He didn't even notice it was sweet, but he thought he'd choke if he tried to eat anything.

"Yeah, we saw it on the wall unit. The King's in Wairoa now, getting people out from the buildings that collapsed. Wineera's in charge of the buried Fish rescue. You got out okay?"

"I wasn't even bruised," Kiri said bitterly. He was beginning to feel like a coward. He had to have done something cowardly to avoid being hurt when so many others were.

"Man, are you ever lucky!" Crowed Sandy. "What would I do for luck like that!"

Kiri stared at the plate. He thought he was going to be sick.

"You'd better eat it, mister. You need something in your stomach. What's your name? I'm Allisandrea, but people call me Sandy, and this long drink of water is Bill."

"Hi. I'm Kiri Amaru."

"Anatoe Amaru's brother, the composer?" Sandy's voice shot up to a squeak, her hands were clasped together, under her chin, her eyes were nearly starting out of her head.

"Er – yes, that is, my brother's the musician, I'm a history teacher."

Sandy giggled. "Ooo, I just love the AA Sound, I follow them all over the islands to see them. I've been to over three hundred concerts, and I've got every one of their discs. I moved here because I read that Nat Amaru is from here, but I've never seen him. D'you think I could meet him? I mean, you could tell him I gave you the pie and all."

Kiri blinked. He looked at the pie and realised most of it was gone, though he had no memory of eating it. Still, it was in his hand with bites taken out of it, he was chewing something, and the warmth of the hot gravy, vegetables, seaweed, and pastry were doing him good. He had to swallow hard to push down the rising urge to burst into hysterical laughter at the image of his scrawny brother having fans who adored him to the point of following his band and moving to where they hoped to run into him by accident. He took a big swallow of tea, clenched his jaw hard to get his twitching smile muscles under control, swallowed again, cleared his throat, and in as casual a voice as he could manage, said, "Nat doesn't live here. Our Dad lives here. But he has a new house, and I can't find it, which is why I stopped in here. I lost everything but the clothes on my back, including my old man's address."

"Oh, well, that's easy to fix," Bill said, pushing Sandy to get off the seat so that he could stand up. "I can find out where Mr. Amaru lives and take you there when you've finished. You have more colour now that you have something in you. Didn't they give you any tucker?"

"Juice, and there might have been tea. They had a kip tent, and I don't know if they had a kai tent, or food in the kip tent. I never went in the kip tent, I helped them get some of the wounded out to get them on the Fish to the hospital, and then I took the Fish home."

"Good-oh, mate, you eat up, and I'll find your Dad."

Kiri took a deep breath, and for the first time said the words out loud. "It's not Amaru. My Dad's name is Hatoe Hetaru."

"Oh, that's why I couldn't find him," Sandy breathed.

Kiri had a sudden image of girls bothering Hine to try to find Nat, and all at once felt protective of her. "He doesn't live there," he said firmly. "My dad lives there. Please don't bother my Dad."

"Oh, I'm not going to bother him. He just might know where Nat lives, you know?"

"I'm his brother, and I can't find him. He's a musician. They're like the wind. Who can catch the wind? Please promise me you won't go to my Dad's house."

"But you don't understand, I really love him. Really."

"Look, Sandy, there's been a big earthquake. My brother's bound to make sure the family's okay. If he comes here, I'll see if I can get him to come in here and see you, okay? Then will you promise not to go to my Dad's house?"

"Oh, I could meet him, really? You'd bring him in here? Oh, oh, oh!" She squealed, jumping up and down.

Kiri thought his head would split open. She wanted to know all about what Nat was <u>really</u> like. He thought saying that Nat was a skinny, weedy little mutant who'd taken Kiri's stuff and wrecked it, and kept his room like a swamp, was probably not what she wanted to hear, so he went with the acceptable line that they'd always known he was a musical genius, and they all adored him, even if they had made him take his share of the jobs around the house. And yes, he had got that lost seal-pup look in his eyes from losing his mother so young and wasn't it all tragical and romantical. At the first sign of Bill coming back into the shop he got to his feet, thanked Sandy hastily for the meal, and took Bill outside with him, ignoring Sandy's pleas to wait until she had closed up so she could come too.

Bill was shaking his head. "Sorry, man, I couldn't find a Hatoe Hetaru. I looked under Amaru, too, just in case."

"Is there a Hinerehia Hetaru?"

"Yeah, nah. No Hetaru."

"I wonder if it's still under Hetaraki."

"The bloke that skippered the Kaumoana?"

"Yep."

"We can look. I heard his widow's new partner is old enough to be her father."

"Not quite." Kiri fell into step beside Bill. "She was left alone with two babies."

"Oh! Don't tell me – I'm so thick. Your Dad?"

"The same."

"I'm sorry, mate."

"She's jake. Please don't let it get around. I'd never given a thought about Nat's fans. D'you think you could help me find that house?"

Bill nodded. "Come with me, mate. I know the general area. You want to look it up in the database?"

Kiri shook his head. "If we get to the general area, I'll be able to find it."

"Don't worry about Sandy, she's harmless."

Kiri didn't answer. He didn't know what the relationship was between Sandy and Bill. He might be just a customer, or he might be family. Best not to say what he thought of Sandy's 'harmless' desire to meet Nat. Kiri didn't want anyone to know where his family lived until he was sure Hine could handle it. It was the first time he'd thought of Hine as family, and he wasn't used to the feeling.

He shook Bill's hand and thanked him very much the moment he recognised the approach to the house and set off at a lope along the path under the Flying Fish, trusting his long legs to take him out of sight quickly in the dim light.

There were no lights on at the front, so Kiri made his way down the side of the house to the garden gate and let himself into the hex. Hine's pet kea immediately set up a racket, though Kiri was sure he hadn't made a sound. Instantly lights came on over the back door, and Nat's curious face appeared through the fruit trees. He was barefoot, clad only in his lava-lava, despite the cool temperature. Kiri's knees felt weak at the sight of him, though what he said was, "You'll catch your death of cold coming out here like that in the middle of winter, stupid."

Then Nat had his arms around his younger brother and was smacking him on the back, hard, "Py korry, man, we thought you were a gonner. Not a word all day. You couldn't've rung?"

"No chance. Honest." Arms around each other, despite the discrepancy in height, they turned to go into the house. "Where's Dad?"

"On the Dolph. Be in pretty blinking quick, I bet."

"Betcha. Hey, lady." Kiri bent down to kiss Hine on the forehead as they reached the door, where she stood, clutching her dressing-gown about her, hair awry, her kea climbing with its beak and feet up the side of her white towelling dressing-gown.

She stepped aside to let them in, closing the door behind them, picking her kea off her dressing-gown to pet it as Nat said, "Look what washed up on the beach." He held his nose. "Stinks like it, too."

Kiri shoved him. "Settle down, you burk." He asked Hine, "Where are the girls?"

"In bed. It's late. Are you alright?"

He dropped his voice instantly. "Sorry, didn't realise. I'm right as rain. No damage here then?"

"Bit," Nat answered him as Hine went into her kitchen to make tea, her kea riding on her shoulder, squawking what sounded like abuse back at the men. "Mostly a roller by the time she got here. Few things fell down, no major breakage. Pretty bad shaker down at Wairoa, though, eh?"

"Don't know. Didn't see it." There was a huge lump in Kiri's throat that made it hard to talk.

Nat gave him a puzzled looked, head tipped slightly, eyes narrowed. "Everyone here's all right, Kiri. We turned off the wall unit to pack relief boxes because Hine couldn't bear to see any more, but if you want to see what's going on, I'm sure she'll let you turn it back on."

Kiri didn't know what to say. He was fidgeting uneasily when Hine carried a tea tray into the room, her kea pretending to hide under her hair on her shoulder. He took the tray from her and held it for her while she cleared the children's toys off the table, telling them, "I've got savouries in the oven. All I really want is little nibbles. Is that enough for you?"

"Perfect, thank you." Kiri put the tea tray down and took a look around the room. It was a very pleasant room in green and lemon, filled with children's toys and white wicker furniture with lots of pillows and cushions. There were cardboard boxes stacked on one side, and others open near piles of blankets and warm clothing. He gave a deep sigh. He still didn't feel as if he were home. He'd thought he'd feel better once he got home, but he didn't.

"We call this room the sunroom," Hine told him.

"It's lovely," Kiri assured her, sincerely.

She dimpled briefly and went back to the kitchen.

"She's still edgy around you," Nat told him, pouring the tea.

Kiri shrugged. "I'm edgy around her, Nat. What does it matter? Dad's happy, that's all that counts."

"It matters," Nat said softly, handing Kiri his tea.

Kiri set his cup down on the table and sat himself down, took up the cup by wrapping his hand around it because his fingers were too big for the cup handle, and took a deep draught, then shivered. He didn't know what he was going to do now that coming home hadn't made him feel better.

"Cold? Didn't bring a jersey?"

"I lost it. And my briefcase. Every damned thing. No idea what happened to them."

"Don't know if they've got anything in the house that'll fit you. I don't think Dad's things will go over that great pot of yours."

Kiri looked down at his stomach. He had no pot belly. It was more likely his Dad's clothes wouldn't go over his shoulders.

"I'll find something," Hine said, coming into the room, putting the food down and leaving again.

"Thanks," Kiri called after her, staring at the plates of food.

"Go ahead, have something," Nat urged him.

He shrugged. "No appetite."

"You sure you're alright? You're all off kilter."

"Don't be such a damned little old woman." Kiri got up in irritation and walked over to a set of shelves that he could see held things for the girls to write with and draw with. He took a pad of paper down and hunted around for a pen. Nat sat quietly, watching him. He took his finds back to the table, drank more tea, moved it out of the way, and started to write music. Nat kept his silence watching. As Kiri became more absorbed in his writing, Nat looked over Kiri's shoulder to see what he was writing. Then he got up very quietly, picked up his guitar, and took his seat again, angling it so that he could watch Kiri write out what he couldn't say.

When Hine came back into the room carrying some clothing, the two of them were completely absorbed, Kiri writing music, and Nat leaning back, his feet up on the table, plucking the music out as it appeared on the page. "You've got your feet up on my table!" she yelped. They both jumped.

"Sorry, sorry," Nat dropped his feet down and sat up straight. "I didn't notice, honest."

Kiri felt as if he were waking up from a deep sleep. He shook his head to clear it, but still caught a significant glance between his brother and their stepmother. It infuriated him. He could see they thought there was something wrong with him. He poured himself another cup of tea and stuffed a whole pastry in his mouth so that he wouldn't have to talk to them.

"Shall we take a look at the wallie?" Nat asked. "Would it bother you, Hine?"

"Yeah, nah, I'm alright, Nat, thanks. Go ahead. Maybe they've found some more people alive in Wairoa, like that little girl the King dug out, eh?"

Nat picked up the clicker and turned on the wall unit, turning it way down so that it wouldn't wake the girls. "Nah, yeah, man old Ronnie's been true blue, eh? Did you hear that speech he made? Bloody marvellous. Perked you right up, right away."

"Yeah, nah. He wasn't making any speeches when I saw him."

"You saw him? You were in Wairoa?"

"No."

A prickly silence fell. Kiri was shocked to see the devastation in Wairoa and the surrounding towns. He'd had no idea. A 7.9 earthquake with the epicentre on the blind fault that ran right under the town. The shattered houses, the people evacuated, the rubble. Thousands of hectares of land lifted up out of the ocean. A six-metre tidal wave had run down south and shared the destruction for thousands of kilometres. He was so transfixed by the pictures that he didn't hear what the announcer was saying about deaths and injuries, and the supplies already arriving from outside the area of destruction, the disaster response working perfectly.

Then there were pictures of the lighted tents where he'd been such a short time before. The sonorous voice of the announcer talking about the landslides that had been caused by the quake. A six car Flying Fish that had been buried. Wineera talking to the people about how brave everyone had been, how they'd all done what they'd been trained to do, which had saved countless lives. The heroism of the people buried alive in the train.

Kiri felt the room spinning around him. He knew they hadn't all been brave, that he'd done nothing, he hadn't even got himself hurt. She was wrong. She was completely wrong.

"She's the hero here, isn't she?" Hine said, admiringly. "What a woman to look up to, eh? Great for the girls to have an example like that."

"She's great, isn't she, Kiri?" Nat added.

"She likes your music," Kiri choked out.

"What's that got to do with it? How do you know?"

"She told me. She wanted me to write something about . . . about . . . this." He gestured helplessly.

"She told you?" Nat was on his feet. "That's where you were?"

Kiri could feel himself crumbling. He tried to tell them to turn it off, but no words would come out. The lump in his throat was even bigger. He was shaking. Hine jumped up and got a blanket to wrap around him, as Nat, shocked, was almost shrieking. "Tane-mahuta! You were in that bloody Fish?"

"I'm not hurt. I wasn't even bloody bruised, and people were hurt, Nat, they were really, really hurt." Tears started to run down his cheeks.

The sonorous voice was giving the number of known dead and injured, explaining that the names couldn't be given out until the next of kin were notified. Suddenly the image of those sheet covered bodies made sense to Kiri, and he started to sob, great wracking, body shaking sobs that he couldn't control. "They were dead. They were all dead. And all I thought about was the grass looked tidy."

Hine was whispering to Nat, urgently, "He'll wake the girls up. They'll be frightened."

Nat put his arm around Kiri. "Come on, bro, into the bathing room. You need a good, hot soak." Together the two of them chivvied Kiri into the spacious bathing room with its tiled tub and shower. They eased Kiri into the hot water, Nat shucked his lava-lava and climbed in, sitting on the seat across from Kiri, who was still berating himself for thinking about the grass instead of the people lying on it. Hine closed the door behind her, leaving them in there where the sound of a man's sobs were less likely to frighten little girls out of their sleep. Finally, Kiri was able to get to the part of how close the tree had come to him and his students. It would have killed Lucy. There'd been a shot of her on the wall unit as they were leaving the sunroom, but none of them had heard what she was saying. Still, Kiri was able to tell Nat how close it had been for her, with the image of her face pinched with pain, her red hair tumbled on the pillow on the stretcher.

Nat let him talk until he'd talked himself out, making sure to keep the water hot, and the jets pulsing until his brother calmed down. "I never got so much as a damned bruise. Not a mark on me."

"You were just lucky, Kiri. It's not your fault you weren't hurt. It's not your fault either that other people <u>were</u> hurt. I'm sure you're not the only person who came through without a scratch. Maybe Mum was watching over you."

Finally, Kiri wound down and stopped. His head ached, but he didn't feel sleepy. "I've got to get out, I'm shrivelling up."

"Nah, yeah, well, we've been in here a while. Let's see what Hine found for you to wear."

Kiri looked around. He remembered back to a time when he and his brother were much younger, when they'd sat in the bathing room of the house they grew up in and raged against the death of their mother, Anakiri, the two of them in the tub like they'd been today, but with their Dad, and at times with his family, or their mother's family, or friends. All at once Kiri was glad it was a different bathing room: different coloured tiles. There were ferns, mosses, and vines growing over the windows outside, taking luxuriant advantage of the steam vents in the same way as the ones in the other house, but it wasn't the same room. This one had Hine's touches all over it: cute pictures on the walls; ferns and orchids in hanging pots; children's toys in baskets beside the tub; a frilly, frilly pink and white dressing-gown that their mother would never have had anywhere near her, hanging on the back of the door; a large vanity counter with pots and creams, pieces of coloured glass and baby plants all tastefully arranged.

They got out, dried themselves off, and padded over the warm floor tiles to the shelves where Hine had put the bundle of clothes she'd found for Kiri to try on. One of her choices actually had them chuckle out loud. It was two of Hatoe's lava-lavas. "There you go, mate. It takes two of them to cover your fat arse."

In the pile was a real treasure, Kiri's old dressing-gown from years before. "Why does Dad still have this old thing?" he asked, with pleasure. A combination of his Dad's two lava-lavas, a stretchy shirt with no sleeves that pulled tight across his chest and left his midriff bare, and his old threadbare dressing-gown had him covered enough to cope until they could clean the clothes he'd worn round the clock the day before. They jammed those in the clothes hamper, pulling faces at the reek of them.

They peeked quietly out of the bathing room. "It's nearly morning. Come on, bright boy, let's see if there's anything left to eat," Nat whispered, tip toeing through to the sunroom. The house was deserted and quiet. Even the kea was sleeping.

Kiri settled back at the table, while Nat made tea.

When Hine got up in the morning, they were back in the position they'd been in the night before, Kiri bent over and scribbling on paper, Nat leaning back in his chair, picking out the music as it appeared. His feet weren't on the table this time, he'd angled them so that they hung in the air, and the only part of him touching the table was one calf muscle, with the other leg crossed over at the ankle and balanced on top. She turned away without saying anything, collected the eggs from her caged birds, and set about making breakfast.

Hine's four-year-old daughter, Ritihia, stood in the doorway and stared, clad only in a night-dress, feet bare, her plush stuffed whale clutched against her with one hand, her blankie held tightly in the other hand which had its thumb firmly in her mouth, her black curls in fifty directions including straight up. She pulled her thumb out of her mouth only long enough to declare, "You got your feet on the table. Mummy's going to be mad at <u>you</u>."

"Then don't tell her, you little magpie," Nat said in mock fierceness that had the child rush straight at him and scramble up on his lap. He dropped his legs down from the table and lifted his guitar up in the air out of the way until she was settled, leaning against him, staring with huge solemn brown eyes at Kiri, while Nat went back to playing, reaching around her.

Six-year-old Bramerehia, Mere, was shyer. She followed her sister quietly and more slowly, skirting the table while keeping her big brown eyes fixed accusingly on Kiri. When she reached Nat she leaned on his arm, her fingers in her mouth, staring around Nat at Kiri. Finally, she plucked up the nerve to whisper, "Who's that?"

"That's my brother Kiri. Don't you remember him?"

"No."

There didn't seem to be anything satisfactory to say to that, so Nat and Kiri carried on until Tia took her thumb from her mouth again to demand, "Whatcha doing?"

"Making music."

Mere told him firmly, "That's not real music."

"Is so," Nat insisted.

"Is not. You can't sing that."

"Can so, listen." Using his thumb to thump out a catchy beat as he played the tune, Nat took an earlier part of Kiri's composition that had been written full of plaintive minor chords, played it in the key of C, whipped up the speed, and suddenly a heart-wrenching lament was a catchy, bouncy syncopated dance tune.

"That's not the same one," Mere insisted.

"Is so, listen." Nat started again, playing the chords as written, then repeating them with the chord change, and again sped up, and again syncopated with his thumb thumping out the beat.

The child was getting on Kiri's sleepless nerves, but he was fascinated with Nat's talent to take a piece of music that he'd never seen or heard before, and massage it without a second thought. When Nat started to thump out the beat, Kiri put down his pen and rapped out a drum beat on the table. Tia took her thumb out of her mouth, and, laughing aloud, bashed enthusiastically on Nat's guitar.

"Whoa, whoa, whoa!" He swung the guitar way up in the air out of reach. Nuzzling her, his nose right against her cheek, he whispered in her ear, "We never, _never_ hit guitars, Honey."

Tia had a throaty laugh that had delighted Kiri. Wanting to bring her laugh back, he leaned around Nat and told her, "You can make the beat on the table, like I'm doing, look."

With his knuckles and fingers, he tapped out a complicated rhythm. Enthusiastically she pounded on the table. Kiri laughed, remembering his own first clumsy attempts to drum. "Attagirl! Here we go, then!" Kiri beat a quick, one, two, three, then said to Tia, "Now, you."

Nat put the child down off his lap, and as she and Kiri got into the beat, he started to play the guitar again.

Mere protested instantly. "No, no! You've got to do it right."

"What?"

Kiri thought he knew what she meant. "Start like you did before, Nat."

"Oh, I see."

As soon as he stuck the first chord, Tia started pounding the table, laughing her throaty laugh. Mere was annoyed. "Don't, Tia, wait 'til the right time."

"Okay, okay, we'll make a new beginning," Kiri announced. "Tia, we'll let Nat start the slow bit, then, when he gets to the fast bit, we'll be the drums, all right?"

They waited for a moment, as she stared at him, absorbing the idea. "Mary too? Mere too?"

"Mary too, right, Mere?"

Nose in the air, Mere moved to stand beside her sister. Nat started the plaintive passage, Kiri held up one finger, Nat changed chords, Tia dropped her toy and her blankie and leaned forward in excited anticipation, and at the first tap of Nat's thumb started enthusiastically pounding the table. Mere, watching Kiri closely, was making a creditable effort to keep time. Kiri added his deepest bass 'bomp bomp, bomp bomp' undertone, which started the girls giggling. In no time they were dancing around the table as they drummed on it, Mere even making little twirls up on tip toe.

Hine appeared at the doorway, leaning one shoulder against the doorframe, a beaming smile on her tired face, a recorder in one hand, her kea making his way stealthily up her trouser leg intent on investigating the recorder with his destructive little beak. As the kea reached the recorder, Hine transferred it to her other hand, and to distract the curious little parrot, crumpled something rattly down at the bottom of the deep, square pocket of her trousers. When the kea's head was right down in the pocket and he couldn't see what she was doing with the recorder, she stepped forward to put the recorder on the seat of a chair and cover it with a cloth.

As soon as their mother moved, the girls reacted. Tia shouted out joyfully, "Mummy! We're making music with Nat!"

Mere stopped cold, pointing at the pad Kiri had used, and proclaiming, "That's mine!"

The music stopped except for Tia pounding on the table. "I'll get you another one," Kiri promised.

Mere's voice went up a notch. "Mummy, it's mine, and he took it while I was <u>sleeping</u>!"

"It's all right, Mere, I gave him permission."

"But Mummy, it's <u>mine</u>!"

Kiri bent down, looking across the table. "Mere." She wouldn't look at him. He tried to be funny "Mere, Mere, quite contrary, how does your garden grow? With silver bells and cockle shells and pretty maids all in a row." There was no response, so he tried to be more direct. "Mere, please look at me, I have to tell you something." She put her head down.

Hine spoke to her firmly, "Mere, look at Kiri."

Reluctantly she raised her eyes a fraction of a millimetre. "Mere, I'm very sorry I took your paper while you were sleeping. I promise I'll never do that again. I'll get you a new pad, and I'll buy my own pad and keep it here so if I come in the middle of the night, I can write music without ever touching your paper again. I'll never take anything of yours again without asking first, I promise. Forgive me?"

Her cheeks went dark, dusky red and she turned away. Not wanting to embarrass her any further, Kiri nodded to Nat, who started up again, instantly garnering Tia's protest. "Not in the middle! Make the new beginning!"

So, Nat went through the whole process again, the girls stared hard at Kiri's finger, so he lifted it again, and they stood tensely poised, ready to pound the table the instant he dropped it, and they were off, with shrill cries of, "You, too, Mummy!"

Hine stepped up to the table and did her best to tap in rhythm, soon dropping into a mid-beat which accentuated the syncopation. Grinning,

Kiri started his basso line again, and Hine added a high descant. The kea popped his green head out of her pocket with a raucous, "Aarr?" looking back and forth, turning his head almost upside down trying to figure out what was going on. He climbed out of the pocket and hopped onto the table, quickly picking his feet up, dismayed by the vibration. The girls started to giggle at the sight off the kea trying to keep both feet off the table at the same time. Then he decided the vibration was fun and bobbed his head in time. The girls giggled at his antics, infectiously, until they all collapsed with laughter.

"I was trying to tell you lot that breakfast is ready," Hine said when she regained her power of speech.

They trooped into the warm bathing room, accompanied by Tia's indignant shrieks of, "No! No! Make the music! Make the music!" and the kea's furious screaming at being shut in his cage so that they could eat in peace.

Kiri scooped up the angrily stamping, tearful child and swung her high in the air, promising her, "We'll make the music again as soon as we've had something to eat." Discovering that, when Kiri swung her up to the full length of his long arms, that she could touch the ceiling with her fingertips if she stretched as far as she could, Tia rewarded Kiri with her deep, throaty laugh. "Cor, she's got some laugh, this kid," he grinned at Hine, swooping the child down to the floor and peeling her nightdress off so that her mother could wash and dress her.

She beamed at him, expertly applying a wet face cloth to the wriggling child. "How did you get so tall? There isn't anyone else in your family who's that big."

Nat explained it in one word. "Mutant."

"What's mutant mean, Mummy?"

Before Hine could speak, Nat said, "Little brothers who grow bigger than their big brothers."

Mere glared at Tia, "You won't get bigger than me."

Tia pulled aside the towel her mother was applying to her face and announced complacently. "I can if I want to."

Washing his own hands, Kiri told Nat sternly, "If you had eaten all of your veges when you were their size, you would have grown properly, too."

"I'm going to eat all my breakfast!" Tia announced, hauling her shirt on with scant consideration for its survival, or her own face, and scampering off with her mother in hot pursuit calling, "Tia! Wait! I haven't done your hair!"

"Now you've done it," Nat grinned at Kiri, who flicked water at him, then looked down to see what was tugging at his dressing-gown.

It was Mere, who crooked her finger to get him to go down to her height. He sat on the side of the tub and bent over. She mumbled something that he couldn't catch, so he pointed to his ear, whispering to her, "Tell me in my ear." Kiri was thankful she seemed to have forgiven him for taking her pad while she was asleep. He really did feel bad about that, remembering how much it had upset him when Nat had taken his things when he couldn't do anything about it when they were children. It didn't matter what was touched, it was the violation that had hurt so much.

She pushed his bushy hair aside, cupped both hands around his ear, and whispered, "Can you make me touch the roof, too?"

"Are you all finished? All dressed, face and hands washed, hair brushed?" She nodded vigorously, eyes down. "Then here we go, then. Stand on my shoulders." He put his big hands around her skinny little thighs and lifted her straight up from his shoulders, then walked with her fingers brushing the ceiling, so that she gasped in incredulous delight.

"Can I be a mutant, too, when I grow up?" she asked.

"Now you've done it," Kiri told Nat, who howled with laughter.

They sat down in the warm, fragrant dining room, thanked Rongo for the cultivated food, Haumia for the wild food, Tangaroa for the food from the sea, and Papatuanuku for sparing them when the Fish of Maui twitched so violently. They asked the grandmothers and grandfathers to take care of all the people who were hurt, and all of the people who had lost someone they loved, then they dived into the delicious feast of fluffy scrambled eggs, crisp toasted flax-bread, fresh fruit and nuts that Hine had provided for them.

In consideration for Kiri's greater size, she had also prepared a feast of stewed wild mushrooms that he piled on the toasted flat bread and ate with delight, pulling silly faces at Tia's shrilly voiced, "Ewwwww."

Their meal was interrupted not once but several times by people from their hex coming to the back door, and people from outside the hex coming to the front door, with items to add to the relief boxes.

"Let's surprise Mummy by having the table all cleared away when she comes back," Kiri suggested when Hine left to answer the door again at the end of the meal.

"I don't have to," Mere said, in challenge.

"Yeah, nah, you don't have to, but do you want her to know you're the only one who didn't do it?"

While Nat got up to carry things for Hine, Kiri made a game out of clearing the table and carrying everything from the table to the kitchen. He was pretending to dance with the wiping cloth, with the girls laughing at him, when the floor shuddered, and the glasses clinked together. Mere screamed in high pitched terror, "Mummy! Mummy! It's coming back!" and raced headlong through the house. Kiri scooped Tia up and followed, casually pretending to dance with her as he did so.

Mere was clinging to her mother, sobbing, when Kiri and Tia danced their way in.

"Are you sure that was an earthquake, and not just Kiri dancing?" Nat asked.

Mere turned tragic eyes on him. "Kiri can't shake the whole house!"

"Can too," said Kiri, taking the cue, and danced his way over to the sideboard where he slammed his foot down hard enough to sting his heel on the rimu planks of the floor, making the dishes piled on the sideboard shift and clink. "See?"

Tia gave out her throaty laugh, wriggled her way down from Kiri's arms, and jumped determinedly across the kitchen, making no difference at all.

Soon Mere was jumping, too, trying to make the glasses clink. "That's enough jumping, girls," their mother told them.

"I don't have to," Mere announced, jumping one more time.

"You <u>do</u> have to," Hine said, putting her hands on Mere's shoulders to hold her still.

She turned on her mother, indignantly. "We made a surprise for you, and you weren't even surprised!"

Kiri bowed, displaying the dishes on the counter.

"Oh, what a lovely surprise!" Hine said, on cue. "The very first time you were big enough to clear the table all by yourself! Thank you, sweetie." She kissed Mere.

"I did, too!" Tia ran at her, was fended off from painful collision with a hand, then gathered and kissed. "Kiri did, too." Tia pointed at him.

Gravely, Kiri bent down, offering his cheek, and Hine gave it a quick peck, adding a hurried, "Thank you," as she ran off to answer the ringer.

They were doing her dishes when she returned, took the dishcloth from Nat, and told them, "That was the Harbour Master. Your Dad will be at the dock in a couple of hours."

"I'll tie the old boy up," Nat said.

Kiri looked at himself and said, "I can't go in this get up."

Hine told him, "Oh, I put your clothes in the washer first thing this morning. They should be dry, now."

"You are a treasure!" Kiri said, leaping towards the door of the kitchen, then hesitating for directions to the wash house.

"Next door past the bathing room," Nat called out, on his way to his room to get changed into outdoor clothes.

Kiri dressed in double quick time, then ran back to the kitchen and sat on the floor to put his shoes on but was hampered by the girls climbing all over him. "Can we come too?"

"Not this time, sweetie."

"You said we'd make more music after breakfast."

"We'll all make music together when we bring Dad home, to show him what we did."

"He's not my real Dad," Mere announced.

Kiri spun on his rump on the floor to look at her, with Tia perched on his shoulders. "Yeah, nah, he isn't your real Dad."

"I don't have to call him Dad."

"Yeah, nah, you don't have to."

There was a silence while Mere looked at Kiri defiantly, her chin jutting out, but didn't say anything more, and Hine sighed sadly in the background. Kiri flicked a quick glance to Hine. He got no inspiration from her, so he tried, "What do you call him?"

Mere dropped her eyes, but she didn't speak.

Kiri told her, "He's my real Dad, so I do call him Dad."

"My real Dad's dead."

"Nah, yeah, he is. And my real Mummy's dead."

Mere's head snapped up. She stared, wide eyed at Kiri for a moment, then turned to look at her mother.

"It's true," Hine told her.

When she looked back at Kiri he told her gently, "Your Daddy's dead, and my Mummy's dead, so we can make a new family together. I don't have to call your Mum 'Mummy' and you don't have to call my Dad 'Daddy.' What do you want to call him?"

She countered with, "What do you call my Mum?"

Nat arrived in the kitchen wearing long pants, socks, long sleeved shirt, jacket, and shapeless old wide-brimmed hat. "Wicked stepmother," he put in.

Kiri rolled his eyes. "I don't. I call her Hine."

"I heard you call her 'Lady' before."

"Nah, yeah. I can call her 'Lady' and I can call her 'Hine.' My Dad's name is Hatoe. You could ask him if he'd like you to call him Hatoe, or you could call him 'Sir,' like I call your Mum 'Lady,' if you want to."

"I don't want to. Can I call him Hatoe-Dad?"

"We'll ask him if he likes that, okay?"

Kiri got up from the floor, pulled Tia off his shoulder, held her upside down, gave her a hug and a kiss, and asked her to be good for her Mum while he was gone, then handed her over to Nat and picked Mere up to do the same, except that he held her right side up. When he'd dealt with the children, Hine stepped up to him. He bent down to give her a hug, and she whispered, "Thank you. That's been a sore point."

He stepped to the door with a smile, calling back, "We'll bring Dad home to you, Hine-Mummy."

Nat sashayed up to her, "Give us a kiss, Hinny-Mummy."

"Oh, you!" She pushed them both out of the door.

As they went down the garden path under the fruit trees around the back door, Nat said, "I don't know if I'll have all that much time to play music when we get back, Kiri. I've got to get going."

"Get going where?"

"When the quake hit my first responsibility was to the family with Dad out. I couldn't leave Hine by herself, eh? She's already been left alone with the two kids once; she gets a bit touchy when things go wrong. Got to keep her company until the old man's home. Once he's back I've got to get those relief boxes off to the needy."

"You have to go with them?"

Nat twiddled his fingers in the air. "Got to take me talented digits to where people need cheering up."

"Right. You couldn't risk them by doing something like helping rebuild or anything."

"Me? Build? Not if you want anyone to be safe in it. I'm bloody useless, mate. Look, I can do one thing. One. I can interpret music. I can't even bloody write it. I'm not like you, mutant Renaissance man, turn your hand to any damned thing and come up aces. I play music. That's it."

"Me?" Kiri stopped on the path, gaping. "I've never done anything right in my life. Can't work on my Dad's boat. Gave it a good shot. Useless at it. Can't play music. Hopeless at it. Got a degree in composition – can't use it for anything. Wasted my Dad's beads. Got a degree in history – can't use it for anything. Wasted time and beadage. Experimented with underwater sound, even got a grant for research – got exactly nowhere with it. Another waste of time and money. Pair of useless twits, aren't we?" He continued down the path at a lope.

"No, man, listen. You knew exactly what to say to those kids. Dad and Hine and me've been agonising over this bit with Mere about what to call Dad. She won't call him anything, you know. "Mummy wants you to come to the table," not "Dad, tea's ready." Months we've talked, worried, read books. You sit on the floor putting your shoes on and come up with something in a moment. Anyway, you didn't get any old degree, you got a doctorate in history. Not everyone thinks that's a failure. Don't sell yourself short, big boy."

"You neither, short stuff. One thing we've got to do, on the way to get Dad."

"Buy the new pad for Mere?"

"Yeah, that, too. We have to pay a visit to Sea, Soy and Soda."

"Why?"

"There's people in there who helped me out when I got here. I promised to introduce you."

"Me? Why me?"

"She's a fan."

"She? She? What kind of she?"

"Oh, about fifteen or sixteen years old. Blonde. Probably cute, but I was too shocky at the time to notice. Shows you how bad off I was. Got a squeal that could etch glass."

"Rangi in the heavens, she's probably got legs up to her armpits, heels a metre high, skirts as wide as a belt, and low-cut tops that show nearly every part of her breast that she jiggles right in your face. I hate that kind. They show up at every concert. They give me the willies."

Kiri almost lost his stride with laughter. "But Nat, my boy, don't tell me you go without!"

"I do all right for myself, thank you very much, but not with the breast jigglers. Can't stand them."

"Well, she loves you, and I promised."

"You'll pay for this, boy."

"All kidding aside, Nat, it was all I could do to get her to promise not to try to find Dad. Honest, if I'd known you had fans like that, I'd never have said my name."

"Find Dad? I don't live with Dad! I live on bloody Motiti Island where that type can't find me!"

"I know, I told her you didn't live here, but she thought Dad could tell her where you live. I had to keep her away for Hine's sake, eh?"

"Yeah. Bloody hell. Let's get it over with. And while we're on the subject of love, who's the girl?"

"What girl?"

"You can't fool me, mate, don't even try. I interpret music, remember? You wrote it last night. You're in love with someone. Out with it!"

"I . . . er . . ." Kiri was taken aback. All he could think of was Calline, but he hadn't thought that he might be in love with her. His face was hot, and his brother was grinning at him. "I didn't think about being in love with her. Her name is Calline Digan. She's a medical doctor. She's very special, but love? I don't know."

"Think about it. She's got you hook, line and sinker, son, even if you don't know it. All your defences were down last night. It showed."

"Thanks for – you know – last night."

"I'll still never forgive you. I'm too tired for this."

"I've been up all night, too, but the weird thing is I don't feel like it. I don't feel like I've had a good rest, exactly, just not as if I've been up since yesterday morning."

"Oh, you're still running on adrenaline."

In falsetto Kiri asked, "What's a drenna lin, Mummy?"

Nat snorted and led the way to the milk bar at a fast jog, saying as they pulled up at the door, before they came into earshot of the people sitting at the tables outside, "If you're wise, you'll never sleep deeply in your bed. One of these days, when you least expect it, I will pay you back for this."

Grinning, Kiri strode into the milk bar. There were people seated at the counter, and several seated at tables and booths. He strode up to the counter and asked a man frying chips, "Excuse me, do you have someone here by the name of Sandy?"

"On a break, mate. Watcher want?"

"Er . . . is she a fan of Anatoe Amaru?"

"Watzit to ya?"

"I'm his brother, and I promised her I'd bring him to meet her."

There was a sudden silence in the place. Kiri looked around. Every eye was on him. The waitresses were frozen on the spot. The man frying chips was looking at him out of the corner of his eye. "You never. You're not his brother. You don't even look like him."

Kiri beckoned to Nat, who slouched in through the door and dragged his feet all the way to Kiri's side, his hands deep in his pockets, his shoulders hunched forward, his hat pulled down low over his eyes.

"That's him?"

"Nah, yeah: ugly, ain't he?"

Nat raised his head to glare at Kiri, the waitress who caught sight of his face gasped, "It's him!" the chip fryer lifted the basket of chips up out of the fat and set it to drain, then came around the counter with a wide, amused grin.

"Great Tane in the forest, this is a kick." He wiped his hand on his apron and held it out to Nat. "Pleased ta meetcha. You wouldn't believe it. She's got whole flaming shrine to you back there. You look smaller in person. Hate to think what it's like at her house – she's only here three days a week and she's got a honking great shrine to you back there." He bawled over his shoulder, "Sandy!!" And grinned at Nat, "She's not going to believe this."

There was a sullen bellow from the back, "My break's not over yet, Charlie!"

Charlie grinned even wider. "This is beautiful. I'm taking bets right now, boys and girls. Is she going to faint, or is she going to wet herself?"

Nat couldn't take it anymore. "Oh, man, I've got to go. Let's just leave this, Kiri."

"I promised."

"You're going to pay for this, I'm telling you."

Charlie roared again. "Sandy! Someone here to see you!" Then asked Kiri, "How'd she rate?"

"I was in that Fish that got buried. I was in bad shape when I got here. She took care of me."

"Sandy did? Our Sandy? After she knew you were his brother, right?"

"Before."

"Sandy!!"

"Coming!"

"I never knew she had it in her. There might be hope for her yet."

Behind him Sandy strolled out, sullenly, pouting. Kiri stepped up to the counter as she came around it, and said, "Hi, Sandy, remember me?"

She looked up, saw Kiri, her eyes widened in recognition, then she saw Nat and started hyperventilating, all without saying a word. When Nat stepped forward, with his hand out, intending to give her a kiss on the cheek, and starting to say, "I wanted to thank you for . . ." she made a strangled sound and fled back into the back room.

The entire milk bar burst out laughing, people started exchanging money or arguing about whether what she'd done was what they'd bet on. Kiri and Nat stood, arms limp, staring at each other, non-plussed. "Oh, the poor kid," Kiri said quietly. "Bill told me she was harmless. She would never have gone looking for you. It was all kid talk."

"Got some paper, Charlie?" Nat asked. Charlie gave him a serviette. Nat picked up one of the waitress's pencils that was on the counter and wrote on the serviette, "To Sandy. Thank you for taking care of my brother. This is a backstage pass for one. Lots of love, Nat Amaru." He drew a heart on it and gave it to the waitress standing nearest. "Please make sure she gets this."

They left the milk bar and jogged off down to the wharf. Nat impersonated Charlie, sarcastically, "You look smaller in person."

Kiri said, "I feel really stupid, now."

"Tell you what, bright boy. Don't count on a career as my manager."

Glendrona Tomptell

Being in the shelter had phases for Glenda. At first, she was too tired and numb to care, as long as she was warm and fed and dry, so that day and the next it didn't matter. Then it became like a nightmare. Some children were claimed by their parents and left with them, bringing the expectation that it was all over, and she would go home any minute. But her parents didn't come that day, or the next. Glenda began to worry that they didn't know where she was and couldn't find her. When she was assured that couldn't be true, she worried that they couldn't come because something had happened to them. They were older than other people's parents. She'd heard someone, somewhere, say this was hardest on the very young and the very old. What if they were ill and couldn't come and get her, ever? Would she live on the floor of this Marae all of her life?

She didn't know how many days passed before her father's voice could be heard one morning. It seemed to be forever that she'd been sleeping on the floor of the Marae on an uncomfortable pallet with none of her stuff and wearing ugly things that didn't fit that came from relief boxes. At first there had been dozens of children there, then the ones who lived nearby were claimed by their families, then the ones from further away, until there was only their group and one other from the north coast of the peninsula left. Finally, parents started to arrive for those children. One by one the children left, until, when Kim went home with her Mum, only Moana, Alan, and Morehu were there with Glenda, who didn't have anyone her own age to play with. Ms. Sergill and Ngaire were talking about returning to their hex with the four children once they had made sure that they had a place to take them to, when Glenda's Dad arrived.

They were all to go back together. At last Glenda was on the Flying Fish on the way home. She curled up close to her Dad, so glad to see his dear old lined face again that she didn't even care who saw her. During the trip he told her how he and her mother, and her mother's mother, Granny from upstairs, had evacuated before the water had arrived, so they were all quite safe. Their home hex was further away from the shore than Ms. Sergill's hex where Glenda went to have her music lessons, so their hex was undamaged, but the hexes closer to the shore had been hit by high water, so Ms. Sergill, Ngaire, Moana, Alan, and Morehu were going to stay with them until they could return to their own homes.

Glenda found that idea completely horrifying. There'd never been another child in her home. She felt protective and anxious of her things. What would Mummy think? It had been Mummy's idea. Well, then, what would Granny think? Granny had been so stressed by the evacuation that she wasn't going to be home for a while, she was going to be in a place that took care of elderly people with special needs. She would be home when she'd had a good rest. Where would everybody sleep? They didn't have places for all of these people. Glenda would share her room with Moana, and she could pretend she had a sister, but it would only be for a day or so, then Moana was going to stay with her aunt until her home was rebuilt. The guest room would be made into a bedroom for Alan and Morehu. They would stay for longer. Alan's father was there, working on repairs, but his mother had been injured, so they were going to take care of him until his family claimed him. It would be a while before he had a home to go to. Ms. Sergill and Ngaire would share Granny's flat. Granny knew about it; she was glad to help out in the emergency.

Glenda stared at Morehu, sucking his thumb, clutching at Ngaire, in absolute horror. She couldn't imagine hearing his high-pitched whine, "Nyree!" every day.

Her Dad whispered in her ear, "Don't be selfish, sweetie. If we'd lost our home, we'd want people to help us. It's not for long, only until they can get themselves set back to rights. Just think how you would feel if you didn't have your nice snug home, and your Mum and Dad."

Glenda tried to picture it. They'd been the last children in the shelter. If her Dad had picked her up, and not the others, they would still be there, by themselves. Ngaire and Ms. Sergill couldn't have taken the others home with them the way they'd said they wanted to, because they had no place to take them to. What would have happened then? Glenda couldn't imagine.

CHAPTER THIRTY-FOUR

Voyage

On board the ship that was taking them back to the island, Joe Mack and Willie Jay were hot bunking with the troops. This made it nearly impossible for them to speak to each other without being overheard.

Ambassador Flint met with one or the other of them two or three times a day, which gave them little chance to say more than the odd word in passing.

Grabbing the first opportunity he saw to talk to Willie Jay, Joe Mack reminded him, "We got to remember what we're here to do." He didn't dare use Sam's name just in case someone was listening in despite all his precautions.

Willie Jay protested, "Shoot, I can't do that! I know we're supposed to find out if anyone got sick when they got back to the islands with Gomer Jordan. Thing is, if I try to remember all that stuff and the Ambassador wants to know something at the same time, I get all mixed up and he gets real mad."

Remembering that Sam had made a point of telling him to watch out for Willie Jay, Joe Mack gritted his teeth and tried to think what Sam would do. This business of biting his tongue was not his style. He'd as soon knock the dumb ass up-side his head and tell him to get a clue. It was for Sam, though. He had to give it a shot for Sam's sake. "What are they going for?"

"They want to know about the islanders."

"Well, duh! That's what it's all about. They ask me about cities. Are they asking us the same thing?"

"The Ambassador got real mad that I never seen no capital city."

"I bet he did! We never believed it when we first heard it, did we? I was only there the one time, and we never saw a city. You mean you never saw even one when you came back?"

"No."

"Gomer took you guys to a different place, huh?"

"Kind of. We were looking for a town, you know, bigger than what we saw the first time. We went into that giant bay Temperance took us past, remember?"

"Oh, Geez! It's years since we were there with Temperance! I can't remember one bay that we sailed past. It's tough enough to remember the island we stayed on, and I thought I never would forget that."

"You don't remember Sunday Island? I'll never forget it. It's like paradise on earth."

"No, you eejit, I never forgot the island! I just can't remember every bay it had."

"I can."

"Why don't that surprise me?"

"Well, we're sure to stop over there on the way, so then you can remember it as good as me."

Joe Mack could feel a headache coming on from not being able to beat some sense into Willie Jay's thick head. "Forget the damned island! We got hardly any time before they split us up for you to bring me up to speed on what Tuffy Flint wants to know from you so we can figure out what's his angle and can make sure we don't cross each other up."

"W – w – well . . ."

Oh, God! Now the eejit was stuttering again! He was worse than useless for their cause; he was the weak link in the whole set up. There was no way out of it. They were on the ship, days away from land, with no chance of escape. Would it be better to give it up as a bad deal, or try again later, or just keep on? He couldn't just walk away . . . if he and Willie Jay didn't get it straight there was too much chance of them saying things that would make the Faithful camp suspicious.

One thing Joe Mack was sure of was that Tuffy Flint wasn't in charge the way he looked like he was. Maybe he thought he was running the show, but Joe Mack's gut told him that Tuffy's security were watching him as much as guarding him. To Joe Mack, that smelled of invisible hands controlling everything. That thought snapped him out of his frustration with Willie Jay. They were dealing with bigger guns than the stupid Ambassador. Tuffy was only dangerous to them while they were on the ship, but Caleb had unknown power. There was no way to tell who he knew or how far he could reach.

Joe Mack's mind flashed a quick memory of Colonel Lycus with a feeling of dread. He paused to think about it for a split second. He and Chuck had served under Jaakobah Lycus pushing the Panhandle through to the sea. They had seen a first-rate Commander who kept more of his men alive than any other officer they had, while getting a job done that the GR had been trying to do for a hundred years. Instead of making Old Jack a national hero and naming the Panhandle after him, the military demoted him and shipped him off to the Southern Front, an engagement so dangerous that they all knew it was a suicide mission. The rumours about Old Jack included one that he had once been Caleb Faithful's son-in-law. If Caleb could do that to someone like Colonel Lycus, a puffed-up toad like Tuffy Flint stood no chance against him. Neither did he and Willie Jay, if they weren't very careful and smart. He had to get Willie Jay back on track right then. "Okay, so you went into the big bay. Then what?"

"Then – then . . . w - well, they . . . she took us . . . she got them to take us on that dinky little train back to that same place where we started when we came with the explorers."

"That's gotta be their capital, then."

"No, I don't think so. They've had an election since we found them, and the old lady that was their President ain't no more."

"What? Say what?" All at once it hit Joe Mack that something he didn't understand was going on. He remembered Willie Jay and Chuck saying something about it after they got back from the trip with Gomer Jordan, but it hadn't made any sense to him then. Carefully, so that he wouldn't set off Willie Jay's stutter again, he asked, "What old lady was their President?"

"Olarine Eidola. The First Servant. The lady with the long white braid that sat at one end of the table with us when we first found the islands."

Joe Mack had a horrible feeling that he'd missed something important. Cautiously, he checked. "She was the President's servant?"

It was what he'd been afraid of. "Ms Eidola ain't nobody's servant. She was the President when we first got there, and a congressman or something when me and Chuck got back."

"They elect women?"

"Yeah."

"What guy votes for a girl to run the country? What man wants a female boss?"

"I don't get it either, but it seems to work for them."

"It don't bug you at all that these guys got everything wrong?"

"I guess right and wrong ain't up to me. I never get none of that stuff right, anyhow."

Joe Mack felt bad about the number of times he'd told Willie Jay that he never got anything right. He changed the subject. "What's with that 'servant' crap?"

"Their government is called servants, so they don't forget they're elected to serve their nation and the people who voted for them. They told me that the people got to remember that, so they won't let the government get out of hand. They said once a government starts to serve itself, it's almost impossible for the people to take the power back again."

"Shit!" It was maddening that the ignorant savages had worked out something that would have saved the GR from falling into the hands of a snake in the grass like Caleb Faithful, when the best people on earth hadn't figured it out. He didn't want to talk about that either, so he changed the subject again. "How come you can get that shit?"

"They told me."

"Yeah, but no one else can make head nor tail of the island gabble. It's worse than the Weskie's. They sound like a bunch of chickens squawking over a worm."

"It ain't all that hard, Joe Mack. They mostly say the same words we do, they just say them different than us is all."

"That ain't right! Some of their words ain't like nothing I ever heard before."

Willie Jay conceded that point. "They got two languages just like us, only it ain't English and Spanish like us, it's English and Maori."

"That's such a load of crap. We don't got two languages, just GR."

"Well . . . yeah, but GR is . . ."

"Forget it. How come you can get this when no one else can?"

"I dunno. Anyone can get it. All you got to do is listen to them."

"If I didn't know any better, I'd say you done gone and found something you're right good at."

"Oh, no, I . . ."

"Ain't a one of us can make sense of that island jabber by just listening, so if God done give you a gift, you got to do good with it." It was annoying that Willie Jay got all bug-eyed, with his mouth moving and no sound coming out. It might have been a bit strong to bring God into it, but Joe Mack couldn't think of a better way to get Willie Jay's attention. "Now, just you mind me, Boy. You got to learn me that island jabber. You got to tell me everything you heard about them weirdos being as how you can talk to them and all."

"They ain't really weird . . ."

"They sure as hell are!"

"But they're real nice folk, Joe Mack. They're kind and polite and all that stuff our Daddies wupped our butts to make us do. Only with the islanders it's everyone everywhere all the time."

"That ain't going to do them no good at all in the real world."

Willie Jay's face fell. "No. I get that. If they lived where I grew up, they'd be beat up all the time like me."

Joe Mack got an inkling of why Willie Jay connected with the Islanders so well. He changed the subject. "So, you figure it's true they don't build proper blocks?"

Willie Jay relaxed. "Yeah. It ain't like square blocks, it's like circles. They call them hexes."

"That means to put a curse on someone. Black magic."

"No, not with them. When they say it, it's short for hexagon."

"What's that?"

"They said it's a six-sided shape like a square is a four sided shape."

"So what?"

"I don't know. You asked."

"So, they build in circles instead of squares and they call them hexes instead of blocks. Must screw with their traffic worse than a polecat at a church picnic."

"Well, you know they don't got roads like we do."

"Ain't no way they can build houses and boats and all the other stuff we saw without no roads to haul stuff."

"I don't know how they do it. You saw what it's like when we were all there with Sam."

"I don't remember their roads."

"You got to remember the only way to get around was walking or that shiny little train thing with no driver."

"Oh, yeah, right. It's all so weird I forgot a lot of it. I was only with the people for a little bit. I remember the deserted island better."

"You got to remember that train running on top of logs that looked like they were stacked by little kids!"

"Yeah, I guess I do. What did they call it? Stupid name. Had nothing to do with trains."

"Flying Fish."

"But they don't say it right, huh?"

"They say everything wrong, like they can't talk right or something. They say 'Fly' like 'flay' and they say the 'ing' part all weird. Not 'in' like everyone else, but sort of, 'eeng,' and the 'fish' part is more like 'feesh.' When you get used to it, it all makes sense on account they do it with everything."

Joe Mack felt a surge of confidence. "That's how you understand them? Just get used to the way they mess up the words? I can do that!"

"Oh, yeah, if I can do it, anyone can. It's easy to tell what words are the same as ours only they say them wrong and what's their own babble like the Weskies got. All you got to learn is what the babble means."

Joe Mack's brief spark of confidence wavered. "How the Sam Hill am I supposed to do that?"

Willie Jay's guileless face had that shining-with-innocent-hope look that always made Joe Mack itch to shake some sense into him. "You'll pick it up easy. Soon as you know the way they say everything wrong you can hear what words ain't like nothing you ever heard before. It ain't confusing like the way they say something, and you know what they said and you know what it means when we say it, but that ain't what they mean when they say it."

"What, what, what?!"

"Like when they say, 'King,' they don't mean an undemocratic ruler like we do; they mean a guy that ain't got no power."

"What's the use if he don't got no power?"

"The People love him."

"How can they 'love' a pantywaist that ain't even got the moxie to get himself some power when he's the head of the government?"

"Their King ain't the head of their government: the First Servant is."

"Now see, that's all wrong, too. 'Servant' don't mean ruler."

"That's what I meant. They got a whole lot like that. You know what they said so you're figuring you know what they're talking about, and just like that . . ." he snapped his fingers . . . "you see that you're talking about two different things and you got no clue what they're babbling on about and no clue if you just said what you thought you said or if the words meant something you never thought about."

Joe Mack's heart sank. It was as bad as he was afraid it was, if not worse. "I'd love to see you tell that load of crap to Tuffy Flint."

Willie Jay face fell. "He gets so mad. He says I'm a stupid, useless tit that don't know my ass from a hole in the ground."

That sounded like bad news for both of them. "You got to teach me all that stuff so's I can explain it to him." Hearing himself say that gave Joe Mack a spark of an idea. "I know how we can do this. They need you to translate for the Islanders, and they need me to translate for you."

Willie Jay started to protest, with an offended look, but Joe Mack cut him off. "Go with it. That way they need both of us. If you can get them to listen to you without getting mad at you, what do you need me for? You'll be on your own."

"Oh, yeah."

"We better split up before they can accuse us of plotting together." Now that he'd come up with a strategy, Joe Mack felt a tiny flicker of hope that he would be able to get some control of their situation.

As he and Willie Jay headed off in different directions, his head was full of plans to get Tuffy Flint to see him and Willie Jay as a unit. If they were always debriefed together, then he wouldn't have to worry so much about him and Willie Jay crossing each other up. All his experiences in manipulating superior officers during his ten years in the army came to his aid as he tried to come up with a sure-fire angle. He had to be careful. The last thing he needed was for those security guys to get what he was up to and let Tuffy know. He was pretty sure he could handle one guy, but a bunch of suspicious guys standing around watching was a big-time headache.

The next time he was ordered to present himself for debriefing, he decided to start with a distraction that he hoped would look like he had no faith in Willie Jay.

Yet again, Tuffy was demanding to know where the island capital was.

Joe Mack tried to find a new way to explain the concept since saying they had no capital was getting them nowhere. "Their Capital is where the First Servant lives."

"Now we're getting somewhere!" Tuffy leaned forward. "And where is that?"

"We won't know that until we get there and find out who's gotten elected."

"What the hell does that mean?"

"Their President don't move to their Capital. Their Capital is where the First Servant lives."

"That's crap! Ain't no way to move a whole city every time they have an election. Don't try to kid a kidder, Boy!"

The security glared at Joe Mack, moving slightly closer to him.

He didn't give any sign that he'd noticed them, keeping his eyes fixed on Tuffy's. "It's like they got a whole nother way to look at things."

"You trying to be a smart-ass?"

The security looked even more menacing and gave the impression of being closer without seeming to have moved.

"No, Sir. I'm answering your question about the Island Capital. They do everything so weird that even when you know what it is, it still don't make no sense."

"What the hell does that mean? You just said you know where their capital city is. Now where is it?"

Joe Mack was strongly aware of the threat hidden in Tuffy's words. Carefully, he explained, "I know how to figure out where it is under their new administration. The way we do that is find out who got elected First Servant since the last time we were there, and then find out where that guy lives. That's their Capital for that guy's term." He deliberately left out that the Public Servants might not be men. One hard to swallow fact at a time.

The silence that followed told Joe Mack he'd got through to them.

It was one of the security who spoke first. "There ain't no way that could work."

Tuffy's voice was almost a wail when he protested, "How in Sam Hill can I jam that in a report? Ain't no way we can hunt down a new Capital every time we make this trip!"

Two facts jumped out at Joe Mack: one, the security were definitely not just body-guards; and two, not only was Tuffy Flint not the master-mind behind this expedition, he was scared of whoever was. Remembering the rumours about Gomer Jordan, Joe Mack had a pretty good idea who Tuffy was scared of and why. It wasn't chicken to be scared of Caleb Faithful, it was just good sense. In the interests of his own safety, Joe Mack thought it was best to lower the level of panic. "It's what we got to do if we come out here again. When we first found those guys, their leader was an old lady who lived on the north corner of the east coast. So, they took us there. The second time some guy was elected, so their government was moved to where he lived, only we never knew, so Mr Jordan went to the same place that they took us the first time. We don't have to find out where their government is to meet with them. Mr Jordan met with them, and he never knew where their Capital was because they came to him."

"Yeah."

Joe Mack caught traces of expressions that flashed across Tuffy's face, plus the glances that flickered from eye to eye. He got the feeling that he'd just given them an edge of some sort. He had no idea what it was or how he did it, but he was going to take advantage of it.

"You on Gomer Jordan's reconnaissance mission?"

Joe Mack thought he'd be better off showing security full deference even if it riled Ambassador Tuffy Flint. "No, Sir. I only came once before, on the exploration."

One of the security leaned forward threateningly. "Then just how do you know this shit, huh?"

"Willie Jay Rimmon's been there more than anyone else." He wasn't the least bit surprised that they immediately heaped scorn on Willie Jay and everything about him, but he continued. "Yeah, I know he ain't the fastest bullet in the clip, but he's the only one who's been there two times. He knows more about those cats than anyone else."

"Don't give me that crap." Tuffy sounded pleasant despite the words, which creeped Joe Mack out more than an open threat would have. "What about all the grunts that were assigned to every mission, huh? Did you think we didn't know about them?"

"No, Sir. The thing of it is, Mr Ambassador, they've been on the ships, but ain't a one of them would've set foot on that land unarmed, even if Major Temperance would okay it, which he never did."

They all stared at him like he'd sprouted wings. "What?!" One of the security demanded.

"They didn't brief you on that? The Islanders won't allow any weapons on their soil."

Security spluttered with indignation: "They better learn real quick who does the allowing around here!" and; "No little panty-waist nation tells the GR what to do and lives!" and; "Somebody's got to teach them savages some manners!" and; "I ain't being unarmed without a fight! No one will."

Then Joe Mack got to see how it was that Tuffy Flint had managed to earn a living as an Ambassador. He didn't pay as much attention to Tuffy's words as he did to the body-language, tones of voice, and the masterful way Tuffy used eye contact. There was no doubt it was a brilliant performance, but the main impression Joe Mack got was slickness. "This guy's oily," he thought. Watching Tuffy do his thing, Joe Mack realised that the man didn't have an ounce of sincerity anywhere in his make-up.

"We just tell them what they want to know. There's plenty of time to smarten them up if they got anything worth having."

He was not intending to deal in good faith with the Islanders. That meant Joe Mack's challenge was different from the one Sam had given him. The tasks he could see ahead of him was figuring out what Tuffy was up to, and finding a way to get the word back to Sam. He wasn't looking out for Willie Jay because Sam asked him to now. Now he was doing it because he had to have someone around who he could trust. No matter what people said about him, Willie Jay Rimmon was the most honest guy Joe Mack had ever known.

Joe Mack figured he'd better jump in there before things went too far. "If you're saying we should carry concealed weapons, Mr Ambassador, it's a great idea, and it should work once a couple of things are out of the way."

They all glared at him murderously.

"What things?"

If Joe Mack didn't know better, he'd have thought Tuffy Flint sounded dangerous. A little niggle in the back of his brain steadied him: the voice of the only commander he'd ever actually admired, Jaakobah Lycus, saying, "Never under-estimate your enemy." Very slowly he panned the room with that in mind. "I'd have been going ashore – and trying to explain how the hidden weapon had been found." He was watching Tuffy's eyes.

While the Security roared, Joe Mack and Tuffy didn't really imprint with it. They were conscious of each other's eyes, not paying over much attention to the men yelling. Finally, Joe Mack gave in, just before they'd caught on. He was not about to get them all interested. "They're bound to get all worked up if they find a hidden one. You'll be best to avoid the markets. Willie Jay can't keep clean when he's supposed to, so we'll be better to keep him out of the supermarkets."

The first response was noisy, but the Ambassador waved impatiently. It was quiet a few moments that satisfied Joe Mack. It answered more of the questions that Joe Mack had about the security.

"We'll do well to leave him on the ship."

Yes, that's what he would have expected. "The problem is that the islanders are expected to be conversing with us."

"That would have you ready, then, wouldn't it?" Tuffy said, equally.

"Yes," Joe Mack, smiling. "The problem is that Willie Jay is the only one who can hold a conversation with the islanders. With enough time to work it out, I will have sorted it out."

"What do you mean?" Tuffy's people preparedness was holding up, but his threatening cloud was showing.

"I need to work with Willie Jay to concentrate on the ways the Island language differs from the GR language."

The GR checked with one another. Tuffy looked at Joe Mack.

Before the GR could reorganise their protests, Joe Mack said firmly, "There weren't enough time place to study the language. We weren't interested in coming back towards the Islands." He noticed the security was crowding around him, but Tuffy didn't move. Joe Mack concentrated on the area he knew, having a good warning not to give them room to manoeuvre. "The Islanders have a weird way about them when they talk: they have changed the sound of the words. You can't make sense of the words. The languages can't be learned by the GR."

"Why can't I get the same chance as you?"

"You could, but think about the reactions to each action: you go ashore with hidden weapons; you try to talk to them when you don't know enough to get what they mean; anything else?"

Tuffy waved impatiently. He wanted it to be left to Joe Mack and himself. "Yeah. What's the answer to it?"

Joe Mack was concentrating as hard as he could on this. "I hope the answer will be completely put off by the Islands." He saw them start to move and rushed on. "There are no changes that can't be worked out by us, but we first must know what they are. Now, Willie Jay told me that the sounds that are changed all have certain tones, which would give us a time to learn. This would work well with us, so long as we remember that other values shift, too."

"What!" Tuffy looked as caught off-guard as Joe Mack had figured.

"It's all the vowels that have shifted: i became e; e became ee; and so on. We can deal with that. What we can't always deal with is shifts in sounds that don't mean what we thought they meant."

Tuffy looked as thoughtful as could be. He's staring around him, not taking much notice of the noise occurring around him. One security finally pushed Joe Mack. Tuffy focused on them. "If you don't see the need to learn all the reality to portray, then perhaps you could get to leave us?" His voice sounded friendly, and his looks seemed genuine, but Joe Mack could swear that an individual barrier was being passed. The security backed down.

Joe Mack felt good to hear Tuffy's voice give an unsettling feeling. It would be cute to see how Tuffy would have played that out to his boss. He was sure that Tuffy had to answer to Caleb Faithful and the security played an important part in it. He rather enjoyed watching the security taking a lower stand, for all he made it look as though he didn't seem to be on to it.

"What's the low-down on what Willie Jay wants?"

"Well, Willie Jay didn't describe the information the way he wanted it. I thought it would help you to learn from him as well as from me. If I were planning to make the move, I'd ask Willie Jay with you in the room, and then we'd both have a chance."

Tuffy grimaced. "I'd actually be happier without Willie Jay."

Joe Mack smiled. "The unfortunate thing is that Willie Jay is the only one who can figure it out by himself." He looked suitably sorry for Tuffy. "None of the rest of us would have been able to sort it out like he did. We'll just have to make as much use of the native talent as God has provided." Tuffy looked as doubtful as Joe Mack was concerned he would. He hurried to provide, "Once we've got the way to make their life real to us, with all of the strangeness understood, then we can put our minds to solving the language."

"And that's it?"

Joe Mack knew not to relax. He said, "Oh, that's a good start. We'll learn together. Willie Jay and I can figure out some answers."

"Hmm . . ." Tuffy hesitated. "What would you like to spend with Willie Jay?"

Joe Mack handled it very carefully, scared that they would run his excuse out. He knew enough not to fall for the obvious trap of money or time. "Well, I would like to study with Willie Jay every day, and I'd like you to be around sometimes so that you can be there whenever we discover something." The little bit of distress in Tuffy's eyes was alerting for him. "It's a long way for Willie Jay to realise the information is useful. It's been a long time since he was told the island information was valuable to anyone. I'm thinking that if I could get some bits and pieces, then he'll begin to come up with some things that might be down-right interesting to you."

Ambassador Tuffy Flint pressed the left hand over his chin in a thoughtful way. "You mean that we could get it all from him?"

"Not that I didn't want to, but no, Sir, I don't think one man can study a whole nation in only two visits."

"Hmm . . ." Tuffy considered things carefully. After a pause, he focused on Joe Mack. "I take it that we won't do well without knowing the Island ways, so I'm going to try this set up. We'll pay no attention to the times you're together, provided you're working on the things that we need to understand."

"Yes, Sir." He decided that the best thing to do was not to question the other items. He hurried off as soon as he was allowed to go. As fast as he could he found Willie Jay and told him the news.

CHAPTER THIRTY-FIVE

Getting Going Again

Kiri and Fedrack

Kiri and Fedrack were cleaning up after one of their bouts of trying to produce sounds that whales can hear. Kiri was quite despondent, saying, "This will never work."

Fresh out of a mod vil session, where the counsellors were trying to teach Fedrack that he had to pay attention to what people were saying to him, he answered, "Don't let it get you down, Kiri. We had success with the noise that releases sphincter muscles. This one is harder."

Kiri shrugged. "We can't sell that one. This one will sell big time, but it's no good."

Scrambling around in his head to find what he should say, Fedrack suggested, "Why don't we take a break from it and do something we enjoy?"

Kiri stopped and stared at Fedrack. "Like what?"

Fedrack also stopped and stared at Kiri. "I ... I ... you have to not tell anybody."

Intrigued, Kiri quickly turned back to cleaning and putting all of their notes away.

Fedrack finished cleaning up, too, watching Kiri warily.

They locked the lab, and went out into the world, with Kiri saying, "Let's pick up some kai and go off and eat it, then you can tell me."

They did that, with Fedrack leading the way to the bush. They sat down, and opened their snacks, and Kiri said, "Okay, then. I promise. What is this?"

Fedrack took a bite, hands shaking. "It's something I like to do by myself. You know the Troggies made tunnels?"

"Nah, yeah." Kiri was cautious.

"They made a tunnel around here that's been boarded up, but I've found a way into it."

Kiri stared. "I never expected anything like that!" he said.

"You don't have to come."

"No, no, I want to! That's marvellous!"

"It's illegal."

"Well, yeah – but right now it'll be a great distraction!"

"I thought so," said Fedrack with great satisfaction for having finally chosen to do something that worked. "You'll need some glow sticks, and good shoes, and something to eat, and we'll have to pick a time when no one will be surprised that we're going off together."

They went off, each to his own life. Kiri thought for a long time about what he should do, and finally decided to tell Nat. He swore him to secrecy, and said he'd let him know when they were going to do it, so if he didn't hear from Kiri in a certain amount of time, he'd know where to look.

He was full of enthusiasm at his school, both in his own classes and when he was teaching others, and in the lab with Fedrack.

Finally, the two of them set off, Fedrack saying that they ought to meet in the forest. Kiri did that, wondering the whole time whether or not Fedrack had pulled his leg. But no, he was there in the woods, waiting when Kiri got there. They headed off and found the filled-in end of the tunnel. Fedrack lifted down some big rocks, and Kiri put them aside, until the hole was large enough for them both to squeeze in.

"Cor!" exclaimed Kiri, looking around at the edges of the tunnel. There were ferns growing around the entrance, but it seemed to be made of bricks. He looked all around. It was high enough for him to stand upright. "Oh, wow, I never expected anything like this!"

"What did you think, then?" Fedrack asked, puzzled.

"I don't know. I thought it would be like a tunnel people dug to hide in, but this is perfect. I can see people living in this."

Fedrack cracked his glow stick and started walking. They came to a door, which Kiri stopped to look at. "What's this?"

"I dunno. They seem to all have doors just inside. Some are old wood, some are ceramic, some on hinges like this one, some are sliding."

"Oh, they've got to shut it off from the weather, then." Kiri was quite decided on this.

"It's not on the outside," Fedrack objected.

"Yeah, nah, it's put enough inside that anyone coming in was sheltered here while they opened the inside door."

"Oh, cool."

Further inside the tunnel they found rooms, which they figured were where the people had lived. They explored thoroughly, getting more of an understanding about their ancestors.

When they left, Kiri thanked Fedrack most sincerely. "That's the greatest thing you could have shown me," he said with deep feeling.

They put the rocks back, making it look as if no one had been there, and each made their own way home.

Kiri was flummoxed. Who'd have thought Fedrack would keep such a terrific secret? But when he thought about it a little more, it stood to reason that Fedrack would think of it, given that he was outside of the general rules.

In fact, Kiri was fascinated by it, and studied the tunnels as part of history, and he looked for them no matter where he was. When he could manage it, he went into them himself, but he kept it secret.

Pete and Ron

One of the things First Servant Pitamete and King Ngaronoa did was take the time to go fishing together. They took the canoe out as soon as they could.

"What's bugging you, Old Son?" Ron asked as soon as they were away from the shore, pitching his voice low.

"I really need your advice, regardless."

Ron pursed his lips and rowed harder "What is it that you're prepared to risk the government?"

"We've been going fishing since we were little kids, Ron. We just want to talk to each other."

"And."

"And what about this business of sending people over there?"

"If they want to go, we can't stop them. It's only for six months, and they can tell us things we're only guessing at now."

"Who are you and what have you done with my friend, Ron?"

"Yeah, nah, Pita, I'm serious."

"I suppose you had to grow up some time. Better late than never, so they say, but I think you're taking it a bit far. Look, going off fishing isn't a crime, just so long as you don't tell me how to do my job or try to influence me, okay?"

"What?" Ron was completely lost.

"What we are doing has to be completely off the record."

"If you're that uneasy about it, we can talk about something else," Ngaronoa said, quietly.

"Yeah, nah. I'm nervous is all. I really need your input," Pitamete, sighed.

"That's the sum-total of it. You pick the ones who go and talk to them when they get back. Now we talk about the fish, or the kids." Ngaronoa was solid.

Pita sighed again. He knew the subject was closed.

They talked about the fish, sports, the kids, and their wives.

Seamore

The visit became yesterday's news, fading off into the mists of memory, becoming unreal. Hardly anyone thought about it or talked about it anymore. The general feeling was that if they were going to hear from them again, they would have by now.

It seemed to Ahnya, looking back on those years as her children grew out of babyhood into busy children, that the sun had always been shining. Life was golden, revolving gently through the daily routines of childcare, playing in the commons, gossiping with the other mothers in the hex, working on her career, attending the meetings of her hundred and then talking them over with Donstan. Together she and Donstan had cookouts and hex parties with the other families in their hex, spent languorous hours on the beaches with their children, and frequently spent weekends with his parents.

She loved the sight of the three generations of boys, her beloved father-in-law, her darling partner, and her precious sons when they sat in a row on the sofa in the evenings to watch the cartoons on the wall unit. The similarities in the faces and hair lines delighted her, and the row of the same grey-blue eyes that had passed from generation to generation warmed her heart. Harry, Donstan, and Wynson all had fair hair, but Ahnstan for some inexplicable reason had black hair. Ahnya didn't understand that, since, from her grasp of genetics he should have had either fair hair like his father or brown hair like hers. He should not have had hair darker than hers. But then, Donya had Rita's dark brown eyes, and that shouldn't have happened, either, according to everything Ahnya had read about genetics. Donya should have had either blue eyes like her father and brothers, or green eyes like her mother. She shouldn't have managed eyes darker than either of them, any more than Ahnstan should have had black hair like Ahnya's mother.

It pleased her, though. Not only did she enjoy puzzles, but it made Wynson look more like Donstan's natural son than Ahnstan. If anyone were to guess which of their children was adopted, they usually guessed either Donya because of her dark eyes, or Ahnstan because of his dark hair. That gave her an obscure pleasure.

But now that Harry had passed away, and Donstan and Ahnya weren't getting along anymore, nothing seemed to make sense anymore. Ahnya went through the daily routine, but it didn't mean the same thing. Donstan was seeing a young woman named Violet, Ahnya knew that, and she didn't know what to do about it. She tried to talk to him about it, but it all blew up and he moved out, leaving her with her mother-in-law. Rita was kind to her, but they still had no place to live.

Ahnya made the move and put them all in a small house, but they were lost. Ahnstan looked for his father, Wynson acted out, and Donya stayed at her friends' homes. Ahnya felt broken. How could this have happened?

She had thought they would cope with everything together – but now he was living with Violet. She thought she would die.

They had said they would go on the cultural exchange, but now she wondered if they would, because they weren't really a family.

The kids all seemed to like Violet, so she concentrated on her work, and tried to tend to the kids as they needed.

They had previously decided to go along with the cultural exchange, and now decided they would go through with it, because they all needed to start over, and thought 6 months away would do it.

Arrival

Tuffy Flint

After the ship arrived in the Islands, the GR settled down quite quickly. There had not been any escorts to welcome them, which Tuffy didn't expect. The translators both warned him not to be too relaxed by it, because the Islanders had done it both other times they had arrived, but Tuffy didn't see any reason to be concerned. He figured the translators were exaggerating.

When he arrived, he was quite prepared to hide the weaponry, but a stern-faced representative came out to see the ship. He asked for Willie Jay, and apologised, but no one could land if they didn't leave their guns on board.

Tuffy gave way smoothly, planning to get revenge in his own way. That was the beginning of a whole long time of finding out the Islands did not in anyway function in the way he expected.

Not a single soldier was allowed a concealed weapon. They started grumbling then, and never gave it up again. They didn't even warm to the job as it heated up, rolling their eyes and refusing to go out on the land without their arms. They had to be ordered to go on duty.

A man or two were picked up with hidden weapons. Tuffy made an example of them by leaving them on board.

Then, his beloved supportive wife and companion, Dinah Rose started to mutter about the conditions.

"Oh, Sweetie, I'm not in the mood tonight. The first few months of an occupation is always hard on the nerves. What we need is support."

But she didn't stop. "We can't even get a break and go off for a hunt. What are we supposed to do?"

"I don't know. All I know is I must be left alone."

"And what am I supposed to do then? It never stops raining. The women never seem to meet, so I can't see how I'm supposed to achieve my own ends."

"Dinah Rose, I'm begging you, drop the subject."

The topic was eased in the next few days by the suggestion that the guests could get to know the Islands by moving into a hexagon. The Island's leaders seemed to go into a kind of shock. They excused themselves and discussed the idea. To Tuffy the decision should have been a simple matter of the one who had the right to make it just making it. He was taken by surprise at first, but then settled in to work on the language. The longer it went on, the happier he got. It didn't matter to him that he was no winner in learning the Island chatter, he was so delighted in seeing the Island's inability to make a simple choice that he didn't even care.

When Willie Jay pointed out the correct pronunciation, Tuffy laughed and kidded, "Oh, well. I never could get my head around that stuff. Don't matter none do it?"

Willie Jay gaped. Joe Mack said, "But Sir, aren't you going to protect yourself from the Island ways?"

"There's no need to worry about that now – the savages can't decide to save their lives. I never could learn the way they talk. I guess I'll miss these." He put his sidearm down. "Come on, you guys, let's go." Tuffy, and the security who were always with him, all left.

The two men were left staring at each other.

Tuffy Flint enjoyed the next few days. While the Island government talked about the idea of foreigners having housing, he entertained himself wandering around and asking questions. He was convinced that he was 'finding out,' but the Islanders assigned escorts to any foray off the ship. The Ambassador had no idea that the idea had been figured out. Even Dinah Rose had suddenly broken out of the state rooms and was running about giggling wildly at the 'funny little bits' she found. The two translators were kept busy by the two of them.

Tuffy thought it wouldn't do any harm to go ashore without an escort, but the Island government wasn't having any of it.

"So sorry," a dark little woman, Quanita, tried to apologise. "You have the best trained translators, why don't you want to use them? You're having a terrible time with the language."

Tuffy's efforts to fawn attention on the woman got nowhere. "She ain't going nowhere like that," he muttered.

Even though Tuffy hadn't clued in that Quanita was the leader of her country, and had a husband, Joe Mack ventured to point out, "Well, she's come as far as she can right here. It might not be in our best interests if you keep chasing the ladies."

There was the usual howl, and Joe Mack was swapped with Willie Jay, so that things went on a little more smoothly.

At any rate, they were informed that the Public Servant's house was a long sail, so they should be ready to leave the next morning. They were all excited.

Under sail, they relaxed into the warm air flow, deep blue sea, and calling birds. The birds swirled up in flocks, calling in sounds that the GR had never heard before. Tuffy came out and sat on the deck watching the birds like everyone else. He took the trouble to warn the men not to spend time on their guns, especially not using the birds as target practice. "They've got boats to show us the way, and others come on out to look at us. We are not going to give them a way to say that we shot a sacred bird."

The little boats of the Islands were so much faster and manoeuvrable that the GR watched and marvelled. "That's a technology we could definitely use," Tuffy muttered to himself. "You know, they could let us meet the natives," he grumbled more loudly.

One of the security went to answer him, but then the whole group of them were distracted by the sight of a huge flock suddenly diving into the water. They raced to the rail to watch, wondering what in the world was going on. Then the birds proceeded to come back to the surface with fish. It turned into an entertaining pass-time.

But once they'd passed the top of the island, the balmy weather was gone. The wind made them cold, even when the weather was looking warm, and the strong current made them stay away from the shorelines. The one advantage that Tuffy could see was to have his sketch-artists note down all the details of the new land.

When they got most of the way there, they pointed out a break in the island. It was true that there was a rain that would obscure the details of the far reaches, but they sure wondered about it.

"Why would they keep a division of the island from us?" Tuffy mused.

The security poured abuse towards the islanders in general, and women leaders in particular.

"Anything's possible," Tuffy said. "But isn't it weird that they left us on our own to make this trip? We can't ask anyone about anything."

People got quiet then and started mumbling in a way that had other people being very glad they weren't on the wrong side.

The talk swelled then until no one knew what to expect. Tuffy would have loved to shut the gossip off, but who knew if the things being said might have some truth?

When they reached Quanita's harbour, they could see through the rain that there were many little boats. In this case they could see that the boats were all stored in boathouses, whereas the ones in the northern ports were all stored on the open water. "Interesting how the local customs vary from place to place," Tuffy mused.

One of the security answered more or less without caring. They were more interested in the local wild life. There were a few desultory boaters out to look them over, but none to welcome them. The security were looking them over for enemies. "Just don't let them see any guns," was Tuffy's only comment.

The ship was duly tied up and Quanita appeared and made a welcoming speech.

Tuffy made an acceptance speech. His efforts resulted in silence, which puzzled him. He thought it had to do with local customs and asked Willie Jay. Bad mistake. Willie Jay told him to be careful when the locals seemed to be commenting on his performance, he stormed around, and Joe Mack ran back and forth trying to calm things down.

It was in that frame of mind that they found their house was not a big establishment. No one to wait on them, they were shown an ordinary house in an ordinary hexagon.

Tuffy decided to accept the house and work with it. They smiled blandly as they were shown around the house, and the food, then they were finally left alone.

"What are you going to do?" asked one of the security.

"I'm going to send the ship back. Let's sit down at the table and hammer out a good solution.

They crowded around the table. The main problem that the men noticed about their planning was the lack of drink. Tuffy sent some he was glad to be rid of to fetch some alcohol and a few bites. "These drawbacks could be a real tripping point if we don't watch for them," Tuffy commented. "But keep quiet about it. We don't want them to realise what we're up to."

As they sat at the table, they sorted out how they would proceed, and what they were going to do.

Tuffy was going to remain in the islands, but Dinah Rose would go home. She would collect their children, was all he told the men, and some servants. He set out the plans for the men to go home, leaving out why he'd chosen some.

Later in the night he snuggled cosily with her to tell her. "Yes, I saw something like that coming," she said. "I thought there was something like this on the way because we just can't make any headway against the mindset here."

"What did you see?"

"I hung around with the women. That's a lot harder than it seems because the men here are interested in the same things as the women, so it's harder to find women on their own."

"Shopping and everything?"

"Yes and having the same days off."

"How could they make that work? Men must support the household, and women have to take care of the house and children!"

"I don't know. I'll find out more when I get back. What I saw was the train. Gomer never mentioned the train, did he?"

"Yeah, he did, remember? It's what made your father so mad."

"Oh, I didn't mean like a train, I meant in the way it is. It runs all over the place, stopping and starting, without a driver. We could use it. But I couldn't find out how it's powered or driven."

"That'll be my job while you're gone."

"Yes. I don't think they are trying to stop us from finding out."

"Well, they did say that we would use it for something dangerous, and they couldn't support that."

"What the hell have they got against what we do? It's none of their concern, and nowhere near them!"

"I tried to tell them that, but they said we haven't evolved enough to understand."

"The gall! Are they going to teach us that? And what's 'evolved' anyhow?"

"Hsst! Ssh, quiet you fool! Some of these men must be spies for Caleb; your father."

"I forgot," Dinah Rose subsided. She picked up the conversation, "As well as the train, I saw patterns and colours in fabrics the like of which I've never, ever seen."

"You mean the bright clothes everyone's wearing?"

"Yes, but they mean things, and soon they won't always mean what they do now."

"No. There'll be no pushing of fashion. Your father won't get the association between coloured cloth and reasons for war."

"Okay," said Dinah Rose, and changed the subject. "Their way of doing things is completely different. They're going to need training in the most basic of functions. However, once they have the training, they have the easy-going ways to make working for us to be worth the effort. I think Daddy should look very seriously at having vacations over here."

Tuffy Flint should have wondered why she'd dropped the subject that easily. She would cause him to regret that he had been distracted by her dedication. In the heat of the moment he said, "How is that going to happen? The GR doesn't have any ships for people to relax in."

In smug self-satisfaction she cooed, "Oh, Daddy'll love building the floating hotels. Of course, he'll have to build over here, too."

"The people weren't very favourable to Gomer when he mentioned it, were they?"

"Gomer was a dead loss. He mentioned it before he knew what was what. No judgement at all. You're not planning to copy him, are you?"

"Copy the firebrand of the family? Are you out of your mind? It's dangerous enough to keep him happy with me as it is! Give me a break!"

"Well, if you aren't going to copy him, we don't need to worry about him, do we? Daddy's going to love it, a whole big building project and lots of profit. In the meantime, we can arrange to have some lovely spending money all our own."

"Oh, I want to make a nest-egg all our own, Sweet-heart, but how are we going to do it? We are so far away; how are we to store it and sell it?"

"Well, the risk is high, of course, but it's part of the deal, isn't it? I store the goods when I get there, and we do nothing. If this post is short, we have a stash, and if it's long we plan to sell."

Tuffy laughed, softly, so no one would over-hear them. "I ain't too worried. I tell Caleb that the Islanders are well-organised and needing careful handling over a long period of time, but I'm not concerned. They're worried about violence; they can't make decisions to save their lives; they allow women to rule; their king's got no power; they don't have animals; and they don't eat proper meals. We don't have anything to worry about: we spend time finding out what else is valuable for our war effort, and then we move. If they give it to us, it's good and we go home. If they won't then we fire on them. They fear shot, so they'll fold when they see people dropping around them."

Dinah Rose smiled. "I got a pretty good idea of what's valuable. And when I bring our children, they'll mix with the local kids and hear a lot of stuff we'll never get any other way."

Tuffy hadn't faced having all three of the children; Jaakobah Lycus's son and his own two. She was right, so he smiled and made agreeable sounds while she got rhapsodic about it. He was concerned about Faithful Lycus. The boy had been supposed to be raised like them and not like his Dad, but he kept on reacting the way Jaakobah would have.

*　*　*

Dinah Rose hummed to herself as she packed away the Island fabrics, dreaming of the amounts of lovely cash she would not have to share because her husband didn't know. When he'd forbidden the sale, he'd played into her fondest dreams of earning her own income. If she was caught, she had a built-in excuse – for Caleb she could share the profit and tell him it was a trial to see if it would really sell, and for her husband she could simply tell him that it was for them.

*　*　*

As her ship pulled away, Tuffy turned to deal with the Islanders. He had a plan to become known as a rather ineffective foreign visitor, bumbling around the island.

He was surprised to find that it didn't work. He couldn't go anywhere without an escort. None of the GR could explore on his own. They didn't have transit fare, and there wasn't any other way around. The Islanders apparently walked everywhere nearby. This began to look like a real pain in the butt.

Not a one of them could find out anything they wanted to with a guard at their side. No matter how nice and polite they were, they sure felt like guards. They were big, too. When they mentioned it, they realised that the GR were seriously outweighed.

"If I didn't know better, I'd say they were putting someone on us that we couldn't do anything about." Tuffy sounded bitter. He was frustrated in getting around the Islands, he couldn't find out what was valuable, and the local authorities didn't become friends with him.

"How can I break this deadlock?" he burst out one morning.

The security responded very seriously. "We've been thinking about that. You know how much easier it would be to have some Islanders in our hands."

"Yeah, but they'd be real touchy about the way we treated their citizens."

"No, this is serious. We must come up with a way to get some Islanders to the GR."

Tuffy grinned and perked right up. "Yes, we do. Now, how do we set this up?"

They talked it over among them and decided between them that it was the normal way in the GR to welcome new cultures. They didn't have to do it right away because of the communications, so that gave them enough time to come up with an unstoppable idea. They planned between them a Cultural Exchange. There would be musicians, political leaders, and working men ready to learn from the GR.

When they were satisfied that the Islanders would accept it, Tuffy presented it to Quanita.

In short order the Islanders were buzzing about it and holding competitions to determine which entertainment group would go.

The GR settled down to wait for Dinah Rose's return. It bothered them no end that they couldn't get any information about the train, but they carried on playing along with the locals to keep everyone in a good mood. No sense getting them all worked up when the time would come when they'd be trying to get better terms from the GR.

Tuffy even tried judging the artistry, though he couldn't tell what was good. He thought he might have been able to see things if he travelled around, but those plans came to nothing. The Islanders wouldn't take a big crowd travelling with them, which put the GR out of countenance, because they had planned to skip off away from the Islanders and poke around by themselves. All they could do was sit and wait.

Maori Glossary

Word	Meaning	Pronunciation
Abeline Eidola	Abernaud and Olarine's daughter	Aber-leen Eye-dola
Abernaud Eidola	Partner for life of Olarine	Aber-naud Eye-dola
Ahnirlynya Seamore (Ahnya)	partner of Donstan	
Ahnirwyn (Ahnir)	Ahnya's father	
Ahnstan Seamore (Stan)	Ahnya and Donstan's eldest son	
Ahriri Lagoon	A lagoon on the coast of	Ah-reeree
Akaloa	An area near Christchurch	Akah-low-ah
Anatoe Amaru (Nat)	Hatoe and Annie's eldest son	Ahna-towee Ahmahroo
Aotea	One of the waka that brought the Maori to New Zealand. It means White Cloud, and the name was given to a large piece of land on the east coast of the North Island	Ah-ow-tee-ah
Anakiri Amaru (Annie)	Deceased life partner of Hatoe	Ahna-kirry Ahmahroo
Aotearoa	New Zealand, The Land of the Long White Cloud	ah-ow-tee-ah-row-ah
Aue	Oh – the opening of a song	Ow-ay
Benatoe Westimaru (Ben)	Hatoe's nephew	ben-a –towee West-i-mah-ru

Word	Meaning	Pronunciation
Bramaroiti Heteraki (Bram)	Hine's life partner, skipper of Kaumoana	Bram-ahroetee Heter-ahkiee
Bramerehia Heteraki (Mere)	The elder daughter of Bram and Hine	
chin wag	A good talk	
Chur bro	Cheers, brother – a form of thanks	
corker	Something first rate	
cuzzie	Cousin, and a good mate that's like family	
Donnurite Grahmore (Rita)	Donstan's mother	
Donstan Seamore	Ahnya's partner	
Donya Seamore	Donstan and Ahnya's daughter	
Emere Turikora	Ngaronoa's partner	
Fedrack Rianploot (Brain)		
Flynirwyn (Flyn)	Ahnya's brother	Flin-er-win
Flynya	Ahnya's mother	Flin-ya
Glendritz Tomptell	A Public Servant	Glend-ritz Tomp-tell
Glendrona Tomptell	Daughter of Glen and Istell	
Half-pai	A mixture of English and Māori: half good. Half and good	Half-pie
Hatoe Amaru/ Hetaru	the father of Nat and Kiri	ha- towee Ahmahroo
Hauraki Gulf	A large area of the east coast from Tāmaki-makaurau to the Coromandel Peninsula	How-rahkee
Heretaunga Bay	A bay on the mi-eastern coast of Te Ika a Maui	Herr-retong-ah

Word	Meaning	Pronunciation
Hinerehia Hetaraki/ Hetaru (Hine)	Bram's life partner, mother of Mere	hinny
horopito	Pepper tree. It means treatment	Horow-peetoe
Hokowhitu campus	The history wing of the university	Hoko-feetoo
hui	A meeting	hooee
Istellona Tomptell	Partner of Glen	
Kahutoe	Hatoe's father	Kah-hoo-tooee
kai	food	Keye
Kapiti	An Island off the coast of Wellington	Kapit-ee
karanga	Ritual call by women	Kahrahng-ah
Karoro	One of the boats; it means the southern black backed gull	Kahroe-roe
Kamautaurua Island	An island in Ōtākou, near Ōtepoti	Kahmow-tow-rooah
karengo	A red seaweed that is eaten	Kah-reng-oh
Kaumoana	a metal hunting ship. Means 'seafarer'	cow- mo-ahnah
Kawakawa berries		
Kia ora	hello	keeahorah
kirituhi	Tattoos that do not fit with the restrictions for moko	Kirree-too-hee
Kiritoe Amaru (Kiri)	younger son of Hatoe and Annie	kirry-towee Ahmahroo
Kiwa	the god of the sea	keewah
Kuia Rock	A rock on the outskirts of Mauao	Koo-eeah
kumara	Maori sweet potato	Koo-mahrah
Kurahaupo	One of the famous ocean-going waka	Koorah-howpoh

Word	Meaning	Pronunciation
Leora Meithei	Piamete's partner	
Mahi mahi	A type of deep-sea fish	
mānuka	a medicinal shrub	man-ookah
Manukau	One of the harbours of Tāmaki-makaurau, meaning wading bird	Mahnoo-cow
Marae	Meeting place	mahreye
Matapihi	a small town on the east coast of the North Island of New Zealand	matta-peehee
Matakana Island	An island at the entrance to Tauranga Harbour	Matta-kahna
Matamata	An inland small town on Te Ika a Maui, means Headland	Mattah-mattah
Mauao	Mt Maunganui, a mountain on the east coast of the North Island	mow-ah -ow
Maui	the trickster god	mowee
Mikitoe Westimaru (Mike)	Ben and Miki's son	Micky-tooee Westy-mahroo
Mikitonia Westimaru (Miki)	Ben's lifelong partner	Micky-toe-neeah Westy-mahroo
Moko	Maori tattoos	mocko
Mohaka	Small town on the coast; means a place for dancing	Moe-hahkah
Mere	Bram and Hine's older daughter	mirry
Mod vil	A behaviour modification village – mostly on land so the inhabitants can be near their families, but those that posed a risk, or refused to stay, were put on offshore islands, 'stranded' until either they posed less risk	
Morehu	A small boy evacuated with Glenda	Moar-ree-hoo

Word	Meaning	Pronunciation
Morena	Good morning	Mo-reenah
Motu Aotea	Great Barrier Island. It means the Island of White Cloud.	
Moumoukai	A mountain on Rangitahua	Mow-mow-keye
Mount Taranaki	A volcano on the west coast of Te Ika a Maui	Tah-rah-nackee
Miki	Ben's life partner	micky
mushies	mushrooms	mushees
Nah - yeah	Means yes	
Ngaire	Glenda's music teacher	Ngeye-ahree
Ngaronoa Turikora (Ron)	The king's son	Ngah-onoah Tooree-korah
Ngāti Kurī	a Maori tribe	ngah-tee Kooree
nikau	A type of palm tree in Aotearoa	Nee-cow
Olarine Eidola	A Public Servant	Olar-een Eye-dola
Ōtākou	Otago, means a village	Oh-tah-go
Otaki	a small town on Aotearoa's east coast	otah-kee
Otanerito Bay	On the other side of Banks Peninsula from Ōtautahi	Ohtah-ner-ritoo
Ōtautahi	Christchurch: the place of Tautahi	Oar-toe-tahee
Otou	a small town on Aotearoa's east coast	otoo
Ōtepoti	A mid-sized town on the east coast of Waipounamu	Otee-potee
Papatūānuku	The god of the earth, wife of Ranginui, mother of 6 major gods	Papa-tuah-nookoo
Pitamete Meithei	A Public Servant	Peetah-metty Meye-tie

Word	Meaning	Pronunciation
pou whenua	a commemorative pole	poo Fen-ooah
Pūrehuroatanga	References the University	Poo-reay-hoo-rowah-tahngah
py korry	Slang; it means by golly	
Raethew Perenara	A casual worker on the boats, Ray	Ray-thew Pe-ren-ahra
Rahari	One of Kiri's students	Rah-harree
Ranginui	The god of the sky, husband of Paptuahuku, and father of 8 major gods	Rahng-ee
Rangitahua	Raoul Island, the largest of the Kermadecs	rahngi-tah-hooah
Rangatira	A seaweed collector, a boat	
Rattle your dags	Hurry up	
Raukawa Moana	the Cook Strait, the water that splits the North and South Islands	row – kahwah Mo-ahnah
Ririno	One of the fleet of waka	rireenoh
Rehutai	Small town in the far north of Te Ika a Maui, means sea spray	Rehoo-tie
Remuera	A small town on the isthmus between the Waitematā and Manukau harbours, meaning a burned skirt hem	Rem-oo-air-ah
Ritihia Heteraki (Tia)	Bram and Hine's younger daughter	Rit-eeheeah
Rotatoe	Hatoe's brother	row-ta-toee
Ruahine	A sandbank of the coast of Mauao	Ruah-hinny
Ruamoko	The god of volcanos	Ruah-mocko
Skite	show off	skite

Word	Meaning	Pronunciation
strand me	The Island equivalent of: 'sue me' Part of a comprehensive system of mental health treatment, people are put on secure offshore islands and treated	
Ta	thanks	tah
Tairāwhiti	A major town on the mid-eastern side of Te Ika a Maui: means the coast upon which the sun shines across the water	Teye-ah-feetee
Tane	An exclamation, such as Great Tane!	
Tanemahuta	The god of the forests	Tah-nay-mahoo-tah
Tāmaki-makaurau	Auckland, means desired by many	tah-mah-kee mah-cow row
Tangaroa	the god of life in the sea	tahng – a -rowah
tapu	Taboo – forbidden, sacred	tahpoo
Tapu Tapuatea	'L Esperance. Rocks sticking up to 70 metres above the deep ocean	Tahpoo tapooah-teeah
Tarawera	A volcano on Te Ika a Maui: means button fern	Tah-rah-wee-rah
Taupo	A mid-sized town in the interior of Te Ika a Maui, and the lake there	tahoopoo
Tauranga	a mid-sized town on Aotearoa's east coast	tow- rong-ah
Tauranga Moana	Tauranga Harbour	tow- rong-ah Mo-ahn-ah
tawhai nuts		
Tawhirimatea	the God of winds	ta firry-mahtee-ah
Te Hiku o te Ika	The northernmost part of Te Ika a Maui, means the tail of the fish	Te-heekoo-oe-te-eeckah

Word	Meaning	Pronunciation
Te Ika a Maui	The North Island, the fish of Maui	Te-eecka-a-mowee
Te Kunenga ki Pūrehuroa	Massey University in Manwatu. It means 'From Inception to Infinity'.	Te koo-nengah kee poo-ree-hoo-rowah
Te Māhia	A peninsula between the towns of Wairoa and Tairāwhiti where the islanders lived in tunnels during the short Ice Age	Te Mah-heeah
Te Matau-a-Māui	Hawkes Bay: the fishhook of Maui	Te-mahtow – a - mowee
Te Tai-o-Rēhua	The Tasman Sea, means the tide of butterflies	Te-tie-oo-ree-hooah
Te Waipounamu	The South Island,	Te-Weye-poonah-moo
Te Whanganui a Tara	Wellington	Te-fung-ah-nooee-a-tahrah
tuawha	Slang term for a quarter bronze kiwi; it means fourth	tooahfah
Tuhara	Small town just east of Tairāwhiti	Too-hah-rah
Tuhua Island	Mayor Island	Toohoo-eeah
Tuitaerua (Tui)	A red-haired girl	
Turitea campus	The administrative area of Pūrehuroatanga, and student housing	Too-ree-teeah
Uetaoroa Turiahi	The King	Ooee-tahoo-rooah Too-ree-ahee
University of Manawatu		
Up the Boohai without a paddle	Up a creek without a paddle: Boohai is slang for Puhoi, a river north of Auckland: it means totally lost	

Word	Meaning	Pronunciation
Veges	vegetables	vegees
wahine	A woman or a girl	Wah-heenee
Wairakei	Mid-sized town on the eastern side of Te Ika a Maui	Why-rahkee
Wairoa	Mid-sized town in Te Matau-a-Māui, the mid-eastern side of Te Ika a Maui: the long water	Wy-ro-ah
Waitematā	One of the harbours of Tāmaki-makaurau, means the obsidian waters	Wy-te-mahtah
waka	Maori canoe. Can be one or an outrigger, or a massive ocean-going ship with two full hulls attached by a building	wahkah
Whakaari	A volcano in the Bay of Plenty, eastern side of the North Island	Fah-kah-ree
Whanau	family	fah-now
Whangarei	A mid sized town in northern Te Ika a Maui, full name: Whangarei-te-rerenga-parāoa, the gathering place of whales	Fahng-a-ray
whare kai	Eating house on the Marae	Fahree keye
whare nui	The largest house on the Marae	fahree nooee
whinge	complain	Win-j
Wineera Rangituri	A Princess of the Islands	Wineerah Rahngee-tooree
Wynlynya (Winnie)	Anya's younger sister	
Wynson Seamore	Anya and Donstan's adopted son	
Yeah - nah	Means no	

Mexican Glossary

Agarrar la onda – you understand, or get it. *¿Aggaraste la onda?* — Do you get my drift?

Aguas watch out or be careful. Used instead of *ayuda*. It comes from when people used to dump their sewage out the window onto the street. They'd say *aguas* to let others know they were about to empty *el bacín* their "chamber pot"

Aguas con los perros. – Careful with those dogs.

Ahora – now

Ahroita/Ahorito – literally *little now*. Used to mean soon or eventually. ¿Puedes ayudarme con mi tarea? Ahorita. — Can you help me with my homework? Soon. ¿Ya nos vamos? Ahorita. — Let's go now? Soon.

A huevo – hell yeah! Of course! Or fuck yeah! The actual meaning is "to egg". In English, we refer to "testicles" as "balls", in Spanish, they're *huevos*.

¡A huevo! Hell yeah! Is the male version. The female version is *hueva*, which can be used to mean 'lazy' *'Tengo mucha hueva'* means 'I'm feeling lazy'

A *huevón* is a lazy person.

albur is a vulgar pun.

alburear

Ando bien pedo – means more or less "I'm very fart". "I'm Drunk"

Antro – is a nightclub.

Antros – what a *narco* would call a nightclub

¡A la verga! – The actual meaning is "to cock", so it basically means the same as "it went to shit" or "shit hit the fan" "Aw, Shit"

A poco – a little, used to mean 'really?!' or 'you don't say!' *'¿Te dieron el trabajo? ¡A poco!'* = 'You got the job?! No way!' *¿apoco?* Really?

Apodo – a nick name

A toda madre: This means awesome, or when about yourself it means you're feeling great, ready for action, as in *Estoy a toda madre.*

Autobús – the official word for bus

A webo – hell yeah

Baros – money

Bien buena – admiring comment on a woman's appearance: *Estas bien buena güera.* – You are hot (have a nice body), white lady.

Bigote: mustache

Bigotona: girl with a mustache

Borrachera – a drinking party or binge

Buena – hot, as a woman with a nice body

Buena onda means a good atmosphere. In a building it means good atmosphere, but a person can be said to be laidback and easy to get along with. *Ella es buena onda* — She's cool.

Buena onda – a nice female, cool waves, cool vibes, good waves

Buen pedo – a nice male

Buenota – a beautiful woman

Cabrón means a male goat, it's an offensive term and the type of word that shouldn't be said in front of children, translating to 'asshole', 'fucker' or 'bitch'. It can also be used in a positive way to say you're 'really fucking good at something', *'Soy bien cabrón cantando'* would mean, 'I'm fucking good at singing'.

Cabrón is slang for 'friend'

Cacharro – anything broken

Chafa – Something that will have you screaming *"¡Que chafa!"* which means "what crap!" *Esa camisa está chafa* – This t-shirt is bad quality (or fake)

Cafres – terrible drivers

Caguama – is a type of sea turtle, said as the name of a 1.2 litre bottle of beer

Caguamón – the biggest caguama

Cámara – I agree or it's a deal.

Camión – both formal and informal route buses, even though it means "truck" in the rest of Latin America. *Apúrate que no vamos a alcanzar el camión* – Hurry up or we won't catch the bus

Cantina – a bar. *Hoy no tengo ganas de ir a la cantina, vayan ustedes* – I don't want to go to the bar tonight, but you guys can go

Carnal really means buddy between close guy friends, but when used by a stranger it's like calling someone out and making sure they know you've seen through them and what their up to. *Carnal* is slang for 'friend' - *¿Qué onda carnal? ¿Cómo estás?"* What's up brother? How are you? *Oye Carnal como te va?* – Hey brother, what's up?

Carcacha – a beat up car

Cebolla: onion

Cebollón: what they call someone who eats too many onions

Cejas: eyebrows

cejón: guy with bushy eyebrows

Chairo – social justice warriors

Chafa – something cheap or low quality. *Este coche es chafa.*

¡Chale! – Shit! Or fuck! When something bad happens.

Chamaca/Chamaco a kid, usually one who's a bit of a punk or pain to deal with

Chamacca/Chamacco – the kids

Chamara/Chamaro – the kid - *Ese chamaca necesita calmarse. Me estoy irritando.* "That kid needs to calm down. I'm getting irritated."

Chamarra – slang for jacket or coat, and acts as a replacement for *"chaqueta"* which is used in every other Spanish speaking country. In some parts of Mexico, *"chaqueta"* is a slang term for masturbation or touching yourself. *¿Me prestas tu chamarra?* – Can I have your jacket for a minute?

Chamba – a difficult or shitty job. An unpleasant situation, or work or a job i.e. something you don't want to get stuck in for too long; *Voy a chambear"* I am going to work: *¡No quiero chambear! Tengo hueva"* I don't want to work! I can't be bothered. *Mañana tengo que volver a mi chamba wey, o me despiden* – I have to go back to my job tomorrow man, or I'll get fired *Tengo que regresar a mi chamba* or ask *¿Que chamba tienes?*

Chambear – the job, with no pride or enthusiasm. *Tengo que chambear mañana.*

Chancla – means "flip flop" It's become a meme for every *madre's preferred weapon* (Jandals) *¡Aguas! Chanclas de mamá!* Watch out! Mom's flip flops!

Chanclas – sandals and flip-flops. *Deberías ponerte algo mejor que esas chanclas para salir* – You should put on something better than those flip-flops to go out

Chancludo – someone who wears *Chanclas*

Chango – a monkey

Changarro – means a small business, a little store or small restaurant. The name given to small, wholesome family businesses; *Ve al changarro*

ese y ve si tienen algunos dulces – Go to the store and see if they have any kind of candy

Chava or *Chavo* – a kid - *El chavo sigue en el colegio, debería buscarlo* – The boy is still in school, I should pick him up. *Los chavos están jugando al fútbol* – The kids are playing football.

Chavoruco is an old guy who acts (or tries to act) young.

Chela and *cheve* are slang terms for beer; '*Vamos a la tienda para comprar la pista. ¿Quieren una caguama o un six de cheves?*' = 'We're going to the shop for drinks. Do you want a bottle of beer or a six-pack?' *Chela* comes from a beer cocktail (*michelada*) that mixes beer with lime, chili and tomato juice. *Dame dos chelas para mi y mi compadre* – Give me two chelas for me and my compadre.

Chicana/Chicano – a Mexican who was born in Mexico, but immigrated to the US - *Hay una población bastante grande de Chicanos en Los Angeles* – There is a very important Chicano population in Los Angeles

Chida means it's cool, great, awesome: '*Esa camisa es muy chida*' means, 'That shirt is really cool!' '*¡Ay, que chida estuvo la película!*' = 'The film was so cool!'

chido – *Esta bien chido ese regalo, gracias wey* – That gift is really cool, thanks man. *Es un vato chido* – He's a cool guy!

Chilangos – people from Mexico City

'*Chinga tu madre*' means '*go fuck yourself*'.

Chingados – madness, mess: *Qué chingados esta pasando aqui?* What the hell is going on here? (or What kind of craziness is going on here?

Chingar means fuck *chinga tu madre* (go fuck yourself) *chingadera* (rubbish, in the sense of an object) *chingonazo* refers to someone admirable: '¡*No me chingues! Vete a la chingada.*' = 'Don't fuck with me! Go fuck yourself.'

Chingarle – to go at something aggressively/to hustle/to work hard: ¡*Hay que chingarle mucho para ganar un buen dinero en México!* You gotta hustle to make good money in Mexico!

¡*Chingadazos!* – bullshit

Chinga su madre – screw your mother: *Si ella terminó contigo pues* ¡*chinga su madre wey!* ¡*Qué idiota!* If she ended it with you well fuck her, bro! What an idiot!

Chinga tu madre – fuck your mother, swearing

Chingón – wicked, far out- in a good way: ¡*No mames wey el festival de house estuvo bien chingón!* Omg bro the festival was so awesome!

Chisme – gossip

Chismoso – a gossiper

Chiste – means the trick, or the way to do something, as in *el chiste es hacerlo así* — the trick is to do it like this.

Chistoso – something funny

Cholo – Commonly heard in the southwest of the United States, "cholo" is a somewhat loosely defined term, but it generally refers to Mexican gangsters, with a very specific look – big white shirts, black baggy shorts, shaved heads, religious black ink tattoos, black shades, etc. *Tengo algunos primos cholos, pero prefiero no meterme en eso* – I have a few cholo cousins, but I'd rather not get involved with that

Chorro – Literally spill, it means diarrhea, as in *tengo chorro*. It can also be used to express that you have a lot of something — not necessarily diarrhea.

Chula – saying a woman is hot in a way which can also mean good in a general sense.

Cochina/cochino – A pig, in the general, metaphorical sense of the word — dirty, disgusting or rude, whatever applies. *Tu casa está cochina* — your house is dirty.

Cochinito – a nicer way of saying someone is piggish

Colonia: neighbourhood

Colonos – neighbour

Conste – I agree or it's a deal.

Chupe: a drinking party or binge

Chorro – a stream of something, meaning you have large quantities of it. *Tenemos un chorro de películas por ver esta vacaciones, deberíamos comenzar* – We have a ton of movies to watch on vacation, we should get started

Coda/Codo - translates to "elbow," but it's is also used in Mexico to describe someone overly frugal or tight-fisted with his or her money. *Juan nunca gasta en cosas innecesarios. Es muy codo.* – Juan never spends money on unnecessary things. He's very frugal. *No seas codo* – Don't be cheap.

Coger – literally means 'to take' but is used to mean 'to fuck'

Compa is slang for 'friend' from *compadre*, or Godfather - *'Es mi compa, mi carnal – ¡lo quiero!'* = 'He's my friend – I love him!'

Compra – Friend. It's short for *compañero* or *compañera*, but it doesn't need gender changes like the whole word. So you wouldn't use it as *compro* for a guy. Everyone is *compra*.

Crudo which means raw, is used to mean hung-over: *¡Estoy muy crudo esta mañana!* means 'I am really hung-over this morning!' *¡Estoy bien pedo! Estaré muy crudo mañana.'* = 'I'm so drunk! I'm going to be hung-over tomorrow.' *Esta mañana amaneci crudo* – I woke up with a hangover today. *¿Cuándo vas a dejar de actuar estúpido? Nunca, pendejo.* "When are you going to stop acting stupid?" "Never, dumbass."

Cuate means fraternal twin, is slang for very close friend, almost a brother

Culero asshole *'Eres tan pendejo.'* = 'You're such an arsehole.'

Culo: ass (vulgar)

Culero: literally ass seller, but actually more like asshole.

Culona: girl with a big ass, possibly complimentary but still vulgar

Cursi – cheesy

Dale – from the verb *dale*, to give, which means 'okay, sure, let's go'

de la fregada – it's fucked up

Depa: flat, apartment

Departamento – apartment

Derechairo – hard rightists, from Dere-, as in derecha, added to chairo

Desmadre: A mess, or a fucked-up situation, is a *desmadre*.

¿Dónde es la peda? – Where is the party?

Echar/tirar la hueva – "*¿Qué haces aparte de echar la hueva huevón?*" What do you do besides sit on your butt lazy you schmuck? "*Ai wey déjame tranquilo, solo quiero echar la hueva hoy.*" Bro let me be, I just wanna chill and do nothing today.

Ei-oh – huh? Eh?

El cine era muy gacho. No lo recomiendo. "That movie was so lame. I wouldn't recommend it."

En serio – Really?

Eres la neta after someone has done you a favour – you're saying "you're trustworthy" "you're amazing" *¡Eres la neta!* – You rock!

'*Eres un pendejo*' means 'You're an asshole'.

Ese – guy

Ese chamaca necesita calmarse. Me estoy irritando. "That kid needs to calm down. I'm getting irritated."

Escuincle – means a spoiled brat

¿Es neta? No way! For real? '*Oí que estás embarazada. ¿Es neta?*' = 'I heard you were pregnant. Is it true?'

Eso que ni qué really means "That what or what." or "That what nor what" it's used to mean no doubt about it

Especial – special, picky, especially for food

Está carbon – he's tough.

Está chingón – it's fucking awesome

Esta crudo – "I'm hung-over" (fem)

Está de la chingada – it's fucked up

Está padre – it's cool, great.

Está padrísimo – it's awesome.

Estar cañón – difficult or hard, as in: *El examen estuvo cañón* – The exam was really hard. *Te extraño cañón* – I miss you so much.

Estás pero si bien pendejo – you're a fucking idiot

Esta vieja – this old lady, could refer to any female, usually with a negative connotation.

Estoy Crudo – "I'm Hung-over" (masc)

Estoy bien crudo hoy – I'm very hung-over today.

Estoy pedo – I'm drunk.

Estoy jodido – I'm fucked.

Feria – can also refer to pocket change.

Fiesta – party

Flaco – thin

Floja: means laziness

Frente: forehead

Frentona: girl with a big forehead

Fresa really means strawberry, but you call someone this and they're snobby or flash: *'Mi jefa es muy fresa'* would mean, 'My boss is really stuck up.' *'Ella es muy fresa, ¿verdad?'* = 'She's a bit stuck-up, right?' *"Ya no quiero salir con ella, es una Fresa".* I don't wanna go out with her anymore, she is a snob. *Sabes que no me gusta salir con hombres como él, es demasiado fresa* – You know I don't like going out with men like him, he's way too stuck up

Gacha or *gacho* is a substitute for *"feo"* (ugly) and is used to describe someone or something totally uncool, or even sloppy. *No seas gacho, déjalos ir al parque* – Don't be so awful, let them go to the park. *No me gusta esta fiesta. Está bien gacha.* – I don't like this party. It has bad vibes.

Gacho not good – *'¡No seas gacho!'* = 'Don't be bad/ mean!'

Güera/ güero – light skinned woman/man

Gúey – an ox (buey), used to mean a guy, a dude, or a dummy by being spelled as it's spoken, wey

Gordito – fat

Gordibuena – fat hot chick

Groserias – bad language

Hablar por los codos – talk too much

Hasta la madre: To be sick of something. *Ya yo estoy hasta la madre, de que me pongan sombrero*

Hay un chingo de tráfico – there's a hell of a lot of traffic

Hermano – brother

Híjole – Wow! or My goodness!

Hola, amigo. ¿Qué tal?

Hola, compa. ¿Qué onda?

Huaraches – used to mean sandals, now a food

Hueles feo – you smell bad (not ugly)

Hueva – means laziness: *'Tengo mucha hueva, ya no quiero salir.'* = 'I'm feeling lazy, I don't fancy going out now.' *¡Tengo que ir al correo pero me da hueva!"* I have to go to the post office but I'm too lazy! *Tanta pendejada me dio hueva.* All of this nameless stupidity impeded my will to do anything.

Huevon literally means a "large egg" but is used colloquially as an insult to talk about an extremely lazy person. For example: *Mario nunca hace nada. ¡Qué huevon!* – Mario never does anything. What a lazy guy!

Jaina – girl, chick or *chica*

Jalada – something that is completely unbelievable or overdone. *No puede ser, que jalada toda esa historia, ¿como quieres que te crea?* – That's a ridiculous story, how do you want anyone to believe you?

Jeta – is a dirty look, a sour expression

Jetona – woman with a sour expression

Joto: Sissy, gay

La banda – the band, and the friends

La chingada – A place really, really far away, i.e., The Boondocks: *"No mames wey fuimos hasta la chingada y el bar estaba cerrado! ¡Qué mal pedo!"* No way man, we went all the way to BFE and the bar was closed! How shitty!

Lana – wool, money

La neta the truth *'La neta te amo!'* which means 'The truth is, I love you!'. Also for emphasis: *'Mi nave es la neta wey!'*, which roughly translates to 'My ride is the shit, man!'. *¡Dime la neta!"* Tell me the truth!

Latón – a container for beer, a big can, a tall boy in English

luego luego – right now, immediately

Madre – mother - *con madre* (awesome); *me vale madre* (I don't give a shit): *'¡Estuvo a toda madre!'* = 'It was awesome!'

Madrear – a simple verb for getting your ass kicked: *Voy a madrear todos estos pinches blogueros que copian el contenido de mis artículos.*

Madrazos – bruises

Malacopa – a person who can't hold his liquor, loses control, fights, and cries. *Creo que el pomo no hacía falta, estos son muy malacopa* – I think the bottle wasn't even necessary, these guys are extreme lightweights. *No seas una mala copa.*

Mala onda or "bad vibes."

Malinchista – a Mexican who someone who symbolically betrays Mexico by talking constantly about how wonderful other places are

Mamá – mummy

Mamada – a blow job.

Mamadas can mean both 'blowjob' and 'bullshit': *¡No mames! Son unas mamadas.*' = 'What the fuck! That's bullshit.'

Mamado – means he is muscular — implying he breastfed a lot and got big.

Mamar – suckle or breastfeed. Also give a blowjob.

Mamón – picky, stuck up man

Mamona – picky, stuck up woman

¿Mande? – Come again? What? Tell me. Go ahead.

Mandilón – a guy whose wife or girlfriend is always bossing him around

Marqueta – market

Me da hueva – something bores you.

Me encabrona (or *me encabrita*) este wey – this guy pisses me off.

Me Vale Madres – "I Don't Care" but it really means "I don't give a fuck" or "I don't care, motherfucker"

Metiche – That person who always has his/her nose in other people's business. Not guaranteed to spread rumors, but still likes to keep tabs on everyone's business. *Hay demasiados metiches en mi trabajo, no los soporto* – There are too many nosy people on my job, I can't stand them

Mi jefa/mi jefe – mother and father as the bosses

Mijo/mija, which is *mi hijo* and *mi hija* ("my son" and "my daughter")

¡Mira qué Cabrón! – Don't try to be a smartass – used when someone is trying to take advantage of someone or something

Mi vieja – wife, fiancée, or girlfriend

Mojados – wetbacks, Mexicans who are in the US illegally

Morenita – dark skinned woman

Moreno – dark skinned

Morra/Morro – the kids

Mucha chamba – lots of jobs

Musica fresona – cheesy, lightweight rock

Naco – someone with a tacky, or poor attitude, and is considered less sophisticated than your regular member of society. - *Naaah, te ves muy naco con eso, mejor cambiate* – Nah, you look really trashy in that, go change

Nalgada – slapping someone on the butt

Nalgas: butt

Nalgona: girl with a big butt.

Nariz: nose

Narizón: guy with a big nose

Negocious – businesses

Neta – If you refer to a person as *neto/a*, you are describing someone who can be trusted or that you can always count on. "*Te lo juro! ¡Es neta!*" I swear to you! It's true! "*No manches! ¿Es neta?*" No way! Really (for real)? "*La neta es que no tengo tiempo para salir.*" The reality (or thing) is I don't have time to go out. "*¡Dime la neta!*" Tell me the truth! *Sí, es la neta* – Yes it's the truth. ¿Es la neta? – Is it the truth? *esta fiesta es la neta* — this party is the best.

Ni madres – No fucking way.

Ni modo – Literally no method, it falls somewhere between "no big deal" and "it is what it is." "It doesn't matter", "it can't be helped", or a dismissive "whatever". Either you have no preference or also to express disappointment at something you have no control over.

Ni pedo – no problem

Ni pex – nothing going on

No Hay Bronca – means that there is no problem – everything is fine. *Claro, yo te puedo prestar algo de dinero, no hay bronca* – Sure, I can lend you some money, no problem

No hay de que – "no problem."

No hay pedo – more vulgar way of saying no problem

No mames literally don't suck. It's used to mean no fucking way, stop fucking around, stop being an arsehole: *no mames* loosely translates to 'no fucking way' or 'what the fuck'. In the presence of elders, the tamer *no manches* expresses the same sentiment. "*No mames wey, ¡no puede ser!*" Come on man, there's no way! No mames, literally don't suck me off.

No mamen – literally, don't suck me off, man.

No manches literally, Don't stain , used for real, or no way - "*No manches! ¿Te dieron la posición?*" No way! They gave you the position!

Ñoños – are nerds, and as an adjective it means *nerdy*.

No Pos Wow – literally, '*no pues, guau*' "Not Good, Wow" mainly used in a sarcastic way, like "You don't say. eye roll"

Obra: work project

Obrero: worker

Órale encouragement, like "Go for it!" or "Right on!" It can be used to agree: "Let's do it!" or "Let's go!" Or it can express excitement, like "Wow!" or "My goodness!" an interjection of encouragement, an expression of shock, surprise or excitement, or agreement with a statement: '*¿Vamos a la fiesta?*' '*Sí, órale, vámonos.*' = 'Are we going to the party?' 'Yeah, sure, let's go.' *¡Órale! ¿Y tu desde cuando trabajas tanto?* – Wow, since when do you work so much?

Padre means father, but in Mexican it also means 'cool'. *¡Que padre!* means 'How cool!' or 'más padre' ('very cool'). *Está bien padre ese juego, ¿como se llama?* – That videogame looks really cool, how's it called?

Pachanga – party

Palabras sucias

Palomita: popcorn

Palomero: popcorn seller, who walks the streets with his cart.

Parque central: the central plaza of a place

Paro – means favour. *¿Me puedes hacer un paro y recordarme eso?* – Can you do me a favour and remind me of that? *Hazme un paro* — Do me a favour.

Parranda – party

Partir la madre: This means kick your ass, as in *te voy a partir la madre.*

Pata de elefante – 4 litres of wine; literally means elephant's foot

Peda: a drinking party or binge

Pedero – a person who causes problems

Pedo: fart which is used to mean drunk and problem: *¡Estoy bien pedo! Estaré muy crudo mañana.*' = 'I'm so drunk! I'm going to be hung-over tomorrow.' *No pensé que fuesen a volver tan pedos wey* – I didn't think you'd come home so drunk, man. *¿Cual es tu pinche pedo?* — What's your fucking problem?

Pelo is hair

Pelón – a bald guy, especially those who shave their head.

Pendejadas – from *pendejo*, asshole, means bullshit

Pendejo really means asshole or pubic hair, but it also means dumbass, stupid, idiot. *Eres tan pendejo.'* = 'You're such an arsehole.'

Peques, short for *pequeños* — is used for little kids only.

Pex – problems

Pinche the worst, ugly, awful. *'Mi pinche nave esta roto'* which means 'My fucking car is broken *'Mi pinche hermano le robó mi sueter.'* = 'My fucking brother stole my jumper.' *¡Jajaja! pinche Ricardo, siempre sales con esas cosas* – Hahahah, fucking Ricardo, you always come up with stuff like this. *Eres un pinche idiota, Ricardo* – You're a fucking idiot, Ricardo. *¡Pinche coche!* – damn car. *Pinche Juan* – goddamn Juan

Pinche estúpido – fucking idiot

Pinche pendejo – fucking asshole

Pista: a generic 'drink'.

Pistear – the vulgar way to say drink

Pisto: the vulgar way to say *booze*

Plata – silver, money

Pomo – a bottle of any liquor that you might find, from vodka to some fine tequila. *Las chelas no van a alcanzar para todo el mundo, hay que abrir*

un pomo – Beers aren't going to be enough for everyone, we have to open a bottle

Prieto – someone with darker skin. *¿Recuerdas quién es Daniel? Mi amigo prieto, estuvo acá el otro día* – Remember who Daniel is? My black friend, he was there the other day

Puta and Puto – a whore and a faggot

Putazos – bruises

¿Qué chingados? "What the fuck?"

Qué hueva – *Ai no, qué hueva! Tengo muchísima chamba y cero ganas de hacerla!* Oh no, I can't even (or too much laziness). I have so much work and no one will to do it! *Que hueva* — how boring.

Qué huevos – what balls! When someone has done something that took guts

¡Que milagro! – Literally What a miracle! This is how Mexicans say Long time no see.

¿Qué onda? What wave which means what wave did you come in on, or how's it hanging, a friendlier way of saying it. "What's up?"

"*¿Qué onda carnal? ¿Cómo estás?*" What's up brother? How are you?

¿Qué onda, wey? What's up, Bro? *'¿Qué pedo, wey?'* = 'Mate, what happened?'

¿Qué pedo? cruder version of what's up which means what fart, and is a little more accusatory

¿Que pedo con esta madre? – What the fuck is wrong with this fucking thing

¿Que pex? – what's up?

Que poca madre: Something bad, wrong, not pleasing for sure. *¿Reprobaste tu clase? Que poca madre.* — You failed your class? That sucks.

¿Qué tal? ¿Qué pasa? Both mean what's up

¿Qué tal, jaina? "What's up, chick?"

¿Que tranza? – what's up

rabo verde – literally green tail — green in the sense of not ripe, is an old guy who dates young women, or chases young tail.

Rata – a thief

Ratero – it's used instead of "*ladrón*" both of which mean "thief". *Pues el teléfono me lo robó un ratero, así que no tengo* – A thief robbed me off of my phone, so I don't have one

Resaca – hung-over

Refresco – sodas of any kind, though if a policeman asks you for a *refresco*, he's asking for a bribe. *¿Quieres beber refresco o te sirvo algo más?* – Do you want to drink some soda or do you want me to serve you something else?

Rodeo – the kind of nightclub that specializes in *banda* music — the cowboy hat-wearing groups with loud drums and big horn sections.

Rola – a song

Romperse los codos – work too hard

Ruco: is an old person

Sale – Okay, yeah, it's a deal, I'm down, let's go! *Vamos al cine a la tarde?* – *Sale* – Shall we go to the cinema in the afternoon? Ok, cool. *Quieres ir al cine mañana?"* *You wanna go to the movies tomorrow?* "¡Sale, vamos!"¡Yeah, let's do it!

Sin broncas – *Bronca* roughly translates to "fight" or "row." to say something or someone is *sin broncas*, you are saying there's no problem (e.g. they're "without fight/disagreement").

six/seis (literally just a six-pack

tacaño – stingy, as in a cheap or stingy person.

Tocayo – Nickname given to anyone who shares your first name. *Ahí va el tocayo* – There goes my tocayo. *somos tocayos*

Te crees muy muy – "You think you are such a big deal"

Tener feria – "to have money", as in: *¿Tienes feria para salir esta fin de semana?* – Do you have money to go out this weekend?

Tengo cruda – I'm hung over

Tonterías – bullshit (suitable for table conversation)

Tope: speedbump

Tu es chismosa or *tu es chismoso* – you're a gossip

un buen de tráfico – there's lots of traffic

un montón de tráfico – there's a awful lot of traffic

Un pedote – is a boozer, a big drinker, although it could also mean a big fart.

Un putero: A fucking ton of: *Un putero de gente* a fucking lot of people

Vale from *valer*, something of value, meaning, 'okay, sure, let's go'

Vales Verga – it means "worth penis" or even "cheap penis". "Worthless"

Valedor from *valer*, someone of value is slang for 'friend'

Valió madre – It's worth your mother – something is fucked

Valió verga – it's worth a cock (penis) – something is fucked

Vamos a chupar – let's drink/get drunk.

Varos – 'bucks' 'loonies' 'quids' *Me pagaron esta semana, puedo poner unos cuantos varos más para la pizza* – I got paid this week, I can help with a few more bucks for the pizza *Esta vale cien varos* — It's worth one hundred pesos.

Vato – guy

Vecinos – neighbours

verdad, – Really?

Verga means penis: *vales verga* means you're not worth dick, ¡A la verga! Gané la loteríá!' = 'OMG! I won the lottery!'

Vete a la chingada – go fuck yourself.

Vieja – Although this directly translates to "old lady", in Mexican slang, this word is used as an affectionate word for your mother. *Tengo que visitar a la vieja de vez en cuando, y darle algún regalito* – I have to visit my mother from time to time, and give her some little present

Viejitas – the diminutive softening the blow.

Viejo – old man, can be used among friends like man

Vocho – the old Volkswagen Beetle. *¿Por qué hay tantos vochos en la capital?* – Why are there so many beetles in the capital city?

Wey, ¿viste eso? Bro, did you see that? *Mira güey, ¿salimos hoy o que?* – Hey dude, wanna go out today? *Wey, ¿viste eso?* which means, "Bro, did you see that?" *Estaba estudiando español, y wey esta frase fue muy difícil* "I was studying Spanish, and like, this phrase was really difficult…"

Ya valí madre means "I'm fucked."

Zócalo – is the main plaza or the central square of a city

$\mathcal{L}$aurie de Vere was born and raised in Aotearoa, otherwise known as New Zealand. She was born in Remura, and grew up in Omanu, Mt Maunganui. She moved to Tauranga to go to Secondary School, because there were no Secondary Schools at the Mount back then.

She has been writing since she was seven, something that was frowned upon by her parents, who did everything they could to stop her 'telling lies.' She kept on, anyway, hiding what she wrote.

No longer writing about fairies and people who could fly, she now writes more serious books. Volcano in the Ocean is the first of four books, called The Fire in the Fern Four. They tell the story of a non-violent society being attacked by a violent society.

The beginnings of the story are post-apocalyptic, 260 years after Yellowstone erupted and nearly extinguished all life on the planet. In the small Ice Age that followed the eruption, the Islanders survived by going underground where it's warmer and building enormous greenhouses to preserve the native plants and birds. Living underground was crowded, and in order to survive, they put plugs in everyone's vas deferens and fallopian tubes, so the only children born were planned, which kept the population stable. They called themselves troglodytes, which was shortened to Troggies.

The Troggies had to be non-violent to survive in the crowded conditions, so they took from their non-violent ancestors, the Moriori, and Te Whiti o Rongomai and Tohu Kakahi and formed what the Troggies called Nunuku's Law – a non-violent way of life.

After living underground for more than 60 years, when they came up onto the land, they built their homes in hexagons instead of grids, and started to live again. With no oil, and no metals, they used what they had – a lot of sand – and invented a silicate society.

When the GR got back on the oceans again, and found the islanders, they thought that no savages could have invented the things the islanders used. In GR thinking, it was invented by them, and they wanted it. The islanders thought they'd use whatever they got to do evil towards other people, so they would not give their secrets over.

In the second book, Ignition in the City, we follow the story further.